SHANE O'NEILL
'The Grand Disturber'
Of Elizabethan Ireland

by
Brian Mallon

SHANE O'NEILL, 'the Grand Disturber'

US Copyright © 2012 Brian Mallon
All rights reserved.
ISBN-13:
978-0692502723
(RedBranch Press)

**ISBN-10:
0692502726**

SHANE O'NEILL, 'the Grand Disturber'

DEDICATION

This book is dedicated to my mother, Dorothy Mallon, who has helped me in every way possible, to my father whom I still miss, and to my Grandfather from Tyrone, who instilled in me an abiding love of Ireland and her history. Also to Sr. Jane Edward IHM, who told me that I would one day be a 'great Irish writer'.

SHANE O'NEILL, 'the Grand Disturber'

Red Branch
Press, Dublin

SHANE O'NEILL, 'the Grand Disturber'

ACKNOWLEDGMENTS

All my gratitude to dear friends who've read, encouraged and advised: Christine Quinlan Gordon, Howard O'Brien, and Robin Howard. Also a special thanks to Noel Lawlor, and to Fionnula Flanagan for her support and encouragement.

SHANE O'NEILL, 'the Grand Disturber'

FORWARD

This is not intended as an historical romance in the usual sense, although I have borrowed from that genre for entertainment value. My purpose here is to tell the *real* story, the actual events in the life of Shane O'Neill as I have discerned them, to untangle the narrative of his life, showing cause and effect, and to explain many of the seemingly unrelated events of those turbulent times. The actual forces at play in the conquest of Ireland are revealed here. The telling of this tale is informed by over thirty years of research, bringing to light many previously unknown factors, both personal and political, that drove these events.

I believe I have used or referenced every snippet that is actually known about his life. The familiar Elizabethans are depicted in their own words, Elizabeth, Sussex, Cecil, Sidney, and even the 'wizard' John Dee. Here and there, phrases lifted from their letters are indicated with single quotation marks. Excerpts from actual letters are included, always indicated by indented margins when they are genuine. The only principle character who is invented is Gillie, the poet's young servant. (And half way through the writing I found a list of Shane's effects, wherein he left three gold chains to one Gillie Dubh MacReachain, so perhaps he existed after all!)

Much of what has been written about Shane O'Neill is simply repetitions of political propaganda from the period. I began with the assumption that the Catholics of Ulster were not barbarous savages who would follow a debauched tyrant. People who intend to colonize

SHANE O'Neill, 'the Grand Disturber'

always assert that the natives are sub-human. I have portrayed them as I know them to be.

Most historians seem to be completely unaware of the Irish custom of 'the wind-up', and they fail to take in the leg-pulling that is so much a part of Irish culture. It's the only thing that could account for Shane's ridiculous overtures to Lord Sussex' sister; he was twitting him. Always repeated is the ludicrous notion that Shane kept Katherine chained to his bed. Had they checked Scottish sources, they would have found in Lord Argyll's journal a reference to his attending Shane and Katherine's wedding. Many of the guests are there mentioned, including Katherine MacLean's family from Mull. They would hardly have attended if such a thing were true, let alone sent him several hundred gallowglass warriors to help him. When you sift through the evidence, there is nothing whatsoever to support the claim that he was a cruel savage. He was fighting bitterly a people who were intent upon expelling the Irish from their lands and colonizing it with their own settlers. In the event, that's exactly what they did, and yet he is blamed for the ferocity of his resistance.

The turbulence of the Reformation plays a hand in this story, as Elizabeth skillfully runs Shane afoul of the Catholic Church, undermining him with his people. The Jesuits, both the Papal Nuncio and the (Anglo-Irish) Primate, collude with the English to ultimately bring him down. A subplot of the Irish (Gaelic) Primate and his martyrdom was found in a Latin history of the Irish Church, 'De Praesulibus Hiberniae' by the native Irish historian Seagháin O'Loinsigh, a book that has shockingly never been translated into English! Irish historical sources are obviously little accounted by our academics. The notorious Franciscan, Myler Magrath, the famous bard, Farleigh O'Gneeve, the Duke of Argyll, and Queen Mary Stuart, all have a part to play in these events, but perhaps none more than the spirited Scottish Countess, Katherine MacLean. She takes her fate in her hands, and moves events by her canny intrigues on O'Neill's behalf. Shane's struggle to protect his people deserves to take its rightful place in Irish History.

SHANE O'NEILL, 'the Grand Disturber'

Shane O'Neill

CHAPTER 1   1559 anno domini

Another dismal Atlantic sky, endless grey. Soft rain blearing the Donegal shore til you wouldn't know sea from foreland, as far as the eye can see. Not bloody far. But near on a half-mile up the coast road a stir of horses, aye. And very probably a carriage, looks to be, and tumbling along at a fierce clip. Surely bound for the castle, for they've passed the turn-off at the stiles. Something dire, hopefully, to shake up this dreary interminable day. Aye, a carriage, so it is.

Katherine turned from the window, and stepped softly over to the oaken trunk at the foot of the bed. As she lifted the heavy lid, a waft of heather and wool, and a deep drawn breath, soothed and settled her just a bit. Burrowing under a mound of tartan mantles and blankets, her fingers felt for the precious frock. Ah! It had been carefully rolled in fur with a wee sachet of dried roses, and as it unfurled across the bed, Katherine smiled to see it as fresh and blue as it was on that last night in Paris. Aye, as blue a gown as ever graced the Virgin Mary, but with a wee bit of decolletage! She hugged the dress across her bosom, when a sharp knock on the open door spun her around all the way from Paris.

"Beggin' yer pardon, M'Lady. The gateman says to tell you there's a coach and a few horsemen on their way in. Is the master in here?"

"He is not. My husband's at his books or his sleeping. Tell the auld man to bestir himself, Mórag, and then come back and lace me into this. Good girl."

"I will, so", she sighed, and off with her down the steep stair.

Katherine set about donning the velvet frock, and she confided in the cat, who was stretching and settling himself cozy in the open trunk. "My husband in here? When O'Donnell crosses *this* threshold again I'll away for Scotland! Oh, aye. It's little you care, Pishogue... And who do you suppose is coming to call? Well, whoever it is will not find the Countess of Argyll in rags. Even in this aul boghole."

O'Donnell was there before her when Katherine reached the courtyard, and he was clearly puzzled to see his wife bedecked in her blue finery on this bleary afternoon. "Who's this you've got coming, woman, that you never gave a warning word?" She raised her brows and shrugged by way of reply. Even in Ireland, surely, a countess would not receive callers dressed like a fishwife!

There was a commotion at the gates and a voice from above shouted through the misty rain, giving him his answer. "Tis O'Neill, Sir. With your daughter in tow." The gates parted and three horsemen bolted into the muddy yard. The first, sure enough, was Shane O'Neill, his black hair glistening in the rain. A tall brawny jack-the-lad with flashing eyes, he rode in the Irish fashion with no saddle, and wore a shaggy mantle over his tunic. Behind them rolled a huge coach with its team of white horses. It was loaded with trunks. Katherine stepped back out of the rain, away from the splattering mud, but still slightly forward of her husband and his attendants. Cullagh O'Donnell was a stout florid man with bushy white brows and doubtful watery eyes that belied the grim cunning behind them. He had achieved his position by imprisoning his father who still languished in a tower above. The carriage came to a halt before the arched threshold, and the driver and two of the horsemen dismounted to unpack it.

O'Neill swung his horse around the yard in a gallop, and reared up directly in front of them. "Here's your daughter back, O'Donnell!" He waved a leather pouch before him, and tipped it with a flourish, pouring a clatter of golden coins onto the stones. "And here's your bloody dowry as well!" He gave a sharp tug on the reins, and stepped

SHANE O'Neill, 'the Grand Disturber'

the horse a few paces back.

The door to the carriage swung open and Moya emerged in a flood of tears and rage. She was a clipped, brittle, stick of girl in a black frock with a starchy collar, haughty and prim, and if she was in a hot temper, the sight of her father's young wife did nothing to cool it. She took in the blue gown spilling lacy cleavage over its bodice, and a certain provocative light in Katherine's eyes; for although Kat was working fiercely to keep her face composed, her blue eyes shone with wicked glee at the spectacle before her. As O'Donnell tried to embrace his daughter, Moya pulled away and spat in Katherine's face. "Bloody cur-bitch!" She lunged at her wildly, and as her father pulled her back, she kicked mud onto the blue gown. A few of the servants came to his assistance and bundled her inside. Shane rode forward proffering a white kerchief.

"This is not a surrender," he said with a wink. "It's for you, Countess." Katherine accepted the linen with composure, wiped her face, and tossed her auburn hair. As O'Donnell edged forward, O'Neill straightened up tall. His eyes narrowed and cooled to a steely grey and he thundered, "All deals are off, O'Donnell. There's not a pope nor a parson could make that marriage stick. You only married her over to me so she could spy for Sussex. I want no agents of the queen at my board or in my bed!" His stallion danced under him as he steadied him back a pace or two. His shining grey eyes were not on O'Donnell now, but on the old man's young wife. She met his gaze, steady and cool, a thing she had avoided on past occasions, as unbefitting, perhaps, for a mother-in-law. O'Donnell stepped between them.

"A man who keeps to the law need have no fear of spies!"

"I keep to *Irish* law!" O'Neill glanced at the waiting carriage, and turned his horse. "I keep to Irish law. And I fear no-one!" Shane O'Neill reeled, and galloped off through the open gates followed by his men. The coach and six made a great circle in the yard and disappeared under the archway, thundering over the cobbles, and leaving the stacks of baggage on the stones in the empty silent courtyard. The rain had ceased.

SHANE O'Neill, 'the Grand Disturber'

Not far from the Great Lough in the wilds of Ulster, a raggedy grove of hazels bend and twist and scrape (and bough!) before an ancient towering oak as they have done since the War of the Trees. They were wintersticks now, wet and black against the luminous moss-green braes of Slieve Gallon. A noontide of winter sun, and a low glowering bank of purple Northern clouds set all in stark relief, with only the flitting of restless jackdaws to mar the stillness. It was they who noted the young intruder, and they threw up a clamour of cries. Their rasp and squawk seemed to give voice to the jagged hazels themselves as they pulled and strained at their roots. A lanky lad of perhaps fifteen summers loped and scrambled through the brush that seemed to shift and shiver at his footfall. His blue eyes puzzled a path before him from under a shaggy glib of tangled hair. He hugged a bundle to his breast, fending off the odd wayward branch as he drew ever closer to the giant oak.

The tree itself rose like a castle from a crag, sprouting massive limbs like turrets above. The exposed roots below would call to mind a mote filled with writhing serpents, where a tangle of limbs stretch and twist before disappearing into the mossy earth. It was avowed by at least one particular sage that all these were one time below ground until the receding waters of the Great Flood swept them free. This wise man never made mention, however, of a certain dark hollow beneath this oaken muddle, for he was a poet, and he took this secret root-strewn cavern as a retreat for the dark visitations of his muse. It is widely known that poets are like cats, and will nose their way into any cozy nook that will accommodate them.

The old conjurer would seal the cave's portal with a broad flagstone, not only to hide, but also to keep the precious darkness within, a vital consideration to any of the Bardic Orders. But if you put your ear to the stone you would hear, just this minute, a rush of liquid Gaelic, rippling in meters and staves in the berryblack hollow within.

SHANE O'Neill, 'the Grand Disturber'

And if you had the Gaelic, his visions would be called before your mind's eye. Darkness is the realm of the ear, and where colors and shapes are banished, the word is all, and phantoms and gods are free to come and go...

> "A bitter vision
> lights my eyes within
> within the black
> that lies about my weary limbs.
> She rides, She rides
> and flashes sorrowed eyes,
>   tossing tangled tresses in the wind.
> That brightest brow
> she raises now
> and breathless she approaches.
> The goddess Eire,
> grey eyed one.
> I hear her say
> He's on his way.
> He's bound to come.
> Her lover, her beloved one-"

A clatter of tumbling rocks halted vision and verse. The voice stumbled, fumbling again at the rumble of more tumbling rocks, as a narrow shaft of light pierced the dark dream. A white haired old wizard of a man lay naked, muttering to himself on a furry hide in a nest of straw. There was a fairly large flat stone resting on his belly. His eyes were scrunched tight in a fury of concentration.

"That brightest brow...now...she raises now...Aaagh! Seven red curses on you! You venomous little squint of a hellfire beam! You have my blessed poem shattered!" He took a deep breath and settled back to recollect his treasured staves. He'd learned long ago to gather his thoughts before turning them to the damnation of squabbling squirrels and badgering badgers that occasionally intruded on him here. He tried again to retrieve the verse. "I heard him say, he's...

SHANE O'Neill, 'the Grand Disturber'

...brightest brow...?"

With a scrape and a thump, winterlight flooded the poet's lair, silhouetting the awkward youth who stood peering into the cave. He inquired in the loudest whisper he could manage; "Are ye awake, Farleigh? Farleigh?" The steady murmur from the straw pallet grew louder at his intrusion, so he brought the full of his throat to bear as he insisted, "Hut! Farleigh! Are ye awake? Get up!!!"

As the old poet bolted upright, the stone popped off his belly onto the disheveled cot. "Up? Up, is it? You lanky wee slouch! A down without up to you! You're a six foot flea that's due for a scratching!"

The boy met this fury with a smile of relief. "Och, Farleigh, it's yourself! I thought you were in a rupture."

"*Rapture*, you lump!" The old man dipped a quill into a pot of ink and began scratching down the hopeless remnants of his poem.

"Aye, Farleigh, aye. That's what I'm after sayin'. You were lookin' fierce wild, the way I thought you were away with '*themselves*'. " The boy knew enough not to refer to the fairies directly, not so much for fear of their dark powers, as for wariness of the hot tempered poet before him."You're a terrible hard man to rouse."

"But you never fail to rouse me!" The poet blew on the scrap of parchment and turned his attention to the lad. "And who has set you on me this time, if I might ask?" He furrowed his bushy brows and nodded toward the bundle at Gilly's feet. The boy tossed it to him and explained.

"Shane O'Neill is waitin' below at the salmon leap. He sent me off after ye with these." He lowered his tone a notch. "Begod, that was a fair while ago, for I went astray in the wood."

Farleigh got to his feet and shook out the massive garment. "But this is my high mantle! What the devil is he at?" A sudden thought took his eyes from the cloak to the boy's face. "Is the aulfella dead then? The Earl?"

"Aye, sure isn't that what I'm tryin' to tell ye!" Gillie swung the pitcher 'round and splashed water into the basin beside Farleigh. A fierce roar parted the white mustache and beard.

"Well, damnit boy, out with it!"

SHANE O'Neill, 'the Grand Disturber'

"Shane's father has died, this week since, and now Shane is going to the stone, to be the new chieftain. The crowd is already gathered at Tullahogue. The hill's black with them. And Shane won't wait for the new moon, like the books say..." He grabbed a fresh-looking linen that hung from a twisty root tendril above, and tossed it to the naked old poet. "You'd best bestir yourself, Farleigh. I'm tellin' you, the whole commotion's in an uproar!"

Farleigh set about his ablutions, and lifting his dripping face from the basin, he inquired calmly, "When will he take the oath then?"

"At sundown today."

"What? This very evening?" Gilly's casual affirmative nod sent the old man into a flurry of motion and bellowing, and set splashes flying like a wet hound shaking off a cold swim. "Balor blink your evil eye! What hour is it now, boy?"

"Ach, it's only goin' the mid day," Gilly replied, in his most soothing tone. "Shane is waitin' on ye below, and they can't hardly start without himself."

"Aye, just so..." Farleigh's alarm gave way to excitement as he relished the boy's news. "And he'll not wait for the new moon! By Crom Dubh, he's the O'Neill right enough. The stars and the planets move too slow for him!" He began wrestling himself into various garments. "Well, what black wind has filled his sails? Tell me all, boy!"

"Sure I always do sometimes." Farleigh's eyes winced at this, but the boy hadn't a glimmer. "Ach, Farleigh, stories are galloping into Benburb nearly every hour. First it was news of auld earl, Conn O'Neill, dying up in Dublin. Then word come in that the new English queen will pick Conn's bastard for the new earl. Well that put the flame to the flax!"

The poet nodded thoughtfully. "Matthew is the baron right enough. But his unblessed birth will not go well for him under English law. Our law is blind to such matters, but the Saxons despise a bastard."

"Ach, go 'way, Farleigh! Isn't it King Henry's get is settin' on their throne beyond? Bejeweled and crowned? Sure, the Saxons bedizen a bastard!"

SHANE O'Neill, 'the Grand Disturber'

"By the blessed book, boy, there's a great deal of sense that never found its way into your head! Will ye listen?" The old man marveled at his own patience for it was second only to his great wisdom.

"Aye, surely, why wouldn't I listen?" A flutter of Farleigh's fingers told Gillie he was sitting on something, so he shifted over a bit and tossed a long pair of stockings into the anxious palm. The poet bent to his task and resumed the lesson.

"Elizabeth doesn't know she's a bastard. Her father was widowed every spring. He made sure of it. Buried every wife that didn't bear a son. Then he changed the religion of his entire realm just to make his daughter legitimate. It's enough to set a cat laughing. The English! There's a tribe for you! Savages -starched and buckled! Henry pulled his whole kingdom into Hell after him."

"But aren't you just after sayin'...?"

Farleigh jumped to his feet. "Will you whisht!" He wound a satin belt about his robe. "Give me a hand with this. Arrah, if your tongue was as idle as the rest of you, I'd have peace. Augh! Not so tight!" The pair of them pushed and pulled, and clasped and laced while Farleigh O'Gneeve explained the intricacies of Tudor politics as they appeared to the denizens of Gaelic Ulster. "Matthew's claim was English. When Shane was still a pup, his father was forced to take the English title 'earl' and forsake his proper title 'the O'Neill'. Henry Tudor gave him a chain of gold for his troubles. A collar for his neck, the like you'd set on a prize hound to bring him to heel. Young as he was Shane refused to stand beside his father. That's when Matthew was dubbed the Baron of Dungannon, heir to the Earl."

Gilly nodded wisely, and inquired sensibly, "Who was Baron before him?"

Farleigh was taken aback. "There was divil a baron!" he roared. This simple question, bringing into stark relief the enormity of the void to be filled with knowledge, and the complexity of the matters at hand, befuddled and bewildered the old sage. He froze in mid-breath, held a quizzical pause, and expelled the canceled thought as a vast sigh. "Ah, Gillie, you're too young to remember, but there was a time... There was a time in this place, when there was talk of neither baron

SHANE O'Neill, 'the Grand Disturber'

nor earl...when only a strange traveler that you might hear discoursing on a Fair Day, would even know the *name* of the king of England. At the hearth, and in the field and forest, there was only news of the O'Neill."

Another field of inquiry had opened itself to Gillie who now had an inexhaustible fund of questions to pose. "But Farleigh-"

The poet raised a silencing palm before him. "Hold yer prate!" He took a long draught from a dusty bottle of wine, turned and pointed the bottle at his young messenger. "This is a day of the world, boy! Shane O'Neill steps into his rights this night. Keep your ears cocked, your eyes keen, and your jaw still, and you will have a story for your old age. One that will draw you a welcome at any fire, and a draught at any pot." With that, he set himself to gathering up the mysterious utensils and implements that were scattered around the cot.

Gillie kept a watchful eye on the wily old scholar while he filched a hearty slug of his wine. "Aye, Farleigh, just so. It's a sweet sound a silent mouth makes. And, sure, mine'll be the sweetest you never heard in your life".

"Whisht!! I heard something!" Farleigh brandished an upraised palm again and cocked an ear for listening, but the boy's mind, if it could be said, was elsewhere.

"I'll be as quiet as an egg in the thatch. People will be wonderin' where all the quiet is comin' from, and I'll not even open my mouth to tell them it's me. Ach, just wait til ye hear!" There was a fierce tug at the back of his neck. The old poet had him by the scruff.

"One more chirp, and I'll split you!" The briefest silence ensued, broken by the boisterous whinny of a horse, followed by a deep and unmistakable voice.

"Farleigh! Farleigh, Are you down there?"

"Here he is, in on us now!" Farleigh drew up a mighty breath and called out toward the cave's bright threshold. "Shane?!" He loosed his grip on the boys collar and nodded. "Bundle up those things." As he went to make his way out, that portal of light was eclipsed by the crouching figure of Shane O'Neill stepping in out of the brightness. His eyes adjusted, moving quickly through every stage, from squint to

SHANE O'Neill, 'the Grand Disturber'

wide eyed wonder as they darted about the cave. For as long as he'd known of his old friend's secret lair in the forest, he'd never had occasion to see it. He clasped Farleigh in a hearty embrace, and pulling back suddenly with mischief in his eyes, he chided him.

"For God's sake, look at the state of you! Festering down here in an auld slaghole. A filthy aul rat's nest." And with a wink to Gillie, "Were you robbed?"

The expected diatribe did not follow. Only three simple statements delivered with a quiet imperious finality. "There is no filth here -only dirt. *Filth* is to be found in cities. We are in the womb of a goddess." He lifted his poets' mantle from the crook of hanging root. "Give me help into these colours, Gillie." He turned and offered the dusty wine bottle to his guest. "Oh, you're a fine one, Shane O'Neill! Taking the oath on a waning moon! I suppose you've come seeking my counsel so you can do the contrary, is it?" Shane gave a laugh and took a swig of the French wine. He settled himself on a stump.

"You picked some time to scarper off to your fairy tree. One crucial conundrum after another, and not one couplet of your sage advice... He's told you about the father, I suppose." Farleigh nodded his head to one side and said in a half whisper,"I'm sorry, boy.""I'm not." His tone was light and energetic. "Not sorry, not glad. Just scrambling to pick up the pieces he left. O'Hagan and his lads brought him back to lie in Armagh churchyard. They tell that Sussex met them in Dublin, and he said that the Baron of Dungannon is to be made Earl. Matthew will not come North now without an army behind him. The divil take their English titles. I'll be the O'Neill from tonight. All of Tyrone will be in my hands before the Baron leaves Dublin."

"It's bold as bedamned!" Farleigh's eyes danced with excitement, then dimmed ever so slightly with a shadow of caution. "You'll have all the tributes? From all the chieftains?"

"Aye, as far as the Foyle. All except O'Donnell and those under him."

The old man shook his grey head and arched a brow. "Oh ho! You'll never get *him* to come in without a fight. And you after sending his daughter back to him? What way *is* the girl? Any news since?"

SHANE O'Neill, 'the Grand Disturber'

Shane O'Neill shrugged his massive shoulders and knocked back the last sup of wine. The all but forgotten Gillie piped up.

"There's a story blowin' round these hills that she's away in the abbey at Clogher... They say some weakness has befallen her." A short spell of silence and a furtive exchange of glances followed, while Farleigh worked up a good steam. He had already butted heads with some local clergy over the matter. He spluttered out a furious defense to the unspoken reproach.

"O'Donnell's as crooked as a ram's horn! He had her settled in on you so she could spy for the English! And vex you from bed to board!"

"Aye, that's so, right enough." Shane nodded, adding, "It was a battle from the first day... or maybe *night*! Moya was ever a delicate girl and you know I'm an awful eejit for the whiskey and the hooring."

"Was there ever a proper hero that wasn't?" You can't wed a chieftain and marry a monk! And if it's in the Clogher abbey with her now, it's where she should have started and not finished. Aye, the black veil for her, and not the white! Gillie, what the devil are you gaping at?" The poor lad was wishing he'd never tossed a word in. "My shoes, Gillie!" The boy was relieved to amble off after the brogues, and Farleigh lit upon a less weighty topic. If he was a sage, he was also a poet, and scarcely above a bit of gossip. "And what of Cullagh O'Donnell's *own* fair bride? She's scarcely older to Moya herself. He didn't take a soft-spun comforter to his bed, if the talk of the women is true."

Shane's eyes shone, and a broad warm smile brightened his whole countenance. He nodded his head to one side, winked, and rubbed his hands together. "Aye, my wee Scottish mother-by-law, with the bonny white bosom. I'd like to take comfort *there*!" He gave a sharp laugh. "Mind you, so would O'Donnell! I have it from his daughter that soft spun, or hard bound, Katherine MacLean is a stranger to his bed."

In an instant Farleigh's eyes waxed full as a harvest moon. "She's never! Go on away with yourself!"

Gillie was back with the old man's shoes. He presented them, and offered his own fair assessment of the matter. "Ach, why wouldn't she be? Sure, what wee girl would want to bump skins with a rickety aul

SHANE O'Neill, 'the Grand Disturber'

grey-hair? Cullagh O'Donnell must be drawing on his three score years!" The fact that this was at least a dozen years younger than Farleigh had been left out of his calculations, but became alarmingly clear as he saw a red fury scorching the old man's face. Gillie started to smile, and when he turned to Shane, they both fell about in a roar of laughter. When he turned back to Farleigh, he was laughing too, but still he clipped the boy with a goodly splash from the basin, shouting, "I got ye, ye little rip!"

Gillie dried his face with his long sleeve, still laughing, and put his oar in once more, trying to steer them back to the matter of the moment.

"Is she as handsome as they tell? The Countess of Argyle?" The Poet was occupied now, tugging one of his shoes on, and the thought of his impending duties cast a rather urgent light on things, so he called him up short and sharp.

"Gillie, gather up those scrolls and raven quills, you spindly little squawk! And stop your yammering. We have a journey to make, and we'll make it faster without your guff." The lad sighed, and looked to Shane for sympathy.

"Sure, it was only a wee question, and I can't listen any quicker than ye can talk." Shane O'Neill's thoughts were still in Donegal.

"The countess? Aye, she's a beauty, right enough. And I'd say she'd be game enough if Cullagh was a rebel. But since he turned for the queen, he can't get the leg over. I'd almost pity the aul bastard. She's a Scot from the isles, and a red haired one. Moya says that when O'Donnell speaks English to her, Katherine spits in his eye!"

"Ah, the Scots are sound. Fierce enough," Farleigh replied absently as he gave a last lookabout. Satisfied, he clutched his leathern satchel, and issued the marching orders. "Are you right? Come away now, Gillie, we're off." He lifted his cloak, and stooped through the cave's narrow portal. The seven colors of Farleigh's high mantle, traditional for a bard, made a vivid splash against the wintry brown oak as the sun shed its luster over them. The bearded bard in his ceremonial splendour would call to mind an Arabian potentate in the Holy Lands. He filled his lungs with the freshness about him. "Ah, well," he said,

SHANE O'Neill, 'the Grand Disturber'

"Glory be for the mild day that's in it!"

Farleigh took little notice of the two great wolfhounds that lay like bristly grey sphinxes on either side of the dark hollow behind him. Flann and Scohaun were as big as ponies, regal in repose and fierce in a fray, and were always to be found standing sentry for Shane. As he emerged now, they bounded forth, wagging their tails gleefully. Farleigh looked about him in puzzlement. A spirited whinny from O'Neill's dark stallion recalled for him where he'd left his horse. Both were tethered to a wayward root, quietly munching the lush wintergrass around the mossy side of the great oak.

Shane's majestic stallion was several hands taller than his own. 'Mac an Iolair' he called it, meaning 'son of the eagle' and it was reputed to be the fastest steed in Ireland. Farleigh squinted up at the sky. "I'll have to raise a right sweat on the mare if we're ever to beat the sun to rest."

Shane threw his leg over the stallion and settled himself. He cast his eye across the scraggly grove to the lush braes, and steep Slieve Gallon towering over them. 'Tirowen among the bushes' it was called, and it would all be in his keeping after tonight. "We've lashings of time," he said, "but this is rough country yet."

"It is." Farleigh followed his gaze. "May the Powers preserve it. It is." He stepped his horse a few paces back where he could see Gilly sealing the cave, covering the flagstone with brush. He turned again to Shane. "Those mighty oak groves near the walls of Dundalk have been felled. It would bring tears to a stone, so it would."

O'Neill's eyes narrowed, piercing some far off phantom in the hills. There was a sharp edge on his voice as he spoke. "Aye, the forests of Ireland carted off to England to build their ships and roove their cathedrals. They mean to flush us out! Like a fox from his lair. O'Moore's country is wasted. O'Dempsey's, and all up to O'Reilly's country has been shorn, to the very edge of Ulster. Well, don't you fear, aul man. The Saxon's axe will never sound in Tirowen while I have a breath."

Farleigh squinted up at the sun. "Signs on it, you've a fine day for the rites! The snows have all vanished for you. More like March than

SHANE O'Neill, 'the Grand Disturber'

January!"

Gillie approached, slinging a bag over his shoulder, and Farleigh extended a hand down to help him up. "Up with ye, Gillie!" he said, and with one good yank, the lanky lad took his place behind the poet. Shane trotted out at an easy pace, the wolfhounds leaping and loping alongside. The poet turned his face back to Gillie. A great light shone in his wild ancient blue eyes, as he confided, "You've never seen an inauguration, boy. Ah, well! There will be a new day before there is a night!" He put his heels to the flanks, and off they went after O'Neill.

The journey was undemanding, with the day holding fine. No obstacles but the Ballinderry, and a fine shallow ford a little ways upstream made for an easy crossing. The ford was paved below with stones; what the English in Dublin referred to sneeringly as 'an Irish bridge'. As they drew nearer their destination, they passed more and more wayfarers on the roads, and all facing for Tullahogue. These were not roads in the strictest sense, but byways, rough and gutted, that were as old as the hills around them.

Although the chapel bell in Derryloran had pealed only three, the winter sun was well into the West when they approached, finally, the village of Tullahogue. The street was thronged with visitors dodging the waggoners and draymen, ponies and traps, and even carriages. Farleigh O'Gneeve's high mantle of brightest motley announced their arrival even from afar, and when Shane O'Neill was spotted, the merry crowds parted to cheer them through.

Makeshift public houses had been contrived in any sizable shelter fronting the street, and the revelers spilled out through the doors to join the commotion. They passed the wee hall where only last night the chieftains of all the septs of ClanFergus had cast their ballots to choose the O'Neill. The bright banners and standards lent an air of grandeur to the shabby structure, for it had weathered nearly forty years since Shane's father's inauguration.   Like Brigadoon, the

SHANE O'Neill, 'the Grand Disturber'

sleepy little village would sprung to life every half century or so, to host again the great inaugural fair with flutes and harps and pipes blazing. Shane's stallion pranced along, high stepping his way up the steep road as he nodded and smiled to all, his right hand held aloft in a grand proud gesture. Even at this time he was known to the people as 'Seagháin an Díomáis', Shane the Proud. With his arrival, it was clear that the ceremony was imminent, so the village emptied in a boisterous throng, as the people fell in behind Shane and Farleigh for the last mile or so up to the fabled Hill of Kings.

n O'Hagan's rath on the mossy summit, there was a great flurry of trifling last details, and a great gabble of worry, as the sun sank lower and lower in the west with no sign of Shane O'Neill. All the clans and septs of Tirowen were gathered and camped all about the western slope of the hill below the stone. They too were growing restless as each new rumour about the delay rippled across the hillside.

The gently sloping hill was covered with rough brush, mostly whinbushes, except in the west, where these had been cut away in straight banks to accommodate the gathering. Above them, an imposing crude stone chair, the 'Stone of Kings', faced down the setting sun, as it had done for over half a millennium. Behind it stood a row of tall posts, each crowned with a stag's antlers, bearing the colorful standards of the clans below. Off to the side, a phalanx of brown-robed Franciscan monks from the nearby friary of Brantry filled rows of benches. The rath itself was a circular rampart of earth and stone at the crown of the hilltop, and at its rim, a ring of mighty beech and fir trees stood sentinel. Within the earthen walls were several fine thatched buildings, one of them two stories tall, with lead-glass windows, the home of the O'Hagan.

The O'Hagans were a legal sept, and its chieftain always held the office of Chief Brehon, presiding over the highest court of Brehon Law. He, along with the O'Mallon and the O'Kane had, since time

SHANE O'Neill, 'the Grand Disturber'

immemorial, officiated in the investiture of each new O'Neill. The O'Mallons were the keepers of St. Patrick's bell in its bejeweled shrine of gold, a treasure put in their keeping by St. Columbkill a thousand years before. The bell had untold dark powers, and the O'Neill could not be created without its striking. O'Kane provided a great force of warriors to the O'Neill, and he was keeper of a golden sandal that sealed the oath.

When word reached the assemblage that it was Shane O'Neill leading the mighty throng that was coming up from the village, a great cheer went up. On hearing it, O'Hagan and the other chieftains emerged from the rath to take their places. Firstly came the chiefs of Clan Fergus; the Donnellys, Devlins, Corrs, Quinns, and Mallons. They shared with O'Neill a common ancestor and were entitled to elect the chieftain. The other clans under O'Neill's aegis followed. They were O'Hanlons, MacMahons, O'Kanes, McCartans, McGuinness, Maguires, McCanns, McCaghwells, O'Gormleys and, by Brehon law, the clearly absent O'Donnells. These clans were vast and burgeoning, and some could put on the field two or three hundred young warriors.

The sight of these underlords brought forth another roar from the crowd. The bearded chieftains stood patiently, each beneath his own crest of arms. O'Hagan, a tall dignified man, whose shaggy hair was only lately more grey than gold, sighed as he looked out over the multitude. "It's little any of us thought that we'd be gathering at the stone again. But here we stand." Friar Magrath gave him a cautious glance. Art O'Hagan ventured more. "When Conn O'Neill took the earldom, he swore to King Henry that he would abolish the chieftainry. I reckon these English will be up here soon with leadshot" The priest shook his head.

"Will there never be peace, Art O'Hagan?" The judge considered the question briefly.

"Only the *eternal* kind, I'm afeard. But there will be plenty of that, and plenty gone to it before we see their backs! This English queen will soon proscribe the two of us. I with my Brehon Law, and you with your Roman Mass. We'll be a queer pair of outlaws then."

SHANE O'Neill, 'the Grand Disturber'

"Brehon Law is still the legal law in Ulster." The priest replied tersely; an attempt, perhaps, to dispel such gloomy prospects.

"But for how long?" O'Hagan challenged. "They've added two new counties to the Pale, and there's talk of nine more. With English magistrates and sheriffs. The Brehon judges *there* only hear cattle raids and stick fights. A matter of time..." He crooked his head to one side, with a warning nod to the priest. "You'll soon find yourself idle, Father Magrath, if this Elizabeth Tudor keeps the throne beyond." The friar's green eyes flashed in a sly grin.

"She'll need a parcel of miracles to last as long as Lady Jane. And we have Shane O'Neill!"

"Time tells a tale best..." Art O'Hagan wished fervently that he could rest his mind on such comforting ballyhoo. Magrath, he knew, was hardly impartial. He had been reared by the Donnellys, with Shane as a foster-brother, and being a Franciscan, he was given to blind faith. The other chieftains had 'left their posts,' what with Shane still so far down the hill, and they had drifted in on the contending pair. They weighed in now, agreeing with Myler. Fergus O'Kane, a huge mountainy fellow, clapped a paw on the cleric's broad back. "True for you, Friar, and well spoke too!" Warming to this murmur of approval, Myler pressed on.

"Am'nt I telling you! Elizabeth will lose Ireland like her sister lost France. We've only to hold fast. The good Lord of Creation has risen up Shane O'Neill amongst us this very day. Shane will stand and Ireland withstand." The judge stood his crumbling ground.

"Sure, we're all behind him! I'm only saying. O'Neill is the strongest man in Ireland. But the world and his mother know he is rash and proud, and if he fails...if he fails, it could well hasten our ruin!" He looked from face to face for a response, but saw that they were all gazing past him in a state of wonderment. Another late arrival, the low-sized burly chief of the O'Quinns was approaching. He was festooned in ruffs and galligaskins, and made a queer sight in his English courtly attire. He was a jovial little fellow in his late years, and he addressed the friar with a grin. "I'm not interrupting a confession here, sure I'm not! The judge would keep you all day, he's that

SHANE O'Neill, 'the Grand Disturber'

wicked!"

"It's never!" the priest exclaimed. "Aul Brian O'Quinn, the O'Quinn! What are ye got up for?"

The O'Kane cocked his head back, arched his shaggy brows, and peered accusingly at the old man in his English doublet and hose. "I wonder how much *news* it takes to buy a rig-out like that up in Dublin... Or is this the latest fashion from the bogs of Lissan?" The others laughed, although they knew he was in deadly earnest, and O'Quinn looked puzzled. Father Magrath patted him on the shoulder and smiled.

"In truth, Brian," he said, "you want to be mad coming to the O'Neill's rites got up like that! Shane is sworn against all English ways." The old fellow stretched out his short arms and examined his garments from his wrists to his ankles. He shook his grey head and shrugged.

"How was I to know they were English?" A mighty laugh was shared from smile to smile, and O'Quinn's voice rose over it. "It was Shane's own father gave them to me not four years ago. I figured ye'd all be wearing them!" When another laugh subsided, he continued. "Ach, I can't keep tally these times. God be with the old days when it was only ourselves alone that was in it. A man knew what way to dress and to ride and to talk. I was above with the O'Donnell this while past, and he ups and starts yammering away to a messenger in some class of gibberish. "What's that?" says I. 'Tis the English,' says he. 'I have business,' he says, 'that carries me to Dublin, so I have need of it. Where have ye been, O'Quinn?' says he, 'Sure, everyone has it but the *hillfolk!*' Hillfolk!!!" No laughter this time, but an indignant round of harrumphs, with O'Kane's voice loudest.

"The low scoundrel! Hillfolk!"

A cheer from below turned their thoughts to the business at hand. Shane and Farleigh had dismounted and were making their way through the crowd, delaying here and there to shake a hand or return a blessing.

O'Quinn squinted into the low sun and pointed down the hill. "Who's that man talking with Farleigh the poet? The dark man."

SHANE O'Neill, 'the Grand Disturber'

"A dark man?" The priest raised a hand to shade his eyes. "It might be Satan. That pompous aul pagan has been out to his fairy tree this long while. The Dear knows what demons he's conjured up out of his black reveries." Fergus O'Kane, in some alarm, chided the cleric.

"Ach, friar! Will ye give over! I don't hold with blackmouthing a poet. There's bad luck in it!"

"Glory be to God, the aul rhymer can't hear us!" The good friar was getting the wind up.

O'Kane leaned in to the priest's ear and confided, "Aye, just so. Yet they say he listens til the wind."

"It's his own wind he listens to!" Myler Magrath was always nettled by the superstitions and pishogues of the unlettered. The priest guarded his turf jealously as the only ordained custodian of mystical powers. "I don't care *in* it or *out* of it if he talks to the squirrels! He's a randy aul heathen. And he puts Shane up to acting the horny ram, and drinking himself crawsick."

"I suppose he tells the tide to flow!" O'Kane was still fixed intently upon Farleigh and the stranger. "It is! That's Black Hugh O'Donnell, so it is! Looking for all the world like a man with no home to go to." The O'Quinn finally had his answer.

"Aul Cullagh's young brother, is it? Has he brought the tribute?"

"There will be divil-all tribute from O'Donnell." O'Kane was up to them all, for he was as foxy as anything in the deep dark woods. "This Black Hugh is a renegade. He's putting in with Shane to help him against the Baron. His brother's likely got wind of his capers. I'd say Black Hugh will *need* more help than he'll give! Shane will regret making so free with him." O'Quinn was still confused.

"O'Donnell refuses to render up? What makes him so bold?"

"Do you not know of the wee letters?" O'Kane looked at him as if he had three heads, and then his eyes took on a sly glint. "Shane sent Cullagh O'Donnell a wee letter that read 'Send me the tribute. Or if you don't-' with just a dash, d'ye see? So O'Donnell sends the messenger back with his own letter. 'I don't *owe* you tribute. And if I *did*-' O'Kane clapped the little fellow on the back and they both laughed long and hearty. "Aye, that's a good'n, so it is. 'and if I did!"

SHANE O'Neill, 'the Grand Disturber'

The skirling blast of a piper put a quick stop to a whole hillside of colloguing and blather. At the sound of his frets and drones all was settled, and Shane and Farleigh quickly made their way up past the stone to confer with the O'Hagan. Farleigh was presented with a long scroll. Just as on the last occasion some forty years earlier, it fell upon *him* to read the long genealogy of O'Neill, so crucial to the proceedings.

Shane removed his tunic and his linen shirt, and his leather boots, and was thankful for the mild evening. He wore now only the long leather breeks, with a shaggy sporran off to one side, in a manner that would raise a frown (or a dirk!) had he been in Scotland. He refused a scroll from O'Hagan, and assured him and Farleigh that he had mastered his short speeches. They would begin by invoking the three goddesses of Ireland, in spite of the long-standing objections of the Franciscans, for this was the oldest part of the ceremony. As the piper's last note faded away, Art O'Hagan stepped forward and called for the rites to commence. "The sun is setting. This is the time!"

Indeed, the sun was nearly at the horizon, and cast a golden glow on the crest of the hill. The crowd below was in absolute stillness. Farleigh O'Gneeve winked at O'Hagan and said brightly, "We'll commence, so, and let the sun to have its rest." He moved into place to the right of the Chair of Kings, resplendent in his colors. Assuming now the ancient druidic duties that had passed long ago to the Bard, he called out solemnly, "There are three women who slept cold last night! Éire, Fódhla, and Banva! Who will come to the Women of the Hill?" He swept his arm to the left, and cast his eyes on the Judge.

O'Hagan took a pace forward and intoned, "In the name of all the septs of Clanfergus, freemen all, who have chosen by open vote, from all those within the first degree of bloodline, I call forth Shane O'Neill to stand before the stone..." To a roar of cheers, Shane moved swiftly down to the Chair of Kings, and stood shirtless and shining before it. His hounds, Flann and Scohaun, followed him warily and settled themselves on either side of the stone. When the din subsided, Farleigh spoke again.

SHANE O'Neill, 'the Grand Disturber'

> "I speak for Eire, Woman of Earth.
> Her swollen paps have covered the plains of Conn
> with rivers of bounty
> to suckle her brood.
> Her children have nestled in this fastness
> Since ever the sun was lit.
> Since ever the stars burned in the Darkness
> The fires of her people have blazed in answer.
> Last night Eire stirred the ashes and found no fire.
> What is your pledge?"

Farleigh turned to the young man on the stone. Shane folded his bare arms and replied. "I pledge her my *loins*!" A boisterous roar from the crowd followed. Few of them had witnessed the rite before, and it had a curious power still, after centuries of use. Farleigh continued.

> "I speak for Fodhla, Woman of the Word.
> Over the blood red lips of Fodhla
> Came forth every word.
> Words
> To breathe a soul into a rock or field,
> Word upon word
> To fix forever the dominion of the Gael
> Over all she saw.
> Name upon whispered name,
> The kingdoms of the Earth and Air
> Fell before the powers of Fodhla,
> And gave forth Learning and Poetry.
> This morning Fodhla woke to stillness.
> What is your pledge?"

He turned again to Shane. In full awareness now of the spell being cast, Shane reveled in it. He unfolded his strong arms and shifted his weight. He spoke slowly, deliberately, a deep resounding promise. "I pledge her my *tongue*!" Again the spectators roared their approval, for those women's names in the Irish tongue signified Ireland itself in her three guises; physical, cultural, and militant. These were not abstractions for scholars, but conversational references, part of the fabric of life. As the crowd settled once again, Farleigh invoked the third of the goddesses.

> "I speak for Banva, Woman of Valor.
> Banva of the bloodrush and battle fury.
> Since the coming of the stranger
> The men of Banva have defended her
> With hero feats and bloodshower.
> Still came the English.
> On every seventh wave they came,
> Until the men of Ireland
> Put aside their hardness
> For the soft word and the soft deed.
> This day Banva tried to stir
> And could not move.
> She was bound in a golden chain.
> What is your pledge?"

Farleigh turned again to the chair, but was astonished at what he saw. Shane pulled from the sporran a golden chain, similar to that of an English earl. He held it aloft and stretched it with sudden jerk. "I pledge her my *arms*!!" he roared, and made a great, protracted show of pulling it asunder. This theatrical impulse worked to great effect, as the throngs below thundered their approval. Sensing the crowd's fervor, the two hounds bayed at his side. When the chain finally broke Farleigh sighed with relief, shaking his old head. Shane spoke again. "The three Women of the Hill will sleep warm *this night*, for I ...am... Shane O'Neill..."

Farleigh unraveled the scroll before him, waited for a reasonable silence, and began to intone the litany of Shane's progenitors. "...son of Conn Bacach O'Neill, son of Conn Mór, son of Henraí, son of Owen,

SHANE O'Neill, 'the Grand Disturber'

son of Niall óg, son of Niall Mór, son of Hugh Mór, son of Dónal, son of Brian king of Ulster and of all the Irish of Ireland, son of Neill the Red, son of Hugh...." He stepped off to the side, lowering his tone, as he continued reading the illustrious list.

Shane stepped down as several attendants came forward, two lovely young women in white frocks. One carried a silver bowl, and the other, a white linen. Shane dipped his right hand in the bowl and held it forward as the girl dried it. This part of the ritual seemed to mirror the lavabo of the Roman Mass. Two other maidens brought forth a woolen mantle adorned with a shaggy fur collar and slipped it over his shoulders. As they moved off, the O'Hagan spoke. "Shane O'Neill, let you take your place upon the Stone of Kings." Shane stepped up onto the stone chair to further applause. There was an ancient hollow footprint on its seat that perfectly encompassed his right foot. At this point, the O'Hagan approached with a white wand, extending it to Shane as he spoke the timeless words.

"From the right hand of the O'Hagan, Chief Brehon Judge of Tirowen, to the right hand of the O'Neill; a whiteness without blemish, a straightness without twisting, and a firmness without bending." Shane accepted the wand in his cleansed right hand, and held it high before the assemblage.

"Upon this hazel rod, I swear to uphold and preserve the Brehon Law, and to deliver it to my successor's hand as white, as firm, and as straight as it stands this day."

Art O'Hagan stepped back, and the Franciscan monks rose as one from their benches. They commenced to sing 'Deus Meus' with its verses in Irish and Latin. This sent a wave down the hill as the assemblage descended onto one knee. From out of the rath came forth a small stately procession of the ecclesiastical dignitaries and their anointed, to put the seal of God on the proceedings. Firstly came the Archbishop of Derry, whose See encompassed the Northern lands of Tirowen, followed by his lay Archdeacon O'Mulholland. Nextly came the Dean of Armagh, Terence Donnelly. He was acting in place of the Bishop Primate of Armagh, as that seat had been vacant since the death of the previous Bishop. After him came the bearers of the sacred relic, the Bell of St. Patrick. In stately procession 'the turbulent O'Mallons in their leather coats' came forth. Leading them was a hooded Franciscan, one of their number, swinging a golden censor of smoking incense that lingered in a hazy cloud about their feet. Over their heads, they carried aloft a purple pall, and on it, glistening in the fiery light of the setting sun, the magnificent bellshrine of the Bell of the Testament.

The relic had been left in their keeping by St. Columkill for nearly a millennium. The golden bejeweled bellshrine was brought forward and presented for the crowd's admiration. When the friars reached the 'Amen' of their plainsong, the pall was lowered onto small table. Cahir Mór, the tall white haired chief of the O'Mallons, archdeacon and steward of the Church's lands, stepped forward and opened the shrine. The precious bell that had been his charge for life, mostly for the administering of oaths. Indeed, he had rung it on this hilltop thirty-six years ago for Conn O'Neill. The iron bell stood nearly eight inches in height and was both round and square like a cowbell. The old chieftain held it aloft to Shane's reach where he stood on the stone. The younger man, still holding the hazel rod to his heart with his left hand, placed his right hand upon the sacred bell. The O'Mallon spoke the oath. "Upon St. Patrick's holy Bell of the Testament, do you Shane O'Neill, swear to preserve and defend the Holy Mother Church, her monasteries and chapels from defilement, her schools and sacred books from the torches of the heretic?"

"I do so swear." The bell felt rough and cold under Shane's fingers, but even accounting for the old man's unsteady hand, he marveled that it seemed to throb with a quavering pulse. The sun was sinking now and reached an incandescence that burnished all in golden red. The chieftain turned and stepped forward now.

"From this day forth, Shane is The O'Neill, with all rights of tribute, and all duties attending. Let the four winds carry forth our tidings!" He rang the bell thrice in each direction. The tolling of the bell sent a fluttering wave down the hill as the assemblage blessed themselves. The relic was restored to its shrine, and the old chieftain took his place among the rest.

SHANE O'Neill, 'the Grand Disturber'

The Dean of Armagh, Turlagh O'Donnelly, now came forward in his splendid canonical robes. He blessed the new O'Neill, 'in nomini Patri, et fili, et spiritu sancti', and took up the Old Testement to read the traditional passage for the investiture. Somewhere back in the mists of time, the Irish had decided that they were the lost tribe of Israel, and so they had a special affection for the Old Book and its strange rites. Now Fergus O'Kane approached with the sandal of Gold and knelt before the stone. Shane sat on the stone chair, stretching out his right foot and O'Kane slipped the bright vesture onto it, as Dean O'Donnelly solemnly read the text. "Ruth IV vs.7 'Now this was the manner in former time in Israel concerning change for to confirm all things; a man plucked off his shoe and cast it to his neighbor. And this was a testimony in Israel.' From Psalm sixty, 'Moab is my washpot; over Edom will I cast out my shoe: Philistia, triumph thou because of me!"

Shane gave his short oath; "By hand and foot, brave deed and brave standing, I swear to uphold our rights and freedoms." He now removed the sandal and held it aloft. "I cast forth the golden sandal!" With that, he threw it far out over the throng who rose as one from their kneeling. Some one of them caught it, and a huge cheer went up. Fergus gave his sword to Shane, and stepping back, struck up the familiar chant, quickly embraced by all. "O'Neill to victory! O'Neill abu!"

The newly invested chieftain raised his sword, and the fiery cheers soon settled to a hush. Into the charged golden evening he poured his words. "We are gathered on this height, in defiance of a foreign queen and her armies. They would tell us that we are illegal in our laws; that our nobility is base. That the father has knelt, and so the son cannot stand. *But we are off our knees!*" Now a great clamour rose again from the crowds before him. "I do not ask war. I claim only my rights. -But I will defend them with blood and spirit! I am...The O'Neill!"

Farleigh the poet, still reading the geneology, stepped out just below Shane, his pitch rising to command the field and the last flaming moments of light. "...son of Niall, son of Feniusa Farsa King of Scythia, son of Baath, son of Magog, son of Japhet, son of Noah, son

SHANE O'Neill, 'the Grand Disturber'

of Lamech, son of Methuselah, son of Enoch, son of Mahalaheel, son of Cainan, son of Enos, son of Seth, son of ADAM, WHO WAS SON OF GOD!"

CHAPTER 2

"We cannot read us these letters, Cecil. It is night at noon in this chamber!" In the oaken Presence Chamber of her castle at Greenwich, the young queen shuffled and squinted through the muddle of state papers before her. Her secretary peered over his shoulder at a drowsy footman, and set him to task.

"Draw back the arras!" Cold winterlight flooded the room and cast the long shadow of William Cecil across her desk. "The casements are draughty today, your Majesty. There are great winds without."

"There have been great winds within! All the morning! Who have we now?" Elizabeth's tone was pointed and familiar, to a trusted older confidant.

"Sussex, Your Majesty. Argyle is not yet arrived."

"Very well," she sighed. Her keen eyes darted about the papers that lay before her, and lit upon the dossier in question. Thomas Radcliff, Lord Sussex was ushered quietly into her presence, while she perused his report. Employing one of Cecil's expedient devices, she read only the last page. On finishing, she raised her eyes. "Lord Sussex, is our retinue in Ireland grown so small in number that you must deliver your own dispatches? We shall read this anon when our time affords us. Since you are come, you may speak."

Sussex was a tall man, quite thin really under his ample doublet of Italian brocade. His ever-arched brows and solemn dark eyes,

SHANE O'Neill, 'the Grand Disturber'

presided over sharp features that gave him a prickly aspect; his long sharp nose and his barbed mustaches, even to the tapered goat's beard on the end of his pointy chin. To add to all this, he now laboured at a mirthless smile, contrived to convey the vigorous self-assurance of a bearer of good tidings. "Majesty, the rebellions in Ireland have been acalmed. In those two new counties that were lately added to the Pale, the lands forfeited by the wild Irish have been planted with English subjects, and will henceforth accrue rents and annuities for the Crown. The rebels are reduced so that even MacCarthy Mór, that was once warlike and wild, has pledged to uphold the crown, and to extirpate rebels in that country. He endeavors to learn the English tongue, and bids me even request an English wife for him to wed!"

Elizabeth nodded slowly. She added brightly, "We are glad to hear it. Is it his suit that brings you to my chamber?"

"Majesty?" His features disarranged themselves in perplexity.

"Do you come a wooing for MacCarthy Mór? Her bright voice had acquired the keen edge of impatience.

"A wooing?" He probed doubtfully.

"God's Wounds, man! What is your suit?" There needs no favorable report of your service in our commission to entertain this court." She flourished his thick dossier before him. "If that realm of Ireland be in such goodly state of order and governance, wherefore have you made request of additional troops and arms? It is clear...the conquest *limpeth*!" In an instant her countenance and her voice softened and warmed. "Come, good Thomas. To matter."

"John O'Neill has gone to the stone in Ulster, and taken in barbaric fashion, the proscribed Irish title of 'the O'Neill." The queen considered briefly and responded lightly.

"He might just as well have taken the title of Caeser to sooth his vanity. An empty honour of past days." She looked to Cecil for assurance but he urged caution.

"Indeed, in that land of Ulster, to be the O'Neill is a name more in price than Caeser. The powers and rights attached to it in former times far surpass those attaining to an earl. There is grave danger in this." Emboldened, Sussex pressed on.

SHANE O'Neill, 'the Grand Disturber'

"There is more. He makes claim to succeed his father the Earl of Tyrone, who is now lately deceased. Certain of his followers did, this two days past, murder the rightful heir, Matthew the Baron of Dungannon, who was entitled by your father King Henry to succeed the earl. John O'Neill now holds by force the country of Tyrone, and in all his deeds shows himself a rebel, although by pretences and words he seeks to cover for winning time." As Elizabeth drew a breath to speak, Sussex surged ahead, resonant and fervid. "My suit is this, Majesty...monies to levy additional troops for a speedy hosting; a show to the rebels in that nation that we are purposed to spare no charge to scourge and subdue him and his complices to very extremity!" A painful silence followed, his intemperate tones still ringing in the heavy air. Elizabeth's response was quiet and sharp.

"We have no monies for a "show" to rebels in the bogs of Ireland. What think you, Cecil, of lord Sussex' suit?"

"It befits him ill. Too costly, with overmuch show." The queen's wry smile lingered on him until he was obliged to continue. "As to John O'Neill, since he is in quiet possession, what I think therein is this. I think good to stir no sleeping dogs in Ireland, until a staff be provided to chastise them if they will bite. Many things in commonweals are suffered that are not liked." A footman entered softly and whispered to Cecil. Elizabeth commended her secretary again.

"Well spoke, Cecil! To the very pith!" Sussex winced to see yet again how easily wit will vanquish reason. He thought that perhaps a metaphorical argument could prevail, so again he ventured his case.

"Majesty, this small wound in the body of the state could seem a signal to verminous traitors and rebels who would infest therein. If it be not staunched, there will anon beneeds much letting of blood." Elizabeth replied in tones final and firm.

"Your physic is too costly, good doctor. Cecil has wisely spoke. We have other needs more pressing far in the ordering of this realm. Henry of France has an army in Scotland to press the claims of Mary Stuart to our very throne. Will we empty our coffers because an Irish cur has snatched a bone? Our happy subjects in this England mayhap will not cheer Our Majesty so hearty when we go a begging in the Commons. Our purse is closed, Lord Sussex".

Lord Sussex, disconcerted and desperate, pleaded weakly, "But your majesty, if we-" But the queen ignored him, her voice and conviction rising to close the issue.

"Prudence commends us this caution; that we not meddle in any small bog until such time as we are ready to reorder all of Ireland. When the treacherous winds that blow from France and Spain are acalmed, then will we raise a sail for Ireland, and make us civil shireland of *all* the land beyond the Pale...with English tongue and English law. Then shall you have your troops, Lord Sussex. Not before!"

"God save your Majesty." He resumed his proud comportment, waving his plumed billycock in a sweeping bow. When he turned for the chamber door, Cecil raised a hand to halt his exit. The secretary nodded to the queen.

"If I may, Your Majesty?" Elizabeth obliged.

"Yes, Lord Cecil, what say you?" He placed a hand on the other man's shoulder and guided him back into the queen's presence.

"Stay you, Lord Sussex. Such a staff as will chastise this cur may be at hand." He looked to Elizabeth. "Majesty?.." Her lively curiosity was peaked.

"What now then? Some new contrivance?"

"Upon brief reflection... perhaps a worthy conceit?" Cecil paused for an instant to collect and order his thoughts. "If O'Neill's enemies in Ulster were advanced over him with peerage, and his rights of tribute spurned, his own followers would more readily desert him. His chiefest rival is Cullagh O'Donnell to his west. Were he created Earl of Tirconnell, and charged to subdue his blood enemy, surely the O'Reilly and Maguire, and lesser clans and septs would rally in his cause to serve our ends." Elizabeth sat back straight in her chair, beaming.

"There is husbandry in this, Cecil. Titles and honours, though they be worth more than gold, they do not diminish our treasuries. And still..." She turned suddenly to Lord Sussex. "Though he oppose our enemies, yet does O'Donnell beshow himself loyal to our crown?" Heartened by this sudden change in his prospects, Sussex again sprang to life.

"Most faithful, of late, in routing rebels. And he undertakes to learn the English tongue. What is more, O'Neill is married to O'Donnell's daughter, whom he has lately spurned and sent back to her father, instilling such rancour in the old man that he will relish his charge." The new light in Elizabeth's eyes emboldened him to chance again his appeal for troops. "And yet I think such honours could not induce him to attack O'Neill without support from Dublin Castle -of regiments to come at flank and rear. The hopes of such a venture-" The young queen bristled at this second grasp at the royal purse, but Cecil's 'brief reflection" had yielded more.

"Just so!" he said triumphantly. "At his flank and rear lies but yet another staff for his chastisement. The Antrim coast is settled with some ten thousand Scots from the Isles. These Savage redshanks could be easily stirred to enmity, and would so plague him at his-"

"But, Majesty, these are *papist* MacDonnells from the Isles, supporters of Mary Stuart's intrigues!" Sussex had twice attempted to oust these intruders and he was horrified at this turn in secretary's scheme. "They increase there daily to the danger of that country, and indeed, of this very kingdom!"

"Enough!" Elizabeth clapped her fists onto the desk with fury. "France and Scotland above and before, and will we tolerate with Scottish traitors at our very back in Ireland? Nay, they must be driven hence!" Undaunted, for he was adept at persuading his volatile mistress, Cecil lowered his voice and gestured toward the door. "Your Majesty, the key to Ulster awaits even now in the next chamber. Since the Lordship of the Isles was abolished some fifty years ago, these MacDonnells are liege to the Duke of Argyll, who comes now to seek your help against the French in Edinburgh. Should we but gratify James MacDonnell's clans, and retain them in our service, we might employ them against the Northern Irish. Thus we undo O'Neill's threat with more speedy effect and less charges; and that complished, we may easily expel the Scots also out of that realm!" Elizabeth was delighted with the prospect of such frugal expedience.

"What folly is this? Hell's Bells, then! Call him in. We will hear of it."

Cecil nodded, turned, and disappeared into the ante-chamber. Sussex bowed and stepped uneasily off to one side. The queen held her expectant gaze on the door, and spoke with relish. "A contrivance most subtle, and like to settle, lest he miss his mark!" Lord Sussex tried to hold his tongue, but at length his indignation prevailed.

"So please your Majesty, be chary of these wiles! Not cunning, but constancy and a heavy hand is like to break a colt. It is long said among the army that Cecil meddles in everything and muddles all."

"Among the *army*!" Elizabeth glared fiercely. "The army knows naught but arms! And draining bursaries to buy them! Our sister Mary took their counsel and lost more than Calais. Therefore are the coffers bare, and still they cry for more!" She turned abruptly and flashed a warm smile upon the new visitor as Cecil announced him.

"Campbell, the Duke of Argyll."

"God save your Majesty! As he rose from his courtly bow, Argyle matched her sunny countenance. He was a tall craggy man, grey at the temples and not yet thirty. Along with his dukedom he held court as a Gaelic chieftain, 'the MacCaileann Mor', with Gaelic bards and intricate Highland law. He straddled both these worlds deftly, as indeed no man ever had. His manner was quick and curt, but jovial, and his speech was refined; spiced with the crisp burr of Edinburgh.

"We welcome you back to court, good Archibald, and to England. We have read us your reports. How fares your good wife Jean Stewart?

"In good form, Your Majesty, all pluck and mettle and cheer," he replied.

"And her half-sister, our own cousin Mary Stuart?"

"She thrives in France." Argyll sought to re-assure her. "Indeed Lady Jean avouches that Queen Mary will never return to Scotland, now she is Queen of France."

"And 'of England'? ...Heard you not so at the coronation in Paris?"

Argyll chose to ignore the implied reproof. He smiled. "French bluster. No more."

SHANE O'Neill, 'the Grand Disturber'

"And her royal seal? She bears a rose in her arms. She'd best be wary lest it may prick her yet!" Argyll regarded it as unseemly. Grown men, the nobility on both sides of Hadrian's Wall, forced to suffer the jealous squabbling of these strident young lasses. Still he smiled. "French fancies only. We have their frippery, fops and courtiers, with papish priests in tow in every nook in Edinburgh. The Lairds chafe to hear their-"

"Your wife is a Papish...and doubtless faithful to her sister. What then at home, Lord Argyll? Do you see eye to eye?"

"Alas, mostly 'aye' to 'nay'!" His unyielding composure had worked a charm, and Elizabeth laughed freely.

"The wits grow sharp from such a 'pairing'!" Argyle's hearty peel of laughter at the queen's wordplay, echoed by Sussex and Cecil made a merry fairday for bartering, and he resolved to broach his business. "For all Mary is Queen of France, her husband is not King of Scotland. I am her loyal subject, but I owe naught to France. The lairds look to you for relief of these French troops." Elizabeth gave a smiling nod, and cocked her head back.

"Mayhap we can assist, as we stand you with ready chance to return in kind." She cast her shining eyes upon Lord Cecil, anxious to hear more of his scheme.

"The matter of Ulster." Cecil stood beside the queen and made his offer. He knew that the Scottish laird was well familiar with the turmoil in Ulster. "John O'Neill's partisans have murdered the Baron of Dungannon, and he has usurped the captaincy of Tyrone. Lord Argyll, you must assure that James MacDonnell's clans stand to, with support from the Isles against this traitor. The crown is willing to cease all hostilities against the MacDonnells, and pending inquiry, will draught such peerage, a baronet or earldom, as will seal their claims in Ireland. Can you deliver them?"

A sudden storm flashed in Elizabeth's eyes as she turned them on her secretary. "But, Good My Lord Cecil, when he accepts peerage, this Scotchman will be duty-bound to host against our rebels. Wherefore do we need the offices of Lord Argyll?"

"Majesty, if I may speak to this?" It was Sussex who now awaited

SHANE O'Neill, 'the Grand Disturber'

the queen's nod, and then lent his support to Cecil. "MacDonnell well may spurn the honour, and will, most like, need to be coaxed to forsake O'Neill. It was but four years ago, when I summoned a hosting against the Antrim Scots, Shane O'Neill did, instead, repair to James MacDonnell, with all his force and power of men, and did combine against our late sovereign, Lady Queen Mary. And in the following year, O'Neill again spurned our advance on MacDonnell, and received into his safekeeping and fostering all of their goods and cattles, and procured an assault, even, to be made in a pass upon Her Majesty's army upon our return. The question indeed is '*Can* Lord Argyll deliver us the support of MacDonnell against his ally?" Argyll looked from one to the other incredulously. He dare not tell them that the MacDonnells were still galled at losing the Lordship of the Isles, and quite unresigned to his superiorities. "My lord, O'Neill's forces could drive them into the sea, which doubtless he intends!" But Cecil was well ahead of him.

"O'Donnell will first assault at O'Neill's west. Your Scots must then beset him from the rear guard. That done, he be easily vanquished." The laird slowly cast his glance from one to the other, a sly grin overtaking his features. "And O'Donnell will get his peerage... Earl of TirConnell?" Seeing the affirmative nods, he laughed. "Katherine will be pleased." In that instant, a wild notion gathered itself in his head, and set him off. "Ah! There's the one! Katherine is the pivot!" The looks of wonder and perplexity about him only spurred him on. "She is wife to O'Donnell in the West, and niece to James and Sorley MacDonnell in the East. And though she's little more than five and a score years of age, Katherine MacLean was for a time my stepmother, the Countess of Argyll!"

Cecil met the happy gaze of Elizabeth and crowed for both of them, "Such a confluence! And to our very purpose!" They turned again to the laird for further illumination, and he happily complied, slowly spelling out what he had in mind. "When my aged father died, his widow, the young Countess Dowager, was left on my hands. For all my father's entreaties, she had never embraced the reformed kirk, and I could find no suitable match for her among the protestant lairds of

SHANE O'Neill, 'the Grand Disturber'

Scotland. As O'Donnell did so entreat me, I betrothed her to him for a sum, along with certain arms of war- for the which I keep his bond still. She is a Lady accustomed to the luxuries of Inverrary Castle and the refinements of Edinburgh. And so, I assure you, she will prove *most* ambitious for O'Donnell's peerage, and will prevail upon her uncles James and Sorley to comply. She is clever and most persuasive. Oh, she will do my bidding in this. Upon my word, Katherine will lead the dance!"

"Tell your lairds, Archibald, that they shall have our aid against the French!" Elizabeth was doubly pleased, since she had already determined to send these troops before his arrival. "And O'Donnell shall be summoned and created earl. Good Cecil, see that his peerage is draughted. Oh, and unto his wife be sent some such gown as we have ourself discarded, for both to beshow their new honour, and to set example of the English fashion for their barbarous kinsmen." She bestowed her smile on each of the company in turn, until alighting on Thomas Radcliffe, who had been silent this long while. The smile vanished. "Good My Lord Sussex, your grim countenance beshows some grave doubt!" He looked up with a wan smile.

"No, Your Majesty. 'Tis naught but sober thought." Elizabeth sighed.

"Poor Thomas, if We may be left with our scant treasury intact, well, this sorrow must you bear. Yet John O'Neill shall be chastised! Let your sober thoughts drink of that!"

The nebulous shroud of grey at last was thinning and melting away to a radiant blue, as the chalk cliffs of Kenbawn sparkled into view. Just beyond it lay Ballycastle and Sorley MacDonnell's fortress. Katherine relished the swell and heave of the rolling sea below her

SHANE O'Neill, 'the Grand Disturber'

feet as she stood on the creaking deck. She savored the briny air, the tingling chill of sea spray on her cheeks. These spindrift winds that tossed her dewy hair seemed to cast away her dark burdens and lighten her heart. She was an islander, and the sea was home.

Favorable winds and obliging waters had swept the nimble galleon from Donegal Bay, skirting the northern coast to the Antrim headlands. Occasionally, when the sun would dispel the mists and haze, the shores of Scotland could be seen from here, shimmering far off beyond Rathlin Island, across the Sea of Moyle.

Since the Lordship of the Isles was abolished some fifty years before, all these shores and the glens below them had been settled by Scots, and presided over by Katherine's uncles. Alistair was ensconced just above those white cliffs in the newly raised Kenbawn castle. James MacDonnell, chief of the clan, resided in Kintyre away across the North Channel. In times of peril, when the warning fires were lit on the cliffs of Torr Head in the night, the chief would sweep in from the Isles with legions of 'redshanks' by morning. Sorley, the youngest but most vigorous of the brothers, kept his home at Ballycastle. He was the only one born in Ireland, and he felt a deep bloodbond with these glens.

Katherine was sure that he would help her. A letter had come to her. A letter! Only a bit of ink and parchment, but it could hold within it the power to change your life, as surely as a war or a tempest. Argyll, formerly her step-son, now one of the most powerful lairds in Scotland, had sent auspicious tidings; news of Elizabeth's scheme to vanquish Shane O'Neill. Katherine marveled that he should apprize her such a fool. Did he think she could not use this knowledge to serve her own ends? She had learned so much since the time she was his old father's "wee ginger bagatelle". Ah, well! Why would he not count her a fool? His father's young widow, that he so blithely sold to the next old man for guns and gold. And now, when she is so many leagues away from Argyll's power, he sends instructions to follow. We shall see!

When the letter had arrived –could it be only days ago? Such elation! A curious sensation that could only be an inkling of power.

SHANE O'Neill, 'the Grand Disturber'

Archibald was right enough; she *could* truly sway her uncles, for unknown to him, they had common cause. Their fortunes would rise or fall by the fate their cousin Queen Mary Stuart, who was rumoured to be returning to Scotland, now that the Dauphin was dead. Upon receiving the letter, she had said not a word to her husband of his impending honours, but took herself off to Ballycastle "to lend comfort to an ailing aunt."

The journey itself was clearly a risk, and all might yet come to naught. Katherine prayed that Sorley Bui MacDonnell would be in residence. He was so often away, and there had been no time to write ahead. If James, the chieftain, were in from Kintyre, it would be all the better, for whatever words would be forthcoming, his would be last. It was only the propitious arrival of this galleon, on its route to Dublin that had decided her on her course. Any sudden opportunity could prove to be an omen. 'The open door is the way in.' Here was a ship leaving within hours. Only a small sum had secured both her passage, and this brief unscheduled putting in on the Antrim coast.

Above her now loomed the familiar fortress of Dunanynie, her uncle's home, looking strangely unfamiliar . For all the stops and sojourns Katherine had made here since childhood, she had never approached it from the West. It towered above the headland that sheltered Ballycastle Bay, and seemed to command the whole North Channel. Just at the foot of the cliffs below it lay the tiny harbour of Port Brittas, and Katherine thought it fortuitous to see the small fleet moored there. There were four longboats, galleys from the Isles, and she quickly determined for herself that they would, indeed, be in - both Sorley Buí and the James the MacDonnell.

The small galleon quickly glided into the bay, turning in to drop anchor among the galleys, as the seagulls raised a shrill chorus of welcome. The vessel's unexpected arrival had attracted, too, a fair crowd of curious onlookers. Katherine was arrayed in a beautiful tweed gown in the MacDonnell plaid that had once belonged to her mother, Mary the daughter of Alastair of Islay, by whose right she wore it. As she appeared above the gangplank, two young cousins sighted her and rushed in to greet her. They assured her that her visit was, indeed, well timed to meet with her uncles.

After assigning their gillies to see to her trunk, they quickly ushered their guest up the steep path to the castle. Katherine ascended with a lighter heart and a lively step, for the violets and budding primroses along the way, the scent of early spring, and the warm afternoon sun, had stirred within her some deep forgotten well of promise and hope.

Her aunts, Mary and Agnes, sprang to their feet with shrieks of delight when Katherine appeared. The uncles and their wives were gathered in the drawing room before the massive ornate fireplace, and its dancing blaze tossed shadows and lustrous shimmers of red from one excited face to the next. The customary roar of "Give us a lumbur!" meant warm hugs all 'round, ending with Sorley, who stepped back and eyed her from tip to toe. "You've forsaken the 'blue and green' of Argyle, so? It was never so bonny as the reds! How are you faring in Donegal, wee girl? Tell us all."

Whiskey was poured and a cook summoned. Katherine asked for news and gossip of kith and kindred. There was speculation as to their cousin Mary Stuart. Shortly before Christmas her husband, the young French king, had died from an ear infection, and rumours were rife of her probable return to Scotland. All were firmly convinced, and most anxious to see it come to pass. Sorley said rightly that it would change everything, but his wife Mary insisted that 'it would still rain in Ireland!'

Katherine regarded her two aunts, and wondered now if they would venture an 'aye' or a 'nay' upon hearing her appeal. Each was bound by blood to key players in this 'grand design'. The old chieftain's wife was Agnes Campbell, sister to Archibald, and though she was eight years older, she had been for some years Katherine's step daughter as well as her aunt. She would surely favor Argyle's plan, but no, old James would hardly consult her. Sorley's wife Mary was Shane O'Neill's half sister by one of the Earl's mistresses, and she was a fair bit older. She had the same grey eyes and black hair as he, but for the grey that was setting in. She might prove helpful, unless she were minded to hold her tongue.

SHANE O'Neill, 'the Grand Disturber'

When asked if she missed her life of opulence in Inverrary, Kat broached the reason for her visit. "I had my full of the place, truth to tell. Auld Campbell was kindly to me, God rest his soul. Your father was a fine man, Agnes, but once he was gone, that was no life for me. I had some word from his son Archibald this week past that I'm bound to share with you, James, for it concerns no-one more." All casual motions and fidgets stilled now, for she had captured their keenest attention. "Elizabeth has a new scheme afoot. She's going to make an earl of O'Donnell and some lesser chiefs, O'Reilly and Maguire, in order to hobble Shane O'Neill. They're to beset him from the west, and she wants all of ClanDonnell to attack him from this quarter."

Mary blessed herself and looked to her husband Sorley. He cocked his head back and peered down his nose at Katherine with a sardonic grin. "Tell Lord Sussex we'll be at his back for him!" His blue eyes glowered with mischief. Twice in the last ten years, Sussex had attacked and failed to rout him. Katherine looked to James.

"Archibald has it that Sussex is minded to cease all hostilities with you, to accept and confirm your titles to Antrim, and to bestow a baronet or an earldom. If it's to be believed." Kat watched as the two men sat silent and stony faced considering the weighty matter before them. The eldest, and the youngest; James was grey, while his brother's hair was flaxen still, an attribute accounting for the sobriquet 'buí' meaning yellow. James set his jaw and peered into the flames, while Sorley gazed intently into his goblet of whiskey. The women exchanged meaningful glances in the tense silence until Agnes, the chieftain's wife spoke. "The title, James. It's the title. It would seal our rights here."

At length, the MacDonnell ran his fingers through his long white hair and looked from one to the next about the room. "What say you, brother?"

"I say... that the one immoveable and imperishable piece on the board is the Queen. O'Neill's standing does not threaten hers, and she will be here long after him. When you are Earl of Antrim, we'll have peace here, and none could dislodge us."

"*If*...you can believe them." Katherine looked from Sorley to James.

SHANE O'Neill, 'the Grand Disturber'

"You'll get neither title to the land, nor title of peerage, until *after* you've attacked O'Neill. Once you've done that, whether they vanquish him or no, they may well think again on their offers. Sussex could attack you then with no fear of Shane O'Neill at your side." James nodded his grey head.

"But with O'Neill gone, we would be free to settle the Route. MacQullan and O'Kane could never withstand us. As it is, they press O'Neill to keep us back. We have more and more coming from the Isles, and more want of land."

"But O'Neill has stood with you in the past." Katherine's tone was dispassionate. "In the assault of '56... And yet again the summer following, didn't Shane bring his armies to your aid? If you stand with him now, the queen's army will surely fail to conquer him, and you'll be gratified with a strong ally." The silent moment that followed convinced Katherine that she was making headway.

Agnes and Mary sat stunned and still, in their state of amazement. They had never seen their niece comport herself so brazenly before her uncles. Mary got up and filled glasses and Agnes whispered to her, out of Kat's hearing. "To speak so to the chieftain!" Mary pursed her lips and cast a sharp glance at Katherine. She turned back with brows raised and whispered "Cheek and brass of your Cambells in her now!" She sat again as all awaited some response to Katherine's appeal.

Sorley broke the silence, raising his glass. "A health to our wee Katherine!" When they had all drank, he continued, addressing his brother. "Ach, we have our fill with the English here. We won't like an O'Neill so powerful as he would be. To overlord us. And a chieftain has no standing in their parliament. Agnes is right, James. The title is what you need."

The MacDonnell looked as if he were about to render his judgement, so Katherine spoke again.

"Mary will come back to Scotland. The story is on everyone's lips. Didn't we all agree? And she's pledged to restore the Lordship of the Isles to you. You told me so when we returned from France. Then you'll not need Elizabeth's title." She could see in their eyes that this arrow had hit its mark. "And let us not forget that Mary may yet take

SHANE O'Neill, 'the Grand Disturber'

Elizabeth's throne, and if she does, you'll have naught to fear from Sussex." Sorley warmed to this new line of reason, and turned to his elder brother.

"If Mary does come to the English throne, you could find yourself the Earl of Ulster! Over O'Neill and O'Donnell both. When we were in Paris, Mary said as much!"

"What did she say?" James demanded. "What did Queen Mary actually say?"

"Little more than little and less than much!" Sorley's wife Mary blurted out, launching a hearty laugh that broke the tension. Goblets were raised again, and smiles flashed in the firelight. Sorley cocked his head and his eyes, eyes filled again with mischief. "The nights must be cold in Donegal Castle, if you're asking us to fight beside O'Donnell's enemy! You're a clever wee lass, and you know more than your prayers. What's your stake in all this intrigue? I think the Kat purrs for her own sake!" Katherine laughed with the rest. She replied simply. "What will hinder Elizabeth will help Mary. And what will help Mary will help us all."

"Well spoke, lassie!" Sorley noted a look of resolution in the chieftain's eyes. "Well, brother, what way is it to be? Will we fight for Elizabeth? Or will we fight for Shane?"

"We needn't fight with either!" The MacDonnell stood now, a tall silhouette before the bright fire. "If O'Neill stood with us before, it was in his interest to do. Didn't we aid him against his brother? No... If we fight for either, we stand to lose men and blood, and gain nothing. Let them to it, and may they spend themselves well and all! Let O'Neill be told that we'll not ride with him, but neither will we raise a sword against him." All looked to Katherine for her response. She knocked back a last dram of her whiskey. Her eyes glistened in the firelight and with a certain sparkle from within. "Well, Elizabeth will never defeat him without you...So perhaps, God willing, the battle was won for O'Neill here today! God save Queen Mary!"

SHANE O'Neill, 'the Grand Disturber'

The thunder of hooves over the cobbles of Dungannon brought eyes to every window and gaping doorway, spilling narrow shafts of light across the dark road before them as they made their way up to Castle Hill. A galloping horse in the night was a sure harbinger of trouble, and the clatter of twelve horsemen drew all but the infirm away from their fires in some state of alarm and inquiry. The fluttering ensign of Fitzgerald, St. Patrick's red cross on its field of white, was discernible above the squadron, and this was re-assuring in some measure. The House of Kildare was the most powerful sept in the South of Ireland and they were cousins to O'Neill. They were well regarded in these parts, for, although they were of Norman origin and held feudal titles, they were staunch defenders of the native Irish, and their Catholic and Brehon ways. Only the late hour and their urgent pace portended some troubles to come.

This castle at Dungannon was not Shane's principal residence, but it was where his father, the Earl of Tyrone, had lived and died, and perhaps ten generations before him. It was as well appointed as any lord's castle in England. While his father was alive, Shane had grown accustomed to the more bucolic environs of Benburb castle, with Easters and short stays at his lodge in Fathan, and Christmases and occasional sojourns here on Castle Hill.

A late dinner had only just been cleared away in the dining hall when Kildare and his party were ushered in. Shane was still at table with his foster brothers the Donnellys, and Father Magrath. It was with some delight and a great deal of surprise that Shane greeted his illustrious cousin.

Along with Garret Fitzgerald was Terence Donnelly, the Dean of Armagh. Back in the fourth century, Armagh had been the seat of St. Patrick, and since then, the see of the Primate of Ireland. Since Bishop Dowdall's death in '58, the primacy was vacant, and Shane's emissaries vied with Elizabeth's to secure the seat for an Irishman. At that time, Pope Pius IV appointed Terence Donnelly "Guardian of the

SHANE O'Neill, 'the Grand Disturber'

Spiritualities of Ireland", so he carried out the duties of the Primate without the title or the temporalities belonging to it. Officially the English knew him as Terence Danyell, but he was the eldest of the brothers who now greeted him around the table.

He was also Shane's foster brother. In accordance with the custom of 'comhaltas' or fosterage, as a young boy Shane had been sent away by his father to be reared by the Donnellys. It was common practice among the Gaelic gentry in order to foster alliances, and their bonds of loyalty to Shane stood proof of its power. Dualta Donnelly was Marshal of Shane's army, and the other three brothers Manus, Éamonn, and Seamus, served below him as field commanders. The cold miasma of distrust that had lingered ever between Shane and his father was another less fortunate result of that fosterage. Indeed, the whole of Shane's struggle for succession could be laid to that cause.

"God love you, Garret. Even if it's black tidings that brought you - and I'm thinking it is, I'm that glad to see you!" Shane turned to a servant. "Ah, good man, Tague, let's get a goblet of wine into his fist before these troubles pour forth." There was no mistaking the Earl's troubled demeanor. Though he was of average height, he appeared small and slight next to O'Neill's massive frame. He was arrayed in Engish garb, doublet and hose of hunting green, with ruffs a bit wilted after a hard ride. Shane embraced the Dean and the Earl, while the Donnellys made room for them at his side. "You've news of Sussex' parliament I'll warrant."

"We have -but little that was unforeseen, Cousin." Fitzgerald's blue eyes were bedimmed by his dark tidings. "I attended there and I had occasion to speak to Lord Sussex. He's a twist in his guts that you've outmaneuvered him, gone to the stone. I've never seen him so vexed. He'd pinned his last hopes on the fair haired Matthew, and he's howling for your blood. Calls it a murder. I told him you were nowhere near, but he's attainted you traitor and ordered you to submit in Dublin. A thing you must never do."

"Divil a fear of it." Shane tipped a sup from his goblet and flashed a quizzical smile. "He's had a knot in his guts since he took up that post. Seven letters I sent him, and he answered not a one...Nor did they ever reach Council! You've sweated your horses for naught, my kinsman, if that is your story. His ill humours are not news here."

"That was prelude only!" The young earl spoke gravely. "He's going to raise up your vassal chieftains over you. An earl for O'Donnell, and even for the O'Reilly and the Maguire."

"Upstarts. They sent no tribute this season. I knew something was afoot." Shane's smile had vanished.

"Sussex will lead us from the South –he has all the five Irish earls, and O'Donnell will beset you from your western flank. And the worse yet–"

"I'll drive them back with redshanks. I have Sorley buí MacDonnell, and he can muster at least–"

"You haven't, Shane." Kildare's abrupt tone brought Shane to a halt. "You haven't. Sussex is making a Baron of him. And an earl of James. They'll be at your back! Six hundred new troops, Sussex will have, to sail shortly from England. We're to assemble the hosting in Dundalk for the twentieth day of May. And I'm in no position to rise until help will come from France or Spain. I've only just been restored."

"That gives us little time..." Shane's eyes now clouded over, showing nothing of the dark ruminations behind them.

"Time for what?" Kildare asked, after a moment's silence. No answer came. Looks of concern, expectation and dread darted about the table in a silent commotion. "Time to do what, Shane?" Still ominously silent, but clear and focused now, O'Neill met his gaze. "Shane, since my detainment in London I have corresponded with Lord Robert Dudley, the Queen's favorite. He is party to a faction at court, along with Sidney, that are fiercely opposed to Sussex. He has the queen's ear in all matters and is, I believe, to be trusted."

A wry smile restored the light in Shane's eyes. "Trusted? The horns of a bull, the grin of a dog, and the smile of an Englishman..."

"Dudley was instrumental in restoring me to favour, and you can make what use of him you will. He thinks you need go directly before Elizabeth, and present your grievances against the Lord Deputy, and your rights to succeed as Earl. In both matters you have a powerful case to put forth. He's convinced you could prevail." Shane shook his head.

"I'll prevail in Tirowen. If they had me to London they would never release me. They would be fools to do, because I'll never rest my sword until the last English ship has sailed." Father Terence Donnelly now spoke.

"You could draw up a list of demands, Shane. Garret and I could negotiate terms for a safe conduct. They would need to-"

O'Neill's eyes blazed alight. "So you shall! So you shall!" He stood up now and laughed to himself as he paced before the fire. Looks of wonder crossed about the table. Suddenly he turned to them. "I'll open negotiations direct with London, and Sussex' hands will be bound tight! So long as the Queen bargains with me, he must hold off his assault. I can spin out time until a fair wind will favor my needs." A spirited laugh from the Donnellys bespoke admiration and some relief for their chieftain. Shane turned to his cousin. "What do you hear from the Continent, Garrett? Is there hope to be had?"

"More empty promises only. The pope still refuses to excommunicate Elizabeth Tudor, and as long as he does so, Philip and Charles can do little." The Dean spoke again.

"Right enough, Shane, the mediation will give you time to marshal your forces. And yet, Lord Kildare must be seen to be acting in good faith. If he's-" The other priest at the table broke in.

"For God's sake, Terence, Shane need only present rigourous demands and a will to parley. This queen is stingy with her purse, and if she can forestall the expense of war- Shane is right, time can be won until chance favours him." Myler looked from Shane to Fitzgerald. "And...if the queen should *meet* O'Neill's demands, he may find it in his vantage to hazard a journey to London. Who knows what winds may prevail in, say, a year's time?" Grinning, Shane settled himself back at the table and looked from Garrett to Terence.

"What about it, lads? Will you undertake this for us?" Kildare sat back in his chair, smiling.

"Ah well, since this is not only the best plan we have, but the *only* bloody plan we have...I will! I'll use my good offices to see it through.

SHANE O'Neill, 'the Grand Disturber'

Dean Donnelly?" He turned now to the cleric.

"Apart from Father Magrath, we're the only two here who have proper English, so I suppose the lot falls to me. If you'll help me sort out your demands, Shane, I'll take them to off to London."

A lively clamour of approval followed with spirits poured and goblets filled. Shane suspected that none of them were truly convinced that his ruse would succeed, but to attempt it, at least, was a course of action in the face of a most daunting threat. Trifling matters were tossed about now, until the discourse inevitably found its way back to Sussex' parliament, and the religious reforms imposed for the new queen's reign.

"It was only dissolved this week past, on Brigid's Day," Lord Kildare replied to Magrath. The priest's inquiry had been casually posed, considering his impatience for the momentous news. "I conferred with Sussex on the day following, and then I set out for Armagh. I thought surely the Dean here should be apprised of the affairs, since no officer or cleric from Ulster had attended."

"Who was there, so?" Myler's anxiousness was plain to see. "Tell us what transpired, man! What sort of coggery and thimble rigging did they get up to *this* time?"

"I made a strict count. Twenty bishops, and twenty three temporal peers including the five earls. The English speaking towns had burgesses there. The chief business, of course, was to establish Elizabeth as head of the church, and to restore the heresies of her father. It was the usual order of things official. There was talking in English and whispering in Irish -from the few who had it. These English are so bloody obtuse. It was little over two years ago that Sussex presided over the same rites in Latin, when Queen Mary restored the Roman supremacy. He's piously condemning people for following the dictums he put before them but two years ago. There was a fair bit of sniggering, I can tell you, but he's that dull, he didn't turn a hair!" A bit of derisive laughter around the table followed, with O'Neill concurring.

"A pompous jackstraw. He hasn't the wit know shame! How many submitted?"

SHANE O'Neill, 'the Grand Disturber'

"All but the first two bishops. They were forced to take the oath individually, and refused. My own devoted guardian, Bishop Leverous of Kildare. I had begged him not to attend. He and Bishop Walsh of Trim. Both imprisoned. After that, Sussex perceived the trend of things and thought it better to put it to a vote. It was clear to all that Elizabeth could no more enforce the measures here than could her father. There are no ministers to speak a sermon in Irish, and no congregations to understand English. And so it was approved. The staunchest opponents hadn't been invited.

"That was most fortunate for them!" Myler filled his goblet again. "To lose place, and perhaps life, when all could be overturned again in another two years time. The faith of this realm has changed five times in the past thirty years!" Dean Donnelly looked askance at his fellow cleric. "You have a nimble conscience, Father Magrath."

"Too bloody right I do!" Myler had the wind up now. "Look at the poor fools who refused to yield under Henry, and were not alive to see Mary restore the Church! In these dark days, can the Church afford to lose it's most devout? These are tickle times, and where politics are concerned, one had best be politic!" Perhaps in deliberate contrast to Myler's agitated tone, the Dean answered him serenely, leaving him to sound desperate and unsure.

"God's truth is a fixéd star, and by it we are bound to set our course, *without* veering."

"And if we would sail into the wind, we must haul close and tack, now windward, now leeward. These are rough waters and deep. Only a nimble conscience will weather the storms that contend about us these days!" He looked about the company for support, but found only sly amusement. Terence Donnelly's dark eyes remained fixed on him.

"If you toss your principals overboard, you were as well to drown."

"There was no oath required of them! The fool who will not duck a blow is as bad an English Puritan. The Lord gave us wits –some of us! And let us use them to defend ourselves!" Winks and waggish grins now, to see the brown and black-robed contenders sparring. Terence Donnelly looked slyly to Fitzgerald.

"Wits is it? Tell them of Father Leigh and his dexterous

conscience, Garret. His feeble wits have nearly scuppered our cause!" The earl's hearty laugh put all once again at their ease. He ran his fingers through his reddish hair and his quick blue eyes darted merrily about the company.

"The opening rites in the cathedral were in the English tongue, from the Book of Common Prayer. Christchurch had that beautiful marble Christ with a crown of thorns on His head. You know the one- Bishop Curwen had re-installed it during Queen Mary's short reign. And as the service droned on, it was observed to bleed!" At this, several of the Donnellys blessed themselves. Kildare smiled. "Oh yes! Indeed and it was! Red blood was dripping down from the crown of thorns! There was gasping and whispering, for many there were inclined to embrace a miracle, especially one as auspiciously timed as this! The mayor himself produced a rosary and went to his knees before the ...bleeding thing. One of the monks who had formerly tended the cathedral- His name was Leigh and his speech was North of England. He cried out that Christ could not but sweat blood since heresy had come into the Church. Well, a great tumult seemed imminent, and Sussex and his suite came rushing out of the choir. But the bishop climbed onto a bench and showed that Father Leigh had hidden a blood-soaked sponge within the crown of thorns!" A roar of laughter followed. Some rejoinder was expected of Myler, and he obliged. He held his cup aloft.

"Let those who have wits use them, and let those who don't ...abide by those who do!" More spirited laughter and flowing French wine. Shane was in high spirits now, enjoying the banter. He had a great capacity for setting troubles aside, in favour of company and libations. In the morning, as always, he would attend to the burdensome duties of his office with clarity and cunning.

"The Deputy was puffed up as a peacock, I'll wager." Fr. Magrath wanted more news of the counterfeit miracle in Dublin. "Sussex is shrewd enough to have contrived the incident himself, but I remember this Friar Leigh. An earnest little Englishman. A zealous fool!" Kildare shook his head.

"Oh, the Protestants were triumphant. And triumphal! The justice

SHANE O'Neill, 'the Grand Disturber'

of their cause so lavishly evidenced before all! We were quite confounded. Bishop Curwen had the statue broken up. And Sussex has persuaded the Queen to have all images and icons removed from all the churches. It's well for you that the Queen's writ is powerless here. Only for the O'Neill..."

With that, a heavy silence settled over the company, as the impending threat posed by the crown forces, Sorley Buí, and Cullagh O'Donnell, possessed utterly, once again, the minds present. The crackle of the fire was suddenly audible in that long moment, and the haunting spectre of this gathering storm dared them to speak. Shane became aware that all eyes were regarding him. "Well, boys, we'll assault them with diplomacy and see what that will get us. Dualta, the time has come to start training the farmers and tillers in the arts of war. We can no longer leave this with the knights and freeholders. Soon enough the people will be fighting for their own hearths and chapels. They have a mighty stake in this. I want you to double my army. In the meantime, my good Fathers Terence and Myler, your prayers would not go astray, for Cherubim, Seraphim, or Thrones, we'll need a powerful angel to shift the constellations in our favor!"

CHAPTER 3

An Atlantic storm had settled darkly over Donegal town, as the small English galleon approached the crude moorings that served as a pier. The seas had been treacherous, and the harbour was a great relief on this last stop of his mission. Only the long voyage home would remain after the day's business –if only he could set about it! The downpour promised an agonizing delay, and he was yearning every minute to put his feet on land, dry or no.

Will Hutchenson was a short man of slight build, fastidious and effete. He had been engaged as an emissary for the queen's secretary, Lord Cecil, on a circuitous diplomatic tour that had taken him, as he thought, well beyond the furthest reaches of civilization. He was dispatched firstly to Edinburgh to consult with Thomas Randolphe, the queen's ambassador; and then off to Inverrary to see the Earl of Argyll with letters from Lord Cecil.

The envoy had been instructed to obtain letters from the earl and sail to the isles, stopping first with James MacDonnell, the chieftain who resided in Kintyre. His welcome there had been little more than cordial, with neither a 'yea' or a 'nay' to report. He had then to cross the channel to the Antrim coast in Ireland with a missive from James to Sorley MacDonnell, and with a letter also from the queen. Although he had come offering a baronet and gifts from her majesty, his reception was again unaccountably cool. These cagey and canny Scots had sent him off with only a promise of neutrality and further consideration of the matters. This unlooked-for turn of events had

SHANE O'Neill, 'the Grand Disturber'

rendered today's mission all the more vital.

After an hour's wait on board, the rains had scarcely subsided, and it was determined that, given the hour, they should venture forth notwithstanding. Two sailers were dispatched to handle the trunk, and to escort him to the castle. In the absence of a carriage, they engaged a local waggoner to carry them the half mile or so up the castle road to their destination. There was no cover or canopy on the cart, and the short jaunt was just long enough give Hutchinson a thorough soaking. The driver, as per usual he thought, had no English, and in the way of such bumptious savages, kept turning his head back to them, sniggering and laughing for no reason whatsoever.

By the time he appeared before them in O'Donnell's great hall, the royal agent looked like a drowned cat. There were snags in his crimson hose, and the shrunken doublet appeared ready to burst. His ruffs were wilted; the plume of his billycock was plastered to his cheek like so much purple seaweed. And his nose was running.

The drenched and disheveled envoy was given a fresh linen to dry himself and ushered up to the fire. Katherine was, at the time, entertaining a friend, Shune, wife to the MacSweeny Fanad, and so they and Cullagh O'Donnell were seated before the great carved stone hearth. Only Katherine knew the reason for this strange visitation, but she let on nothing of it. The two ladies exchanged looks of sly merriment as the diminutive Englishman postured and prattled his royal tidings before them. O'Donnell had only the most rudimentary grasp of spoken English, but he nodded sagely each time the wee man would pause for air.

When Hutchenson finished his oration, he handed over to O'Donnell the sealed letter from Her Majesty. An awkward stillness followed as the mysterious missive was opened, so Katherine spoke sharp and quick in the Gaelic, apprising him of what was in it. This set off an effusion of grateful gibberish from the new earl, each spate of which ended in "yer honour, sir!" Katherine could see scorn in the little man's eyes, so she spoke in Latin to her husband, advising him to do likewise. After this, they had the advantage. Apparently another letter would be forthcoming from Sussex, with a date for his

SHANE O'Neill, 'the Grand Disturber'

investiture in Dublin.

By and by the agent turned to Katherine. "Her majesty has not forgotten *you*, Lady O'Donnell." The trunk was opened, and in it was a musty gown of velvet, with voluminous skirts and a beaded bodice that appeared a bit threadbare along the edges to Katherine. The little fellow held it up to himself, topping it with the silliest grin Kat had ever seen. "A formal garment from her Majesty's own wardrobe," he crowed. "It has actually graced the royal person!" Seeing her doubtful smile, he quickly added, "Yes, my lady, for *you*!" He tilted his head and extended a sleeve, as if he were modeling it. He was oblivious of the fact that the Countess of Argyll was wearing a much finer gown there as she stood; a Venice blue brocade, with a fawn colored shawl –one of six gowns she had acquired in Paris. She squinted at the dress and turned to Shune, smiling incredulously. "It must be ten years old!"

The royal envoy held the dress out for her inspection, the daft smile frozen on his little face. "You can touch it! It was worn by Queen Elizabeth and now it is for you!" Kat held it out at arms length when she got wind of the fusty gown. Perhaps it hadn't traveled well at sea. She examined the buttons and beading, and looked on the inside of the skirts. She was shocked to see on the front panel inside the dress, a deep red menstrual stain! She held it up for Shune, and the two women exploded in laughter. Both men were appalled. Cullagh reverted to his broken English, as he attempted his profuse apologies. Hutchinson mused again on the irony of his assignment; investing honours and superiorities on rude savages who possessed not even the civility of English domestic servants.

When the sniffy little man had been appeased, he presented Katherine with yet another letter from Archibald, and told her of the unsatisfactory response of her uncles. "Indeed," she said, "I shall write most earnestly to persuade them to combine in this urgent campaign against O'Neill."

While Hutchinson was being fed, letters of acceptance and humble gratitude were written by Katherine and O'Donnell's secretary. A carriage was brought round for him and his escorts, and a fine hooded cape was given him to wear against the rain that showed

SHANE O'Neill, 'the Grand Disturber'

no sign of abating. When he had disappeared into the storm, O'Donnell unleashed a great fury on his ungrateful wife. He then apologized to the wife of MacSweeny.

Shune had come to invite them to the 'Bards' Contesting' to be held in a fortnight's time. Cullagh said he would be happy to preside, and would bring Katherine and his bard, MacWard, and the fledgling poets of his entourage. It would be a lovely mid-May feast of women and poets amid the blossoming gardens of Kildonal Abbey on the western shore of Loch Foyle.

Shune assured him that, although it was true, the abbey was some twenty-three miles into Shane O'Neill's country, there would be no danger. Even if O'Donnell were sighted, it would be a two day journey to inform Shane, and a further two days before he could reach the abbey. They would be home by then. He concurred, said he would be pleased to see her there, and excused himself from their company. The new earl went off then with his secretary to study the royal letter, and to toast it with port wine.

The storm blew and rumbled through the night, but had vanished by first light, and the morning was glistening bright and fresh. When Katherine had seen her friend off, she repaired to her chamber to compose a letter. She was just sealing it with wax when Mórag returned with her brother Colin. They were a part of the youthful entourage who had accompanied the countess from Duart in Mull. With their speech and their ways, they were a comfort from home to her, and were fiercely loyal.

Neither Colin nor his brother who would accompany him knew the byways of Tirowen, so Kat gave him explicit instructions. Anyone meeting the pair of kilted striplings would assume they were Galloglass mercenaries, and they would pass freely through the Sperrins, and on to Shane's castle at Benburb.

"Wake up, O'Donnell, it's morning! Or is it night? Ah, well, I

SHANE O'Neill, 'the Grand Disturber'

suppose it makes little difference to you here." Shane O'Neill settled his fiery torch into the iron sconce and turned to his prisoner. The old man scrambled to his knees, for his irons were chained to the stone floor of the dungeon. He squinted up at his captor who towered darkly over him directly before the flaming torch. O'Neill's tunic of glittering chain mail cast tiny stars of firelight dancing about the cold chamber. "God love you, you're still on your knees! Near to four days. The longest submission of all." O'Donnell spat into a dark corner.

"Where is my wife?" he growled.

"And the tribute! A princely sum!" Shane's eyes and teeth glistened in a wicked grin. "It well reflects the nobility of the noble O'Donnells."

"Where is Katherine?" the old man barked, and he kicked his tin cup over the stones, splashing away the last of his water. The cup was also chained to the floor and it swung back 'round to his feet in a clatter of futility. Shane kept at him with a breezy tone.

"I suppose it isn't much, if I tallied the winters since last it was paid."

O'Donnell's face was raging red, but he spoke low and steady.

"Your father lost those rights of tribute for ever and all time, when he knelt in Greenwich under King Henry's sword. He foreswore his claim to our fealty when he took the golden chain."

"The Earl of Tirowen is in his grave, and *your* father is imprisoned in your own keep. We have *both* buried the arrangements of Greenwich." As he raised his voice, Shane's deep timbre struck an echo off the vaults of stone about them. "I am the O'Neill and you are the O'Donnell, and you have paid your tribute. Paid handsomely..."

O'Donnell's churning blood drummed in his ears under the silence until he heaved a weary sigh. His watery eyes clouded in a listless stupor, barely regarding the shapes before him. "What tribute did you take, then?"

"All you had grazing upon the slopes of Laggan. Cattle. Ten thousand head." The solid image of his massive heaving herds dispelled the vagueness from O'Donnell's mind. "I'll get them back. Ten thousand head... And your head into the bargain. Sussex will soon

SHANE O'Neill, 'the Grand Disturber'

march North, with O'Reilly and Maguire. They-"

"Aye. They march North tomorrow...in irons. Both are taken by my men. If they were marching to your aid, they didn't stir far from home. O'Reilly in the Breffney and Maguire among the reeds." Shane laughed and produced a leathern flask of spirits. "That's what brings me down here to your door, Cullagh. You see, we were all celebrating, and I knew you wouldn't refuse a toast to the 'Earls Undubbed', the 'Knights of Never.' And Matthew, lest we forget him, the bastard pretender who is lately *late*." He swigged a hearty slug from the flask, and bent his knee to the damp stone floor to right the metal cup. He poured into it a goodly measure of whiskybaugh.

"Where is my wife?" The old man growled through his teeth, his eyes smoldering like a cornered wolf. Three days of night it had been, his torment in this dark dungeon, the grim sequence of his capture playing at his mind with halt, without respite. The walled monastery in the shadow of Hugh MacHugh's castle at the fall of night. The winning bards had been chosen. The friars had only just filed out for evensong, and the poets still commanded a rapt silence. Suddenly in every doorway of the hall, rough warriors appeared, silently filing into place along the walls of the room. Some one of the monks must have opened the gates, he had thought. A gasp, and a terrified murmur silenced the poet just as O'Neill entered. He called the bard by name and told him to carry on. He bid him even recite 'Oh, You Who Follow English Ways.' O'Neill's smirking stare had brought all eyes onto O'Donnell, and when it was finished, the warriors seized him.

Shane O'Neill explained to the company that O'Donnell was delinquent in his tribute under Brehon law. He then bestowed lavish gifts upon the winning poets. These lands, he said, were within his domain, and though it were several day's riding from Benburb, he would ask of them to extend an invitation to the next such occasion. All this elaborate mummery was really an attempt by O'Neill to purchase the goodwill of these bards. They were the chief purveyors of news in the land, and their account of these events would prevail in the public memory. In the event, most of them being in the service of O'Donnell, the story of O'Neill's savagery went duly forth from hall to

SHANE O'Neill, 'the Grand Disturber'

hearth through the western hills.

O'Neill's war party numbered less than sixty men. O'Donnell had been bound and carried off by half that number for the long journey east. But what of Katherine? He had looked for her in the hall at his capture, and had seen no trace of her, until a fleeting glimpse at the gate, as he rode off in shackles with his abductors. O'Neill towered over him now, smirking, waiting for him to take up the cup of spirits. O'Donnell's ears were hot, and his breath laboured. "Where is my wife? What have you done with her? I saw her in your custody at the gate." Shane considered briefly and determined that the matter could wait.

"Your good wife is safe." He raised the flask, and slowly shook his head, his eyes sad with mock pity for the prone peer at his feet. "To the slippery doorstep of the House of Lords!" He drank once again, while O'Donnell stared sullenly at the cup before him. Shane wiped his mouth with the back of his hand. "I've won tribute from every chieftain north of the Pale. All but the Scots."

"Spend it quick, O'Neill."

"Ards, the Glens, the Route... The Bann to the Blackwater and beyond. If you had stood with me, Cullagh, you'd be standing still."

"A short standing it would be, to stand with you." The old man regained his composure. Pride was the only weapon to hand. "You may be cunning, my boy, but you're a cunning fool if you suppose you can stop the future from coming."

"I make the future! Look at your wrists, old man, and see the future I've made for you." As O'Neill turned about and paced, the stars of firelight from his chain mail swirled in the darkness, marking an eon of changing constellations. "My broadsword is keen, and it cuts fine, and I'll hack and hue the day until it is a tomorrow to my liking. Oh, aye, the craven lot who serve the strangers always must sniff the wind before they bow to their most profitable 'inevitability.' And how right they are. For the man who surrenders, defeat is inevitable."

Cullagh O'Donnell, drew some faint comfort, perhaps, from seeing his young captor engaged in the futility of justifying himself. He flashed a derisive smile. "The septs and clans can pay your tribute,

SHANE O'Neill, 'the Grand Disturber'

O'Neill, but they can no longer give you power. Power is in the scepter of Queen Elizabeth to bestow or to withhold.

"My power is here!" Shane beat his mailed chest with new fury. "And while my red blood courses within, I need look to no-one's scepter but that between my legs. Elizabeth Tudor's scepter will not keep your wife in your bed...*old man.*"

"Where is my wife, O'Neill?"

"She's above in the Hall...dancing." Shane's eyes flashed with wicked glee. Strains of piping could indeed be heard, if ever so faintly.

"You're a liar," O'Donnell growled, but with an audible trace of doubt. He peered up at his captor now, searching his eyes for the truth of it.

"Lying is a game that weak men play." After ten years of bitter bilious warfare between the two men, Shane savored this sweet moment of pure revenge. Cullagh's old father, Manus, was uncle to Shane, for on the death of Cullagh's mother, he had married an O'Neill. Cullagh's young half-brother, Black Hugh, was actually Shane's cousin, and when Cullagh went to the English to usurp the his father's place in '55, Shane had sided with Black Hugh and Manus. The memory of a bitter defeat at his hands still galled Shane. He gazed down with supreme satisfaction as the flaming torch cast its flickering light on the old man's face, marking each stage of awakening to his wife's betrayal as it played across his features.

"You knew- she *sent you word* that I would be at Kildonal Abbey. Your troops were waiting..." His face and his limbs now twisted in a convulsive fury, jangling the heavy chains that bound him. "The hoor! The filthy Scottish hoor! She'll dance in hell if I set my grip on her! God's curse on the treacherous slut! I'll send her back to Mull in a pine box! Or two, or three, aye." His flaming eyes lit upon the tin cup of spirits, and he seized it. He gulped it down with the low heaving growl of a wolf. Once again Shane raised his flask.

"To women, then! No secret is safe with them..." In the shadows behind him, Katherine watched in silence. She had been recounting her husbands numberless cruelties as she sipped from a goblet, tasting something sweeter than wine. When O'Donnell had drained the cup,

SHANE O'Neill, 'the Grand Disturber'

he looked up at his grinning captor, and down again at his gyves and chains. As he calculated, they were just short of allowing him the scope to trip up his tormenter. Shane was still leering down at him, nodding his head. "Ah well, auld Cullagh got a different chain than he bargained for."

"I'll have my gold chain yet!" The old man drew himself up, his chin forward, striking a defiant pose.

"Oh? Oh? Can you be a posthumous earl? Ah no. If we can change the future itself, we can't change the past." O'Neill now brandished a short dirk that glistened in the torchlight. He bared his teeth in a snarling grin, and jerked the blade at him with a menacing twitch of the wrist. O'Donnell flinched, and then recovered his poise of defiance. "You think to kill me, then? I don't fear your dagger, O'Neill, for I know you daren't use it. You would be killing your feeble hopes for an earldom. As much as you'd like to, you can't!"

"To the weak as he can. To the strong as he *will*!" As Shane lunged in on him, the old man tripped him with a sharp jerk of the chains at his feet.

Shane quickly wrestled him to stillness with the dirk poised at his throat, as Katherine rushed from the shadows screaming.

"No! Don't kill him! Don't kill him!"

'Kill him?" Shane looked up, with some surprise to see her. He pulled back his dirk and got to his feet, laughing. "Just a bit of sport is all. I may need to barter him...and you can't take a dead horse to the fair. Not even a gelding!" The old man's face twisted now like one of Dante's demons. He writhed in his chains and shuddered with seething fury.

"Slut! Rutting bitch of a she-wolf! God's curse on you! Your legs in the air for every mangy cur!" Katherine was gratified, at least, that someone else was there to witness his fiendish tantrum. Although she had never carnally betrayed him, she now took a perverse delight in twisting the knife of shame that consumed him. She drank deep from her goblet of wine, and put her arms around Shane, kissing him in mock passion. If Cullagh was blind with rage, he was well able to see this spectacle before him. "You dockside hoor! A pox on your filthy

SHANE O'Neill, 'the Grand Disturber'

slit! On your womb! May it dry and shrivel as barren as dust!"

Katherine now was laughing hysterically at his impotent rage. "Ruff! Ruff! Ruff!" She barked and sniffed at Shane. "Oh, beware of the she-wolf!!! She howled as well as she was able, for all her teary eyed laughter. She wagged her finger at Shane. "Beware of the filthy slit!" She took the flask from Shane and swallowed the burning dram. Kat handed it back to him, giggling, her eyes alight with a new cause for mirth. "Aye, mine is filthy. But not Elizabeth Tudor's! Oh, he's a howl! Wait til I tell ye! The English messenger came with news of his peerage, and what do ye think? He brought a wee gown for myself- to set the fashion in the bogs, d'ye see? One of Elizabeth's aul frocks...that had never seen the side of a washboard, by the stink off it! I swear to God, Shane O'Neill, the flies were dancing on it! Swooning and staggering!"

"Treacherous Scottish hoor!" O'Donnell was still growling. O'Neill was laughing. Kat was warming to her story.

"And this wee fellow here! -the one in the irons! -was that pleased...I thought every minute he was going to wear it himself! Oh, he was panting, and wagging his wee tail! Well, I was in a stoney temper...until I saw the forepiece inside. It was slobbered. Stained all across the forepart inside. And it was not blue blood, I can avow! Ach, if you had only one laugh, you'd have used it that day! I nearly broke my heart laughing!"

"There's a lesson in English refinement for the savage Gaels!" Shane was enthralled by this wild woman cavorting in the torchlight. He had never suspected such spirits could burn within the haughty countess.

"Wait til I tell you! The wee Englishman was that horrified at me... for I wouldn't take the gown. He finally offered to cut out the piece, and stitch in a fresh cloth. But the bold O'Donnell throws in his oar. 'Divil the stitch,' he says. Isn't the gown that bit more precious with traces of the royal personage upon it?"

"The O'Donnell's are a proud family." Shane, nodded his head as he laughed. Kat shrieked with laughter as a new notion caught her fancy.

SHANE O'Neill, 'the Grand Disturber'

"Wasn't it great good fortune there was only blood! Oh, it would set a cat laughing! 'Traces of the royal personage!' He has them himself- on his nose!" As the echoes of laughter faded in the dark hollows of the vault, O'Donnell's shackles rattled and the old man sat up. He spoke slowly, a low quiet voice.

"Laugh your fill, Katherine MacLean. There will be no laughter in hell."

"There will be when *you* arrive!" Kat drained her goblet. She folded her arms about her shoulders and shrugged, looking over to Shane. "I want to dance. It's cold down here." Shane put his powerful arm around her.

"I'll warm your blood for you." As he did so, she turned with his arm, spinning slowly out of his reach. Katherine smiled mischievously, and wagged her finger once more.

"I might stop under your plaid, Shane O'Neill, and I mightn't."

He descended again on his knee and emptied the flask into O'Donnell's tin cup. "There's a wee snout-full for you, your grace. Drink to the inevitable future." He lifted the fiery torch from its sconce.

"Guard!" As the heavy iron door opened fully, the wild strains of a harp could be heard from the hall above. Shane held the torch aloft and led Katherine up the narrow circular stair. They heard behind them the creak of the great door and the clank of turning bolts. As they approached the Great Hall, the soaring tune rolled and tumbled to a finish, and the revelers within burst forth a mighty ovation. It was Shane's captains and trusted sub-chiefs, all in the highest of spirits after the day's victories. They had smashed the grand alliance that the English had worked so hard to forge against O'Neill.

When Shane and Katherine reached the great oak doors of the hall, he stopped. Instead of opening them, he ensconced his flaming torch on the wall, and turned around to face Katherine in the narrow passageway. "You might stop under my plaid, is it?" He put his arms around the woman and kissed her fiercely. She responded momentarily, and then drew back and slapped him loud and hard. He laughed and pulled her close again. "There's a bold captive!" When he

SHANE O'Neill, 'the Grand Disturber'

saw the fury blazing in her eyes, he released her. Shane was clearly bewildered.

"I am not your prisoner, O'Neill. My husband is. You have a prisoner of him because it suits me that you do. I am the Countess of Argyll." Katherine, at her most imperious, could wither the most ardent or threatening of men. But Shane, towering over her feigned fury, could only smile –a sloppy, warm eyed, twinkling grin, that at once disconcerted and disarmed his militant red haired adversary. He had her fairly cornered in the close confines of the passageway, and he lowered his grinning face, bearing down on her, trying to coax a smile from her.

"Aye, a lovely fierce barking countess!" Katherine turned her eyes away.

"That was only a daft bit of pranking inside. A last blow to settle a score!" A sudden cold draught stirred the flaming torch above them, and she folded her arms over her bosom. They were both suddenly aware of the haunting slow air from the harp behind those great doors."You're shivering," he said. "And I've a fine warm plaid to stop under." It was the deep low voice of secrets.

"No.. Not under your plaid, no." Kat spoke loudly to break a spell. "I'll stop under your roof, and then I'll return to my father in Duart."

"No." His intimate tone persisted. Their eyes were locked.

"I'll go to my uncles in Ballycastle, and then I'll away for Scotland "No..."

She felt his grey eyes probing the deepest depths of her being, and she lowered her head. He gently raised her chin with the tips of his fingers, and kissed her passionately. Even then she made a fleeting half-hearted show of resistance before finally giving in. After, she laid her head on his shoulder, then suddenly drew back with a teary smile.

"You haven't heard a word I've said, ye great beast!"

"I've been listening to your eyes. They've told me all I want to know. Since first I saw you. The Lady O'Donnell." Katherine drew a breath, and denied all indignantly.

"I never spoke to you!"

"Not a word. No," he said. "Just these blue eyes. Regarding me in secret. At table, in the field -even at my back I'd feel them.. at the point of kindling. You'll stay with me now."

"How can I?" Kat's eyes were misty now, her voice pleading. "I would be a monster! The names I would get on the market hill! And I'd warrant them all!"

"You are my prisoner. That's all. The other names are for me." They kissed again, to the strains of the sweetest and saddest air ever coaxed from a harp.

The first full moon of summer cast its lustre over the castleyard of Benburb, tracing in deepest cerulean those patient dark horses that gleamed in the shadows. Only one of the dozen or so stirred and whinnied, as a young groom tethered the last of them to the hitching post. Across the courtyard, a towering bonfire leapt and danced behind the lively black shapes of Shane's army council, who were gathered around it awaiting his arrival.

The officers were mostly seasoned warriors with some grey in their shaggy manes. Dualta O'Donnelly and his brothers were there, along with Devlin, O'Quinn, O'Kane, and Black Hugh O'Donnell. Father Myler Magrath was always to be found at such conferrals, as Shane had an abiding reverence for his cunning. Various matters were being bandied and wrangled, contending for focus among the men. Several methers of ale were being passed about. A mether was a large square wooden mug with four handles, and the custom was to take a draught and pass it along. In the midst of all this was Farleigh the poet, snoring evenly into his white beard. Fergus O'Kane was fulminating, as usual, about the Scots that were pressing in on his holdings.

"It's all these Scotch redshanks pouring into the Route, driving all before them onto my lands. They've built another castle at Kenbawn, and they've no notion of leaving. We've got to put it to O'Neill to-"

"You haven't a hope, Fergus! Will you give over with that?" Dualta

SHANE O'Neill, 'the Grand Disturber'

Donnelly was weary of these distractions. "We need their truce, until we settle these English that are coming. Enough! Rise out of it." Father Magrath saw that O'Kane was getting the wind up.

"Now Fergus, these Scots are of the True Faith still. That's a weighty matter these times, with this new Protestant queen on the throne. The MacDonnells are Catholics." The huge lumbering chieftain turned on Myler now, with a roar.

"Catholics is it?" He spat angrily into the fire. "Ach these Scots would ate you without sayin' grace! They're more savage nor the English!" The wily cleric was deliberately engaging him on trivial points until his temper would abate.

"And they speak our own Gaelic tongue, if they mangle it itself. Didn't they come out of Ireland to begin with, away long ago?"

"That was not the day nor yesterday. They must have been the snakes that Patrick drove out with his bell! Aye, that's come slithering back into O'Kane's country." Myler laughed amiably, and took his turn at the mether of ale. He passed it along, and wiped his mouth on the sleeve of his cassock. He nodded his head to one side with a wink to O'Kane.

"I'll tell you why you haven't a hope of Shane attacking the Scots..." His voice was low now, and Fergus leaned in with an ear for listening. "O'Neill has taken into his bed the wife of Cullagh O'Donnell, a Scotswoman, and she's a niece to Sorley Buí MacDonnell! You haven't a whore's prayer."

"Ach, do you tell me?" Fergus drew back, eyes wide, and nodded with a crafty smile. "Sure that's good! He's the proudest cock that ever roosted! But, listen to me...Is Shane not married to the O'Donnell's daughter?" Myler Magrath shook his head.

"He sent her back to her father. That marriage was never blessed in church nor chapel!" Fergus O'Kane stared at him now with vacant wonderment, and suddenly burst forth with a roar of laughter. He reached over for the approaching mether. "Oh, you're a cute lot, ye are. And Shane's sword arm was never baptized -anymore nor was mine!" He laughed again, and drew forward to the friar. "Your true faith is as crafty and cute as the untrue faith beyond in England, so it

SHANE O'Neill, 'the Grand Disturber'

is!" With that he took a drink of ale. Myler was livid. He spoke loud and deep, with the weighty tones of a magistrate.

"This forest has wolves. It is no place for a sheep!" O'Kane exploded, spluttering ale in all directions.

"Who are ye tellin'? Who are ye tellin'? O'Kanes is no sheep! If we was, ye lot would have been run out by Scots long ago! No place for a sheep!? These forests is no place for a tree! Them same English are cutting down every bit of woods in Ireland. The whole island will be a barren stubblefield!"

Only Shane's arrival deflated the blustering winds of his rising temper. A ragged but spirited chorus of "O'Neill!" brought all eyes forward. Shane looked a bit rough, but all smiles, and the first thing he did was to dip his head into a trough of water and shake it. Gillie rushed in to hand him a thick linen cloth. He gave his eyes a quick wipe, and welsh-combed his black hair.

"Never mind 'O'Neill', ye blaggards! What have ye brought me? My poet needs victories. Auld Farliegh O'Gneeve can't ply his trade without victories..." His gaze fell upon the snoozing bard. "God Almighty, you've put the man to sleep!" Shane's face lit up with a sly grin. He dipped the cloth in the trough and swaggered over to the auld fellow. He gave it an almighty twist over Farleigh, wringing a drenching torrent of water onto the dreaming sage. "Get up out of that, ye dozy aul druid!!"

"Augh! Thunder and shite!!" All of Farleigh's limbs were flailing the air, like a cat on its back. "Gillie, I'll scorch your arse for you, ye little..." The great laugh that rose around the fire, brought Farleigh to his earthly senses. Shane stood over him smiling.

"A bad sign. A sleeping poet in a war council is a bad sign..." Farleigh sat up now, wringing his wet white beard.

"Sleep, is it? It was divil the sleep! I was composing. A poet closes his eyes to see!" At this point, Katherine appeared. Some few of them stood, with "God save you, Lady Katherine!" She sent Gillie off to fetch a towel for Farleigh. She was introduced to those unknown to her. Black Hugh was her husband's young half brother, and they eyed each other like two foxes. The young lad returned with a dry clout for the old man. Katherine took it and gave Farleigh's head a good rub, until he took it from her and continued to dry himself.

"There's a good man, Farleigh O'Gneeve! We don't want you taking ill. There's a bit of a chill in the air."

"Aye. Gillie, take Lady Katherine up to the Hall. Tell the harper to twist some Scottish airs for her."

"He'll do nothing of the kind!" Katherine's brows arched in magisterially high dudgeon. "I have delivered up the O'Donnell to you, and I have stayed the swords of ClanDonnell. Which one of these hairy-arsed heroes can do as much?" She looked the company from face to face, settling finally, her challenging gaze upon Shane. "I'll take the airs of the east yard, if you don't mind. Otherwise I'll have a wee war council of my own!" Shane laughed.

"It was Katherine who kept Sorley MacDonnell from joining in Sussex' combination against us. This wee woman is a mighty persuader. She'd coax a sheep from its lamb." There was warm ovation then, as she took her seat.

Dualta Donnelly, marshal of the forces, spoke next. "We've taken the Queen's O'Reilly and the Queen's Maguire. Set up their brothers to replace them. Good rebels, both. Just as we should do with O'Donnell here. He patted Black Hugh amiably on the back. A sound man!" As the cheers subsided, Shane raised his palm.

"That is a matter that will have to bide. The O'Donnells have rallied around Cullagh's son. But they'll not stir while I have their Chieftain below. We'll put Hugh in his place soon enough. But we've pulled Sussex' beard rightly this time. And that's our fight." Black Hugh stood.

"I have enough, and more than enough to keep my sword arm busy in your cause. My scouts have only just returned with their story. Dublin Castle is mobilized. Sussex has got the wind up, rightly. He's marching his army north. With cannon. They should reach the Newry by week's end. He's proclaimed you traitor, O'Neill, and warranted for your arrest. You're for the tower, cousin, if you're taken!"

"-Alive!" Shane's teeth glistened in a bold smile. The old poet raised his voice.

SHANE O'Neill, 'the Grand Disturber'

"A great honour for an Irishman, the tower! The highest laurel!"

"An honour I shall respectfully decline." Bright laughter crackled around the fire. "How many are they?" He turned again to Hugh.

"Twelve hundred horse, and eight hundred foot. Two cannon." O'Neill looked now to his marshal, Dualta.

"Near as I reckon, we have two hundred and fifty horse and three hundred foot. Five hundred and fifty in all, against their two thousand! And more than four score of them are but woodkerne, lightly armed and barely trained." The startling odds would have brought a dispiriting silence, but Katherine spoke.

"Although the MacDonnells have chosen not to ride with us, I have engaged a few bands of gallowglass, mostly MacLeans, MacKays, and MacLeods. Their long boats are sailing across Lough Neagh tonight." There were a few gaping mouths and even gasps at this unexpected revelation. The north of Ireland was awash in fierce Scottish mercenaries called galloglass, 'foreign warriors', who would often find themselves fighting against each other, and were known to switch sides at the glint of a shilling. "We'll have leastways a hundred and twenty by morning. And I promise you, they'll fight like twice their numbers!"

A rowdy cheer went up, in spite of the still daunting odds facing them. Shane smiled and cocked his brow at her, but she shrugged, affecting a routine indifference. She was, indeed, a marvel, and a sneaky one!

"Let the Saxons come!" Black Hugh's voice rose over the rest. He looked to Shane, and the others followed suit. Shane stood now. His fires were lit and they shone in his eyes.

"We'll wear them out! Lead them a lapwing's chase- away from the nest. Through the bramble and into the bogs! And when they're rightly wasted, we'll meet them in the open field." A muted cheer followed, that bespoke uncertainty and doubt. Because of their smaller numbers, the Irish had always relied upon guerilla tactics. Fergus O'Kane was as fierce a warrior as any since Ferdia and Cúchulain of the Golden Age, and yet he was cautious as to strategy and position. He knew that he spoke for many.

SHANE O'Neill, 'the Grand Disturber'

"In the open field? At these odds? With a raggedy band of woodkerne? Would we not be best to keep to the uplands? Hit them, and hit them, and then get away to hell out of it, same as them before us did. And not be scattering our bones across a field!"

"If we don't put a halt to their march, the heretics will rule here as in Dublin!" Myler's voice rang as from a pulpit. "Who will stop an army of heretics by sniping from the trees?" O'Kane was not to be gainsaid by a windy 'brown-frock' in matters of war.

"If the Pope won't abide these English heretics, still he never changed his law agin' self slaughter. We'll lose the here and the hereafter!" There was uneasy laughter. "We haven't the numbers for to meet them head on. A good run is better than a bad standing!"

"We can make a *good* standing!" Black Hugh O'Donnell spoke over the uncertain murmur that followed O'Kane's words. "We can make a good standing on ground of our choosing, with gallowglass at our side. If we meet them on the high plain, their shock will fight harder in our cause than those few legions they have over us!" A hearty cheer this time. Shane stepped forward.

"We'll not face them til we have the edge, but this time and henceforth it must be the English who scatter into the wood. These are our hills and our fields, and they must no longer be let to tread upon them! I've seen you fight beside me, and I know that we can drive them back to the Pale in fear of their lives!" A massive cheer rose up now, and someone dashed spirits into the fire, for the flames climbed high into the night. "Together we will destroy Sussex' forces and capture his arms. He's brought his cannon into Ulster and here they shall stay. If Elizabeth Tudor would put her paw in the fox's den, it will be a meal for the fox!" A lively roar now, and Fergus stepped forward again, and raised his sword in the air.

The sword of Fergus O'Kane is the edge we will have over them. When you've stepped in behind it, we'll meet them in the field and we'll take the day!" As the cheering faded, Shane turned his back signaling that the rustic conclave was adjourned. All around the fire there rose the cry 'O'Neill abú!' (O'Neill to victory), and the company broke up into quiet chat.

SHANE O'Neill, 'the Grand Disturber'

Shane brought a mether of ale over to Farleigh, who was peering up at the night sky. "O'Gneeve, you'll have a victory to set your quills scratching for a twelvemonth!" The old poet nodded, and motioned with his merry eyes to Shane's side. Back a few paces stood Katherine, with an enigmatic smile, and a gleam in her blue eyes. Shane turned and faced her. "Katherine MacLain is in a loud hush this while. Or are you just sharpening your tongue for the next volley?" She stepped slowly past him, then turned with a toss of her reddish hair.

"If you're inquiring after the shape of my tongue, you'd best see for yourself. It's cold here under the stars." With that, she moved through the crowd, and Shane watched her until she disappeared into the castle keep. When he turned back, he saw that Farleigh's eyes were closed.

"Farleigh, old man, are you dreaming again?"

"You may rely on it." The old rhymer sighed, and winked. "The waking dream that we dream together. And it's a good dream." Shane offered him the mether. Farleigh gave it an indifferent sniff, and peered up at him with a wicked glint. "Get along with you, ye randy hoor. Go tend to your 'prisoner.' She's cold under the stars." Shane laughed, took the mether in both hands for a mighty swig, and handed it on as he moved to the door. Farleigh gazed up again at the clear night sky. "Aye, the sun to warm the body...and the stars to warm the soul."

SHANE O'Neill, 'the Grand Disturber'

CHAPTER 4

Outside the towering walls of Dundalk, boisterous crowds were gathered, clamouring to see the Lord Deputy's army, as it marched off to war. Bright banners flashed and fluttered in the early morning haze, as the endless parade spilled forth from the narrow gateway. On and on, over a mile in length, shuffling and snorting, the deadly serpent snaked its path through the dark drumlins north into O'Neill's country.

Each local chieftain, upon seeing the massive force, sent runners off to Shane O'Neill with news of its whereabouts and its 'whereabound'. The best guesses in his camp supposed the Deputy to be heading for Dungannon for an assault upon O'Neill's castle there. Cannon were not commonly used in the field as of yet, and the 'Wilde Irish' kept very few fortifications in their domains, as they presented such irresistible targets for the predations of the Strangers.

With the Deputy's forces invading Ulster, Shane ordered a small guard unit to move his prisoners, O'Donnell, O'Reilly and Maguire, from his castle at Benburb to the safety of a cranogue. A 'cranogue' was an island fortress found in many a secluded lough. The island was created from nothing, with a ring of stakes in the water, filled in with earth and stone, and then built upon as a defensible bunker to hide prisoners or treasure. He sent these men to keep Cullagh O'Donnell out of the way of the Lord Justice, moving him from one island and islet to another, in the wilds and recesses of Tirowen, until Sussex should leave the country.

Never venturing so far as Dungannon, Sussex instead brought his forces to Armagh, where he burned the town to ash, just as he had done three year previously, driving its inhabitants off into the forests.

SHANE O'Neill, 'the Grand Disturber'

This time he seized the cathedral on its lofty hill, and billeted a garrison of two hundred troops within its massive walls. The church made a fine storehouse for his arms and provisions. As it was the seat of the Roman Catholic Primate of all Ireland, he knew that the insolence of the gesture would be a bloodcurdling taunt to the 'disloyal savages' not only in Ulster, but in all the wild regions beyond the Pale. Occupying it would prevent the new Primate from presiding there, or conducting his Romish rites within. He boasted that its chiefest defense lay not in its strong walls, but in the Papish superstition of the Irish, for *that* would deter them from attacking the blessed cathedral. Having secured this bastion in the heart of O'Neill's country, the Deputy fell back into Meath, where several days later he was joined by Lord Ormond with more troops from the Pale and flying columns of Scots galloglass.

Sir George Stanley had been left in command at the cathedral garrison. Upon seeing a scattering of Shane's woodkerne drifting into the smoldering town, the officer sallied out after them. Suddenly, on the crest of a hill outside the walls, appeared a force led by Shane himself. With him was a Roman Catholic Archbishop in his mitre and robes. It was the new Primate of Ireland, Donagh O'Tighe, riding alongside the Irish chief on a white horse. He had received the pallium in Rome on St. Patrick's Day, and his preferment represented not only a huge victory for Shane's long diplomatic offensive in Rome, but a bitter defeat for London. His presence with Irish forces in the field was unprecedented, and shocking to the English. Stanley and his company turned on their heels, and raced back to their cathedral fortress.

Now the whole Irish army appeared over the crest of that hill, led by a procession of Franciscan monks, and 'every man of them carrying aloft a blazing faggot' to burn the cathedral over their heads. The monks sang a Latin Mass, and the Primate galloped three times around the Irish army, sun-wise, in the ancient druidic manner, to steel them with his blessing. He invoked the Archangel Michael, and exhorted the men to 'go forward in the name of God; to put right the abasement of his sacristy by foreign heretics!' The old chieftain of the

SHANE O'Neill, 'the Grand Disturber'

O'Mallons rang the sacred ancient bell imparting St. Patrick's celestial encouragement to the forces. Shane swore a mighty oath not to turn his back, and with an eerie bone-tingling howl, his legions came on. The Irish assailed the cathedral on the lofty summit, shattering the stained glass into deadly showers of glittering spikes and splinters, but the garrison proved too well fortified. The well-armed citadel of stone and slate withstood the barrage of fire. After some sharp hand-to-hand fighting under a strafing of lead from the towers, the Irish army fell back to the friars' quarters outside the cathedral close. They set them ablaze, and marched back over the rise to their camp.

A few days later, Sussex and Ormond arrived back at Armagh with their main force in search of an enemy to fight. Shane held back, biding his time for a propitious moment. The Ulster skies glowered and growled over all, and a ceaseless torrent of rains flooded the rivers and byways. The English army languished, idle and weary, in their fusty moldering encampment, as disease set in and provisions ran low.

For want of any discernible headway, Sussex sent Ormond to treat with Shane. The Butlers of Ormond were rivals to the House of Kildare in the South. They were shirttail relations of the Queen through the Boleyn line, and could always be counted among the staunch supporters of the crown. In their brief parley, it was clear to Shane that Ormond was quite ill. Still he blustered and threatened, but Shane refused to give up Cullagh O'Donnell. He offered to tender some worthless hostages and to depart forthwith to the Queen, but he would nowise submit to her Deputy.

When Ormond arrived back at camp, Sussex was elated. He had expected nothing to come of the parley but time, perhaps, for some opportune chance to arise. It had. Some of his Irish spies had brought word to him of O'Neill's vast hoard of cattle and its secret hiding place. Shane possessed massive herds of cattle, numbering in their many thousands, a commodity that, in this Irish pastoral society, represented true wealth and power. He had driven his kine into secluded pastures in the Breffney of Cavan for safe keeping while the crown forces were about. Sussex was delighted with himself over this momentous bit of tattle. Cattledriving was a traditional war manouvre

SHANE O'Neill, 'the Grand Disturber'

that carried great weight among the Irish, and Lord Sussex determined to have them.

Now, as it happened, these spies of the Deputy's were Shane's own men, acting under his orders, as he played upon the credulity of Lord Sussex. O'Neill merely wanted to draw the English forces into the bogs and brambles to have at them.

Lord Ormond had indeed taken ill, and Sussex "in an evil hour" as he said later, remained behind to attend him. The Lord Justice sent out from the camp at Armagh a company of captains, Sir George Stanley, Fitzwilliam (Sussex' brother in law), and Wingfield, with two thousand men, both horse and foot, to take the preys and spoils. His Irish spies led them into the hills of Cavan. O'Neill was kept apprised of the movements of these troops; and he marched silently and stealthily to meet them. They were to have been attacked at night at their first halting place, and it was only a chance turn off from their planned route that spared them. The herds of kine were driven off, and still no Irish enemy appeared.

Early the following morning, after they had collected their preys, they marched out in loose order back towards Armagh. Fitzwilliam, with a hundred horse in his train, was over a mile in advance. Behind them plodded five hundred men-at-arms, with a few hundred loyal Irish from the Pale trailing them. Another hundred horse under James Wingfield brought up the rear.

O'Neill's troops, greatly outnumbered, waited behind the rise of a low hillock along the brakes and thickets of a brambly stream, as the long straggly line of soldiers and cattle passed slowly by. When at last his scouts saw the backs of Wingfield's rear guard, Shane gave his signal.

Over the rise they charged, setting upon them from behind. Wingfield had allowed himself to be surprised. Instead of holding his ground, he galloped forward upon the men-of-arms, and as the horses and men struggled in a melee of confusion, on came the Irish. From out of nowhere, in a savage onrush they came, howling their fierce battle cry 'Lamh dearg abú!' [Lauvderrig aboo] Red hand to victory! Wingfield's cavalry, in panic and terror, rode down his own men.

SHANE O'Neill, 'the Grand Disturber'

Finally, breaking free of the seething crush, they fled the field and made for the crest of an adjoining hill, as Shane's warriors rode into the broken ranks hacking their way through footmen on all sides.

Over a mile ahead, Fitzwilliam rode blithely forward, unaware of the pandemonium in his wake. Suddenly an uneasy murmur behind caused him to turn his head. A lone horseman in a mad gallop was tearing up alongside his line, wildly waving a red kerchief of distress. Fitzwilliam brought his men to a halt, and suddenly, in the silence that followed, the screams and cries of battle could be heard on the misty morning wind. He wheeled his charger and galloped to the rear, followed by Sir George Stanley and the rest of the advance horse.

They charged into the bloody fracas, and sent a captain to rally Wingfield's horsemen on the crest beyond. As those forces converged on the battle, Shane saw no further gains to be had, and sounded the recall note. His men turned as one and withdrew from the field, unpursued. O'Neill's kerne had driven off the stolen herds during the welter of battle, and his army now followed, to restore them to hidden pastures.

Of the English, more than a hundred lay dead or wounded, a scatter of scarlet over the field. This was the first time the Irish had ever seen English soldiers in red livery, and it was known as 'Catha na gCotaí Dearga', the Battle of the Redcoats. The survivors straggled back to Armagh without the precious cattle and without their honour. They were so dismayed, it was said, as to be unfit for further service. Sussex and Ormond returned to Dublin without Cullagh O'Donnell, but with much to explain to (or conceal from) her Majesty.

A fortnight later, on St. John's Eve, there was a joyous midsummer's feasting on the rise above Benburb, celebrating the wondrous outcome of the bloody affair. On the crest of the hill, before the towering midsummer bonfire, Shane presided over the open-air feasting. He had slaughtered many of his beeves to feed the multitude that assembled there. Small fires burned here and there surrounded by hungry kinsmen, and the air was sweet with the aroma of roasting oxen. Each fire was straddled by three posts, from which was suspended an ox hide filled with meat and stew, simmering over the flames.

Under a beech tree at the crest of the hill, where steady breezes kept the smoke at bay, Shane and Katherine were seated at the centre of a long low table. At his left hand was Father Myler Magrath, the tonsured Franciscan in his place of honour. It was customary for him to speak while the company ate, and he did his best to amuse and inspire them. His theme on this occasion was the Lord's bounty, and His divine favour of their cause, as witnessed by all in the great victory at Armagh, as well as a stirring tribute to the fallen.

The usual entourage took their places beside the long victual-laden board. Along with the great platters of beef and broth, the table was covered with fresh ferns, on which were piled loaves of oat cake, wheaten cake and bannocks, parsnips, carrots, and watercress. Wicker baskets of yellow butter, wooden bowls, tankards and goblets covered the rest of the table. Apart from those at the O'Neill's board, the people ate with 'shligawns', a kind of mussel shell that served as both spoons and knives.

The full compliment of O'Neill's household was in attendance along with Shane's two champion wolfhounds, Flann and Scohaun who mingled freely, and were well looked after by the company. The enormous hounds had a merry hunt, flitting in and out through the crowd, spilling ale, as they dragged off their trove of greasy bones and meaty joints. Pipers piped and harpers harped.

After the meal, when dusk had settled to dark, the great bonfire was lit, and Farleigh O'Gneeve was called before it to give his account of the battle. It was a new ode, epic and lyrical, and, as poetry was the principal medium of drama, it was eagerly awaited by the crowd. The objective was not literal truth but epic truth. The harper strummed quietly, giving wild twists and turnings where the verses paused. Farleigh stood before the fire and cast a word spell, stirring

SHANE O'Neill, 'the Grand Disturber'

the senses of the throng. His powerful voice rose and fell, quickened and slowed, so that the listeners' pulses beat as one, one great beast, tamed, enthralled, and thrilled before him.

> "A shiver of pain
> rolled through the soft fair hills of Eire that day,
> like the shadow of a low cloud racing,
> darkly tracing shame across the startled hills.
> The gentle hills and braes
> bundled and hunched hard against the grey,
> like proud flesh at the touch of the stranger,
> the touch of the stranger.
>
> Crow by crow,
> the skies emptied and stilled
> and the twitching trees kept watch
> with a thousand crow black eyes that day,
> that day,
> when into the Gap of the North
> surged forth
> the blood red column of Englishry.
>
> Aye,
> Once inside the wheat sewn womb Of Ulster hills,
> The brands were lit and raised.
> A score of miles apart they paced
> And scored a searing gash.
> Burned to blackened ashen waste
> Each standing field
> Or fold or fallow,
> Height or gentle hollow
> Where the English legions trod.
> They left nor stake
> Nor scollop in their wake.
> Each chapel, shrine, and sacred well

SHANE O'Neill, 'the Grand Disturber'

Debased,
They hacked their plodding path
Toward that blessed place,
Toward the holy city of Armagh.

The hosting of O'Neill Road out then,
Marched out then
To the smoking hills,
And turned the English forces
From their road,
To trudge the fens and drumlins
With their load.
Drudge of iron cannon wheels
On a course of mire And bog,
Gorse and bramble
Snapping at their heels
Like a peevish hungry dog,
and arrows whirring blindly
Through a fog.

Rumbling clouds burst through the nights,
flooded the days and narrow ways
Of Ulster's thorny heights.
A stag of seven tines,
 swift and silent through the pines,
O'Neill, through the fastness of the wood.
Then he stood.
Some one of his liegemen raised the cry,
a fearful cry,
to trace that line of smoke across the sky.
He reeled upon his stallion when he saw
the city of St.Patrick
blazing like a house of straw.
Above the fire ,
the ancient spire

SHANE O'Neill, 'the Grand Disturber'

in the holy city of Armagh.

The grey eyes of O'Neill
sharpened in a twisted grin
and flashed and kindled them
a raging fire within.
Then a demon marvel did begin.
The trees of Ulster
shook their twisted limbs
and scattered to the skies
those startled rooks
that roosted there.
A feather storm of crowblack wings
beat the heaving air
and raised a hellish din.
And the death screech of the Morrigu
writhed and danced upon the wind.

The unbaptiséd arm of Shane O'Neill
raised aloft his sword of glinting steel
and stilled the very clamour of the crows.
He swore an oath upon his sword
Above his battered shield,
To feed each crow his fill Of English guts,
A princely meal!
To lay a feast of blood upon the field.

Onto Macha's smoldering plain,
That level place at Emhain, came
The legions of the stranger
In the company of death.

Like a lightening cloud
He thundered through the raging battle flood,
and bolts of vengeance

SHANE O'Neill, 'the Grand Disturber'

ploughed the field of blood.
The heart of O'Neill
Boomed in his breast
Like a drum of war.
And rocked a fiery pulse
Among the Irish hearts,
Behind him and before.

Hooves pound hard ground.
Swords ply, spears fly,
Bones break, earth shakes,
Arrows strike, piercing pike.
Saxons fall. O'Neill takes all.

Routed! Running!
Standards down!
In disarray
They fled the fray.
Reeled and fled!
And left their dead!
The forces of the crown!
The air resounds
With victory's sounds,
Shrill and loud
For Shane the Proud,
A victory of blood and steel,
For the red hand of O'Neill."

July was cold and rainy, with the raging Blackwater flooding its banks, an impassable angry bulwark for Ulster. With armies at bay, words were flying. Scripted messages of terms, demands and conditions were sailing and galloping between Benburb and Dublin

SHANE O'Neill, 'the Grand Disturber'

and London. Having driven the English out of his lands, Shane now proposed to treat with Lord Ormonde as a deliberate humiliation to Sussex. He sent his secretary Neil Grey with letters, accompanied by his seneschal Cantwell, to Dublin to speak for him and to present his terms. Shane made a point of flaunting the conventions of courtiers, and he enjoyed writing in mock humility of their great wisdom and of his rude ignorance, as he pulled their reins and turned their heads.

Shane O'Neill to Lord Sussex, Viceroy:

My humble duty premised. I wonder very much for what purpose your Lordship strives to destroy me, the faithful subject and the steadfast liegeman of Her Majesty the Queen, without any ostensible cause, but that you wish to aggravate her royal Majesty by unnecessary expenses in commencing an unjust war against me. And I have more to say on this subject, if it were necessary; but I say this only, that, until you take away your said soldiers from Armagh, I will not go anywhere else, but will, to the best of my ability, by God's favour, defend myself against your unjust war; but since you have unjustly levied soldiers to place them against me at Armagh, I being driven to it will approach the sacred presence of my Lady the Queen, which I have long wished to do, and which I shall never desist from accomplishing, viz., to present my person before my most serene Mistress.

But to prevent my journey, you, as soon as you came to Ireland, without any just reason, sent a force of soldiers into my country, you, who ought to have advertised me friendlily of your arrival in Ireland. I call the Most High God to witness that I have nothing more at heart, and that I wish for nothing more anxiously, than to present my person before Her Serene Highness; and although she may learn that I am mendacious to those dwelling in Ireland on account of your Lordship, nevertheless you have proved yourself more mendacious in word and deed than I am considered to be. And I beseech your Lordship, if you do not desire to do injustice to me, that you will,

SHANE O'Neill, 'the Grand Disturber'

as you ought, send my messenger with my letters into the presence of Her Majesty; which if you do not do, I will send a messenger to Her Highness by the way which is in my power; and in the meantime I will seek no security from your Lordship unless on this condition, that you withdraw the said soldiers from Armagh. And know for certain that by the journey in which your Lordship intends to thwart me to make my appearance before my Lady the Queen, I have lost three thousand marks of my property. And I am not more certain of this than you are yourself, and many in the English districts.

Farewell. 1st July, 1561.

I am,

O'Neill.

Shane to the Lord Deputy Sussex:

My humble duty premised. I have read your proclamation against me, and I would wish, if it were agreeable to your Excellency, that you would not delay to send my messenger with my letters before Her Highness the Queen, that I may, as I well can, take exception to every single article contained in the proclamation. And in the meantime, please to say if it please you to withdraw your soldiers from Armagh, and to have the peace between us which I wish for, til the return of my messenger from the presence of Her Majesty; or whether you rather wish for war, which I do not decide upon, because I would prefer peace. And I call the Great God to witness that you desire, without any cause, to withdraw my subjection and my obedience from her Gracious Majesty. And be it known to your Lordship for certain, that whatever shall be ordered by my mistress the Queen, agreeable to justice and reason, and which may be transmitted to me by your ambassador, be it war or peace ye wish to have with me, I will accede to without doubt. Fare ye well.

From my woods, this 17th of July, 1561.

SHANE O'Neill, 'the Grand Disturber'

I am-
O'Neill.

The long dim days of that rainy July at the fireside, dictating to his scribes, left Shane restless, and when August brought its sunny sultry days to Ulster, he took himself off to the Glenconkein wood to hunt with the Donnelly brothers and a few other mates. He was away from the feast of Lughnasa 'til Crom Cruach Sunday, little less than a week, reveling in the heat and the hunt. He was a keen shot with his longbow, and when he had chased down his quarry, he seldom missed his mark.

With a stag of seven tines slung behind him across his horse, Shane approached Benburb castle feeling pleased and heroic, and trying to fend off thoughts of the heavy concerns that would await him there. His retinue departed with a boisterous farewell, and headed down the hill to the army's encampment. As the gates drew open before him, Shane saw two large wagons being unloaded into his keep. A low sized wedge of a man carrying a trunk appeared behind the second wagon, and gave a quick nod to Shane.

"A fine roe stag you have for you!" His clothes were Irish, but his speech was Scottish.

"What are ye's at here?" Shane nodded to the wagons.

"The lady Katherine. Her goods and her gear out of Donegal Castle. Shane glanced at the great wagon piled high with trunks and carpets.

"I'd say there are fierce echoes now in O'Donnell's keep." It occurred to him that this delay was clearly adding weight to young fellow's cumbersome burden. "Go on along with that. Tell her the O'Neill is returned."

The fellow's eyes went wide. The shirtless shaggy man on the horse could have been any hunter. He nodded again. "I will, aye. It's only the goods and chattels as she listed in her letters." He turned and lumbered off, just as Katherine appeared out of the shadowy archway. Her simple yellow frock and her auburn hair shone like a flame in the glare of noonday sun. Shane laughed to himself, as he had never seen her in an apron before. She smiled brightly as she hurried to his side.

"I see you've brought the supper! Aye, well, you were long enough about it! Did you wrestle him down?" He laughed, and she stepped into his shadow so as to avoid squinting. "Your secretary's been waiting on you this while with messages. The stout one."

"Aye, Neil Grey. He's back from Dublin, so. How are the boys?"

"They're chasing each other about the stables, the last I saw. Your sons are coming round to me, Shane! Wee Éamon brought me a handsel of wildflowers, and Turlagh was reading off for me one of Farleigh's poems yestere'en."

"Didn't I tell you they would? Where is Farleigh?"

"He and the lad are down the mud flats, slithering about. Where else do you suppose in this heat? He tells me it cures his pangs and twinges." Shane's eyes brightened.

"The mud, aye! We'll have some wild muck below after the torrents of the past weeks. Put down your apron, woman, and we'll bathe!"

"I will not. I've work to do, Shane O'Neill."

"Acting the scullion? In this heat?"

"It's cool enough inside the Keep. And there's dirt enough inside your castle if I were minded to wallow in it! You won't know the kitchen or the great hall! We've been at them for days." She tossed a quick glance over her shoulder at the Keep. "Your auld aunty is none too pleased with me, I can tell ye. She's forever lurking about behind me like a wee ghostie, giving me the fish eye. And always the sour gub on her!"

"Ah, Poor aul Bríd! She's done the keeping here since my first wife left me, and she always tended the servants. Sure, Moya paid them no mind." Shane's horse snorted and whinnied, shifting weight under him, and Katherine took a step back. He glanced down pointedly at her apron, nodding. "She likely reckons you're treading on her toes - mistress of the house and char-maid too!" He beamed at her now, his smile and his voice as bright as the day. "But I'm sure you can coax her to you. Use one of those smiles that set *my* wits astray!"

"Smiles? I've tried them all! She didn't see anything she fancied!"

SHANE O'Neill, 'the Grand Disturber'

"Find something for her to busy herself with, and she'll come round."

Katherine tossed her hair, and with a wry smile, she spoke it blunt and blithe. "She'll not come round til I'm shrived and wived. That one takes a dim view of connubial bliss without the nuptials."

"Aye, she's devout, -but she's devoted. And when she knows how much I love you, she'll make peace with the devil. Aul Brid nearly reared me herself when I was fostered out to the Donnellys." He leaned down to her and suggested with wink, "Why don't you leave *her* to the house-chores and slip off with me now?"

"Go 'way with yourself! I've all my parcels and appurtenances to sort!" Her face was suddenly radiant with joy. "Och, Shane the place will be that bonny you'll be dazzled and dazed! Wait til ye see! And now I have my tapestries!" She looked with sudden concern over to the wagons, where the lads were struggling with pieces of a massive canopied bedstead.

Shane tried again. "But it's Sunday; you mustn't work. It's sinful wicked." He was determined to coax her. "And it's Crom Cruach Sunday. If one god doesn't get you for it, the other will!" Crom was one of the old gods, malevolent and crooked. He was said to have occupied a massive carved stone in Killycluggin, until St. Patrick split it with his crosier, unleashing bolts of lightening. Somehow his day in high summer has held its place in the Gaelic calendar even to this day.

"Och, Shane, my girls are come from Tirconnell, and didn't they bring my wee cat Pishogue! And those lads as well. My grand retinue from the isles! They're sorting out the chambers above the east hall for themselves. I'll feel that much more to home here now, with them about."

"All the better! *They* can unpack your things for you! Will ye not come down? It's near onto a week since I laid eyes on you." His voice was pleading.

"Oh, it's your eyes you want to lay on me, is it? I will not, Shane O'Neill!" A sudden gust of haughty airs, perhaps in answer to his pleading tone, possessed her demeanor now, and she took the opportunity to scold, but not without a saucy glint in her eye. "I'll not

SHANE O'Neill, 'the Grand Disturber'

be slipping into the mud with you any time soon. In the company of these wooly mates of yours. And you with the horn, poking out of the mud and acting the wild man. And pawing me in sight of all! Oh, you're mad! Too free with your friends; too fierce with your foes! Respect comes of distance! You want to learn that much by the English!" Shane laughed heartily.

"Yes, your Ladyship!" He looked down at the stag's head behind his foot, and brought his horse around to face the butchers gate. "Well, I'll not detain you. I need to go up the river and cool my blood."

"So you do!!!" Katherine smiled and tossed her flaming hair. "If ever anyone's blood needed a cooling!" She regarded the ruddy tan of his glistening chest and arms. "And you've a queer fiery hue on your pelt! You look like a wild red man from the New World! Barring only the feathers!" They laughed, and she faced for the loaded wagons. She turned back. "I'll tell Neil Grey you'll hear his news after the dinner!" Shane halted.

"Tell him to bring his letters down to the mud flat. And his quills. And a flagon of wine!" Katherine shook her head after him.

The Blackwater was swollen high over its banks, swirling darkly around ancient trees that appeared to be wading into its cooling stream. Indeed the day was fairly sweltering for Irish weather. Shane hiked the quarter mile upriver to the rocky bend where the mudpits lay. A swirl of drifting smoke just beyond it told him that Gillie would be stoking up the sweat lodge, and he reflected that it was hardly needed on such a day as this!

Shane smiled as his thoughts returned to another sultry day more than a dozen years before. Young Henry Sidney was acting Lord Deputy at the time, and he had brought his troops up to Dundalk on the edge of the Pale. He sent his messenger to summon Shane to appear before him there, and Shane had refused. He wrote Sidney that his "timorous and mistrustful people" would not allow him to go, for

SHANE O'Neill, 'the Grand Disturber'

fear of his safety, but would he not come to the lodge at Fathan, and stand gossip for his new son's christening? And, fair play to the big fellow, he relented and came. Shane had reversed the summons, and the mountain had come to Mohammad.

Shane was married that time to Tríona MacDonnell who, after some stormy years and a brood of children, left him for his philandering, and returned to her father. They had entertained the Lord Deputy lavishly in the Great Hall, with fine French wines in crystal glass, and even fleshforks on the table! Unlike Lord Sussex, Sidney was a genial fellow, known among the Irish as 'Anraí Mór na Beorach' or 'Big Henry of the Beer.' They had reached an understanding –noninterference, for the most part –and things had remained quiet enough until Sidney was replaced in office.

Shane was thinking back to a day, the morning after the christening, when he had brought Sidney out to a mudpit beside the lodge. He told him it would clear his head. While that much was true, he had also wanted to shock him. And perhaps to test the limits of his cordial bonhomie, which Shane regarded as but another device to reduce him. In truth, Shane took a perverse glee in unsettling these grey-faced foreigners. It never hurts to act the wild man. Let him know that he is leagues away from the ruffled courtiers and powdered faces of London, and that their codes of dubious honour mean nothing here.

One would not soon forget Sidney's look of stupefaction and discomfort, as he stood dumbfounded, facing the naked muck savages of O'Neill's court. When he'd regained his composure, he affected to laugh and commend their rude health, but he never loosed his stiff collar or doffed his warm coat in the sweltering sun. Shane smiled now to think of him reporting the spectacle at court. "Learn by the English," Kat had said. "Respect comes of distance!" These people were laughed at in the meanest hovels in Ireland! Respect comes of fear alone.

Shane doffed his trews and tossed them onto a bush next to Farleigh's. That was the only sign of the auld wizard, for he was most likely above in the sweat lodge. It was a low bothy with walls of sod, built over a trickling rill that billowed up in steam over the hot stones. A great comfort in cold weathers, but not for today.

Shane plunged into the mud with a splat and a thump, sending splotches of earth flying in every conceivable direction. The cool mud was fresh and bracing after the morning's journey from Glenconkeen Wood, and he laid back and kicked his long legs about, listening to each gush and thunk in the mucky mud. He stopped of a sudden and opened his eyes when a great roar issued from a rock near to his feet.

"Are ye mad, or what ails you?" The voice was Farleigh's. "By Crom the Crooked! Is it wild fits you're taking?" Two piercing blue eyes glowered in a muddy black lump maybe a yard's distance from his feet.

"It's yourself, is it?" Shane laughed. "I never saw you. You look like you're melting into your elements there!"

"Time enough for that, thank you very much..." Farleigh knelt upright now, so that his shoulders could be discerned on either side of his molten mass of muddy hair and beard. "What way was the hunt for you, then?"

"Great sport altogether. Labor for the limbs and rest for the mind. And a fine roe stag for the dinner." Shane dunked his head in the mud and came up looking like Farleigh, bedrabbled and black. He filled his lungs with the musky pungent air and savored the fresh earthsmell about him. He opened his eyes to see the dark oozing form of Farleigh, red mouth agape with laughter, the bright eyes twinkling like gemstones in a dark mine.

"Ah, we're a right pair!" the poet said.

"Pair of what?"

"Insatiable *voluptuaries*!" Farleigh thundered his verdict like an Old Testament judge, then a merry laugh. "The man who can luxuriate in God's simple elements has wealth that can never be lost. Not even time or hoary old age can rob him of it!"

Shane looked intently at the old man, and the bright fervor in his eyes peering out of the mud. This was the clearest image of the human soul he had ever witnessed. An animated spirit shining forth in the molten muck! A wily old saint with the divil in him. Shane lay back

SHANE O'Neill, 'the Grand Disturber'

now, and closed his eyes against the sun that was burning brilliantly directly overhead. The buzzing of a fly...the faint hum of bees in the...breeze in the trees...riverrush of the Blackwater...

"Hoigh!" The voice of Neil Grey. The secretary. A heavy mantle on a hot day! But a flagon of wine would not go amiss! Shane raised his hand and waved to acknowledge the approach. Gray was a portly fellow of a nervous disposition, but amiable enough. A Dublin man by birth, of an English father, but his mother was Tirowen bred. He had both languages from the cradle, and it was said that his writing and learning came of a failed try for the priesthood. Kat's hasty assessment was that he was equally uncomfortable in both worlds. "Lady Katherine sent me down to you, although I've nothing urgent to report." He was a bit winded, by his voice.

Shane stood, and high stepped through the sucking mud to the grassy bank. He strode purposefully up to Grey, and as he approached him the stout man backed away, his eyes wide. The towering muddy naked man reached his hand out, and the stout man flinched. Shane laughed. "Give us over that flagon, for the love of God. I'm not going to kill you. Or kiss you!"

Grey gave a nervous laugh and slid the strap from his shoulder. Shane took the flagon and stepped back into the ooze, as Neil Grey followed him to the edge of the grass. There was a sizable log nearby and he rolled it closer and sat upon it. He opened his leathern case, and peered intently at its contents. He looked up furtively, and drew a deep breath as he reached into it. Grey shivered now, as his fingers touched the cold steel of a loaded pistol, and instantly drew away from it, clenching into a tight fist. He sighed, and managed to compose a taut little smile, as he carefully extracted a few papers from the case. Shane settled himself near Farleigh and looked up expectantly. "Well, what news out of Dublin?"

"Will I read the letter out?" He was donning his spectacles.

"No, no, man! After the dinner. Just tell me how it stands."

"Ormonde was nowhere to be found. His officer said I must speak to Lord Sussex, so I did. The Deputy says you've been attainted 'traitor' and there will be no talks until you release O'Donnell and the

SHANE O'Neill, 'the Grand Disturber'

others." As he spoke, he slipped the letters back into the case, and took out an inkhorn and quill, and a sheet of vellum which he laid carefully over the leathern case on his lap. He knew he would get much of his first draught here. "He never said, but I heard reliably that their robes and collars and coronets had arrived over from England for their investitures. So he's in a stew about that. He says he'll not treat with a traitor; that you need surrender at Dublin Castle forthwith!"

"These men -Are you inked?" Shane awaited his nod. "O'Donnell, O'Reilly, and Maguire are my liegemen. They are lawfully detained for nonobservance of duties. I will *in me arse* repair to Dublin to answer these empty charges." The secretary looked up with a dubious squint. Shane winked. "Fix it!" He waited til Grey looked up again. "Yet there will be charges aplenty to level for your unprovoked and wanton wasting of my lands." When Neil Grey raised his quill, Shane asked, "And what of my demands that he withdraw from Armagh?"

"Not a man, he said"

"Tell him this. 'If you remove your soldiers, I will repair the cathedral at my cost, but I will not make peace while they remain on my lands. No one in his senses would believe in the peace while such a sign of war remained. As long as there shall be one son of a Saxon in my territory against my will, from that time forth I will not send you either settlement nor message, but will send you my complaint through some other medium to the Queen.' He awaited Grey's look. "What of my going to London?"

The secretary hesitated and swallowed. "He laughed. Said if you go to London, it will be in chains!"

"As for Dublin...the only visits I shall make to the Pale will be with fire and sword. In future, I will parley with headquarters, and not with hindquarters!" This drew a big laugh out of Farleigh, who had been listening intently to this 'business in the bog'.

"Oho! You're some can of piss! 'The hindquarters!' I wonder would that be lost on an Englishman?" Shane gave the flask to Farleigh, and turned again to Neil Grey.

"Pack your papers away til tonight. Had Sussex any other bargains on offer? Some dark undertaking for you, perhaps?" Neil Grey started visibly. He raised his thunderstruck eyes and spluttered, "Most certainly not!" He stood up and swallowed. He inspected his person and papers now, jerking his head from point to point like a bird. "Perhaps I've misunderstood you?"

"I think not. Murder and such. Dirks, poisons, and pistols; that sort of thing..." Shane stood up, a pearly grin shining out of his muddy face.

"No, no. Nothing of that sort." He carefully blotted the sheet and blew on it. The stout man closed his case now, and began backing away. "Well, I-"

"Why don't you kick off your breeks and take the mud with us? You look to be stifling!" Shane tipped a wink to Farleigh. "We're about to bathe in the river."

"Ah, no, Sir. I couldn't, Sir. I've a touch of a chill. I'll be rightly in a while if I take rest."

"Tell me this, Grey. Did you see the Dean?" Neil Grey expelled a deep breath.

"Father Donnelly had gone off to London before I arrived." He looked up suddenly with forgotten news. "Oh! Lord Kildare's peace party is making headway. A crowd of the Dublin gentry have been petitioning against Lord Sussex, and all are saying now that Kildare will be commissioned to negotiate with you! I haven't heard any official word, but I've left you letters from him and Dean Donnelly up on your desk. And evidently Lord Sussex believes it, for it threw him into a raging fury."

"Oh ho!" There was a tumult of laughter and splashing mud. "I think I can come to terms with cousin Fitz! Give us a sup of that, ye spindly old mudlark!" The secretary called out to him, over the muddy commotion.

"If that will be all, Sir?"

"Go on away with you, so!" Shane picked up the wiry old poet and dropped him with a splattering splunk into the ooze, and the portly dark figure disappeared into the trees. Shane laughed and staggered up through the mud onto the mossy bank. He drank from the flagon as he watched Farleigh O'Gneeve tottering on his skinny shanks, lurching slowly onto dry land. He looked decidedly top-heavy, with his mud-soaked hair and beard. Shane held out his hand and the old fellow grasped it. It took a mighty pull to extract his feet from the stubborn sucking mud.

Farleigh was winded. He gave Shane a sideward nod and wink, and reached for the flagon. When he had swallowed a gulp, he heaved a sigh. "What was all that about poisons and dirks? That was wild queer stuff! Your man near to fainted!" Shane cast a glance to where Grey had disappeared into the wood.

"We'll have to keep our eye on that one. Every other envoy I've sent to Dublin Castle has come back with reports of secret offers, to spy for them or worse. He's the first of them not to tell me of it! And he was prickly and skittish. I'd say he's taken the shilling."

"I wondered what you were at. He's a quare duck right enough! But I'm thinking he hasn't the guts in him for such capers." He shaded his eyes with his hand, and squinted up through the brake and bramble to the white whisp of smoke that still twisted its way into the sky. "Where the blazes is that young skitherer gone off to? Gillie!" He waited and heard nothing. "Do you fancy the sweat lodge?" Shane shook his head. "I suppose the day is sweaty enough. All the same, it puts a powerful thirst on the skin, to drink in all the richness out of the water. The Blackwater is full of turf and minerals! That's why it's black. Teeming with the stuff of life!" He saw Shane starting to amble downriver. "With the floods, I had to find out a new wee spot for bathing." He pointed up to the rocky bend.

Shane followed, and they swam in the sunbright clearing. Some frisky otters had claimed the spot before them. 'Waterdogs' they were called, and Shane had sport chasing them around the swirling white water, where the mossy rocks and boulders make their brave stand against the tumbling flood. With all traces of mud dissolved into the river, Farleigh stood on a crag to dry in the sun. Shane fancied he looked like a ghost; a tangle of white hair and beard over the pasty white skin that covered his wispy frame.

When Gilly arrived, they made their way back to the castle. Neil Grey was nowhere to be found, and word was that he had left Shane's

SHANE O'Neill, 'the Grand Disturber'

letters on his desk, and galloped off along the Dundalk road as though he had demons at his heels. Katherine ventured her theory, and at least half in earnest. "It was likely the sight of ye lot, lepping about in your pelts like the madmen of Bedlam!"

Farleigh nodded to Shane. "I'd say now, he was a man who wouldn't like to get his hands in the mud." Katherine smiled.

"Your Éamon was that excited over Neil Grey's new mount. A clever wee lad. He seems to know everything about horses."

"Oh?" Shane gave a knowing look to Farleigh. "What sort of horse is he riding now?"

"Éamon said it's a fine black Arab stallion. Very costly, he reckons." The men exchanged meaningful nods at this revelation. Katherine put her hand to her mouth. "My God, Shane! Wait til ye hear. Grey told me that the story is everywhere in Dublin that you have me *chained to your bed!*" Katherine's eyes were wide. "Chained to your bed!" Shane laughed.

"You should have told him 'No, that's another woman!'" More laughter followed.

"Oh, ye think that's great sport? Of course, he told them it was lies," she added hastily, over the bright cacophony of mirth.

"You shouldn't refute such tales!" Farleigh's eyes lit brightly. "Such a story could win you battles!" Katherine gave a quizzical look to Shane.

"Farleigh is right. Would you want to fight a man who has a woman chained to his bed?" Shane laughed and nodded to Farleigh.

"Such tales of fierceness will ward off challenges, and play in the minds of your enemies to weaken them when they face you." Farleigh lowered his tone with great reverence. "Words are a powerful weapon!"

CHAPTER 5

Far away in London, Queen Elizabeth sat with her secretary Lord Cecil in the privy chamber at Whitehall. A late summer shower drummed steadily against the high leaded glass window behind them as they puzzled over the latest dispatch from her Lord Deputy in Dublin. She gripped the letter tightly, tensely, with both hands, and held it up before her to best capture such light as availed her on the gloomy afternoon. She squinted and frowned, and then protested aloud, "He furnishes not the vaguest detail of what befell there. Ah!" Some new outrage had presented itself. "This beggars belief! 'The forces of settled government are afforded little credit for small victories over rebels, for as they are expected to gain them; whereas rebels acquire prestige for the very slightest successes at the expense of governments.' Aye, you may tell him, Aye!" There was fire in her eyes as she turned them on Cecil. "Aye, victories are expected of him! This 'slight success' for O'Neill at Armagh was likely of some slight magnitude, else he would hardly need belittle it!"

She resumed reading the letter before Cecil could respond. He could see only her deeply furrowed brows overtop the page until she lowered it revealing a sour smile. "It seems the Almighty is to blame!" She read on, "Man by his policy doth propose, and God at His will doth dispose.' So you see he is hardly to be blamed when God is labouring for O'Neill! And still no accounting of losses!"

"A prior letter has perchance gone amissing." Cecil had the difficult task of trying to calm the royal temper, without seeming to take Lord Sussex' part. There had, indeed been prior letters; written

SHANE O'Neill, 'the Grand Disturber'

privately to Cecil himself, wherein Sussex gave a detailed account of the matter. Cecil later confided in his journal that when he heard the evil tidings of the disaster at Armagh, he was so appalled that he had much ado to hide his grief, for there was no-one with whom he could share it. 'There was not a person at court, no –not a person, not one, who did not either wish so well to Shane O'Neill, or so ill to the Earl of Sussex, as rather to welcome the news than regret the English loss!' He could not betray Sussex now. He suggested brightly, "He writes as though a full account of the battle had been dispatched heretofore. Oft times these missives go–" Elizabeth's raised palm bid him to stillness, as she read on in silence, grinding her teeth.

"After conference had with John O'Neill's seneschal Cantwell, I entered talk with the secretary Neil Grey; and perceiving by him that he had little hope of O'Neill's conformity in anything, and that he therefore desired that he might be received to serve Your Highness, for that he would no longer abide with him, and that if I would promise to receive him to your service, he would do anything I would command him. I sware him upon the Bible to keep secret what I should say to him, and assured him that if it were ever known, during the time I had the government there, that besides the breach of his oath, it should cost him his life. I used long circumstance in persuading him to serve you to benefit his country, and to procure assurance of living to him and his forever, by doing of that which he might easily do. He promised to do what I would have him do."

She looked up, bristling, and affected an ironic smile. "It seems We should have saved us our armies and sent you in their place, Cecil. Lord Sussex has engaged a 'secretary' to complish what his legions can not! He has fumbled in the field, and now resorts to dagger and cloak. He writes, 'His secretary, Neal Grey, affected to dislike rebellion, and by his manner gave me to believe that he might serve as the tool wherein we should have quit of his master. In fine, I brake with him to kill John O'Neill, and bound myself by my oath to see him have a hundred marks of land to him, and to his heirs for his reward He seemed desirous to serve your Highness, and to have the land, but fearful to do it, doubting his own escape after. I told him the ways he

SHANE O'Neill, 'the Grand Disturber'

might do it, and how to escape after with safety; which he offered and promised to do. I assured him, Your Highness, he may do it without danger if he will; and if he will *not* do what he may in your service, there will be done to him what others may. God send your Majesty a good end. Signed, Thomas Radcliffe Lord Sussex." She turned her frozen smile again to Cecil for his response.

"A fortnight and more is passed since he put his hand to this. Mayhap this secretary has 'complished the deed, and O'Neill is no more to be feared. And this defeat at his hands is of no consequence. At this remove, we can but hope."

Only days had passed, when Shane got word of his secretary's fate. The O'Hanlon, whose demesnes encompass the furzy hills outside the walls of Dundalk, sent news of Neil Grey. "I have a kinsman well placed within the town, who avouches that he witnessed with his eyes the capture of your secretary Grey as he put his foot on board of a ship bound for France. Three Englishmen, strange to that town, seized his person, and carried him off into the mountains of Mourne. They were later to be seen drunken in a dockside tavern, boasting and gloating of his murder there, and counting out gold coins got from Pierce, the constable in Carrickfergus, for payment. They called him a rank coward, in that he had renigged a promise to slay O'Neill."

Shane summoned his other secretary Garret Fleming and fired off his charges against the Lord Deputy to the queen herself. He professed to believe that she could have known nothing of the plot, and that as a loyal subject, he was apprizing her of treachery in her ranks. As to the ongoing contentions, he maintained that O'Donnell and the rest were legally detained, that Sussex incursion into Armagh was unwarranted and illegal, and that the continued occupation of the battered cathedral was an act of war.

His letter's arrival sent the Queen into a fury. Firstly, it was the first indication that Shane was still alive; secondly that Sussex' ill-conceived plot had failed; and finally that news of these dark intrigues would cast a pall of suspicion over her administration in Dublin. She dictated a short response, accusing Shane of slander against her officers, citing the paucity of evidence, and suggesting he produce a body before taking 'the legal proceedings that must be pursued if he be in earnest.'

Elizabeth wrote in her own hand to Lord Sussex, castigating him for his clumsy and unsuccessful attempt on O'Neill's life. This, along with recent revelations about her army's defeat at Armagh, prompted both a new stroke in policy toward her nemesis in Ulster, and a furious rebuke to the Lord Deputy. "...By your blunder, O'Neill has captured two cannon, fourteen military drums, seven standards and enough horse and weapons to arm every rebel in Ulster. This must we hear from the Spanish ambassador, when our very captains would deceive us! And you are probably hiding yet worse news! Lord Sussex, you have failed. Your failure has been a direct encouragement to the disaffected. You have confessed yourself powerless to carry matters with a high hand. There is nothing for it but to temporize. We shall summon O'Neill to London."

In Dublin Castle, upon reading the queen's castigations, and her resolve to receive O'Neill in London, Lord Sussex pounded his desk and flailed the air in a growling hissing fury. He was alone in his chamber, cursing O'Neill and the coward Grey, and his enemies at Court. "Sidney and Dudley are at her ear again! Blast them into the bowels of Hell! Cursed knaves!" Sir Henry Sidney, who had preceded him in office was the brother of his wife Frances, but family ties did nothing to soften the enmity between them as rivals at Court. Sidney was married to Mary Dudley, and was firmly in the camp of her brother Sir Robert Dudley, the queen's favorite. Sussex had an abiding hatred for Dudley that rivaled in passion his hate for O'Neill.

He poured a small port wine for himself, and stood a long while at the window watching the dark low clouds scud across the Dublin Mountains. He waited until his blood had cooled, 'lest his pen utter

SHANE O'Neill, 'the Grand Disturber'

somewhat of that swell in his stomach.' He tamed his passions and ordered his thoughts, and when he was ready he sat with quill and ink.

"...So please your Majesty to but stay the course. Our nation in this realm is likened to the French in Scotland. We be railed on at tables with terms not sufferable. The people are incensed to wax mad. Here in the Pale all are prophesying a total change of policy and religion, and so refusing to obey any law. I pray your Majesty be constant. Your policy now is as useless and unprogressive as Penelope's web; woven by one governor only to be picked to pieces by the next. It would be for the Queen's honour either to support her representative cordially, or to recall him honorably in some other place where I can do better service. At the least, so please your highness, for so much of my dignity as remains, receive O'Neill *not* until I am come to witness."

Shane's cousin Lord Kildare was, as predicted, charged to negotiate with O'Neill, and the insult to Sussex was widely conceived. The feeling on the border and in the South was in Shane's favour. It was said that Sussex would soon be replaced. The hundred tongues of rumour were busy everywhere naming first this lord, and then the other to his office. Everything was believed but the truth, and naturally orders were disobeyed and rulings disregarded.

For some months bartering went on to lure Shane to London. He resolutely refused, until Sussex' threats gave way to coaxing and generous inducements from the higher powers in Whitehall. At FitzGerald's suggestion, Shane had begun a correspondence with Lord Robert Dudley, and sent him some highly prized falcons and hawks. Dudley told Kildare in London, that Shane should hold out for the most propitious terms, and that Kildare should simply grant them at the last possible moment. A bit of mummery, brash and bold.

Dean Terence Donnelly found his diplomatic mission a trying ordeal. He blushed shamefully as he put forth O'Neill's deliberately

SHANE O'Neill, 'the Grand Disturber'

outrageous demands to Lord Cecil. The brazen insult of such disingenuous negotiation in clerical garb! He asked for £7,000, and laboured to keep his face composed, as Cecil, looking quite dumbstruck, asked him to repeat it. And then, to repeat it once again!

Shane's demands were shocking at a time when a farm labourer earned £5 a year; a school headmaster or a shipmaster £20. A prominent barrister or a landed gentleman would see £1,000 in a year's turning. One pound would purchase a cow, or a pistol, or a coat of plain cloth. Most people's weeks were counted out in shillings and pence. £7,000 for the journey? Cecil knew when he was being hoodwinked. Shane was assessing the value of his own majesty, as a rival king!

Ultimately Cecil was prepared to vouchsafe whatever would bring the recalcitrant chieftain to London where he could be dealt with. He knew his challenge was to pare down the stakes of the deal until they could be presented to her frugal Highness, without fear of the gallows! Finally, with tentative terms on offer, and a carefully crafted letter of safe conduct, Dean Donnelly and Kildare made their way back across the Irish Sea.

Accompanied by Viscount Baltinglass, and by Lords Slane and Louth, Kildare rode out from Dundalk on the edge of the Pale, to the windy gap of Carrickbradagh, the usual place of parley. It was a small castle guarding the Moyry Pass between Dundalk and the Newry. Its name means 'the rock of the robbers,' and it was thought to be apt, for someone was usually robbed in the wrangling negotiations that echoed in its draughty hall. This time it would be Kildare, albeit quite willingly.

Fitzgerald was acting on behalf of the queen, so all formalities were observed. The presence of the other lords precluded any undue familiarity between the 'contending' cousins. On the first day of negotiations, Shane affected to be in bad humour and would listen to nothing. On the crucial point of the English garrison at Armagh, he would give not an inch. He finally bellowed his demand for their withdrawal with a stony face, turned his back and galloped off to his lodge at Fathan, his train of followers behind him. He was many miles

SHANE O'Neill, 'the Grand Disturber'

gone when a messenger overtook him. He was to have his way in the matter.

Upon his return the following day, O'Neill deigned to sit at table with the delegation, the Dean of Armagh at his side. After spirited deliberation, they reached agreements on the Articles of Peace, as well as the terms of pardon, conditions for his journey to the Queen's presence, and the stipulations of his safe conduct.

Kildare acceded to all his demands, and agreed even to remove the garrison of soldiers from Armagh Cathedral. In the interest of good will, Kildare convinced Shane to accept that their withdrawal would await his actual departure for England. As to money, Kildare assured him of the lesser but still incredible sum of £2,000 sterling, 'that he might conduct himself abroad in a manner fitting to his station.'

Sussex had raised the cry that were O'Neill to be provided with a great sum of money, he would surely renege on the journey to London, and resume his rebellion. To prevent such a temptation to perfidy, it was agreed that £500 would be paid him by Kildare at the start. £1,000 awaited him at Chester, and a final £500 would be got in London. He was compelled to offer up three hostages to Dublin Castle for his good conduct, although he protested that he himself would be little better than a hostage in London.

Upon his return to Benburb Castle, Shane found it thronged with his dependants and their messengers, all awaiting news of the Articles of Peace. Dean Terence read them out in the courtyard for all to hear, and then Shane's more intimate retinue retired to the Great Hall to hear of the safe conduct, and the Queen's letter summoning him to Court. Among them were O'Kane, O'Hagan, Farleigh, Black Hugh, and the Donnelly brothers. Katherine welcomed them in and old Bríd Donnelly seated them. As it was a crisp autumn day, she had the servants pass around steaming tankards of mulled ale. Each table was plenished with baskets of apples and bowls of hazelnuts. The Dean read out the terms, and finished with her Majesty's closing. "...signed before and after, sixth day of October in the third year of her reign; Elizabeth R."

There was a stunned silence, only the crackle of the wood fire, sounding, perhaps, like the frayed and snapping nerves around the table. Shane's eyes went wide and swept the company, and then crinkled in a boisterous victorious laugh. "There is nothing in it but an invitation to supper!"

Uneasy laughter followed, and Farleigh spoke over it with deep commanding tones. "Aye. Every night for the rest of your days...in the Tower of London! Like many's the guest before. What are they at? She knows you'll never go to London."

"Does she? Does she indeed?" Shane sat himself up on the end of the table with feet on his chair. "She'll withdraw the garrison from Armagh, and give me safe conduct, and two thousand of English pounds for the journey. The Queen of England has met my terms. She wants to parley!"

There was some amenable nodding. Only Farleigh ventured to speak.

"A trick and a trap! That's my own good opinion of it for you."

"Sure, anyone would think you don't trust them!" Shane turned his sly grin to the others, prompting a ripple of laugher, and the O'Kane stepped forward. Brandishing his sword, he spoke his spoke.

"Put your trust in God and your sword." He raised his shaggy brows, squinting, and lowered his tone conspiratorially. "And keep your eye on God! That's what the O'Kane says." Mock cheering now, with sly winks and drumming on the table, for they knew he was in deadly earnest. Dean Donnelly stood, smiling and holding up the Papers of Conduct, bringing the room to attention.

"This is the key to our security! Now this is a matter of great consequence. She has to honour a safe conduct, or she'll not be able to offer it to the next man." He looked to the chief Brehon for support. O'Hagan nodded sagely.

"True for you, Reverend Donnelly. Their English law is a powerful

SHANE O'Neill, 'the Grand Disturber'

weapon. They'll not cast it aside lightly. A safe conduct will stick." He looked around to a murmur of assent, but the poet was not about to abandon the hard bought wisdom of his many years on the planet. He spoke with passion, holding aloft a bony finger for emphasis.

"Like any weapon, they'll toss it aside when it fails the job. There's many a man known to all here that left his mortal life without a 'whereas' or a 'wherefore' of English law on him, but only quick-poison! English law is a crafty snare, and if you come through it safe, they have daggers aplenty for your back!" A loud gabble of doubt and dissension echoed through the hall. Shane slid off the table, swallowed back a slug of the mulled ale, drawing all eyes to himself. He slammed the tankard down onto the table, and wiped his mouth on his sleeve, as the room fell silent. "I'll not *turn* my back. I'll face them!" He flashed his roguish smile across the company. "This young Elizabeth needs to hear what the O'Neill has to tell... Elizabeth Tudor is a woman of twenty-five years who has no man. And if I can't get around her, I'll go through her. Up the middle the way she'll like it!" Raucous laughter again, with drumming and cheers. Shane hoisted his tankard. "If I don't come back...you'll know that Shane O'Neill is King of England!"

A merry commotion of cheers and laughter swelled and echoed back upon itself in the vaulted hall, and in a trice died eerily away. Katherine MacLean had risen from her seat. Her presence had clearly been forgotten. She walked proudly to the great doors and then turned to face the room. Her tone was firm but her voice was easy as she faced her lover across the room. "This English queen is not a blushing fool. There's many a proud man's head adorns her battlements. And Mary Stuart is in Scotland. She has warned you and even forbidden you to go to Elizabeth's court." He smiled.

"This is not Scotland yet, my Lady. And even there her commands are but hopes and wishes." Behind her, she could hear the heavy doors parting for her, and then a tense silence.

"Right. Go you then to Elizabeth. There's a saying in Scotland, Shane O'Neill, that if you would sup with the devil, you must use a long spoon." Her eyes swept over the seated company of men. She bowed her head. "Gentlemen," she said brightly in farewell, turned, and took her leave as some of them leapt to their feet. All heads turned back to Shane expectantly. His eyes shone as he held his gaze after her at the doorway. He smiled broadly again.

"There's one that knows well the long spoon of Shane O'Neill. That lovely woman carries my child!"

More cheers, with cries of 'Fine woman!' and 'Good on ye!' Farleigh raised his tankard. "A health to Katherine MacLain! She's more than a lady; she's a woman. And a damned fine handsome one!" Tankards clinked and ale spilled under a chorus of 'God bless her!' 'Lady Katherine!', and 'Katherine's health!' Old Bríd Donnelly bit her lip and quietly blessed herself.

Shane sat again, his eyes afire, calling out his plans for the journey. "There's money enough to keep a retinue of forty. Farleigh old man, you're coming to London!" Farleigh still looked doubtful, but he was smiling. The chieftain turned to his marshal, Dualta Donnelly. "I want a guard of the biggest galloglass, lads of comeliness and mettle. We'll put the tailors to their task. I want all after the Irish fashion that's outlawed. And the hair in a shaggy glib. Not a word of English from any as might have it...our best harper,...and Farleigh the Bard. If she wants a submission, I'll give her an Irish submission made of Irish defiance!" A thunder of cheers. O'Hagan turned to Farleigh to see if he was as yet resigned to the news.

"Would ye credit it? Our Shane is bound for London!" Farleigh gave his sidelong nod and wink.

"Aye. So he is. But he's going as a King!"

Heretofore the voyage to England had been a phantom to threaten Sussex, or a ruse to spin out time. Now it loomed before Shane, a dark ship in a murky fog, ever darker, ever closer, towering higher and higher before him. As the details and dangers of the venture clarified,

SHANE O'Neill, 'the Grand Disturber'

Shane thought more coolly about the enterprise, and repented of his blunt words to his future hostess concerning the Neil Grey affair. Although he had taken care to level all blame on Sussex, he had spoken of his outrage. After all, Elizabeth was not accustomed to communications of such undisguised defiance. Even the other potentates of Europe employed diplomats to shade their messages with nuance, and to dissemble on points of contention, so as not to arouse her displeasure. Perhaps, as she put aside his letter, she had savored anew the prospect of seeing him in custody, away from his fastness in Ulster. He would dictate to MacKeever another letter to her Majesty. This he did in the late morning with goblet of fine wine, when his powers of flattery and deftly concealed irony were at their peak.

> "To Her Royal Highness,
>
> And now I am going over to see you, I hope you will consider that I am but rude and uncivil, and do not know my duty to your Highness, nor yet your Majesty's law, but am brought up in wildness, far from all civility. Yet have I a good will to the commonwealth of my country.
>
> Please your Majesty to send over two men that you can trust, and will take no bribes or otherwise be imposed upon, to observe what I have done to improve the country, and to hear what my accusers have to say, and to judge of Tirowen and the Pale, which country is the better governed. Let them hear also the complaints of the families of the Pale, what intolerable burdens they endure of cess, taxes, and tallages both of corn, beefs, muttons, and porks. Not only do the soldiers live at free quarters, but they have their dogs and their concubines all the whole year long in the poor farmers' houses, paying in effect nothing for all the same.
>
> Within this year and a half, not less than 300 farmers have come into my country out of the Pale. These men were once rich and had good houses, but they dared not so much

SHANE O'Neill, 'the Grand Disturber'

as tell their griefs to the Queen, yet the birds of the air will at length declare it unto you. It is a very evil sign for your kingdom that men shall forsake the Pale, and come and dwell among wild savage people.

I am
O'NEILL

In the upper quarters of Benburb Castle, the faint wash of first-light was stealing into the nooks and corners of O'Neill's bedchamber, sketching out the dim shapes of the room, and slowly overtaking each shade and shadow of night. Katherine lay awake, nestled up against her plush eiderdown bolster, peering out at the vague colorless world before her. If only the night would linger! A frisky morning wind was whistling about the creaking casements, trying to find its way in. And the jackdaws! She was determined to banish from her mind the insistent rasping plaints of those troubled jackdaws in the courtyard below. It was surely they who had wakened her! Roused her from a wonderful dream that now eluded her memory.

She closed her eyes and tried once again to recall it, but instead she became aware of the slow rhythmic swell and sigh of the slumbering man beside her. With each heave and roll of his chest, and the low rumble and purr of his breath, the bed itself seemed to breathe like a warm living thing, and soon a kind of quiet lazy rapture settled in upon her, to feel so cozy with the heat of him under the quilts and coverlets. Like a womb. She laid her palms flat upon her swollen belly. Near onto five months. She had felt him today – *yesterday* now. 'The quickening' they call it. Not a kick as yet, but a stirring. Life.

Yes, felt *'him'*. Old Farleigh *must* be right. How queer it was! Before she knew, herself. He told her she had a right broody look about her, that she was flushed and glowing with new life. And she had instantly accepted his verdict, for there *had* been a strange elation those weeks that she couldn't account for. And Farleigh said 'he' would be fine and healthy. So that was that.

A little catch in Shane's breathing now hastened the drowsy tempo of his soft bellows. Kat noted a sudden tremble, and even a furrowing twitch in his brow, and she smiled to think what sort of dream possessed him here at her side. He was leagues and miles away. Already. In just a few short hours she would watch from this window as he and his men disappeared into the far hills beyond the Blackwater. By tomorrow this bed would be still; a cold barren expanse with little comfort for a lonely heart.

But, no. Such notions only weaken the spirit. She let her thoughts flit from perch to airy perch, considering first her French tapestry that graced the wall before her. Its colours could just be discerned now in the faint morning light, but they were still a mere whisper of the vivid hues that she loved so. She could hear Pishogue purring outside the door. He would be some wee comfort round the bed, settling into the pillows, preening and waiting to be petted and stroked. It had taken everything to coax Shane to keep his two hounds out of the room. "Smelly aul beasts," she thought, "all fleas and slobber. Not fastidious like Pishogue. He'd let the pair of them lie across the bed with him, drooling and scratching!"

"Still, he's coming 'round. London will smarten him up to refinements. Thanks be to God Kildare is going along. You couldn't trust them. Who would be up to them? For treachery. Two months of a journey, he says. We'll see. Elizabeth would be mad to let him escape her clutches. And she's not mad. Not by a long taper. He's never been to London. Even if he doesn't come to be locked in the Tower, it could be the ruin of him. Just seeing the scope of that city, the fleets, and the riches. It could well slacken his resolve. He's that cocksure, charging over these hills, but perhaps if he knew the leviathan that lay beyond them, he would lose his mighty spirit." Still there was no more question of stopping him than the tides. Or the cool grey morn that was, yes, that was settling into the room. Below in the courtyard, a cock crew now to put its seal on the matter.

SHANE O'Neill, 'the Grand Disturber'

Shane stirred with a single long snore, stretched and turned the broad of his back to her, then fell back into his even slumber. As the blankets shifted she could smell the salty sweat of him. She sniffed at her own soft shoulder, wondering did she smell of last night's exertions, but it was mostly a rosy remnant of her French perfume that lingered still. "Will he take me again this morning?" she wondered, and slowly ran her fingers through her hair, freeing the silky tresses that were bunched flat against the pillow. "He will of course, for he's a brute! But I have a wee power over him, all the same. He'd go through hoops in Hell to get me stirred up for him. I waited long enough for it. After those two pasty paunchy old men, I couldn't abide the naked touch. Small wonder! Now I long for it. When he was away last, I *ached* for him! And now when I need him, he's off again for the Dear knows how long, and the blackest days of winter closing in." She ran her hands lightly over the swell of her belly. "He'll not worry himself of my fidelity while he's gone! Leaving me in this state. And he's off to hoor his way through the brothels of London. I'll be fat as a broody aul hen, scuttled in the high heaths of Tirowen, without so much as..." The cock crowed again. And again.

Shane rolled over onto his back, heaving a long drowsy sigh. Suddenly he opened his eyes and bolted upright. Kat gave his back a gentle stroke. "Be easy for yourself, love. It's only second cockcrow. The world is only beginning to stir."

"Aye, the wagons are packed." He yawned and stretched his massive shoulders. "There's naught to be done 'til the boys are assembled and the drays are harnessed and hitched." He turned his drowsy eyes to Katherine and she could see the sleep leaving them, as they grew bright and piercing. Her disheveled hair seemed to capture all the light in the room, and her face was fresh as dew. Her blue eyes regarded him with softness, and she watched as the first flicker of a wicked glint met her tender gaze. He lay back and reached his arm under the coverlets til his big hand rested lightly on her belly. Katherine smiled.

"Aye," she said, "he's still there." She sighed and tilted her head. "*He's* not gone off to London on me, at any rate." Shane laughed low and quiet. "What manner of husbandry is it, Shane O'Neill, to sow your seed, and leave your field to the wild winds?"

"Will I tell you to stay out of the winds now? Or is it a fine shawl you're after?" His hand gently stroked her belly, finding its way to the warm moist flesh below, and Katherine trembled under his touch. He laid his head on her shoulder, his short rough beard scratching against her fine silky white skin. She breathed deep and nestled her head against his tousled black hair. She spoke into his ear with a lazy little voice, chiding him playfully.

"A fine shawl, is it? You had better bring me more nor *that* from the high shops of London! Leaving me lumbered with this great belly, while you go off catting about …"

Shane sprung up onto his knees, and drew himself over top of her, his two strong arms outstretched above her shoulders. His grey eyes glistened as he bore slowly, slowly, down upon her. He spoke in the deepest whisper.

"Do you think I can bear to be parted from you? It's little you know me, Countess Kat!"

On that cold grey morning in late November, Shane and his party set out upon the first leg of the momentous journey. On his right was his cousin the Earl of Kildare, and on his left was Black Thomas Butler, the Earl of Ormond, leader of the pro-English faction in the Irish Parliament. The man who had accompanied Sussex on his foray into Tirowen. Both were occasionally political enemies of Sussex. Shane had been adamant that he would not stir without the assurance of their company.

Each of the earls' ensigns rode before them with their bright colors fluttering above them. MacCaffrey, the hereditary standard bearer of Tirowen, flourished the 'red hand of O'Neill', keeping a few paces to the fore. Behind the earls were Farleigh and Gillie, the chief Brehon Art O'Hagan and the tonsured chaplain Myler Magrath, Will Fleming the barrister, O'Devlin the sword bearer, and Blind Colm

SHANE O'Neill, 'the Grand Disturber'

MacCuarta, with his harp strapped upon his back. There were the three designated hostages for Sussex, various grooms, stewards and squires, two Arabian stallions, three wagons loaded with trunks, and MacSweeny, captain of the guard, with his magnificently turned out gallowglass, numbering some forty in his train.

Shane had left a cousin, Turlough Lynnach O'Neill, to act as chieftain in his absence. Turlough resided on the western side of the Sperrins, and he had been chosen 'tanist' (successor designate) to Shane at Tullahogue, on the evening before the investiture. He aspired to rival Shane, but in fact, gave him little cause for worry. The safe conduct precluded any interference in Tirowen in Shane's absence.

The splendid procession twisted its winding path through the drumlins and hills to Dundalk, and then followed the Dublin road along the coast of the Irish Sea. The sight caused quite a stir among the denizens of the Pale, who were more accustomed to O'Neill's fire and sword, than to this stately progress through their villages. Word of his coming had preceded him, and men, women, and children lined the roads to glimpse the fierce Gaelic chieftain of the North.

Just below Malahide in the county of Dublin, they turned inland a short ways til they came upon Balgriffin Castle. The estate of about three hundred acres, known for its fine watermill, had been granted in 1545 to Shane's father Conn, the Earl of Tyrone, for services rendered to King Henry.

It had a turbulent history that was not yet history. Conn's brother in law, an uncle of Kildare known as Silken Thomas, had lost the estate after his failed rebellion, and Conn had been granted it for not having joined in that rebellion. It was now a bone of contention between Shane and Brian, son of Matthew the late Baron. The young pretender was currently in possession of Balgriffin, having the support of Lord Sussex, but this evening upon Shane's arrival, the estate was deserted.

Brian 'MacBaron' was not in residence, and at the sight of Shane's gallowglass, the retainers and servants had fled, and could even now be seen scurrying over the hills. Although smoke was still curling up from the chimneys, the manor was empty, and the gates were

SHANE O'Neill, 'the Grand Disturber'

unlocked. The O'Neill and his party settled in for the night and helped themselves to the abundant provisions that had been reluctantly left them.

The following morning a lone rider galloped into BalGriffin with a letter for the O'Neill. He was winded, and his horse was well sweated, for he had ridden all the night from Tirowen. He said that the letter had arrived shortly after their departure, delivered to Benburb by a Franciscan monk. He looked at the other two Earls, and determined to say no more. Shane sent the courier off to be fed, and repaired to his private chamber to read it.

The letter was from Mary Stuart in Edinburgh. In it, she pleaded with him not to go to London. She warned him of the treachery awaiting him there. She bid him to stay fast in his demesnes; that she had written on his behalf to the Holy Father in Rome, and would afford him aid when her kingdom was secure and the time was propitious. She exhorted him to release her good cousin Katherine MacLean from sinful bondage, 'to conform to the precepts of our Holy Church in his personal affairs, and to beshow a moral standard commensurate with his exalted station, that he might yet prove himself worthy of the Divine Providence that he will surely need in future.' Shane crumpled the letter, then reconsidered, folding it and slipping it into his satchel. A measured response would secure her good will. "The missive came too late," he thought. "It came to me, alas, in London."

When he was ready, the two earls escorted Shane into the city of Dublin. Behind them rode the three hostages. Henry O'Neill was Shane's son by his first marriage, raised in fosterage by the Donnellys since his mother's departure. He was fourteen years of age, tall and thin, with already a stubbly beard heralding his coming of age. He relished being in his father's company, and standing hostage for Shane's return. Only those of highest blood could take on this noble task. He had never been south of Drogheda, and longed to walk the lanes of Dublin. Beside him were Dualta O'Donnelly's son, Donal gorm, and Shane's cousin Phelim O'Neill. They would be kept in comfortable confinement for the month or so that Shane would be in

SHANE O'Neill, 'the Grand Disturber'

England.

Bright banners fluttering before them, they crossed the Liffey not far from the glorious cathedral of Christchurch, entering the city at Bridgegate. From there, they made their way along High Street to Dublin Castle amid the cheering throng of Dubliners who pressed in to view them. The Catholics of the Pale were very apprehensive at this time, and the sight of the fierce Catholic champion of Ulster, along with the staunch Lord Kildare, aroused their simmering disquiet to a fevered passion. The cheering could be heard even within the great stony towers of Dublin Castle.

Upon reaching the castle, the hostages were given over to an official named Master Shortall, a brusque wiry fellow, more short than tall, who promised to look after them and see to their needs. Lord Sussex, of course, deliberately kept the three earls waiting for two hours and more, before he deigned to grant them audience. This in spite of the fact that O'Neill had been summoned to appear. His abject loathing of Shane, his resentment of Lord Kildare's commission, and his disdain of Irish peers as a rule, had him pacing in the next chamber, impatiently marking the degrees of their humiliation as it compounded in grains of sand, sifting slowly through the hourglass on his desk.

His sister Frances had arrived from England to stay with him, and she had chosen this day to visit him in the castle. She was fair in coloring, even discounting the white powder so fashionable in London, with light hair that Katherine would have called mousy rather than blond. Rather tall and thin, with the angular features of a Radcliffe, she possessed the dark almond shaped eyes of her brother, but she used them demurely. He explained to her about the debauched savage warlord in the next chamber and bid her depart, but much to his consternation, she was all the more eager to view the legendary chieftain.

When finally they were ushered in, Sussex was seated in a grand armchair of carved oak, his sister standing behind at his shoulder, in what appeared to be a laboured tableau. Five towering guards loomed behind them along the wall, eyes forward but peering off into some far abyss beyond the three Irish nobles. Shane turned back to see a further six guards standing at attention along the wall at his back, one of whom had stepped into the doorway where they had just entered. At the sound of the Lord Deputy's nasal English tones, he faced forward again. Since it was widely believed that Shane had no English, Sussex' choice to speak it now was a pointed breach of diplomacy.

"We thank you, Lord Ormond and Lord Kildare, for delivering John O'Neill into our custody. His submission here will obviate the need for his journey to London. Her Majesty has more important matter to attend to than squabbles in the bogs of Ulster!"

Kildare was taken aback. He answered in Latin. "Good my Lord Sussex, I am commissioned direct by the queen's order to conduct him hence, without regard to the rulings of Dublin Castle. He is here in my custody and that of Lord Ormond. I have his papers in my possession."

Shane spoke now in rough Irish. "Tell this dog's bollocks that I am not a prisoner! I travel of my own volition at the queen's invitation. He's detained us long enough."

"Conduct him where you will, you are under my jurisdiction while in Dublin. Lord Kildare, you will be so good as to bid him save this gibberish for his bogmen in the bushes of Tyrone!" Truth to be told, Shane understood plenty of English. He responded again in Irish.

"Tell this oaf I would not sully my tongue with his clacking English!" Kildare gave Shane an impatient squint and turned again to Sussex, reproaching him again in Latin.

"Since you address O'Neill in English which he has not the speaking of, he responds in Irish."

"I did not address him. And I shall speak the Queen's English at my pleasure. If it offend him, well and good! Mayhap he will endeavor to learn it. He would have us believe that he aspires to be a peer of this realm." Kildare drew a breath to reply, but Sussex forestalled him with a louder, angrier reproach. "Your commission, Lord Kildare, ended with the signing of those treasonous Articles of Peace. An abject surrender! Wherein you yielded all, and demanded nothing. With no regard for the Queen's honour, you have surrendered

SHANE O'Neill, 'the Grand Disturber'

Armagh, a garrison dearly won with the lives of Her Majesty's loyal infantry soldiers!"

Kildare remained impassive and uncharacteristically taciturn. "I was invested with full authority to treat, and I have induced O'Neill to surrender unto the Queen's Majesty in London. The thing is done and cannot be undone."

"That remains to be determined." Sussex continued in Latin. "John O'Neill. We will be pleased to hear your submission, when your knee is bent."

"That is a thing you shall never see." Shane's head was tilted back, as he looked down upon the 'rancorous upstart' whose seated vantage now seemed more a posture of supplication. "Only before my sovereign lord, Her Majesty, will I kneel, to pledge my faithful service unto her. And I shall tell her of your malfeasance, that she may know the true cause of the troubles in my country."

Frances Radcliffe stepped quietly in behind her brother's tall chair. Her head was bowed, but her eyes wide, and transfixed upon Shane. He unfurrowed his brow, smiled and made a courtly bow. "Please forgive me, my Lady. I've not made your acquaintance. This business at hand is perhaps something too pricklish for your delicate refinement, I'll warrant."

Sussex rose to his feet indignantly."Gentlemen, this is my sister, the Lady Frances Radcliffe. She regrets that she is unable to stay." As the three men bowed, he took her hand. "Farewell, my dear. Algood will see you to your carriage." The heavy oaken door was heard to open as she made her way to it. When she had reached it, she peered back at Shane, her dark eyes wide and quite shocked to be caught out, as he smiled broadly at her over his shoulder. She turned her head swiftly and disappeared through the low stone portal.

Lord Sussex was fuming, and Shane tipped a sly wink at FitzGerald, enjoying their host's discomfiture. He had a sudden inspiration. "Be assured, Lord Sussex, that it is not for fear of war that I attend on Her Majesty, but to yield to her honour that I might enjoy her grace. For in that grace alone will I bring the wild lands in my keeping to civility and prosperity, and bring my people to know their proper service to the Queen. I shall prevail upon her Majesty to marry me to some English gentlewoman of noble birth meet for my vocation, to teach me in civility and manners. Such a one as your beautiful sister Lady Frances." He wet his lips and cast a backward glance to the door. "She would make a fit wife for the Earl of Tyrone, and I'll venture she could bear me fine healthy sons."

Throbbing veins appeared on Sussex' temples and his lips appeared to be wrestling one another. Shane flashed a quick smile to Kildare, eyes gleaming with sly malice, and continued all the louder. "Oh, yes! A sweet little bundle. Mark you, by her good civility and breeding my country would soon grow civil, and my seed and blood would be so mixed with yours that my posterity would ever after know their duties to-"

"Enough! You forget yourself, O'Neill. You have not been pardoned of your crimes until Her Majesty so decrees. And you will not see Her Majesty until I release you." He rose now, and took from the desk a sheaf of papers, which he held out to Shane. "When you have signed these, we shall send you to Her Majesty to crave a royal pardon." Shane grasped the papers and began to read them. "An amended draught of our agreement. You'll find but little change in the terms."

Shane's eyes flashed fire as he ripped the papers in two and let them fall at Sussex' feet. "You will not mollify one iota of the agreement. What I have written, I have written." He folded his arms. "As I shall put no more in writing than is written already, I shall look for the performance of all things written and of nothing else!" He spun on his feet and tripped up the guard who stood before the doorway. As he leapt over him, the other five guards descended upon him. After a fierce struggle, they had him pinned down, and one began to kick him. Kildare pushed him aside, and was set upon by the rest of the guards. He came to order with a swordpoint at his throat.

"Put him in irons!" There was no mistaking the glee in Sussex' eyes, as they shackled O'Neill in a handlock that appeared out of nowhere, too handy for happenstance, and Kildare winced to see that all that had gone before had been a trap. As they pulled Shane to his feet, Sussex turned to Kildare with smug disdain. "As he is unrepentant, and has already tried to escape, he shall make the voyage England in irons."

CHAPTER 6

"The tower? Put him in the Tower, say you?" Elizabeth's radiant smile had vanished; her cheeks suddenly tight and ashen; her eyes were fire and ice. "Good Thomas, methinks you show sudden brave to turn our thoughts to the tower. You bluster at court and blanche in the field!" His ears burned red under her fiery gaze, and Sussex felt long moments pass as he groped for a rejoinder. He had only now arrived in London, and had thought the matter closed.

"Alas, Lord Sussex was not *in* the field." Sidney could not resist such a silence. "Had he but ventured there with his army, he would doubtless have acquitted himself nobly." The malice of Sidney's hollow defense was not lost on Sussex, but it gave him cause to shift his eyes from the Queen's withering glare, and he found his speech.

"Lord Ormonde was deathly ill, your Majesty, and I could-"

"And so he stayed abed!" Elizabeth thundered over him. "Wherefore had *you* cause to shirk the fight and foray? Was it to hold his hand, and mop his brow? You sent our army abroad without a captain, to convulse like a headless chicken in the field!"

"I sent George Stanley in my stead, with Fitzwilliam, and Wingfield. I judge them able officers to lead the-"

"Wingfield? Will you look us in the face and call an ass a stallion?" She held her stare, a basilisk peering into his soul. "Is this why he stands unpunished for his cowardice? Ill fortune in battle may be put to 'chance of war', but when cowardice stands cause there must be penalty!" When at last Sussex parted his lips and drew a breath to make reply, she cut him off once again. "If you will abide this white

SHANE O'Neill, 'the Grand Disturber'

feather in your ranks, I will not. You will answer for it, my Lord Sussex!"

"My soldiers were beset by pestilence. And the engagement was most strange. And sudden. Out of keeping with all custom and habit! Experience, that great tutor of generals, has taught us *not* to expect a charge in the field from these rebels. Never before durst Scot or Irishman look an Englishman in the face in the open plain!"

The brief silence that followed as the Queen considered allowed Sidney to strike again. "And now John O'Neill -in a plain *three* miles away from any wood- has, with scarce half your numbers, charged our whole army; and was like in one hour to have left not *one* man of that army alive!

"There is enough, good Harry!" Her eyes flared and just as quickly softened. "We are advised of this. 'Though *not* by our *captains*!" Sussex ignored this reproach, and made his plea.

"Provisions, your Highness. Supplies and proper soldiers. We disburden the prisons of thieves. We rob the taverns of tosspots and ruffians. We scour both town and country for rogues and vagabonds. Ill used and ill payed, they cannot but fail against these wild Irish, who skip like goats through those very bogs. They fight in companies of brothers and cousins, and make a great show of valour before their clans."

Elizabeth looked from Cecil to Sidney for a reply. Sidney obliged, after shaking his head and expelling a weary breath. "Your Majesty's soldiers are indeed ill used if this be their lord deputy, for on the field and in the Court he has used them ill. I shame to hear it!" Lord Cecil, suddenly aware of the Queen's impatient glare, stepped in to defend the Lord Deputy.

"Was that kingdom in such goodly state of governance when you tended it as deputy, Lord Sidney? I recall it not so."

"My troops were used seldom, and only when victory was assured." He turned to the Queen. "Not only has this defeat cost us cannon and weaponry and faithful soldiers... But yet the *tidings* of this loss have taken from us that very dignity whereon loyalty does fix its yoke. Such a defeat will breed more rebels, and embolden those malcontents who chafe and grumble to take up arms and fight for O'Neill." Sussex' dark eyes narrowed and he threw his head and shoulders back. "Like Lord Kildare, you *purchased* your peace –and paid dearly for it with the Queen's honour! When O'Neill spurned – and most publicly spurned, your summons to Dundalk, you deigned to attend upon him at Fathan, and to further appease him, even stood gossip to his infant child! And this contravening the Statutes of Kilkenny, a law of some two hundred years standing."

Sidney countered with a low, even, victorious tone. "And thereafter had we peace from him! And peace from those who feared him, for he pledged to uphold the Crown. And this *not* at the Queen's expense!"

Some sudden commotion took their eyes to the double doors leading to the next chamber. It was the Long Gallery at Whitehall, filled with an expectant crowd of courtiers. There was an uneasy murmur like distant thunder, and audible gasps portending some calamity or wonder. Cecil bowed to the Queen and disappeared through the massive portal. When Elizabeth returned her gaze to Sidney, he turned to Sussex and continued his calm tirade.

"Not my diplomacy, but your defeat has cost the Queen's honour. Even within the Pale is heard the mockers laugh. Sorley MacDonnell's Scots have taken CarrickFergus which was a loyal English town. O'Neill did follow hard upon this battle with more raids, exacting tribute, and adding legions to his force til now -but for the Scots- he is sole captain of Ulster."

"*Sole* captain he is not!" Elizabeth could abide no more. "Has he not come to London to submit to his sovereign queen? We have many captains, Henry Sidney, to order our provinces, and most like Ulster is quiet today, and our treasuries undiminished for some hours." The great doors parted again, and Cecil bustled in brandishing a large scroll. "What is the hurlyburly? Is O'Neill come then?"

"Indeed he is, Highness." He cast a backward glance at the doors, and shook his head. His eyes wide, he lowered his voice to a half whisper. "And lo, what spectacle he makes! A magnificent train of Irishry and a guard of galloglass arrayed in the richest habiliments of

SHANE O'Neill, 'the Grand Disturber'

their country. I would-"

"Is the Court assembled?" Elizabeth peered into her looking glass and patted a wayward curl.

"Filled. And never have I seen such 'stonishment here. All imagine that they behold a potentate from such distant quarter as China or wild America. They stand amazed, and gape as before a wild beast of the desert!" Cecil saw the Queen's gaze fall upon the scroll in his hand. "O'Neill bids me bring your Majesty this parchment he has fixed with his seal."

"God's teeth! Does *he* summon *us*?" She took it, absently laid it on the desk, and looked intently at nowhere in particular. Then she demanded, "Is the ambassador of the King of Spain present?"

"Yes, Highness, Bishop DeQuadra is in attendance. So also are most other envoys and ambassadors to court. Perhaps it will be best to seem unmoved by the spectacle before you, now you stand warned of it."

The young queen tugged at her bodice, and turned smiling. "Melikes this well enough! A splendid submission out of Papist Ireland will make a nice show to those courts that would undo us." She looked to each and let her smile rest upon Sussex, who supposed foolishly that a response was warranted. Once more he plead his case.

"This is no submission. The horse is not yet broke. I do implore your Majesty to withhold this pardon, and in the tower to withhold this traitor!"

She froze. Her eyes flashed with rage.

"Get out!!! Dare you presume to tell us our office? There is sealed safe conduct. With thanks owing to your bungling! We must needs do what is fair and just!" When no-one moved she raged the louder. "Out! Both of you! Would we had such resolute men as John O'Neill in our service, we would not be forced to treat with rebels in our court!" Sussex and Sidney scrambled awkwardly out the door bowing behind them. The secretary pulled out a chair for her. She sat for a moment with her hands over her face, finally dropping them as she heaved a sigh. "Cecil, I am undone by this dogsplay! Each to chase the other's tail, and all snapping at the crown!"

SHANE O'Neill, 'the Grand Disturber'

"With your forgiveness..." He bowed his head and looked up expectantly. Her voice was tight and controlled, but her eyes bulged with impatience.

"Speak your counsel and fill your office! What say you then?" Cecil tilted his head and stroked his grey beard.

"You said that you must *do* what is fair and just. But your Majesty must do what is expedient in the ordering of her realm. She must be *seen* to do what is fair and just. Therein cuts the edge of statecraft. The lustre and flash of virtue's sword does well to please the heady crowd, but they like not its dull edge. So must you brandish it high...but hue your path with the darker blade, the keener edge of statecraft." She smiled.

"Well taught. But you would teach a Tudor." Now her voice climbed in decibels of impatience. "Do you think me a fool in a child's frock? To matter, Cecil. Speak you!"

"In O'Neill's absence from Ireland something might be cavilled against him or his for nonobserving the covenants on his side; and so the pact being infringed, the matter might be used as thought fit..." His raised brow awaited her approval, so Elizabeth nodded slowly without taking her eyes from his. "You have agreed to withdraw the soldiery from Armagh Cathedral when O'Neill sailed for England. This you have done. The terms do not prevent you from returning them there. Different soldiers...?" Elizabeth's radiant smile urged him on. "In like wise, his safe conduct says only that he will return safe to Ireland. It does not stipulate how long you will keep him at court..." The smiling young queen sprang to her feet and kissed his cheek.

"Sage counsel. And 'twere folly not to heed. Let us turn this visit to account!"

The Long Gallery was thronged with courtiers in their velvets and brocades, shuffling and swirling their rich hues in a sparkling tapestry, vivid and mercurial. Stealthy glances, sharp glares, winks, nods, and

SHANE O'Neill, 'the Grand Disturber'

meaningful gazes darted over shoulders and starched ruffs, as jealousy, ambition, and vanity stirred the heady crowd. It was the sea of velvet, perhaps, that muffled the surging and rolling din to an indistinguishable throbbing buzz.

"Do you hear that sound, boy?" Farleigh raised a hand before him and halted it, and his pale eyes roved slowly about until they came to rest on Gillie's. "We're in the middle of the hive!" He cast his searing glance over the crowd. "These puffed up creatures are the drones. They're stingless. And they make no honey. They've only to keep the queen happy."

"Why did they make us move back here? We'll see divil all from here." Gillie bobbed up onto his tiptoes as he craned his neck from side to side. "If we were any further back, we'd be in the moat! Did you not tell them we're with Shane O'Neill?"

"Don't come that with me, ye little rip! It's your own fault I lost sight of Kildare and the others! You and your blasted capers. Once we were separated from the herd, we hadn't a chance. I suppose we must have been spoiling their fine picture." Farleigh looked down at his embroidered robe and mantle. It was always a source of pride at home, but now it looked almost shabby amidst the bejeweled opulence of the English Royal Court. Certainly Gillie's tunic was eliciting stares and smirks, with its long fluted sleeves and its short waist; his long hairy legs on view, as high as decency would allow, and his eyes almost hidden behind that shaggy 'glib' of dark hair. If there was such a thing as 'kempt', he was certainly unkempt...Farleigh tried again to look for Shane through the crowd before him. "Right enough. We've come a long road to look at the backsides of these fops and dandies!" He glanced back at Gillie, but the boy had vanished.

Gillie had spotted, above the crowd, a young lad mounting a short ladder of three steps. He was making a progress along the walls, replacing the withering garlands of holly with fresh boughs. It was Twelfthnight, and evidently there would be a hooly of some kind to mark the end of the Christmas. Gillie slipped through the crowd and, when no one was looking, gave a sharp tug at a hanging garland causing a small length of it to topple. The English lad stepped down

SHANE O'Neill, 'the Grand Disturber'

sulkily and, muttering, trotted over to see what had happened. As soon as his back was turned, Gillie swiped the wee 'steps' and disappeared into the crowd. He made his way to the back, and presented his plunder to the old poet. "'And behold! The last shall be raised up!' Sit your arse down on this, Farleigh. We can step up ontil it when the shindy gets started."

"Good on ye, boy! My old shanks are worn out." Farleigh settled himself on the 'steps' and they disappeared under his mantle.

"These is some wild crowds over here. Every day is like a fairday every which where you go!" Farleigh didn't answer. He was lost in his ruminations, stroking his long white beard. Suddenly Gillie burst forth with a rollicking volley of laughter. Farleigh looked up and smiled to see the teary eyed youth caught up so in his mirth.

"What is it, boy?" The auld poet scanned the sights around him, turning his head slowly around like an owl, to see what had tickled the lad. Gillie nodded in the direction of three portly gentlemen in broadstriped tunics of amber and black. As he winked the tears trickled down his merry cheeks. Farleigh scrunched up his features, and arched his shaggy white brows by way of silent inquiry.

"The *cut* of them!" Gillie answered in a throbbing staccato catching his breath and laughing. "They *do* look like bumbly bees! Their big wobbly arses all bloated out -atop their spindly black legs! And the...and the bumbly *stripes* on them!" Now Farleigh was laughing too, his head thrown back, and his eyes tearing up in the contagion of merriment. Gillie pounded on the aul fellow's knee to direct his attention. "Them are the most comical pantses I ever seen a man wear!" He cast his mocking gaze, now, at a tall gangly fellow whose blousy pleated galligaskins more than doubled the size of his hips. As if sensing their mocking eyes, the man turned around sharply, and sniffed disdainfully at them. The rosy circles on his white powdered cheeks, and possibly the dangling earrings, set Gillie off again into a peal of bright laughter. "God help us if we can't beat these English! They're a right shower of 'butterflys'! Our Shane O'Neill is the only proper man here!"

Farleigh shook his hoary old head and sighed, as he cast his pale eyes over multitude. "Only the drones. These are only busy buzzy little drones in the queen's hive."

Up near the front of the Long Gallery, every move and gesture of the Irish chieftain was being scrutinized and speculated upon. Every version of every rumour was tossed about and traded upon as social capital. Each knew more than the next of this savage Ulsterman and his mad ways; two hundred tuns of wine in his cellars at Dundrum; the forty bastards; the unhappy Scottish adulteress who found herself chained to a bed; errant messengers with their ears cut off; drunken orgies followed by naked wallowing in dirt and muck. His wild eyes and demeanor, to say nothing of the spectacle before them, seemed to confirm all.

To the fore was the empty throne, flanked by four royal guards awaiting her Majesty. Off to the far right side, also awaiting the royal presence, was the huge retinue, in all their rude magnificence, of Shane O'Neill. Some forty of the chieftain's galloglass were kneeling patiently, huddled before him like a pack of hounds. They were enormous men, bareheaded, with long fair disheveled hair flowing onto their shoulders. They wore deep golden colored shirts of saffron-dyed linen, with wide fluted sleeves, covered with long shirts of mail down to the knees. Across their shoulders were flung shaggy wolf skins, and in their brawny hands were short broad battle-axes. To the assembled courtiers and envoys of Elizabeth's court, it was a sight of medieval splendour from centuries past.

Over them all, towering upright, stood Shane; a powerful man, some six and a half foot tall in height, his saffron mantle sweeping round him with its broad collar of fur; his shining black hair curling down his back, and clipped short over his eyes, "which gleamed from under it with a grey lustre, frowning, fierce, and cruel" as reports Campion. Shane wore a gold chain and a handsome cross round his neck, said to be a gift of the Pope. It was further related that the

SHANE O'Neill, 'the Grand Disturber'

magnificent ring he wore was a present to him from King Philip, presented on the Kings behalf by DeQuadra, the Spanish Ambassador in London, only the day before.

When Sussex and Sidney entered, they exchanged brief bitter words and parted. Sussex made his way to his great ally and uncle, Lord Norfolk. Sidney presented himself to Shane, who had spied him immediately across the room. "Well come! Welcome to London, O'Neill!" Shane extended his hand.

"Lord Harry!" Sidney clasped him in a hearty handshake.

"It's been quite some years. How fares my godson? And namesake! Grown to a man now, if memory serves!"

"Young Henry is coming of age. He's in Dublin Castle this while, standing hostage to my fortunes here. He'll be a man worthy of his name." Shane pulled him in closer with his handclasp. "Was that Sussex came in with you just now?"

"He's only just arrived. And he appears to be rather perturbed!" Sidney followed Shane's line of sight to see Lord Sussex in a highly animated conferral with Lord Norfolk.

"It's an urgent mission that brings him sailing in my wake!" Shane regarded his old friend intently, awaiting further news of Sussex, and of what might be 'perturbing' him. Though they had roughly the same tally of years, Sidney had thickened about the waist, a prosperous belly to show his high estate. Under his tilted billycock, a few whisps of grey had crept into his wavy brown hair, and the sharp little 'goat's chin' had become a lavish ruddy beard nestled in the broad ruffs of his collar. He wore a narrow ermine stole over his broad shoulders, a flourish allowed only to the very highest of rank, with a bright chain of gold across his chest. Very grand altogether. Would he be forthcoming with confidences about his rival? Sidney turned back to Shane.

"I've been down in Penshurst looking after the family. How was your crossing?"

"Wintry and foul. We sailed for weeks til we reached Chester."

"When did you arrive in London?"

"We reached London on the second; early Monday evening, just

SHANE O'Neill, 'the Grand Disturber'

after dark. Went direct to York House in the Strand. Lord Cecil and Bacon met me. Aye, that Secretary is a right sly-boots... Lord Cecil..."

Sidney nodded gravely. "Oh, he's deep as water. Knows all, sees all."

"Tells divil all!" Shane smiled in his *own* sly way. "I keep my secretaries dark; use them by turns, so each knows only a part. Fair dues to Cecil, he gave me the sum that was owing. Chastised me something fierce to see was I was properly contrite. And his staff of scribes took some hours draughting this submission for me -with my legal councilors O'Hagan and Fleming. It's all accordingly." He held up a crumpled parchment. "Cecil was very keen on the 'scale of the gesture." Shane swept his gaze over the gallowglass before him. "Sure, we'll beat them all for a grand gesture! If it's a submission she wants-" He stopped short and grinned expectantly at the approach of two tall prepossessing gentlemen, both sporting broad smiles. Sidney turned to discover two of his closest friends and allies at Court.

"O'Neill, allow me to introduce you to the acquaintance of my dear friend Sir Robert Dudley!" Shane reached out to greet him.

"We've corresponded. You know my secretary's hand. This is mine!" They shook warmly.

"I thank you for the splendid hawks and falcons! The very finest I've seen. I'm most grateful!" Dudley's was a striking countenance of fair manly features with rosy cheeks, raven hair curling over his noble brow; his bearing slim and elegant. He sported a broad auburn mustache with a narrow strip of beard from his lips to his chin. His apparel was singular as well. He was clad in a powder blue tunic with high collars, and a matching plume in his cap.

His bright attire was widely noted this day, as he was only lately back at Court after the highly suspicious death of his wife. And he, known to be the queen's lover! Elizabeth had banished Dudley to his manor at Kew until the inquest was complete. A verdict of 'death by mischance' had cleared him, and he had recently received new apartments in the palace, -adjacent to Her Majesty's, if the rumours were true. The powder blue garments left no doubt that he was out of mourning. Robert Dudley was indeed the dashing paramour of the

SHANE O'Neill, 'the Grand Disturber'

Queen, and a useful friend to have at Court. "I wish you only the best of fortune today; that you will find the Queen's favour as lavish and warm as mine own! I have spoken to her on your behalf. This is my dear friend and boon companion Thomas Stukeley."

"Sir, you're the talk of all London today! And your visage most certainly exceeds the report! I'm honoured!" Another hearty shaking of hands. This man was arrayed in more somber tones of brown and black, with a high dark collar framing his strong face. A double chain of gold looped carelessly across his chest, and a golden ring glistening rakishly on his right ear. Stukeley's beard was short, encompassing the whole of his chin, but his cheeks were bare. His nose was regal and his eyes at once piercing and engaging. "How was your crossing?"

"The winds blew and the ship sailed. I was put aboard in irons!" He looked from face to face as smiles vanished. "With safe conduct signed and bearing the Great Seal, sureties from the five Irish peers, and hostages left for my keeping- for all this, Sussex scorned the law and compelled me to sail in handlocks!"

Robert Dudley shook his head. "The Scurrilous whelp! This demands reproof! But tell me, O'Neill, who freed you of these shackles? Shane smiled wryly and tossed a pointed glance at his gallowglass.

"I had forty honed battle-axes at hand. When the chain was severed I entreated the ship's smithy to dispose of the cuffs. Forty battle-axes can be a mighty persuader! I shouldn't travel without them." They laughed heartily, freed now to leave the matter rest, and greatly relieved of that.

These four men, this conclave of rakes, had the eye of every woman in the Long Gallery. They were indeed well met and well matched, and each delighted to be in the company. A sudden flourish of trumpets signaled the Queen's entrance, and halted this brief genial convergence of heroes. With a clap on the shoulder and hasty farewells, Dudley, Sidney, and Stukeley withdrew.

The buzz and hum of chatter hushed to a tense stillness. Gentlemen bowed, ladies curtsied, and the musicians played on with their bright fanfare until Elizabeth seated herself upon the throne.

SHANE O'Neill, 'the Grand Disturber'

Splendid and bejeweled, her red-gold curls nearly outshining the crown above them, framed by a lavish collar of luminous white lace, she seemed to radiate an aura of light; the incipient 'Gloriana' of her eternal fame. Lord Cecil took his place standing at her right. In his hand was the scroll wherein was written the English transcription of O'Neill's submission.

From an archway on the left, Kildare appeared with Myler Magrath, O'Hagan, O'Devlin, MacCaffrey, and others of Shane's retinue. Myler was dressed as the others, without collar or cassock, and he wore a cap to hide his tonsured scalp. They advanced silently to the fore and knelt beside the throne. Somewhere a massive door was heard to close, and its thud and clank reverberated in the stillness, compounding the air of tension and expectancy in the hall.

The Herald's footsteps could be heard as he stepped forward to the docket. Many fancied they could hear him drawing his deep breath as he was about to commence. "On sixth of January, Twelfthday, in the third year of the reign of Her Highness Elizabeth Queen of England and Ireland, sits this court at the pleasure of the Queen's Majesty. First order the submission and indentures of O'Neill the Great, Cousin of St. Patrick, friend to the Queen of England and enemy to all the world besides..." Tittering could be heard among the courtiers, but it was soon overtaken by the clank and thunder of forty mailed Irish warriors rising to their feet and marching into place. They moved to their formation in tight lockstep, then came to halt in rows of eight, each one a full pace from the next. Shane called out an order.

"Úmhlaigí!" The huge warriors now marched in place with a short syncopated step, well drilled for the display. They swung their battle-axes over their heads, left to right, with a loud whoop, and struck the floor as they as they descended together onto one knee. Shane stalked out before them and faced the throne. His deep voice called out in Irish "Is mire Ó Néill!" which means 'I am O'Neill.' He dropped now to his knees, and as he did so, the gallowglass lay forward, prostrate before the queen.

Shane now launched into a most extraordinary exertion of

SHANE O'Neill, 'the Grand Disturber'

histrionics for the delectation of the crowd and queen. His arms up before him, fingers spread wide, his head thrown back as he rocked back and forward from his knees. He howled and shrieked his 'mea culpa' in Irish, and if there was some sly mockery in it, the fierce conviction of his 'keening' left him beyond reproach. Elizabeth had a fair notion of what the miscreant was required to say, and she held the scroll before her but never gave it a glance. The wild spectacle at her feet was far too riveting. The Court heard only a frightening spate of strange wailing Gaelic.

"Ór fud é gurbé an chéad mcinn agam 'riamh ná mo dhul-sa i gceann mo bhanríoghna,' glacadh go h-úmhal 'r dualgach lena mórgacht-sa, -i ngeall rm a chruallar ina ceann, ɼ ni d'eagla chogaigh, ach le gnádh 'gur le h-úmhlacht agur le támreacht dhíre a chánara- téimre an mo glúmibh i bhriaohmuire gráŕ na banríoghna, ag glacadh leire 'bheich 'mo bheanciarna cheannaraigh man dhea. ina cheanca ra, aomhaim go rroeachar i n-earonóm agur i moghbhail don bhanríogham, agur agriamre parróún ríogach domhra agur do mo muincire. Geallaimre rearca mo rheimbhír d'éilír banríonn Sarana, óʼreann, agur Fraince man dhea. Ní beag rm."

His actual words in Irish, as he spoke them before his delegation and his gallowglass, were a good deal less abject than his tone or posture, and certainly less so than the text in the still unseen scroll, which read as follows:

"Oh, my most dread Sovereign lady and Queen, like as I, Shane O'Neill, your Majesty's subject of your realm in Ireland, have long time desired to come into the presence of your Majesty to acknowledge my humble and bounden subjection, so am I now her upon my knees by your gracious permission, and do most humbly acknowledge your Majesty to be my Sovereign lady and Queen of England, France, and Ireland; and I do confess that for lack of civil education I have offended your Majesty and your laws, for which I

SHANE O'Neill, 'the Grand Disturber'

have required and obtained your Majesty's pardon. For that I most humbly, from the bottom of my heart, thank your Majesty, and still do with all humbleness require the continuance of the same. I now, in the presence of the Almighty God –Father, Son, and Holy Ghost– faithfully promise that I intend by God's grace to live hereafter in the obedience of your Majesty as a subject of your land of Ireland. And because this my speech, being Irish, is not well understood, I have caused this my submission to be written in English and Irish, and thereto have set my hand and seal."

When he came to the end of his impassioned oration, Shane threw himself forward flat out before the Queen and begged mercy of her, howling, "Déan trócaire orm!" This was followed on by his recumbent Gallowglass, who echoed the Irish word for mercy, "Trócaire!" After a moment of stunned silence, Elizabeth handed the scroll to Lord Cecil, and rose from her throne, tall and regal. She clasped her delicate white hands together before her, and dropped them to rest at her waist, with a wan smile, warm and sad.

"We do accept your oath of fealty, John O'Neill." Shane rose up onto his knees. A tearful smile brightened across his face, and he brought his right knee up to rise. A sudden gasp from the assemblage stopped him short. He looked to Elizabeth in inquiry, and she spoke. "But we cannot yet grant that pardon which you seek...for, though you plead on your knees, yet your offences do stand against you. We are apprised that our good and loyal subjects O'Donnell and his Lady, with Maguire and O'Reilly are imprisoned in your keep, contravening our Lord Deputy Sussex. Your deeds do mock your oaths, O'Neill, as hollow oaths do mock this court!"

Not a gasp, not a whisper, not a breath could be heard in the Long Gallery. Shane's smile never dimmed. He held up his right hand and spoke with conviction and sincerity. "Your Highness, I swear before you, I've not traveled these many leagues and miles to mock your court. But on this Feast of Epiphany, like the weary Magi, I come but to honor and witness your radiant majesty-"

"Have a care in your travels, wise man. You are nearing the rocks of blasphemy!" The queen's tone was dark and threatening, but bright laughter echoed through the gallery, easing the fraught atmosphere. Shane, himself, laughed appreciatively, his eyes shining with confidence.

"When I have told your Majesty a *true* accounting of the treachery of her captains in Ireland, who use her seal and office in certain blasphemy, and keep that state from civil order, my offences will prove kind offices in her dutiful service!"

"We do not doubt it...if the tale were the deed. But tell us of the matter at hand, O'Donnell and the rest."

"They are lawfully detained, Highness. It is my bounden duty for your honor, to uphold the law of that kingdom. It must be remembered that my territories have never been shired, nor has English law been established in these lands beyond the Pale of Dublin. Should the Brehon laws be flouted with impunity, that realm would be *without* law. Any man who would see it so does no service to your Honour."

"Yet you daily flout the rule of our Lord Deputy there." She unclasped her hands and rested them akimbo atop her skirts, her chin forward in a challenging posture. She was prodding and testing, without anger. Shane sat back on his heels and folded his arms, a brazen pose for a kneeling supplicant.

"I had no word from him 'yea' or 'nay' since he arrived in Ireland. He answered not one of my nine letters to his person, nor did he forward my letters to Council. He entered my territories in arms. He made attack on your loyal subjects there. He burnt their crops and their homes. Had I been sluggish in my office, in protecting her Majesty's subjects and the law that represents her justice there, I should hardly be fit to serve your Grace."Elizabeth now folded her arms and nodded slowly as her faint smile grew brighter and brighter. "We will grant you this pardon which you seek, John O'Neill, and we do bid you to rise." Shane rose to his feet, and his recumbent retinue of gallowglass rose to bended knee. A rustle and murmur stirred through the hall like a sudden gust through the trees. A sharp turn of the queen's head and the quick flash of indignation in her dark eyes brought all to stillness.

SHANE O'Neill, 'the Grand Disturber'

"You are well and fit to plead your case. We will hear more of this anon when our time affords us. In the matter of your claim to succeed Conn O'Neill as Earl of Tyrone over the claims of Brian MacBaron O'Neill, your remittance and indentures shall await our further considering." She turned to her Lord Secretary. "Cecil, let the Baron's son be summoned hither to plead the validity of *his* patents. Meantimes, you will have liberty within this court and to the bounds of the city of London." She paused for an instant to collect any stray thoughts. "Though your Latin is bright and ready, still you would do you well to learn the English tongue, and to school yourself in the civilities attaining to your station. We do welcome you to Court!"

"I thank your Majesty! Might I be allowed to attend your master of horse, Lord Robert Dudley, that I might learn to ride after the English fashion? I should like to learn to run at the tilt, to hawk, to shoot and, oh, to use such other good exercises as that good lord is so apt unto!" Her quick glance at Dudley's affirmative nod settled the question.

"If dear Robin be amenable, we shall be well pleased withal!" She turned, smiling, and made her way from the dais as the players struck up their fanfare. The murmuring of the astounded crowd rose to a frantic din that resounded through the Long Gallery, waves of fevered pitch rising and falling, surging and seething, like the buzzing of a hive.

By the time the Queen's fanfare ceased, it was barely audible under the giddy clamour of the holiday court. Farleigh and Gillie made their way slowly to the fore, weaving and dodging through the excited courtiers, until at last they caught sight of Kildare and the others. Shane was thronged by well-wishers and ladies of the Court waiting to be introduced.

Art O'Hagan waved Farleigh over. "Where did ye's get off to?"

Myler Magrath peered over his shoulder, spotting them. "Ah, there they are! We turned around and you had both vanished!"

SHANE O'Neill, 'the Grand Disturber'

"I wanted to stay back and have a proper gawk at these goings on!" Farleigh saw that Gillie was about to pipe up, so he gave him a swift dig with the elbow. "Oh, we had a fine perch up the back. We could see it all! Gillie and I are the only two that journeyed to London on the Queen's shilling, and never so much as bent the knee to her! Where's another man can say that?"

Myler and O'Hagan laughed. As the monk in mufti turned back to his conversation, the judge's eyes darted over his shoulder quickly and he bent in to confide. "I don't mind telling you my heart was in my gullet there for a short spell. If she hadn't relented with the pardon where would he be? Did you see those severed heads above Traitors' Gate?"

"No bother to our Shane! He was bold as bedamned." Farleigh winked with a quick nod. "And he had forty battle-axes behind him if his charms let him down short."

"Lord Kildare insists that we're all meant to stay on for this Twelfthnight Revel. Music and food and dancing and mummers." The judge drew his head back to see where Shane was in jovial conversation with the Queen's favorite. "Kildare and O'Neill are going off to Grey's Inn later, for some class of mad frolics. They hold a masque in what they call 'The Inner Temple. It seems Robert Dudley was elected 'Lord of Misrule' for the yuletide season and he's 'commanded' them to go along."

"Lord of Misrule? Sure, who would be up to them? As *I* can see, it's Sussex and Elizabeth should share *that* title. Lords of Misrule, indeed." Farleigh shook his head. " I don't know, I couldn't be arsed to stay, but how would I ever find my way back. This palace is like a rabbit warren. And every corridor looks the same. Food and dancing?"

"And drink! English ale, I'm told, and punch." The old man grimaced and rolled his eyes to the heavens.

"English ale! Bitter as bile." O'Hagan laughed.

"I'm sure there will be lashin's of drink. All sorts of potations." Farleigh welsh-combed his beard, his long fingers untangling the white fleece, and his old blue eyes brightened.

"Maybe we could all do with a right piss-up…"

SHANE O'Neill, 'the Grand Disturber'

The festivities got underway as trays of sweetmeats appeared; gingerbreads, tarts and cakes, marzipan conserves, marmalade, and sugarplums on tiered silver platters. Farleigh was happy enough when a goblet of Jerez wine found its way into his fist, for as he was fond of saying, "Fine sherry, though it sharpens the tongue, it softens the heart."

Most of Shane's gallowglass were dismissed to explore the taverns and knocking shops of the city. By and large, the rest of this relatively elite Irish contingent, having been schooled by the Franciscans, had enough Latin to parlay with the denizens of the Court. Even so, for the first while, O'Neill's Ulstermen kept mostly to their own company, as only a few had the English, and Shane had forbidden them to speak it. "Use it by all means," he had said, "use it to listen!"

The exception was Will Fleming the barrister. Although the Flemings resided in the Pale, their mother was what was called 'mere Irish', the word 'mere' taking its original meaning of 'completely', signifying unmixed blood. He and his brothers were partisans of O'Neill, and often helped with legal matters involving English law. He made his way about the room, his sharp ears attuned for court gossip and remarks concerning the Irish delegation.

Lord Kildare introduced his English wife Mabel and her family to 'his wild countrymen'. Her brother Montegue, Earl of Southhampton, and her beautiful unmarried niece, Eleanor Somerset, were clearly fascinated with these exotic outlanders in their midst. This was an event they had looked forward to for months. All the talk and speculation! Kildare's coming over to present his legendary cousin had added a mounting suspense to the usual excitements of a Yuletide at Court. The Countess Kildare's diminutive blonde niece was quickly surrounded by smiling Irishmen replying to her polite inquiries -with a rapt solicitude they would not have afforded the Queen. When asked how they were finding London, Farleigh said graciously, but with sly ambiguity, "It is all they say it is! And we've *not* seen the best of it, to be sure!"

Soon Shane joined the company with Thomas Stukeley and more introductions were made. Tall and robust, Stukeley had the air of an adventurer about him. His left hand was firmly planted on Shane's shoulder, and it was plain to be seen that the two had found a kindred wild spirit in each other. Indeed, he only left Shane's side to dance with young Lady Somerset when a galliard was called. He had hardly shifted his fervent gaze from her since he coaxed Shane to bring him over and make the introduction for him. She made Shane promise the next galliard to her, when she would teach him the dance. "It's only five steps and hop!" she said. "Simplicity itself! Watch us and you shall see!"

When the dance was ended and the couples began to amble back to their various companies, the musicians struck up a fanfare, and all sprang to their feet for the Queen's return. She wore an elegant crimson gown and a beaming smile for her holiday Court. "Carry on with your wassail," she called out merrily, "for the snows are blowing, and Spring's cheer will be long in coming!" The company cheered her, and the sprightly strains of "The Hunting of the Fox" set the couples queuing up for a trenchmore. Elizabeth stepped out onto the floor on the arm of the Swedish envoy, Duke John of Finland. He was said to be wooing her for his brother the Crown Prince Erik of Sweden, but it was whispered through the Court that he was making headway on his own behalf. They took their place at the top of the row of smiling couples, and the dance got underway.

As the Irish turned back into their company, they saw that Dudley had joined their circle. He stood transfixed, his dark eyes following each twist and turn of the dancing couple, as they glided to and fro through the elegant patterns of the set dance. He watched like a cat poised before a mouse, unaware of the smirks and winks about him. Tom Stukeley thrust an arm over Lord Robert's shoulder and brought him about. "Your Lordship of Misrule! Will you not welcome your Irish subjects?"

Introductions were made, hand over fist in all directions. Dudley smiled graciously, extending warm and profuse welcomes to all. He came at last to Farleigh. "I daresay I know who *this* is. I needn't see the wings of Orpheus to know one of his own. The great wizard and bard Farleigh! O'Neill tells me you're conversant in the Greek as *well* as

SHANE O'Neill, 'the Grand Disturber'

Latin!"

"So I am. The Grecian muses often attend upon me in my cot! However could I fathom their secrets without the Greek?"

"I must acquaint you with my friend John Dee. He was my tutor in my youth. Although he's not a poet, he's a sage and philosopher; advises the Queen on all manner of things. And he's a very learned wizard. I shall bring you out to Mortlake to meet with him, before he sails off to the Lowlands." Farleigh nodded brightly to Shane.

"Until O'Neill's affairs are concluded here, I can assure you, I have nothing but time! I'll see him, so." FitzGerald's wife Mabel laughed sweetly.

"Wizard! That's what my family have named Garret! They've dubbed him 'The Wizard.' And all his friends in London call him so!" All eyes now on Kildare, blushing and shaking his head, as he faced the curious eyes about him.

"Oh, it's simply that I dabble...I try my hand at alchemy."

"Alchemy?" Shane's eyes went wide with wonder. "Isn't he the dark one! Could you not do us a great turn, then, Wizard, and turn our Irish sovereigns to gold. They're not worth an English farthing since Her Majesty devalued them! I suppose she's a wizard too. The scratch of a quill and the stamp of a seal, and Irish gold is dross!" Laughter and bright eyes eager for banter.

"It looks as though you've been changing *your* sovereigns for gold. I've been admiring that cross!" Kildare lifted the golden ornament from Shane's chest, weighing it in his palm. "That's a heavy burden to be dangling from your neck."

"A wee gift from his Holiness in Rome." Shane brandished his bejeweled fist. "DeQuadra also presented me with this ring yesterday at Durham House. He said it's 'but a small token of great esteem from King Philip of Spain.' And so it is. He wants us all to Mass on Sunday and he'll receive us after."

O'Hagan drew his head back and peered at him with an incredulous squint. "How can that be? Is the Mass not proscribed here? They told me there are no Roman churches in London." Lord Dudley shook his head. "No, no. He has diplomatic privilege.

SHANE O'Neill, 'the Grand Disturber'

He's an Ambassador and the Bishop of Aquila; we could hardly forbid him. The Queen has made provision for him to rent the chapel in Ely Place, St. Ethelreda's, from the protestant bishop of Ely."

"But, cousin, you can hardly oblige him." Kildare smiled as he cautioned the unseasoned visitor. "You've just sworn yourself a subject of her Majesty. How could you claim diplomatic privilege? It would be very dangerous to go." Shane laughed.

"Hellfire and eternal damnation are a greater peril, don't you think? Do you suppose I'm not up to them? This is child's play! We'll be there. All of us. And, Garret, I'd hate to think what might be said of you in Kildare, if they heard that you refused to join us..." FitzGerald protested again, but with a note of resignation now.

"I'm telling you, they'll go mad!"

"Good! This one will be great sport. She can't win without offending the Courts of Europe." There was laughter from the Tirowen men.

"Tell him, Sir Robert." Lady Kildare pleaded now. Surely you will advise him to reconsider the matter!"

"On the contrary, I fancy I shall enjoy this. O'Neill seems rather adept at this sort of thing, if this afternoon's performance is to be credited." There was more laughter, and as the music came to its end, the dancers scattered their separate ways. A young page appeared from out of nowhere and formally addressed Sir Robert.

"Her Majesty has summoned the Lord of Misrule to master the entertainments." He bowed and sprinted off through the crowd.

"If you'll excuse me." Dudley turned and paused suddenly. He turned back and asked excitedly, "Will he play the harp for us?" They all turned to Colm Dall and O'Hagan put it to him in Irish. His reply was clearly hesitant, not to say unwilling. O'Hagan explained.

"He says he wouldn't play unless you could get him a proper whisht!"

"A whisht?" After a moment of perplexity, Dudley smiled warmly again. "This is only dance music, so they have leave to talk," Dudley assured him, "but you shall have our rapt attention! Her Majesty most expressly wishes to hear you."

SHANE O'Neill, 'the Grand Disturber'

O'Hagan translated Dudley's assurances and Colm took up his small harp of golden yew and willow, relenting to oblige the Queen. Gillie rose with him to guide the blind man up to the dais. Art O'Hagan went along to translate. He announced that the harper's name was Colm Dall or 'Blind Colm MacCuarta' and that he would favor them with the song 'Cailín ó Chois tSúir Mé', or The Maid from the Banks of the Suir. Colm sat onto a stool and balanced the lavishly carved harp upon his knee. His pale blue sightless eyes swept the crowd in a gesture of engagement. "Behold me now" he was saying "and hear my song." His light wispy hair that stood out in every direction, framing his ruddy face in a halo of light, and his angelic smile, to say nothing of the harp on his knee, all conspired to give an impression of pious innocence. This thoroughly amused his intimates who had seen him often 'with the divil in him and lashin's of porter as well'! He closed his eyes and began to play.

Like a blind man feeling the face of his beloved, his hands traced the intricate tune across the glittering wires of the harp. But the gentle elegance of his motions obscured the true wonder of his artistry. The long nails of his slender fingers plucked with precision and force as those hands flitted delicately, rhythmically, and swiftly over harpstrings that were visible only in his mind. The air he played was by turns lilting and melancholy, sliding deftly from major to minor modes as he sang of the maiden's love and the painful loss of it. The effect was mesmeric and stunning. Blind Colm's light tenor poured from his heart with an unmistakable yearning; a yearning that seemed to settle over the crowd and possess them in its brief spell.

Shane and his men watched him in sheer bliss, moved by Colm's song, and welling up with pride to see the English Court so enraptured by it. The old poet in their midst was thrilled to see what he deemed 'the intangible and ephemeral art' of their ancient culture rendered so beautifully in this London, the very epicentre of progress, materialism, and modernity. The Ulstermen beamed at one another, and marked with a nod or a wink each grace note and flourish, notes that danced on the air or quavered and slid down the scale so plaintively as to raise gooseflesh. They kept careful watch on the

SHANE O'Neill, 'the Grand Disturber'

Queen's face as she looked on in a blissful serenity. Farleigh was astonished that the mere *sound* of words, bereft of all meaning for these listeners, could move them so, and he marveled too, that Colm Dall MacCuarta had been blest with such a gift in place of his precious eyes. His own endowments had come to him at no such cost.

When the song ended, in the unassuming traditional manner, without a rise in pitch or a sustained final note, it was met by silence. Farleigh's brows furrowed in mounting apprehension of an insult to Blind Colm, and indeed, to Ireland. But when, at last, the harper opened his pale blue eyes, a tumult of applause erupted through the gallery. Elizabeth took his hand in hers and presumably thanked him, for neither he nor Gillie could understand or recount her words. The other musicians crowded around him and were eager to learn the air. He promised he would teach them, and he must have done, for some years later in Henry V, Shakespeare's Pistol quotes a popular Irish tune called 'Calen o Custure Me'.

More music followed, and then everyone was ushered into the next hall for supper. When the roast venison was carried in on long spits over the shoulders of strapping servant lads, it was met with greater applause than all the fine music that went before. The Tirowenmen ate their fill and were glad of it. After supper a strange mummery was performed in elaborate costume. There were crows in the habits of Cardinals, asses habited as bishops, and wolves dressed as abbots. The Irish found this pantomime quite disturbing, but they quietly decided among themselves to feign ignorance as to its meaning, and to make little of it.

As the early winter's evening began to cast its shadows through the hall, the myriad candelabras were lit, one by one. The sheer number of glowing tapers and the brilliance of their collective light inspired the Irish visitors more to awe and wonder than all the palatial splendour about them. At length, Shane and Tom Stukeley, and Kildare with his entourage moved off to mingle and greet 'the great and the grand.' There was a great press to make the acquaintance of this 'contrite rebel', and he drew to his side, by turns, the Earls of Arundel, Huntingdon, Bedford, Warwick, and other English peers, as

SHANE O'Neill, 'the Grand Disturber'

well as the Duke of Savoy.

The evening drew on, and there were madrigals and carols, and then Sir Robert Dudley danced with the Queen. Now it was the Swedish Duke's turn to scowl. Tall and fair and well favoured, he stood with his Ambassador, Gyllenstjerna a small dark man by contrast, both of them brooding and fuming as Elizabeth and her favorite danced. As the smiling couple moved with grace and high spirits, gliding and swirling across the floor, they exuded an unmistakable intimacy, most galling to the envoys of her suitor in far off Stockholm.

Will Fleming the barrister returned from his stroll-about and settled himself next to Farleigh, who had a light in his eyes and a glow in his heart owing to the fine Spanish sherry. "Ah, Farleigh O'Gneeve! I've a bit of idle gossip that will singe your ears!"

"It isn't gossip unless there is malice, and malice have I none." They clinked their goblets and Farleigh continued. "But if it's idle you can keep it to yourself. I want the lethal stuff, boy! What have you heard, then?"

"It concerns this new friend of O'Neill's...Stukeley the pirate..." Fleming sipped his French wine, not a bother on him, waiting to be drawn.

"Pirate?" Will nodded his head slowly and raised it slowly to meet Farleigh's incredulous stare.

"I heard Lady Kildare warning her niece to spurn his advances. "A notorious pirate' she said, 'and a thorough cad!' And this is the tip of the top of it; he's a bastard son of Henry the Eighth! Half brother to Elizabeth herself!" Farleigh's beard and mustache parted as his jaw slackened.

"He's never! Go 'way with yourself!"

"It's a well known fact,' she said. Her Majesty can't abide him at Court, and wants him to go back to the high seas." Will settled back in his chair looking smug as 'the source of all knowledge.' Farleigh shook his head.

"He a Tudor! Could it be so? He has the nose right enough...true to the portraits, at least..."

SHANE O'Neill, 'the Grand Disturber'

"If it isn't so, Lady Fitz is a fierce liar. She told her niece that Stukeley married twice for estate, and each time he drained the poor woman's fortune and abandoned her. His city property is mortgaged into ruin." Fleming shot a furtive glance over his shoulder. "And he's lately come to court to manage the dark intrigues of Robert Dudley. Now there's a fine companion for our Shane O'Neill!"

"He's certainly made it his business to beguile our Shane. And Shane looks to be drawn in..." Farleigh's eyes narrowed with consternation as he peered into the empty air. For a long moment the two were silent. Then Fleming's green eyes flickered anew.

"Stukeley's at some conniving and connoitering, to be sure. I noted him earlier, skulking about outside the jakes. When I came out, I saw that little Swedish Jew man, the Ambassador, slip a note into his fist as he walked by him. Not a word passed between them. Very hugger mugger!"

"A pirate! Just the sort of madman that he *would* take to his bosom! But a desperate rogue will sell his confidences, and as you say he's desperate..." Farleigh heaved a long sigh and shook his head. "It's on *me* now to warn him, and he'll not like it! Look at them. The pair of them!" He lifted his head and nodded toward the window embrasure where Shane and Stukeley were in boisterous form, all backslapping and hearty laughter. Easily seen, the two men were up for roistering this night. They knocked back their drinks now and Shane drew his mantle about him. Farleigh turned back to his confidant. "Ah! There! You see? They're off!"

"To the Inner Temple for some Bacchanalian rites with Dudley. Now... you'll *never* credit *this*..." Will Fleming dangled yet another shocking revelation before the old poet.

"Oh, you're a master spy, Fleming! If you were working for *them* we wouldn't have a hope! Well?" Farleigh found this sort of baiting tiresome. "You look like 'the cat among the feathers and divil a bird in sight!' What is it now? Another royal pirate I suppose?"

"Do you mind I told you I'd seen him *before* somewhere?"

"Seen him whom?

"Stukely the Pirate! Well, I have him now. He's a nephew of my

SHANE O'Neill, 'the Grand Disturber'

father's cousin Christopher Fleming -who was Lord Slane before the title passed to my uncle. I saw him there all of fifteen years ago, and he was acting the goat even then. I seem to recall that Sir Christopher's wife was a Stukeley. Of course if it's true that he's a royal bastard, then he's hardly a Stukeley himself."

"Well if he's old Lord Slane's nephew, he'll have told Shane by now. Sir Christopher often confided to Shane the private business of the Council in Dublin. He was a sound, and a trusted ally. This will make it all the more thorny a task to warn Shane off him." The old poet absently ran is fingers through the white locks round the back of his neck as his eyes darted purposefully about the room. "I've not seen O'Hagan or the others this while."

"I didn't see Owen, but some of the others have gone back. Just as well, I'm thinking, for some of them were none too steady, even Friar Magrath. He's a bit frisky without his brown robes to warn the women off! And did you see Blind Colm? Acting the randy goat, with his 'enchanted fingers' finding every bodice within reach of him! And him with the longest nails in Christendom! They took a rake of drink with them, so I'd say it will be a night til morning." Farleigh lifted himself onto his feet.

"I'm feeling a bit light in the cranium myself. Do you mind the way back, Will? To *our* end of the Palace?"

"I do, I do. Of course."

"Now that's a great wonder!" The old man heaved a deep sigh. "A great wonder..." He gathered up his mantle and drew it about him. "It's like a rabbit warren. And all the passages look the same. You turn a corner and there's three ways to go without turning back. All alcoves and chambers. It's a blasted honeycomb... Aye! The honeycomb in the queen bee's hive!" He laughed heartily, and Fleming put it down to a surfeit of Jerez wine. He gave him his arm and led the auld poet back to their rooms, turning and twisting through the six-acre maze that was Whitehall Palace. It would be their home for some time.

CHAPTER 7

"Damn blast it all to hell, they're *all* blagards over here! And if the bloody Queen mislikes him, he must be sound as the Savior!" Shane's tirade stopped suddenly at the muted chime of the Lambeth steeple bell from across the Thames. He listened intently. "There's the quarter hour rung, so we're rightly if we hasten. His valet draped the fur-collared mantle over his shoulders, and jangled a ring of skeleton keys from its hook near the door. Shane tucked them into the small leathern satchel at his side. Farleigh backed out into the hall where Gillie was waiting restlessly, clomping about in his new boots, and thrilling to the din of his steps.

Shane appeared, still glowering, and as the bolt clanked in the massive door, the three strode quickly down the long corridor. O'Neill had more to say, but he lowered his tone from a roar to a rumble, mindful of echoes along the stony hallway. "He's a rogue with the women like myself, and any decent auntie would not spare a slander or two to steer a young one away from him! He's a nephew of old Lord Slane's, for the love of God!"

"It's only by way of a caution for you." The storm was likely past, and Farleigh decided that he had done the needful, and would be happy enough to wash his hands of it. "You can ferret out the truth of it for yourself. But what would you be saying if you found I was withholding somesuch word from you? Something loud and cross maybe!"

"Well, put it from you now. The gossip and rumours that blow

SHANE O'Neill, 'the Grand Disturber'

through this palace would spin your head like a weathercock!" They came to a halt as they entered a vaulted chamber with several doorways to choose from. After a moment's pause, Shane led them into a bright arcade that opened onto a courtyard blanketed with snow. The early morning sun had pierced through the heavy grey above, and it sparkled and shimmered on the white shapes in the topiary gardens before them. Farleigh stopped in his tracks.

"What are these great lumps meant to signify? Are they covered statues or what are they at all? Shane stopped and looked back.

"What are you on about? These? Trees and bushes, they are. It's the way they do gardens here. We've no time to tarry; they'll be waiting on us in the boats!" He resumed his great stride.

Farleigh shook his head and furrowed his brow and stepped his way once again through the snowy garden. He swiped at a spherical shrub he was passing, scattering its cap of snow and gripping the soft evergreen needles just to test were they actual living trees. They were. He hastened his steps, scampering through the snow til he caught up with Shane and Gillie, and they all squinted as they stepped back inside. Their footfall echoed through another long hallway as they hurried along in silence. The old poet harrumphed, and sighed, and when that failed to elicit a response, he tisked.

Shane looked to him, smiling finally. "Will I slow down for you? Are you right?"

"It's the gardens. They're hideous!" Farleigh shook his head.

"What sort of garden looks beautiful in the dead of Winter?"

"A natural one. Isn't it just *like* them! Just the *price* of them! They'd reduce the sumptuousness of Nature to little cubes and pyramids! Simple shapes for their tidy little minds to grapple with. It's a sacrilege! An affront to God. To *several* gods in fact!" Shane's laugh resounded through the corridor.

"You'd want to mind your wicked aul tongue. Sunday morning. And on your way to Mass! Lord save us!" Gillie blessed himself and laughed too.

At the end of the dark corridor, they turned and descended a short stair into another passageway. It brought them to large tiled chamber where the shrill plaintive call of gulls echoed, and grey light from the river flickered and danced on the vaulted ceiling above. The cold light was flooding in through the lancet doorway of the watergate, where Myler and some of the lads could be seen waiting on the steps outside. More were waiting in the tilt-boat below that Will Fleming had engaged. Eleven in all; the full compliment of O'Neill's entourage, barring the gallowglass troops. They quickly stepped aboard.

Thankfully, it was rather a large tilt-boat, with a colorful but winterworn canopy, four watermen at the oars and a very talkative steersman. For all his disdain of opulence and luxury, Farleigh was delighted to find upholstered cushions across the bench-seats and he settled himself at the chief's side, and watched the changing array of vistas on either shore.

The Tirowenmen were all attired in their Gaelic finest, to hear Mass and to be received by the Spanish Ambassador. They presented a curious spectacle even before these ferrymen, who had seen all manner of foreign attire, from turban to tarboosh . The steersman, a quick wiry fellow from the West Country, kept scratching his short greying hair, and stealing glances at his exotic passengers, as he regaled Will with the concerns of his trade.

"This 'ere be winter floodtide. That's why the waters be so dark and muddy. My good missus is praying morning and night the river don't freeze up like as it done last Winter. A hungry time that was! See all them wherries?" Fleming's blank expression was answer enough. "Wherries is them small boats, with but two oarsmen. Well, there be two thousand of them betwixt 'ere and St. Katherine's t'other side of the bridge. That's three thousand watermen certified, and a thousand and more apprenticed was all put idle when the Thames froze over. And this Winter 'ave only begun to blow!" It was indeed a bustling waterway, with wherries, tilt-boats and barges crossing to and from Southwark, and ferrying Londoners up and down along the river. The crisp air resounded with calls and cries from the banks, where anxious arms waved, hailing the few unoccupied vessels; "Ahoy! Oars! Westward ho!" In truth it was an exhilarating sight.

SHANE O'Neill, 'the Grand Disturber'

Along the sides of the river was a succession of splendid townhouses, mansions, and monastic estates, all frosted and gleaming, and behind them an array of towers and steeples fading into the horizon. On the dark water beside them, a pristine flock of some three score white swans glided gracefully upstream.

When O'Neill's company had ridden into London town upon their arrival the previous week, the squalor and stench of the crowded lanes and ditches they passed had afforded the Irishmen a comforting disapproval of the city. Now, at this slight removal, with just enough distance for glamour's luster to work its spell, the full magnitude and magnificence of the city was undeniable. And no one was more impressed, and less delighted to be so, than the sage and scribe Farleigh O'Gneeve. Although he would be loath to see such tame sights in his wild Ulster hills, the old bard's refined aesthetic senses found much to admire, in betrayal of his deepest convictions. But the pleasant vistas that morning also evoked fear and dread among these rustic Irish gentry as they glided down the Thames. The scale of the city, and the enormity and complexity of its achievement bespoke a terrifying power; a power that boded ill for the future of their little world in the struggle that surely lay ahead. Consequently, Farleigh held his tongue, as Shane regarded the city in silence, and little was said by the others.

As they rounded the bend in the river, the steersman pointed out the various mansions along the Strand. One was of special interest to his fares. Above the embankment stood the tall limestone manor that served as residence for the ambassador, Bishop DeQuadra, known as Durham House. From the river, it appeared fortress-like, a blockish townhouse with broad square towers at either end, behind which loomed a battlement, with its square merlons like a row of teeth against the winter sky.

It was only a short jaunt, really, downriver to Whitefriars, where they disembarked, and made their way through a small crowd jostling to board. The pressing throng of passengers parted and stilled as O'Neill stepped from the boat. Astounded, the crowd pressed back, and a whisper of "O'Neill!" swept through them, for his much

SHANE O'Neill, 'the Grand Disturber'

heralded visit was the talk of the season. Many turned to watch the strange troop as they ascended the slippery rise of Water Street up towards Holburn. They trudged the snowy half mile or so past more ornate four and five-storied mansions. Whitefriars itself had been seized from the Carmelites by Henry VIII, and was now a manorhouse, and as Friar Magrath said, "a monument to greed." Farleigh could not resist an unbidden reply. "Perhaps it was a monument to greed before it was seized."

To their right towered the spectacular Salisbury Court. At the top of the street in the middle of the intersection loomed the Fleet Street Conduit with its lofty ornamented water spire, glistening with icicles, and along Shoe Street the parapets of Bangor House caught their admiration. At Holburn Highroad they faced the magnificent Ely Palace and an astonishing vista of open fields and countryside. This was only a half-mile from the Thames! They poked their heads into the Olde Mitre, a tavern just off the highroad, to take a quick gawk, and as they set off again, Farleigh was missing. Will went back inside to look, but the old bard was found standing at the Palace gate with his eyes shut tight, muttering what they took to be a sort of incantation. Some hooded crows had been disturbed in the bare icy trees above, and, over their rasping clamour, Shane called to him.

"Farleigh, old man, are you rightly? We've divil-all time to spare."

"What place is this?" Farleigh opened his eyes, and they had a wild look about them. Shane glanced up at the high gables.

"Ely Palace, it must be, the church is very near."

"Ah...An evil place. Aye...Sixteen years ago it was, in the autumn of the year. Ormonde's father, James, the Tenth Earl, came to supper here. They must have come up this path, as happy as we. He, and his steward, and sixteen of his retinue were poisoned to death inside this cursed place..." Shane clapped him on the back.

"Aye, Farleigh. Aye, there's a power of ugliness behind *all* these grand facades. Come along now, man. I'd say the holy Mass will do us all some good."

Just behind the palace stood St. Ethelreda's, the last outpost of Rome in old 'Londinium.' On the steps of the church was a small group of prosperous looking Spaniards including an old woman in a black lace mantilla. Behind them, at the very top of the steps, leaning against the threshold with arms and legs crossed, was Tom Stukeley, sporting a lively grin. Shane's eyes brightened as he spotted the rogue, and a hearty handshake was shook. "The bold Tom Stukeley! You never said you were a Roman Catholic! Could it be so?"

"It could, if the rumours are to be believed. Anyone who avoids the Common Prayer Service is suspected of being a Papist. Indolence and indifference are seldom even considered!"

Shane matched his grin. "Then are these rumour mongers to be trusted?"

"Truth to tell, my parents kept by the Old Religion, so I was reared in the Romish rite." Stukeley nodded to Farleigh who had joined them at the doorway, as the others went inside. "As there are no churches, and Mass is illegal, it proves to be a very undemanding allegiance!" Even the wary old poet laughed at that, being in full sympathy. Shane turned to him, smiling.

"So you see? He's one of us!"

"If you mean he's a hoor in his heart, then he's one of our number indeed. Oh, ye's are well met! I can see you'll be able to instruct our Shane on the finer points of roguery! Well! My aul bones are frozen. But for that, you'd never see me rushing into one of these temples to misery." As he turned to enter, a pipe-organ commenced to play, bringing the rest of the stragglers in from the cold.

They joined Kildare and his attendants up near the chancel. The small handful of worshippers in the vast towering nave of the church was a stark reminder of the dark powers arrayed against them; powers that could topple the oldest and most pervasive institution of their world. A tinkling of bells marked the entrance of the Bishop in white gothic vestments, and to most of those present, the faithful and fervent few, it was a moving ceremony, charged with defiance. When the choir began to sing, heads turned, and necks craned to see up into the choir-loft. There, seven or eight of the embassy staff filled the enormous chamber with harmony; the simple harmonies of plainsong. It had been chanted by the faithful for half a millennium, and now that it had been cast asunder by the ravenous forces of Protestant 'reform', they cherished it all the more. To Farleigh's dismay it was a High Mass, and although at one point he had to be nudged from his snoring, he later conceded that it was all quite beautiful.

Afterwords, they were greeted by a stout priest and led down an adjoining hallway to await the bishop. The priest was dark, with piercing brown eyes and a grim demeanor. He wore a long black cassock, and a large biretta that covered his forehead, resting on his shaggy dark brows. "Shann O'Neill? I am Father Borghese, Bishop DeQuadra's secretary. His Grace will be finished in the Sanctuary shortly, and he would be pleased if you will await his presence in the Receiving Chamber."

He opened a pair of intricately carved doors, and ushered them into a sumptuous chamber of crimson and dark oak. He drew back the heavy red curtains, and turned to them. "Please to make yourselves comfortable." He started visibly when he saw Tom Stukeley. The only Englishman in their midst, Stukeley supposed it was because his attire contrasted sharply with the rest of the company. The priest made a quick awkward smile, and then he opened the doors of a large cabinet, filled with decanters and sparkling goblets. "You will take a drink! I know that you are Irish!" He filled a glass with dark red wine and placed it beside a large plush velvet chair, evidently for His Grace. "The ambassador will see you presently." With that, he bowed and stepped back into the hall.

Myler poured for Shane and Stukeley, and when they had stepped away, the others crowded in to avail of the good bishop's hospitality. Some of them drifted over to admire an elaborate table clock that loudly ticked away the few minutes until the Ambassador appeared. Borghese was at his side. "Ah, Lord O'Neill! And you are wearing the cross from His Holiness!" He extended the back of his hand. Shane descended onto his knee, and kissed the large diamond ring that sparkled before him.

"Your Eminence!"

"How fine it was to see the papal cross shining on you at Whitehall! And such a display of artful diplomacy! I have sent glowing

SHANE O'Neill, 'the Grand Disturber'

reports abroad of your subtlety. I believe you shall be of great service to His Holiness."

"Thank you, Your Grace." Shane rose, and introduced the rest of his party to the bishop. One by one, they knelt and kissed the ring, exchanging pleasantries with the exalted diplomat. When Tom Stukeley stepped forward, he was surprised that the bishop knew him.

"Captain Thomas Stukeley, we are most surprised to find you here. Am I to believe that you are a Catholic?"

"That is so, Your Grace." He kissed the ring and stood quickly. "I was baptized in my infancy, and I cherish the Old Religion."

"I have many friends at Court. I can assure you that none of them are aware of this..." The bishop moved over to his chair and sat, without taking his eyes from Stukeley.

"Yes, Your Grace. There are many scoundrels at Court who would use such knowledge to thwart my ambitions." Stukeley sighed and lowered his baleful eyes. "Some have tried to ruin me for the sake of it, so I conceal my devotion. I fervently hope that chance will favor me with an opportunity whereby I might do some...*good turn* for his Holiness, and for His Majesty, King Philip."

"Yes, yes, yes. I quite see..." DeQuadra looked up at the others. "Please, won't you be seated." They took their seats as Shane opened his satchel and produced several letters.

"I have these few letters-" DeQuadra raised his hand to silence Shane, and looked back at his secretary.

"Thank you, Borghese, you may leave us. Oh, and if you will tell the others to join us for wine." The monk turned abruptly in quiet fury, and stalked out of the room. The bishop waited until the doors had closed, and smiled over the company. "My modest little choir! I think you will enjoy their company." He rose, and took up his goblet of wine. "O'Neill if you will come with me? Please excuse us for a short time, gentlemen. There are matters of private concern."

He led Shane into an adjacent room, his study. More plush crimson velvet and dark oak. DeQuadra nodded at a large chair and turned suddenly back to his guest. "Yes, yes. The letters. I will see to them." Shane handed him the four letters and settled himself in the chair. He saw that the bishop was reading the destinations of each.

"There is one for Mary Stuart in Edinburgh." Shane waited until DeQuadra looked up. The others, addressed partly in Irish, would mean little to the Spaniard, and he thought it best not to refer directly to Katherine. "Two are for my castle at Benburb, and that one is to the Dean of Armagh."

"Dean Terence Danyell, yes, he is most able, and quite devoted to your interests. Queen Mary is not in Edinburgh. No matter. She will receive it directly." The bishop held his eyes on Shane with a questioning arch of his brow.

"I had a letter from Her Highness. She was most insistent that I not come to London. But it arrived too late for me to...to give serious consideration to her warnings." The bishop nodded.

"Alas, Queen Mary is right! It was madness to come! You are in grave danger here. Perhaps you do not realize it?"

"I'm not afraid of them. If they-" The bishop continued raising his voice.

"That is a pity! A man without fear is a careless man. You have handed yourself over to your most bitter enemies! Oh, yes! They want you dead." He sat behind his desk. "You have cost them dearly, in both treasure and prestige. You have humiliated their armies, and do you know? They are furious still about your diplomatic coup in Rome. Lord Cecil sent a large delegation, offering substantial concessions to His Holiness if he would appoint their Englishman Primate of Ireland. Even I was surprised when your ...Donatus O'Tighe was chosen. And he has missed no opportunity to spurn their superiorities!" He noted a sudden flash in Shane's grey eyes.   "-Or their 'pretensions,' possibly. I'm afraid that you have pulled the lion's tail and then stepped into his den."

"I would be a fool to argue. You are right, of course. But in fairness, they've afforded me every courtesy since I reached London. My rooms at Whitehall are palatial and grand; the courtiers have been friendly and even fawning at-

"The palace is a snake-pit. Trust no one. Only the most ambitious and ruthless come with its walls. Your difficulties as well as your

SHANE O'Neill, 'the Grand Disturber'

strengths will feed the voracious maw of someone else's ambitions." DeQuadra took up his goblet and relaxed back into his chair. "There. Now you are warned. I hope my words will be of more consequence than those of Queen Mary." He raised his glass, and Shane reciprocated. "To Her Catholic Majesty, Queen Mary! Queen of England, Scotland, and Ireland." They drank to Mary's health. The Spanish bishop wiped some glistening wine from his mustache, and smiled warmly at Shane.

"Tell me, O'Neill. Why did you come?"

"I want to be an earl." Shane saw a glint of doubt in the dark eyes that faced him. "For my *own* purposes."

"And what are they?" DeQuadra held his smile.

"It would disarm my enemies. Give me legal status and rights under English law in addition to those I hold under Brehon law. All of these I will use to drive the English into the sea."

"His Holiness could knight you. A Papal Order of Knighthood. You would be an earl. Why go to Elizabeth?" His tone was casual and curious.

"I would be happy to accept a papal knighthood. But it would not increase my powers under law. My father was the Earl of Tyrone; no one else must hold that title. May I?" At the kindly inquisitor's nod, Shane took the decanter from the desk and filled their goblets.

"Yes, yes, the rival claimant. Do you know I think, perhaps, when the baron's heir comes, they will find in your favour. He would be an expensive toy. They would need a large army to enforce his pretensions over the people." He sipped from his wine, and smiled again. "Well perhaps your plan is good. But I assure you the peril is real. Your best hope of safety lies in the good opinion of the Courts of Europe. You stand now, O'Neill, in the great arena of London, for all to see. We must keep you in the light, for it is in the shadows that danger lurks. I want you to keep very close to me while you are in London. Yes?"

"I shall, Your Grace."

"Yes, yes, yes. My watergate at Durham House is most discreet at night -if you are not followed. Come to me in the dark and I shall keep you in the light!" DeQuadra's laughed, and his dark eyes danced and sparkled. "My reports have been most efficacious in garnering interest in your plight. All Europe watches for news of you. A 'League of Catholic Powers' has been drawn up. -by Catherine de Medici and the Duke of Alva and His Majesty King Philip. Elizabeth is quite wary of them."

"I've heard report of this, but I know very little about it." Shane expected the bishop to elaborate, but he only smiled knowingly. He glanced at the pile of correspondence on his desk. "Has there been some reply to my request of His Highness?"

"No, no. And there will be none. Like Queen Mary, His Highness is most concerned right now with matters in France. This business with the Huguenots! These French Protestants could light a fire that will set all Europe ablaze in religious warfare. Again we are urging Elizabeth to remain neutral. But she spurned such entreaties in the matter of Scotland and she prevailed. France was driven out. Why will she heed us now? It is most worrisome."

"But King Philip has promised to send me troops!" Shane's amiable smile had vanished.

"And so you must wait!" DeQuadra stood suddenly. "I need hardly explain to you such priorities!" The Spaniard's sudden flash of temper cooled as quickly as it had flared. "I am sure that both France and Spain will be eager to send their armies to you when the time is apt, and as things stand, you are hardly in a position to use them. You understand that they can do nothing in this matter without the approval of His Holiness." He cocked his head back and looked accusingly down his long aquiline nose at Shane, who had remained seated. "In the meantime, you could do much to gain the Holy Father's blessing."

"Ireland has given beyond measure to the Church! When Europe was barbarian-"

"Not Ireland, but O'Neill! Your personal affairs are far from exemplary. A married countess as concubine... Hardly suitable for a champion of the Faith." The bishop's benign smile now appeared to be one of serene condescension. For an instant Shane was provoked, and then suddenly, he found his 'patron' quite ludicrous.

"Ah, the holy princes! Your Grace, I promise you. I have the virtue of a Borghia and the chastity of a Medici." DeQuadra appeared quite stunned for a moment, and then threw his head back in hearty laughter.

"Yes, yes, yes! Quite! Very shrewd! He tipped his head forward, his dark eyes peering up at Shane to strike a cautionary note. "His Holiness is most anxious that Elizabeth should create a Catholic earl at this time. His nuncio has spoken for you at Court. He must tread very lightly-"

"*Why* must he tread lightly?!" Shane's deep voice rumbled with undisguised fury. "She has outlawed the Mass! Why does allow the Irish to be delivered over to the dominion of heresy? Will nothing induce him to excommunicate this hellhag Elizabeth?"

The ambassador paused for a long moment, his piercing gaze held upon Shane in silence. When calm and restraint had returned to Shane's features, he responded quietly, with a beatific smile. "He is a man of Faith. He hopes yet to win the young queen back to the Holy Church. England has changed religion five times in the last thirty years. Who is to say a new wind will not blow her towards Rome?"

"I will say it." Shane matched his composure, but spoke with conviction and force. "If Elizabeth embraces Rome, she acknowledges her mother to be stigmatized a concubine, and she herself a bastard; establishing the right of Mary Stuart to the Crown of England." DeQuadra considered for a moment.

"Time, O'Neill. Perhaps His Holiness will come to that. God will choose his moment –not you and not I."

"The pope is old. Perhaps a new pope..." For a long moment, Shane's unfinished question hung in the air, unsettling the Spanish diplomat. He collected himself, and lifted his sparkling goblet in a toast. "The wheels of divine justice turn slowly, but they grind most fine. 'Rejoice; for patience shall prevail!" Shane raised his glass to the noble sentiment. "And now I must see to my other guests. Come."

The mood in the large chamber was genial enough by now, the Irishmen chatting happily with the young Spanish staff of the

SHANE O'Neill, 'the Grand Disturber'

embassy. Two young nuns were also present, seated together primly, conversing sweetly to their tippling guests. Although Myler Magrath felt deeply the want of his Franciscan habit, he was gratified to be in this ecclesiastical and most Catholic enclave for the day. Deeply ambitious, after having spent several years in Rome, he was eager to build upon his acquaintance with Bishop DeQuadra. When Shane and the Ambassador appeared in the doorway, Myler made his way quickly to their side. They would accept his intrusion, for he had a message to impart to Shane from his friend. "Cousin, I was asked by Tom Stukeley to extend his apologies. He had to keep an appointment." He added in Irish, "He asked me to give you a rather queer message. He said he's 'gone to supper with naught before him at the table, but a *dark little turnip*'. He insisted you would understand." Shane smiled.

"Good man, Myler! Indeed, and I do."

"I do as well, so I do." It was Farleigh, with a sly grin just visible through the white mustache and beard. Myler stepped away, engaging His Eminence on the religious turmoil of the continent. Shane splashed more wine into the bard's glass.

"You do in your arse!"

"A turnip is a Swede. And *I* know *which* Swede. Oh, I have a network of spies and informants too!"

"You know more than your prayers; I'll give you that!"

Tom Stukeley stepped his black charger nimbly through the bustling crowds along the broad thoroughfare of Cheapside, to the more genteel environs of Lyme Street Ward. Here were the fair houses of the merchant classes, whose wares were sold in the stalls and shops he had just passed by. He tethered his horse at the top of Cornhill Street. Before him stood an imposing stone edifice, adorned with the Arms of England graven in granite over its door, with a stalwart angel chiseled on either side. He took himself down the dark narrow footway that led him into Lombard Street. There, at the rear of the building, hung a large painted wooden sign that creaked with the winter winds. On it was a benign beardless face under the triple tiara of Rome defiantly bearing the legend "The Pope's Head". Reformation or no, a good tavern was not to be trifled with.

Inside was cozy, with warm fires, candles, and lanterns flickering, tossing shadows that fluttered about the room. The air was laden with with the aromas of cooking, mostly from a roasting ox that turned on a huge spit in the great stone hearth at the back. The genteel crowd was mostly wealthy drapers from nearby Birchover's Lane, quaffing their wine at a leisurely pace on a slow Sunday afternoon. This was no alehouse, but a tavern, where fine wine and well-heeled tipplers were served. By evening there would be a rowdy din, but now, only the rumble of low voices and whispers could be heard, as wary patrons guarded their intimacies and dealings from the ears of strangers.

"Good day to you, Master Stukeley. What's your pleasure?" The stout ruddy-faced publican appeared over the low bar, and with a clank and a clatter, he settled two clusters of glistening wet tankards before him. "Do you know, you haven't finished off that butt of claret I pierced for you? It may be you've gone off it, but I'd wager there's more nor a bellyful there, without stirring the dregs."

"No, I still have a taste for it, Jack. The claret will do nicely. And when you're below again, I'd ask you to find the best tun of Rhenish, and set it aside for me." Thomas glanced down past the end of the bar. "Is the first snug vacant? I'm meeting with a gentlemen."

"Aye, you are and all. He's in there waiting on you. Been there since before the last bells. Will ye be taking supper?"

"Yes, indeed we will." Tom made his way toward the back, to a finely carved wooden door that enclosed his customary table in its cozy snuggery, peaceful and private. He paused for a moment at the door, and a voice from the other side greeted him. Perhaps his boots were spied under the door.

"Ahoy! Captain Stukeley! Come in." The door swung open with a harsh piercing creak, then a rasping screech as it started back, like the braying of an ass. Thomas caught it and stepped into the snug, towering over the low table.

SHANE O'Neill, 'the Grand Disturber'

"Chancellor Guildenstern!" He flashed a bright smile, as he doffed his cap and cape, and fixed them to the hook, over the long black gabardine coat of ambassador.

"Nils Gyllenstjerna. But as you are so English, you will call me Nicholas!" Guildenstern was a slight man with a large head, his thin and graying hair stuck flat and close, as his tight cap had left it. His dark eyes were lively and bright, with deep circles about them. Apart from his swarthy complexion, his appearance was also quite singular in that he bore no facial hair, and possessed no discernable lips. But when he smiled, as he did now, his fine teeth were quite impressive for, at that time, straight white teeth were a rare commodity in all but children. "It is so difficult to make acquaintance in the bustle of the Court. These receptions and revels are most tiresome." He noted the dubious crook of Stukeley's brow as he slid in beside the table. "Well, for a diplomat of course, they are work. And Whitehall is so dark, and thronged with crowds of petitioners and such. A man like you, Captain! How you must miss the sea!"

"On the contrary, Chancellor, I-"

"Nicholas. If you please."

"- Nicholas, then. I miss nothing. A man who goes where he lists, pines not for whence he came! I keep my eyes to the fore, and the wind at my back."

Over Guildenstern's shoulder, the wooden sash of the bar-window slid back with a clunk, and a crystal jug of claret appeared with two goblets. The smiling barmaid settled her elbow on the counter, cradling her chin in the palm of her white hand. A welter of long ginger curls nearly hid the sprightly pair of blue eyes that boldly addressed themselves to Stukeley.

"Well! Master Tom..." She peered over the shoulder of the dark Swede to inspect his features, and wrinkled her nose to Stukeley. Too old for her liking, certainly. "Now, gentlemen, how are your appetites today?" She licked her lips and winked. "We have hot succulent meats." She turned quickly to Guildenstern. "-and turnips and mushy peas if you're able!"

Tom rose and set the drinks on the table. He turned back to her

SHANE O'Neill, 'the Grand Disturber'

with a grin, calling in a loud voice, "Two dinners then, Miss, nice and handy!" and he shut the panel with bang. When the goblets were filled he sat, and a quick squint jogged his memory back to the matters in question. "No, in truth, I don't miss the sea-faring. My sea-legs manage quite fair on the cobbles of London. Perchance you miss your fjords, Nicholas."

"Fjords? No, I am a Dane from Copenhagen; we have no fjords. But we have birds. And I have heard from a little bird that it was the tide of your *fortunes* that left you stranded, stranded high and dry among the landlubbers as they say..."

"As the *little birds* say?" Stukeley's curiosity was piqued now as to just what this clumsy 'diplomat' was digging at.

"Indeed, it has been said quite plainly that you are at Court only to recoup the price of a sailing vessel. But how could that be? Anyone can see it that the wages of servitude –even for Robert Dudley's footman or henchman– will hardly purchase a sea-worthy ship." He sipped at his wine, keeping his dark eyes steady on Thomas.

"Yes, I must own that I do know this little bird you've been consulting. It's Mistress Kat Ashley, one of the Queen's ladies. Nicholas, a gentleman betimes will tell all manner of tales to a fetching maid, with little regard for truth, and with no other object than to snaffle her into a bed! Even the men of Sweden or Denmark, I daresay. But perhaps you wouldn't know of such things..." Stukeley knocked back his wine and leaned in, his gaze brash and challenging. After a moment's awkward pause, Guildenstern laughed.

"My friend, I think...Ya, I think you mistake me. I want only to help for you to acquire a fine ship. His Majesty can afford to buy you much greater treasures than Robert Dudley's scant purse can offer." Thomas sat back, grinning.

"And what will be his bidding? Would he have me to mill with Dudley in a bout of fisticuffs for him?"

"His Majesty challenged Sir Robert to fight him in his own royal person in France or even in Scotland! Dudley refused to take the challenge."

"Everyone knows that Dudley told him he would face him in

SHANE O'Neill, 'the Grand Disturber'

England. Wherefore comes he not? Only a feint heart or a fool will send his brother to woo a maid! Oh, I know well that Cecil and the rest have bid him come to Court. He's a Protestant Prince and rich one. A fine physic for their ailing treasury."

"Precisely so. And he will furnish the Russian markets and the trade of the Northern States. What great boon will come to England from this 'jumped up stable boy', the Master of Horse?" When Stukeley declined to answer, he continued. "She will never wed a commoner."

"Sir Robert is knighted."

"That is meaningless. She could never take a man whose rank was lower than Earl. He is a plaything. And a scandalous one." Stukeley bristled at this.

"The Queen is promised to make him Earl of Leicester, a thing she could do on whim, and so your objection is 'meaningless!' The dark Dane shook his head slowly and tisked.

"And yet he remains a Master of Horse..."

"If His Majesty be so smitten with our Queen, why stays he in far off Stockholm?" Thomas filled the goblets.

"Prince Erik will not come while she keeps this odious consort Dudley at her side. How can he court her while she courts a courtier? A courtier she avows never to wed? A courtier who did kill his wife to make room in the marriage bed!" Stukeley's smile faded, and he drank deep. "Cecil and the Council are not to be gainsaid by such a man. Have you pondered what will befall your master when the Queen at last is wed? He will be sent afar from the Royal Court, to the wild Americas most like. And what shall be your lot then?" Thomas gave no answer, but gazed intently at the vacant air. Guildenstern took this as a heartening response. "This time you and your buccaneers have boarded a sinking ship, Captain Stukeley!" Thomas looked up at him. "Ya, it is true. I know you are a pirate. And I suggest it is time to jump ship. The Crown of Sweden has untold wealth, and Prince Erik will soon be at the helm of England."

"What does he want of me? Will I woo the Queen into his bed for him?" Guildenstern sat back and peered down his nose at Stukeley, allowing the mockery of this feigned innocence to infuse the silence.

"Am I a fool? So coy a pirate I have found..." Stukeley summoned up his smile once again.

"Beggin' yer parden, Squire." He raised his voice. "You want me to kill him?" The ambassador started to rise.

"You misconstrue me, sir. And I waste your valuable time. You could be running errands for the Queen's favorite." He reached for his gabardine greatcoat. Thomas stood, with a repentant smile.

"Forgive me Chancellor, I'm a pawky aul salt I was only trifling. A jape is all! Sit down and tell me the tasks and terms of it." The dark Swede turned sharply and looked him sternly in the eye, cold and commanding. Thomas offered his hand. "Don't mind me, Nicholas. I've got the devil in me is all. And judging by what you're asking of me, it may be I've need of him." They sat again, and Thomas splashed more claret into their goblets. "How much is in it?" His voice was low and earnest.

"I've been consigned to pay as much as ten thousand pounds to eliminate the 'impediment' to the royal match. More than enough for a fine sea-worthy galleon."

"The wage is fare. How does he want him topped? Poison?" Thomas peered at the dark envoy over his goblet.

"Discretely. A credible misadventure. Perhaps he might take a fall from a stair, like his unfortunate wife at Cumnor Place." Clearly a dark jest, Stukeley responded with a malevolent grin.

"I'll need the ship at anchor, ready to sail."

"There will be no need for that, Captain, if you are discrete. Anything less would reflect upon His Majesty, by reason of motive." Stukely folded his arms and sat back.

"No, mate. Cautious in the deed, and cautious in the deal. I always see the purser first. His Majesty can stump up half my price, and tender the rest on completion. A few servants will need greasing."

The sash above Guildenstern rumbled open, and two trenchers appeared, heaped with savory food. "Sunday dinner, gents! Tuck into that now!" The ginger barmaid leaned over the steaming wooden plates, with a meaningful look for the sea captain, had he but seen it.

SHANE O'Neill, 'the Grand Disturber'

He spat on his palm and held it out before the ambassador.

"Are we of one accord in the matter then?" Guildenstern glanced quickly at the barmaid with visible discomfort, and then clapped his hand in Stukeley's.

"Ya. We're agreed, sir." Tom shook his hand strong and hearty, and bounded up to retrieve the dinners.

"Commerce and trade on a Sunday! A venial sin." He winked at the barmaid. "But then, even a King's bastard has got to earn his daily bread!"

CHAPTER 8

The next few days passed quickly, short winter days filled with the myriad tasks of 'settling in.' Outside, the skies darkened, and snow settled ever deeper and higher in drifts. For those Ulstermen huddled about the fire within the palace walls, the mounting apprehension of a long stay was unspoken, a dark shadow that settled over every silence like the glowering winter sky. What they had referred to at home as 'a fortnight in London', now promised to keep them seven weeks or more, as it was clear that nothing could be settled, or even broached for some time. No, not until the arrival of the Baron's son with his claims to succeed the Earl. The summons would surely take ages to reach him, and then his sea journey and the endless delays of winter travel could keep them here until spring.

Lord Kildare paid a call upon Shane, and spoke frankly of these gloomy prospects, and the possibility of even longer delays. He cautioned forbearance, and urged him quite simply to make the best of it. He suggested that Shane replace the English domestics and kitchen staff in his palace apartments, and the very next day sent over Irish speaking servants, "more like to serve than to spy." After that, the communal Dining Hall of the palace was avoided, and the Tirowenmen took to gathering at O'Neill's rooms each afternoon for a proper Irish supper. The ballads and banter afterwards would engage and divert Shane, who was growing restless and prickly in his new bearings. It was a circumstance he was already coming to regard as 'captivity.' What is more, his new friend Stukeley had been strangely absent from his side for many days. Not a word had come since he slipped away from the bishop's reception for some nefarious meeting.

SHANE O'Neill, 'the Grand Disturber'

No-one had ever known Shane to 'wait' for anything. He would ride into a storm if he had set his heart on a journey. And now he awaited 'word' to see the Queen's secretary. By Thursday he had resolved to call upon Cecil unbidden. After lengthy conferral, he and his legal counsel, Art O'Hagan the brehon, and Will Fleming the barrister, made their way through the maze of Whitehall to Lord Cecil's office chamber.

As they reached the antechamber they saw a pair of tall footmen snap to attention, crossing their halberds before the great doors. At the Irish party's approach the guards stood stock still, staring quite vacantly before them. Shane's deep voice resounded in the spare stone hall. He spoke in English "Shane O'Neill for the Lord Secretary."

Still averting his eyes, one of the guards responded. "Perhaps you have misreckoned the appointed day, Squire. We have us orders to admit none this day, as none is expected by his Lordship." Will Fleming spoke up.

"We are here at the Queen's command. You will tell him that John O'Neill has arrived."

The guard looked them up and down, shook his head and sighed. He turned, pushing the heavy door open a bit, and disappeared behind it. The other footman took a thundering march-step to his side, and clanked the halberd down at arm's length across the portal. Still he held his empty gaze aloft, and stood rigidly at attention.

Shane squinted at him derisively and turned to O'Hagan. "I'd sooner have Blind Colm guarding my tent!" He spoke loudly in Irish. "I could have had their halberds in a trice, and lopped their heads without a scuffle. Any guard of mine who played at dumbshow like these louts, I'd cut the ears off him!"

Art O'Hagan shook his head. "It's a queer thing, right enough. All these palace guards. They move like the figures on a mechanical clock." Fleming smiled. "Tis only display. It's little they worry about trouble here, this deep inside the palace. These men are symbols, I'd say, to show you how exalted is the lordling behind the door. How unapproachable he is, and-"

"Symbols me arse!" Shane's patience was fraying. "A guard is a

SHANE O'Neill, 'the Grand Disturber'

guard, and those halberds are sharp enough. These English are thicker nor clabber and clay! And too clever to shite!"

The weighty door creaked open a bit, and the footman before it pulled in his halberd staff. A slight young fellow in black with a square white collar, presumably a clerk, leaned out through the opening. "His Lordship was not expecting you to call today, and he is engaged with an ambassador. He will summon you when the depositions are ready. If you will be good enough to come back when you've been sent for-"

"His guards told us he has *had* no visitors today. Did the ambassador come through the window?" At the sound of Shane's deep voice, the clerk shrank back into the doorway, and Shane called out, "Tell him the O'Neill is come-" He stopped at the sound of Cecil's voice, calling from within.

"Nay then, I shall see him! Stand away!" The door pulled back and Cecil stood before them with a sour smile. The clerk disappeared behind him. There was no sign of any ambassador. "O'Neill!" He stood back and swept his arm before him. "Come in, O'Neill, come in. I trust your rooms are sufficient?" William Cecil stepped back, silhouetted against the snowy brightness of a huge latticed window that towered over his massive desk. Vast windows were a recent innovation, and the Irish were silently disapproving, marking the cold draughts as the Secretary ushered them into the cluttered chamber. He cleared some books from a chair and indicated that they be seated. "What brings you forth today?"

"The same mission that brings me into England." Shane sat and smiled cordially. "I have many grievances to present against the Lord Deputy Sussex."

"Unhappily, O'Neill, we are ill prepared to hear of them as yet. Of course, there is no urgency. You shall be with us for quite some time. We have only now summoned the Baron's heir, and those orders will be weeks in reaching him. When he arrives, there will be hearings regarding the peerage of Tyrone." He noted Shane's barely perceptible nod, and forged on with great speed and energy. "But, surely you know as much! We shall have no want of time for these matters of the Lord Deputy. Have you been attending Sir Robert Dudley?"

SHANE O'Neill, 'the Grand Disturber'

"I'm to see him again tomorrow. He's invited me to-"

"Good! Quite right!" The Secretary was all smiles and bluster now. "Her Majesty was pleased that you were amenable to...that you would be instructed by him in the civilities of Court. Good! I think it meet to tell you...that you would please Her Majesty in no small measure were you to attire yourself in the proper apparel for the Royal Court. And your...'entourage' as well. A matter of vital concern! Now that you are here. For your own sake! It would stand you well when the matter of peerage is weighed." Cecil shook his head and lowered his voice. "You really must amend this. I should say, in all frankness, that Her Majesty was grievously insulted by your rude garments at Court on the occasion of your submission."

"Shane's grey eyes narrowed under a twist of his brow. He straightened his back. "On the *contrary* lies the truth of it! It is I who am insulted. I came to Court upon Her Majesty's invitation. I am not an English courtier. I am an Irish nobleman, and I have come dressed befitting my station. If I went to the wild Americas, would she have me don feathers?"

Cecil smiled amiably now, and he spoke as to a child, in forceful tones of patient reason. "Yes, that is so. But it is also true that you are not in America or even in wild Ulster. You are at Court. Her Majesty's Court. And the fact remains that you would honour Her Royal Highness greatly, *and* win favour to your cause were you to acquire courtly apparel, and acquit yourself according to the manners of this Court!"

"I shall consider your words." Shane stood abruptly, as did his silent legal advisors, Owen and Will. His demeanor shifted suddenly, and he grinned at Cecil with an engaging tilt of the head. "If I must- If I should wear English robes, your Lordship, I would that Robert Dudley should accompany me...attired in *Irish* garments, so that the mirth and amazement of the courtiers might be fairly divided betwixt us!"

The Lord Secretary smiled and stood. "Thereupon you must needs confer with Sir Robert! Oh, there is another small- well, no *trifling* matter, as it stands... Upon your submission, Her Highness allowed you freedom to the limits of the City of London. You violated the terms of your stay as set forth, when you and your party traveled to Ely on Sunday last. That is a place that is outside the city of London. St. Ethelreda's is off bounds to you and to your attendants. I trust I shall not have to speak of this again!" Shane folded his arms.

"There now stand *two* grievances of yours you have presented, since you advised me that mine must wait." Cecil held out his hand.

"Very well. I shall take them from you. They will be examined in due course, and we shall arrange a hearing where they can be adjudged. *If* they are found to have merit, they shall be redressed." Shane looked to Will Fleming, who stepped forward.

"We'll want a few days, your Lordship, to revise them as depositions. I'll send them 'round for you then." Cecil moved toward the door.

"And now you had best to take your leave, for there are most urgent matters of state that I must attend upon."

Behind them in the dim corridor, they heard the rumble of the closing doors, the clank of the footmen resuming their station, and then the din of their own footfall as the three men trudged along in uneasy silence. Shane was bristling, his chest heaving, his nostrils flared, and his jaw grinding. "By Christ, it was Stukeley!" he roared. O'Hagan and Fleming were greatly relieved to hear him say what they both were thinking. How else, indeed, could their visit to the Bishop have been known of at Court? "I've not seen sign nor light of him since Sunday Mass. Didn't I wonder at his disappearance? Another treacherous little Englishman!"

They adjourned to Shane's apartments, and began immediately preparing the petition of grievances. O'Hagan had drawn up a list of atrocities and injustices, all set forth in trenchant fiery Irish, and their task was to present the issues in terms less charged, words drawn from English jurisprudence. This was scarcely an easy task, with Shane in a simmering fury. But it was very much Fleming's forte, and since most of the legal terms were Latin, they managed their deliberations in that language. They could quickly see that there was a good week's labour in the task, as they would need to anticipate all the various rebuttals that would be forthcoming. But somehow it was a relief to be occupied with such vital labour. It served to stave off, for a time, the languor and futility of their thinly veiled captivity in London.

On Friday evening, Shane went round to Robert Dudley's lavish rooms, where he was expected for late supper. Sir Robert's man Robert Blount greeted him, and led the Irish guest through draughty halls and regal chambers to a warm and comfortable drawing room where he was asked to await his host. Shane sat before the blazing crackling fire while a chambermaid moved silently about the room lighting candles and oil lamps. She turned at the door and said, "Begging your pardon, Sir, will you have the mulled ale, or do you prefer spirits?"

"A crock of whiskybaugh!" He turned and saw her curtsy and disappear through the velvet drapes of the doorway. From just behind those drapes, Dudley's voice called after her.

"Ho! The very thing! I shall echo O'Neill's call. Whiskybaugh!" The velvet parted again, and Sir Robert strode into the room, flashing a bright smile. "That barrel of spirits you sent me has made me the envy of all London. And, I must own, it has doubled my share of late-calling visitors!" He extended his hand and gave Shane's a mighty shake. "Well come, John! Let the damned blizzards blow, for you've always a warm welcome at my door!"

"Good man yourself, Robert! In a land of strangers, a friend is a fine comfort, indeed."

"It's a pity you've arrived amid these wintry blasts. The falconing and hunting will have to wait." He settled himself in the great leather chair across from Shane. The chieftain leaned over, as if confiding.

"Aye, so they will. This is weather for drinking and hooring!" This brought on a good laugh, and the arrival of a decanter of whiskey with

SHANE O'Neill, 'the Grand Disturber'

Dudley's cupbearer did nothing to dampen the high spirits. He poured a goodly measure into two crystal glasses, bowed, and disappeared through the velvet portal. Dudley's glass sparkled amber in the firelight as he held it up to toast.

"A favorable and felicitous issue for your visit to Court!" Shane stretched his glass forth to clink it.

"Justice be served, and peace in the realm!" Dudley raised his brows at this toast that sounded more like terms of truce. He smiled and clinked, and both drank the fiery dram. Sir Robert winced as he swallowed it.

"Ah! You Irish are well braced against the winter's chill. And your wooly mantle trimmed in fur! I do envy you it on such a night as this!" Shane laughed, and was delighted by the perplexed look on his friend's face.

"You may yet come to wear it yourself! I called upon William Cecil yesterday, and he castigated me roundly for my Irish attire. I told him I would dress the English courtier, perhaps, if Sir Robert Dudley would accompany me dressed in *Irish* robes! -So that the mirth of the courtiers might be divided fairly betwixt us!" Dudley's eyes blazed with merry excitement.

"I shall do it! I shall do it! Cecil will squirm, but Elizabeth will laugh a bellyful!" Shane raised an open hand in caution.

"Now...I've not settled on this notion of English garb. It can wait. I may need it to sweeten the pot when we're haggling over final terms. These matters of show can often trump matters of substance in diplomacy."

"You shall engage my tailor! It must be splendid, and such a garment will keep him stitching for weeks upon weeks. By such time as it is ready for *you*, you may be also ready for *it*! To coax some concession from Her Majesty..." O'Neill pursed his lips and squinched his eyes as he considered. He shook his head, but his smile looked quite amenable. Dudley pressed on. "I could send my tailor to you tomorrow!"

"You'd best not. I want to keep this dark, and he would be noted coming to my door. I'll go to him."

SHANE O'Neill, 'the Grand Disturber'

"You can meet with him here! Anyone will suppose he's about his usual business with me. He often calls here." Shane nodded, and Dudley clapped him on the knee. "Aye, that's it, then. He'll bring his tapes and measures, and samples of stuffs." A sudden inspiration flashed in Sir Robert's eyes. "Then you must have a portrait commissioned!"

"Steady now, steady on!" Shane laughed. "A portrait in hose? I think not!" He belted back a slug of the whiskey. "Cecil will know of this suit before ever a stitch is drawn. His newsmongers are everywhere."

"Aye. His net is cast wide and drawn tight. I've dismissed several servants whom I found were in his pay." Dudley turned to Shane in sudden alert. "Why? Has he caught you up on something?"

"We heard Mass in St. Ethelreda's on Sunday, and Cecil had it all straight away. 'I've violated my terms,' he says. 'Ely is outside the walls of City of London."

"So also is Whitehall, -where you reside! What 'terms' are those, exactly?"

"Something she said at my submission. 'Liberty of the palace and to the bounds of the City of London,' she said. It was nothing I put a quill to in my terms of Safe Conduct."

"He's looking to find something against you, some minor infraction to justify withholding you here." Dudley raised his voice now in stern but friendly warning. "I pray, give him no peg to hang you from! Defy him in the spirit, yet keep always to the letter!"

Shane drew himself up. "Will he or nil he, I will hear Mass of a Sunday!"

"Indeed. Cecil doesn't care a fig about Ely Place. He niggles over your crossing the Holburn Highroad! It's a blind. His true quarry is the Mass and your defiance there." The glint in Sir Robert's eyes brightened now. "But since he *has* aimed his censure at your whereabouts, you've only to move the Mass. Bishop DeQuadra has a private chapel in his residence. Why not attend him there, and hear your Mass at Durham House in the Strand?"

"Good man yourself! We'll save us a journey into the bargain.

SHANE O'Neill, 'the Grand Disturber'

When Cecil's spies report that I've bested him he'll be confounded rightly." Shane took good swig, and poured again. Dudley looked pensively into the fire for a moment, then spoke brightly.

"Who saw you in Ely?"

"Apart from my own? Spaniards mostly. And Tom Stukeley."

Dudley's eyes went wide. "How did Tom come to be there?"

"You'll have to ask him. I can account only for my own. He would never...?"

"Tom?" Dudley winced with incredulity and shook his head. "Cecil loathes him."

"It might buy him favour. I've not seen hide nor hair of him since."

Dudley laughed easily. "He'd far prefer *your* favour! No, John, I've kept him hard at it of late. A bit of skullduggery of my own with these bloody Swedes!" He took a belt of the whiskey, swallowed hard, and sighed, short and sharp. "There's a dark scheme afoot –Cecil and the Council. They all conspire to compel the Queen to marry with this Swedish prince."

"Why does she not simply refuse?"

"She *has* done -to many of these royal suitors. But this is difficult. She has a duty to wed, to have issue, a royal heir to the throne. The Privy Council has grown impatient, for Elizabeth has turned away many. Such-a-one is a papist, another too fat, too old, and now comes this wealthy fair-haired Protestant prince from the North who brings with him the markets of Skandia and Russia. And what is most in his favour; he is not me!" Dudley shook his head. "Oh, Cecil and the Council are firmly set upon him. No matter that he is half mad. His brother rides through Cheapside tossing coins at the crowds there, leaving hurly-burly in his wake."

"Aye, my own men have jumped after it, scrambling in the slush and muck for his gold. 'The Swedes are coming!' he shouts. 'Prince Erik loves you!' Shane leaned forward, resting his arms upon his knees. "He's as mad as a March hare, by all reports. Surely that would be grounds enough for the Queen's refusal!"

"They mark it down to his 'zeal'." Dudley's eyes rolled heavenward in disdain. "Such an ardent suitor! And he has lavished gifts upon her. An endless array of gifts; eighteen piebald horses, tapestries, several chests of uncoined gold and silver, strings of Oriental pearls, exquisite furs... She dare not refuse them, though she swears she would do." Shane's doubts on that matter were hard to conceal. Dudley smiled broadly. "Her Majesty's keen diplomacy forbids her to return any token or gift for fear of offence, -to her treasury!"

Shane laughed. "I am the O'Neill, and I would never be advised on such business as marriage by a council, if ever there were men so bold as to attempt it!"

"Neither will Elizabeth be compelled, and yet she cannot appear to be capricious in this matter. She needs a solid reason to banish Prince Erik's embassage from Court. Cecil and his minion Keyle, and even some of her own Ladies, all conspire in his scheme. We know they are in correspondence with the Prince, and have taken bribes from his ambassador, Guildenstern. Elizabeth wants proof of their meddling, and so I've put Tom Stukeley onto them." He smiled and nodded at his Irish visitor. "Therein lies the reason you've not seen him lo these many days and nights! Even now he meets with Guildenstern, -a credulous fool by Tom's reckoning. He tells me he has him baited and hooked, and he swears that he will draw him in tonight. I must confess I'm feeling the torments of Tantalus waiting to see what the rascal has caught on his line! He's promised to call here with his fine catch this evening."

"I'm happy enough to keep vigil with you." Shane raised his glass and tipped a nod and a wink to his friend. "He's kept himself so scarce of late. It relieves me to hear that there's good cause for it." His smile faded as he gazed into the faint blue billows of the drowsy fire. "Every man jack scurrying through this palace is shoulder to the wheel, working and scheming, while I crack nuts at the fire!" He sat back again and stretched out his long legs until his boots rested in the ashes.

"Ah, I see. Of course. Life at Court would hardly suit a man like you. And you've no interest in scheming?"

"Cecil's desk was a mountain of parchments and vellum, all

awaiting his deliberations. He's up to his neck in it, and I envied him his labours. Most of the which are likely for my undoing!"

"Aye, John, Aye! You've hit the mark *there*, I'm afraid. Lord Sussex took little rest on his journey back to Dublin. He dispatched a letter from Southhampton before he sailed. More stratagems and ploys to unsettle you. He urges Her Majesty to shire Ulster and form a provincial council. A council that *he* would rule as Earl of Ulster. It's a title he covets, one that would long outlast his rule as Viceroy." Shane drew himself up, taut and tense, at the edge of his seat.

"Aye, behind each slanderous report of me he sends to the Queen, is the shadow of his own greed and dark ambitions. I am told often and often that nothing will please him but to plant himself in my lands; that he desires to be styled 'Earl of Ulster.' Even if I succeed to my father's title of Tyrone, I would be liege to an Earl of Ulster under English law."

"They are shiring Connaught at present, and Ulster soon thereafter. In Elizabeth's privy chamber is a map of Ulster that Lord Sussex has drawn up. I have seen it. Your vast Ealdom of Tyrone is shired into three counties. He has severed off the lands North of the Ballinderry River, and those South of the Blackwater to make the three. He will preside over all the province through his council at Armagh."

"He will in his arse! He wouldn't live a week in Armagh. What says the Queen to his scheme?"

"Her Majesty will be advised. Norfolk and his faction back Sussex, of course. Lord Cecil speaks for him, but many are opposed. He has powerful enemies at Court!"

Shane smiled slyly, darkly. "So it would *seem!*"

"You must come to proper terms with Her Majesty before you leave, so that she will find no *need* for his costly reforms." Shane nodded thoughtfully, looking daggers into the waning fire, as he considered his bitter adversary in Dublin Castle and the evil designs for Tirowen. Dudley's eyes, drawn to the fire, marked its flagging state, and he rose to stir it. He prodded and poked until a crisp black log split asunder, and a shower of sparks went whirling up the dark flue. The long red gash of ember blazed again, casting long shadows up the walls behind them. Shane felt the heat against his brow and it matched the searing fury in his heart. Still on his knee, Dudley turned to his friend who seemed to be mesmerized by the leaping flames. "There is yet another plan afoot! Sussex has thrown down the gauntlet where your new Bishop of Armagh is concerned. Donatus...?" Shane looked up.

"Donogh O'Tighe, is it? Bishop O'Tighe?" Sir Robert met his eyes and spoke on.

"It seems the Primate's defiance of the supremacy of Canterbury will not be brooked. He's-"

"But surely, in its very essence, that's what a Primate *is*! He is the head of the bishops of Ireland, and takes his counsel directly of the Pope." Shane's ears burned hot and red, though his voice remained steady. "And the primacy of Armagh predates Canterbury by hundreds of years. Are they mad altogether?"

"This is but a watchman's whistle, my friend. A quiet warning from the parapet." Dudley rose, and seated himself again. He spoke softly and slowly, looking calmly into Shane's eyes. "Sussex prevails upon Her Majesty to refuse to *honour* the papal appointment; to declare the seat vacant, and to appoint his own chaplain, Adam Loftus, as Bishop of Armagh and Primate of Ireland. I need hardly tell you that he is an Englishman of the reformed rite." Seeing that his words had hit home, Dudley sat back with a wry smile. "Now you are forewarned, you may think fit to leave off 'cracking nuts at the fire' and lay up plans to thwart him. Mind, you've heard no word of this from *me*!" Dudley turned suddenly to a noise at the doorway, where a smiling chambermaid curtseyed.

"The table is laid, your Lordship, and the dinner is served."

Shane thought it a wonder that dinner was served not in the grand dining hall, but in a small salon, at a round table set for four. Perhaps Stukeley would arrive soon. Certainly there was no suggestion of waiting for him. Above the table was suspended a ring of flickering tapers that cast of circle of shadow fluttering on the table below.

The fare was roast pheasant with parsnips, leeks, and gravy. The savories were pickled herring and brandied fruit, and the wine was French.

It was served in fine crystal, and there were silver fleshforks at each place. On the platter beside the roast was a long carving knife with a bejeweled handle that resembled a ceremonial sword. Shane was suitably impressed, though he let on none of it. He thought that Katherine would delight in such refinements, and then he smiled to himself, for he decided that his lady fair would probably say that she was accustomed to better, and even disapprove the ostentations of Whitehall. After the whiskey, he had completely forgotten about eating, but the savory aromas that filled the air in this small salon quickly whet his appetite.

The two men fairly hacked at the glistening fowl until their plates were full, and then diligently set about the business of eating. No words were spoken for some time while this ravenous dining ensued. At length, Dudley sipped his wine and, looking across the table, he noticed the prodigious knife stuck upright in the roast, looming over it, sparkling and shining in the circle of light from the candles above. He smiled, just as Shane glanced up with a curious expression, so he nodded at the skewered bird. "The sword in the stone!"

Shane regarded the chance tableau before them and laughed. "Sure, aren't you just the boy *for* it!" He took a swallow of wine. "Will you wed the Queen, then? The story is everywhere!"

"The question is rightly 'will the Queen wed *me*?" Dudley's smile faded and he added earnestly, "She is *promised* to do."

"Publicly?" Shane instantly regretted having let slip this challenge, but Dudley evinced no sting. He half-smiled, sighed, and shook his head.

"For my ears alone she is avowed. Albeit in whispers. But I believe her. That is when she is most true. Publicly Her Majesty has said only that if she marries an Englishman, it is Robert Dudley she will wed." Shane nodded, and then he resumed eating. He would inquire no further, but Sir Robert preferred to allay the silence. "Some few years ago, before she came to the throne, -a *lifetime* ago, perhaps, we were both prisoners. In nearby confinement. We could talk to each other, and oftimes we did. Just two voices escaping the iron bars and mingling. I suppose our hearts grew intertwined in just that way, and now, only the exigencies of her high estate stand between us. But they are bars still. Oh, we shall wed. But we must bide our hour."

"What is it you wait upon?" Shane posed the query casually as he tore a hunk of bread. In truth, he was titillated to share such intimacies about the Queen's affairs, and charmed by Sir Robert's frankness.

"What, indeed...What will make the hour propitious? Dudley pushed his plate away and filled the crystal goblets. He pursed his lips and shook his head, and then took a good swallow of wine. The candlelight danced in his dark sad eyes as he reflected. "Not so long ago, a tragical accident befell my poor wife, God rest her soul, and stirred a torrent of foul rumour that lingers still. As it would, of course... It feeds upon a poisonous miasma of envy that wafts and seeps through every corner and nook of this Court. Calumnies spread far and wide by my enemies." He tossed a glance toward the door, and lowered his tone discretely. "Indeed, my dear Amy had a deadly tumor in her breast near the end, and would have soon left me a widower. It has come to my ear that these enemies at Court may have contrived this 'accident'. Yea, that the cloud of suspicion should fall upon me, to dash my prospects of wedding the Queen after her passing." He sipped again and turned his eyes to Shane. His voice sharpened. "Time must pass. We must await fresh winds to sweep the air clean. But Elizabeth will take no other husband than me. I would venture to say-

A sudden ruckus in the hallway shattered this quiet moment of confidences. It was a voice that they both instantly recognized. A certain familiar strain of 'Heave away and haul away!' briny and bellicose, that could only be Stukeley, with another unsteady baritone compounding the damage. Shane laughed. "He's bagged his quarry, I'll wager. And quaffed a lake of ale on the head of it."

The doors parted and, shoulder to shoulder, the two tipsy buccaneers lurched in, Stukeley and a massive younger fellow both raising their dissonant voices in song.

SHANE O'Neill, 'the Grand Disturber'

"Heave away and haul away,
Walk the plank and fall away,
Down and down and all the way!
Bones for Davey Jones!"

As they launched into another verse, Dudley stood up, smiling.

"Tom!" He slid a chair out from the table. "Tom!!" The raucous verse fractured and faltered at his interruption, so he pressed on. "What have you got there, you blaggard? Under your greatcoat?" Clearly something was concealed under the folds of his cloak. "Tom!" The pair stopped singing altogether, and swayed unsteadily in middle of the room. Sir Robert tried again. "Tom!"

"Tom, Tom, the piper's son, stole a pig and away he run!" Stukeley bundled and jostled his mysterious burden, squealing like a pig as he capered about the room. "Ooweeeeeee! Wheeeee! Wheeeee!" Laughing, he plopped himself down onto the chair, settling the hidden cargo on his lap. He reached over it, and seized the bottle of wine. With a noisy 'glug glug glug' he filled a goblet, and gurgled again as he drank deep. His friend settled himself back against an oaken press, breathing like a bellows and grinning. Dudley pulled out the other chair and motioned him to sit.

"Settle yourself now, Master Allen, and fill your belly. I'll venture the pair of ye have taken no dinner but skins of wine and pots of ale! The big fellow sat, still grinning, and filled his cup. Stukeley turned to smiling Shane then, and clapped him on the knee.

"Ho! What says the King of Ireland?"

"The O'Neill is bursting to know what booty and plunder did you heave away and haul away? And where have you been at all, this long while?" Shane folded his powerful arms across his chest and leaned back in his chair.

"I've been about some ticklish business with Auld Nick! One Nicholas Guildenstern-"

"That's Shwedish for 'gilded turd!'" His mate Allen could not resist sharing his insight in the matter. Stukeley spoke over him.

" –Guildenstern! -who serves a prince; a prince who is rival to King

SHANE O'Neill, 'the Grand Disturber'

Croesus of Lydia in riches, and bides in the far North. And a rival, too, of one closer to hand!" An ominous nod to Dudley now. "He's hired me on to remove *this* lively impediment to his royal match. What could I do but oblige?" Stukeley opened his cloak, revealing a middling small sea-chest, and heaved it up onto the table with a thud. He produced a small key and made a protracted show of inserting it and tumbling the lock. As he lifted the lid, there was an audible tempest of gasping and sighing and whistling at the glittering hoard of gold. He raked up a handful of ducats and let them slip through his fingers. "All fresh counted and weighed before our eyes by Master Daniel, the goldsmithy in Gutheron's Lane. Five thousand pounds!" Stukeley turned his head and smiled up at Sir Robert, who was peering over his shoulder. "Your princely rival Eric allotted *twice* this sum to have you 'put out of the way'..."

"Out of the way?" Dudley preferred plain speaking threats.

"Aye. 'Out of the way,' the man said. That is to say, stowed safely under a churchyard!" Stukeley laughed gleefully at his own wit. "Guildenstern promised all to be paid upon delivery –or upon 'dispatch' shall we say, but I haggled and stickled him so...that he stumped up this half -on nothing more than 'my sacred word of...word of' ...*What* was it?" As the others laughed, Stukeley knocked back a swig of wine and beamed at the faces around the table. Shane shook his head.

"The Swedes are a mad lot! Gloomy and ponderous, and fierce gullible!" Dudley stepped nimbly round behind the table and sat back in his chair, looking a bit doubtful.

"He took no surety?"

"Naught but a shake of the wrist! He as much as named me pirate, and then bade me to 'board his ship!' He fancies that Prince Erik will soon be 'at the helm of England." Stukeley quaffed again, and dried his mouth along his coat-sleeve. "I never saw a Jewman part with gold on such feeble terms. He must be the Simple Simon they tell of! He's wont to say he is a Dane, and I think his simple dealing stands him proof of it!"

"Yet he is not so simple as to set it out in ink?" Dudley's hope was faint, but eager. Stukeley shook his head, and Dudley rolled his eyes to heaven. "If he be Simple Simon, *you* are Tom o' Bedlam!" Shane laughed heartily, and Master Allen snickered into his cups. Stukeley tisked.

"And all this for your own dear safety!" Tom affected to be deeply wounded. "When first my ears perceived this hazard to my friend, my heart gave stern command; that Guildenstern's purse must perforce be made the lighter of this bounty, else it might prove too tempting an enticement -to some wretch more like to *honour* the hellish bargain." Laughter around the table now, and expectant smiles. Sir Robert stood and bowed deeply.

"And so I am in your debt! Such unsparing devotion to my cause! Such unstinting sacrifice! If you would persist in attending so to my defense, even unto sparing no thought for your own peril, I fear you may yet grow fat and rich!"

"Aye, you jest! You jest! But this bounty was once a ravenous threat upon your very life, and now it is tamed like a pussins, to be but some little comfort for your faithful protector. It cost me dear in honour...and yet perhaps... Perhaps, I might yet keep faith with my promise..."

"Might you?" Dudley sat and leaned across the table. "And how do you propose to discharge such a pledge?"

"I shall kill you with kindness!" A mighty laugh now, and Stukeley spoke over it. "It may take me a lifetime, but no matter. He never did set forth an hour for the deed, nor fix upon a weapon to effect it. Aye, some may choose the poisonous glance, or lethal stare, but kindness will be my chiefest weapon!" He reached for the decanter and splashed out a measure to the brim of Dudley's goblet. "Drink well of this fine wine, my friend, for it is ever said that toping will shorten your years!" Shane raised his glass.

"Fair dues to the blaggard! He's on the job already!" Dudley sounded a cautious note amid the merriment.

"Of course, Tom, you must perceive that this bit of sport will swell the ranks of those discerning fellows who seek your death!"

"Only incrementally. And as it stands, they are legion, so no

SHANE O'Neill, 'the Grand Disturber'

matter! I keep close watch behind me." Stukeley sat back, blissful and smug. "Will I tremble at the glowering of a pack of peevish Swedes? They are-" Dudley raised his hand to interject.

"And once they have tumbled to your betrayal, you can hardly partake of their company. There ends your espials in our cause! I sent you among them to catch out Cecil's meddling schemes in the matter of queen's betrothal. All your labours to inveigle yourself-"

Now Stukely's massive hand reached out to bid him hold, and behind it, a grin as broad as a longbow. He held up one finger, then reached inside his coats, fumbling for a breast-pocket. He produced two letters of vellum, each wounded with the crimson blotches of their wax seals, and he slapped them down on the table before Dudley. "After all the tallyho, I forgot me the prize of the hunt!"

Dudley snapped them up and read their markings of address. He looked up, smiling. "Perhaps you've *earned* your fat purse! But have you ensnared the *foremost* stag of the wood?"

"Cecil's name is not writ, but his man Keyle is all about it. That should implicate his master, should it not?" Dudley was hastily scanning the documents. He shook his head.

"Nay then, he will disavow all knowledge, and slip easily from the snare. But Keyle is prize game still." He read on. "And Dymock!"

"Aye. One is from Cat Ashley of the Queen's Ladies, and the second from her friend Dorothy Broadbelt. Keyle and Dymock called on them here in Whitehall before the Christmas, plotting to bring Prince Eric to Court. They speak of bribes for some lords of Council to the very farthing and pence." Sir Robert folded the letters, and laughed from his belly, and the others followed suit. He flourished the letters before him.

"Here is a fine fat cat to set among the pigeons!" He looked to Shane O'Neill. "So! You shall learn something of politics here at Court. Your time will not have been wasted!" Shane shook his head.

"Oh, I know well the tricks that pass for politics! They're as old as the first lie told in Eden. Dissemble. Distort. Disown. Discredit. Distract!" Shane unfolded his arms and raised his cup. "I prefer the honesty of a battlefield." Stunned faces all round, then laughter.

SHANE O'Neill, 'the Grand Disturber'

Dudley raised his glass, and spoke over the merry din.

"Blow out your lantern, Diogenes! We've found an honest man in London!" The tipsy laughter rippled and plashed about the table. "And even within the walls of the Royal Court!" Stukeley's hand fumbled and probed once again in his cloak. "Aha! Well, boys! Will we rattle the bones?" He slapped his hand with a mighty thwack upon the table, and withdrew it, revealing a fine bright pair of bone dice. "Ye shan't let a dishonest man and his fortune leave together now! Ye'll all play me for a piece of this swag! Stakes and wagers! O'Neill, here's another of our 'courtly pastimes' for you to learn for her Majesty's sake!"

"Would you teach an Irishman to gamble, would you?" Shane grinned and rubbed his palms together. "Clear the board, and I'll show you how it's done. Ye lot are only pikers. In Ireland, you'd not get the name of 'gambler' on you, until you've walked away from a table stripped to your pelt!" He considered the frolicsome crew around the chest of gold, and thought to himself, 'Aye, if gambling be the sport, I have this lot beat! For in coming to London, I've gambled all. Life and limb and liberty.'

CHAPTER 9

As January wore on, the snows grew steadily deeper and banked higher and higher along the roads and narrowing footpaths. Heavy glowering skies pummeled the land with piercing winds, and slowly choked the mighty river with ice. Nothing melted, and the winter squalls never relented. Soon the weary city lay quiet and frostbound under the mounting white mantle of snow. Frozen too, were the affairs of Court and commerce. No word had come from Cecil regarding Shane's depositions, no day appointed for hearings, and no hint of impending negotiations in those crucial matters that had demanded his presence at Court.

Kildare had departed for Dublin with a quiet mission from Dudley and his faction. He was to send over a delegation of students with a roster of legal complaints against Sussex in order to further hamstring the Lord Deputy there. Although Shane had professed himself to be politically savvy, he was impressed by the extent to which such seemingly random events were being carefully orchestrated by political factions.

It seemed that the greater part of a courtier's hours were devoted to correspondence, sealed and secret, to effect ends also covert. To labour at your cause was, quite simply, to conspire –as Cecil's agents Keyle and Dymock found to their cost. Stukeley's stolen letters had produced their intended effect, and the two men were swiftly confined in the Tower. This had a cooling effect upon Cecil and the Council as regards their advocacy of the Swedish cause. Dudley was hailed as the

SHANE O'Neill, 'the Grand Disturber'

Queen's protector, and all affected to be shocked and dismayed at the presumptions of these rogue elements within the Court. It served as a caution, too, for Guildenstern as he resigned himself to the irredeemable cost of Stukeley's swindle.

Shane, too, busied himself in correspondence. Letters to Katherine reassuring her of his safety, and of his love and concern for her, sharing his conjectures on the negotiations to come, and, at her insistence, full reports on Court gossip with full details of Stukeley's 'Swedish swindle'. He wrote to the Dean, Terence Danyell, to alert him to Elizabeth's plans to name a rival Primate of All Ireland of the 'reformed' persuasion to the See of Armagh.

Two bishops in the one see! One for pope and one for queen. This was a step none had anticipated, and it was met by incredulity, even by such a crafty old hand as Bishop DeQuadra, the Spanish Ambassador. He argued that such a plan for the primacy would entail placing rival claimants in *every* diocese in Ireland, and perhaps in every diocese in Christendom. He could not envision such madness being seriously entertained by the Court. Even so, he duly passed on the ominous report to Queen Mary of Scotland, the League of Catholic Powers, and to His Holiness, the Pope.

Shane and his men arrived each Sunday evening under cover of darkness at DeQuadra's watergate for Mass, and to confer, and also to send and receive correspondence free of the Crown's surveillance. The Irishmen were amazed at the succession of English Catholic gentry coming and going under cloaks and hoods. When Shane inquired discreetly of the bishop about the reason for their visits, he was told "Spiritual concerns. The same as your own."

The wintry blasts subsided around Brigid's Day, and February's thaw quickly restored life to the city. The dingy residue of trampled sooty snow vanished into bright puddles and thirsty wintergreen grass. Londoners ventured forth from their firesides, and the lanes and markets were quickly thronged and bustling again.

Sir Robert Dudley was good on his word, and on the first mild day, he escorted Shane and his followers across the Thames to Southwark.

SHANE O'Neill, 'the Grand Disturber'

The Queen's permission had been granted him to bring the Irishmen beyond the legal bounds of London that they might savor the dubious entertainments confined to the Liberties of the South Bank. His first notion was to show them the latest theatrical offering of the Queen's players, but when he considered that they had so little grasp of English, he determined that the thrilling spectacle of the Bear Pits would be more to their liking. In the event, he was mistaken.

Dudley had the use of a Royal barge for the day, and there was quite a stir as they moored at Bankside until it was clear that the Queen was not aboard. Just up the stairs from the banks, in sight of the river was the round three-storied wooden structure known as Paris Gardens. It was eight-sided with a central arena under the open air.

As the day happened to be Sunday, the old forum was thronged with excited Londoners, delighted to be let out from their cramped winter quarters for a day's frolic and an early taste of Spring. The rhyming calls of peddlers and mongers could be heard above the noisy crowd, hawking sweetmeats and nuts and other dainties. "Two a penny, two a penny, hot crossed buns!" "Warnuts, warnuts, sixteen a penny, part with a little and feast upon plenty!" "Sheep's trotters, pig's feet, piping hot and good to eat!" Farleigh remarked, discretely in Irish, that English poetry was making great strides!

A bell rang as the gates opened, and upwards of a thousand Sunday revelers jostled and swarmed about them, a penny in each fist to buy admission to the wild spectacle. Sir Robert's chief attendant, a tall gaunt fellow called 'Blount' warned them to beware of pickpockets and cutpurses, as he led his party around the crowd to a special entrance for gentry. They filed up the steps and took their seats in a box just above the arena.

First off was a cockfight. Bets were placed, and the heady crowd shouted and roared as the feathers and blood flew. Cockfights were common enough in Ireland, so the lads were more amused by the wild carry-on of the crowd than the shrieking squawking little skirmish in the arena.

SHANE O'Neill, 'the Grand Disturber'

At last the drum rolled and the real show began. A massive sable brown bear lumbered out into the arena, followed by a little man in a leather jerkin. He capered along behind the beast holding aloft a chain that was affixed to the bear's hind leg. In the centre of the arena were several large wooden stakes, and before them had been placed a glistening chunk of honeycomb. The bear ambled over to the honeycomb and sat, licking and chawing it while behind him the little man fixed the chain securely to the stake with a large bolt. He then stood and bowed with a flourish. "Ladies and lords and gentles all! *And* you lot!" Laughter and cheering rang from the galleries. "I present to you the king of the Black Forrest, King Ursa Major! And the prince, Ursa Minor!"

Cheers and jeers now, followed by laughter as a lively brown bear cub came scampering on. The man following behind him gave a sharp pull at the chain on his hind leg, and the giddy crowd laughed to see him roll and tumble and paw the floor as he was dragged backwards to the second stake. The first man took hold of the brass ring at the end of the short chain, slipped it over the stake, and fixed it with a bolt. He faced the crowd and bowed again. The big bear dropped his honeycomb and sprang to his feet, letting forth a mighty roar as he strained at his fetters and pawed the air.

"These ferocious beasts of High Germany...these fierce brutes of the Black Forest-" Whistles and hoots greeted the cub as he tried to scramble to the big bear and fell on his face at the end of his short tether. Growling and yelping could be heard now from behind the curtain, like hounds in the hunt. "-these grizzly German bruins will try their savage might against the yeoman strength of our own little English curs!"

On came the bandogs. Slavering and barking, they leapt upon the bear cub with vicious fury. There were eight of them in all, mottled brown and white, low and squat, with short legs and pug snouts. Two of them began springing up at the great bear as he swatted them off with his mighty paws. The rest of the pack snapped and bit at the cub as he shrieked and rolled, kicking and clawing them off. The crowd

SHANE O'Neill, 'the Grand Disturber'

howled with glee as the squat little dogs savaged the bearcub in a frenzy of blood and fur. All the while, two of the dogs would run back and come bounding up at the snout of Ursa Major, springing up to be batted away.

At one point, the great bear caught one of the curs under its arm and squeezed the life out of it while it while biting its tail. As the dog was squealing out its last breath, some wag shouted out, "He's a bloody Scotch bear!" and this tickled the frenzied crowd to convulse with laughter, for they fancied it looked like the bear was playing the bagpipes. He let go the crushed dog and swung him by the tail until the bloody carcass went flying off into the crowd, only to land on a woman's lap. She jumped to her feet and screamed hysterically as the ringside crowd shrieked with delight and thundered its approval. Soon the gory carcass was being tossed around the stands for sport.

These curs were a new breed of dog bred in England for just such displays as bear and bullbaiting, and in time they would come to be known as 'bulldogs'. The body is short and stout, allowing it to crawl in under the beast. It's lower jaw sticks out further than the top one, allowing the bulldog to grip onto the snout of the bear and still be able to breathe due to the lay-back of the nose. The wrinkles on its face allow the blood from the other animal to run down its face, instead of streaming into its eyes.

When one of the pack had locked its jaws about the bear cub's snout, the leather clad man stepped in to protect his investment. He pulled the dog off with his huge gauntlets, and with his hobnailed boots, he kicked away a few persistent attackers that yelped and snarled and panted. The bloodied cub curled up in a ball, and stumbling and rolling, he was dragged off to great applause. The dogs now assailed the great grizzly, Ursa Major. Seven pugs in rabid fury, leaping and snapping, several biting at his tethered hind leg, some at his back. As he lunged down on one, the others sprang at his head tearing his bloody ears. The bear's eyes were soon drenched in blood, and he thrashed and swung blindly at his attackers.

The Irish delegation was stunned to silence, while the rest of the crowds howled with glee. Farleigh noted Friar Magrath stealing a glance at Shane, and he looked back himself to see what way the chieftain was disposed to this barbaric display. Of course Shane could wade through gore and blood on the field of battle without a bother, but a noble nature delights in poetry and song for disportment. To imply otherwise is a scurrilous indignity that would never be brooked in Ireland. As for O'Neill himself, he stood impassive but stern, peering intently at the carnage before him. His brows were gathered and his jaw was set, but neither poet nor priest could discern what humour was on him. When they saw him cast a sidelong squint at their host, furtive and suspicious, they could only conjecture that perhaps a fury was kindling within him at the insult of such a depravity being presented before his crew.

Shane regarded Dudley's cheerful face beside him. 'The smile of an Englishman...' This spectacle was no chance entertainment. There is another message here, like the grisly heads spiked over Traitor's Gate. How all-fire savage and fierce are these powdered English lordlings in their hose and ruffs! Oh, look upon our might and tremble! Shane resolved to be unmoved, and perhaps bored by the shoddy gambit. He stretched his great shoulders and sighed audibly, blowing through pursed lips, eyes straight ahead, intent upon the English 'heroics' in the arena.

Now five leather-clad men appeared with whips, and formed a circle around the great bruin. They kicked the dogs away, and the great bloody bear rose rampant, towering over them, on his hind legs. With a ferocious roar that seemed to shake the rafters, he pulled and strained at his shackles. The five men turned their backs to the beast at a safe distance, and as they cracked their whips in unison over and over, the dogs backed away yelping and whimpering.

Then the men turned in upon the bear. By turns they whipped the bear from alternate sides, so that he swung about spun in a blind fury. His roar was unearthly in this torture, and the visitors from Tirowen were considerably unnerved, looking to each other, aghast at this spectacle of cruelty. In truth, they felt some deep bond with this

SHANE O'Neill, 'the Grand Disturber'

shackled forester beset by its English captors. Farleigh scowled and fumed, and Miler Magrath blessed himself and began to quietly recite in Irish the prayer of the founder of his order, St. Francis of Assisi. Some of the others blessed themselves.

"Blessed are you, Lord God, maker of all living creatures of the earth and air. Oh God, who called forth fish to swim the sea, birds to mount the air and beasts to trod upon the land; who inspired St. Francis to call each of them his brother, we ask you to behold and bless this beast before you. By the power of your divine love, let it to live and bide according unto to your plan. Praise be to You for the beauty of all creation. Blessed are You, Lord our God, who shines forth through the eyes of each of these your creatures, wild or tame!"

While no-one could decipher this spate of Irish, there was no mistaking the quiet chorus of 'Amen!' that followed it. Shane's temper was indeed rising, but not in defense of bears. He was vexed at this show of delicacy from his men, for it could only subvert his reputation of power and menace. Such mawkish qualms at court would soon diminish that dark forbidding shadow he had so successfully cast as a figure of brutal Irish defiance. A further shame was the seeming affront to Sir Robert's hospitality. When finally Dudley noticed the troubled Gaelic murmur down the row, and the disapproving scowls of his guests, he shook his head and laughed. He stood up, and nodded at Blount who jumped to his feet at the end of the row. He said simply, "This day is too fair to squander in the stench of this old barn. Shall we be off?" Shane rose and turned to his men, admonishing them in Irish.

"Hump off with ye's now, ye pack of sainted devils! Onto the blasted barge." The others sprang up and followed Blount clumping down the narrow staircase. Once outside, Shane said loudly to Sir Robert, "You'll have to excuse the ladies their squeamishness, Robert, for they have most fine and delicate feelings, -although they are churlish enough to spurn your hospitality! If I had Sweeney and the lads here, now there would be savage sport altogether! My gallowglass boyos would be tossing about the bloodied corpse of your man, that scrawny coward in the leather breeks! And pulling and twisting a long rope of his guts after him! You want to cut the shackles off the bear, is what you want, and let her at them! A bit more blood, splashing and splattering, would suit the crowd. Then you'd have a proper show. Aye, it's a mighty show, all the same...although in fairity, it's not for the likes of poets or priests." Dudley laughed.

"Ods bodkins! I never recked your Irishmen for Puritans! You took me by some surprise indeed! The Puritans are agitating furiously to ban these disportments. But, of course, it's widely noted that they object not to the cruelty, but only to the people enjoying themselves!"

There was easy laughter, and as it faded the riotous din of the bear pits behind them surged and rang in the air. A dark frenzy of laughter, devoid of mirth, like a deep rumble of thunder on the wind. Farleigh spoke.

"Enjoying themselves, is it? The people are enjoying wanton cruelty. As the base appetites are fed, so they will grow and fester until only the most sordid sensations will appease them. The heart itself becomes blasted and defiled. No, Sir Robert, this is not merriment. It is a poison to the very soul!" Farleigh raised his palms before him to forestall argument. "I am no Puritan, my boy. Let there be laughter, and dancing, and tumbling in the hay! Sport, and lusty frolics, and lashings of porter! Feed the belly. Feed the soul. But not on cruel depravity!"

There was silence again, with still the dark din hanging on the air. All waited to see what way Shane or Dudley would respond. Farleigh spoke again with a sly glint and a hint of a smile under his beard. "And poetry! Let there be poetry! Merry laughter now and the tense spell was lifted. "Sir Robert, there are three great wells of bloody-mindedness; the bear-pit, the bullpit, and the pulpit!" Even Friar Magrath laughed at this. Dudley clapped the old poet on the shoulder.

"I'm not fool enough to dispute an Irish philosopher! And poet. And wizard!" He glanced over his shoulder at the barge, squinted up at the sun to check the hour, and smiled. "Do you mind I promised that I would acquaint you with our great English wizard John Dee? Well, what say shall we take us to Mortlake now, and pay him a call before he ventures off to the Lowlands?" He looked to Shane. "It's but a trifling journey upriver. What say you, O'Neill?"

"We're aboard your ship, captain. Set what course you will! Come along now, ladies. And mind your step. Don't be harming the ants and snails underfoot!"

They filed back up the gangplank, and began the pleasant sojourn to Mortlake, past their domicile at Whitehall, past the steeples of Lambeth, past Robert Dudley's estate at Kew; a serene journey of just under two hours. It was shortened for them by the sweet strains of a musical quartet, and an abundance of mulled wine. Sir Robert invited Shane to join in a hunting party two days hence with the Duke de Guise and Queen Elizabeth. This brought on a lively spate of boasts and challenges, and toasts.

After the Thames looped its bends North and South, the steeple of St.Mary's could be seen towering over the tiny hamlet of Mortlake. As they approached, Shane and his men could see the tall stately house beside the church that Sir Robert pointed out as their destination. A small barge was moored at the dock below it, and several figures appeared to be boarding. A tall slender man stood back and waved them off upriver. He then turned and raised his arm aloft calling out to Sir Robert's barge with words that were lost upon the wind. It was the great wizard himself, John Dee.

He was clad in a long snug black cloak, and the purple scarf under his chin brightly framed a long pointed black beard that danced in the river breeze. His black hair was cropped short, and atop it was a skullcap of purple silk that caught the sunlight in such a way as to make him appear incandescent. His nose was long and fine, and his deep-set eyes of hazel were piercing in their intensity, bright, yet somber and forbidding. Farleigh was struck by the wizard's youth, for Dudley had spoken of him as his tutor, and yet he seemed to be scarcely five or six years older than he. And, strange to say, all around him, the breeze seemed to hum with the queerest of sounds!

SHANE O'Neill, 'the Grand Disturber'

The gangplank was secured, and Sir Robert led his guests onto the dock. John Dee stepped forward without the faintest hint of a smile to greet his friend. "I hoped that this was you, but I feared it was only Her Majesty on the river, making a progress to Hampton Court." He shook his head slowly, gravely. "Oh Robin, such relief! To see that her green Tudor standard was not aloft! That you had kept your promise to call!"

"Whenever have I failed you?" Dudley clapped him familiarly on the shoulders. "Have faith in your old pupil, Master John!"

"Indeed, you've come, with scarcely a nick to spare! I sail on Thursday from Southhampton!" John Dee faced the others now, and nodded. "You are all most welcome." Abruptly turning his back to them, he strode down the creaking dock that bounced underfoot, and led the party up onto the lawn, where he stopped and stood aside. He quickly spotted Shane, towering over his companions. "And this will be John O'Neill! The Tamburlaine of Ulster!" He warily accepted Shane's grip and acquiesced to a vigourous shaking. "Robert tells me you've set about to conquer London!"

"Aye, so I have! And then a hasty retreat across the Irish Sea will suit me grand! No prisoners I'll take! This time! And, here is my chief poet who's come to confer with you!" Shane looked, smiling, over his shoulder, but Farleigh was not to be seen. And most of the others had their backs to him. They parted quickly enough with a murmur of 'Farleigh!' He and Gillie had wandered a small ways off, and the company was treated to the curious spectacle of the two of them lepping and pouncing on the green.

Now, beyond the dock lay a marshy inlet of tall reeds and cattails from which a loud low-pitched buzzing sound emanated. A small laneway separated the lawn from the marsh, and across it a bubbling brown stream of creatures was swarming and teeming into the marsh; a flood of twitching flitting life, dark and effervescent, like the spit and sizzle of a griddle pan.

"Ah, the toads!" John Dee tilted his head back and peered down his nose at the blackened lane beyond. "Indeed. It's a marvel! On the

SHANE O'Neill, 'the Grand Disturber'

first fine day of Spring they make their way to mate and spawn. They're off early this year and it may yet cost them dear, for we've not seen the last frost of winter!"

For his visitors it was a far more wondrous sight than he knew. With the exception of the widely traveled cleric, Myler Magrath, none of the Irishmen had ever seen a toad, or a frog, or a snake, and so this pestilential vision was quite astonishing. St. Patrick was known to have driven them all into the sea a millennium ago when he routed the old gods of Ireland and banished the serpents.

Gilly caught a toad in his cupped hands, and when they turned round, he and Farleigh were both surprised to see the bemused company waiting on them. They strode back proudly with Gillie holding his squiggling quarry aloft by the leg. Farleigh was beaming. "Is St. Patrick come to England now? Or has someone lifted a plague of toads? They're streaming into the rivers! It's bloody biblical!" It was Shane who answered.

"John Dee says they're off to mate and spawn. They've only gone a wooing!"

"We'll leave them to it, so. It would be unseemly to interrupt that!" The wind was playing with Farleigh's white beard, so he pulled it down onto his chest and folded his arms over it. He smiled brightly at his sombre host. Shane stepped in beside him.

"This is the wizard of my court, Farleigh the Poet." Sir Robert swung his arm over John Dee's shoulder and tipped him a quiet word. Dee nodded his head slowly, and spoke to Farleigh in the ancient Greek.

"Poets utter great and wise things which they do not themselves understand.' -Plato!" All eyes now turned to Farleigh to see him meet this mysterious challenge in the strange tongue. He unfolded his arms and nodded sagely.

"But that is the very essence of profundity. For even great Poseiden could not fathom the depths of purest Truth! And truth is but the clay from which poems are fashioned." The poet beamed with victory, and the mystified crowd turned again to Dee. His brows arched in wonderment, then furrowed in perplexity.

"Sophocles?" Farleigh shook his head.

"Not at all. T'was Farleigh O'Gneeve said it. And, although he's a poet, he understood it, too!" He gave a great laugh, and the others joined in, for, whatever had been said, they sensed that he had bested John Dee in his Greek challenge. Sir Robert Dudley looked to his friend for an accounting, but Dee only shook his head as he twisted his beard, and said, "Indeed, he's a marvel! I fancy I shall enjoy this." He looked up to the great doors of the house, where two servants stood waiting to attend his guests. "Come now. I must present you to the mistress of the house. Aye, respects to my mother, and then I shall show you about!" With that, he turned and strode across the great lawn, and the rest hastened to follow.

The usual pleasantries were exchanged with the lady of the house, Jane Dee, who fussed and pressed upon them a spirited hospitality, sending her cook off to the larder to set about preparing a Sunday feast. She apologized for the cluttered hallways, explaining that her son had only recently given up his rooms in London, and was lodging all his books and belongings here while he foraged through Europe to acquire even more! He was bound to fill her house with all the knowledge of the world, she said, until she wouldn't have a place to sit! Indeed, contrary to appearances, the house was not large, boasting little more than a hall, a scullery, three bedchambers, and a few other rooms cramped with trunks and presses.

Dee led his visitors through the cluttered chambers and out the back to an outbuilding, which he had taken for his study. Here was a sight to see! Like an alchemist's laboratory, the walls were lined with bottles and clay jars and tubes and funnels. Books were stacked everywhere, and atop them were charts and lists and scrolls. Mysterious symbols marked every closed chest and trunk. There were skulls, birds' wings, splendid butterflies pinned in rows, and scientific implements of all kinds; globes, both celestial and terrestrial, a five foot long quadrant, a wavy distorted looking glass, a tall cross-staff, a ten foot long 'radius astronomicus' for peering at the heavens, a nautical compass, and ticking away patiently in the corner, a large portable watch-clock. In the middle of the muddle were three stills, bubbling away in a most un-fragrant cloud of sulfurous steam, beside a bowl of eggshells and horse dung.

"And what, if I might ask of you Doctor Dee, says the 'reformed church' to all this magic of yours." Father Magrath's patronizing tone was in jarring contrast to the awe of his compatriots. "Surely the black arts would arouse some opprobrium at Court."

"I do not practice what is vulgarly accounted 'magic.' Real magic has naught to do with superstition or witchcraft. My magic is knowledge; the study of the mysterious hidden forces –spiritual as well as physical- that rule Nature. Indeed, I know naught of curses or hexes, and I keep the Sabbath. And what manner of sorcery do Irish wizards practice?" Dee turned to Farleigh now, glad to relinquish his chilly place in Myler's inquisition.

"Oh, I'm a poet. I ply only the magic of words and visions. Insights and outsights. I see and I say." Farleigh glared at Myler through a broad smile. "Ah, no. We must leave the incantations and miracle-mongering to the Holy Church." He suddenly noticed Gillie fumbling with the various implements beside him. "Put that down, boy! Use your eyes! A glance never broke a glass. The eyes can gather up what knowledge is to be got, and never disturb a mite." The wizard came to Gillie's aid.

"Indeed, a sage instruction for the lad! But I would give him leave to take that up again. It's only a lodestone." John Dee nodded to Gillie, who gave an edgy glance to Farleigh, and then tentatively held up the strange heavy block of ore. "It's magnetized iron," the wizard explained, "and its properties tell secrets of the whole world. Bring it here to me." He took from the shelf a small tin box and rattled it, as he led them to a round table covered with charts and papers. As they looked on, he emptied the box of needles onto the table. "Now. What do they call you, boy?"

"I'm Gillie, sir."

"Now, Gillie, touch the lodestone here, and raise it ever so slowly, and let us see what marvel is here."

Gilly did as he was bidden, and a long string of shiny needles glistened from the stone down to the table, met by an airy chorus of 'ahhh!' He and many of the others had never had occasion to see the like. Myler, of course, was well familiar with such stunts, and spoke again with a skeptical challenge.

"And what great wisdom has this wee trick to tell us of God's creation?"

"From my trials and tests, I've come to believe that every object or entity in the universe emanates invisible rays of some force, a force that influences the objects that it nears or touches."

"People as well? These rays?" Farleigh was intrigued. He'd been puzzling over the small shifts and twists in Shane's manner since coming into London. John Dee's dark eyes locked on Farleigh's, and he nodded gravely.

"Every object! Every man! From the smallest atomy to the great celestial bodies of the heavens. That is why the placement of constellations at birth will determine the fates of man below. Indeed, one day I shall prove that it is the shifting orbs of the night sky that cause the very ebb and flow of tides!" Farleigh laughed now.

"You'll be a long time putting proof to that, John Dee, for it is known and testified since the Druids that the heave and draw of the Tides is the breathing of the Earth." Dee stopped himself from speaking, befuddled now. Then he brightened and nodded sagely to Farleigh.

"Ahhh, I see! The poet will speak poetry! Orpheus will have his say. The Earth breathing, indeed! A whimsical conceit!" Of course, Farleigh had intended no metaphor, but he resolved to make light of the matter. Madness can be most unsettling. Best not to dwell on these wild theories.

"No harm to you, John Dee! For even Aristotle himself failed to gain an understanding of three things: the work of the bees, the coming and going of the tides, and the mind of a woman!" The wizard laughed at this, and Farleigh decided to broach the 'business' at hand.

SHANE O'Neill, 'the Grand Disturber'

"Upon what manner of matter is it, John Dee, or on what powerful conundrum is it that you wished to confer with me? Surely to God it wasn't invisible rays! Or the tides! I would be divil-all use to you there, so I would."

"Manuscripts and seals in the Irish tongue." He turned to Blount, Robert Dudley's steward. "If you'll be good enough to see our new friends to the Hall, they might avail themselves of wine and sweetmeats there." He looked to Dudley. "You've not yet seen my library! O'Neill may like to look on it, though it be only a bare start to the mighty archive that shall be." Farleigh came round the table to join them.

"All beginnings are weak, but a smart start is half the task!" O'Hagan and Fleming also stayed at Shane's side. Fleming customarily served as both translator and secretary, and, as Shane's legal counsel, both were keen to browse the library texts. Myler Magrath, too, would not be left behind. Blount led the others back to the house.

The chosen six, then, followed John Dee through his wintry orchard along a path of planks that slid and gushed in the mud under them to yet another farm outbuilding. This one was older than the main house, with a high pitched gable and timber cladding that had only recently been repaired. Inside, the walls were lined with shelves, newly hewn and filled with books, with piles of trunks, and stacks of books everywhere. There were two rough chairs with rope seats, a rickety desk, and an old bedstead with a straw mattress also piled with books. Farleigh shook his head at it.

"I don't know how under Heaven a man could sleep in such a room as this! With all the knowledge of the world about him, and books everywhere chattering at him and beckoning to tell their story!" He cast a smiling glance over his shoulder to the wizard, but Dee was in some serious conferral with Dudley in English. Beside them Fleming was perusing some text, but Farleigh could see he had an ear cocked for listening. Dee was agitated to some degree, and was absently clutching the bloused sleeve of Sir Robert's doublet.

"No word, say you? Or no funds? And what of your word that you would plead my suit?"

"When I broached it, I found myself admonished. She bid me not to beleaguer her treasury. She would see firstly a list of the books, and she would know why each is vital to the state. Would you not-"

"When last she spoke, she made promise to bear the charges of the journey, else I should not have endeavored..." Dee closed his eyes and shook his head slowly. "All is lost... I dare not sail." Dudley clapped his hand gently on Dee's shoulder.

"Keep heart now, John. I shall give you a letter of credit -on mine own estate. But you must send straight the tallies and sums on each purchase, with some word wherefore it be needful to Her Majesty, and of the hard bargain she has won. Else I shall never redeem the charges!" He held out his hand, and John Dee shook it vigorously, nodding his head. He turned to his guests now with his first true and natural smile since they had clapped eyes upon him. Farleigh even noted 'a touch of the brine' glistening in his eyes. Dee suddenly recalled the matter at hand.

"The Irish manuscripts!" He wagged his finger absently as he looked from pile to pile. "Ah. Here is the trunk to a certainty!" They helped him shift boxes and books until he could pull forward a dusty black trunk marked with mysterious symbols in chalk. Upon opening it they could see that it was nearly filled with scrolls and books and parchments. All were in Irish or Welsh script and many were illuminated with vivid colours twisting and twining in animal shapes around the text. Farleigh had never envisioned finding such an astounding hoard of Irish treasure in a remote English village. His first response was in Irish.

"Thunder and shite! By Crom the Crooked, they would steal your teeth and sell you an apple!" He shook his head and inquired in English, "Wherever did you strike upon this trove of learning, John Dee? It's a great wonder altogether!"

"Oh, I've found it incrementally, by ones and fews. Rescued whatsoever I could come upon. Alas, when King Henry dissolved the monasteries twenty years ago, he unleashed a hoard of villains and ruffians to despoil them."

"That's no word of a lie, John Dee." Farleigh had reconsidered, and was warming to his host. "They are a crowd of crawthumping blaggards that would rise a blush on the cheek of Attila the Hun!" Dee nodded gravely. "Dark days they were, alas. All the art and precious learning sundered and razed. The works of the ages reduced to smoke and ash. What few manuscripts they failed to burn or shred were sold to grocers and soapsellers. The rest were set by for menial usage; some to scour their candlesticks, some to rub their boots, and some to serve their jakes!" There was an audible gasp.

"Blasphemous heathens." Myler whispered over the hush. "No more than beasts to defile the Holy Scriptures so." He carefully extracted a sheaf of illuminated pages from the trunk and took it to the desk to examine them.

Farleigh unraveled a scroll and examined it closely. The others looked on over his shoulder. "A chronicle of the bloodline of the O'Byrne. And look you here. Hugh of Glenmalure is lastly entered, and he's said to be scavaging in the mountain wastes now!"

"A man who is known to you?" Dee was elated to see the first of his mysteries unravelling. Farleigh looked to Shane to elaborate.

"Only another ancient line of Irish nobility who've been run off their lands. I fear you'll hear of many a sad tale before you see the bottom of your trunk." O'Hagan murmured something to Shane, and he nodded. "John Dee, my counselors here would like to have a look at your Law tracts, if such books are in your keeping."

"Behind you there you will find those shelves lined with tomes and texts of Law. Some are quite old and will test your Latin." The wizard turned back to see what manuscript Farleigh was perusing now. "Ah! Does this have meaning for you? Take care! It's brittle, and the margins have nearly crumbled away."

"Aye, this one is ancient, by its Irish text." Farleigh squinted his way down the page. "I judge it to be a fragment of an account of the 'Voyage of St. Brendan the Navigator.' He is said to have sailed to the North islands of America in the ninth century."

SHANE O'Neill, 'the Grand Disturber'

"Yes, I know of him! I have seen such a text in Latin! This is truly a marvel, for it is my contention, -and I shall prove its verity- that his discoveries, and those of Madoc the Welsh prince who crossed the Atlantic Seas four hundred years ago, provide manifest proof of Her Majesty's title of claim to the sea coasts of America, and all its islands from Florida northerly!"

Farleigh looked up still squinting, but now in utter disbelief, at this staggering display of English presumption. Dee took this quizzical expression to be a request for elucidation, and responded accordingly. "By prior discovery! And by that they are next unto us. And here is the crumbling parchment in evidence!" He looked over to Robert Dudley, who was at the desk. "You must tell Her Majesty of this discovery, that she may think on the prospective profits of my library to her realm and treasury.

"Indeed, John, I shall. Her Highness is most anxious to strengthen her claims to the North lands of America. This will bode well for her support." Dee glanced again over Friar Magrath's shoulder.

"What have you here?"

"More scripture. Psalms they are, with fine knots and flourishes." Myler found in the desk's drawer a quill, ink horn, and vellum, which he passed about. Lists were listed, and sorts sorted, as the room became a hive of industry and inquiry. O'Hagan and Fleming were copying passages from a legal tome when John Dee's curiosity brought him to their side.

"Ah, 'The Donation of Constantine'! You're delving into weighty matters, I should say." Robert Dudley looked over.

"Which treatise is that, John? 'The Donation', I've heard mention made of it."

"Issued by the fourth Century Roman Emperor; it grants the Pope dominion over all the Western Empire and over these western islands too. It underpinned the sovereign rights of many princes who received of the Pope. Of course it was a forgery." The squeaking and scratching of quills ceased abruptly. O'Neill's two legal scribes looked up from their pages, in a state of wonderment.

SHANE O'Neill, 'the Grand Disturber'

"A forgery? It's not accredited in Law?" Fleming looked crestfallen.

"Outside of the Roman Curia, it is inadmissible. The Italian scholar, Lorenzo Valla exposed it as long ago as 1440." Dee turned back to his shelves. "I have it to hand. It is...here! Yes, 'Defalso credita et ementita Constantine donatione" Valla examined the Latin forms, and the many anachronist references within it. For nearly a century his treatise gathered dust in a collection in the German States until Martin Luther took it up so vehemently. And, of course, King Henry cited it when he broke with Rome. 'The Donation of Constantine' is now accounted a piece of classical fakery."

Fleming sighed and put down his quill. He closed the heavy tome with a thump. O'Hagan whispered excitedly at Will's ear and rose to his feet. If Fleming was downcast, his Brehon law partner was elated. O'Hagan put out his hand to John Dee. "Might I see the treatise? Ah, good man yourself! Your library is astounding! When you have scoured Europe for its treasured books, I've no doubt but you'll rival the great library of Alexandria, right here on the RiverThames."

He and Will Fleming dipped their quills, and resumed their furious scrivening, citing the principal passages to refute all they had just copied of 'The Donation.' Shane thought it curious, and inquired discretely with an incredulous squint, but got only a sly wink for reply. Farleigh and Myler sorted through the rest of their trunk, and when dinner was called, Owen and Will insisted on staying behind to study Valla's treatise. This sudden disregard for a Sunday supper piqued the curiosity of all, and presented an opening topic at table. John Dee speculated that perhaps they wanted to defend the papal position on the validity of the 'Donation'.Farleigh thought best to make light of it.

"Who could be up to the shifts and dodges of brehons and barristers? They're like three-penny-trickmen, dazzling the world by twisting and picking apart knots of law."

"Yes, perhaps, but what sort of legal knot would require 'the Donation of Constantine' to unravel it?" John Dee looked from face to face around the table. "It's all rather mysterious."

"Nearly as mysterious as those mystical cyphers marked on all the boxes and trunks in your library!" Farleigh had decided to engage the wizard in his own curious concerns, but it was Myler who took the bait.

"God pity your auld grey head, O'Gneeve. Those 'mysterious cyphers' are letters of the Hebrew alphabet! I hope your Greek is better than your Hebrew!"

"Aye, your hopes are small and easy granted." Farleigh turned to Dee at his side. "The question is 'Why Hebrew?" John Dee's somber dark eyes were suddenly alight.

"In the beginning was the Word!" He looked again from face to face in a silence that stilled all eating and movement. "St. John has imparted that clue unto us. The 'word' was in Hebrew. To learn Hebrew is to uncover the very structure that underlay God's creation. The laws of nature make its verbs; the stuff of physical reality, its nouns. This is why I have immersed myself in the Kabbalah."

"And what have you learned of this eternal 'structure' from your Hebrew grammar?" Myler's condescension was palpable, but Dee seemed unaware of it.

"The Kabbalah tells of a three tiered universe; the divine level where angels reside, below it the celestial level of the stars, and at the bottom, our physical world. Thusly does the Hebrew language hold three parts of speech. Twenty-two letters comprise the Hebrew alphabet, which are divided into two groups of nine letters and one of four. These correspond to the nine orders of angels, the nine spheres, and the four elements: earth, air, fire, and water. Oh, yes, letters and cyphers have much to tell us. They hold many secrets. Cryptography and codes form a great share of my studies. But Hebrew is the key to all."

"Irish is nearly as old as Hebrew." Farleigh would not have his own tongue dismissed or diminished. The Irish are a lost tribe of Israel, and our language is not without its mysteries and secrets, and all bound in the magic of creation. Each letter of our alphabet, 'ailm, beith, luis', and so forth, is the name of a tree. A druid's grove can tell a story, can spell a story if approached from the East."

SHANE O'Neill, 'the Grand Disturber'

"That is astonishing." Dee was captivated. He looked to his mother. "Isn't that a marvel, Mother? Each tree a letter!" Farleigh paused, and considered, and decided to elaborate.

"When I was a lad, there was a poet dwelling in the wood beside us. He had a great age. I couldn't judge of his poetry for I was that young, but he was of the old religion, and a great man for a withering curse. We were much afeard of him, but I came slowly to his acquaintance, and learned a power of the old knowledge from him. It was his way to send short messages to his few learned colleagues by way of leaves. A wee stack of precisely ordered leaves, each of a different sort, and a stick poked through them. They would be meaningless to all but those versed in the old knowledge."

Myler Magrath harrumphed, and tore a hunk of bread from the loaf before him to break the stillness of the table. "Pish, posh, and piddle to that! Writing exists to elucidate, not to obscure. Let us praise God for bringing us His Word."

A feeble chorus of 'Amen' followed. Looks were exchanged about the table, and eating was resumed. 'Fierce eating', as Farleigh later recounted. At length, John Dee spoke again, perhaps to appease Myler.

"I have embraced the study of Hebrew so that I shall be able to talk to the angels." He twisted the tip of his short beard with his greasy fingers, one may suppose, to refine its point. As no-one spoke, he turned again to the old poet beside him. "You made mention of your visions. Tell me, have you spoken to angels?"

"Divil a one!" Farleigh's retort evinced mild laughter, and banished the tension that lingered around the table, but Dee failed to understand his Irish phrasing.

"What is that? Alas, my ear was not quick enough to attend."

"I said nay then, John Dee, I've not spoken to angels." Farleigh raised his voice just a bit to oblige his host. Dee's eyes were wide and wild now.

"Well, that is my resolve! I intend to confer with angels!" Farleigh raised his goblet.

SHANE O'Neill, 'the Grand Disturber'

"Well, I suppose that I intend to confer with the angels too. But I'm in no blasted hurry!" There was laughter now, hearty and free, and as the wine flowed, replenishing all cups, Shane lifted his voice.

"A noble call now, Farleigh O'Gneeve. Give us a toast to our host!"

The auld poet raised his cup aloft.

"Ach, why wouldn't I? I shall oblige." He cleared his throat, as the table settled. "Here's a health to you, and God's help to you! And may you never be a corpse until every curl of your crotch is as long as a goat's beard!" More laughter and high spirits around the table, and Farleigh leaned across to John Dee's smiling mother. "My apologies to our hostess! Of course, it rhymes better in the Irish." She smiled sweetly.

"Oh, I've been fair warned about your Irish roguery!" Her son tilted his head back, smiling at Farleigh.

"Much have I heard of Irish blessings and of the curses, of their extravagance and wild language. They are said to exceed the grandeur and malice of the Sultans of Araby. Surely that toast was but a pale pleasantry, perhaps in deference to my mother. I should like to hear the most disagreeable curse in your roster!" Farleigh shook his head.

"My maledictions are too powerful and potent to be tossed about at supper. Perhaps it was just such a frivolous curse that brought this plague of toads down on you! But here, I suppose is mild one, that you might get the taste of it.

> A down without without up to you!
> Empty hands to you!
> And a heavy foot to you!
> A staggering upwards!
> A floundering downwards!
> A driveling outwards!
> And a sniveling inwards!
> An often going out
> And a seldom coming in to you!
> A thirst without slake to you!

SHANE O'Neill, 'the Grand Disturber'

And may your mouth be as dry
As the welcomes before you!"

Farleigh cleared his throat, and smacked his lips, and, with merry laughter, his cup was filled again. The banter was convivial, and wine plentiful as the Sunday callers lingered at table. Eventually Myler slipped a quiet word to Shane that the evening was wearing on, and that it was indeed Sunday, and they were expected by the bishop at Durham House for late Mass. This prospect was more welcome than one might imagine, for as always, there would be important letters and parcels awaiting them there, and the hospitality would be lavish.

Shane brought all to their feet. A servant ran off to fetch O'Hagan and Fleming, and returned with a book for the wizard. As they all gathered at the door, John Dee presented the book to Farleigh with a short statement in the Greek. It was tattered surplus copy of 'The Voyage of Odyseus', that he deemed his library could spare. The old poet, however, chose to answer him in Irish. He held John Dee's hand aloft in both his hands, and recited a 'blessing' that Myler was obliged to translate. Farleigh intoned his blessing, sonorous and solemn, with the customary glint of irony under his white shaggy brows.

"May the hand that gives never falter!
Or come to some terrible harm!
And may it not
Fester and rot,
Or wither and stink,
And shrivel and shrink
And fall off your generous arm!

SHANE O'NEILL

CHAPTER 10

"The lambing end of March. Aye, by my reckoning I'll come to term in the week of Lady Day. Have you leave to stay as long as that?" Katherine swept a stray lock from her forehead and smiled hopefully at her sister.

"Leave is it? I'll stay til I go! And I'll not go until your wee'un is in your arms." Úna turned to the young lads who were gathering up her bags. "Not that one. Leave the wee parcel down. Or no, then, you can bring it here to me." She was soft and round, nearly stout, with dark wavy brown hair cropped to frame her face. Her face too was round and fair, with rosy cheeks and quick blue eyes. The boy laid the bulky cloth parcel beside her on the settle.

"Where will I bring the cases, M'Lady?" He looked to Katherine.

"You may leave them in my bedchamber, Colin." As the boys lifted a large trunk, she looked to Una. "Will that suit you? You'll be in with me like the aul times."

"Aye, that's the way. That'll be grand, then..." She managed to slide the straps away, and laid the frieze bundle on her lap. "Wait til ye see, girl." Úna smiled as she ever so carefully unslipped a row of buttons and opened out the bundle, revealing a stack of gowns and bonnets for the baby. She fingered through them, and produced a delicate lace gown of tawny white. "Do you mind this, Kassie?" She raised it high to show the length of it, and flourished the wee cap over her hand. "Four generations it has served! It's only just come from our Mary's christening in Sleat [slate]. He's a lovely bairn, her wee Donal gorm, so he is. And sound as a trout!"

"God love you, Úna, you've brought a fine blessing under my roof!" Katherine leaned forward to feel the gown, and turned to a servant who was poking the fire. "Morag, bring us a candlebranch, for the light is failing."

"Aye, M'Lady, these rainclouds bring on an early dusk, so they do."

"And the fine state of it!" Kat slid her white hand under the delicate lace. She tilted her head and marveled. "A lovely gossamer whisp of a thing to endure so! And even to outlast the wee wearer of it..."

"Some of that mending is yours. The best of it! And you were only a wee slip of a girl, with your clever hands. Even Julia says you could spin silk from goat's wool!" Úna lowered her tone portentiously. "I was surprised to see her at Mary's christening so soon after the funeral. In her very elegant widow's weeds."

"What is our dear sister's estimation of me now? I'm sure you told her you were coming. Does Julia send her blessings? Or had she none to spare?"

Una laughed, for they both knew their eldest sister's ways. A branch of flickering candles was set before them, and she waited until the servant went off with fresh instructions to bring wine. "Aye, Julia's shocked and appalled, of course. Publicly she holds it was an abduction, and it's 'our poor Katherine the hostage', but she knows well of your hand in it. Thinks you've lost the head entirely. And *I* wouldn't hear the worst of it, for my own marriage was never blessed. Another 'handfast marriage' to shame her into an early grave!" A hearty laugh rolled back years for the two sisters, who were but one year apart, and had shared many a secret, and many a tattle of gossip over their pillows.

"A 'handfast' was never disparaged by the Gael! It holds before God, the same as a cathedral wedding. This is English fashion creeping in, with their prudery and snobbish ways." She held up a wee tartan bonnet. "Lovely! Úna, these are precious! Ah, well, now she's widowed, we'll see what mighty match she'll make."

SHANE O'NEILL

"Her son Rory Mór was elected the McLeod, so she wasn't unsettled entirely. But I could see her teeth were on edge. Firstly, our Mary wed the MacDonald of Sleat. Nextly, my Donal Dubh became the Cameron of Lochiel, when his brother died. And there's nary a sooth-sayer could see that coming! And now 'poor wee Kassie' is the lady of Shane O'Neill, the mightiest prince in the three kingdoms! Aye, she thought you'd come to little when auld Campbell died, and she said as much. And she was pleased to pity you when you wed the aulfella O'Donnell. Now she's the 'dowager'."

"Well, I wish her a fine match. And I pray God I'm not next to don the widow's weeds!" Katherine held a wee gown up to the light, admiring the embroidery.

"Unless they're for auld O'Donnell! That would set you rightly..." Úna's tone was sly, like the devilish glint in her eye.

"Sure, Shane is married still! And I wish no harm to any." She blessed herself hastily. "I'll leave them both to the God who made them. I'm sure they'd more to speak of at Mary's than my wicked elopement..." Kat noticed a furtive shadow pass over Úna's face that seemed to portend some trouble. "What are you not telling me, girl? Has something gone amiss? It must be dire, when you daren't broach it."

Just then Morag entered, carrying on her tray a lidded tankard and two mugs of mulled wine from the kitchen, with a whispy ghost of steam over them. She set them down and, noticing that she'd brought a silence, she made a half curtsy and skipped off. Úna took up her cup and blew on it. "Aye, just so. I was only making my way 'round to it. It's news that needs a bit of softening. They told me, 'Don't be piling woe upon worry for Katherine, when she's near to her time, and troubles enough to fret!' but I said our Kassie is made of sterner stuff nor that. I said-"

"That's enough softening, girl. I've a stone in my throat from it. Tell the tale!"

"Aye, well, the tale to tell is not who was at the christening, but who was not. Hector Mór, nor Hector Óg. Our father and brother refused to come. His own grandson! Because he's a Kintyre MacDonnell and there's been trouble..."

SHANE O'NEILL

"It must be great trouble for him to refuse poor Mary!"

"Aye, it's dire, right enough. There have been several clashes, but only the one death that started it all. Thus far, anyroad."

Kat put her hand to her mouth. "Who has died, then?"

"There you are. I couldn't tell you rightly. A MacLean. Near kin of father's, and it went unpunished. But it's all about the Rhinns, and who holds them. That's those lands in the north of Islay."

"The MacLeans have been bailies there since Noah had a boat! I recall Grandda saying that about the Rhinns." Kat shook her head and sighed. Her brows were knit. "My God, a bloodfeud!"

"Not as yet, but tempers are high, and blood is spilt. A clash of claims. Lord Argyle is stepping in. Archibald's called a Highland Council to put a stop to it, and, please God, he will! Ach, it's the madness of men, isn't it? Thank God we've only to bear and raise their childer. Until they're old enough to join the slaughter..." Úna took a cautious sip of her mulled wine, and Katherine did the same. The driving rain and blustering wind at the casements made themselves heard now, as the sisters considered the matter. Kat spoke.

"Still...Still, the man who keeps peace when his fences are broached will soon find his neighbors crowding in on him. Even if it's close kindred encroaching, the men are rightly on their guard. And we must bide." Their eyes met, and they shared the dark ominous burden of this news from home. The MacDonnells were cousins and dear to them, and there was sure to be sorrows ahead if peace could not be found. "God help us! If trouble isn't coming down the road, it's coming *up* the road!"

Úna laid down her cup, and put her hand on Katherine's. Her eyes flashed with dark merriment. "There's only one place has no troubles, wee girl, and that's the churchyard. And I'd liefer fret myself the odd time, than share their peace!" Another moment passed, silent, but for a rumble of distant thunder on the wind. Katherine looked around her before she spoke.

"Una, love. Thank God you've come. I've been that worried. I have this dire feeling, a presentiment, that I'll never see him again. He's in London still, and no sign of even a hearing." Kat's voice became small

SHANE O'NEILL

and unsteady. "She'll never let him go. Never! She'll have his head on her battlements. Last night...last night I was certain sure I heard the banshee keening and wailing for him. Nan Roe they call her. It was an unearthly wailing. It near took the life out of me. I got no sleep at all."

Úna stiffened. She spoke slowly, with urgent deliberation. "Did anyone *else* hear her?" Kat looked away, and slowly shook her head.

"Not a soul. I asked them all..."

"Of the O'Neill blood?"

"Two of Shane's sons are here. They heard nothing!"

"Twas no banshee, so. What sons are these?"

"Wee Turlough, and Éamon, of Tríona MacDonnell's brood. You'll meet them at supper. His daughters Moraed and Rósa are away at the convent-school, and the other lads are in fosterage. I've only the two here. But the boys were abed and asleep!"

Úna softened, and fetched a deep sigh. "Any 'blood O'Neill' would have heard her, asleep or awake." She blessed herself. "And you should thank God and his Holy Mother they didn't." A sudden inspiration brought a burst of merriment. "'Twas more nor likely some aul cat in the throes of heat!" She laughed heartily. Katherine rolled her eyes and summoned up a weak smile, so Úna tried again. "Och, you're over wrought, Kassie. It was only your fears strumming through your taut nerves you heard. You shouldn't be alone... And you're *not* alone. What are the miles and leagues between if you're in his heart? Surely he writes?"

"He does, aye. Father Devlin will bring letters tomorrow. I count the days and hours til they come, just as I dread them lest the tidings be bad." Kat saw a flicker of doubt in her sister's eyes. "Oh, I have others of his party pledged to write to me, for Shane's letters are spare of the dark news. He withholds whatever is worrisome, and fills them with tattle of the Court. Last week he wrote of a hunting party with the Duke of Guise who is on his way home from Scotland. Shane saw the duke's brother kill two stags with a single arrow! Would *you* ever credit such a tale?" Katherine followed her sister's eyes, and turned to see Mórag awaiting her attention. "Yes, girl, what is it?"

SHANE O'NEILL

"Beggin' your pardon, M'Lady. The Tanist and his men have arrived. Only just now. They number some twenty two. I gave word to the cook and the chief steward. Will I tell him you'll be in to him, or would you rather he came up?"

"Ask him to come here to me, Mórag. At once, if he would spare me a moment. Tell him I'm anxious for his news. Good girl."

"Aye, gracious like. I will, so." She bobbed her head and hurried off on her mission.

"Turlagh Lynnagh O'Neill it is." Kat turned back to Úna's inquiring smile. "He's cousin to Shane, and his designated successor, and I fear he may be a bit too eager to take the reins. He swaggers about the place like Shane is only a memory. He's just made a progress through all of Tirowen, to settle disputes and keep the peace. Shane told him to let them all see that if the cat's away, there's another cat still! –No, not a drop for me. The one wee bowl was plenty." She saw that Úna was pouring more wine from the steaming tankard. She slid her hand slowly over her belly. "I can feel him kicking now, and if he's akin to his father, I wouldn't like to have him in a drunken stew!"

Úna laughed. "I'll have another -to drown my envy! I've been hoping to conceive this long while. My Dónal dubh will want an heir now he's chieftain. And it would surely be one way to get us blessed in chapel!" She took a swallow, and settled back in her seat. "I mind you were always that keen for the babies, Kassie. You would often muse on the great brood of childer you'd have, and as the years passed I feared you'd never bear a child." She blessed herself again. "And look to you now! Is it all as you fancied?"

"Aye, *fancied*! I hadn't an *inkling* of all that would come over me. It was all beyond my ken, and I'd say I've a few wonders yet in store. A rosy picture is seldom a true likeness."

"Tell on, Kassie. There must be more to the tale than a rosy glow!" Úna saw that Kat was rubbing her arms, so she reached over and tossed a few sods of turf on the smouldering fire.

"Well, right enough it started with a glow. It was well beyond the elation of wine. Aye, a sort of 'bliss' you might call it. And scarcely a few weeks later it was a weakness, and an uneasiness. A curious drained feeling, as if my very lifeblood was being stolen away. The next month my senses were afire! Tastes and smells were overwhelming me. I had to draw back from the fire. There were pungent vapours, and a queer taste in my food. *Sickly* smells! I had the girls tormented with cleaning, and even my garments troubled me. And I began to crave things that I never had a taste for. You get the notion that it's not yourself that wants them, for there's another spirit dwelling within you, and it's a queer feeling all the same. Perhaps had Shane been here it would have taken my mind off of it. Loneliness can draw phantoms to you."

"Aye, there you are, my girl, banshees and all!" Úna nodded sagely and sympathetically.

"Still, the peculiar shifts and turns, and the odd wee adjustments had only but begun-" A rattling casement and the howling March wind behind it interrupted Katherine's thoughts. "Would you ever fetch me that shawl, love?"

Úna draped the shawl over her sister, and poured a bit of the hot wine for her. "There's a cold draught coming in. This damp chill in the air will do you more harm than a wee drop to warm you!"

"Aye, cheers, love. That will take the chill off."

"What strangeness came upon you then, Kassie?"

"You've only to look and behold." She opened the shawl out, flashing a broad smile, then wrapped it tightly around her. "My own flesh, my very form altered so that I didn't know myself. My bosom swelled and drooped. 'Twas like a second go of puberty! It would turn your head around, so it would, when you feel the burgeoning of your own flesh. Of course, my belly grew round and swollen, but it was more nor that. It's firm and hard, with muscles that were never there before. I'm like a changling. It isn't me at all. Look you!" Kat made a grimace that curled her lip up over her teeth, and leaned in before the candles. "Do you see? The shine of my teeth is vanished."

"I'm sure they'll glisten again. You've lovely white teeth still. I'd no notion! Perhaps had you been forwarned of these things, you'd have taken them in stride."

SHANE O'NEILL

Kat threw her head back and laughed. "I did take them in stride! I'm not daft, girl. This is the first word I've breathed of any of this. And only for your asking! I'm only saying that life is a strange thing, and carrying life is a queer business. And I'm sure you'll know all about it soon enough!" They heard the sound of quick steps in the hall, and Mórag appeared through the portal drapes. "Yes, Mórag. What is it?"

"The Tanist is here to see you, M'Lady."

"Thank you, girl. Send him in." Katherine blessed herself quickly to banish her fears. The girl disappeared through the drapes, and soon they parted again as Turlagh O'Neill stepped into the room. Tall and dark he was, with a rough complexion and small grey eyes. He wore a long glistening shirt of mail, and his hair was soaked against his skin. He nodded to Katherine, and tossed a quick glance at her sister. Kat smiled warmly. "Och, forgive me, Turlagh, there was no great need for such a haste! You're soaked to your pelt. Stand over to the fire! It's only that I'm longing for news, and I wasn't expecting your return for another week or more."

Turlagh grabbed a chair and settled it in near the fire. He dropped into it heavily, dripping and exhausted from a hard ride in hard weather. "A dirty aul night!" He glanced again at Úna.

"This is my sister Úna. She's wife to the Cameron of Lochiel." She turned to her sister. "Turlagh Lynnagh O'Neill. He's tanist for Shane, and he's minding the 'kingdom'." They nodded at each other. He swept the wet hair from his brow.

"The news I bring will be a comfort to no-one, Lady Katherine. I was below in Slane with Sir James Fleming who is fresh back from Dublin. Has that priest come and gone, then?"

"Father Devlin?" Katherine moved to the edge of her seat and spoke quickly. "No, you've not missed him. He'll be here in the morning, and you can send your news on to Shane. What has happened then?" Úna handed the tankard to Turlagh, for there was enough hot wine left to brace him.

"Lord Slane said that Fitzwilliam read a letter from Lord Cecil in Council; a letter about Brian McBaron O'Neill, the bastard's son. He said

SHANE O'NEILL

that his orders to repair to London have been secretly 'contravened'! So there's our Shane waiting on him, and they've told him *not to come*." Katherine closed her eyes and blessed herself, patting her breastbone softly as she listened. "We must tell Shane. Sir James said the letter referred to Brian as 'the *lawful* Earl of Tyrone', with no word of deliberations or hearings about it. They're keeping Shane on a lie! Fleming thinks the baron's son will try to re-take Dungannon soon." He took a goodly slug from the tankard. Katherine glared into the fire.

"Shane must escape! Before they know he's on to their deception..."

"It was madness to trust them!" Turlagh stood, and turned his back to the fire. "When I was above in Dundalk, one of Sussex' men, a wheedling oily knave, name of Smith, he called me aside with an offer from Sussex. 'We'll make you O'Neill,' he says. I told him to go to the Devil, for no one can make an O'Neill but the men of Tirowen. 'And if I *was* the chieftain, I'd soon make you rue the day that Turlagh O'Neill stepped upon the stone!' But how many others are they approaching? Sussex is a treacherous viper. Lord Slane tells me that Kildare is contriving a delegation from the Pale to bring charges against Sussex before the Queen. More power to his elbow, say I!"

"In Dublin? Surely Kildare is not in Dublin!" Katherine's face was flushed, and she could feel heat rising in her, bringing a throbbing pulse of fear to her temples.

"He is, aye." Turlagh was taken aback by her consternation at such trivial news. "Are you rightly, woman? What is it?"

"Kildare has come home without Shane..." Her voice was weak. "He was pledged as his surety. And he has left him behind in their clutches..." She looked to Úna in disbelief; a look of shock and dispair. Turlagh stepped over to Katherine and patted her hand gently where she gripped the arm of her chair. He spoke softly, coaxing gently.

"Have sense now, woman. What could Kildare do if they want to keep him in London? You're frighting yourself for naught."

"But you've hit the very mark! Do you not see? What could *any* man do? For they *do* want to keep him! All this long delay, awaiting the Baron's son; it was a ruse to keep him. And Kildare acting as surety;

another meaningless ruse. She'll never allow him to return to Ireland." She turned to her sister, pleading. "I couldn't stop him going! Didn't I try? Didn't I try..." Her throat was closing on her and her eyes were tearing. Úna put her arm around her.

"Wishhht now. Mind your courage now for the baby's sake."

"Lady Katherine, sure, you know that Shane is well able for them." Turlagh dropped to one knee, and looked her in the eyes where she sat. "Shane has fierce wits in his skull, and these are only Englishmen. He could take them to the fair and sell them dear. We've only to warn Shane of what we know. And didn't you say yourself the priest is coming tomorrow?" Úna gently patted Katherine's shoulder.

"Keep your heart high, Kassie. Things will come aright. We've seen many a dark cloud that's brought no rain!"

"Aye, ye's are right. It's my being in this delicate way is all." Katherine wiped her few tears with the back of her hand, and looked up smiling. "I've fierce wits of my own, and now is soon enough to use them. I'll pen another page to my letter. He'll be put wise to their treachery." She sat up straight, pulled her shawl tight about her. "Shane must tell Elizabeth everything she wishes to hear. No matter how it galls his tongue. When your hand is in the dog's mouth, you draw it out slow and easy, with a fine soft smile..."

Shane arrived at the Privy Council Chamber just as the others were shuffling in. The distant bells of Lambeth could still be heard fading under the voices and sounds of Whitehall. The atmosphere was lively but muted, with a tipsy air of expectation that called to mind for Shane those queues at the Paris Gardens in Southwark. With his brehon and his barrister beside him, he took his place behind the last of the lot, two elderly gentlemen bedecked in sombre finery; sombre but for the trim of showy ermine that proclaimed their high estate. The older, taller one tottered along, bending in to hear some confidence, and then suddenly his shoulders shook in a wheezing laugh. He smiled back over his high-ruffed collar to see who was behind. As his little watery eyes beheld O'Neill's towering figure, all mirth drained from the gaunt old face. He coughed and cleared his throat and turned swiftly to the fore, passing between the grim guards at the chamber's threshold.

The room was bright but also strangely muted, bathed in bleak winter light owing to the vast expanse of leaded windows, and the turbid grey sky behind them. The councilors stood behind their chairs, arranging themselves around a long oak table, and the lively murmur of deep bass voices quickly faded to stony silence as Shane stepped into view. His demeanor was fierce and proud. As his bold glance swept around the table, the wary statesmen averted their gaze, mostly casting their eyes to the top of the table where an ornately carved high-backed chair awaited the Queen's arrival.

After a few creaky seconds that sounded like minutes, Shane broke the stillness. In brazen full voice he addressed his two companions. His Irish was deliberately rough and gutteral as he suggested they take their places behind the three chairs at the bottom of the table. "These are the bold heroes of the Kingdom, then. I've met some of these auld hoors, and listened to their prating, and now of a sudden, they'll turn into a pillar of salt if they meet my eye!"

"That's the 'blind justice' they boast of." Fleming quickly scanned the faces to see if anyone might have Irish. He was re-assured, but spoke quietly all the same. "They'll not look you in the eye. That's to shield the conscience, lest it hinder them in the treachery they know they will be obliged to commit. Why is Lord Dudley not here?" O'Hagan surveyed the stern faces arrayed before them.

"Aye, he would be a warm comfort in this blizzard of hospitality." Indeed the only advance word of this hearing had been a quiet tip from Sir Robert in the tavern two days before. Shane shook his head.

"The Queen has promised him a seat in Council, but he has yet to attain it. I don't see Cecil as yet, and he is the chief councilor." As they spoke the murmur rose gradually again around the table. After some few moments, a door was opened by the guards and all talking ceased, for behind it were the Queen's private chambers. In came Lord Cecil carrying the Royal Mace, a silvergilt staff adorned at the top with a crowned orb of gold. He was followed by two young clerks, solemn little acolytes, in their black attire with square white collars, who perched themselves at the high desks beside the windows. The door was left open, and Shane watched for the Queen to appear, but all that was visible within was a glittering drape of Italian brocade across its threshold.

All stood to attention as Cecil recited the call to order for the honorable Privy Council 'meeting at the pleasure of the Queen's majesty.' He said that the order of the day's business would commence with a hearing of the charges and plaints of John O'Neill against the honorable Lord Deputy of Ireland, William Radcliffe Lord Sussex. He then sat himself beside the vacant royal seat, and the others took their places with a rumble of chairs and a murmur that quickly settled into a creaky silence. Cecil winced and squirmed in his chair, and looked quite peevish. His colleagues assumed rightly that his old complaint of gout was troubling him. Although, at thirty-eight, he was the youngest of the council, his demeanor and his grey hair gave him a gravity and authority well beyond his years. He peered expectantly across the long table at Shane, who bristled as he apprehended the intentions of the Council.

"Lord Secretary, you had best carry on with the remainder of your docket," Shane announced, "for my matters will await her Majesty's presence." His tone was easy but pointed.

"Alas, her Highness will not be in attendance. She has directed us to hear of your business in her stead."

"I have traveled many leagues and miles, to the peril of my country, with one purpose only: to plead my suit before my sovereign Queen." Shane stood, and Owen and Will followed. "We must set another hearing date that will be amenable to her Majesty."

"Just as you say, O'Neill, there shall *be* another hearing, in a fortnight's time, when the Queen's majesty will attend your suit. The Lord Deputy, too, will be present to answer to these grave charges that you bring. Today's proceeding is a preliminary airing of your charges

SHANE O'NEILL

for the edification of Privy Council, many of whom have traveled miles to accommodate you. Stay you then, and let us to your business." Shane nodded.

"What I have to say, I will say before any man. Aye, in any court in Europe. As you are to advise the Queen, let you hear the truth of what is done in Ireland in her good name." He nodded to his advisors, and they took their seats once again at his right side. Will Fleming opened the leather folio and placed several sheets before Shane, who quickly glanced over them. Cecil cleared his throat.

"Perhaps you will begin by telling to us your reason for refusing to attend the Lord Deputy in Dublin upon his summoning you..."

"Aye, I'll tell you rightly why! My people would not suffer me to come into the Lord Deputy's presense...because many lords and gentlemen have been slain and tortured upon their coming unto him!" A low indignant rumble of disapproval was quickly checked by Shanes's sweeping fiery glance. "I will enumerate these outrages, for even the precious ears of courtiers must on occasion hear the truth, however they may mislike it. Firstly, the instance of Dónal the O'Brien who, with his brethren and his son, came to the Lord Deputy in Limerick. They appealed to Sussex to settle the controversy betwixt them and the Earl of Thomond. A dispute over succession, not unlike mine own. The O'Brien required the benefit of her Majesty's laws, by which he asked the matter be tried. This was denied him, and, contrary to all protections, he and his brothers were taken, proclaimed traitors, and all their lands and possessions confiscated. Thereafter Thady O'Brien, the grandson, came unto the Lord Deputy under the like protection to plead for them. He was imprisoned for a time, and *his* estate is now in the hands of the Earl of Ormonde. Upon his release, he came to Limerick and made appeal to the Justice Marshal. He was brought before the Constable of Dublin, and was there imprisoned for two years and a half, until, *with God's help*, he broke prison." There was not one at the table whose breath did not add to the loud gasp. "This was the bitter fruit of their recourse to English justice and Law!" A troubled murmur followed, while Shane looked down at his papers. He looked up, and spoke over it.

SHANE O'NEILL

"Item." A searing glance restored the silence. "Donagh O'Connor came in, under Lord Kildare's protection, when *he* was summoned. In the presence of the Lord Deputy he was shot by an Englishman called Digby. The ball missed his flesh but tore through the sleeve of his shirt. This same Digby escaped punishment, while O'Connor was imprisoned. He was kept until he had delivered up six hostages for the Lord Deputy to keep in his stead. These pledges were all later put to death at Dangan. Item. Art O'Cavanagh was sent for by Captain Hearne, the Lord Deputy's man. After partaking of dinner in Captain Hearne's house, he was traitorously murdered. Item. Randall MacDonnell's two sons, good servitors to her Majesty, were sent *upon the Lord Deputy's word* to the house of Sir Andrew Brereton in Ardglass. After they had supped, young Gillaspick slept in the chamber where he was appointed to lie, and was there murdered by Brereton. His brother Alistair was that same night slain by Brereton's men in the next town. Sir Andrew Brereton was ushered safely back to England without punishment. These evil practices and more did all transpire within this nine or ten years past, and I have furnished to you the particulars of these offenses in a written deposition. If you desire more knowledge of them, you have only to ask at any hearthside in Ireland, for in even the meanest hovels, the true deeds of the Lord Deputy are known and recounted. Even as the Queen's Council hears naught of them." Shane folded his arms and sat. A clock ticked loudly over the briefest silence, and then a deep loud furor erupted about the table. Cecil pounded it to silence with his gavel. Art O'Hagan whispered at Shane's ear, and he stood again, raising his hand out before him. "There is more."

Cecil regarded him coolly, and cast a quick glance at the thick dossier before him. "I dare say there is. Indeed, you would seem possess a boundless fund of offenses and charges-

"And affrontery!" It was old Sir William Petre, Cecil's predecessor in office, who was clearly chafing. He didn't trouble himself with Latin. "My Lord Secretary, this is an outrageous indulgence of Irish insolence. It would never have been brooked in King Harry's time. Nor, indeed, even in Queen Mary's reign. What the devil does it matter what words are passed in hovels in the bogs of Ireland? These are things that must not be uttered in the Royal chambers! I shame to hear it." He won for himself a clamour of approval from his colleagues." Cecil cleared his throat, and raised his bearded chin, peering across the long table at Shane.

"Speak then, John O'Neill. We are here to see that justice is administered."

"Item." Shane paused again, with a challenging glare for the councillors. He folded his arms and spoke out over the table. "The Earl of Sussex did promise in writing that, upon my coming with Lord Kildare to this Court of London, all troops and garrisons would leave Armagh, where they occupy the Cathedral of the Primal See of Ireland. Here I stand before you. I kept according to my promise. And yet those troops were but *one day* removed from Armagh, and then garrisoned again. In breech of a solemn and signed treaty! Item. Contrary to all signed protections and securities granted, when I came to Dublin with the Earls Kildare and Ormonde, the Lord Deputy did have his men to seize me, and shackled me in a handlock. I was carried as prisoner until I came unto her Majesty...and this in breech of all lawful covenants. Item. Only six months have passed since this same Lord Deputy did entice my secretary Neal Grey to murder me, and upon his failure to complish the deed, did have him foully murdered in the mountains of Mourne!"

"Let him prove these slanderous bruits or withdraw them!" Old Lord Howard's temper was white hot, and his voice a low growl.

"Lies!" "Slander and calumny!" Others of Sussex' faction cried out now, only to be silenced by Cecil's gavel. At once Shane resumed his chronicle of misdeeds.

"Item. Conn O'Neill, the Earl of Tyrone and father unto me, came forth to Dundalk upon the summons of the Lord Deputy. This same Deputy told him...that were it not but that he was old, and such a one as did no service in his years illspent, he would have off his head, there and then, and see his blood poured in a basin! And this ill use of my noble father was undeserved. Indeed, my people are timorous and mistrustful of the Lord Deputy for all of these treacherous proceedings.

SHANE O'NEILL

And it is only by *reason* of this mistrust I have escaped his traps, by the help of God... and that I have lived to come into the Queen's gracious presence." Shane took his seat.

"These are grave allegations." Cecil's tone was cautionary. "Lord Sussex has been apprized of them, and will be pleased to consult with our inquiry. But I must own, O'Neill, you have put forward precious little to substantiate them. If they be false, it will stand to bolster the Lord Deputy's case against you, and will likely ensure the Baron of Dungannon's succession to his father's estate, not withstanding your claims thereto. Do you wish to recant or alter your testimony?"

"What I have said, I have said. It is not for me to uphold her Majesty's law in Dublin when it be abused by her ministers. My rights to succeed to my father's estate owe nothing to the question of Lord Sussex' misuses of office." Old Sir William Petre leaned in across the table, and spoke in low tones to his successor, inquiring as to the intentions of the 'Irish upstart' before him. Cecil looked up and addressed the others.

"O'Neill disputes the succession of the son of his half-brother Matthew to the Earldom." The Lord Secretary glanced around the table to see that he was understood. "He has petitioned her Majesty that his father's patents wherein he was created Earl be amended forthwith.

"Not amended, but draughted de novo." Shane spoke and all the anxious hoary heads turned as one from the top to the bottom of the table. "The treaty was invalid...in that it provided for the succession of a bastard son over the rightful progeny of the Earl of Tyrone. As accounted in the depositions before you, Matthew Kelly took for himself my father's name of O'Neill, and proclaimed himself to be a bastard son of the Earl, which was not denied. Could any of Good King Henry's bastards, though they be noble and male, challenge the rights of our gracious Queen to the throne of England? Surely they could not. The king married six times to beget legitimate issue! Such a precedent would undo the rule of princes. Had I not challenged the Baron's son, there are a hundred other legitimate O'Neills who would be entitled to do so, and would prevail if law were honoured."

SHANE O'NEILL

"That is a matter which must await the arrival of the young Baron of Dungannon. Upon his coming to London we shall conduct an inquiry as to the validity of his patents."

"That will hardly suffice." Many mouths were open, and eyes wide, as the council listened, quite aghast, to O'Neill's objection. "As the treaty at Greenwich was invalid, the process ought properly to be commenced anew. My father was created Earl because he was -under Irish law- the acknowledged prince of Tirowen. So, in like wise, am I the O'Neill, his son legitimate, come likewise unto her Majesty to pledge fealty to my sovereign. -As the acknowledged prince of Tirowen. And this is a thing that Brian Mac Baron could not claim, for he holds no part of Tirowen, nor the allegiance of its men, nor of its tributary chieftains."

"This 'allegiance' from what you call 'tributary chieftains' ought properly to belong to their sovereign Queen. It is a matter which shall require clarification." William Cecil sat back, nodding, with a wry smile for his councilors. "Indeed, Lord Sussex tells us that it is simply a kind of 'black rent' demanded of weaker lords by a more powerful one." A ripple of laughter, smug and derisive, gave way to a loud murmur around the great table. O'Hagan and Fleming spoke at Shane's ear, and then Will Fleming stood; a surprise that quickly silenced the room.

"The O'Neill has longstanding rights of tribute from all the other septs of Ulster outside Tirowen as well. They are enshrined in Irish law for nearly a millennium. If he would hold under English feudal law, the O'Neill ought rightly to be styled not 'Earl of Tyrone', but 'Earl of Ulster!'" An audible gasp greeted what was perceived as yet a further insolent demand. Cecil responded.

"Kindly introduce yourself to council!"

"I am William Fleming, barrister of the Dublin Bar, and council to Lord O'Neill."

"If you are versed in law, you will know that this is hardly a question of 'rights'. For all its great pomp and its pledges of mutual trust, the settlement of 1542 was not a *treaty*. Not an agreement betwixt kings, but simply the full submission of the rebel Conn Bacach O'Neill before his sovereign king; a king whose rights over Ulster the O'Neills had usurped

SHANE O'NEILL

for many hundreds of years. Conn O'Neill's accession to the Earldom of Tyrone was not a contract but a matter of grace, for it was with King Henry's power to raise up any man he chose to such rank. These rights of tribute, so long usurped by the O'Neills, belonged properly to the Earl of Ulster, a title held in the Crown since King Henry II." The satisfied murmur of harrumphs and 'Hear, hear!" at this long awaited rebuttal had to be gaveled to a silence. Will looked quite unperturbed.

"And from whence did King Henry II acquire such title to Ulster?"

"As is well known unto you, King Henry II did receive the Kingdom of Ireland as a papal grant from Pope Adrian IV in his bull of 1157 entitled Laudabiliter. This is undisputed."

"No man but a fool would dispute that Pope Adrian IV granted Ireland to the Crown of England, for that his name was Nicholas Breakspeare, and he was the only Englishman ever to be made Pope. And yet, from whence did the Pope of Rome acquire the kingdom of Ireland to bestow it unto Henry II?" The insolence of the query brought an astonished silence. Cecil was clearly piqued, and mocked the question with a tone of long suffering patience.

"In the 'Donation of Constantine' the Pope was granted by the Roman Emperor Constantine the dominion of *all* the isles of Europe." In spite of his best efforts to conceal his glee, Will's eyes flashed like a pouncing cat.

"Unlike England, Ireland was never a part of the Roman Empire, and therefore was not in Constantine's power to grant, no more than the emperor of far China!" Tempers roiled about the long table, and Will spoke over the dark din. "And yet...And yet...The voices simmered to give way to the speaker, as curiosity overcame outrage. "And yet, leaving that aside, our own good King Henry VIII attested that 'the Donation of Constantine' was a forgery, a papal forgery, and henceforth not binding in law! The pope had no right to bestow what was not in his keeping. And therefore the rights of tribute held by the O'Neill in Ulster were not usurped, for the crown held no rights to them until Conn Bacach O'Neill submitted in 1542 at Greenwich. I submit further that the O'Neill has *not* come here to dispute the rights of the Crown. He has not come to dispute the rights of the Crown, but to affirm them! He has pledged submission to her Majesty before her full Court on the feast of the Epiphany. He has implored her Majesty's grace to grant him feudal title to the dominions that he holds now legally under Irish law, in a province unshired, where English law is not established. All this...that he may more perfectly serve her serene Highness." The voices of outrage and shock had only begun to surge again when Shane stood and brought all to stillness.

"That is sufficient for this time. If this was a hearing, you have *heard*. I shall take my leave, and use no more of the Privy Council's time. I await the hearing a fortnight hence, for you may be assured, there is more to hear." Without waiting for a 'by your leave', Shane turned and strode out the door. O'Hagan jumped to his feet as Fleming gathered up the folio, and the two men hastened after him.

Into the brief stunned silence tore the sharp rattling clank of curtain rings, as the portal drape to the Queen's chambers was snapped back. A guard held them open and Elizabeth stormed into the room. She did not stand upon ceremony, but shrieking with rage, she hectored the old men as they scrambled to their feet. "Ninnies! I have a council of feeble ninnies! Would that I had *one* man in my service to match this pompous hellion! He would topple the heavens in his pride! God's teeth! His very submission is a challenge!" In her rage, she had even forsaken the royal 'we.' Elizabeth covered her ears and shook her head in anguish. "To witness such a drubbing in our very Privy Chamber! Ninnies all!"

All eyes were lowered, each fearing to engage the royal wrath. Lord Cecil pulled out the Queen's chair and held it for her. She beheld the gesture with disdain. "We have sat for too long! We have sat for too much! Weary old men waiting to rest their bones! Had we but one stout heart to match him!" She paced now angrily, turning her skirts as the others stood back. "And all this muddle will be noised abroad by that ghastly Spaniard! Laid before the courts of Europe like a broadsheet! We have us letters from every court and capitol asking news of this O'Neill, yet showing us they are informed verse and chapter of his every move." She turned back to Cecil. "When shall we see Lord Sussex at Court?"

SHANE O'NEILL

"He is on the sea. The Lord Deputy will reach London within this week coming, barring ill winds."

"Ill winds indeed! He blusters and blows, and bungles all! He is a fool! To leave such a reckless trail of blood in his wake, without recourse to our justices! What does he suppose the courts are for? Such miscreants must be dispatched legal and clean, else the law may lose its edge. Let him labour to account for these clumsy murders before your Board of Inquiry before he be aquitted." She suddenly stood stock still, her gaze piercing the empty air. "There shall *be* no hearing. There shall be a report from your Commission of Inquiry to bind up these matters with no course of appeal."

"Yes, your Majesty."

"Set my retinue of barristers to the task of refuting each of O'Neill's arguments. Should they fail against these bogmen lawyers, they shall be deemed unworthy to face a judge, and disbarred!" Again she stopped suddenly, this time to regard the abashed faces of her Councillors. She found no eyes to meet her stern gaze, and with sudden revulsion she shrieked. "Out of my sight! All of you! We are cursed with feeble old men. How shall we weather the storms to come in this creaky old vessel? But one stout heart in all the Court!"

As the councilors shuffled out, the Lord Secretary waited at her side. She held her white hand to her brow and paused, her eyes shut tight. At last she looked to Cecil and spoke, her voice low and grave. "This man is the very Lucifer of pride. If he be not broken, we dare not set him loose into Ireland. Ever." With that, she turned away and disappeared into her chambers.

SHANE O'NEILL

CHAPTER 11

Kneeling so close, he squinted before the glare of the small flames. The ascending rows of votive candles flickered and licked the darkness, shimmering like a starry stair into the night. Towering over him, a statue draped in purple pall stretched out its arms to the Heavens. He was vaguely aware of a procession of hooded monks behind him, shuffling slowly past as they chanted their plainsong dirge. He knew it to be the Stabat Mater Dolorosa.

The grim figure above him began to move, stretching the taut purple draping into grotesque shapes, and moaning away some deep hurt that seemed to ebb and flow. Then came the insistent whisper that he strained to hear. The purple figure bent low to him, calling him with its breathy voice. He tried so to make out the desperate whisper over the deep undulating chant that throbbed and receded in waves around him. As the whisper grew stronger and more insistent he knew that the voice was Katherine's.

"Turn away! Turn away and take ship, for the tide will not wait! Turn away, Shane O'Neill"

A hollow thundering boom and a shrill clank that resonated in the vaulted shadows around him made him turn to look. A cold blast of wind followed, and when he turned back, the tapers were extinguished, and he could see only thin coils of paraffin smoke rising into the darkness where she had disappeared. A quick footfall echoed in the

SHANE O'NEILL

towering nave, and he followed it, moving in and out between the columns of what he could see now was a great cathedral. Before the altar rail the brown-robed friars were huddled in a crowd. They appeared to be troubled, as they jostled and swarmed around something in their midst. Around *something*. As he moved up towards them, the bright altar shone over them, and he could see that the sanctuary lamp too was extinguished, with only its wispy trail of smoke to tell of the vacant tabernacle below, and of the apparent departure of God.

As he approached, he saw that the brilliant light before the altar was not from the silver candelabras, but seemed to emanate from Queen Elizabeth who sparkled there in her jewels and lace. She was drinking from a golden chalice and laughing with the mummers who danced and frolicked around her. There were crows in the habits of Cardinals, asses habited as bishops, and wolves dressed as abbots.

Upon seeing him, the hooded monks backed away in each direction revealing a coffin set upon its bier before the altar rail. There was a sharp knocking from within! Standing over it, he was shocked to hear the muffled voice of his father calling out to him. The knocking and banging became louder and more insistent as Shane struggled to free his father from the coffin. But something was stopping him. He found that he could not move his hands, for they were bound in a handlock!

He closed his eyes, and in the darkness he heard birds twittering and a dog barking. When he opened them, it was to brightness; his pillows and bedclothes, and what he soon recognized was the four-poster upstairs in his rooms at Whitehall. Still came the knocking! He swallowed to allay the dryness of his throat, and called out, "Come in, for the love of God!"

Here was a new day. His nightworld had vanished, leaving his memory with no vestige of its murky terrors. Only the world before and after sleep. Shane held the dreams of others to be wild curiosities, and set great store by them, for he firmly believed, as he would attest, that he never dreamed. Again came the knocking.

"Lift the latch up above! And come in to hell out of that banging!" A jangle, a clank, and the door creaked open, revealing the voluminous

SHANE O'NEILL

white beard and locks of the bard of Benburb. "Ah...Good man, Farleigh." Shane winced, and cast a curious squint around the room. Farleigh watched with a sly grin.

"Looking for someone? The bird has flown. She nearly toppled me on the stair this morning in all her finery, when Gillie came to take the hounds. I was going to knock then, but I thought better of it. Do you know who she is, Shane?"

"Ah, give it a rest, man. Lady Something of Somewhere, I suppose. Give us over that jug." Shane sat up properly and Farleigh delivered the waterjug. As Shane gulped and gasped by turns behind the jug, the old poet gifted him with his sage counsel.

"Lady Something of Somewhere! Only too bloody right she is! They'll have your head on a pike at this rate, my boy! Tupping all the wives at Court, and taking their monies at dice. We'll never see Ireland again!"

"Do you suppose I'm troubling myself over the stuffed codpieces that mince about this Court? Sure, they've no power at all." Swinging his legs over, he planted his feet on the floor with a thump. He put down the jug, and stretched his limbs. "There's one queen in this deck. The rest are knaves. And I know how to play them." Shane moved to the washstand across the room with plodding 'morning after' steps.

"Aye, well, someone's knavery is keeping you here. The fortnight is past, and nearly a week more! Fleming said that you twisted her lawyers into knots. Where is this hearing she promised? Whenever will we have leave to go our way?" He could hear Shane behind the screen, splashing a whole ewer of water over his head and into the basin. Looking somewhat brighter for his dousing, he emerged toweling off his hair as he pondered the matter.

"Sussex is here now, at any rate." Shane considered again. "They say it was a bad crossing, and there's little cause to disbelieve them, for haven't those same tempests delayed our post?"

"But the hearing." Farleigh folded his arms and tilted his beardy chin. "When is the hearing?" Shane shook his head and shrugged.

"Sure, last time there was no forewarning. No warning at all. That

SHANE O'NEILL

must be one of the rules of power. To divulge nothing; leave only darkness and mystery around you. What did my steward below tell you, then? Was there still no word from Cecil?"

"Divil all... It's well past the midday. And the rest of the day is in a tatters by the look of you..." As Shane washed himself, Farleigh ambled over to the window and gazed idly down at the courtyard below where some young lordlings were teasing a dog. "The men are restless too. Fighting in the taverns. There's scarce a publican left that will take their custom. By Crom the Crooked, we're the queer haul of fish in that woman's net, flopping and gasping. I haven't seen a vision, or dreamed a dream, or coupled a couplet since I left the banks of the Blackwater. That was before the Christmas. There are daffodils standing there now, and they will be withered and wintered again before I see those hills."

"Put it from you now, will you. Give my head peace..." There was silence now, save for the barking below, where the young boys were beating the dog with a stick. Its shrill yelp echoed and rang through the crisp spring air of the bare courtyard. Farleigh was thinking about what sort of comeuppance he'd like to administer to the young buckeens, and he turned from the window with a scowl, a scowl that Shane assumed was a reproach for him. "Well, what am I to do? When I came to Sussex with a safe-conduct, he put me in chains. And when I spoke to Elizabeth, she said the safe conduct guarantees my return but states not when; that the hearings could not be held til 'Brian mac Bastard' arrives to press his rival claims." With a devious wink, he added, "Don't be getting grey hairs over it now, Farleigh. When he comes, my suit will best him." But, grey hairs or no, Farleigh was in no humour for jesting.

"I'll say nothing, so. Pride is a holy shining thing, but as it dazzles your foes, it blinds you to danger." Shane had wrapped the long white linen over his shoulder and round his waist, and he paced near the fire now, looking like a Roman orator, and declaiming like one.

"Two and a half thousand Pounds sterling it's cost her to buy peace with me. I'll take back with me all the favours I can part from her. I have only to spare her honour. I'll submit to her authority on the sole condition that she never use it. 'Queen of England, Ireland, and France',

SHANE O'NEILL

I said in my submission. I might have added Fairyland for all her pretensions!" He halted and grinned at his friend, his grey eyes lit with fiery zeal. "Farleigh,...well *more nor half* her English subjects hold by the Roman faith still. Nearly every night the Catholic lords of England skulk in and out of Durham House under hoods and cloaks, conspiring to undo this queen. When the Pope excommunicates her, he will loose the bonds of allegiance for all Catholics in England and Ireland. There will be ructions, man! I've only to build my force and bide my time. I've only to-"

"Whisht! Hisht! Someone is listening!" In the silence, the rustling of someone behind the door could, indeed, be heard. Shane's fervent words hung on the air, mutinous and subversive, and most certainly incriminating! Although the servants had been sent by Kildare, they could well be in the pay of Cecil's agents. Clearly *someone* was spying at the door. Shane's garments were heaped over a chair close to hand. He pulled his sword from its scabbard, and motioned to Farleigh to open the door. As the auld poet flung open the door, Shane stepped forward brandishing his steel blade in the face of a petrified Gillie. His look of frozen terror gave way to frantic pleading.

"It's me! It's me! I swear to God, it's me!" After a moment's pause the three fell about laughing. At last Farleigh caught his breath.

"Blazes, Gillie! Why are you creeping about?"

"Sure, I wasn't creeping about. Didn't I knock the twiced?"

"We never heard you, boy!"

"Sure, I knocked quiet, so's I wouldn't disturb yez!" Shane roared laughing again, and the other two suddenly twigged to Gillie's unintended jest, and laughed along. Shane was normally quite impatient of fools, but he had a warm spot for Gillie, whose illogical logic always amused him. Farleigh shook his head.

"You nearly got that wild wee head of yours split in two! Well, what the devil is it? What have you got there?" Gillie had an ornate leather satchel slung over his shoulder that Farleigh had never seen before. The lad slipped it off, and unfastened the flap to reveal a goodly parcel of letters. Shane dumped them out on the bed and was flipping through them, as Gillie explained.

"Aye, I took Bran and Scohaun for a wee dander along the Strand, and as I passed Durham House, a priest come running out to me. I *think* he was a priest. He said the Bishop wanted to see me, and wouldn't I come inside? He must have seen me from the window. I tied up the hounds and went up. Th'aul bishop had a lot to say in Spanish, or English maybe, but all I could make out was 'O'Neill.' But, sure, I knew it was the post ye were waitin' on these long weeks, so I just nodded at him and I brung it."

"Good lad! You did rightly enough, boy." Farleigh turned to Shane at the bed to see him hold up a sealed letter, smiling anxiously.

"Katherine's hand!" He broke the red wax seal, and sat on the side of the bed, fervently reading the pages. Gillie fastened up the leather satchel, and hung it over his shoulder. Farleigh held out his hand fluttering his fingers.

"I'm sure his Grace will want this back come Sunday. That's likely what he was telling you." Gillie sighed and gave it up to him.

"Sure, there's nobody has the Irish here, and they be always sniggering at you." They both turned as Shane bounded to his feet.

"She's born me a son! Her sister has written it in on the side here. 'A bonny wee lad' she says, 'with lungs of leather and fists of steel." Farleigh laughed and hurried to his side. He threw his frail arm around Shane's massive shoulder and clapped him heartily on the back.

"Ah well, where acorns fall, it's oaks that grow! Good on ye, Shane O'Neill!" Gillie motioned to Farleigh that he was leaving. "Aye, go on with ye, boy. Did Hermes e'er bear such fine tidings? And you nearly got yourself killed for your troubles!" Gillie paused at the door.

"God bless Lady Katherine! Health and long life on your fine son, Shane O'Neill!"

"And on yourself, Gilly lad." Shane thought of another wee task for him as he was closing the door. "Send my valet up to me. You know him, the ginger fellow." Gillie stuck his head back in.

"I do, aye, surely," he said. "Egan Roe. I'll send him in." Off he went as the door shut behind him.

SHANE O'NEILL

"Kat will be heartbroken, for I'll not be there to attend the Christening." He moved over to the bright window, and returned to reading her letter. A furious twist in his brow soon appeared, and without looking up from the page, he exclaimed, "The conniving hellhag! Elizabeth! I knew it! It's all a lie." Farleigh looked on with alarm.

"What is it, lad? More of the Queen's treachery, is it?"

"Our friend Brian mac Baron is not on his way to Court. Kat has it that his public summons to London was privately countermanded. And he's been making moves against me in Tirowen. That's another breach of the safe conduct. Turlagh paid a call on Lord Slane, and he confided that Fitzwilliam read out a letter from Cecil in Council contravening those orders. He bade him keep the Baron's son safely in Ireland. So we are kept here on a lie. Captives!"

"Didn't I say their words were worth nothing? Fine words, stamped and sealed, and worth not a farthing. I said it all. Words to the winds! Callow youth will defy the wisdom of age, and the lessons of the world must be learned over and over again, to man's eternal cost! You should consult that wily auld Spaniard about this. And lose no time about it." Alas, Farleigh's sage counsel was again wasted, for Shane was solely intent upon the letter before him.

"Katherine pleads I must tell Elizabeth only what she wishes to hear. She bids me save all defiance for when I've come safely out of the lion's den. 'Make any gesture,' she says, 'that will assure them of your loyalty. Any gesture...' Shane shook his head slowly. Some angry voices drew his gaze out the window to the courtyard below, where a dapper young courtier in his doublet and hose now stood admonishing two boys with a dog. "That's *it*!" Shane laughed quietly to himself. This bewildered Farleigh, for their dire circumstance hardly warranted levity. Shane went on now, speaking excitedly to himself. "A *massive* gesture! Good man, Dudley! And it's only just finished and ready. Providential, to say the least!"

"What the devil are you on about?" Farleigh watched as Shane pulled a mysterious box from under the massive bed. He carried it behind the dressing screen that stood beside the wardrobe at the far end of the room. Shane laughed a sly little laugh.

"But have patience, my learned friend, and all shall be revealed!" He cast an anxious glance at the door, and muttered to himself, "Where the devil is he?" His curiosity piqued, Farleigh drifted over to the window to see what had inspired Shane to this mysterious lark. Nothing appeared out of the ordinary and he was none the wiser. Shane was now seated at the writing desk, pouring over his letter, still bedecked in white linen. Farleigh perched himself on the edge of the bed, and sorted through the rest of the post. When he saw Shane look up from his letter, he spoke.

"Well...they've broken every letter and word of your safe conduct. Whatever you do, you'd best do it quick and get us back to Ireland."

"The place is in an uproar. Turlagh Lynnagh is skirmishing with the Baron's son. He told Katherine that an agent of Sussex approached him in Dundalk and offered to make him the O'Neill. Turlagh held a dirk to his scrawny throat and bade him go to the Devil. And mark this! He told him, "Were I the O'Neill, I would so plague you, that you would wish tenfold that you had Shane O'Neill back in my stead!"

"Wasn't that bold!"

"Aye... Aye, but there may be something *in* that... A stick to threaten them." He glanced down at the page, and looked up with more news. "Sorley MacDonnell's building another castle in MacQuillan's country and...and with the MacDonnells pouring in, he and O'Kane are spoiling to-" Shane stopped abruptly when he saw Farleigh jump to his feet, holding his hands over his eyes, panting with terror.

"Stone the crows!"

"What is it, Farleigh? Are you right?

The old man moved his hands to cover his mouth now, as he muttered "No, no no no no no no..." His eyes were scrunched tight.

"What *is* it, man?" Shane went to him and sat him back on the edge of the bed. He trembled and his hands were shaking badly. "What's ailing you, Farleigh?" At last he opened his eyes. They had a strange gleam about them as the old man peered wildly into the far reaches of his mind. He swallowed hard and took a breath and he spoke.

SHANE O'NEILL

"I tell a lie! I said I'd no dreams here!...I woke up last night in a lather. But I never took it for a dream! I thought it was some black memory." He quickly blessed himself, a thing Shane had never seen him do. "Safe be the telling! ...Scots, all of them! The MacDonnell plaid... Walls spattered with your own red blood, Shane! Dirks rising and plunging into your breast.. Your eyes glassy and still...glassy and still. And your blood tracing a red web among the cobblestones..." He heaved a deep sigh, and turned to Shane, his eyes clearer now, as a level sense returned. "A horror it was. I couldn't get a breath into me til I doused my head in the basin. I splashed it all away. Couldn't recall a splink of it til now. Just a dark cloud in my head." Shane patted him on the head, and gave it a quick playful rub, scruffing up his white hair.

"A dark cloud, is it? Well, you've brightened *my* day considerably! Where's that whiskybaugh? Shane poured a wee dram and placed it into Farleigh's hands, hands that were somewhat steadier now. He knocked it back, gulping loudly, and then squinted wisely at Shane who was also tipping back the golden drop. The old fellow gave him a quick wink with a sidling nod.

"You must tell it to dispel it, lad. Put words on a thing to tame it."

"Is there anything in it, d'ye reckon?" He looked inquiringly at Farleigh, his head tilted back. The auld fellow pursed his lips as he considered seriously Shane's query. He relaxed suddenly and smiled.

"A warning only. It'll not come to pass if we heed it." Now Shane returned the wink with a devious smile.

"Well, it could hardly come to pass, if we didn't come safely out of London, could it? So you can give over your fretting; we must be going home after all!" There was a sharp double rap on the door that he knew to be his valet. "Come in, ye dozy git!" The door opened and the young man entered.

"It's sorry I am, sir, for the delay, for I was attending to the-"

"Nevermind where you've been, you blaggard, aren't you here now?"

"I am, sir." Shane threw off his few ells of linen and marched naked to the vestuary screen. "I've a full docket of solemnities, sport, and feasting today, and I can't attend them in my pelt." The two disappeared

SHANE O'NEILL

behind the screen, and Farleigh wondered what could be in Shane's mysterious box from under the bed. Some sporting habit, most like. He drifted idly about the large chamber, regarding whatever was unfamiliar, and, ignoring his own dictum, picking up sundry objects to examine them. Of course, he was listening all the while. Shane's voice was a low rumble, but Egan could be heard plainly.

"These, is it?"

Now Shane's voice, his words quite indistinguishable.

"Sure, they're scarcely new tricks for me. No, Sir, I'm a better hand at this sort, for I'm well use to such. I attended Lord Kildare. Put your arm through here." Shane was shushing him now. After a moment, he called out to Farleigh.

"Sorley will betray me. That's plain as a pikestaff. And I was certain sure of him! But I've not forgotten that the MacDonnell turned away when I called upon him. Didn't I save his herds of kine for him in '56? And I saved his hide when Sussex came at him again in '58. This time Sussex came for *me*, and the MacDonnells sat on the ditch and made enemies on both sides of it. I'll put my mark on them yet. Betrayal and treachery everywhere."

"You thought your father a betrayer because he came to London...and here you are..." Farleigh called out his idle challenge to the voice behind the screen.

"That was a different kish of brogues, old man. My father knelt here and never stood again. My submission is pure cunning. Every soft word and bow she smiles upon today will pierce her heart."

"If she has one. Is she a woman at all?" He could hear Shane's dark laughter.

"If she's incapable of pity, she's amenable to flattery."

"She's a cold painted cadaver!" insisted the bard, getting a bit worked up.

"You're no gentleman O'Gneeve! Sure, she's lovely! The English find that white powder 'most fetching'!" He was baiting the aul fellow, and Farleigh's hackles were up just thinking about her.

"The boundless vanity of the woman! Do you know that before she will issue forth from her palace, she sends out a wee squad of guards -I saw it for myself, now, and I inquired. They're commanded to disperse from before her eyes any 'hideous or deformed people.' The lame, the hunchbacked, any whose appearance might shock her fastidious sensations. And, sure, she's no beauty herself! She's a hatchet-faced crone. They even say that her blood is blue. She's ghastly! No nature in these people!"

"Aye, well, she's set her cap for her stablemaster Dudley -so she's fond of the stallions... There's bad blood between Dudley and Sussex. It was Lord Dudley convinced the queen to bring me here. To confound Sussex, I suppose. He's proving to be right handy." This gave Farleigh pause.

"Is he a lord then, or what is he at all? Fleming tells me he's not."

"He is, aye. He's knighted only, but she's promised to make him Earl of Leicester."

"Huh! She's making a lord of her stablemaster, and she balks at the O'Neill!" Farleigh scratched his head, and then gingerly lifted Shane's shaggy mantle, uncovering a glistening marble statue. It was a naked figure of Achilles, the Greek hero. "Thunder and shite! What is this? Is it plunder you're at now?" Shane's face appeared over the screen, as he looked to see what was the object of this wonderment.

"That's civilization, Farleigh. A gift from Dudley, the very man in question. Probably for the falcons I sent him. My Katherine will like it. She thinks Tirowen could use a bit of culture." Shane disappeared again below the screen, and Farleigh draped the cloak back over the marble hero, his blood stirred by this inadvertent slight to his dignity.

"A bit of culture? Does she? Does she indeed! Pish to that! Civilization is in the mind. It's not wrought in stone or wood. Culture is a refined vision of life, my boy. Of rapture in its mysteries! Joy when the blood is hot, cool contentment in the sounds and stirrings of the elements. Words breathed in company, mixing and tossing, wrangling and raucous, or heaving and hushed. It's ideas and ideals conceived in the mind, and born forth into the flesh of words, recited or sung or scratched upon a page. All this frippery and finery in marble and brass is cold and still. It's nothing to the swirling cathedral of the forest, the star vaulted blazing dome over columns of oak... the lush flowering and falling, winging and crawling wood-" His hands in mid-air, waving and gesturing in the passion of the moment, he suddenly noticed Shane's astounded face above the screen, watching and marveling at his extravagant tirade. Farleigh slowly lowered his arms, and rolled his eyes under his shaggy white brows. He shook his head and smiled. "I need to get home!" Shane laughed, and vanished once again behind the ornately carved screen. Farleigh started at a single loud clap of hands from the same quarters.

"Now!" Shane's cheerful voice again assailed the bard in his restless despair, sounding grand and plummy. "I am requested to attend Lord Dudley this afternoon. I explained that I'm desirous to learn the English fashion of riding, with halt and stirrup. Or side-saddle, is it?" Farleigh sighed and shook his head.

"That will be much funnier when we're back in Tirowen. I haven't a laugh in me." As he looked up, Shane appeared from behind the screen in doublet and hose, starched ruffs and all. He flourished his plumed bonnet in a courtly bow. Farleigh roared with laughter, and squealed when he tried to speak, catching his breath. "Augh, ye... ye...Ah, ye crafty hoor! You could escape in that rigout, Shane, for your own mother wouldn't know you!"

Shane proceeded to the looking glass, capering about and affecting English airs for Farleigh's amusement. In actual fact, the courtly apparel was quite stunning on him. The exquisite scarlet doublet and hose complimented his wavy black hair and fair skin, and it showed to fine effect his long legs and heroic build. He declaimed his day's actual itinerary now, in a haughty nasal voice. "Her Majesty demands that John O'Neill averse himself in the civilities of the courtier. To whit: At three of the clock this afternoon he shall train in English riding and he shall 'rrrun at the rrring'." He minced about, in a mock 'run at the ring', as Farleigh and Egan tittered away. "This evening he shall dine with the queen's favorite at St.John's Head in Cheapside!"

"St. John's head! A fine name for an inn!" That would put you off

SHANE O'NEILL

your dinner! Take care the head on the plate isn't St. John O'Neill's."

"Dudley advised I wear them to attend Court. I'll give her the soft eyes, and ask her for an English wife to civilize me."

"Sure, who would be up to you? What if they oblige?" Farleigh shook his head. Shane laughed wickedly.

"I've been pulling Sussex' beard rightly, asking for his sister's hand, and some of the rest of her as well! And like the credulous grim little Englishmen they are, they suppose me to be in deadly earnest. If you could but *see* the Deputy squirm when I speak of co-mingling our blood! He thinks I'm fair lusting after this spindly sister of his, who is *the spit of him,* the very likeness!" Farleigh's face scrunched up in horror.

"*Like* him? What a dreadful thing to say of her! You're no gentleman either!"

"That would serve my haughty lady at home!" Shane poured out two wee drams of whiskybaugh, and settled one in Farleigh's anxious hand.

"To my Katherine! Her news may very well hasten our return. And to my son!"

"To your son! May you see him before he's grown!" They tossed back the fiery dram, and Shane clapped Farleigh on the back.

"It'll not be long now. You'll see, Farleigh old man! I have a devious little shift in mind. If it proves a trump, Elizabeth will bid us farewell at the pier as we cast off. You'll see! And you'll see your cursed daffodils!"

"Shhhh...shoheen, shoheen, a vickeen ohhh...My wee laddybuck..." Katherine was cooing softly to the bundled baby in her arms. A heavy highland mantle of rusty MacLean reds tucked around her, and bolstered with plush pillows, she huddled in the grand carved oak chair beside the hearth. Golden shafts of afternoon sun pierced the umber shadows of the chamber, and their swirl of tiny sparkling motes cast an ethereal lustre upon the cozy room. Perhaps it was only the enchantment that is always found in the presence of new life.

SHANE O'NEILL

At her shoulder, beaming, was Lady Jean Stewart Campbell, wife of Lord Argyle, and sister to Queen Mary of Scotland. She was near to Kat's age, but her tight prim coiffure and her somber attire, taut and starched, conferred on her a more matronly aspect. All this was belied, however, by a warm smile and bright twinkling eyes.

"Ach, He's lovely, Katherine. I do often think there's such a smell of sweet freshness about a newborn babe."

"Aye, by turns, I suppose!" Kat laughed softly, and sniffed deep over the wee one's head. "Aye, I don't know is it my own milky fragrance from nursing him? My wee hero is nodding off." She raised her head, and smiled at her chambermaid, who appeared at the door in a timely happenstance. "There you are, Mórag! Into the cradle with him now. He's had his fill to drink, and he's drowsing for his nap. When you've put him down, ask Colin to bring up a Cabernet from the cellar for Lady Argyle. Good girl!" She handed up the napcloth and Mórag draped it over her shoulder. Kat unwrapped him, and ever so gently held up the tiny infant in his long trailing gown. Like any young lass, Mórag relished such a task, and she took up the babe with a blissful smile.

"*Up* a dandy! Shhhh!" The sleepy lad gave no protest. "Her ladyship's bags have been placed in the Southeast chamber for her, and auld Bríd sent Tague in to lay a fire that will take the chill off the room. There will be fine sun there if the morning is clear." Kat watched as she went off, and turning to Jane, she noticed a look of alarm.

"What is it, Jean? I'm sorry. The servants are from home and they've no English. She says your room is prepared." Lady Campbell reddened ever so slightly. She closed her mouth, and shook her head."

"It's nothing, aye." She saw Katherine's determined look, and quickly relented.

"It's not for me to...I was only surprised that you've no swaddling on the child. Are you not concerned that his limbs may grow crookedly?" Katherine smiled.

"Och, we don't hold with binding the limbs in this part of the world, Jean. And if you look about you while you're here, you'll see naught but comely straight forms and figures. I was never bound, myself! Sure, God

SHANE O'NEILL

will mould him and prosper him like his father before."

Lady Jean smiled now as she recalled the gesture she had made upon her arrival but a short while ago. After the custom, she had put a golden coin into the baby's fist to see if he would grasp it. "Aye, well...He took a fine grip of that gold sovereign. He'll surely prosper! You'd swear he knew the worth of it!" They laughed freely.

"He has a Scots temper as well! Oh, Jean, how was your crossing? I know how you dread the sea!" Jean settled herself on the high-back chair, and folded her hands demurely in her lap.

"The seas were choppy. And little wonder for the rough and gusty day we had. But I never lost sight of the land, so it wasn't as bad as the high seas. I'd never dreamed Ireland was so close to the Western Isles! But the roads here! Glory oh!" Kat rolled her eyes.

"Roads? They're naught but cow paths!"

"Heath, and bog, and forest!"

"And bog, and *bog!*" Kat used a deep slow voice, and the two laughed merrily. She pulled back the tartan from her shoulders and draped it back over the chair. The nursing had left her frock disheveled, so she tidied it, and tossed back a few stray locks of auburn hair. Lady Jean sat forward in her chair. Her voice was low, in the half whisper of a conspirator.

"Oh Katherine, does your heart not ache for Edinburgh?"

"Ah no, Jean, not I. This is far more like my home in Duart. I only miss the sea. The odd time I'll see Lough Neagh in tempest, when it whitens under the wind, and I long-" She cast her glance to the door where Colin had arrived with the wine and crystal goblets. She nodded him over to the small table nearby. "No, no, the briny air is what I miss." As she rose from her chair, she addressed the lad. "Thank you, Colin, I'll pour. That will be all."

He nodded and barely muttered, "Yes M'Lady," as he turned on his heels and sauntered off. Katherine decanted the wine liberally, and wore a saucy smile as she presented Jean with her glass.

"I've had weeks upon weeks of buttermilk! Salubrious, but dreary!" Lady Jean took a wee sip, and when her hostess was seated, assailed her again with sedition.

"Would you not come back, Katherine, now while he's away? Mary says you needn't return to your husband. You could go to your father in Duart."

"I would *not*!" Kat was quite taken aback by the suggestion, but she supposed that Jane would know little of her true circumstance.

"I would coax you back to Argyle, but Archebald is still in a temper!" They both laughed now with wicked glee. Kat leaned forward, playfully combing her long tresses with slow claw-like fingers, and declaimed slowly in a voice of sly witchery, "I spoiled his wee plan!" She rubbed her hands together, and then clasping them round an imaginary ladle, she churned the air before her. "Stir the pot! Stir the pot!" Jean shrieked with laughter, and as it subsided, she wiped away a few stray tears.

"Oh, how could you *do* it, Kat? I would *die*! 'This is never our Katherine' I said. Och, he was fit to burst! Said you made him look the fool in London. Even the Lairds were howling for his blood. What came over you, girl?"

"Came over me? Mary wants me to leave Shane?"

"Don't be cross with me, Kat. I have her letter here. I thought it was a chance to see you." She quickly shuffled through the embroidered bag at her side, and produced a slim book. Pressed within its pages was the letter from Queen Mary Stuart. Katherine accepted it delicately with her fingertips, and crossed over to the window to read it. She broke the seal, and was not impressed to see that the missive comprised barely half a page.

"A bit scant! Barely a scrape of the quill!" Katherine read silently at the window as Lady Jean watched her face. Kat looked up with an indignant frown and quoted from the royal dispatch. "A disgrace before all Europe!' 'Your scandal has set back the Catholic cause!' Is she mad? The courts of Europe know nothing of these bogs. They've never *heard* of Shane!"

"Oh but they have! That was Elizabeth's great blunder. By parading him at Court, she's made him a Catholic champion. His name is uttered in every court in Europe now. Even Mary has hopes for him!"

SHANE O'NEILL

"Can that be true? If he comes safe home to me, perhaps some good may come of all the risk he has braved in going there."

"And yet in your very bed you are risking the support of Catholic Europe. These intimacies of yours have a political price." Katherine's eyes narrowed as she read again from the letter.

"Shameful adultery'...'Damned for eternity!' Bloody hypocrites!" Her lips were pressed white as she read on. "Ah! A royal command! '...or you shall never have leave to return to Scotland!" She tossed the letter aside and drank again of her wine. After a moment's thought she pronounced her response with a cool smirk. "Sail said the Queen. Stay said the wind!" With that, she went back to the sleepy fire in silence, and poked at the turf until a bright flame flared in the grate. She took her seat, and saw that Jean was looking mortified. "Oh, Cousin, it's a fool's errand that brought you to my door...but I'm that glad to see you!" Now her face brightened with a flash of inspiration. "You could...Jean, would you ever stand gossip to the child? Stay for the Christening?"

"Oh Katherine! Archibald would never forgive me!" She looked remorsefully to Kat, and saw a sly sparkle in the eyes of her otherwise serene face, a wicked gleam that emboldened her. "I will, of course!" They both laughed heartily over this wee conspiracy of defiance. Then she said, with a hapless smile, "But I must bring you back. It was a royal order."

"Let Mary look to her crown and her Kingdom, and I'll tend to my imperiled soul. I was bartered for policy, but she'll wed for love!" Katherine sat back. She watched the fire flicker through the crystal of her goblet for a quiet moment, and then she looked to Jean with lively curiosity. "And what of her own good self now she's a widow? I'm told that you're biding in Edinburgh these times. Has she a suitor?"

"Aye, so she has. All the Catholic princes of Europe! And even a mad Protestant prince from Sweden, who pesters her to peevish distraction." Kat sat forward now, her eyes wide.

"Erik? Is Prince Erik courting Mary?" Lady Jean was surprised that she knew of him.

"That's his name, aye. He showers her with lavish gifts, but Mary's having none of it. He's 'queer daft and fit for Bedlam', to hear her tell it."

"Does she know that he's wooing Elizabeth Tudor all the while?"

"*Is* he?" Jean's jaw dropped, and her eyes grew round with wonder.

"Shane wrote to me of his intrigues at Court. His brother, the Duke of Finland is at Whitehall, pleading his case, and pledging Erik's undying love. And even bribing officials to espouse his cause. I'm sure Elizabeth knows nothing of his attentions to Mary! But I can promise she will!" Lady Jean concurred, with a look of stern reproof for the prince.

"He has no hope of a betrothal in Edinburgh. Mary would never consider a heretical prince, even if she fancied him. She's keenly aware of her duties as a Catholic monarch. A crown is a heavy burden for a woman to bear." Kat's eyes flashed in a sudden show of pique.

"Mary will follow her heart! And so shall I. Twice I was wed for policy, and now I shall follow my heart, for I know well the tyranny of duty." Jean sipped her Cabernet, and considered her friend's intemperate remark. She tilted her chin, and rendered her judgement.

"There's a fierce change in you, Katherine. Your mother wouldn't know you."

"Aye, the daughter of the MacLean. Second youngest of nine. I was seventeen years when my father gave me to old Argyle to wed. Sixty-*four* he was! I was traded off to him so that my eldest brother could wive his daughter. Oh, aye! Archibald's sister Janet. That's how she came to be betrothed to our Hector Óg. She has my lost youth to thank! Sixty-*four*! Floods and torrents of tears I wept." Indeed, Katherine's eyes were brimming even now at the memory of her travail. Lady Jean's hands were again folded primly on her lap. Strangely, this emotional outburst elicited from her distance rather than empathy.

"He left you a fine title."

"When auld Campbell died and left me 'Dowager Countess' I could have made a match. But Mary and your Archibald had a wee plan. Did you know that O'Donnell paid your husband 400 Scots marks per anum for this tidy wee countess? I begged Mary not to let him marry me off to O'Donnell. I went to Paris and pleaded with her. Another withering wilting auld pisscock of a man!"

SHANE O'NEILL

"Och, Katherine!" Jean crossed herself hastily. "God save us!"

"Our Mary! I begged her! She talked of 'duty', 'personal sacrifice'. Well, I've made the sacrifice. I've *been* the sacrifice. I have a man now. Here I stay."

"Have you? My husband tells that O'Neill is married to your stepdaughter. Could that be true?"

"Aye. Cullagh's snivelly wee daughter..." Katherine sipped again at her wine, and sighed to think on yet another 'brier in her garden'.

"It's true, then?" Jean's arched brow only spurred Kat to shock her with further revelations. She nodded boldly.

"But that could be annulled. Moya O'Donnell could bear Shane no children. She's a dry peevish wee thing with no hips. They say she's in a convent now, and that her wits have gone astray since Shane put her aside. But he tells me that she was tightly strung, and near to madness always."

"How dreadful!" Lady Jean's hand covered her mouth.

"I have a son. My wee Hugh. A fine healthy son. And I'll bear more sons for Shane O'Neill. With or without royal leave! Or a priest's blessing!"

"I'm casting no blame, Katherine. You know yourself, that I was born out of wedlock. 'The king's bastard' and then, 'the queen's bastard sister,' I understand these circumstances, but I know well the cost of them. What of the church? You can't take the sacraments. Where will that leave your immortal soul?"

"It's different out here, Jane. The Gaelic church. They would never deny me the sacraments. You see, not all marriages here are blessed. We have older laws. Marriage is a matter for the Brehon Law, rather than Canon Law. And maybe that's as it should be, for I'm told that Jesus spoke little of such things." Jean frowned, and shook her head. With a single tisk, she quoted from scripture, slowly enunciating each word.

"What God hath joined together, let no man-"

"That was all St. Paul! And sometimes I think his noddle took a knocking when he fell from that horse! Old Farleigh, our bard, says that morality has naught to *do* with sex. 'It is the mastery of Love over greed,' he says, and I'm inclined to agree with him." Kat laughed, but clearly her guest was not amused. "Ach, I know little of such things, Jean, but I know that a marriage can be more than a bondage contract of dowries and alliances."

Lady Jean put down her goblet. She looked quite stunned. "You've not gone over to the reformed kirk! Surely, you've not!

"I have *not*! God knows they're worse still." Kat folded her arms and sat back in her chair. "He hates women! This John Knox and his angry book...The First...?" Kat looked to her friend to jog her memory. Jean obliged.

"The First Blast of the Trumpet-" Kat chimed in.

"-Against The Monstrous Regiment of Women!' He even rails against the Blessed Mother because she's a woman. That crowd! They're dry as dust! And I've heard that he's quite mad. A raging berserker they say!"

"That he is. Aye, I know him well...to my cost!" Jean went silent for a moment, as she coaxed aside her pride and resolved to speak of her own heartbreak. "I've no doubt you heard something of our great row last year." Katherine nodded solemnly. "Archibald and I, well it had been building for some years...in truth. Last Whitsuntide, in the kirk, he accused me publicly of adultery! Of course it was a lie, and he's a great whoremonger himself. You can well imagine my devastation, Katherine! His pastor, this mad preacher John Knox, intervened, as he said, to save our marriage. He put his bony hands on my face...on my *face*, and called me a filthy whore. He said I was in league with Satan and his minions in Rome. He spoke of 'shameful Eve', and of the 'foul pestilence of the weaker sex', and tried to banish some demonic spirit from my soul. I can tell you, I was frightened to death! He publicly reconciled our marriage, but he made Archibald pledge never again to sleep with me, to punish me for my wickedness!"

"Oh, Jean! I had no idea! Such madness!" Katherine was genuinely shocked. "And all this because you refused to give yourself over to their heresy!"

"No, then, Katherine. It's something quite else." She averted her eyes, and swallowed hard. "It's a childless marriage. I'm barren, and he'll not forgive me for it."

"Perhaps it's *himself* that is unable to beget, and he's wont to blame you! Wouldn't that just be the price of him!"

"No." Lady Jean shook her head slowly, and then raised her eyes. "No. His many bastards prove that the fault lies with me." Her voice was a bit choked with emotion, so she took a deep breath, and managed a wan smile. "Thank God our Mary came back to Scotland last August. Since her return, I've been at Court with her in Holyrood. They tell me he has taken a mistress." She laughed weakly. I suppose I hoped that I could coax you to Edinburgh, for we're in sore need of your light heart, and your winsome ways!" Katherine's cold words about Moya O'Donnell's barren hips came back to her now, and she blushed with shame.

"Oh, Jean! Will you ever forgive me? Here am I, with my healthy babe, crying in your ear! I never bethought myself!" Jean closed her eyes and shook her head.

"Don't spare it a moment's thought. You've not had an easy road!"

"But there's nothing, no royal summons, that could take me from Shane's side. If Mary doesn't understand that, then it's a lesson for the learning."

"But you'll be exiled forever." Lady Jean smiled, and coaxed with a soft voice. "Come back for a wee while. I'll take your part with Archibald and Mary!"

"Archibald? If Archibald is vexed at me so much the better! Shane took Donegal. And I spoiled their wee plan." Katherine's face softened now, as well as her tone. "Right enough, I *have* changed, Jean. I'm no longer a pawn. That's what I was. Square to square, shunted blindly across the board. But no longer, my girl. Now I shall play with the best of them. And I have a King. Tell that to Queen Mary!"

SHANE O'NEILL

CHAPTER 12

It was a fresh spring morning in Londontown. Sprouts, and sprigs, and tender shoots speckled the ways and byways of the city with their delicate green promise. The markets of Cheapside were bustling, thronged with scurrying shoppers, nimble errand boys, strollers, draymen, dogs, and vagrants. Shrill morning sunlight slid and sparkled down the bright-colored awnings and bounced on the cobbles, dappling the vivid motley of the crowd. The brisk air, too, was astir with the eager calls of the higglers and hagglers, gawkers and hawkers, and the clipclopping traffic that jostled and trundled along the thoroughfare. Farleigh beheld it all with a crinkly smile.

"Well, it was a relentless hoor of a winter, and 'glory be' to the Powers above, we've seen the last of it! Just when my creaky aul bones were about to give out." Will Fleming cocked his head to survey the brilliant blue skies.

"A grand day, aye."

"When I was a lad, winter was a green drizzly affair, with seldom even a hoarfrost. You're too young to recall it so. But each year it blows colder, Will, and I'd hate think on the blizzardy times to befall when my days are done." Farleigh closed his eyes tight and filled his lungs with the lush fragrant breeze that was tossling and thrumming his beard. He smiled again. "But still and all, on the shiny side of the shilling, a hard winter gives you a wild taste for the springtime. My blood is singing like a mountain stream!" He turned and halted now, for Will was adjusting his small bundle of purchases, mostly silks and brocades for the wife at home. With a shrug and a shift, Fleming resumed his pace, and offered his own thoughts on the matter.

"I'd say it's lifted O'Neill's heart as well. He was under some woeful dark cloud this while back, and now he's light and easy and whistling jigs."

"Was he?" The old poet pulled in his chin, and raised his shaggy brows. "I thought he was holding up grand! Would you say that, now?"

"I would. If you'd gotten the rough side of his tongue, you'd know to the differ." Will turned to him with a doubtful squint. "Do you not see the change in him this week and more?"

"Ah, well...He had a great worry on him over Lady Katherine. She's all of twenty-six, and that's a bit long in the tooth to be bearing a firstborn. Now she's delivered of it, healthy and whole, he's settled in himself again." Farleigh was about to dismiss the matter, when he hit upon the crux of it. With a sudden light in his eye, he added portentiously, "And he has some *plan* afoot!"

"Is that the way of it? What sort of a plan is he at then?

"There I leave you. Not a word have I heard of it. He was talking some notion about 'power and secrecy' the way of the Queen's ministers, so he's keeping close to himself. It's little good he'll learn by the ways of this Court!" Will harrumphed, and followed on with a sly wink.

"Secrecy is a fine thing when you're doing what you aughtn't! That's why it's so rife about the Court. This little 'plan' would account for Shane's restored humours. Returning from Mass yesterday, he was lilting one of Blind Colm's airs, a thing I haven't seen him do since we crossed the Blackwater."

"Right enough, Will, now I think back upon it, you're not wrong. This last month and more, waiting on these hearings, he was like a man adrift in a dead calm at sea. Huffing and puffing to raise a wind. But now he's struck upon this plan, and it's put a sharp gleam in his eye. He fired off a spate of letters filled with orders and instructions for Dualta Donnelly, and the tanist Turlagh and the rest, so I'm thinking it's some

SHANE O'NEILL

foxy maneuvers against the Pale. What's this he said? He said 'now that they've broken the safe conduct, all covenants are in the fire! What the devil is going on up here?"

Farleigh halted abruptly. The thoroughfare up ahead was congested, for the traffic had stopped, and the crowds seemed to be milling and dawdling. "We'll never get through this throng. Will we cut through the lane?"

"They're cheering someone. Do you suppose it's that mad Swede, tossing silver about?" Just then, two fairly genteel men came jostling past. One of them butted against Will's shoulder, and his plumed cap went tumbling onto the cobbles. Will retrieved it, and handing it back to him, inquired brightly, "Beggin' your pardon, what's all this hurly-burly in the road above?"

"They say that the wild Irishman O'Neill is approaching. He's abroad with the Lord Mayor, and the Queens favorite is at his side." He brushed the cap along the hem of his doublet, blew on the feather, and clapped it on his head. "Much obliged. This will be a rare sight! He is known to exceed the King of Barbary for savage splendour! He goes bare-legged as a highlander, with wolf-skins on his back!" His portly friend looked on impatiently.

"I have heard honest men swear that he eats of human flesh! Come you, or we shall miss his passing!" They nodded farewell as they turned, and hurried along to join the milling crowd. Fleming laughed and turned back to meet Farleigh's grin.

"Come on with you, O'Gneeve. Let's follow them. We'll see how the Saxon's will like this bloodmad barbarian in his frippery and scarlet hose!"

They scurried after the others, and shuffled in among the crowd. In the centre of the broad street there loomed an elaborate three-tiered water conduit adorned with stone sculptuary, and little else could be seen over the plumes and bonnets around them. Now, a crowd is a fluid entity, with its sudden eddies and its slow serpentine currents to be maneuvred, and the two Irishmen soon found themselves quite at sea. Will grabbed Farleigh by his long fluted sleeve, and tugged him along

SHANE O'NEILL

out of the heaving mass, til the pair staggered up onto the broad stone steps of a church, like so much flotsam washed upon a shore.

As they stepped up, they were delighted to be looking out over the crowd where the whole vista could be enjoyed. The street was lined with ornate four and five story tudor dwellings, with timber cladding and steep gables above, and shops and stalls below. Approaching from the west, Shane and his illustrious entourage could indeed be seen, with standard bearers before, and a guard of stern gallowglass following closely in their wake. Farleigh scratched his head.

"Now, where do you suppose he's off to?"

"He's dining with the Lord Mayor today in Lombarde Street up beside 'the Pope's Head.' Will relished his bits of news as an insider, and he loved to get one over on Farleigh, who was so clearly an intimate of O'Neill's.

"A bit early for dining!" Farleigh shaded his eyes with a crooked salute.

"How did that come about, I wonder."

"Sir William Harper, the mayor is called. O'Neill met him when he was knighted by the Queen a month ago. Around the feast of St. Valentine, as I recollect. He's a droll little fellow, and O'Neill was quite taken with him. Did you not *know* that?" Farleigh's eyes rolled, unseen under their shaggy white brows.

The crowd was roaring its approval, and among those close at hand, Farleigh noted a familiar voice. He peered over his shoulder, and who should be standing on the steps above but the two gents who had tipped them word of O'Neill's approach. When Will Fleming saluted them, they smiled and made room, beckoning him and Farleigh to join them on their loftier perch. Being a Palesman, and a barrister at that, Fleming's attire did not betray him as an outlander.

"The town's astir!" Will clapped his arm. "You've found yourselves a fine crow's-nest to see the grand procession."

"Aye! They're thick as flies, but we'll escape a crushing here!" The tall man had evidently given up on his cap, for it was not to be seen. "Godsblood! Could that be him?"

SHANE O'NEILL

Shane could not be missed in his scarlet doublet astride a shining black Arabian stallion, his own black hair tossled in the breeze and his right arm aloft in a proud greeting to the cheering throngs. The bejeweled hilt of his sword sparkled in the sun, and he was indeed a sight to behold. The Lord Mayor and Lord Dudley rode a few paces back on either side of him, so there was no mistaking the object of the crowd's excitement. Even Shane's ensign with its bloody red hand preceded the Lord Mayor's flag, and Dudley's banner as well. Will Fleming smiled.

"Aye, that's the O'Neill riding to the fore!" He winked at Farleigh, his silent companion, who would eagerly await his report of all that was said here in the strangers' tongue.

"In truth, he's a valiant looking man!" The tall fellow turned to his friend. "If this be the savage barbarian, there will be a new mode among the courtiers! He bears himself as stiffly as any lord. And he wears the high fashion most comely."

"He's a rascally looking churl, with a scornful eye." The stout fellow took a more dubious view. "And he struts with the airs of a Castillian Don. 'Tis said the Queen is partial to a handsome face, but God forbid she lay her trust in *him*! His heart is wolfish. That's plain to be seen! Look you his roguish scowl!"

Shane passed by now, smiling only in his eyes. His jaw was set firm and his demeanor was proud. Farleigh and Will waved with the rest, and Shane's clear gaze seemed to fall directly upon them, but if he saw them, he gave no sign of it. The cheering reached its crescendo and began to ebb. The taller gent peered scornfully now at MacSweeny and his fierce company of gallowglass.

"A frowsy lot, these savages! If O'Neill has learned his manners at Court, these kerne are unhampered by such graces. But still, their lord's mien bespeaks nobility. Now he is reconciled to his duties and his Queen, she may well have luck of him! He has as brave an eye as any true man! His every action does beseem him well! She may yet need him to vanquish the Spaniards."

"Aye, tis very like we may sweat with the Dons, and if there be valor in this wild Irishman, we shall have need of it. And of his savage heart withal." The tall man stepped down before them, and turning back to take his leave, he looked up at Will Fleming.

"Did I not tell you it would be a rare sight?" Will nodded.

"You did, aye. We're most grateful! Good day to ye both."

"Now you have seen him! The most boisterous blade in Christendom!"

The roaring din subsided as the Lord Mayor's cavalcade turned into the shadowy narrow streets of Cornhill Ward, leaving the heady crowds of Cheapside behind them. Sir Will Harper and his aide rode forward to lead the way, and Dudley trotted along next to Shane. He looked over, and nodded approvingly.

"In truth, you've fair won them over! Such a clamour is rare indeed! And without tossing silver among the throng!"

"Oh ho! I have news of this hapless rival of yours, Robert! And I think that silver will not save him!" Shane's grin was triumphal. "Jean Stewart, sister to the Scottish Queen, avows that this same Prince Erik is also courting Mary Stuart!"

"He is undone! He is undone!" Dudley laughed heartily. "Is it so?"

"I have it sworn. He has been wooing her with gifts and promises since before the Christmas."

"I will have Randolph in Edinburgh to confirm this, though I fear he will take fire from Elizabeth for not uncovering it." Dudley laughed again. "Oh ho, indeed! This is all she will need to send the Swedes apacking! I promise you, John, her Majesty will be most grateful for your news! And bestly, we shall have Cecil and his faction confounded! Yet another of his schemes to miscarry so!" Dudley threw his head back and laughed again. "They are already deep in turmoil with this delegation of student petitioners from the Pale. Could you but see them, John, I swear you would piss yourself proper! A gaggle of pale scrawny young Dublin law students, wet behind the ears, and they are holding Sussex' feet to the fire with their twenty-four articles of malfeasance. They press and press, and will not cease to hold him culpable for the miserable state of the Pale!"

"He would be a fool to underestimate the little Dublin squireens! Cute hoors they are, like their sires, devious and sharp-witted."

"When their hearings are done, I shall entertain them in grand style! They must be afforded the honour of your company, John, with your harper and the rest. But it would hardly be prudent before that time, for Cecil would surely cry collusion."

"Aye, they would be scuppered altogether. My barrister's nephew, Christopher Fleming, is among them, and I have given Will strict orders to stand aloof. But what of my hearing? I was told that when Sussex arrived, my grievances against him would be heard formally."

"There will be no hearing on your charges, alas. A private inquest is underway. They will review the accusations you've leveled in your deposition, and issue a report of their findings." He could see a flash of ire in Shane's eyes. "But her Majesty wishes see you this week! An audience in her Presence Chamber, to consider those issues wherein you seek redress. Your courtly attire, and your news of the Swede's double dealings will surely stand you in good stead!"

"Oh, here is a sight! Our wild Irishman makes a proper comely English gentleman!" Elizabeth beamed radiantly at her Court in the presence chamber of Whitehall Palace. Seated on a broad Roman chair with its inverted arches of oak, she was surrounded by her smiling ministers of state. Lord Cecil stood at her shoulder, with Sidney and Sussex at either side, along with Bacon and the rest, all planted firmly on the plush red carpet. Her ladies were present, as well as a number of courtiers. Noticeably absent was Sir Robert Dudley.

SHANE O'NEILL

"Mark you what goodly effect John O'Neill's time at Court has wrought! The tailor, too, must we credit for plying his art, with stitch and snip and needling done, til outward show does now conform to the noble spirit within!" There was soft laughter and gentle applause. Shane stood proudly before her, with his genial smile. "Good John, tomorrow being the Sabbath, you would do us much honour to accompany us! Will you escort your Queen to the Service of Common Prayer?" With this prickly challenge, the eyes of her smiling courtiers narrowed now, betraying perhaps just a tingle of bloodlust. Such a covert opening thrust by the Queen signaled that they might soon have at him. Shane replied with artful diplomacy, breezy and bright.

"It does her Majesty honor and wins her grace to attend such service, and yet...for *me* to breach a precept of my church would imperil my soul. I must decline." Elizabeth smiled coldly and tilted her head.

"And when you attend mass each day in the Spanish Embassy, does Bishop DeQuadra discuss the state of your soul? Or is it matters of state that require his conferral and blessing!" Shane flashed her a roguish smile as intimate as a wink.

"We are sinners all, every son of Adam.' Her eyes flared.

"*Are* we? Are we *indeed*! What says deQuatro of whoring and wenching? Is it true that your queen is the only woman at Court that you have not wooed?"

"I have not yet departed, your Majesty!" Elizabeth laughed in spite of herself, and Shane continued. "My office is not to be a saint. The mild chief who would store up graces would soon have need of them. Indeed, he would find e'er long that his kingdom were not of this world!" Elizabeth laughed gaily now, and looked smiling to her ministers.

"Is this Irish charm, or more of Blarney?" They laughed obligingly, and she turned back to Shane with a coquettish smile. "You have a ready wit. A ready wit, for fair!" Shane shifted his weight with a subtle hint of physicality. He lowered his head and looked up at her with a sly grin.

"I stand ready from toe to top to serve my queen." There were gasps and giggles from the Ladies, but dark murmurs from the men, compelling Cecil to chance a thrust.

SHANE O'NEILL

"How does your Spanish confessor acquit you of sottish inebriety?" The others laughed, and, emboldened by the Queen's acquiescent smile, Sussex added *his* rebuke.

"Whoring and drunkeness do not trouble the Romish soul. His priest will absolve all!" The Queen rounded on him, stilling the incipient laughter of the crowd.

"Enough! We will not countenance a Puritan inquisition." Sussex' smile vanished. Shane's did not.

"Majesty, the matter is thus. My humours need the occasional combustion brought of spirits- and if this bloodless coxcomb mislikes it, so much the better. The fops and dandies of a Lady's Court in London will not make the fashion in the woods of Tirowen. In despite of these refineries, I am no courtier. I am the O'Neill."

"Ah! To matter! *Now* we come to it!" She sat back, her elbows out over the arms of the chair, tilting her head back so that she peered down her regal nose at him. "You have taken to yourself the proscribed title of the O'Neill, a title renounced for all time and ever by your father in this very court!" Her ministers edged in closer around her, leering with malice. Shane folded his arms, but his smile remained.

"Upon my father's submission, it is true that he did forfeit the lands of Tirowen unto King Henry, and renounced the ancient right of O'Neill-"

"Upon his rebellion!" Sussex' outburst was checked by a stern glance from her Majesty. When Elizabeth turned again to Shane, he continued in patient tones to explain the issue.

"The King did then grant to him those lands as the Earl of Tyrone- making him *owner* where he was before but an officer."

"But an *officer*?" She was genuinely perplexed. "He was the O'Neill, was he not?"

"The O'Neill is but a *captain* of his lands- by election of the people of Tirowen- from among the direct line of O'Neill blood. Under the law of the Brehons, *the only law* thus far established in Ulster, authority and power of his office is conferred by the people- so that the lands belonged to the people of Tirowen and *in keeping only* to my father's office.

SHANE O'NEILL

Legally, he could forfeit no more than his own interest which he had but during his life -and then, upon his death it was in the country to make a new O'Neill." After a momentary silence, Elizabeth turned her head and looked, smiling, over the high sparkly ruffs at her shoulder, to engage her expectant ministers. She spoke with caustic merriment.

"The power of governance is conferred by the *people*?!" Reassuring laughter filled the chamber, derisive and darkly excessive. "This barbarous system were not Law, but its very undoing! A base usurping of divine appointment! Lucifer was banished from Heaven for lesser affront!" Her riposte was met with a burst of genteel applause. Shane stood proudly, his composure undisturbed, awaiting silence. He nodded to acknowledge the Queen, and answered blithely.

"English Common Law is not established in my lands." The Queen turned to Cecil to explain or refute. He bent to her ear and spoke quietly.

"Ulster is not yet shired, your Majesty." Shane pressed his point.

"Even in the Pale and shireland, its writ does not allow protection to the Irish clans. We are not let avail of it, though it is commonly invoked against us." As the Queen considered, Sussex stepped boldly into the breach.

"Still, your assuming title of O'Neill upon your father's death did *usurp the rights* appointed by legal patent to Matthew O'Neill the Baron of Dungannon. There can be *no* dispute in this."

"Matthew's rights were themselves usurped." Shane turned back to Elizabeth and explained. "He was a bastard. He was fully sixteen years in age when his mother brought him forward." Sussex edged closer to directly engage Shane.

"Were he or were he not Conn O'Neill's son, yet he was so accepted and declared to be by your father." Again Shane addressed his remarks solely to her Majesty.

"My father considered it mannerly never to refuse such claims. And yet under English law *or* Irish law, this patrimony cannot be sustained...for this woman was married at the time of his birth. He was called Matthew Kelly until her husband's death, and only *then* presented

SHANE O'NEILL

to O'Neill. He is a Kelly. Any farmer in England will avouch, "The calf belongs to the owner of the cow- not to the owner of the bull."

Elizabeth raised her outstretched palm at her side to stay Sussex from responding. She sat forward, engaging the argument with spirit. "Yet he was granted a legal patent to succeed. Made not 'to male in tail' but directly to him. What say you now?" A sprinkling of tentative applause. Shane leaned back, his arms akimbo, and his eyes merry.

"That King Henry was deceived in the claim, and therefore it was not legally binding. No more nor should your Majesty be tricked, would she be bound to uphold a perjured claim." With a raised brow, Elizabeth turned to her courtiers, now this side, now that, to see what answer might be had. Finding only bemusement, she smiled at Shane.

"There is more in this than Irish glib. Your claim, if it bear closer study, mayhap might merit you an earldom!" Cecil cleared his throat, and her bright smile vanished. In its place appeared a smile of pity and condescension. "Alas, nothing can be determined until we examine the patents of Brian O'Neill, the undisputed heir, certainly, to the Baron of Dungannon, if not the Earl of Tyrone. He has been summoned, and will not be long in coming."

"You Majesty, I-" Elizabeth silenced Shane with her raised hand.

"Again, we see that you have made request to return into Ireland, and again we must bid you be patient. These matters demand a sound hearing and you must, perforce, bide with us for some time longer. We will submit these depositions to Council and consider us by their instruction. For now you may withdraw." Shane made a courtly bow.

"God save the queen's majesty!"

As Shane exited the room, Elizabeth whispered to Cecil, and he stepped forward to address those remaining in the Presence Chamber.

"Her Majesty thanks you all for attending this noonday audience." An attendant clapped twice, and all quickly made their way out, with an excited murmur that passed into the hall outside. The heavy oak doors closed with a dull clank, and the chamber fell quite silent. The queen's councilors moved casually down front where they faced her in a state of expectation. She cast her gaze serenely from one to the next, and

SHANE O'NEILL

stopped on Sussex who was clearly perturbed.

"And now, good Thomas, you may untwist your brow and loose your tongue." He clasped his hands tensely before him, white knuckled, as he tried vainly to muster his composure, and then he swung his arm out wildly in oratorical gesture.

"The man is a liar and a traitor!" He shook his head, as he settled upon a line of reason, and then suffered to explain, as if to a child. "If O'Neill is let prevail over the Baron, other chieftains will press their ancient dignities to rival the new peerages created by your father. To advance him were to imperil the entire stratagem of 'surrender and regrant', the first policy ever to bear us result in subduing Ireland. He must be extirpated. If O'Neill be overthrown all is settled. If he be settled, all is overthrown!" Elizabeth listened, huffing impatiently as he made each point. She stood now and faced him down.

"Could you but raise your eyes from the Irish bogs, my Lord Sussex, you might see what dangers loom to imperil our very kingdom! Look you East, where the princes of Catholic Europe conspire to undo us. Look you North, where sits their hope, Mary Stuart in Scotland, waiting to take our throne!" Elizabeth looked gravely to Cecil, who nodded solemnly. "We are *lately* informed that the Catholic lords of England do nightly conspire with Bishop DeQuadra at Durham House to foment a rising-up in this very realm against our Crown. And will you talk to us of Irish 'dignities'?" She turned now and paced. "If we spurn O'Neill's claims, he will surely combine with the Stuart Scots, and we shall find us besieged on three sides! Nay, then, my Lord Deputy, we have *other* plans for him. If he be drawn on with some honours, he can complish our ends for us. While yet he hopes in us he is our tool- and we shall ply him to good effect against the Scots." She looked to each now, as they nodded their agreement, but Sussex stood firm.

"My Lady, he will never forsake his Scottish alliances. He -above all other Irish captains- is tangled in their fortunes. His sister is wed to Sorley Boy MacDonnell. He keeps the Countess of Argyle as concubine. She has forsaken O'Donnell, and born a son to O'Neill only this fortnight past. Scotch galloglass have made his front ranks in every battle. Indeed it were fair to say that the combination of Scots and Irish have kept Ulster the most Gaelic province, and have kept it from the civility of English governance."

"The greater reason to part them company!" She glared fiercely at Sussex, and quickly surveyed the fraught but acquiescent faces around her. Satisfied, she took her seat once again. "O'Neill affords us two strong reins to turn his head withal; ambition and pride." With a gentle voice, Sussex bravely ventured once more to dissuade her.

"But he has also charm and cunning. He has even now-" Elizabeth interrupted him with a hearty laugh, to the surprise of all.

"My doubting Thomas! Did you really think your queen to be cozened by the wiles of this Irish rogue?" They all laughed now, and with some relief, if truth be told. She looked up at him, with her brows arched in a condescending smile. He answered sadly, with resignation.

"Nay then, your Majesty. Your wisdom and prudence are known to all. And yet it grieves me that the ordering of that nation be deferred awaiting more propitious times, and yet again we must temporize with rebels and traitors."

"Have heart, Lord Sussex. When this danger to our realm is passed, then will we turn us to Ireland. And there will be lands and honours aplenty for Englishmen. We will plant it with loyal subjects, and till it with husbandry and zeal til it be another England -in dress and tongue and habit, and like also in conformity to the reformed Church." She sighed, and rose again from her chair. "For today there is matter enough to fill our docket. And We are weary. When you have finished your testimony before the tribunal on Tuesday, take you hence to Ireland, Thomas. We will keep the grand disturber with us for some while -in his state of expectation. You may find him grown civil and English on his return into Ireland." Upon seeing that he was about to respond, she raised her chin and glared. "*Godspeed!*"

SHANE O'NEILL

CHAPTER 13

"Jesu! Here is the very spark to set all Europe aflame!" Elizabeth's bejeweled white hand was pressed firmly to her brow. When she opened her eyes, they were moist and fearful. "And 'massacre' was his word?" Cecil nodded solemnly.

"Throckmorton writes from Paris that the toll of death swells at each telling, from many hundreds and even unto thousands. And yet, by his own reckon, it stands but three score dead, and several hundred of wounded." Elizabeth's tense hands curled into fists before her, the knuckles whitening in fury.

"There is massacre *enough!*" She turned sharply to her ladies in waiting who were seated at the window embrasure. "Leave us." When the doors of her privy chamber had closed behind them, she turned her eyes to Lord Cecil. "A massacre of Protestants! Mary Stuart's uncles by their burning papist zeal will bring all Europe to cinders!" She lowered her voice portentously. "And who can know what sparks may blow from Calais to stoke the hateful embers that smolder hereabout. What befell there to incite the fray?" Cecil laid the embassador's letter on the writing desk before her. Her brows raised, she picked it up and read it with pursed lips and a growing scowl.

Elizabeth slapped the desktop with a loud thwack. "We have no monies to fight war in France, else we should have Calais long ago! The Duke de Guise has ruffled his feathers, and so must every prince rally to war! Nay, then, we shall sue for peace." Her burning eyes peered off through the grey spring rain that pattered and trickled down the windows, as she passed a long moment in her dark ruminations. Cecil knew better than to intrude upon her thoughts, and he gazed idly upon the sumptuous trappings of her bedchamber, noting the discrete door that was said to lead to Dudley's apartments. At length, she sat back with a triumphal smirk.

"Aye, we shall sue for peace. If Throckmorton be so bent upon war, we shall send Sir Thomas Smith to treat for us, and we shall sue for *peace*. But e'en so, we shall firstly level a broadside, such as our scant treasure will afford us. Send you word to his niece Mary Stuart that this interview she so craves is rendered null. We do decline to see her! And give as reason the bloody war her family wages against the Protestant faith. Aye, and let you publish it forth so that her Calvinist subjects may know of it, that she might totter some small bit more on her wobbling throne in Scotland."

"A wise decision. Indeed, your Majesty, such deft strokes of policy can oft outweigh a cannonade!" Cecil stood patiently before her desk, nodding his approval.

"Here is further cause to banish her Scotch legions out of Ireland. We shall force John O'Neill to complish *that* end for us. And so doing, he will sever himself from the kindly graces of Mary Stuart for good and all! Thus shall we scotch them both. And undo this cursed threat at our back, this dark cloud rumbling always, *always*, in the West." Her bitter smile faded. "And still must we keep wary watch, leeward and windward, fore and aft, with papist plotters on every side!" Elizabeth looked up with sudden purpose. "What of DeQuadra's peevish little monk? Where is this letter he has furnished? We must hope that it is genuine."

"We are satisfied it be so. I have the translation to hand. In truth, I think it more damning to King Philip than to his Ambassador." Cecil shuffled through the folio before him and quickly produced the document. "Third of April, 1562. To Cardinal Grenvelle." He squinted over the page. "Ah, here! 'Shane O'Neill and ten or twelve of his principal followers have received the Holy Sacrament in my house with the utmost secrecy, as he refused to receive the Queen's Communion. He has assured me that he is, and will be, perfectly steadfast on the question of religion. *As to the rest*, if his Majesty should intend to mend matters here radically, as he writes me from Spain, this man will be a most important instrument!" He laid the parchment before the Queen, but she did not examine it.

"Ha! Philip would 'mend matters' in our Kingdom! And make an 'instrument' of our Irish rebel! O'Neill's papistry and his 'secret' Mass are known to all. But this evidence of King Philip's scheming shall prove a trump, when next we take a hand with him! Has he furnished further revelations of these popish plots?" She saw that Cecil was fidgeting with his old complaint. "Sit your gouty bones *down* then, if you be ailing so!" He drew up a chair and seated himself before her impatient gaze.

"The bishop's secretary? I fear there is little more to be gained there. After bestowing upon me this letter, the friar undertook to resume his office in Durham House where he was pledged to make espials in our cause. But alas, the crafty bishop was forewarned of his betrayal. Though I am loath to say it, DeQuadra has planted spies within our very Court. Friar Borghese relates that when he resumed his duties, the Ambassador, feigning amity and forgiveness of their quarrel, directed him to undertake a mission to Spain, doubtless to be killed, as he insists. Thereon the fearful monk fled the Embassy to bide here at Court for a time. My men are pressing him for details even now." The Queen tilted her head and arched her brows in a dubious smirk.

"What then, will he reveal aught now in cool temper that he withheld in his hot rage?" The Secretary nodded gravely.

"Aye, most like he divulged all he knew with the letter. But, as for the rest, the comings and goings, he was privy only to names. DeQuadra is too shrewd a hand to entrust vital confidences in a waspish and prickly servant."

"That vile bishop is sent by Philip to spy for Mary, and for the League of Catholic Powers. And now he has set his spies rustling in our very skirts, that they do hear our secrets, even to espy our spies! *You*, my Lord Secretary, have entrusted in our service some secret Catholic in the pay of Spain." Elizabeth challenged him with a cold menacing stare.

"Rest assured, we will find him out, your Majesty!"

"We will rest assured when you have done so!" She smiled warmly now, and sighed deeply. "Oh, my Spirit! We fear your duties are too broad and numerous to fully attend to this web of intrigue that is spun around the Court. It is out of hand. For want of a cat the mice are dancing underfoot! Find us a cat, we charge you, Lord Cecil, who will match his cunning. And find him out!" She layed her finger over her lips for moment of concentration, and then looked up brightly. "What of that devilish dark young imp, that I spoke of?"

"Walsingham?"

"The slyboots, tall and lank. 'Tell a lie, and find the truth', he said!"

"Aye, Walsingham. He is on a diplomatic mission for me. I shall recall him, and set him to the task."

"Something must needs be done! Smart and quick!" Her eyes softened instantly, as did her tone. "Still, this monk has given up names of the Catholic peers who consort with DeQuadra, has he not? Who does he name?"

"Westmoreland, Northumberland, Montague, and possibly Derby."

"Is not Montague brother-in-law to Kildare?" She looked to Cecil's nod. "O'Neill, too, is doubtless party to this intrigue. King Philip's ready 'instrument'!" Elizabeth's jaw was clenched, and a shadow twitched in her cheek. Cecil thought best to strike a more encouraging note.

"We have the names. And more important still, those other foul things not agreeable to the office of an Ambassador; the grievous insults to your Majesty, written in DeQuadra's hand, in letters bearing his seal! This were no trifle, as diplomatic affairs are counted." Elizabeth sighed, and relaxed back into her chair, her face alight with a devious smile.

"Aye! We are *glad* to suffer his spite! For the discovery of such a breach of diplomacy shall serve us nicely as grounds for his prompt removal to Spain! We shall soon see the last of this meddling bishop!" A sudden notion brightened her smile. "That is two! Mary Stuart turned away, and Bishop DeQuadra turned out!"

"And your erstwhile suitor, Prince Erik of Sweden! Is he so soon forgot? You may count his minions too among the banished!" At this, the Queen laughed and clapped her hands together.

"Ha! They too are turned away! A goodly swat to all pests that would pester us!" Cecil smiled bitterly at his dashed hopes for the Swedish prince, but to assuage his volatile mistress he was obliged to cheer the misadventure as though he had effected it.

"The Chancellor Guildenstern and Duke John of Finland have been served of their papers. The diplomatic mission is closed, and they sail for Skandia on the morning tide!"

"Huzzah! But for Robin Dudley's vigilance I should never have known of Erik's double-tongued courtship! Oh, he is 'my Eyes'!" She saw the mirthless smile fade from Cecil's face. "-As *you* are my 'Spirit'!" Elizabeth was jubilant now. "That is three! Out! Out! Out!" Elizabeth laughed gaily as distant bells told the turning of the hour. "When does our Privy Council sit?"

"At two of the clock, your Majesty. Shall I withdraw til then?" The Queen nodded.

"We shall have much to settle anon. We must send an embassage to treat with Catherine De Medici that we may quell the growing flames of Vassy. For now, you may withdraw." Cecil made to speak, and then closed his mouth. He nodded his perfunctory bow, and turned to leave."

"Lord Cecil!" The Secretary spun back around at the sharpness of her tone. "There is something more. Tell us straight what is left unsaid."

"I thought best to leave it await the Council's attention. A small matter regarding John O'Neill."

"There are *no* small matters where O'Neill is concerned! What, then? Some further mischief we must endure?"

"I have word from Sussex of troubles out of the North. And... O'Neill's hostages have excaped Dublin Castle."

"God's teeth! Again we are undone! We are foiled by papish spies and bribed guards! Betrayed on every front! These hostages were Lord Sussex' charge, and once more he has failed us!" Again the Queen's white hand lay across her brow, with eyes shut tight against the world. When she opened them, she looked up with fire. "Go to! Go to! Let the

SHANE O'NEILL

Irish mice scurry away then, for still we have the rat in our keeping! O'Neill -that 'instrument' of King Philip- is little more than hostage here, and *he* shall not stir for quite some while! If, indeed, he shall *ever* be loosed!"

The stables of Benburb Castle were already full, when a mudspattered but elegant carriage rolled through the gates. Braving a sudden downpour, two grooms hurried to attend as the team came to a halt before the arching entrance of the keep. The horses were blowing, and a haze of steam rose from their withers after a hard ride. The carriage door swung open, and the distinguished Dean of Armagh emerged, followed by the two young clerics who assisted him. They dashed inside, to be greeted by his aunt, Bríd Donnelly, who ushered them into the Council Chamber.

The room was more than full, with many standing against the walls and huddled into corners. The close air was heavy with the smell of wet wool and sweat, mingled with the spicey scent of burning turf. The tanist Turlagh O'Neill was speaking, but heads turned sharply as the Dean's presence was perceived. Those seated stood. Turlagh halted now, and turned his attention to welcoming the Dean.

"God bless you Dean Donnelly, we were afeard you weren't coming. We've only begun to broach our business."

"You've only begun? Then I'm sorry I've caused you such delay. The roads were quite impassable. I should have come on horseback, but I'm overing a cold. Caution over valour, alas!" Room was made beside the tanist, and the crowd parted before him as he stepped up to the head table. Upon reaching his seat, the cleric reached across and shook the hand of each of the three newly returned hostages, and a wild cheer was raised. The room came quickly to order when he raised his hand to offer

SHANE O'NEILL

a benediction. "God save all here! We offer our thanks to the Almighty for restoring to us Henry and Phelim and Dónal Gorm from their late captivity, and we ask that He bless us in our business here this day! In nomine Patre et Fili et Spiritu Sancti."

With a flutter of hands, the crowd blessed themselves, and murmured as one, 'amen'. Turlagh whispered to the Dean. He cleared his throat, and turned again to address the assemblage.

"His Eminence has been colloguing with O'Neill in a constant stream of letters since the day the chief departed, so he knows all the thorny details of the matter. He's made a hard journey coming to us today because what we do now will be crucial in solving this devilish impasse in London. Let us hear from him before we proceed." With that he seated himself, and all looked to the Dean. He was a figure to inspire confidence, a tall man of fine features, grey at the temples, with piercing dark eyes that told of ascetic depths, as well as compassion and strength.

"I bring you the blessings of Archbishop O'Tighe, the successor to St. Patrick in Armagh. He has asked me to tell you that you are all very much in his prayers, and that his special intention at Mass this morning was the success of this meeting, and of our mission here. These are dark days for the people of Tirowen, days of uncertainty and fear, when the O'Neill is held against his will in the land of the stranger. We have all stood powerless these many months, awaiting word of his return. And yet, today we may find some solace and cheer, in that it has fallen our lot to help him! I have before me Shane O'Neill's letter. He has bidden his tanist to assemble here the true and the trusted of Tirowen, so that we might act as one in strength and purpose to break this deadlock in London. The Queen has deceived O'Neill. She forbids him to return, in spite of a hard won safe-conduct that bears her seal. She has bidden him await the arrival of the Baron's son, even as she has instructed the Baron's son to remain in Ireland!" A dark murmur arose at this disclosure, a sound of anger and concern. "In short, the Queen has cast a cold eye on the O'Neill's offer of peace. The men of Tirowen will offer war, and she will look again to the terms of O'Neill." Deep whispers of alarm rustled through the crowd. "We need not *go* to war. We need only

SHANE O'NEILL

meet her deception with one of our own! We shall take measures to make the English believe that Turlagh here has usurped the office of O'Neill. That Shane O'Neill has been supplanted by a man who will come to *no terms at all!* When faced with the choice, this Queen will choose the devil she knows, and will send him home at once. If nothing else, she is frugal, and she will relish the thought of O'Neill and his cousin destroying each other in a dynastic feud, with no expense to her coffers." He leaned over to hear a quiet word from Dualta, the Marshal of Shane's forces, and looked up smiling. "Captain Éamon Donnelly will tell you of the plan we've contrived to do this, and of the part you must play." There was applause as Éamon, the youngest of the Donnelly brothers, stood now and turned to face the room. He was ruddy and craggy, with a wild look about him, for all his military bearing.

"Ye lot are here...because when word starts flying about that Turlagh has stepped into Shane O'Neill's rights, that he's made himself chieftain, we don't want ye taking up to defend Shane. As we know ye rightly would. What O'Neill wants is a bluff, and if it does the job, it needn't last but a month or two, and when he's back with us we can have a right good laugh. We need to give a fierce jolt to these hoors in London. Now, this sham can only work if they believe it, so ye's are all bound to secrecy. And it has the Dean of Armagh's blessing, so ye needn't trouble your conscience over deceiving the lyingest pack of hoors that ever lived. Ye's would not be here if ye were not trusted, but still ye should be advised... We have our own spies in Dublin Castle, so if anyone tips them word, we will know who that man is, and I needn't say more." Sly laughter rippled through the crowd, with nods and winks. "Here's what we'll do. There will be two great bonefires, wild massive, that will rise columns of smoke in the sky. They'll be seen for miles around. One here at Benburb, and the second at O'Neill's fortress on Inishdowel. That one will show clear across the lough. We'll fire off harquebus and set the big guns blazing and thundering. Turlagh and his captains from the West will lead a force marauding through the hills hereabout, so there will be bonafide witnesses. Sure you know, yourselves, they'll be busy telling all they saw, and more than they saw. There's divil a man, however prying

SHANE O'NEILL

or meddlesome, will stick his nose into a welter of gunfire, so we'll get no intruders, and the only story that will go out is the one our runners will tell. We'll want some men to scatter south. We'll need some fierce liars for that, and I see a few of ye out there!" This brought a good laugh, and several names were called out in jest. "We'll need women and children to flee into Dundalk in wagons, all with the one tale of a fierce battle here, and of the savage Turlagh stealing the reins of Tirowen. The story will *fly* through the hills. Ye have all heard it said that one dog will set all the dogs of the village barking! Aye, well that's our mission."

There was rowdy applause and cheering as he turned to his brother to see who would speak next. As it was settling, a familiar voice from the back called out, "Ho, Éamon, you're some crafty hoor, boy!" There was laughter then, but it settled when Shane's marshal, Dualta Donnelly, rose to take the floor.

"Aye, we'll set them all barking. But not only will we bark, we'll bite too! For, once that story is in the wind, Turlagh and his men will attack the Pale!" Cheering and whistles erupted at this prospect. "O'Neill has given orders for him to fire the Pale, and to demand the old 'black rents' from those outside the town. He'll demand it as the new O'Neill, and word will fly to Dublin Castle." There was more cheering now, and in the midst of it, Dualta saw Fergus O'Kane step forward from the doorway to speak. "Welcome, Fergus. Let us hear what the O'Kane has to say."

"Aye, I'll tell ye what he has to say. This scheme is good, and ye lot are the wily hoors to pull it off! But tell me this! What is the thing that is keeping O'Neill in London? Is it not the claims of Brian Kelly O'Neill, the bastard's son? Saving your presence, Dean Donnelly, but I say we Tirowen boys should send him to London. We should send him to London in pieces! Fine collops for the hounds!"

On the first clear day the charade was commenced, with ominous black smoke billowing high into the sky over the castle and the Lough.

SHANE O'NEILL

The thunder of guns echoed in the hills around, setting people to flight. In the castleyard itself, this was, inevitably, an occasion for sheer revelry and sport. A rake of drink was consumed, and there was mayhem all around, with the rowdiest competing to set off the biggest charges. Katherine had been taken to Shane's lodge at Fathann with the rest of the immediate household, so there was little to restrain the pandemonium. Less gleeful, of course, were the runners, and the wagonloads of ragtail refugees who crowded into Dundalk seeking shelter and telling their tales of woe. The resulting alarm was astounding, and the explosion of talk in that small seaport sent word flying in every direction by land and sea. The local Chief Constable lost no time dispatching a messenger who went galloping off to Dublin Castle.

Once the news was firmly established of this *coup d'etat* in Ulster, Turlagh unleashed his terror on the Pale. The northern skies were dark with smoke, and the wary denizens of the Pale looked to Dublin for help. Sussex was truly confounded, with few troops or provisions to send.

In a dockside public house in Dundalk frequented by soldiers and sailors, a stranger bellied up to the bar. His gait was unsteady and his English was chancy, laden with a heavy Gaelic 'brogue' that marked him as rustic from the Sperrins. He put good money on the bar, and called porter for those around him, an ingratiating gesture that assured his welcome.

As he fell into amiable discourse, he inquired earnestly about the next ship out to England. He was told by a sailor that a ship would be sailing on the next tide in little more than two hours time. It was noted by some that he had no luggage, save for a cloth satchel that he clutched tightly under his oxter. He called for whiskeybaugh for his new friends, and toasted to 'her gracious Majesty!' He told them what he knew of the

SHANE O'NEILL

fierce row above in Benburb. He told them that this new O'Neill was a wildman who would make Shane O'Neill look like a monk. He spoke strangely about all manner of things, and hinted of his important business in England.

As the drink flowed, the lads there were happy enough to humour the fellow, and winks were passed. 'A wild taig', as they said, 'but harmless enough.' He was putting it away at a fierce clip, growing less and less steady on his pins. After a time he made his way out the back to 'relieve his paunch', and when he returned, he staggered past them out the door, muttering about catching his ship to England.

After a fair while had passed, one of the soldiers discovered the fellow's satchel on the floor against the bar. Whether he had made it aboard or not, it was a certainty that the ship had sailed, and so the satchel was given over to the publican for keeping. By the usual way in such matters, he opened it to inspect the contents. It was nothing but a packet of letters, and as they might easily be sent on, he held one up to the lantern to make out the destination. He checked another, and another. Looking up with astonishment, he announced in hushed reverential tones, "These are letters to Shane O'Neill, for secret delivery in London!" The men were struck with wonder at the magnitude of the find. These very letters would be of great import to Lord Sussex, or even to the Lord Secretary in London. The publican himself was filled with feelings of destiny and grandeur. "*I'll* put a hobble on this boglord savage! See if I won't! Mind the shop for me, lad, whilst I run these across to the Chief Constable. He'll want to get them onto a fast horse for Dublin Castle!"

This was all the talk of the alehouse now, and as word spread, the place filled with dockers and townsmen wanting to hear the story first hand. There was conjecture as to who had written the letters, and what might be in them concerning the recent upheavals out there in the dark hills beyond the Pale. There was speculation and mocking jibes, too, about the poor fool of a courier, the drunken bogtrotter, waking up from his stupour out on the high seas, and finding his precious charge gone a missing. "Woe betide the poor besotted bastard! O'Neill will surely cut the ears off him if he be cought! The poor sod had best to jump overboard!" But the 'poor sod' was not on board the ship. He was galloping back to Benburb, whistling a merry jig.

A bright sickle moon slipped in and out behind low swift-moving nightclouds, casting its fleeting silvery gleam upon the river. At Shane's request, the wherryman hugged the shore, passing quietly through the shadows, with only the rhythmic slap of oars to intrude upon the stillness. Such sounds as did arise seemed strangely magnified over the lapping waters; the distant bark of a dog, and the squeak of water rats scurrying and sleeking about in the squalor along the banks.

As they reached the watergate of Durham House, Myler paid the oarsman his due, and fixed a time for his return. He did not moor the boat, but sculled alongside the submerged stone steps until the two Irishmen hopped nimbly up onto the narrow wharf. The wherry disappeared into the night, and O'Neill and his chaplain slipped discretely into the dark recesses of the doorway. A single knock brought the watchful attendant, who hurried them inside. He held the door ajar and gazed out over the river.

"Ha! Still they are there." Shane peered over his shoulder.

"Where?" From the dim vestibule he could see the dappled silver trail of the moon upon the water, and in its path, bobbing gently, the dark silhouette of a skiff with two men aboard.

"Those men are fishing, but not for fish. They have been there most every night since Borghese forswore the king. We must be mindful, Lord O'Neill, for some of our late visitors have been seized and held." He closed the heavy door, and took up a small candle that was flickering in a glass cup.

"Father Diego will see you up. His Eminence is expecting you." He led them between puddles across the damp tiled floor, and opened the arched inner door to the brightly lit reception chamber. A young Spanish priest, with eyes and hair as black as his biretta, was there to greet them. He smiled warmly, and gave a nodding bow to each.

"Lord O'Neill. Father Magrath. His Grace will be most happy to see you. If you please." He took their heavy frieze mantles and hung them in the massive oak wardrobe. "Come with me." He led them through various corridors along the customary path. "I hope you are both faring well." Shane disregarded his pleasantry.

"The messenger spoke of some urgency?"

"Everything is urgent now. That is all I can tell you, for that is all I know. Since this unfortunate business with His Grace's secretary, we are visited by crisis upon crisis. Letters and missives flying to every principality, and always urgent. Messengers coming and going until my head is spinning like a potter's wheel!" As he opened the door, Bishop DeQuadra could be seen rising from his desk to greet them.

"Come in. Come in." They stepped quickly into the chamber, and nodded respectfully as they shook DeQuadra's hand. He looked sharply to the priest. "Leave us." When the door had closed silently behind the young cleric, the bishop turned his back and walked casually and slowly to the liquor cabinet. He chose a decanter and poured an amber splash into three crystal glasses. "Brandy?"

"What is it, Your Grace?" Shane curiosity and mounting impatience were getting the best of him, for his tone was brusque. "I was asked to come immediately on some urgent business."

"I thought that this might be my last opportunity to speak with you." He handed a glass to Myler, and Shane appeared at his side to take the other. DeQuadra eyed him closely. "You haven't heard then."

"I've not. Have you been recalled to Madrid? All in the palace are laying wagers as to when you'll depart!"

"Are they indeed? No, no, no. Nothing of the kind. King Philip has instructed me to 'brazen it out' as they say. No. I think perhaps it is not I who will be departing, but you. I have several matters of grave concern to you. Sit. Sit." They both took their seats alongside the massive desk. Behind it, the bishop settled himself in his throne-like chair. "I received a letter today from your Dean, Terence Danyell, bearing some rather serious news. Your rival, the son of the Baron of Dungannon, is dead. Yes. Slain some days ago by certain of your followers." Shane was truly astonished, and quite elated. He cocked his brow at Myler, who was stunned as well. They both laughed, and Myler blessed himself in his laughter, saying, "God forgive me! Rest his soul." Shane looked to DeQuadra, who appeared somewhat bemused.

"But these are grand tidings, Your Eminence! With the Baron's son safely under sod, they have no-one to champion against me, no serious challenger to rival my succession! Myler Magrath raised his glass.

'To the Earl of Tyrone!" They all three drank, and Myler inquired further. "Your Grace, did the Dean say who killed him?"

"Yes. Yes, of course. I have his letter here." He unfolded the letter on his desk, and skimmed down the page. "Here! 'At length their false dealing has produced a cruel and bitter fruit. That boy who was used as pretext for this delay, Brian MacBaron O'Neill, is lately killed. He was waylaid two days ago, in a wood near Carlingford by John's deputy, Turlagh O'Neill, who pursued him with a hundred horse. The boy fled for his life, the assailants behind him, until he reached a riverbank. He stripped off his clothes, but being unable to swim, he hid himself in a thicket. One of his followers who was taken, to save his own life, offered to betray the better person. And so the boy was discovered, and he was there slain." Myler looked knowingly to Shane.

"The very spot where his father had the like friendship of his men!" He turned back to DeQuadra's inquiring gaze. "Dungannon's line is held to be false by the people, and neither father nor son could command the loyalty of his men."

A sudden concern darkened Shane's countenance. "The Queen has summoned me to appear tomorrow. I knew there was something in it! I will be held accountable for this. But *tomorrow*...If she were sending me to the tower-"

"No, no, no. She can say nothing!" The bishop's dark eyes glistened with cunning. "Officially the Baron's son was in defiance of a royal summons to London. Your safe conduct, O'Neill... The Dean said it was an armed foray, well within your lands. He was where he ought not to have been." He raised his glass. "To Her Catholic Majesty, Mary Stuart!" Shane and Myler clinked his glass, with a merry chorus of assent.

"To Queen Mary!" The three men drank it back, and DeQuadra took their glasses over to pour again. At the desk Father Magrath was perusing the Dean's letter, when he caught the bishop's eye upon him. "Your Grace, I was curious, was there any mention of the Baron's other son? He's but a child."

"The English have taken Dungannon's other young heir. Doubtless to protect him from your partisans. Dean Danyell believes they intend to raise him in England as an English O'Neill." The Ambassador turned back to Shane, taking an ominous tone. "That is not all, you know. There is much more. Did you inform the Lord Secretary of this upheaval in Ulster that you told me of?"

"I did. I begged Lord Cecil to allow me to return. I told him that my lands were in grave danger from the attacks of an ambitious rival. I warned that my people were fickle and angered by my submission to the Queen. He was unmoved. He said the province would hold without my keeping and-"

"Yes, yes, I see. I am sure he supposed you to be bluffing. My sources inside Whitehall inform me that Lord Cecil has lately captured a number of letters written to you by your captains at home." Seeing Shane's look of disbelief, DeQuadra nodded slowly, knowingly. "They were intercepted by his agents in the Pale. I daresay another triumph for his clandestine ventures. His spies are everywhere. But such is the irony! What they have learned from this prized capture will no doubt *help* rather than hinder you! It seems this deputy of yours has seized control and proclaimed himself ruler in your stead. What is more, he makes war upon the Crown, assaulting the northern outposts of the English Pale." He paused suddenly, and furrowed his dark brow. "How odd that Terence Danyell says nothing of this!" He cleared his throat of a cough, and continued. "These tumults in Ulster have brought great consternation to Whitehall. So much so, that my informant tells me Elizabeth has determined that she can no longer afford to keep you here.

SHANE O'NEILL

And now, with your rival slain, she must perforce release you!" The wily bishop sat back now, and regarded them both with a devious glint. "But tell me, O'Neill, do you expect great difficulty in subduing this deputy and his mutinous forces?"

"I'm not greatly troubled, Your Grace. When I am restored to my country, I'm sure his support will melt away like snow from a ditch!" Shane looked to Myler, who concurred, adding his assessment.

"While the cat's away, the mice will play, but upon his return..." DeQuadra nodded with a dubious smile.

"Yes, that is so...The ways of God are most wondrous and mysterious. All forces seem to conspire towards your release. Even within the Pale there is unrest. Someone put rumours abroad that you had been beheaded! Oh, yes! Raised a terrible stir, a great outcry. The Catholics were horrified. They are, of course, very nervous there just now...of Proscription. They dread the priest hunting, the confiscations, and all the other perils it will bring. Everyone is waiting for heads to roll."

"So I was the first martyr! Who set these rumours abroad?" The Spaniard shrugged, his dark eyes dancing with sly merriment. Shane laughed. "Machievel must have been a Jesuit!"

"He hadn't the requisite subtlety!" DeQuadra laughed softly. "There is general clamour for your safe return. An 'urgency', yes? She will *have* to send you back now." Myler gave a sidling nod, and smiled darkly at the bishop.

"Perhaps the ways of the Lord are not so very mysterious after all!"

"Yes, yes, yes. That is quite possible." The sly Spaniard regarded them both with some amusement. "And perhaps my news for you today was not such a revelation as you would have me to believe. No matter. There was something else...Yes. The Dean of Armagh writes also of this new Archbishop of Armagh-" Myler was happy to prompt him.

"Donatus O'Tighe."

"Yes, it concerns the Pope's great Council in Trent. His Holiness had petitioned Elizabeth to send delegates from England, but she refused in no uncertain terms. Whereas, your Archbishop O'Tighe sent a full delegation of three bishops to the Council from Ireland. My sources tell me that the Queen is livid!" Shane clapped and rubbed his hands together.

"Good on you, Donagh!"

"I'm afraid matters are a good deal more serious than that, Lord O'Neill. She and her ministers are furious, and, if my informant is to be believed, determined to put an end to his defiance by extreme measures. No gesture he could have made would stand so flagrant and public a proof of Armagh's primacy and independence. The insolence of the Primate's move, -for so it is conceived, has so compounded the malice and spite of her Majesty that I fear he is in grave danger. I feel compelled to warn the Dean that they must be most vigilant for O'Tighe's safety. Lord Cecil has cast his net of informants and agents even within the offices of the Holy Mother Church. The Primate must surround himself with his loyal Irish Franciscans, and be wary even of the continental orders and *Jesuits*. Oh, yes! There are anointed priests who are no strangers to political intrigue!" The hypocracy of this angelic warning against political clergy was not lost on Myler Magrath. Indeed, he searched the bishop's eyes for some trace of irony, but finding none, he simply concurred.

"Aye, Your Grace. I spent six years in Rome, and I *know* whereof you speak. Political intrigue is rife. Caution would hardly go amiss." Struck by DeQuadra's genuine concern, he ventured further. "So many Irish bishops have died in the last year, and all had refused to forsake Rome. Do you believe the rumours to be true then? The Irish are cute and suspicious by nature, and so they will make sly inquiries about the physician attending. But with poison, who is to say? There is many a bane, belladonna or monkshood or such, that will leave less trace than a serpent's tooth!" Knowing looks passed between them, and DeQuadra shrugged and sighed.

"From what I know to be true, none of these things would surprise me. But I know that the threat to the Primate O'Tighe is a serious one. Elizabeth is determined to appoint her young chaplain Adam Loftus in his place, and she will stop at nothing." Myler looked doubtfully to

SHANE O'NEILL

Shane.

"He will resist such precautions. O'Tighe is a very trusting soul, and will turn away none. But his physician certainly must be Irish. And Catholic." DeQuadra raised his hands and shook his head.

"No, no, no. He must be wary even of Catholics! I have made inquiries. And I find that many of my own order are quite out of sympathy with the Irish-speaking partisans of the Church. Everyone desires to win England back to the Faith, and they fear that some Irish measures of resistance will push Elizabeth further from Rome." Shane bristled at this, as a sudden heat rose to his temples.

"This is why His Holiness has abandoned Ireland to the tyranny of heretics! How can he justify his refusal to excommunicate her?" DeQuadra looked coolly into Shane's eyes for a long moment of silent reproach, as the proud chieftain's scowl faded to calm.

"I might remind you, O'Neill, that upon *your* word, his Holiness appointed the first Irishman to the Primal See of Armagh in two hundred years! He gave unto you the ecclesiastical patronage for Ulster, and your other bishop in Clogher. In doing so, he spurned the long-standing prerogative of the English Crown to name the Primate, bringing upon himself untold diplomatic assaults and pressures. And will you dare to question his concern for Ireland?" Shane could hardly deny this, and he fetched a deep sigh.

"Aye, your Grace, that was churlish of me. It's only I'm impatient for help from the Catholic princes of Europe, and they look to His Holiness."

"As for why he has not excommunicated the Queen, I can tell you that precisely. I had a letter from the Holy Father, since last we spoke of this, wherein he writes of his concern for the suffering in Ireland. He declares, and I think rightly, that *were* he to excommunicate Elizabeth, it would unleash a persecution of Catholics unlike anything the world has seen. Such a ruling would render the Faithful disloyal and seditious under law by the mere practice of their Faith. His Holiness is quite resolute, and will discuss it no further." The bishop's eyes challenged Shane to respond, but he only nodded gravely, as he considered the

SHANE O'NEILL

Pope's reasoning. A crushing disappointment, certainly, but sound considerations that had not occurred to him. He had thought only of the great rising such a Papal pronouncement would engender. DeQuadra searched for some consoling thought. "Those matters are truly in God's hands. We cannot know. Elizabeth could be dead in the morning and Mary would rule." A distant bell struck the quarter hour, and Shane got to his feet.

"I'd best not depend upon that! I'm most grateful, Your Excellency. These reports will stand me well tomorrow when I face the Queen. I pray that you're right; that she has summoned me to send me home to Ireland."

"Oh, I am quite sure of it. I'm afraid I shall not see you again." He rose and clasped Shane's hand. "But you will go with my blessing. Perhaps Father Magrath, you will be good enough to keep me informed of O'Neill's progress? And of your own! I am certain that you will achieve some distinction in your service to the Holy Church." Myler cherished this small tribute to his unspoken ambitions.

"I will write, surely, your Grace." DeQuadra put his bejeweled hand on Shane's shoulder as he led him to the door.

"Yes, yes, yes. Elizabeth has no choice but to bid you farewell. But she will firstly try to wrest concessions from you. She will have indentures to be signed. She will ask you to assent -perhaps even to *assist* in the establishment of the Common Prayer in Ulster. Your hand is strong, O'Neill. You must give her nothing!"

"You mustn't, you shan't, you daren't, you can't' and all between is Blarney! This is the Irish for '*no*'!" With an angry shriek, Elizabeth pushed back her great chair and bounded to her feet, prompting Lord Cecil to rise as well. Both now glowered down at Shane where he sat, alone at the great table of the Privy Council's Chamber. A parchment bearing the indentures lay waiting before him, with quill and inkpot to hand. The Queen's head was trembling slightly, and her eyes wild, goaded into near frenzy by his cool demeanor. "By heaven, you do mock our patience!"

"Majesty, all the-"

"Mark you, your *won't* will not o'erstep our *will!*" Elizabeth shouted over him. "The articles will be signed!"

"If your Majesty will but hear me out." She pursed her lips and raised her thin brows in grudging assent. "All the powers of my office I will expend in your service, but those powers are *temporal*. A chieftain cannot impose a new liturgy, or disestablish the Laws of the Brehons whereupon he derives his office. I have no peerage. If I cease to be chieftain, I *have* no office. Another would be chosen. If I were an earl I would have the authority to-"

"An earl! Shall we reward your villainy with an earldom? Nay then, mayhap a crown! So deserving...for such disservice! For decimating our armies and our treasuries, for taking captive of our new Irish peers, for combining with Scotch rebels against our Lord Deputy, *and for murdering* Brian Mac Baron O'Neill barely a fortnight since!" Her eyes narrowed to a searing squint of fury, riveted upon him. "Do not feign astonishment! Doubtless it was done upon your word!"

"In Faith, I am astonished. For that your Majesty told me a month and more ago that the Baron's heir was summoned to London. If such royal orders were issued and ignored, then he was surely in rebellion - and liable to prosecution! For my part, I sent no such word. I cannot answer for what my deputy has done in his foul mutiny. Never would such chance have befallen him to rise in rebellion against me, had I not been kept from my people these many months! Long beyond the terms of our signed accords!"

"Ha! If there be rebellion in your ranks, it is divine justice long overdue! It is your *own* rebellion stands cause of all!" With this stinging rebuke, Elizabeth drew in her skirts, and Lord Cecil hastened to adjust her chair as she once again took her seat. The Secretary then followed suit, and Shane took up his appeal with a calm deliberative tone.

SHANE O'NEILL

"Were I truly in rebellion, I should never have come to pledge my fealty to your Majesty. *I* was not compelled by royal summons. Not only was Brian Mac Baron in breach of your royal summons, he was within my territories with a force of arms -a grievous violation of the terms of my safe conduct. Wherein is also avowed the removal of your garrison from Armagh -which was but one day removed, and occupied again the following morning."

"Enough!" Elizabeth slapped her hand sharply onto the table. "The garrison will remain until MacDonnell and his seven thousand of Scots are settled back into the isles. James and Sorley MacDonnell and all their wild Scots abide there in violation of our royal edict; an edict banishing all Hebridians out of Ireland. They are clearly there by *your* grace, to disprove before all the world your false oaths of loyalty!"

"It was not upon my word they came to Ireland."

"If you were a true leige of your Queen, you would have enforced our edict long ago, and driven them hence. Instead, you daily consort with them, and make forbidden marriage alliances with them." Elizabeth sighed, and regarded him with a gaze of pity. "And for all this they laugh at you. A proud Irish peacock whose pretty plumes will grace the cap of Mary Stuart when his throat is cut." She shook her head wistfully.

"I *am* your leige, I swear!" Shane appeared to be contrite and sincere. Elizabeth smiled bitterly. She raised her chin and arched her brow, peering down her nose at him.

"Your vanity has dimmed your ready wits, O'Neill. We are not deceived. Argyle sends no troops, though you hold captive of Katherine MacLean. Her kindred MacDonnells, and even McLeans, rise out in your service. She is no captive. Mary sent her, that you would rise in her cause. And yet were Mary Stuart seated upon our throne, then would Ulster be granted to her kinsman James MacDonnell. She has pledged as much to him!" Elizabeth's jubilant smirk dared him to reply.

"Saving your presence, that rumour is long abroad, but it is far from true. Queen Mary is promised to restore the Lordship of the Isles to them, which will *relieve* Ulster from their predations." At this, Elizabeth threw her head back and laughed.

SHANE O'NEILL

"And there is rumour long abroad that *you* are cunning..." She tisked now, and her eyes shone with gleeful malice. "Argyle holds the Lordship of the Isles; he would never relinquish it! And Mary needs him, for he is the only Protestant laird that will support her. Nay then, she has long held the Throne of Scotland, and the Isles well within her providence. She could long ago have restored that title unto them." She looked slyly to Cecil, and he handed to her a letter. She slowly unfolded it, moving the second page forward, and handed it to Shane. "Just here at the top, look you. You know the hand, we are sure of that!" He saw, on the page before him, Mary's pledge to James MacDonnell to confer upon him the Lordship of Ulster. He felt at once a flush of shame and fury. He quickly skimmed both pages, and looked up to Elizabeth's mocking smile.

"But there is no word of Katherine MacLean. She is blameless!"

"She has cast aside her wedding ring. What trifle then your unblest tokens when Mary's piper calls?"

"She has born me a son."

"Have a care she does not bear him again -into Scotland. Mayhap he will furnish the Scots a tidy claim to Ulster when your head adorns a gate." Elizabeth laughed slyly. "Mary plays upon you like a bagpipe, all wind and bluster! And she sounds every stop to play a Stuart air!" She smiled sadly, her brows aloft in a teasing inquiry. "A glint of light in the East? Has the dawn yet come to wake my Irish cock?" Shane clapped his hand to his heart, and filled his moist eyes with all the sincerity he could muster.

"I can but avow my abject loyalty, your Majesty. What more? My words are a poor physic for the poisonous slander of enemies at Court. What words can-"

"Words! We will have deeds! Since the Baron's heir is slain, we can no longer justify the cost to our treasury of keeping you at Court. We fear that these troubles that rage so in Ulster are owing in some part to your long absence from that country. And so we shall return you into Ireland on these terms; that you put down the present disorders there, and capture and turn over to the Lord Deputy the murderer of Brian MacBaron O'Neill. When order is restored among your own people, you must raise a hosting and enforce our edict to banish the Scots. We know that Sorley MacDonnell is wed to your sister, but *you* are pledged to your Queen! He has displaced our true and loyal Irish subjects in the glens of Antrim, and he conspires with Mary Stuart to our undoing. He has attacked the English at Carrickfergus and Dundalk. Either he is one of yours -under your command, and you have broken our good covenant, or you are my honest liegeman and, as he is mine enemy, so is he yours...And therefore you will undertake to capture him and dispel his followers." She sat back, still and silent for a long moment, her imperious smile and fearless eyes commanding him to yield. Shane nodded, and held his right hand aloft solemnly.

"I will subdue him...and drive the redshanks to the sea. I am sworn."

Elizabeth nodded to Lord Cecil, and looked sternly again to Shane. "When the Scotch are banished, we shall withdraw our English soldiery from Armagh. As for your prisoner Cullagh O'Donnell, you shall each of you choose two peers to arbitrate. The council of four shall hear the disputed matters and make their deliberations. All shall abide by their judgement."

"Yes, Majesty." The Queen turned for a brief whispered conferral at Cecil's ear, after which he nodded gravely. She sat back again.

"When you undertake to rout the Scots, O'Donnell's wife will go back to her father in the isles. This you must let her to do. Perhaps we can then find for you a suitable English wife. And yet we counsel you to keep the child, lest he shall later provide the Scots a claim to Ulster." Shane gave a deep nod of assent, and looked up dutifully, eager to hear the rest. "As to the Book of Common Prayer, that shall bide until such time as the province be shired and an Earl be named. As to the matter of your peerage, we shall consider us by your actions if you be loyal or no. Meantime, you may fashion yourself 'Captain of Tyrone' with all rights and pre-eminances of the O'Neill. You will answer, not to the Viceroy in Dublin, but directly to us. Let these indentures be so amended, Lord Cecil. And when he has signed them, he is free to depart. Be it known that John O'Neill is our good and natural subject! To Ireland, now, and keep our covenant!"

SHANE O'NEILL

Shane glanced down at the still unsigned parchment before him. He rolled it up and smiled as he handed the rejected indentures over to the Lord Secretary. With a tilt of his head, he nodded jauntily to Elizabeth. "God save the Queen!

SHANE O'NEILL

CHAPTER 14

"Land ho!" A rousing call from the masthead stilled the chatter over breakfast, and O'Neill and his men scrambled up to the quarterdeck to see. It would be their first glimpse of Ireland since early winter. This was the last of May, and there was not one among them whose heart did not ache for home. The rain was still falling, but lightly now, barely noticeable in the sea spray that was blowing over the bows. Through the drizzly grey mists in the west they could just barely discern the dark peaks of the Wicklow Mountains, and a hearty cheer was raised. Shane's wolfhounds barked and howled with the excitement, and set to chasing each other, leaping and splashing about over barrels and rope-coils on the slippery deck.

Shane O'Neill moved off silently to the foredeck, to avail himself of the wet and windy solitude of the ship's prow. It had been a stormy crossing, nearly a week since the ship left Southhampton, yet somehow, the leagues he had put behind him had eerily compounded the passage of time, as London receded and faded like a long-ago memory.

In truth, but a fortnight had passed since he had been summoned to her Majesty's privy chamber to sign the amended and final draught of the indentures. Even then, in the Queen's own bedchamber, there had been more haggling. Shane agreed not to molest the garrison at Armagh, on condition they be victualed out of the Pale. For this concession, he was given a 'loan' of 300 pounds for his return, with no stipulations as to its repayment. He was enjoined to deliver a copy of the indentures to Lord Sussex in Dublin Castle, after which he would be free to return to Ulster. When the ink was blotted and blown, he and his men had taken a carriage, and, with a full escort of gallowglass, paid a brazen visit to the Spanish Ambassador in Durham House to show him the accords. After all the surreptitious night-calls at the watergate, this bit of coat-trailing seemed to lend dignity to their departure.

It had been a memorable afternoon. Myler Magrath concelebrated a Mass with the archbishop in thanksgiving. Afterwords a lavish banquet was laid on for them, with an impromptu concert that included Blind Colm and his harp, all to celebrate the great success of the journey. The following week was spent in preparations for the return voyage, and included a good deal of roistering with Tom Stukeley and Robert Dudley. All very congenial...

And yet, now, as London seemed so very far away and so very long ago, what remained of the visit was heartscald, a smoldering fury for the many indignities he had been obliged to suffer. Chief among them was the galling shame of mendacity. The finest of wines could never wash away this bitter aftertaste of feigned smiles and courtly flattery, such ignoble gestures for a man of his blood, gestures that surely betokened servility. Shane filled his lungs with the fresh briny sea air. There would be no more lies.

Wet winds chilled his face, as glistening drops of brine rolled down his brow and his ruddy cheeks. They tasted salty and clean. His scowl had vanished now, but for a dark glint that lingered in his wry smile as he gazed out upon the shores of Ireland. Unawares, he spoke aloud his resolve, casting his words upon the wind. "Aye! They thought to give me a lesson in statesmanship. I'll give them a lesson in war!"

The travel weary Ulstermen never lost sight of the land now, for the ship hugged the coast all the way. This Irish shoreline was straight, unbroken by inlet or bay since Wexford. At long last, they sighted Bray Head and Howth Head, those lofty and commanding promontories that rise like dragons, straight out of the sea, to guard Dublin Bay.

The winds were with them, and as the three-master rounded the

SHANE O'NEILL

headland and sailed into the bay, the clouds were beginning to scatter over the Dublin Mountains. Sunlight broke through, and spilled onto the lush green hill of Dalkey above the bay so that it glittered like a trove of emeralds. Below it was a forest of sailing masts, for some fifteen ships were anchored there. It was from here they had departed a half year ago, so there was some surprise aboard ship when they sailed on past. The boatswain explained that would not be putting in there, for although Dalkey had served as Dublin's port for hundreds of years, it was no longer the nearest approach. No, they would 'lengthen the voyage, but shorten the journey,' by making for the new port of Ringsend at the very mouth of the river, where the turf-black waters of the Liffey spill into the blue bay.

Offshore, there were several small vessels at anchor, awaiting a high tide that would let them sail upriver to Merchant's Quay at the very walls of the city, but this big three-master, with its heavy draft, would need to unload at Ringsend. Mooring so close to Dublin was a recent innovation, and the dockage was still rough. Although one end of it was newly enclosed in lime and stone, most of Ringsend wharf was little more than a steep earthern bank bolstered by a palisade of logs. Above it a row of sturdy treetrunks served to coil and anchor the mooring ropes. It was hardly ideal. At low water, the ships lay on hard sand and were exposed to every wind. But Dublin was less than two miles away!

Shane's 'Red hand' standard was fluttering proudly from the masthead, and it caused quite a stir on the waterfront. While the ship was being berthed a crowd gathered, mostly mariners and dockhands, and as word spread, the wharf filled with rapturous throngs from an adjacent settlement called 'Irishtown.' Like Ballybocht (poortown) across the river, Irishtown had grown up in the last hundred years, after the Gaelic Irish were forbidden by law from dwelling within the walled town of Dublin. A welter of thatched hovels, vast and densely clustered in the scrubby shorelands,   Irishtown was home to fishermen, fishmongers, cocklepickers, and dockers. As these rustic Irish cheered and welcomed O'Neill, the Tirowenmen were astounded and delighted to hear so much Irish spoken in the very heart of the Pale. The crowd

SHANE O'NEILL

was jubilant, and giddy with relief to see their Irish champion restored to them after all the frightful rumours that were blowing about during his captivity.

When Shane appeared atop the gangplank, there was an uproarious clamour. He addressed them briefly in Irish, with a homely blessing that one might utter upon returning to a wee cottage. He tipped them a nod and a wink. "God save all here!" There was laughter and cheers. "It's a great blessing to be delivered out of the lion's den, and to be here among my own once again! I can tell you I did not come back empty-handed. I went to London to get, and not to give. The journey has been a triumph, for I have given nothing and gotten all! The Queen has recognized me to be 'the O'Neill', with dominion over all the other lords of Ulster. I have been authorized to treat directly with London, and absolved of any duties to the viceroy here in Dublin. In my lands beyond the Pale, the heretics shall hold no sway, and the good friars will keep to the Holy Mass, as they have done since St. Patrick lit the great fire of Slane!" The crowd erupted in a wild swell of cheering now, and Shane had to wait for it to ebb. "Our day of deliverance draws ever nearer! So let you keep your eyes to the North! There is a fixed star in the North, a lodestar that will not shift to please the gloomy Strangers in our land, with their heresies and their clacking English. Like the helmsman of a ship, look you North to set your bearings, and we shall come safe through this storm. And when the constellations are moved aright, and the hour is at hand -as St. Patrick drove out the slithering snakes long ago, we will drive these greedy hoors into the sea!"

A thunderous cheer was raised, and one of Shane's gallowglass blasted forth on his pipes with a triumphal air, a skirling anthem to raise gooseflesh and quicken the pulse. Shane stepped down the plank to move among the crowd, embracing young and old, exhorting them in Irish to keep faith and 'bide their hour to rise with us.' Although stormclouds lingered in the west, the skies were clearing in the south, and the midday sun had dispelled the rainy morning gloom. Farleigh and the others looked on brightly from the quarterdeck rail, for this boisterous welcome below was truly a heartening sight, after all the

SHANE O'NEILL

doubts and dispair in London.

The unloading of the ship's hold was bound to take ages, with dockers lugging and hauling litter after litter of trunks and bundles down the gangplank. After a while had passed, Shane was delighted to see his horses appear on deck. As they were led clip-clopping down the ramp, he resolved that he and his men would set out immediately for home. MacSweeny and half his troop of gallowglass would stay behind to see the train of wagons and baggage-carts North, for that would be a slow and cumbersome journey.

The horses were unsteady and wild after their long wave-tossed journey in the darkness of the hold. They had to be put at grass for a short spell until they settled. When all was readied, O'Neill and his entourage mounted, and the crowds parted to cheer them through. MacCaffrey led the way brandishing high the red hand banner, and behind him O'Devlin held aloft his bright sword.

Shane looked up to the clearing skies, and cast aside his shaggy mantle. His new black tunic was trimmed with gold, and it showed to fine effect the magnificent golden cross that had been bestowed upon him by the Pope. Beside him rode the tonsured friar, Myler Magrath, in his brown Franciscan robe. He had donned it joyously, the moment they cast off from Southampton. Art O'Hagan and Will Fleming were close behind, and following them was Farleigh, with Gillie and Blind Colm, his harp slung over his shoulder. In the rear guard rode a score of gallowglass warriors, and one of their number struck up a stately march on his pipes. The steeds were skittish still, inclined to bolt and frisk, and the party set out for Dublin with a tight rein on their horses.

The only obstacle to the journey in was the Dodder, which was nearly in flood, but the road brought them to a ford that was easily managed, since they were unencumbered by wagons. The rest of the way was 'slobland', a stretch of low wet heaths covered with bracken and furze, with a few lonely cottages along the boreen casting up their wispy banners of turfsmoke to mark the way. Above it all, looming ever more prominently in the West, was Dublin Castle.

An imposing Norman fortress, Dublin Castle was essentially the four massive round towers connected by its great stone walls. There was no keep within. The castle comprised the South East corner of the walled city, which stretched along the south bank of the River Liffey. On this day, as the Tirowenmen drew near, the dark rain-drenched stones of these walls, seen against the heavy glowering western skies behind, gave the castle a foreboding air, and, though it was little remarked, O'Neill and his men were anxious to put it behind them and head north.

The rough boreen soon became a road, and the road became a street as they rounded Hoggin Green. They clipclopped along the cobbles of Dame's Street, casting their gaze ever upwards to regard the great towers before them, little knowing that they were being spied upon from high above.

In the shadows of a narrow window of the eastern tower, Lord Sussex had been keeping watch. Only a short while ago, a runner from Ringsend had brought word of the 'Red Hand Banner' sailing into port. The Lord Deputy was undecided as yet on just how he would receive this haughty chieftain, and was considering the various indignities that might be offered him after he had cooled his heels with waiting. He nodded slowly, and under his breath he muttered his verdict. "Aye, we shall let the swine bide a while below. A day's delay or more! We may teach him manners yet!" His dark eyes smoldered now, as he watched the procession narrow to single file to traverse the causeway over the River Poddle, that 'dark pool' that formed the castle's moat. How easily might a marksman, from this very perch, put an end to the Northern wars!

One by one, the wary Ulstermen entered the city. Emerging from under the arch of the portcullis, Friar Magrath blessed himself, and raised his eyes to the statue of St. Mary les Dames for whom the gate was named. He was quite shocked to see that she was gone. It had been several years since he had passed the way of Damesgate, and it was a jolt to encounter such a trenchant sign of the new order. Apart from the English born officials, the people of Dublin were staunchly resisting the Reformation, but clearly they were powerless against such sacrilege, and, indeed, such affrontery. St. Mary les Dames! There, in the niche of stonework over the gate's arch, was her pedestal still, and even a fragment of her foot remained, with the serpent writhing beneath it. Myler reflected that perhaps the serpent had prevailed after all. Perhaps the serpents *would* prevail.

No sooner had the fluttering 'Red Hand' appeared through the narrow gate, than a great stir began to reverberate through the streets of Dublintown. Word passed from door to door, and from lane to lane, and the excited populace crowded into Castle Street to see the great Northern Chieftain. Within these town walls, the people were of mixed Irish and Old English blood, and the recent security policies, that reserved *all* official positions to those English-born, had bred a strong resentment of the 'Castle', and a high regard for this Catholic champion of Ulster. They were jubilant to find him in their midst.

When Shane reached the imposing drumtowers of Castlegate, the swelling crowd was cheering wildly. In a move calculated to offend, he sent Will Fleming inside to summon the Lord Deputy. Shane waved to the throngs, and chatted amiably about London with several Aldermen who had approached. At length, Fleming emerged, not with the Lord Deputy, but with Sir William FitzWilliam, the Lord Justice. He was brother-in-law to both Sussex and Sidney. A tall slender fellow with dark brown hair and a tidy ginger beard, FitzWilliams strode purposefully across the drawbridge and bounded down the steps flashing a bright smile.

"I bid you welcome, O'Neill! The Lord Deputy is most anxious to see you! He regrets that his duties detain him at present, and would have you stop within, and betake yourselves of rest until he can attend you." Shane met him smile for smile.

"Ah, now, there's a great pity, FitzWilliam! For, alas, I've no time to tarry! This is ill fortune indeed, for I wished to tender him thanks for his hospitality when *last* I called upon him!" Shane shook his head slowly, and turned his eyes to the North. "I must make my way north to vanquish the rebellion of my deputy there, and to restore the Queen's order." He cast a cold eye on the grinning Englishman below. "Had Lord Sussex done as much, I should be at leisure now to await his good offices." The lustre faded from FitzWilliam's smile, until only the ghost of it remained. After a brief silence, he spoke sternly, endeavoring to take command.

"I *must* entreat you, O'Neill, to halt but a while with us in Dublin! Well you know that those disorders in Ulster will bide some hours more while the seals of state are tended to."

"And my long detainment at the Royal Court is well known to the Deputy. My journey homeward is long overdue. He will forgive my haste! If he does not, you may inform him that, upon her Majesty's word, I am no longer bound to attend him, but in hostings."

"Be that as it may. Still, the settlements you received of Her Majesty in London *must* be lodged proper with her Lord Deputy of Ireland."

Shane looked over to Will Fleming, gave a slow nod, and said in Irish, "Give this churl the thieving papers, so, and we'll rise a dust behind us!" Will opened his leathern satchel and retrieved the scroll. FitzWilliam watched him cautiously, and then turned again to Shane, pressing further.

"His Lordship was most adamant, and you will save you a tedious return! The indentures, *by law*, must be proclaimed abroad to her subjects here, else they be not binding." He smiled engagingly now, as he thought to coax them inside. "I have fiery whiskybaugh within, to fortify your spirits and respite your journey!"

Upon hearing this feeble ruse, and conceiving the insult implied, Shane gave a pointed look to his men, so charged with both scorn and pained forbearance that they burst out with hearty laughter. He nodded once again to Will Fleming, and spoke again to him in Irish. "Read it out, so! Fill your lungs and blast it forth, man. Haven't we the town assembled?" He glanced at Will's horse. "Get up with you on the horse's back, the way they'll see you clear." Shane turned back to the bewildered FitzWilliam, smiling broadly. "As we have Dublin assembled before us, we shall oblige you, and comply with the strictures of law."

With that, he turned about and looked out over the crowds, bringing them instantly to stillness. He flashed again his smile, and called to them in slow deliberate English. "My blessings and salutations to the good people of Dublin! I'm most grateful for this welcome from the heart that you've put before me, as I return from London to keep the Queen's peace! I bear with me the accords I obtained in London after months of fierce negotiations that kept me so long away. List you now, til they be read unto you!"

Will Fleming read out the document, slyly omitting that one rankling clause that forbade O'Neill to levy tribute upon his sub-chieftains in Ulster, outside of Tirowen. The edict was a cause of great wonder among the people, for the highly favourable terms won by O'Neill. When Fleming finished, a long rousing cheer was raised. Shane raised his hand for stillness, and then he held up the heavy golden cross that hung suspended from his neck. "I bear also this Sacred Cross of gold sent to me by His Holiness Pope Pius IV in Rome, who prays daily for the Faithful in Ireland. He too, sends you His blessing, by way of his humble servant, Friar Magrath!" He looked to Myler, and nodded.

Myler lifted his hand with two fingers extended, and a rustle moved like a rippling wave over the throng as hats were removed, a murmur of excitement rising for this shocking gesture of defiance at the very gates of the Castle. The friar moved his arm broadly in a slow sweeping sign of the cross, as he solemnly intoned the Roman benediction. "In Nomine Patrii et filii et Spiritu Santi." Seeing the great flutter of hands among the multitude in every direction, Shane looked down at Lord FitzWilliam, who appeared very small, and very disconcerted.

There was a sudden stir in the crowd, as they parted to let someone come forward. It was an old woman with long unkempt silver hair that caught the sun in its tangles. She wore voluminous skirts and motley shawls, and some were coaxing, "Go on, then, Bridie!" as she stepped forward out of crowd, holding aloft a bit of greenery.

Her pale eyes were alight with rapture as she beheld the famed chieftain from beyond the Pale. Shane looked down from his charger, grinning, for she had a wild look to her, right enough, and a beaming prankish smile like a young girl. Approaching him, she called out, "Yer honour, Sir! Lord O'Neill, Sir! Would you ever don the aul bayleaves, now, like Caesar Augustusus! Sure, aren't you the red hand hero of the

SHANE O'NEILL

North?" She held up to him a laurel crown of bay. "Haven't you a right to thim, Sir? After all yer triumph beyond in England!"

Shane took it from her and laughed as he held it up to show the people. There was a thunderous ovation, and he looked to Myler, who nodded sagely. He looked then to Farleigh, who spurred his mount and moved up beside him to advise. "You must oblige them, lad! 'Vox populi, vox Dei!' It's only the *people* who can bestow such an ancient honour! By the Powers! A victor's laurel! In the English Pale!"

O'Neill clapped it on his head, and gleeful cheers resounded against the towering walls of Castlegate. High above, from a narrow turret window, the Lord Deputy looked on, his temples throbbing a furious pulse that drummed in his ears. The crowds surged forward now, closing in around the O'Neill. He shouted down to FitzWilliam that he was 'away now', and whatever was said between them, they were neither the wiser. FitzWilliam waved his arms as he backed away onto the drawbridge, quite thunderstruck at the sight he beheld before him. He appeared quite agitated until Will Fleming tossed him the scroll of Indentures as he passed.

The sea of people parting before him, Shane and his splendid cavalcade made their way slowly up Cork Hill into High Street, waving and nodding to the throng. He held his right hand aloft in a proud gesture, but in place of the haughty regal demeanor that was customary on such occasions, he smiled warmly at the eager exultant faces that welcomed him along the way. His piper let blast with a stately march, and the crowds fell in behind as they moved up through the town. With nearly all of the townsfolk following the procession, High Street was lined, for the most part, with small clusters of women and children. Old people waved from windows and doorways, and a gaggle of prosperous looking *gentlemen* were gathered before the steps of St.Michael's, craning their necks and gawking, some waving their plumed hats, but not a peep out of them.

The Tirowen delegation was filled with warm feelings for these denisons of the Pale, a people hitherto not close to their hearts. Farleigh waved blissfully to the crowds, his sharp eyes watchful, as always, for

SHANE O'NEILL

those glimmering elusive snatches of beauty and spirit that can leap out from a passing vista to play on the memory ever after. The Dubliners were dressed, for the most part, as in London, but the faces were wild and Irish, he thought, and full of holy divilment.

The night's shower had given the town a thorough soaking, leaving bright puddles along the Highstreet, dotted with the roundy tips of cobbles. Above the glistening thatch, dark billows lingered in the Western sky, and the shrill midday sun cast a radient glow over the town, infusing its damp colours with vivid depths in splotches, like fresh pigments splattered on an artists palette. Smiling Farleigh filled his lungs, and thanked the mysterious Powers for the fine day that was in it.

The town followed Shane's highstepping stallion around past Ormond Gate, and progressed slowly along Bridge Street until they reached the two lofty turrets of Bridgegate. Here the chieftain halted and turned around to bid farewell. His cavalcade parted to each side, and he galloped through them until he faced the cheering throng who had followed behind. He raised his arms aloft, his white teeth flashing in an ecstatic smile, his eyes nearly closed. He resembled a holy prophet in the transports of religious fervour, and his black tunic and golden cross did nothing to dispel the illusion. He called out in English. "May the Lord bless Dublin! Stand by me in the times that are coming!" he said. "Stand with O'Neill, and Ireland will prevail! Stand with *Ireland* and our Holy Faith shall triumph!" With that, he reeled his mount, and hastened back to the gate. Disappearing then, into the shadowy arch, the cheers re-echoed around him as he led his men under the portcullis, and out onto the bridge across the River Liffey.

On the north bank, more crowds were gathered before the Inns of Law, waiting to cheer them through. There were but a few streets this side of the Liffey, streets lined with two story houses, and these soon gave way to low cottages, where rustic families waved and shouted 'hurroo!' and 'O'Néill abú!" Several young lads were perched in the trees, laughing and waving, and it was a merry farewell to Dublin. In no time at all, Shane and his men found themselves in the twittering quietude of furzy glens and rambling meadows, on the long northern road.

SHANE O'NEILL

At Drogheda, Will Fleming made his departure from the crew, setting off for his home at Slane. He gave his promise to come to Benburb in Shane's service as soon as he had tended to his family, and to whatever pressing matters had emerged during his long absence.

The weather was holding fine, and by late afternoon the following day, O'Neill and his men could at last see before them, through the hazy summer air, the high walls of Dundalk. They drew to a halt in a leafy bower beside the road, to rest the horses and 'relieve the paunch.' Farleigh had Gillie cut a branch of fresh bayleaves, and he wound them around the dry remains of the laurel crown. The old poet was uniquely attuned to the power of such symbols. Shane donned the garland once more as they entered the gates of Dundalk, the northernmost settlement of the Pale, and his piper's skirling anthem brought eager crowds forth from shops and dwellings along the highstreet. The welcome this time was wary but spirited. The townsfolk were hopeful that Shane would put a stop to the predations of his upstart cousin Turlagh, and that, having reached some understanding in London, he would at last keep the Queen's peace.

As O'Neill and his men emerged through the western gate of the town, the dark ramparts of the English Pale towering behind them, a great sense of relief and excitement quickened their pace, and they galloped forth across the fields into O'Hanlon's Country. To their astonishment, over the first rise, a band of Ulster warriors appeared, silhouetted against the sky. Fluttering over them was the 'Red Hand'of O'Neill. The rowdy crew came roaring down the hill to welcome their chieftain, and as they drew near, Shane was delighted to see his fosterbrother Manus Donnelly in command.   It was a warm reception, rollicksome and frolicksome. Manus reported that Turlagh O'Neill and a large contingent of the men were waiting only three leagues away in the Fews, camped around Shane's lodge at Fathan. With no further delay, they were off. Shane led them over the rough drumlins and through the ancient wood to the lodge.

These Ulster hills stirred the heart of Shane. The heady air of freedom, the exhilaration of power and command, and a deep yearning to see Katherine and his infant son, fired his pulse, and urged him to rally the men and press on to Benburb. Upon reaching the glade at Fathan, however, he marked the long shadows and the weary trod of the horses, and he resolved to halt for the night and set off again at the first streak of dawn. Farleigh coaxed him, yet again, to don the laurel crown as he entered, so there was no mistaking who got the better of London. Once more, the welcome was jubilant, and this time nearly frenzied, after all the months of suspense and worry.

The great oaken hall of Fathan rang with giddy laughter, and boasting, and praise for the triumph of their mighty ruse that had befooled all the crafty schemers of the Royal Court. Tirowen had bested the Crown! And hadn't they 'made a right hare of the Deputy' into the bargain! The home-again heroes supped well on their familiar Ulster fare, and if 'hunger is the best sauce', absence made them fonder still. News was first and formost, though little of London was recounted, for the returning men wanted all the reports of home and hearth. Shane inquired after Katherine. Turlagh smiled.

"Aye, that's a brave wee woman you took for yourself! She and the child are thriving, and they'll be the better for your return. She's had her Scots coming and going to keep her spirits high. Her uncle is with her now."

"Sorley MacDonnell?" Shane started, ever so slightly, at this news. "He's at Benburb?"

"Aye, just as we were setting off, he arrived with a company of his Scots. We near came to blows!" Turlagh paused with a sly twinkle in his eye, but Shane said nothing. His steady gaze was fixed on his cousin, with little patience, just now, for the tricks and flourishes of storytelling. Turlagh didn't need a nod or a wink to see how things were. "Aye, he rared up on me! The hoor was spittin' bile and breathing fire, giving out about my 'mutiny'! 'I'll stand by Shane O'Neill', he said, 'and I'll do for you! Ye thieving Judas! I'll have your heart's blood!' But in fairness, he had a right laugh when I set him straight about our wee charade! Sure, we had them *all* deceived."

Shane nodded, and laughed to himself, but it was easy seen he was

SHANE O'NEILL

deeply troubled about the MacDonnells. Manus Donnelly spoke up.

"Sorley put a power of questions to us as to what way you're minded, O'Neill. All this amity betwixt yourself and the Queen of England bodes no good for them Scots, if you take my meaning..." There was a silence then, and Manus and Turlagh exchanged a quick glance of concern. Shane heaved a vast sigh.

"True enough. It bodes no good for them. No good at all..."

It was nearly midday when a sentry in the tower of Benburb spotted the ranks of O'Neill's cavalry approaching through the far-off hills beyond the Blackwater. There was a deal of commotion and concern until the 'Red hand' was identified with certainty, for, had they been Crown forces approaching, there was but little defense on hand. Word of Shane's arrival struck like a bolt of summer lightning, charging the place with energy and excitement. Tasks and tools were dropped with abandon. Men from the encampment, and crowds from the village below hastened down the riverpath to put a welcome before O'Neill at the ford. People were singing, and spirits were high, for, even beyond their natural elation at the chieftain's safe return, they knew to a certainty that there would be wild feasting this day, and roistering til morning.

Inside the keep, a different spirit prevailed. The servants and footmen were scurrying about from chore to chore, to put all in readiness for the chief's return. Auld Bríd Donnelly was in a dither, harrying the staff like a sheepdog, barking orders and digging up new tasks, and sniffing about too, as she tried to oversee it all. "Don't skite that broom! Less scatter and more sweep! Fetch more chairs til that table yon!" She set the cooks to work on a proper feast, sumptuous and savory, with pots boiling and roasts turning in her mighty galley of a

SHANE O'NEILL

kitchen. As she bustled her way through to the hall, the roar of the cheering crowds outside told her that the master and his retinue were home, ready or no. She sighed and swept a grey lock from her brow, pressing it in place as she surveyed the room. "Aye then, there's every lick of it sorted and swept."

Bríd cast her gaze down to examine her frock now, and after brushing away a few wisps of straw, she looked up in sudden alarm. "Katherine!" She could hear the porter opening up the great doors for Shane, and she spotted young Mórag idling at the window. "Get ye above and tell your mistress to shake her feathers! There'll be the divil to pay." She could hear himself approaching down the hall, and Mórag was barely stirring. "Och, Glory be to God! Get up them stairs, girl! Raise some dust!" She turned to see Shane and Farleigh at the doorway, and her frown gave way to a beaming smile.

"Hail and welcome O'Neill!" He was not smiling. Shane was in a fierce temper, and his scowl looked just a bit silly under a leafy crown of laurels. Behind him were the worried faces of Farleigh and a few attendants. Shane's blood was up, and his eyes darted sharply around the vast chamber.

"Bedamn the welcome. Is she here at all? And my son!" Auld Bríd stuck her chin out, and glaring up at him with a glint of humour, she matched his fierce tone.

"She is. If you're a lion itself, Shane O'Neill, you'll not be roaring at me! Or I'll clip your ears for you! Now give us a kiss and I'll tell you all." Armed with a smile, bold and bright, she charged forward, her arms outstretched. He smiled sheepishly and gave her a powerful hug.

"Och, *Bríd!*"

"She's above. The Countessa will be down in her own by and by and that's the way of her. I hung her colours from the window above and she had her servants pull them in." The stout wee woman folded her arms and stepped back to regard him. "Begod ye must've taken well to the climates beyont in England, for I see you've sprouted leaves!"

Beside the chief a servant was ever so fastidiously decanting wine into goblets. Shane grabbed the bottle and splashed a brimming cup for himself. He spoke forcefully, but without anger. "Tell the woman to come down. With the child." He looked up at Brid, and realizing what she had said, he snatched the laurel from his head and tossed it aside. "We've been feasted and cheered since we landed, and never got a mean welcome til I reached my own doorstep." Farleigh picked up the leafy crown and donned it himself, on the thought that some boasting and high spirits would not go amiss.

"Triumphal! Like Alexander or Caeser! Dublin was roaring for him - in English! All 'hosannas and hallaloos'. They're terrified of this Protestant queen. It was 'Hurrah O'Neill' from the Liffey to the Blackwater!" Auld Brid took up the theme, and the bright tone too.

"God bless you, Shane. Sounds like Palm Sunday for you! We got the odd word of it up here." Farleigh capered about in his laurel, with grand rhetorical gestures.

"Not a stir from Dublin Castle! Afraid to show banner or shield! Not with all the hurlamabuck in the streets. The people were wild mad for our Shane O'Neill!" But Shane's demeanor had not brightened. He nodded to himself, and then shot a look to Brid Donnelly, grave and apprehensive.

"Ye got wind of more nor *that*...by the look of things. When did Sorley clear off?"

"The Scots broke camp two days ago." Her arms folded still, Brid met his dark gaze, and spoke what she knew, straight out. "Aye, they had some word. It was nothing good. They had it that you'd betrayed them, Shane. That you sold out Mary Stuart and Ireland too. God's curse on them for liars." She looked from one to the other, searching their faces. "Of course they had it wrong. Katherine told them as much."

"Katherine? What had she to say?"

"It near took the life out of me!" Brid blessed herself quickly. "They were all gathered round the castle...like a siege! A piper skirling, howling away! Waiting on Katherine to ride with them. My heart was in my throat! Your Katherine was fierce. Roaring from her window that it was all English lies and treachery, and that they'd be back soon, and she wouldn't stir on a lie! And divil the stir out of her. She hasn't been down since." She held her eyes upon Shane, tilting her head back to regard him. He nodded once more, gazing into the depths of his goblet. When he raised his eyes to her, she could see that they had softened just a bit.

"How is wee Hugh?"

"Ohhhh!" Her face lit up now, and her voice filled with cheer. "Och, he's a grand sturdy wee baby! Sure, *I* can't get near to him. *I'm* only Irish! She has a Scottish wetnurse, and these impudent girls from the isles. Will I go and fetch her down?" Shane nodded, and off she went. Farleigh crooked his brow, and offered his opinion.

"'Twas an English bird brought that story here. 'Twas none of our own."

"Or Spanish. DeQuadra. Mary Stuart's runners brought word to Sorley." Shane drank deep of the wine, and wiped his mustache on the back of his hand. "Tis just as well he scarpered. If he'd been sure, he'd have taken the castle. I'll choose the ground for *this* battle." The poet's hoary brows beetled at this, and then relaxed into a queer mock-up of a smile. He spoke as to a child.

"The battle! Aye, just so! We'd want to find just the right spot to kill them all. Whatever can be done to delight the lovely English queen after her six months of hospitality. Katherine and the child! We could send their heads over first!"

"You'll believe me yet, wise man." Shane tipped more wine into his goblet and drank. Farleigh picked up a gleaming silver plate, and held it out before him to see his laurel-crowned reflection. He assumed a breezy air now.

"There's no use trying to get a rise out of me, lad. I know you'll not attack the Scots. Apart from ties of kith and kindred, they've-"

"I signed a pledge in London."

"Pish to that!" Farleigh straightened his back, and turned to face Shane across the narrow table where he stood. "A prisoner's oath doesn't travel well. She only freed you because she fears Mary and the Scots."

"Let her fear them in Scotland. When I have them routed, she's sworn to remove the English garrison from Armagh. That's both of them gone out of Ulster." The old fellow folded his arms over his long beard, and tilted his head to one side, assuming an ironic treacly tone of wonderment.

"Who would be up to you? The *both* of them gone..."

"Oh, I'm a good scholar. And I've a good lesson learned in England."

"You may have taught them a few tricks too." When Shane said nothing, Farleigh took the bait. "What did you learn?"

"Sovereignty!" Shane's eyes were bright with triumph, but Farleigh pished again.

"That's a wispy sort of a notion!"

"Not to Elizabeth Tudor. She has it, and she knows *exactly* what it is. Now I've seen it. I know the look, the taste, and the smell of it. The solemn pronouncement, the hint of regret, all in dutiful compliance to the will of God, which only *happens* to comply with the interests of the king. It's clean and lethal, with parchments and drumrolls, but it's cold blood on bright steel-for anyone who threatens the power. Even a barren wife! Dispatch with dispassion! Farleigh was wincing and gurning at this, as if he were encountering various wafts of stench, but Shane pressed his argument. "It's absolute. A man who is not loyal is a traitor. Either I am loyal to Elizabeth, or I am her enemy. Either Sorley MacDonnell is loyal to me or he is my enemy..."

"Either or! This or that! Such English foolishness! The world is seldom 'this or that.' The world is mostly 'this *and* that'." Farleigh laughed triumphantly. "Oh, ho! The English have many things for a man to steal, but *wisdom* is not one of them." Shane held up his goblet, as a toast.

"The English have logic." He smiled smugly, and drank.

"Logic indeed! Life is not logical! It is random and explosive, like roses and clouds!" The two contenders leaned in to each other over the table.

"I used logic in London, and I won the day from her lawyers! Logic is a powerful weapon. A kingdom is ordered with logic."

"With *law*. A kingdom is ordered with *law*."

"Law is logic." Shane gave him a smirking victorious nod, but Farleigh was unbowed.

SHANE O'NEILL

"Our Brehon law is not based on logic. It's based on fairness. And fairness is not logical! 'Power takes all.' *There* is logic!"

"Ah! Now you have me! 'Power takes all!' That's my plan." Farleigh looked at him for a long moment, then shook his head.

"Oh, you're very glib, Shane O'Neill. But you've stopped listening to your heart, and there's no good can come of it. Sacred blood ties and sacred oaths cast aside for a golden chain-"

"God blast the damned oaths and pledges!! They're only words, man! Do you think the English crown gives a thought for oaths? Or blood ties? Her father shifted Heaven and Hell, burned cathedrals and wives to ensure his dynasty. A dynasty that was but *fifty* years old. The House of O'Neill has stood for a millennium. Til I can set it aright, *all* my oaths are captives' oaths! My pledges are weapons. My words are knives!"

Farleigh's pale eyes started. Shane saw that the old fellow was looking past him to behold some alarming sight. He turned to see Katherine standing against the door, her hands behind her. Her foxy hair was longer now, tumbling onto her shoulders, and the light summer frock showed that she had already recovered her shapely form, more fleshy and buxom than he recalled. There was a wild look on her. Her face was flushed with anger, though there were tears standing in her eyes. She laughed bitterly.

"Amn't I the fool of the world! Prisoner of a prisoner. Intriguing with Elizabeth's menials." She stepped into the room. "And poor O'Donnell! I've delivered up one hopeful courtier into the hands of another. Earls, is it? Of *what*?"

"The 'Countess' is entitled to laugh..."

"A Scottish title for a Scottish noble. Not honours begged from a foreign queen, a bastard usurper!" Katherine moved past him and stopped suddenly. She closed her eyes, and as the tears spilled onto her cheeks, she quickly pressed her hands to her face. With a bitter shriek of laughter, she dropped them, and shook her head, tossing her flaming hair as she turned to him. "Oh, God forgive me! I laughed at *her* for believing you. And all the while... *I* was the fool!"

"Katherine, I never had planned to-"

SHANE O'NEILL

"Don't speak to me!!!" Her glistening eyes burned into him. "Your words are knives. That's what you said. And well I know."

"I was left no choice. I'll not be at the mercy of the MacDonnells! If *I* hadn't betrayed *them*-"

"The devil take the MacDonnells! You have betrayed *me*! You great besotted bastard, do you not understand? *Me*! *I* stayed their swords when Sussex called upon them, offering title and peerage. *My* people. I delivered up my *husband* to you that you might defeat the English forces. *The Baron's get* would be Earl of Tyrone but for that. And I brought you all of TirConnell." Her voice quivered now as it softened. "I've shared your bed, and borne your son. Elizabeth has given you *nothing*. Not even that shiny chain that you covet so." Katherine tilted her head to find the right angle of scorn. "She'll never make you an earl. *Never!*"

"I will rule Ulster. Not Elizabeth. Not Mary. And *not* the Clan MacDonnell." Shane's tone was low and firm.

"The Irish! Treacherous to all but your enemies!" She sniffed, and pressed her sleeve to her wet cheeks, composing herself. "It may be you'll not defeat the MacDonnells. One Scot is worth two Irishmen on a battlefield. Your head will adorn a pike, and it will not have cost Elizabeth so much as a man!" Katherine looked around her now. The servants had fled the fray, and Farleigh had retreated to a shadowy nook among halberds and shields. She could see Bríd peering in at the hall door. In the queer silence, she could hear her own breathing. Some hint of amusement in Shane's eyes drove her to new fury, and impelled her to surge on. "Well, I'll not be here to mourn you! I'll not stop here any longer than it takes to pack." Shane gave a sidling nod and a sly wink.

"You're free to go your road. You always were. When O'Donnell's ransom is paid, I'll send him after you."

"Have a carriage readied." She spoke this to Bríd, but it was Shane who answered.

"The child stays."

"What are you saying?"

"Your ears are quite sound. The son of the O'Neill is not away to

SHANE O'NEILL

Scotland. Are you daft, girl?" Katherine opened her mouth to speak but nothing would do. She felt a heat rising into her face and her eyes brimmed. Her breath came in quick little huffs, and the tears came in torrents with no sound. Feeling a weakness under her, she sunk down onto a chair, and laid her head upon her arms over the table. Shane came and stood over her. He spoke softly.

"Aye, weep then. But save some tears, love. Lots of tears for all of us. These are savage times...and it's rough winds blow on the highest hills." He turned to Brid at the door. "Where is my son?" They disappeared then, and Farleigh hastened to follow. She called out after them in a weak tremulous voice.

"*My* son! He's a fetter for me now. In a cage of my own crafting. I *am* a prisoner, so, in the end of the tale!" She wept bitterly now. And as the tide of anger and dispair slowly ebbed, she puzzled over this sudden storm that had left her here in tears, on what should have been the most joyous day. What had come over her? Oh, how she had yearned for his return! She had swallowed whatever vestiges of pride remained. For him! Pining for him. Tossing and worrying through the nights for him. The hours in chapel, with every taper ablaze, wafting her prayers to Heaven. She had put her immortal soul in jeopardy to have him. And then, and then to suffer such bitter humiliation before her own people. Her uncle surely counted her a fool, that she would suffer O'Neill to betray her, betray her to satisfy the scrawny English bastard, Elizabeth. As though she were a trifle, a streel! How could she face her sisters?

A passing thought of Úna's visit troubled her now, and she tried desperately to put it from her mind. Her own *father* had attacked the MacDonnells over the troubles in the Rhinns. Her words to Úna came back to taunt her now. 'The man who keeps peace when his fences are broached is a fool... Even if it's close kindred...he must fight, and we must bide!' But surely that was different...A whisper of doubt now tormented her all the more. What had she done? She shuddered to think on the comfort of Shane's arms, for it made her feel all the more weak and alone and bereft. A sudden yearning to hold her wee babe welled up within her. Wee Cuey, her poor helpless bairn. She would go

SHANE O'NEILL

to him.

Katherine sniffed, and swallowed hard, and blotted her tears on the sleeve of her frock. She raised her head, and as she tossed her hair, she saw something out of the corner of her eye. She turned in her chair to look at Shane where he stood, by the doorpost. His eyes were moist. He spoke in a quiet voice, as though there had never been a shadow between them.

"He's beautiful."

Katherine's delicate white hand flicked and straightened her tresses, and she sighed. Her face was placid, and her blue eyes opened wide to meet his gaze. "Do you suppose I'm in the habit of making ugly babies, then?"

Shane's eyes glistened with merriment. He nodded. "Oh, I'd a fair idea he'd come by some share of your beauty. I suppose he's a temper as well." He winked. "Sure, he's half a Scotchman." He smiled now, full out, and then his demeanor shifted for his serious tidings. He had reconsidered. "I'll have word with Sorley MacDonnell. If he will meet my terms, I'll leave them bide where they are. But there will be tribute, and some restitution to the MacQuillans. And James and Sorley will not like it. If it comes to the clash, I'll do what has to be done."

"Aye, then, that's fair enough." Katherine could feel her eyes welling, and she wasn't pleased about that. It couldn't be helped, when all her feelings were so close to her skin. As she searched for the right thing to say now, Shane tossed a red velvet pouch onto the table before her.

"You'd want to take this with you, wherever it is you're going. It'll be divil-all use to me."

Katherine looked up with wonder. His face was impassive, but his eyes were full of roguery. She took from the pouch the most stunning necklace of diamonds and emeralds that she had ever seen. She leapt to her feet and threw her arms around him. They kissed passionately, and not without fresh tears from Kat. They clung to one another now, and after a long moment their hearts and their breathing had found the one rhythm, and she pulled her head back to look him in the eyes. She found there a certain wild glimmer that she knew. Katherine held up the glittering necklace that was wrapped around her hand, and spoke in a small teasing voice.

"Take it with me where I'm going, is it? Well, I've a fair idea of where I'm going just *now*, and it will be divil-all use to me there either!"

SHANE O'NEILL

CHAPTER 15

Shane was in high good humour these early days of summer, as life drifted back into its familiar patterns in the hills of home. He was more settled in his mind since he had met with Sorley MacDonnell and laid out his terms for peace. Sorley had yielded, though sullen and sore, assenting to all demands, and pledging to rise out with O'Neill against the English when word came down. He then took sail across Lough Neagh, with a promise to journey on to his brother in Kintyre, where he would convince the chieftain to ratify and keep to the accords. Katherine watched from shore as her uncle's galley faded into the horizon across the great lough, her moist eyes belying a deep sense of relief that swords would not be raised against kin.

She was relieved too, that Turlagh Lynnach O'Neill was no more to be seen, swaggering about the castle. No sooner had Shane returned than his cousin gathered up his men and headed back west, to tend to his lands beyond the Sperrins. Shane spent his days hunting, and his nights in endless conferrals with his officers, mostly the Donnelly brothers, plotting out strategies and ploys for the wars to come.

As beautiful and mild as were those days, they were lost upon Farleigh O'Gneeve, for he spent them in the dark realms under his towering oak. He laboured happily at his idylls, never wanting for company, as he was called upon by a strange succession of muses who arrived in dreams, visions, and bright reveries. When he would emerge,

SHANE O'NEILL

he invariably made his way to the castle, for Shane's table held its own charms, with convivial banter, and intoxicating spirits that never vanished.

It was shortly after lamplight on a lingering June evening, streaks of pink and gold still smoldering in the western sky. Katherine stood at the open window, the baby in her arms, gently rocking him to sleep. Only the evening star could be seen shimmering in the heavens. Venus, it was. Not really a star at all, Farleigh had said. She wondered if a wish would be wasted there. Kat looked out over the drumlins and purple hills that rolled and faded into the far horizon, and she thought of all the others casting their secret wishes and silent prayers into the gloaming, to be squandered upon a star that was only clay...

A sudden clatter of hooves on the cobbles brought her eyes to the courtyard below. Three horsemen were arriving. Cowled Franciscans, they looked to be, trotting in through the castlegate. But for the hour, this was hardly a wonder. Such monks and priests often arrived unannounced. But they would seldom call without news...What sort of tidings had brought them? God forbid anything dire! Wee Hugh was only just nodding off, and if she put him down now, he would surely rouse and bawl again. She sighed and crooned softly an old lullaby:

> 'Shoheen sho ho, I'll whisper low,
> My bonny wee babe rocks to and fro.
> Dry your tears, shoheen sho ho,
> For there's no harm can befall you.
>
> You shall have the Golden Fleece,
> The staff of Pan from the King of Greece,
> The spear of Finn, and the shield of Naoise,
> And no harm shall befall you.
>
> The rod of Moses shall be yours,
> And you shall have Cúchulainn's horse.
> Come tempest, blight, or bloody wars,

SHANE O'NEILL

There's no harm can befall you.
Shoheen sho ho, I'll whisper low...'

Wee Hugh was in a fine soft slumber by now. Katherine laid him in his cradle, and tip-toed from the room, gently drawing the door closed behind her. She had been strangely disquieted by these hooded messengers from the dusk, and as she entered the dank narrow stone passage and descended the dark spiral of steps, this growing sense of dread seemed to capture her breath, so that she had to stop and exhale, steadying herself against the cold stones. She told herself that Shane was home, and safe, that this unease was no more than habit, a holdover of that long travail. But still her steps were heavy.

As she approached the banquet chamber, the sound of bright laughter could be heard! Laughter! Oh, the power of it! Laughter that instantly banished her dark fears. An image from an old tale came to mind, and she could feel the black wraith of a scaldcrow that had settled upon her suddenly taking wing, startled at the tinkling sound of laughter. The talons of fear loosed from her neck, and the taut clench of her shoulders gave way. Katherine filled her lungs, and as she expelled the breath, she laughed at herself. Her step lightened, and she entered smiling, lithe and lissome and gracious.

Seated with their backs to her, the friars were nodding in agreement, and they made a queer picture, with those three bright circles of their tonsured heads, each sporting a ring of fringe over the ears, bobbing down and up. Shane was holding forth boisterously on the subject of Philip of Spain, so Katherine lingered in the shadows at the door. Several branches of candles graced the table with a blaze of light, an extravagance Shane had acquired in London.

Most of his retinue had drifted off early, odd for such an evening in high summer. Only a few intimates remained. On either side of him were Myler Magrath and auld Farleigh at the foot of the table. They had been tippling for some hours, but, from where she stood, no one seemed fuddled, thus far. Well, perhaps! Katherine noticed that someone was curled up in his mantle, softly snoring on the long settle at the window,

SHANE O'NEILL

and Shane's two hounds were keeping a drowsy sentry for him. A flicker of light fell across the glistening wires of a harp, perched at his feet, and the mystery was solved. Kat looked to the table again, and saw that all heads were turned to her. Shane had spied her at the door, and he gestured her over, smiling.

"Lads, this is my Lady Katherine, daughter of the MacLean of Duart." The monks jumped to their feet, and bowed with stiff formality. "Katherine, me love, would you ever hazard a guess...would you ever hazard a guess, and tell us which of these fine young men is my brother?" So they were not messengers after all! She laughed now, for Shane's riddle was no challenge. One was a thin gawk of a fellow with a hooky 'Galway' nose, and another was foxy haired and short. The third was clearly the youngest, with barely a score of years put by him. He had a wizened fledgling look to him, she thought, but for colouring and features there was no question, and a proud demeanor that marked him an O'Neill. He did not meet her gaze, a dodge she supposed, to put her astray. She smiled at the three friars, and winked at Shane.

"If we were staking wagers, now, I couldn't lose. But for the halo, and a few years wanting, he's the spit of you! This will be young Hugh, is it?"

"Oh ho! It's *Father* Hugh now!" Shane gave a sly laugh. "He was only just ordained in Salamanca. Those hands have been turned to every class of mischief you can name, and some you couldn't! And there they are now, anointed, imbued with all the queer powers of the priest. I'm thinking he'll make a fine pope! Won't that be a great ease for us?"

Friar Magrath winced at that notion, even as the others laughed. He stood, a bit unsteadily, to give place to Katherine beside the O'Neill. She took her seat, and assented to a glass of Madiera, as Hugh introduced his quiet companions. Shane nodded to the servant, and he poured liberally.

"Hugh has been labouring at his studies these long years in Spain. He brings to me this grand silver flagon, and a cask of Madiera from the King of Spain-"

"-Who sends with it his highest regards, and his most fervent prayers that you shall prevail in the Catholic cause!" Hugh held up his glass for a bumper, but Shane had more to say.

"You may tell him that next time I will prefer troops, and guns, and more troops, but I thank him none the less." He raised his glass, and looked to Hugh for the toast. Hugh stood, his sun-tinged features burnished all the more by the flickering blaze before him. On the wall behind, a towering shadow mimicked his grand gestures.

"To his Royal Highness, and Roman Catholic Majesty, King Philip II of Spain! Salud!" There was a spirited chorus of 'Salud', and a clinking of cups, and Hugh took his seat again. "This wine was pressed and fermented in Madiera, to be sure, but would you ever believe it? This cask of wine has traveled all the way to India! There is some...'alchemy' in the voyage that alters the wine until it savors of spice! Only upon its return, is it truly considered Madiera!" A wonder was made of that round the table, and Myler bristled.

"Alchemy indeed! Sure, isn't a *man* who is traveled seasoned in just the same way? Not in the ports of call, but in the journey itself, it is, that the change is wraught!" Katherine smiled. Indeed, Myler's pedantic tone was over-wrought, and clearly heightened by the alchemy of Madiera. She turned to the young priest.

"Do you have the Spanish then, Hugh? It's a lovely language, I do think! All lickity clippity!" He responded with a tight little smile.

"'Father Hugh', so please you. I have. My friends will tell you that my Spanish is better than my Latin!" Myler would not let this pass. His tone was teasing, but his 'jest' was in earnest.

"*That*'s a pale ghost of a boast! I hope your bog-Latin is improved since!"

Father Hugh looked at him with sheer disdain. "It's five years and more since you tutored me, Friar Magrath. I should think I've learned something in the colleges of Europe." Katherine stepped in again with the excitement of fresh inspiration. She put her hand on Shane's shoulder.

"He would make a grand ambassador for you, Shane, in the Spanish Court!" She turned again, beaming, to Hugh. As she did, she noticed him avert his eyes, and she was suddenly aware that he had not once met her gaze. She addressed him again to test this strange inkling. "Were there other Irishmen at the college, Father Hugh?"

"Aye, there were, and plenty. Every year there are more. There is even talk of setting up an Irish College there." His eyes darted around the table as he spoke, never so much as lighting upon Katherine. "Since the proscription of the Church, these young Catholic scions of the Pale can no longer attend Oxford or Cambridge, and there has been a flood of them into the halls of Salamanca. Two of the Dons are Dublinmen. But the Palesmen are all quite aloof to the *Irish* scholars. They'll not abide our company, and we hear that they slander us to the Spaniards." There was tisking and pishing to be heard. "We've little time for *them*, truth be told. And our scholars shame them with learning."

It's very like our Lowlanders, with their English ways." Katherine saw now that none of the three friars would engage her eyes, and she suspected some moral opprobrium was behind it. A dim view, and a narrow one, that did not encompass Shane in its censure. Indeed, the Spanish Court would be a grand place for this callow wee prig! She sidled closer to Shane and leaned on his shoulder. He put an obliging arm around her, and she lolled and wriggled in closer still, as provocatively as she could for her clerical guests. Myler was squinting at the young priest, and Farleigh seemed lost in his thoughts. She turned her words directly to the young clerics. "Aye. The English tongue it is. Like our Lowlanders. It brings with it an insufferable arrogance and disdain! I can't abide them. They revile our people, and impute every class of savagery to us. I think, perhaps, your Palesmen are of the same ilk." Farleigh smiled up at her. He had been quiet this while, but he'd been listening, and he put his spoke in now.

"If they are, they belied themselves nicely with their fine welcome, for they turned out in Dublin howling and cheering for himself." He nodded to Shane. "By Crom, I never heard the like of it! And it will stand to you when comes the clash!" Father Hugh looked to his brother, and lowered his voice portentously.

"Perhaps it was *peace* they were cheering. And your submission to their queen. Will there not be peace now? After London?" Shane smiled darkly, and drank deep.

"There will be peace until there is war." The table stilled. All eyes fixed upon him, waiting to hear what the future would bring. "I had another scrape from Sussex, two pages of his prevarications this time. He assures me that I still hold the Queen's favour. A great comfort to me, that! 'The Queen's *fear*' would be nearer the mark!" His eyes moved slowly from face to face around the table, regarding the apprehension or feigned indifference he found there. His own eyes betrayed some dark glee. Perhaps it was simply a tipsy delight in teasing out the suspense of the moment. "By the terms of London, I allowed him to keep his garrison at Armagh, on condition that they be victualed out of the Pale. But, by Christ, they never stopped plundering those hills, taking preys. I sent him word that he had broken the accords. What did I get but more demands! He wrote commanding that I restore to him three hostages. He's still rankled since my young colts bolted on him last Spring. Only when they are returned, he said, could the indentures be enacted. Aye, well. I delivered up the hostages, and still they are plundering at Armagh. Perhaps they are due a wee reckoning." Fr. Hugh looked up with concern.

"Who did you give them, then?"

"Henry and young Turleigh and one of Manus Donnelly's lads."

"Ach, Poor wee Henry!" Katherine shook her head, and tisked. "Sure he's only just home!"

"His own choice, it was!" Shane laughed. "And I consented. Our Henry holds it no great affliction to be confined there, in the company of the sons of all the Great Houses of Ireland. There are twenty-one of them in it! These lads will one day be chieftains and Lords. And they forge bonds of friendship in their captivity that will serve them in times to come." He laughed darkly, and lowered his voice to a conspiring rumble. "These swaggering fops in Dublin Castle haven't a notion! The truth is...the truth is that every grand alliance they face in the field was forged under their own thatch." Farleigh considered this, as he licked Madiera from his shaggy mustache, and he rendered his reckoning.

SHANE O'NEILL

"Still, a prisoner's life is no joy! And at the end of the day, they *are* prisoners..." Shane pished again.

"Aye, 'at the end of the day,' maybe. They're locked up each night, it's true, but otherwise they're free to roam about the Castle, whoring and roistering for themselves. When will they have it better? No worries on them..."

"No worries, is it?" Farleigh spluttered at this. "No worries? There's many a hostage has gone to God when his sire broke the bonds of good conduct. Hangmen are kept in work by the like of that, and there's few of them idle. If *I* were Henry, now, not a *flutter* of a wink would I sleep for fear of your own good promises going awry! If Sussex avows you hold the Queen's favour today, still, you'll hardly stay long in her good ledgers!"

"And perhaps the Deputy is only half a fool." Shane's eyes suddenly burned like embers, and he spoke as to Sussex. "He knows that if harm would come to my sons...if harm comes to my sons, I will hack a river of blood through the Pale until I reach him, to slit his scrawny throat!" The dark temper vanished just as quickly, and he tipped a sly wink. "Sure, Henry knows we have our men placed in the Castle, and by this, he knows who they are. When I am ready to provoke Sussex beyond his natural restraints, there will be another timely escape. No fear." The young priest raised an inquisitive brow.

"And when will that be?"

"When all of Ulster is firmly in my grip, I'll have a free hand to smite the English. Between that day and this, I need to put some manners on Con O'Donnell." He noted Hugh's questioning look. "Cullagh's son is acting the O'Donnell in his place. And there's a few of his followers need to be brought to heel, Maguire, O'Reilly, and MacMahon. Conniving hoors they are, all of them bought and bound to Sussex." Katherine wondered and worried now about a long campaign.

"In the *far* west is it?" Farleigh leaned in to explain to her, his finger tracing a wet line in the spills on the smooth deal table.

"Their lands are all end to end, twisting along the southern borders of Ulster, either side of the Black Pig's Dyke and into the west. Each

SHANE O'NEILL

abutting the next: O'Reilly, McMahon, Maguire, O'Donnell. From the Brefney to Tirconnell, until they're like a long snake, hissing at our back." Shane nodded.

"Hmmm. If they are, O'Donnell is the head and the tail of it. When I have him rightly chastised, the rest will be tripping on each-other's heels to come in." Fr. Hugh sat back, folding his arms under his long brown sleeves.

"When will you put them to rights?"

"Soon enough! I've called a hosting in Dungannon at the Feast of Lughnasa, in a few weeks' time. Word has gone forth to every sept in Ulster to be accounted there. I sent down the hard word to O'Donnell and Maguire. If their faces are not seen at my fire that day, we'll rise out, the lot of us, and pay them a neighborly call. With fire and sword. Come Michaelmas, I mean to have tribute from every chieftain north of the Black Pig's Dyke!" A spell of silence followed, as wine was sipped. Katherine smiled and put down her goblet.

"How did the border of Ulster come by such a queer name?" They all looked to Farleigh. He took a long draught of Madiera, and a sigh of contentment fluttered through the shaggy white fringe of his mustache.

"Not hard to tell..." A gust of laughter whirled round the table until the flames danced on their tapers, for they all knew this to be the start of a hoary old wonder tale, and Farleigh was the very devil for them. He had seldom got such an excuse to launch into one.

"If you were to stand upon a height and look out over it, Lady Katherine, you would see a long ditch with ramparts stretching for many long miles, and it is there since the days of Cúchulain and King Conor MacNessa. Even *then* it was called 'the Black Pig's Dyke.' There was that time a schoolmaster who had the 'old learning' in him. And he must have had the devil in him too, for now and again a queer dark humour would come over him. And when it did, there's nothing would do him but to turn his young scholars into hares with a wave of his hazel wand. And then he would set his hounds on them! Oh, he held this to be great sport, altogether! Now there was a red-haired widow nearby, in the hills of Kiltyclogher, and she had a share of that learning as well. The

SHANE O'NEILL

schoolmaster never bethought himself, and when the humour was on him, he turned one of her sons into a hare, and the other into a hound. What would a hound do, but chase a hare? So the red haired widow's son chased his brother and savaged him. Killed him. In revenge, the woman turned the master into a spikey, bristly, black pig. The herds of swine thereabouts shunned his company, until a raging fury overtook him, and he rampaged across the country heaving up a huge track in his wake. It's little wonder, then, that it would be known as the Black Pig's Dyke!" The heads turned to Katherine now, to see was she satisfied with her answer.

"Sure, what else would you call it?" She laughed with the rest. "Och Farleigh O'Gneeve, you're the source of all knowledge!"

The short reddish monk inclined his head back and whispered to Fr. Hugh, who shook his head and answered in full voice. "No, no...that was Maguire's Country we came through, across the lakes." Shane raised his brows at this.

"Did you land at Galway, then? That's an awkward journey."

"We did, aye, but we sailed again. There was a northbound galleon that brought us as near as Sligo. We spent last night in the abbey at Clogher." Fr. Hugh's words set Farleigh off again with lore of that place.

"Tell me this. Did you see the golden stone of Clocher, then?" They shook their heads. "It's embedded in the Cathedral steps, and it still glistens with veins of gold. That stone was one time as famed as the Delphic Oracle of Greece, and it was consulted by Druids from every-" Farleigh stopped suddenly, silenced by Shane's upraised hand. Hugh was leaning over the table to his brother, murmuring to him. Shane appeared agitated.

"What? *What* are you saying?" Hugh spoke up.

"I say I was greatly agrieved to hear about your poor wife, God rest her immortal soul." He blessed himself quickly, as did his companions. Shane squinted into the candlelight to see him clearly across the table, and his voice was gruff.

"What's this you're telling me? Is she dead? Is Moya dead, then?" Fr. Hugh's eyes opened wide, and he nodded solemnly.

SHANE O'NEILL

"She is, aye. I thought surely you knew! Perhaps it was only recent, when I thought it was old news. I never heard the 'when' of it. The Abbess at Clogher gave me her sour condolence when we arrived yesterday. She was bitter, and she said only that Moya had died of a broken heart at the hands of my O'Neills." The others blessed themselves now, and Farleigh sighed.

"God bless the girl, but a brittle heart is easy broken!" On hearing him, Katherine caught her breath.

"Oh, Farleigh...Every heart is easy broken." She straightened herself beside Shane, who looked a bit shaken. He was nodding slowly, and his look was far away.

Friar Magrath blessed himself and murmured, "May God grant her peace." Auld Farleigh echoed him.

"May God grant her peace...which is more than *she* ever granted to any man!" Father Hugh glared at him. Myler spoke again.

"Sure, we all know...there's many a one, old and young, is *living* with a broken heart. At the end of the day, if she was taken to God, it was because God willed it so."

The young priest nodded thoughtfully. "Aye, it *was* God's will. And maybe it was the Almighty's blessing upon Shane O'Neill, for he is free now to wed. He could make a fine match now, one that would credit the house of O'Neill, and bless him with proper *legal* heirs." The others glared at him in disbelief. Katherine felt the colour rising in her face. She could see that Shane was lost in his thoughts. Now, at last, Father Hugh looked her in the eye. His voice was low.

"Where is your husband, woman? Where is Moya's father?" Katherine stood abruptly, drawing Shane instantly from his reveries.

"My husband is beside me. If you are seeking O'Donnell, let you ask my husband. I shall bid you goodnight." She looked to the others, and they parted to make way. "Gentlemen." As she passed Shane's brother, she stopped and turned. "Indeed, Hugh O'Neill, one *might* have thought you would learn something in the colleges of Europe. Civil manners, if nothing else." With that, she turned and walked proudly from the room. Shane glared at his brother. His mouth curled into a smirk, and he answered Hugh with a jeer.

"O'Donnell is atoning for his sins, Father. In my dungeon on the little isle of Inishdowal. A bit of Purgatory that should win him a grand indulgence! So, you see, I'm looking after his soul as well." His eyes narrowed, and he demanded sharply. "What is it you've said? What did you say to my Katherine?"

"I spoke the simple truth. I said that you are free to wed now. And, plainly, she is not."

"Are we fools, then, that we didn't know as much? You may spare me your pious snuffling, Hugh. I don't recall you heeding *my* advice. I counseled you to take a wife!"

"Who will speak the truth to you, if your brother will not? Even as you strive to restore the very name and power of O'Neill-" Hugh shook his head derisively. "To see it *fouled* and besmirched by this sordid coupling! There is dark talk all through the hills out there. Talk of chains and irons! They say she is a prisoner, and they call your son 'wee shackled Hugh', and 'fettered Hugh O'Neill'. Even were he not my namesake, I would shame to hear it!"

"What is a fireside without gossip?" Shane drank his wine, glaring over the rim of his goblet. Fr. Hugh pressed on.

"A fireside without gossip is a quiet fireside, indeed. But must the House of O'Neill be cockshot for their talk?" Shane set down his emptied goblet, and he huffed.

"Talk! What are words? There's divil-all in them but air." He turned to Farleigh to bolster his defense. The old man tugged at his beard, shifting his eyes from one to the other.

"Words are more than air! Much more than air. But you have the right of the matter, O'Neill. The moon is not hurt by the dogs barking at it."

"They will not respect you." Hugh fixed a cool challenging gaze upon him.

"So long as they fear me! These dark tales make me fearsome and wondrous to them. Anyway it is not *my* people who tell such tales. The O'Donnells and their clans must have it so, or their chieftain will be without honour. Cullagh the cuckold! The English will have it so, to claim virtue for their heretics over the impious savages. And the Scots take up the chorus, so to clear the Countess of her part in the abduction."

"But what of your sons? Will you sire a string of bastards to sulk, and skulk, and envy all their days? This great quest of yours! For years now! Has it not been to put aside the baseborn heirs of our father? You went to London to proclaim your rights over just such an illborn contender. I must own, Shane, I don't understand it."

"On that point, we can agree. When you are my age, you'll understand a good deal more...I hope to Christ!" There was silence now, but for the snoring of a certain forgotten minstrel who was sprawled out on the far settle. The less-than-dulcet tones of Blind Colm. Shane drank again of the Madiera, and peered vacantly into the constellation of candle flames before him. His lips whitened as he pressed them together, rallying his powers of concentration. He sighed, and spoke in a quiet listless voice. "This is most unforeseen, Moya's death. It changes a great deal. I'll have to ponder it out." He turned to Myler Magrath, who looked a bit the worse for wear. His elbow was propped up on the table, his chin resting in his palm, and a weary look about his features that betrayed unspoken misgivings. Shane laughed aloud. "Here's a man could use a dose of sunshine! You crafty hoor, ye! You must have been praying to St. Christopher! Aye, for there might well be a journey in your future, Myler Magrath. I may have some small business for you in Rome."

SHANE O'NEILL

CHAPTER 16

Even the leaden grey morning sky and its misty showers couldn't dim or dampen the spirits on 'gathering day' at Dungannon. Shane's word of summons had brought not only hosts of cavalry, but crowds of revelers, all roused from home and hearth to celebrate the first fruits of the harvest on the Feast of Lughnasa. In Irish, the month of August takes its name from this festival that marks its beginning, and it was eagerly awaited as the high point of summer.

Shane and his household had come down early, in carriages and wagons laden with baggage, for they would be in residence through September. The castle was far more grand than Benburb, and Katherine preferred it. Shane's father and forefathers had tended it with great care, and it was very much a lordly manor, with its heavy ornate furnishings, but he found its trappings too stodgy and, truth be told, too English. He insisted upon residing at his more rustic fortress on the Blackwater. It was Kat's fond hope, nevertheless, on occasions such as this, to win Shane over to this more sumptuous and genteel residence.

The keep at Dungannon had five floors, that served most of the year as the quiet preserve of a certain peevish ghost, if the servants were to be credited, but now its halls were lively and bustling. Chieftains from every part settled in for the week with their families in the nicely appointed suites. By custom, these Irish nobles formed marriage alliances among those of their rank, regardless of distance, and these were great occasions for the matchmaking and courting. To be ensconced in O'Neill's Castle was the 'crow's perch' of social distinction.

The crowds had been arriving all week, and the green hills around Dungannon were a motley clutter of brightly coloured tents and banners. There was barely a nook or a patch, a height or hollow, without its tent or shack or shieling. The wee town below the castle was teaming with revelers, and every class of huckster and hawker, and three-penny-trick man was there waiting for them. Wagons trundled in from the far hills loaded with poitín and other potations, and did a brisk business wherever they stopped. Right from the start there were circles of musicians holding forth, and revelers jigging and twirling in set-dances. There were hurling matches, and weight tossing, wrestling, and footraces. Young people would amble off in pairs or bands, traipsing into the hills to pick bilberries and steal apples, and sing, and court, and maybe swig lashings of poitín, if they had managed to abscond with that. It was a fine time for mad frolics.

On Castle Hill a marvelous feast was held that evening for the nobler sort. All fairly grand by Irish standards, with fine plate and fleshforks and such. This was one of the few formal banquets on the calender, and all the more so under Katherine's courtly 'menage.' Attired in their finery, the guests were led to their places by Shane's chief steward, with his black staff of office that was 'tall as a mill-shaft.' The seating order and placement was extremely hierarchical, and such details were rigorously attended to.

Lady Katherine presided over the evening with lighthearted grace, moving easily among the guests to bid them welcome, and to hear their news. She wore a gown of sea-green silk, with her most precious jewels, the emeralds and diamonds, sparkling over her bosom. Her lips and cheeks were lightly blushed with elderberries, and she looked ravishing.

It was unthinkable for a married woman to appear hatless, but Kat's only concession on the matter was a small beaded cap on the crown of her head that was barely discernible behind the waves of her lustrous hair. She had given no thought as to how this reflected upon her questionable marriage status before the ladies of Ulster. When it was

SHANE O'NEILL

remarked upon obliquely by the O'Quinn's wife, Katherine laughed merrily and replied that she was only delighted to show that she was "not festooned with chains and shackles as *some* would have it!" In truth, her French fashions evoked both admiration and envy. The Irish custom was for married ladies to wear a swath of bright linen elaborately folded and tucked around their heads, so the contrast she made was quite stark. With wit and charm, however, she won them over, and her exotic ways and 'floutings' were put down to the simple fact that she was foreign.

The victuals arrived from the kitchens, greeted by cheerful applause. The merry crowds parted for a procession of servants bearing huge joints of beef and venison on spits and trays. These were presented before Shane that he might carve the first portion, for, as the Jesuit Campion tells us, "it was ever O'Neill's custom when sitting at meat, before he would put one morsel to his lips, he would slice a portion, above the daily alms, and send it to the beggars at the gate, saying it was meet to serve Christ first."

When the lavish meal was about to commence, Katherine seated herself beside Shane at the centre of the head table. Towering behind them like the Praetorian Guard were three fearsome gallowglass in their long tunics of glistening chainmail. Candlebranches were everywhere, of course, with enough flickering tapers to rival the Milky Way. Seven harpers were on hand, and most of the chieftains had brought their bards, with singers and jesters in tow, so there was no want of diversion.

O'Hanlon's bard, Ruarcan O'Hamill, took the honours with his timely harvest ode. Before he began, the servants carried in the warm 'first-loaves', Irish brown bread, the very first made from the new harvest of grain. O'Hamill won over the crowd as he twisted forth his clever staves, invoking the old pagan god Lugh, for whom the feast, and indeed the month, was named. Lugh and Crom Dubh were matching their powers against those of St. Patrick in a dispute over sheaves of wheat. The resourceful saint used the Stone of Crom as a quernstone, and in the end, of course, the fine fresh loaves of bread served as communion for his High Mass. Farleigh gave him due praise, although he considered the piece a craven stunt to win favour with the Franciscans, who seemed to him to be *everywhere*. Indeed, it was Friar Magrath who blessed the first loaves. This was a key part of the evening's rituals, for it was held bad luck to partake of a new harvest until it had been duly blessed.

Songs were sung and dances were danced. The men huddled together over their drams and draughts, and wagers were placed and taken on the great race to be held on the morrow. The sleekest and fastest horses in Ulster would be running, and that was the juicy bone that was chewed over all the night, with boasting and wild speculation. It was a spirited evening, but fairly civil and genteel, due to the unstinting vigilance of the wives. These ladies were ever mindful, of course, of the dignity of the occasion, but mostly wary of the stealthy glances and begrudging smirks of rivals. Only Flann and Scohaun disgraced themselves, by tipping a table for a meaty joint. Now and then a brattle of thunder would intrude upon the cozy gathering, hinting vaguely of darker powers to be appeased, for out beyond the castle walls a more pagan spirit prevailed, and the night belonged to the old gods.

Once darkness had fallen, bonfires blazed up in the hills, casting their eery glow across the black racing clouds that scudded overhead. The heavy skies threatened rain all the night, with Lugh the Long-arm throwing thunder on the hills to stir the winds, and his grandfather, Balor of the Evil Eye, hurling his fiery bolts into the darkness. But the rain never came.

As the night wore on, the massive bonfires climbed higher and higher into the night air, the flames lurching and leaping and licking the sky, and around them whirled mad dancers, mad dancers driven by the frantic throbbing pulse of goat-skin drums and hard spirits surging through the blood. Around them teamed staggering crowds, reeling and swaying. Swaggering packs of lads were roaring out songs to drown out rival anthems. There were skuffles and rows, rumbly thump and roolybooly. A proper shalloo! It was a savage night, all told, and there was many a maid undone by cockcrow.

The grey morning found few stirring. It was nearly midday when the crowds assembled at Castlehill for 'Loaf-Mass'. The clergy would *only*

SHANE O'NEILL

speak of this harvest celebration as 'Loaf-Mass' or 'Lammas.' This 'Lammastide' was their way of arrogating for themselves the pagan feast of Lughnasa. After all, more than a millennium had passed since Patrick vanquished these heathen gods, and his Christian dominion was unassailable. At least by daylight.

O'Neill's Castle stood on a lofty height, affording a view of Slieve Gallon to the north, and Slieve Gullion to the south. Directly below the walls of the castle, a cluster of cottages huddled, snug and humble, on a crescent-shaped sward, and all was ringed by a wide protective moat. Across the moat-bridge, a tall make-shift cross had been erected for this day, and before it stood an altar dressed for Mass. Just below this, on the grassy slope, sheaves of wheat and barley were piled, with a cish of turnips and carrots, and other such bounty as had come to ripeness. The hill was thronged, with the congregation stretching all the way down to the road below. Above it all, the dark skies rumbled softly, charging the occasion with an unwelcomed air of suspense.

As the long procession of Franciscan friars shuffled and tramped over the creaky planks of the moatbridge, a hush fell over the crowd. Behind the monks came the grey nuns of Ardtrea who seemed to drift across in a celestial silence. When they had taken their places at either side of the altar, the fervent voices of these brown and grey-robed ranks rose and blended in a solemn symphony of plainsong. Now came the nobility of Ulster, slow and stately, to take their places nearest the altar, the last of them being the O'Neill and his Lady.

With stately simplicity, too, the Latin hymn stepped its way up and down the Gregorian scales, attesting to the order and unity of creation, even as the heavens glowered and grumbled of chaos from on high. As the last plaintive note of 'Amen' faded on the wind, the Introit bells tinkled, and all rose to their feet. Over the bridge came six young acolytes, and there was a stir down the hillside when the people saw who was behind them to concelebrate the High Mass. It was young Father O'Neill, the chieftain's brother, alongside him the Dean Terence Donnelly, and behind them was the Primate of All Ireland, Archbishop O'Tighe. His tall mitre, over his lank frame, gave a mystical stature to the

SHANE O'NEILL

Primate. With the green gothic chasuble draped over his shoulders, and the crook of his glittering Crozier curling above him, he looked every bit the proper heir to St. Patrick. O'Tighe was a man of warmth and simplicity, and a great contrast to his English predecessors, so that the people regarded him as little less than a saint. For all the lowering skies, the rain held off through the Mass, and that was put down to the Prelate's piety, and the wondrous spiritual powers it conferred upon him.

It was a beautiful Mass, and its hillside setting imparted a vaguely biblical air to the proceedings. The people were charmed by the lilting Limerick tones of O'Tighe's Irish, and his blue eyes glistened and flashed with fervour as he gave his stirring sermon. His theme was thanksgiving and the Harvest.

"Blessed be God for the beautiful harvest that stands afresh in our fields, unblemished and golden, before us. For this we are truly blessed! It is right for us, as we look upon His bounty, to reflect upon the sacred design of our Creator. For within each heart God has sewn an immortal soul, to be tended with Faith and love, one day to be reaped and taken, wholesome and unblemished to His Harvest Home. So too, have we a harvest of Faith in Ireland. There is a new spirit abroad in the land. The seeds of Faith sewn by Patrick over a millennium ago, and tended by the generations, are come to a ripening in our time. In one of God's mysterious ways, the sordid religious convulsions in England have brought a miraculous blessing to the people of Ireland. For both the children of the Gael and the Old English of the Pale have renewed and fortified their Faith in his Holy Church! Our brethren in the Pale have turned their hearts to us, and we shall embrace them in the name of Christ. Oh, it is easy to love those who are familiar to us, those who speak the language of our fireside. But our Blessed Savior asks us to do more than that. In this time of hope, we shall set aside our differences and stand together with the Palesman to achieve our deliverance. Yes, our day of deliverance draws ever nearer, with this ripening in our hearts. For God hears our prayers. We know that even His Chosen People were asked to suffer long and hard at the hands of their enemies.

SHANE O'NEILL

And just as God delivered the Jews from their bondage in Egypt, so He will deliver us from the tyranny of England. Has He not raised up among us Shane O'Neill? Has he not delivered him unto us from his captivity in the land of the Stranger? Almighty God has sent to us a prince of the royal house of Ulster to cast away our shackles, and to face down those heretics who would lead us to eternal damnation. But the Harvest is not yet in. A harvest is the fruit of labour, and there is yet much labour to be done. There must be a gathering in, and a marching forth, for a hard threshing season is upon us. Let us steel ourselves for the work to come, as we give thanks to our Heavenly Father for his bounty, and for his precious blessing of hope. After long ages of darkness, we live in a time of hope, and that is the greatest blessing of all! In the name of the Father, and of the Son, and of the Holy Ghost."

"Amen," sang the choir, over the murmur of excitement that rustled over the hillside. There truly was great astonishment, for the Primate had spoken aloud things that heretofore were only whispered by the priests. The highest spiritual authority in Ireland, the voice of divine guidance, was actually speaking to them in Irish. And for once, they had not been admonished to 'render unto Caesar the things that are his!'

At the Offertory, there was a benediction of the 'first fruits', and, as was custom, the communion was unleavened bread made from the new wheat by the nuns at Armagh. When the Mass ended, a crowd of children gathered around the archbishop, and he appeared very much in his element, teasing and testing them, and doling out apples from a barrel. The sound of their bright laughter seemed to auger a new day, for his English predecessors had mostly never dared to venture outside the Pale, even to visit the Episcopal seat. With an Irishman as Irish Primate, the people felt that a great wrong had been righted.

It wasn't long before the heady crowds dispersed, hurrying off to line the roads for the afternoon's races, and the O'Neill's guests assembled in the Great Hall for a mid-day meal. After a quick repast, Shane and the Dean adjourned to his office chamber to confer, accompanied by the Dean's secretary, an earnest young priest. An attendant decanted port for them, and quietly withdrew. The heavy door clanked shut, bringing a silence that made all suddenly aware of the bustle and noise that had been banished from the chamber. All was stillness, but for the faint twittering of birds from the window. Shane unfolded a parchment that lay on his desk, and handed it to Dean Donnelly in silence, but with a meaningful flash of the eyes. He stood beside the Dean's chair, waiting. As Donnelly perused it, his brow furrowed. He looked up, nodding sympathetically.

"Ah, yes...I see. I might have known. It is his shrewd usage of 'praemissa.' The summons was crafted in this ambiguous way to allow him to sieze you. You were right not to oblige him." He folded the letter and handed it back to Shane, who took his seat behind the great desk. The Dean shook his head. "Another contemptible ruse -that does no honour to Sussex, *or* the Queen. Of course he's furious that you eluded him!"

"Oh? When did you see him?"

"But three nights ago. I've only just returned from Dublin. For *five* nights, he says, they waited on you in Dundalk!" Shane laughed.

"As long as that? He's a fool. If I were coming, I'd have appeared on the day appointed. And I'm sure he *looked* a proper fool, with the Earls at his side."

"Aye. Each day's disappointment adding fire to his fury. When I spoke to him, oh, he certainly was dashed that his little trap had miscarried, but I think he was cheered in your providing him this new pretext for war. He relentlessly assails the Queen to mount a new offensive, but, thankfully, Elizabeth will hear none of it. She's jealously guarding her scant treasure."

"She can't afford a war. Isn't that why she brought me to London!"

"The army's pay is so far in arrears that recruitment has all but ceased. She demands that Sussex keep the peace. And, of course, he's beset by this new High Commission in Dublin! Kildare's little delegation has paid off handsomely there. She's sent Sir Nicholas Arnold over to investigate the charges, and now they're even delving into the false muster rolls. Drawing pay for dead soldiers. Regiments of straw-men on his books. Sussex is rightly tethered and fit to be tied."

SHANE O'NEILL

"Good enough, so. He'll not stir then while I'm in the West." He saw a questioning crook in the Dean's brow. "I've called this hosting to settle young O'Donnell. And old Maguire!"

"Aye, aye, aye...It was no surprise to see that O'Donnell's son had spurned your summons today...but Cúconacht Maguire is a seasoned auld spear! Why would he bring such an onslaught to his door?" Shane looked at him with some surprise.

"Sure, wasn't his daughter Judith wed to the Bastard!" The Dean appeared to be somewhat perplexed. "That was *his* grandson killed at Carlingford, my wee rival, young Brian O'Neill, rest his soul. Ah, no. Auld Maguire will not yield without blood."

"*More* blood." The cleric sighed, and sipped of his portwine with a troubled twist in his brow. "And what of O'Reilly? What's his interest in this rash challenge?"

"Cullagh O'Donnell's mother was his kinswoman. His aunt. He will have to make a show of defiance. But O'Reilly is of small account."

"Sussex will hold this a further violation of your covenants." The priest's tone was cautionary. "He said that all disputes you hold with O'Donnell and the rest must be arbitrated by the four earls in counsel."

"Did he? Did he, indeed? Then *he* has violated the covenants by not sending them to do so."

"Aye. He wants war. That's plain as a pikestaff." The Dean sighed again, and sat back in his chair. "Cruel times indeed...God grant us peace." He blessed himself absently. "His Grace should be along shortly. This new trouble with London is a terrible vexation. I hate to burden him with it when he's in such good spirits."

"Is he?" Shane was thumbing through a sheaf of papers on the desk.

"Aye, he's in great form. O'Tighe knows his horseflesh. I saw him place a shrewd wee wager on one of Egan O'Quinn's sprinters, so I did the same." Shane held up another document, with an enigmatic smile. The Dean reached out his palm.

"What's this, then?" Shane withheld it, nodding with a sly grin until Donnelly twigged. "It's never!!" Shane offered it now, and the Dean's young aide jumped to his feet to retrieve it. Terence Donnelly examined the paper, his mouth open with wonder. "Impotentia Coeundi...Calvatus O'Donnell!" He looked up, smiling. "Impotence! How did you get him to scratch his name to such a thing? He must be half dead!"

"By Katherine's account, there's no word of a lie in it. I explained to him, nice and handy, that since his daughter has gone to her reward, I am now free to wed, but for the impediment of his marriage to Katherine. That being the case, I offered him either an annulment or a funeral, and in the end, he chose to petition the Holy Father for a dissolution of the marriage."

"If Lady Katherine stands by it, I suppose he's been asked to do no more than what is due and proper, however much he mislikes it. Will I send it off to Wolfe with a commendation?" Shane's quizzical squint drew a further advisement from the wary Dean. "The Papal Nuncio in Limerick is *very* jealous of his prerogatives. If he feels he has been overstepped, he might urge against you among the Curia." Shane shook his head.

"I don't like the cut of him. Wolfe. He's well named. I wouldn't trust the shifty hoor. No, we'll not call upon his good offices. Not at all. Your letter of commendation would not be amiss. But I'm going to send Myler off to Rome to broker the annulment directly. He's acquainted with Cardinal Moroni, and several auditors in the Holy Roman Rota."

"Ah, our foster brother! No better man, with all those years he spent in Rome. Resourceful, and sound. And devious! A diplomat."

"I'll have him advocate for the brother while he's there. The Diocese of Down and Conor is vacant."

"A bishopric?" The Dean took care not to betray his shock at this suggestion. "Ah...Now, *there* you will have difficulty. By Canon Law, a bishop must be fully thirty years of age. Hugh is little more than twenty." Shane's voice deepened ever so slightly, with a bristly edge that made it clear he would brook no denial.

"Hugh is the son of an Earl. You seem to forget that I hold the ecclesiastical patronage. Since His Holiness spurned Elizabeth, and upheld my nomination of O'Tighe, the choice is mine. And I recall Myler saying that some of those Italians, those Medici bishops, are barely

SHANE O'NEILL

sprouting whiskers. The Pope's grandson is a Cardinal at the age of fourteen, for the love of God! I'm sure *something* can be arranged...Hugh could be a formidable ambassador for me in the courts of Europe, like Bishop DeQuadra in London. In the meantime, he's residing at Brantry. Perhaps you will have a place for him on your staff at Armagh?"

"Indeed, Shane, I will surely. I'll find something for him. He'll learn the rigours of administration with us, for most every matter in Ireland comes through my- Ah, here he is!" With a clank, the great door opened and an attendant stepped in.

"His reverence, the Archbishop of Armagh, would see you O'Neill."

"In with him, so." Shane and the two priests rose to their feet, and the Primate entered, bowing his head under the low lintel of the doorway. He wore no mitre, but a tri-cornered biretta over wavy grey hair that was still dark in the back. His cassock was purple, with a stole of the same that covered his arms and buttoned down the front. The crucifix that rested on his breast was nearly as large as the one Shane had received of the Pope. A man of some fifty years, his face was craggy and clean-shaven, with bushy grey brows over blue eyes that were kindly and quick. His prominent cheekbones and his rangy frame gave him an ascetic look, but with nothing severe or abstracted about him. He smiled brightly.

"God save all here."

"Your Grace!" Shane gestured to a large ornate chair, cushioned with leather, and the Primate sat, wide-legged with his hands clapped upon his knees. Shane nodded to the decanter. "Will you take a small port?"

"No, no. Not for me. But perhaps another cup of buttermilk from the pitcher, Fr. Keavney, if you would be so kind." His assistant made for the door, but Shane sent his own attendant.

"Tague will see to it. Have a seat, then." Dean Donnelly gave a sidling nod.

"His Grace is a great man for the bonnyclabber. There's said to be a power of health in it. But a dash more port will do me no harm!" His aide did the honours. The bishop fairly beamed at his host.

"Well, God love you, Shane O'Neill! You are to be commended

rightly on this fine Lammastide festivity! It's grand to see the old customs upheld so splendidly. And that's no small matter! It heartens the people, both high and low. And it heartens *me* to see that Ulster will surely flourish under your bold command."

"Your sermon was a fine one, Your Reverence. 'Steel yourselves for a hard threshing!' That will put courage into them!"

"Aye. No more, and no less, that the truth, as God has seen fit to reveal his world to me. Now. What is this all about? What is this new demand from London that has caused you such concern, O'Donnelly?"

"Aye, well, as you're aware, Your Grace, the Queen has refused to recognize your primatial appointment. She has declared it null, and-"

"That is immaterial! I did not receive it of her. Such overweening pride and presumption!" His tone was low and even, but his eyes flashed. He slapped his hand on his knee. "The Primacy was not hers to bestow. I received the pallium from His Holiness in Rome, as did each of my predecessors back to Patrick. She possesses neither the authority, nor –so long as the O'Neill prevails- the *power,* to annul the appointment. Her writ does not run beyond the walls of Dundalk. Maybe we should only smile, and thank the Almighty for that!" The wary Dean nodded slowly, and raised his hand in a gentle cautioning gesture.

"Aye, for that we are thankful. But she *can* render impossible your jurisdiction within the Pale. That much-"

"Ah, now, there's truth in that. No word of a lie..." He shook his head, and, for a moment, the bishop seemed to lose himself in thought. He looked up at Shane then, and poured forth his darker concerns in a confidential tone. "I do greatly fear she's done as much already. From the first, not one of my letters were answered or acknowledged. I satisfied myself in as much as I knew that they had been read. But now she disrupts my administration in the Pale. In November, I called my clergy to assemble for a provincial synod, the English-speaking pastorate, and nearly a third were missing. They had all been threatened by that greedy English lout, Bishop Curwen, in Dublin. I'm told that he is daily pressing others to flout my directives. More and more English upstarts are being sent over to enrich themselves on the temporalities of holy office. All espousing the heretical reforms. Where will it stop? Like her bloated debauched father, she is bound by no conscience! Not a *glimmer* of doubt or remorse. How small a matter to dismiss a Primate, for a woman who will deny the Pope!" His eyes shone with bright fervour. "This is why you must stand against her, Shane O'Neill, and why you must prevail!" The door clanked open, and Tague appeared with the cup of buttermilk. O'Tighe accepted it with an eager smile. "Thank you." He took a hearty swallow. "That's grand. I feel the want of it on such a day. So sultry and close." The Dean gently called him back to business.

"Your Grace-"

"Yes, of course, forgive me, O'Donnelly. I'm making it so very difficult for you to impart your news. Tell us, so. What is this new offensive from London?"

"I have orders to assemble the Chapter of Armagh. A Conge d'elire. Letters patent arrived from the Chancellor-" Shane interrupted him.

"I'm only a layman, now. You'll have to Irish that for me."

"It's a royal warrant to the Dean and Chapter to elect her nominee to the Primacy of Armagh. As if the seat were vacant! She has named Adam Loftus."

"Sussex' chaplain." Shane recalled this from Sir Robert Dudley's first warning in London.

"The very man. An English heretic." The Dean gave a quick glance to Shane. "His age is 28, two years shy of canon law's strictures. A dapper young scoundrel, by all accounts, who has won the Queen's favour and fancy. A very prodigy of ambition and avarice." The bishop sat back in his chair, and regarded O'Donnelly in a moment of stillness.

"And what will the Chapter do?" The Dean was surprised by his question.

"Of course there is *no* question of obliging London! But we must choose the most diplomatic course in our refusal." He smiled knowingly. "I hardly dare broach this with the Chapter. I don't like to rile them." The bishop's raised brow bid him to explain. "The Chapter of Armagh has always been comprised principally of the O'Mallons, and if I so much as give them word of this, there will be ructions from Lurgyvallen to Drogheda." Shane laughed aloud, and the Dean nodded, smiling. "O'Neill knows whereof I speak!"

"But they have been so helpful to me, so devoted to the Church."

"Of course being from Limerick, Your Grace, I expect you'd know little of this long war betwixt the Chapter here and the English heirarchy."

"Ah, well. Perhaps you'll redress that, now, and tell us the tale that has you tittering so. I should know something of these local tempests."

"It was in the time of the five Johns, about a hundred years ago. There were five English bishops who succeeded one another in your office, all of the name of 'John'. They all resided at Termonfeckin Castle in the Pale, and, as they had no Irish, it was more or less left to the Dean of Armagh to administer the Church outside the Pale of Dublin –barring the few English speaking towns. Even so, these Primates were ever and always enacting statutes banning our Irish usages and customs. The Dean had the divil's own job of fending off these meddlesome rulings, - mostly by obfuscating, and befuddling his English superior, as it were." O'Tighe winked a sly wink.

"I'd say, now, you've done a fair bit of that yourself, O'Donnelly!"

"Indeed and I have, your Grace, but not since you took the See! Now, the Dean this time was Charles O'Mallon, and he was particularly adept at keeping Bishop Prene in the dark, and maintaining the Irish ways of Armagh. John Prene dismissed O'Mallon, stigmatizing him a usurper – much like what Elizabeth is doing to your own good self. He appointed his new man, Dionysius Cullen, to the deanery. O'Mallon held his ground, for he had the support of the O'Neill, and the clergy, and the Culdees, and indeed, of every Irish fish in the primatial see! And so Bishop Prene excommunicated him. He then turned his rage on Charles' father, the chieftain of the O'Mallons. Now, there was a long-standing dispute over Church revenues, for this English Primate wanted to take the temporalities and monies from Armagh off to his castle in the Pale, a thing that was rightly resisted. He brought charges against the O'Mallon for withholding of funds associated with the Bell of St. Patrick, and excommunicated him and his whole sept into the bargain. He not only consigned them to Hell, but he deprived them of their stewardship of the Bell, and gave it over to the Mulhollands."

"Well, they got it back. That much we know!" O'Tighe grinned at Shane.

"Oh, they did. To their credit, now, the Mulhollands returned it two years later when the Primate died. They knew to await their turn. You see, when the chief of the O'Mallons dies, it goes to the Mulholland, and when he dies it goes back again, for nearly a millennium now. Well, this interdict against the Mallons remained through all the years of the next Primate, John Mey, but Charles O'Mallon was not to be shifted. He held his post as the Dean of Armagh. Bishop Mey's successor was Bull, a loathsome English partisan."

"John Bull is it?"

"Indeed, this is the man. His name is still reviled outside the Pale. He was not content to sit quietly at Termonfeckin and leave Armagh to the Irish, for, after nearly *thirty* years, the Dean administrating the Church was still Charles O'Mallon. In the spring of 1466, for the first time in a hundred years, the Bishop of Armagh actually journeyed north to visit Armagh. Well, I need hardly say, this was like waving a red flag to a bull where the Chapter was concerned. Two brothers, Shane and Toal O'Mallon, thought that they might instruct John Bull in Irish ways. And, by way of instruction, didn't they steal his traveling horses!" The primate laughed.

"Ah fair play to them! That's sound instruction! Better than a catechism!"

"Well, Bishop Bull was furious, and when they were detected in the act, he pronounced yet another public sentence of excommunication against all the seed and breed of the O'Mallons, and against the O'Neill for supporting them. There was a further sentence of Interdict on the whole city of Armagh, which might not be lifted until the horses were returned to him. That Interdict was never lifted! For the story goes that John Bull had to hire a nag to get him home to Drogheda. Off he went on the nag's rump, calling down curses on the city of Armagh behind him. So you'll see my concern, Your Grace, in stirring up the turbulent

O'Mallons. It would be taking a stick to a hornet's nest, so it would." The Primate laughed and nodded.

"I do, aye." He shook his head with wonder. "Arrah, God help us, it's a prickly seat for a bishop, this Armagh! Well, perhaps we'll not mention the 'conge d'elire' to the Chapter. That's the lesson here, surely. But there's more, I'm thinking. For who has prevailed? The five Johns are old bones making dust in the churchyard at Termonfeckin, and the Dean and Primate are conferring in Irish. There is hope to be taken there." He tipped a wee wink to Shane, who turned to the Dean for some resolution.

"What will you tell the Chancellor?"

"To refuse outright would be courting trouble. I must give him some fanciful reason why it is *impossible* to convene the Conge d'elire. Illness, perhaps?" He looked to his superior, who was scratching the back of his head. His eyes were nearly closed under his raised brows, and he had a sly look to him.

"I recall Thady O'Brien back home, giving out about pardons. And if anyone would have such knowledge in his head, he's your man! Sure, isn't he a prisoner again in Dublin Castle! He said that if you would assuage the English authorities, you've only to affirm for them their lowest estimation of the Irish, attest to the truth of their most cherished slurs, for *that* will sweeten the deal. So, rather than insolence, let us put this refusal down to 'fecklessness', say, for that will please them. Hit a dog with a bone, and the dog will not bark!" Shane laughed at this, but the Dean had reservations.

"Still...I wouldn't like to malign the Chapter for failing to carry out orders I did not convey to them."

"Such an order is improper grounds to *convene* the Chapter. And you would not be altering the Chancellor's low opinion of them one whit! We must preserve a most fragile peace." Just then the strain of pipes could be heard on the wind. The two clerics looked to Shane."

"Aye, that will be the race starting." O'Tighe's face lit up.

"Should we not start down, so?" Shane gently raised his palm, patting the air before him.

SHANE O'NEILL

"We've time enough, your Grace. There's another small matter that needs airing." He looked to the Dean to broach the thorny issue.

"Your Grace...we both feel it would be most unwise for you to be going out to Drogheda this week, or for some time to come." The bishop seemed taken aback for a silent moment. He then spoke forcefully.

"Nonsense! There is work to be done." His eyes darted from one to the other, and he shook his head slowly. "Ahhh, no. I'll not relinquish my authority in the Pale. I am the Primate of All Ireland, from the centre to the sea. These are sacred duties conferred upon my by the Holy Father." Shane met his objection with a conciliatory nod.

"Aye, there *is* great work to be done. Important matters to be attended to. That is why I'm certain sure His Holiness would not wish for you to be placed needlessly in such grave peril."

"Peril, is it? Not at all! Not at all, man! The people love me there, and I must not abandon them to-" Shane spoke over him.

"You could be *arrested* and *imprisoned* as a usurper."

"I must not abandon them to an heretical usurper of my holy office! The people are devout, and they will protect me. We must have faith. Our Blessed Savior has brought me this far, and I must trust in Him to see me safe."

"Our Good Lord required nearly two years of my embassy to Rome to attain for you this holy office, your Grace. With letters I petitioned and begged from the Cardinal of Lorraine and Mary Stuart. Perhaps he requires me now to see to your safety as you carry out these duties. You have aroused great rancour and fury in London! You defied the Queen by attending the Council of Trent, and by blessing my troops, and exhorting them to attack her Deputy's forces. That is no trifle to her! She has no conscience where matters of state are concerned. Didn't you say it yourself! And, the world knows, she has a black temper."

"I will not forsake my trusted friends, my physicians, my colleagues, simply for that their tongue is English. I am a wiser man than you apparently suppose me to be, and I will judge these matters." With that, he rose to his feet and smiled again warmly. "I will give serious consideration to your warnings, and I shall pray most earnestly for

SHANE O'NEILL

guidance in this matter." He downed the last gulp of his buttermilk. "I might also say, O'Neill, that I am most truly heartened by your deep concern." Shane and the others were on their feet by now.

"Aye, your Reverence. If you think it through, I'm sure you'll see the wisdom of caution."

"Caution is a wise thing, surely. But the races?" There was very definitely a twinkle in his eye, and he clasped his hands together tightly. Shane nodded to his attendant, and the door was opened.

"No worries there, your Grace. The horses will not stir until we arrive. We'll stroll down now, at our ease."

"I've a small wager placed. Only for the sport of it. Sure, where is the harm? Only for sport!"

It was ever the custom on the feast of Lúghnasa that all livestock be driven through the waters of loughs and rivers to ensure their health in the year to come. This tradition, strictly observed throughout the land, accounts for the strange course of the afternoon's race. It was a long arduous route that sent the horses splashing through the shallows of Lough Ballysaggart and Lough Killymaddy, and every pond or puddle between them and Dungannon. It was a close race from the start, and there was a roar that seemed to follow the horses all along the route, with excited spectators at the roadside urging on their favorites. The people thought it a great wonder that the race had no sooner begun, when the clouds parted above, perhaps to give a view of the proceedings to a certain interested deity...The sunshine was surely counted a blessing from on high.

The winner was a thoroughbred belonging to the O'Kanes, but it was the second place winner whose name was on everyone's tongue. Whatever the horse's name had been, it was called from this day out 'the Paddereen Mare', for 'paidrín' is the Irish for 'rosary', and there was a holy rosary dangling around the horse's neck. Furthermore, it was widely noted that the Dean and the Primate had backed her, and more than a few wondered and speculated as to why indeed this triple spiritual boost had not given Paddereen a first!

On 'Scattering Day' the crowds of revelers pulled up stakes and faced for home, where the mighy job awaited them of bringing in the harvest. Like an uprooted garden, the colorful panoply of tents and pavilions disappeared bit by bit, restoring the surrounding hillocks to their lush summer greenery. The departing throngs were hardly on the roads when the furred and feathered denizens of those hills returned to scavenge among the leavings of their unwelcome guests. The hare and the fox, the lark, snipe, woodcock, and plover, the wagtail, the wren, and the humble sparrow, all delighted to see the last of them trundle off down the road.

The next morning, at the first glimmer of day, Shane assembled his army in their ranks, and set off from Dungannon into the West. On such a misty dewy morning, even from the highest window of the castle, Katherine had difficulty marking his progress through the hills of Tirowen. Now and again the mists would thin, and the long line of marching men could be seen crossing a hill or clearing. Her mind was not at rest, for Katherine was well past her time. The moon was nearly in its next quarter, and she was chiding herself for not confiding in Shane her strong suspicion that she was with child again. If, God forbid, something dreadful were to happen, he would never know. As the army disappeared into the far hills, Kat fetched a deep sigh. Her logic and her good sense availed her little in such matters, and she knew she would not draw an easy breath until his return.

SHANE O'NEILL

CHAPTER 17

Through the shadowy corridors of Dublin Castle, Lord Fitzwilliam's weary footfall echoed, all too familiarly, as he made his way to resume his duties as Chancellor. He paused at the open doorway of his office chamber, for he could not as yet bring himself to enter.

The curved stone walls of the Record Tower stood (and stand yet) nearly twelve feet thick, and this chamber had but one narrow window, high up in its deeply splayed well. Yet even through those course slabs of ancient leaded glass, begrimed and weathered, the September sunshine had managed to cast its yellow lustre over his cluttered desktop. Fitzwilliam stood silent in the doorway, regarding the daunting array of sheaves and scrolls, warrants, reports, letters, and documents that had accumulated during his short stay at Court. The noontide bells were fading in the air, and the clatter of cavalry horses could be heard, carrying out their midday maneuvers in the courtyard of the Castle. Had he made landfall but a few hours later, he might have left all this panoply of troubles wait until the morrow...

"Will she live?" At the sharp commanding voice of Lord Sussex, Fitzwilliam started just a bit. Stepping into the chamber, he saw the Deputy seated at a desk in the shadows, peering anxiously over his shoulder.

SHANE O'NEILL

"Godwilling, Sir Thomas! Godwilling, her Majesty shall live. But who will dare say more?" He lowered his voice. "It is the smallpox, without question. The London air is sharp with the smoke of pyres. The plague is on all sides."

"But what of her condition?" The Deputy's dark eyes fixed upon him, imperious, insistant. "There must be some word."

"Upon my first hearing, she was in the deepest throes of fever, but there has been no word since. Mary Sidney attends her by night and day, but Mary keeps her counsel. Doubtless, at the Queen's command."

"Mary Sidney is scarcely a sphinx! So often is she want to unboom herself to our good wives. Surely *they* are privy to-"

"Even unto her own dear sisters-in-law* she confides nothing of the Queen's condition, but counsels only prayer. The doctors, too, are mum." Sussex' disappointed scowl prompted the Chancellor to venture a more promising notion. "But...therein lies a clue, I fancy. For while yet they do fear her Majesty's temper, there must perforce be hope of her recovery!"

*[Fitzwilliam and Sussex were both married to the sisters of Lord Sidney, who was married to Mary, the sister of Robert Dudley.]

With a weary sigh, the Deputy sank back in his chair. "And lo, it is Mary who attends the Queen...Well, therein the fog is lifted, and all is revealed! Mary Sidney is at her side, and so Robert Dudley is at her ear!" Sussex turned again to Fitzwilliam, waving a letter before him. "The Queen is under Dudley's spell, else she would never embrace such folly! Cecil writes that she sends troops into France. Troops into France!"

"Alas, the 'Favorite' has outflanked both you and Cecil, for *this* much I *did* hear through my wife's inveigling; that daily did Sir Robert importune the Queen, even in her fever, that she might execute his ambitious scheme to recover Calais. And, alas, in her dire infirmity, she at length did yield."

"He is a pestilence unto himself!"

"He is relentless! And our dear brother Harry Sidney is ever at his side. Dudley will squander her treasure in France, and shake from her purse those scant funds so needful to your impending campaign against

SHANE O'NEILL

O'Neill."

"That is doubtless his intention!" Sussex started to turn back to the papers before him, but he stopped. Lowering his voice, and raising his hand, he offered stern words of caution. "You must utter *no word* of her Majesty's illness here, Will. News has not yet reached the general ear in Dublin. My secretaries are sworn to silence, and I have divulged naught of it. *Nothing* will unsettle a commonwealth so much as uncertainty, or the hope of change. Such rumours would unloose all the fiends of this hellish kingdom. Most especially within the Pale!"

"A prudent course. At least, for so long as we might forestall it. In England, among the adherents of Rome, the rumour is bruited that upon her deathbed Elizabeth has recanted her 'heresy.' Such a word would move like very wildfire through *this* realm." Fitzwilliam shoved aside a stack of dossiers, and placed his leathern satchel before him on the sun-gilt desk. A sudden thought turned him again to Sussex, and in a quiet, but somewhat alarmed tone, he confided more. "In London, the talk of the alehouse is that Elizabeth has named Dudley to be Lord Protector!" But, to his surprise, the Deputy was unperturbed.

"We can safely assume that *he* is the source of such a rumour. And the alehouse is a fit place for such bilge." Fitzwilliam sighed quietly, and took from his satchel a hefty packet of letters and documents bound with a blue ribbon. He presented them to the Viceroy.

"Missives and such from Whitehall."

"From Pandora's box, to be more precise!" Sussex took them, and placed the bundle before him on the desk. Fitzwilliam watched over his shoulder as he snipped the ribbon. The Deputy turned to him with impatience. "If you are come to stay, be so good as to take a seat! You are still wobbly after your voyage, I think. Did you arrive last night?"

"Only this morning, It was a rough crossing, but I came here direct." He sat then, wearily, at his own desk, and turned his chair to Sussex. "I sent Lady Frances out to Ardbracken. She will see you this evening at-"

"My sister is come?" The prickly Deputy bristled again, and glared accusingly. Fitzwilliam appeared to be quite stunned by his tone.

"But she assured me that she had written to advise you of her coming!"

"That she did. And I sent prompt reply, forbidding her to depart from England!" Fitzwilliam was momentarily flustered, but his wits did not fail him.

"The pestilence! She said *only* that you were deeply concerned for her safety, and that she will encounter far less peril here at Ardbracken. For my part, I knew naught of your interdiction. Alas, I expect you'll have much to talk of at supper! How fares the 'hellish kingdom', I am loathe to ask. What of Arnolde's hearings? Have they pinned you to the wall as yet?"

"You haven't heard?" Sussex' dark eyes brightened at this turn of topic. "Bermingham, that stooge of Robert Dudley's, is unable to prove his allegations against me! Since you so valiantly refused to yield up your accounts, your many captains have followed suit. Without such records to check against, no assessment of the Muster Rolls can be essayed." The Chancellor was greatly relieved at this change of tone, and anxious to encourage it.

"A thorough dousing! This may still those dogs that howl for your blood!"

"The gentry of the Pale are sniffing the wind, and it seems to blow in our favour." Sussex' countenance had changed, affecting a smile now, albeit a bitter one. "Those who testified are now *most* anxious to persuade me that they had no hand in Bermingham's doings, that they now perceive that the musters were but a cloak for intrigue."

"Ha! But, now he is routed, the rogue must be chastised. The Queen must command Bermingham's ears to the pillory to set example!"

"Oh, he shall find the Queen's Lord Deputy is no person to suffer to be threatened by a varlet." Sussex' smile was now complete, and his dark eyes shone with glee. "I have leveled charges of my own against the Master of the Rolls, for compiling libelous pamphlets against me. And now he is spluttering and stammering before a harsh inquisition. Unseemly wrangling, all of it, of course, and in the presence of Arnolde, who, I would venture to say, is losing his stomach for the fight! Dashing the fondest hopes of Dudley and Kildare, who are behind *all* of this."

SHANE O'NEILL

"But these are fine tidings! A rare commodity in this chamber! And you will surely come aright."

"Indeed, I shall. Of that you may be sure!" His voice lowered an octave and more. "But for my good name..."

"You bear it still!"

"Aye, though it be sullied, bruised, and tattered from the brawl."

"Who has ever 'scaped these Irish bogs free of muck and mire?"

"It is these malicious practices of Ireland!" Lord Sussex stood now, and looked vacantly across the chamber. He raised his open hand before him, fingers splayed, as he arranged his thoughts. When he had slowly closed it into a fist, he spoke quietly, eerily, as if ravelling the pieces of a great mystery. "They seek first, by secret and sinister means, to utter slander, that... going from hand to hand will breed to a common rumour, and so, helped with time, will endure credit, and leave the honest man besmirched and ruined!" His dark eyes smoldered, as he turned again to his Chancellor. "There is but *one thing* that will restore my good repute, and prove me fit and *fittest*, still, to hold high commission."

"O'Neill."

"I must extirpate him. Utterly!" As his fiery words hung in the air, a cloud chanced to cast its shadow over the window above, leaving the chamber suddenly dim and forlorn, and, curiously, lending a hollow hopeless ring to his grand words of resolve. The Lord Deputy was visibly ruffled by it, and, after a brief pause, he struck his fist down upon the desk with an angry groan. He sank slowly down, settling himself, once again, into the massive oak chair. He put his hand to his chin, and absently gave his pointy beard a twist. After a moment, he looked up to Fitzwilliam's wary gaze, and spoke slowly. "In *all* I have advised of him, *I* am proved right, as Dudley is proved wrong! A vindication unseen and unsaid, of course. More bootless service, accruing only blame!"

"O'Neill has failed to make his submission?"

"Precisely according as I *warned* her Majesty! O'Neill is unchastened by his stay at Court. He refuses all summons to submit in Dublin. With full compliment of Irish peers, I went so far as Dundalk, and even unto the Moyry Pass to meet him! And there received only mockery at the hands of his messenger. A missive, writ in boggy Irish, stating that 'his duty to the Queen forbade him to leave his province in its disturbed condition." The Deputy's mouth twisted in a sneer, and he spoke with strained patience. "He writes that his lawful wife, O'Donnell's daughter, has lately died wherefore he is free to wed...and the slavering beast is lusting after my own fair sister, Lady Frances! Even unto his entreating Lord Cecil to sanction the courtship! My dear sister! A Radcliffe! It is a vile threat, thinly masqued, that sets my flesh to crawl, and my gorge to rise. And now *you* have brought her into Ireland!" Sussex' icy glare charged the long moment of silence, leaving little doubt as to the object of his blame and reproach. "You must see that her visit be concealed, lest this rutting brute might hear of it."

Fitzwilliam, however, was unbowed. He met the challenge with a wry smile, and leapt to his feet. His tall, slender form charged with excitement, he loped some paces across the room, deep in thought. He turned suddenly, approaching now with extravagant gestures. "Nay! Nay, but to the contrary, good my Lord! Your sister's visit might serve to some *advantage* where John O'Neill is concerned! As it was ever your purpose to lure him into your meshes, kind Providence has intervened! Aye! And furnished you with *just* the dainty bait at which this wary fish might rise! Oh, fret not for Lady Francis; abiding within the confines of your estate, she would be free from all peril. I'll be bound, Sir Thomas, you might *easy* coax O'Neill into such a snare!"

As he contemplated this new possibility, Sussex' features slowly shifted, moving from a presentment of abject horror to fiendish delight. When he spoke, his hushed tone savored of both wonderment and stealth. "Well conceived! Marry, this may prove a most fortuitous proposal...lest O'Neill be too cunning a fish! I shall write that my sister is come to stay with me, and recommend that he call to Dublin if he would woo the lady..."

"-That you dare not promise to *betroth* her against her will, but if he were come to Dublin, he might see and speak with her. And that *if* he pleased her and she him, they should both have...your blessing and

SHANE O'NEILL

goodwill..." At this suggestion, Sussex slowly nodded in approval, his dark eyes aglow with guile and spiteful glee.

"Just so...And if he will rise to my bait, he shall have a short shrift for a blessing, and a rough nuptial knot about his neck!"

Sir William laughed with wicked relish. "Aye, something more constricting, perchance, than wedlock! O'Neill will not be the first who's lost his head a wooing!" He chuckled quietly at this jest, and it was only then he noticed that the chamber had brightened once again. He stepped smartly over to his spirits cabinet, and quickly decanted two small sherries. At the Deputy's gladsome voice, he turned.

"By S'n George, we shall do it, Will!"

Even sporting his thin hopeful smile, Sussex looked drawn, and strangely older than he had, barely two months prior, when they had parted. The Deputy was in somewhat better spirits by this time, but it seemed to Fitzwilliam that his absense had taken a toll. So vital, it was, to disburden him, and to bolster his flagging spirits. As he handed him the cordial, Lord Sussex sounded quite restored, even cheerful.

"Mayhap this 'wooing' will entice John O'Neill to leave off his raids in Maguire's country! And furnish some relief to those loyal Irish captains there who serve the Queen."

"Huzzah!" Fitzwilliam exulted at this news of O'Neill's latest infraction. He clinked his crystal glass to the Deputy's, and winked. "Then he has broke his bond of peace!" A quick toast was imbibed, but Sussex' grave demeanor was unremitting. His smile had vanished.

"Peace? The hellion rampages through all the province!" He read aloud the dire account of Maguire's plight, and Fitzwilliam turned his sharp eyes to the Deputy. "Piteous indeed! Such a dire and woeful warning of O'Neill's threat is like to stir a certain frugal heart at Court, and might pry from her purse a proper sum to aid our cause. Is there some *further* word of this business?"

"Upon the last telling, O'Neill had crossed the Erne at Beleek, and burned corn and houses, falling upon the harvest people. Three hundred women and children were piteously murdered." Noting Fitzwilliam's doubtful smirk, he added emphatically. "-*it has been said*...And Maguire

SHANE O'NEILL

is clean banished. He took refuge with the remnant of his people in the islands of Lough Erne, where Black Hugh O'Donnell was making twelve boats to pursue him. John O'Neill then entered O'Donnell's country, *though being upon a sworn peace* before commissioners, and has taken at the least 10,000 head of cattle during the time that Con O'Donnell was here with me."

"Wasn't it most improvident to leave his country unattended at such a time!" Sir William sat back in his chair, folding his arms, and listened with one brow cocked as Sussex put forth his case.

"He contends that he could do naught to stop O'Neill, lest we come to his aid. He pleads, also, that we remedy the miserable captivity of his father and mother, and recounts with bitter anguish his mother's indignities, wherein she be kept chained to a bed, and nightly is ravaged by her captor." Fitzwilliam's brow furrowed in puzzlement and disbelief, and his blue eyes narrowed defiantly.

"His '*mother*' say you? The old man was but *one year* wed to this Scotswoman-"

"His father's wife, *ergo* his *mother*," Sussex snapped peevishly, "-as Lord Cecil has prescribed for its recounting- and he bids us to adhere in such details! O'Neill demands he deliver up the castle of Lifford for the enlarging of his father and mother. That fortress is the chiefest defense of O'Donnell's land, and whosoever possesses it will rule all TirConnell."

"If O'Neill is in O'Donnell's country as you say, the castle of Lifford is most like yielded ere this! I'll wager he will plant Black Hugh there to guard his interests." A baleful glare from his superior prompted Fitzwilliam to add blithely. "But all need not be lost. What odds to us which of these O'Donnells holds Donegal Castle? If we would gratify Black Hugh's ambitions to rule his clan, it should take precious little to set him against O'Neill, and so to serve the Crown."

"I shall do nothing of the kind!" The Viceroy snatched the letter, and tossed it back on the pile. He spoke again slowly, with an edge of impatience. "We must restore Cullagh to his place, and chastise O'Neill, to redeem the good credit of *our word*, that it will stand as currency until we might prevail in arms. In any case, we can do little without a

SHANE O'NEILL

proper disbursement and commission from Whitehall. Let us convey Maguire's letters forthwith unto Cecil, and press for a spring campaign to rout O'Neill. Therein lies our one hope. And Maguire's too, I daresay." Sussex ventured a triumphal smile. "This time we shall prevail! I have the pledge of James MacDonnell to send into the field a legion of his lusty Scots." Fitzwilliam evinced some surprise at this.

"And what of Captain Pierce's report? He writes that Sorley Boy MacDonnell gave assurances to *O'Neill* that they would stand with *him*."

"James cautions me to count for naught his word to O'Neill, for it was not given freely, and he intends not to honour it. We must assail the Lord Secretary, and pray most fervent for the Queen's recovery of her health." Sussex' eyes rolled heavenward. "And of her sound *judgment...*" Fitzwilliam countered with a devious smile, and an air of supreme confidence.

"In the meantime, O'Neill's lecherous appetites may trap him in our snare! And render *all* this vast enterprise needless!"

"Godwilling. If kind Providence be in accord with our design, it shall come to pass!" Sussex began sorting through the letters from Whitehall. "Let us look to the tasks at hand..." Quickly and methodically, he stacked the letters for priority, according to the precedence and rank of each sender. A sudden thought interrupted his calculations. He did not look up. "Is my sister aware of O'Neill's attentions?" When no answer came, he peered up at Fitzwilliam, who looked to be quite dumbfounded. "It would not be unlike her to revel in such a grotesquery. My discomfiture is an unfailing source of amusement to Frances." His brother-in-law shook his head reassuringly, but the Lord Deputy's doubts in the matter persisted. "She has always been possessed of mischief, I'm afraid, and was so thoroughly sheltered in her keeping, that she has little apprehension of real danger."

"She knows naught of it, Sir Thomas. Of that, you may rest assured. She made no mention of O'Neill all the long voyage. Relief from the contagion of London was her sole concern. -And there shall *be* no danger."

"Good...good." Sussex turned back to his business, opening and reading the correspondence. Fitzwilliam repaired to his own desk, and did much the same.

The chamber fell silent for a time, but for the breaking of seals, and an occasional tisk, or huff, or sigh. At length, upon examining the contents of a folio, the Lord Deputy turned to his colleague in exasperation. "God's wounds, twenty-three appointments! Still *more* of our unfledged little English cockalorums to be nestled into the vicarages, prebends, and rectories of this troubled realm...Small wonder that I can muster so little support among these Palesmen!"

"Ungrateful wretches, these Palesmen! The alleged 'gentry' of the Pale..." Sir William folded the letter before him, and tossed it to one side. He sat back and looked to his superior with one disapproving brow raised. "But for our stewardship and protection, they would be overwhelmed by those teeming hoards of bogmen out there in the marches."

"That much is beyond dispute. But Cecil has aggravated the Palesmen needlessly by sending over officials of small parts or credit, far inferior to those born in Ireland, whose positions they are expropriating. I must own, Will, I am a*weary* of the ceaseless blundering of Whitehall."

"I shouldn't doubt it." Fitzwilliam nodded sympathetically, and sighed. "The state here is both fickle and strange. The malefactors increase and are emboldened, while the chief ministers are discouraged. Lord Cecil understands but little of this place." Sussex' dark eyes flashed, and he was infused suddenly with roiling indignation at the delusions of Whitehall.

"Lord Cecil misapprehends everything that *befalls* this cursed island! Betwixt England and Ireland there gapes a chasm wider far than the Irish Sea! How could the Royal Court *fathom* such a kingdom? Where every man would be king! With men and women both, so *unlike* her Majesty's good and civil English subjects. The Irish are addicted to sedition, desirous of alteration, contented with *nothing but will and liberty!*" Fitzilliam regarded the myriad documents and scrolls that covered the desktop between them.

"The Law is of little consequence in such a land..."

SHANE O'NEILL

"Laws in *this* place are like good lessons set for a lute that is broken and out of tune. To keep civil order here is an endless and unavailing task. But a Gordian knot, that will defy the keenest blade, is the task of reforming the Church in this cursed realm!" At this, Fitzwilliam sat back, grinning, and threw his arms in the air.

"Hah! Then be of good cheer, my Lord! For *that* is a task for Adam Loftus! The new Primate will be charged with those duties. And smoothing over the new appointments will be first among them. I'm certain he shall prove most able to loose your Gordian knot, for he is discrete, cunning, well learned, and hath a goodly gift of utterance in the pulpit that will- What, then?" Fitzwilliam's merry effusion was stopped short by an ominous shadow that darkened the already grim countenance of Lord Sussex. "Is something gone awry in his elevation?" Sussex affected a smug ironic air.

"We have received us our answer from the Dean of Armagh. He advises that the Chapter there is so 'sparkled and out of order', as he can by no means assemble them to proceed to the election of Adam Loftus. The greatest part of that Chapter are temporal men, and Shane O'Neill's horsemen. Most like, they are occupied with the torching of churches in Maguire's country! The people in those parts are savages, far disordered in religion." Fitzwilliam shrugged.

"A trifle! The Conge D'elire is a piffling concern. It was little more than a courtesy to the Chapter, a token of the great zeal and favour that her Majesty bears to the common quietness of her Realm. Failing that, it is a simple matter of the Queen's warrant, which shall be forthcoming as soon-

"I have received it. Just here, among your letters from Whitehall!" Sussex leaned across to hand him a scroll, which Sir William quickly unraveled and perused. "As you will see, the exchequer has called in the revenues of the bishopric of Armagh, as well as the spiritualities thereof, which *by no means* the Chapter will let come to the Queen's Majesty. Loftus has obtained a grant of all power to determine Ecclesiastical causes in his Diocese. He is now Primate of Ireland. Whereupon *we* must deliver unto him, by her Majesty's warrant, all the *possessions* of the Archbishopric, effective from the date of her Majesty's letters." Fitzwilliam nodded, as he rolled the parchment, and tossed it back on the desk. He looked up, smiling.

"Acquiring the monies and temporalities of the See may prove nettlesome...ultimately requiring force, I should think. But the Bishop's palace at Termonfeckin, and the Drogheda manorhouse can be got without let or hindrance. Again, a simple matter."

"Quite so. But you had best send up a large force of infantry and light horse to take possession. And to forestall any challenge. Bishop Loftus has requested to take up his quarters there immediately, so I had best detail them this afternoon, to mobilize for an early morning start. They must purge the palace of all Romish icons, and commandeer the manor for his Grace. They must also capture that papish pretender, O'Teig, who usurps his office. *You* shall issue a warrant for the man's arrest." A solemn nod from Fitzwilliam, as Sussex leaned in confidentially, his somber black eyes riveted upon his subordinate. After a long trenchant pause, he added a further directive. "Not *only* must this false Primate be deprived and dispossessed, but we must mete out stern punishment, both for his profanation of holy office, and for his defiance of the Royal prerogative in that episcopacy."

"A chastisement as befitting High Treason..." Fitzwilliam met his dark gaze with a cruel glint of his own, and an icy smile. "We must bear hard upon him, and shut the gates of mercy, lest we shall find a Romish rival in every See. Have no fear. My warrant shall encompass *'all those who maintain, aid, and support, contrary to the laws of this Realm, the renegade traitor come from the Bishop of Rome to pose as Archbishop of Armagh, Donatus O'Teig.'*

SHANE O'NEILL

CHAPTER 18

Dark blustery clouds billowed and blew, all the morning, rolling over the hilltops with inexhaustible torrents of pelting rain. The gusting sheets fell in slanting drifts before the intrepid coachman, making a grey blur of the path ahead, which was, after all, no more than a sodden rutty boreen, overhung with brambles and sloe bushes. No road for a fine carriage.

By the time the skies relented, and the storm had at last swept out to sea, every dyke was flooded, and each rivulet and gurgling stream rushed and roared, dashing its frothy music through the lush green hills on either side of them. The horses plashed through the dips and hollows of the road, and the Primate's mud-spattered carriage tumbled along, lurching and wobbling, and shaking the bones of its pious, forbearing passengers.

Archbishop O'Tighe filled his lungs with the cool moist air, and thanked God for the storm's passing, and for the dewy freshness that lingered in its wake. He managed a kindly smile to meet the fleeting glance of Father Keaveny across from him, who was putting the time away sensibly, murmuring through the prayers of his Breviary. Yes, the bishop was resolved to keep his heart high, although, in truth, he was beset by certain misgivings that concerned the present ordeal. Why had he relented, even given his solemn promise, to abide by these mad precautions?

SHANE O'NEILL

In the end, he had pledged to Lord O'Neill that he would travel within the Pale *only* by back-roads, that while he would attend to his duties and uphold his authority here, he would do so with as little display as could be managed. Even to residing out in the draughty keep of Termonfeckin, a full six miles from his fine warm manor within the walls of Drogheda! Such a pointless concession, really...Oh, not to O'Neill, but to the English heretics, who, for all their sway and swagger, numbered but few in that city. As the carriage lurched over some devilish rut, providing the two clerics with a particularly egregious shaking, he sighed, and wondered again what might have possessed him to consent to this. Perhaps it was some vague imputation of vanity. In truth, he had never really come to terms with the pomp and ostentations of Holy Office.

But this skulking through back-ways and byways was surely begetting more peril than it prevented. What O'Neill failed to grasp was that the Primate enjoyed the patronage and protection of the old Catholic gentry in these parts, the O'Mores, the Plunketts, the MacMahons, and the rest. In fact, it was a visitation to Lady Plunkett for the sacrament of Extreme Unction that had brought them out to Kilsaran last night, to brave these storms and muddy by-roads. Even upon her deathbed, the pious old soul had not failed to endow the Church. No then, so long as the old gentry of the Pale kept to their Holy Faith, Dublin Castle would be obliged to turn a blind eye to his ministrations.

The skies had brightened in the West, where a stand of copper beeches caught his eye. As they tossed and fluttered in the gusting October winds, the huge trees seemed to be shaking dry their glistening yellow boughs after the tempest. The carriage was nearing home now, for the other window afforded a sweeping view of the storm-swept sea, and O'Tighe was drawn to the edge of his seat to observe it. Like a malignant black shadow, the heaving bank of clouds teamed and billowed low over the churning waters, dashing squalls of rain against the sea. Yet, far out beyond this tumult, a bright grey mist sparkled on the horizon. He was moved by this spectacle to muse upon the sheer might and power of God, for he was naturally inclined to such habits of reflection, and he felt warmed by that bright promise of clemency that was sure to follow even the darkest of storms. That would do, now, for a grand sermon on Sunday...

The Primate drowsed for a while, and the gentle slopes and level swards of shoreland accommodated him nicely as they rolled homeward. He was jolted awake when the coach came to a sudden halt at the top of Castlecoo Hill. There was a mad thumping sound.

"The tower is afire! Your Reverence!" The coachman was banging on the carriage roof. "The castle is burning in Termonfeckin!" Father Keaveny scrambled out to see, and O'Tighe leaned out over the open door. A haze of smoke was rising about the castle, whipped by the winds that were still churning behind the storm. He called out to the pair of them.

"Get in, Father, for the love of God! Lanty, put a haste under you til we see what calamity is underway down there." As the door slammed shut, the carriage sped off down the hill, but it hadn't gone far when the coachman pulled up his reins once again.

"Whoa! Shass! Shasssss!" They slowed to a plodding halt, and a stocky red-faced priest came running up to the coach. He was one of their own at Termonfeckin, and was in a hectic state of alarm and panic. Behind him O'Tighe could see a gentleman dismounting, and a young barefoot lad holding his reins. He flung open the coach-door.

"What is it, Father Conroy? What has happened?"

"It's the English, your Grace!" He was winded, and spoke between gulps of air. "Soldiers everywhere! They've taken the house! They've made a pyre of all your things! The holy paintings, and your books! Your books!! Burning everything! Oh, the blasphemy is shockin'! Every manner of sacrilege!" Hastily blessing himself, he followed O'Tighe's eyes, and cast a quick glance over his shoulder at the gentleman who was striding across to them. "Fleming, the attorney...He came to warn us, so Father Healey was able to consume the Blessed Sacrament, lest they should profane it. And he took the monstrance, the chalice, and your ledgers out to the Augustinian Priory. Even your Pallium, he managed to spare. We got out through the tunnel, by torchlight. I was only able to save some vestments, but I took the best of them." There was a sudden catch in his breath, as he recalled more. "Oh! They beat poor Father Killeen something fierce when he wouldn't tell them your whereabouts. Covered in blood, he was, and I'd say-"

"Will he live?"

"Cass Neary is looking after him, and she says that, barring festering or the ague setting in, he'll over it, surely." By this, the gentleman was at his side, a tall fellow with fine chiseled features and sandy hair that was tossling in the wind. His demeanor was grave, and his eyes burned with purpose.

"Your Grace!"

"You're a Guardian Angel, Master Robert! To be looking after-"

"You mustn't stop here! Even through the smoke, they'll have seen this coach from the tower!" He shouted up to Lanty, the driver. "The Primate must come with me, if he is to live! You can turn round just past those trees. Then fly back over that hill like the divil is behind you! For he *is*!" He reached his hand up to help the bishop. "Come along then, your Reverence, til I get you to safety!" O'Tighe bid a quick farewell to Fr. Keaveney, and scrambled down, dislodging his biretta which went tumbling under the carriage. He stooped to look after it, but Fleming called him up quick.

"You'll not be needing that!" O'Tighe cast a rueful glance over his shoulder and hurried along. An old adage crossed his mind, and he sighed.

"The hat while she lasts, but the head forever." Father Conroy fetched a bulky sack from the bushes and climbed into the carriage. He blessed himself and called out the window.

"God speed you, your Grace!"

At the sound of Lanty's 'Hup!' they were off. Fleming hastened the bishop over to where the young lad waited quietly with his horse. He took the reins, and slipped the boy a farthing. "Good man, Felimy! Tell my brothers I have the bishop, and we'll meet them at Knockbown!" The boy nodded, his eyes wide with wonder, and ran off straightaway across the fields. Robert foraged in his saddlebag. "Garret and Patrick have been keeping watch up the stoney lane, and in the boreen beyond Sun Hill. Isn't it well you never took the high road, for they've infantry posted there. Here! Throw this over you for now." He tossed him a gentlemen's cloak. "Can you discard the cassock?"

"I can, surely. Haven't I the long breeches under!" O'Tighe began unbuttoning the line of thirty-three purple buttons down the front of his cassock. Upon seeing the exasperated frown on his new companion's face, however, he quickly tore the rest asunder with a mighty rip. Fleming mounted his steed, and when O'Tighe had fastened the gabardine cloak about him, he gave him a hand up, to sit behind him.

"Hold on, now! It's 'divil take the hindmost!" With that, he bolted out into the boreen, and rode like the wind that was still huffing and howling after them over the fields and the tossing trees.

Once they had put Castlecoo Hill behind them, and were shielded from the view of any new sentry in the tower, Fleming veered off down a narrow path through the thick russet wood that lay beyond it. If the carriage ride from Kilsaran had been jostling, this little jaunt was doubly so, but O'Tighe used the interval to assail the powers of Heaven with his fervent prayers. There was a prayer of thanksgiving, a prayer for the injured Father Killeen, and most fervent of all, a prayer for safe deliverance, for the fact had not escaped him that his escorts would be liable to prosecution should they be caught. Fleming made his way westward under the shade of ancient autumnal trees, galloping the mile or so through the brindled wood, to a narrow sheep drover's lane where his brothers were to meet him. Upon reaching it, Robert reined his horse back into the shadows.

"Are you right, your Grace?"

"Not a feather astray. I'm a fair horseman myself, now, and I'd ride with any."

"They'll not be long in coming. But I suppose a bit of a rest would be no harm." He held out his hand to steady him, as the bishop dismounted, while *he* remained in readiness astride his horse. "We'll stop in Listoke until nightfall. The moon is barely waxing, so, cloudy or no, we'll have plenty of dark. We'll get you some clothes, maybe, to disguise you. If we can get you to my uncle's castle...You'll be safe there for a time!"

"Aye, for a time. I'll not be the first fugitive to find shelter at Slane Castle. The Baron is staunch and stalwart. He keeps faith with the Faithful!" As O'Tighe clapped his hand over his heart, he felt cool metal against his chest. It was the silver pyx that hung suspended there beneath his shirt, and in it was a consecrated Host from his call to Lady Plunkett. The 'real presense' of God...So long as it remained about his neck, he would deem the loss of his cassock a trifle. He took some comfort recalling that his pallium, too, had been spared. It was the white stole of office, received of the Pope upon his elevation, and thankfully, it had been saved by young Fleming's warning. He looked up at him. "Tell me this, Master Robert. How did you come to know they would raid Termonfeckin? What occurred in Drogheda?"

"The soldiery appeared out of nowhere, and suddenly they were *everywhere*. I saw a squadron of them charging into St. Peter's, for my law office is just there beside it. They surrounded the episcopal manor, and then burst in. Oh, you've no notion of the danger you are in! They've a Protestant Primate installed, and he's taken possession. With all his truck and his gear! They've closed the gates of Drogheda, and they're rooting and rummaging through the town for you, til everything and everyone is turned arse over heal. The Lord Mayor challenged them for the writ and warrant, but they had their papers, and the charge is - you're up for *treason*, God help you!" After a moment of stunned silence, O'Tighe's face softened into a kindly smile.

"God *is* helping me, and I'm most grateful for you. The good Mayor will take a hiding for that challenge I've no doubt. Elcock was ever a devout man, as brash and brave as any..."

"You dare not return to Armagh, your Grace, you *do* realize that? The garrison there will be under the same orders. O'Neill would come to your aid, but..." O'Tighe took his meaning, and nodded emphatically.

"There would be a fierce battle, more blood spilt...It would be wicked to bring bloodshed into that holy city on my own account."

SHANE O'NEILL

"I'm sure, in time, we can smuggle you off to Spain. That will all be arranged, once you are safe."

The bishop looked to be stunned by this unimaginable prospect. He had not yet seriously considered the implications of his predicament, and the thought of impending exile was like a blow to the belly. He felt a tightness inside, a fearsome dread that wrung his heart. He raised his eyes, and seeing the look of concern on Fleming's face, he mustered a weak smile. "Aye, Spain for the sunshine..." He nodded. "If the Lord wills it so...Perhaps a prayer wouldn't go astray."

He cast his glance over the ground, thinking to find a place to kneel, but there was no spot that was not sodden. He turned then, and slowly blessed himself as he shambled a few paces off. Staring absently through the wood at a brightness among the sear and yellow leaves, O'Tighe tried to think of a prayer that might do. Those of a more skeptical age would suppose, perhaps, that he was groping for a formula of sacred words to engage his troubled mind, only to keep at bay the bleak realization of his utter ruin. And yet, they would be deceived, for it was not comfort he sought in prayer, but strength. After a time, he resolved to seek the intercession of St. Colmkill who had born the cross of banishment so long ago, that he might be granted the same fortitude and virtue that had sustained the holy saint in his 'white martyrdom' of exile. O'Tighe lost himself in prayer then, with no thought of time, and was puzzled when Robert's brothers seemingly arrived so quickly.

"Oho! Here are the lads!" Fleming called to him. "Your Grace!" The bishop blessed himself as he hurried back, and, with a bracing grip up from Robert, he was quickly astride the horse once again. To his surprise, there were *three* men galloping up the narrow boreen. They trotted to a halt, and sidled up without nod or greeting, but quickly shared what they knew of the army's whereabouts.

It was easily seen which were the brothers. O'Tighe recalled meeting the older one, Garret, at Armagh where he had been on some service for Shane O'Neill. He was sporting a dark velvet cap with a smart plume, and, at Robert's prompting, he tossed it over that it might serve to masque the bishop's identity. With a sly grin, his Eminence clapped it on his head, whereupon the lads laughed heartily, and assured him that, 'cutting such a dashing figure, he would *never* be caught out as a stodgy aul cleric!' It was decided that they had best become accustomed to calling him 'Sir Donagh', lest, somewhere down the road, they might slip and say 'your Grace' when they aughtn't.

Although the three brothers all possessed the fair colouring of their mother, there was no mistaking the fine features of the Flemings. All shared a staunch devotion to the Faith, and, indeed, to the O'Neill, whom they occasionally assisted in legal matters. Their eldest brother William, although not a part of this convoy, was also known to the bishop, for he had famously accompanied Shane O'Neill to London, and still another, Thomas, had been raised in fosterage with Shane's cousin Turlough O'Neill. This other fellow beside them was a local roustabout mate of their's, known as Foxy John O'Carroll for his flaming red hair, and he assured them that he knew 'every bridal path and pack road betwixt here and Slane, or near enough to it!'

After this brief parley then, the men set off on their clandestine journey, galloping hither and yon, through every patch and stretch of rough country following after 'Foxy John.' Near Listoke, they came to a lonely cabin known to them, where a welcome was put before them that included a blazing fire, a nip of whiskybaugh, and a fine hot supper. The woman of the house was moved to rapture that she should be so blessed as to shelter the holy Primate under her thatch. Smiles and winks were passed when, in her excitement, she swithered, to and fro, between poetical spates of tearful compassion for the Primate, and peals of bitter malignant curses. She damned for eternity his English tormentors who had driven him 'like a beggar' to her door, consigning them to the black demons of hell! These thundering blasts were taken in good part, and those few hours spent awaiting the cover of darkness afforded O'Tighe a much-needed respite before the hard ride ahead.

When the lamps were lit, he gave to the humble home his solemn benediction, and they set off again into the night. This time, in spite of his considerable misgivings, a serviceable horse was provided him, paid for out of that charitable endowment from Lady Plunkett from the previous night's ministrations. The Flemings managed to convince him that it had been the Almighty's way, in His divine prescience, of bestowing upon His servant a modest viaticum to sustain him on this unexpected journey.

They rode west, facing, over the horizon, the last fading glimmer of that woeful day, under the deepening darkness of night. Robert Fleming's chief concern was not fear of being overtaken by cavalry, but of being sighted in a part of the country where he and his brothers were widely known. It would take little to deduce that Slane Castle was their destination True to his boast, Foxy John knew where to ford every river, and how to skirt every village. He led them up and down dale, choosing always the obscure paths that would be untraveled by gentlemen or Protestant squires. Any rustics they might encounter would be more likely to help than hinder, and would certainly never betray them.

The night was dark, and swift clouds sailed across the starry sky on a blustering cold North wind. The pale crescent moon slipped furtively in and out of the shadows, not unlike her fellow travelers of the night in the hills below. Near the Hill of Rath, a beggar repaid their alms with news of a 'drove of English night-riders' that had passed him up a short while before.

"They gave me dog's abuse, and nearly trampled me, God's curse on them for blaggards! Heading north over that ridge, beyond. And well armed too, they were!" But, for their part, the prelate's band never caught sight of the Crown forces in all their six hours of journeying, and the only real threat to their enterprise was waiting for them at Slane.

They arrived just after midnight, and Garret Fleming called them to a quick halt when he spotted a grand coach and four waiting before the great doors of the Castle keep. He recognized it as that of the zealous Protestant knight, Sir Frauncis Asgard, a confidant of Lord Sussex, and member of his Privy Council. Garret led them quietly into the shadows behind a spinney of oaks, lest they be seen by Asgard's footmen. After a brief conferral, they turned back to avail of a route through the lower ward, that would take them around to the gated postern at rear of the keep.

SHANE O'NEILL

The men were given a warm, but suitably muted welcome by their aunt, Lady Éilish Fleming. She was, coincidentally, a niece of Lady Plunkett's, so she inquired of the Primate as to the old woman's failing health, and thanked him profusely for his difficult journey to her bedside. He assured her that, as it happened, that journey had very probably saved his life. Lady Eilish instructed the servants to say nothing of their presence to the Baron until his official visitor had departed.

The cook was summoned back into her kitchen, and, after resting themselves, the men partook of a fine repast. O'Tighe was delighted when his humble request was obliged, and a bracing cup of fresh buttermilk was provided him. They hadn't long to wait until Lord Slane appeared, and, after his hearty and heartfelt greeting, they adjourned to a more formal chamber. This was thought to be a bit more in keeping with the dignity of the esteemed Primate of All Ireland, however reduced in circumstance he might be.

Their spirited host was known widely as Black James. Although now, in his early fifties, grey had overtaken the original cause of that appellation, his piercing dark eyes rendered it most apt even yet. He was roughly the same age as O'Tighe, and he cut a fine figure still, with his long limbs and aristocratic bearing. Over glasses of port -wherein *this* time the bishop did not abjure- they recounted for him the troubling events of the day, and he confided the reason for Asgard's call.

Sussex had requested him to muster thirty men for the crucial business of apprehending this 'renegade agent of Rome,' lest he should escape the confines of the Pale. Similar calls had been paid to Lord Dunsany and Lord Roche, but as they were also partisans of Rome, Black James foresaw but little serious efforts coming from those quarters. Much was made of this news, and they all agreed that the greatest difficulty for their beleaguered guest would be crossing out of the Pale.

When a yawn made its way from one to the next through the company, it was resolved to get some rest. Surely things would look brighter, and, indeed, they all might look at the problem afresh after a good night's sleep. Lord Slane rose, and tossed back the meager remains of his port. As the others got to their feet, he bowed to the prelate, and spoke effusively in a warm confidential tone. "You're welcome to bide under this roof for so long as you desire to remain with us, your Eminence. And let there be no hurry on you, for, I promise you, my home will prove a safe haven from this storm...a quiet refuge wherein you may bethink yourself of just where it *is* you wish to go." With a guileful glint in his eye, he hinted of some intrigue. "Once you've determined *that*, I'd say that, with a bit of cunning and a simple ruse, we'll have little problem spiriting you out of the Pale! And we shall see you guarded, then, on to your destination. In the meanwhile, you will let *me* look to your safety, for I hold it to be as dear to me as my life." He reached for the Primate's hand, and bent to kiss his ring, which, in all the precautions, no-one had thought to remove. "I bid you rest well and easy! Good night!"

In spite of that long day's exertions, the bishop was on his feet early the next morning, or on his knees, to be nearer the truth of it. Once he had finished his morning prayers, he made his way through the castle, where only the servants were stirring, and out to view the fine fresh dewy morning that was twittering and fluttering in the sunny courtyard gardens. He did not linger there, for he felt deeply compelled to make a small pilgrimage up the great hill that loomed high over the castle, the fabled Hill of Slane. After a word with the reluctant gatekeeper, the bishop acquiesced to his condition that he be accompanied by several guards. They, in turn, promised to keep such distance as caution might allow, so as to afford him a measure of solitude. The portcullis would remain open, pending his return, lest there should be trouble.

For all the concerns that weighed so heavily upon his mind, Donagh O'Tighe's heart was light as he ascended the lofty hill, for he knew that God was with him, and had brought him here to this place. It was an arduous climb, and fairly steep, as the hill rose some five hundred feet to its crest. He smiled to himself as he passed a barefoot shepherd who lay stretched on the grassy slope, his crook beside him glistening with dew. It called to mind for him his own forsaken crozier. Wouldn't that have been handy, now, for this climb? The lad was dozing there among his wooly flock in the morning sun, and Donagh was struck by the timelessness of this simple scene. St. Patrick, in his youth, would have looked much the same, herding his sheep on Slieve Mish. And it was atop *this* hill, in the year of our Lord, 432, that Patrick had begun his mission to bring the Word of God to the Irish people. In his heart, O'Tighe knew that he would receive here the knowledge of God's holy will, a divine inspiration as to where he must go.

Upon reaching the windy summit, the humble prelate felt, as he thought, a curious elation. But one could scarcely feel otherwise, beholding such a view! His gaze swept the far horizon, and he marveled to see the purple Mountains of Mourne so very far off, huddled low against the northern sky. He turned his eyes eastward, where the shimmering Irish Sea stretched endlessly out beyond the towers of Drogheda. On the western horizon, Trim Castle shown brightly, golden with morning sun, against the blue October sky. Here on this blessed height, the vast world below was rendered visible as only the soaring eagle might behold it!

He turned, now, to see what wonders were arrayed behind him. Far off to the southeast, the sharp peak of Slieve Coolann was tattering the low clouds that drifted over Wicklow, and the Dublin Mountains stood like a mighty rampart shielding the Pale. Lowering his gaze, the Primate saw his bastion of refuge, the mighty Norman keep of Slane Castle, perched there on the banks of the Boyne. It looked far less imposing and secure from these lofty heights. And the Boyne, that ancient river known even to Ptolemy! It flowed like bright shining quicksilver, wending its way through the mottled patchwork of forest, heath, greensward pastures, and the plotted and pieced fields that covered the bright plains of Royal Meath. Raising his eyes he saw, some ten miles beyond the river, that other fabled hill, Tara, rising majestically to command the horizon. Tara of the Kings was the ancient capitol of Ireland, and even at this far remove the Mound of the Hostages could be seen like a shadowy dome atop its broad ridge. Donagh O'Tighe recalled for himself a story he had learned at his grandfather's knee in the warm glow of the turf-fire, so many winters ago. Indeed, it was a tale known to every child in Ireland.

SHANE O'NEILL

In that bygone age when pagan Ireland was under the dark sway of the druids, a great festival was held each Spring at Tara to mark the Vernal Equinox. It was the law, that time, that every fire in Ireland be extinguished on the eve of Bealtaine, in every hearth, be it cot or castle. Only the stars were let to burn in the heavens. On this night the chief druid would set alight a new bonfire on the high Hill of Tara, to be seen far and wide blazing in the darkness. From its flames, torches were lit, and the High King's horsemen would gallop forth, carrying their fiery brands to every neighboring height where they would set alight a tall pyre. Each hearth thereabouts would be re-kindled from its embers. From all of these raths and villages, more torch-riders would sally forth carrying aloft their flames, and so would this continue until, for every star flickering in the darkness above, a fire blazed below. Before the night was gone, that one druid fire burned in every hearth or forge, in every glen, or height, or hollow in Ireland.

On the Eve of Béaltaine, Patrick and his small band of disciples were gathered here, on this very spot, atop the Hill of Slane. As it happened, that night was also the vigil of Easter, so the saint was determined that Christ should triumph over Crom, and Lúgh, and all the other pagan gods of Ireland. When the land was dark, and the sky was black above, Patrick boldly flouted the precepts of the druids, and he lit a mighty Paschal fire on this lofty height before ever a flicker was raised at Tara. The druids there, upon seeing the blaze at Slane, were livid, and they cried out to the High King. They warned King Laoghaire [leera] that if the fire of Slane were not quenched forthwith, it would burn forever in Ireland!

Laoghaire took to his war chariot, and led his band of warriors to arrest the mysterious rebel at Slane. The king's horses thundered up the Hill, while Patrick calmed his few disciples with prayer. Even as the warriors seized him, he greeted the king with warmth and joy. When asked to explain himself, he told the King of this new God, and gave forth in eloquent raptures his compelling gospel of Love. When King Laoghaire was puzzled by his beliefs, Patrick plucked up a shamrock to make plain to him the complexity and power of the Holy Trinity.

SHANE O'NEILL

The High King took Patrick into his chariot, and returned then to the Hill of Tara, where they discoursed of these things all through the night. By morning's light, Patrick had won Laoghaire to the new Faith. He baptized the High King, then and there, on Easter morning, and his disciples were spared, and bidden to go forth and preach Christianity throughout the realm of Ireland.

Donagh O'Tighe laughed aloud now, as he recalled his father's sly remark upon hearing that story all those years ago. When his grandfather had finished the tale, that deep roguish voice was heard from behind the bed curtain. "A night til morning? Sure, there must have been a power of drink consumed that night! And Patrick stoney sober! 'Tis small wonder he convinced the aul king!" Donagh thought of his family, now, of those gone 'the way of Truth', and of those living still. They were all there in his mind's eye, as he remembered his boyhood in Desmond. He gazed out over the rolling plains to the southwest, and wondered if that dim haze at the edge of the sky mightn't be the hills of home.

The pensive cleric was suddenly aware that he was being observed, and he turned his head sharply to see. It was only the guards, whose presence he had forgotten, awaiting him patiently in the shadow of the ruins. The crumbling Franciscan friary, its gothic windows pointing to Heaven like so many hands folded in prayer, its high gabled walls aflutter with blood-red ivy...even in this state, he thought, its ravaged beauty bespoke a nobility of spirit, and an abiding devotion that the flames of those English torches could never consume. The monastery wasn't ancient, or even old. Black James said that his grandfather had built it back in 1512. Only thirty years later, King Henry laid it waste in his war on God. O'Tighe blessed himself, and thumped his fist thricefold against his breast, as dark thoughts of his own ruin assailed him once again. Now King Henry's daughter had sent her soldiers to capture him...Donagh was filled with a longing for home, a deep yearning to be among his own people in Desmond...But would he be bringing armies in his wake? Visiting destruction upon kith and kindred?

The sun was well up over the far hills by now, and it was time to start back, none the wiser, maybe, as to God's will in the troubling matter of his destination. He nodded to his guards, and when he was sure they had seen, he turned and made his way back down to the castle below. Both the courtyard and the keep were bustling by this time, and most of those stirring had not as yet broken their fast, in hopes of receiving the Blessed Sacrament. O'Tighe gave word to the Chief Steward that he would celebrate Mass in the chapel at the stroke of nine, and instructed him to gather the Faithful.

The spare austere chamber was quickly transformed. From out of nowhere, there suddenly appeared a tabernacle, candelabras, and even statuary and paintings. Soon the tiny chapel was full, with every servant and, indeed, nearly every soul in the castle attending. It being a martyr's feast by the liturgical calender, red vestments were worn, and the sermon addressed the daunting and perilous demands of bearing witness to the Holy Faith. As O'Tighe recalled the sea-bourne tempest he had witnessed, he was inspired to eloquence with a stirring message of hope, hope that these dark perilous storms that assailed their blessed isle would soon abate. He exhorted those assembled to lash themselves to the mast of Faith, and ride out this hellish tempest, for the Catholic monarchs of Europe would surely send aid to Shane O'Neill, and he would yet deliver them from the greed and tyranny of this heretical English Queen. As sure as Spring will follow a hard Winter, sunshine and fair winds would follow this test of faith.

The Primate found comfort and reassurance in the timeless ritual of the Mass, and in the true communion of those present. With the rise and fall of these voices in their crisp Gregorian responses, Donagh O'Tighe marked the rapt concentration of spirit in the little room. This congregation was stirred to a pitch of feverish piety such as he had never known in those far off days before King Henry had outlawed the Mass. Here was a 'breathing together', a conspiratorial fervor, occasioned by the very forces that sought to destroy the Faith.

Some time later in the great dining hall, as his intimate company lingered in idle chat after the mid-day supper, Black James rather abruptly turned the conversation to the Archbishop's uncertain future.

SHANE O'NEILL

The rosy glow of 'last night's port' had vanished, and he seemed to have reconsidered the matter, for his words were fraught with a new sense of urgency. He felt it was incumbent upon them to mark out a course for his Grace as soon as possible. "To put it quite simply, your Grace, for so long as you remain within the Pale, you are in grievous danger. I've been pondering this all the morning. Tell me...What has become of those two bishops who refused the oath? They were deprived of their sees, of course, but where did they go?"

O'Tighe was impressed with the Baron's line of reasoning. It had not occurred to him to consider these precedents, and he did so now eagerly.

"Walsh was imprisoned for a spell, for the great crime of preaching against the oath and the Reforms. And thereafter, he was banished. He's now in Spain, as I believe." Across the table, Garret Fleming cleared his throat of a cough, and concurred with the bishop.

"I seem to recall some word of him teaching at Alcala. There's a fair few Irish studying there."

"Is he?" For a fleeting moment, O'Tighe wondered if that mightn't be his own future. He turned back to Lord Slane's quizzical patient smile.

"And Bishop Leverous of Kildare?"

"Bishop Leverous fled to the protection of the Desmond FitzGeralds. I'm told that he teaches school, these times, tucked away in a small village outside of Limerick." The Baron's curiosity was clearly piqued.

"Limerick?"

"Adare. About seven miles west of it."

"And he is unmolested since?" At the prelate's affirmative nod, Lord Slane's dark brows arched in doubious amazement. O'Tighe explained.

"He is. To my knowledge, James, he is. They've left him unhindered. Well, 'tis a remote place, from the standpoint of Dublin Castle. Oh, I know it well, for, would you believe it, now? I was reared in that very spot. Strange to say, the Papal Nuncio himself lodges in the district. And there are charges aplenty on *his* head, treason among them! He's obliged to be on the move from time to time, but...it's a queer thing. He manages to carry out his duties as Papal envoy with little interference."

SHANE O'NEILL

"Could you not go to him?" Black James smiled hopefully.

"The Nuncio?" O'Tighe's eyes flashed wide, and then crinkled in a sly half-smile, as he shook his head. He searched for a delicate way to explain. "He's a good man, and a holy man, but there would be a frosty welcome before me at his door. David Wolfe is from a wealthy Old-English family in the city of Limerick, and, for all his devotion to the Church, he has scant regard for the Irishry. I had several sharp letters from him, concerning Shane O'Neill, and I'm told he has sent poisonous reports of me off to Rome. These Jesuits, now! You see, they have their own ideas of winning England back to the Faith. And they suppose foolishly that Irish measures of resistance are the great impediment to their aims. No, then, I wouldn't like to be beholden to him."

"What of Leverous? If any man would understand your plight, surely he would."

"That's true for you, James. I was still in Rome when he was deprived, but his letters to me bespoke a kindly heart...a good man with natural ways. And he's a staunch Irishman, of course. Wasn't it himself that rescued Lord Kildare in his youth, the time of the rebellion!"

"Was that Bishop Leverous?" Robert Fleming was truly amazed, for the escape was legendary.

"It was. Oh, it was. He wasn't a bishop back in '37. When Lord FitzGerald and his five uncles were hung, drawn, and quartered at Tyburn, the blaggards came then for young Garret. But Leverous took the boy into hiding, and managed, even, to spirit him off to the continent, until good Queen Mary restored the holy Church for those few blessed years. Sure, Desmond's protection is no more than he deserves by right!" Robert pressed on, to coax the Primate, for he was convinced that this would be their best recourse.

"Surely he would shelter you! Hasn't he a rebel heart?"

"A rebel heart?" O'Tighe looked to Lord Slane, with a wink. "Youth is a fine thing, but then the buds of May could know little of April's showers!" He looked back to Robert. "It was Leverous, and it was no-one else, who put the Confederacy together that time against the English! He enlisted Desmond, O'Brien, Kildare, and even coaxed Manus O'Donnell to ride with the O'Neill. He's a sound man, and he's as true as the sun to the dial!" Black James spoke softly now, but with a grave and deliberate tone of resolution.

"Then you must go to him."

"Oh, he'd not turn me away, no. But, what of his own safety? Would I not be bringing troubles to his door?" O'Tighe lowered his eyes, and heaved a quiet sigh of dispair. It was Garret who answered this challenge.

"Are you known in the district?"

"Not by sight, no, apart from those belonging to me. I was only a strip of a lad when I set off from that place. But my name is a great boast for Adare, since I became Primate of All Ireland."

"If you take a false name for yourself, the English authorities would never detect you in such a remote quarter. You might easily be another itinerant schoolmaster! There's many of that lot are known to drift from town to town. Those who know you will keep your secret. And surely Desmond's protection would be extended on your behalf as well."

"And you would be home with your kith and kindred!" Master Robert noted a sudden flickering of amazement in Donagh O'Tighe's eyes. He had no idea that this point would strike so close to the bone, for the Primate wondered now if maybe God hadn't spoken, after all, up on the Hill of Slane. Perhaps He had reasons for sending him home...The young attorney ventured what he hoped would be a closing argument. "Sussex will suppose you to be in Ulster. They'd not be looking down *there*, in the back of beyond, for you..." Donagh O'Tighe looked up to see the expectant faces, all eyes upon him, awaiting his verdict. He nodded.

"I'll go to him. I suppose I'm bound for Adare, then, boys. Back to the fair hills of home. But, sure, God help us, how am I to get there?" They all looked to Black James now, and his dark eyes glistened with a most reassuring sparkle. He folded his arms, and stretched back in his great chair with a sly smile.

"It's a simple matter. We'll run with the hare, and hunt with the hounds!"

SHANE O'NEILL

CHAPTER 19

Although it had been an arduous campaign in the West, Shane's army was flushed with victory, and spirits were high. With all challengers and holdouts to his rule vanquished, O'Neill brought his force eastward, making a progress through the province to take pledges of fealty from the local chieftains. When the last of them departed from Shane's lodge at Fathan, he and his horsemen made their way northward through the steep wooded glens of the Fews on the long trek home. An ancient byway known as 'the Bull's Track' took them over the Carrigatuke Hills, and into the drumlins beyond.

As night fell, those who had not drifted off to their homes, some three hundred men, made their encampment just south of Armagh on a hillock near Drumconwell. The tents were pitched, the men were fed, and the fires blazed brightly amid a clamour of rowdy voices. Barrels were spiked, and foaming methers of ale sloshed and splashed from hand to hand in every direction. Flagons of whiskeybaugh, too, made their way around the fires, fueling the banter and raucous war-songs, and the tussling and the laughter.

A guard of hulking gallowglass parted to either side as Shane emerged from his tent. Before him, a great crackling fire leapt and climbed into the night, its red blaze flashing and flickering over the lively faces gathered around it. Here in this rustic encampment, the

SHANE O'NEILL

chieftain little resembled the reluctant courtier of his London days. His dusty jerkin had a distinctly martial cast, with its studded leather and course blue wool, and the bristly grey wolfpelt draped over his shoulders was a match for his restive mood.

O'Neill seated himself quietly before the fire on a speckled bull's hide that had been laid down for him. His rough handsome features were composed in a broad smile, but for his eyes. His grey eyes were pensive and distant, in spite of a firm resolve to join in the merriment. He had no wish to dampen the spirits around him; the lads deserved a good frolic, but still he was unsettled, for no good reason he could think of. A dripping mether of ale appeared before him.

"Put yourself outside of that, man! Here's the lad will sort you!" One of his commanders, Cormac MacArdal, fixed him with a grin as he held the huge square mug up to him. Shane grasped it, and guzzled a good share of it. Cormac licked the foam from his own sopping mustache, and winked. "Begad, that was sorely wanting! Sure, I was farting dust!" Shane laughed, and passed the huge wooden cup along, but his smile quickly faded, and his eyes settled once more on the dancing flames before him. MacArdal caught the eye of MacKenna, another commander at Shane's side. He nodded to him, marking the chief's flagging spirits, and made another try to engage him.

"Begad, O'Neill, aren't you due for a rest! We've toppled every jumped-up Shawneen from the Atlantic to the Sea of Moyle. And *this* time, they got no reinforcements out of the Pale! There's divil-all left to be done. Amn't I right, MacKenna?"

"No word of a lie. It was wild crack to see it, too! MacMahon, O'Reilly, MacGuinness, the O'Hanlon...All of them came in, nice and handy, once they got word of Maguire and O'Donnell's troubles. All the waverers sworn to O'Neill, and every man jack of them eating crow, and pretending to like it! Aye, it's you're the man should be laughing now!" Shane nodded slowly, and MacArdal reached for another mether that was heading his way. He lowered his voice to a coaxing tone, and held out the frothy cup.

"Arrah, give that black dog a kick, man, and drink a cup of cheer for yourself! Haven't you all of Ulster now, settled and sorted?"

"Aye, MacArdal. Aye, that's *nearly* so. Every mountain and glen, and hollow and hill of it. All but the hill of Drumsallock." Shane's eyes narrowed slyly, and his brows arched as he tipped a sidling nod. "There's a shower of 'sallowjacks' lodged in that cathedral, barely a league from this spot. English soldiery...profaning that sacred temple! Built by the O'Neill, it was, by my father's grandsires who are all buried there. Built for the Primatial Cathedral of All Ireland...on the same patch of earth as the first wee stone church built by St. Patrick himself. The bones of the High King Brian Boru and his son are resting within the north wall...But how could they be? How could they be at rest?" He took the mether in both hands and drank deep. MacKenna took up his theme with gusto.

"No word of a lie, O'Neill! And the hoors are still plundering Armagh, taking preys, reaving cattle for their provisions, and-" Cormac MacArdal's dissenting shake of the head halted the litany of transgressions.

"The way I hear it, they may be mending their ways. The O'Hanlon saw a drove of oxen going out from Dundalk to the ward in Armagh. The herd went through his country a fortnight ago with a wagonload of provisions, under a mighty guard. Fine longhorn steers, he said." Shane peered at him, eyes wide, brows aloft, over the brim of his mether. He lowered the vessel, revealing a dark smile.

"Wouldn't it be a blessed shame, now, if those same cattle were ever to break loose and stray on them...Or fall prey to wolves! Those hills about Armagh are the very devil for wolves!" Cormac tisked, with mock concern.

"Ah, it would. Begad, and it would, O'Neill. They'd be rightly scuppered if their livestock took a flit!" Shane's grey eyes narrowed, the sly glint plain to be seen. He spoke slowly, in a low portentous tone.

"Not *all* their livestock. They'd need their horses to round up the cattle. For they'd have to come out off after them, so they would. And *that's* a dangerous manoeuvre in the dark of night! Sure, you never know who'd be out there laying for them!" MacKenna nodded sagely.

"No word of a lie. A situation *fraught* with peril!" Shane tipped his head back, and his eyes darted from one to the other, significantly.

"Or...what might befall the garrison itself, while they're away out chasing their steers!" His tone suddenly sharpened. "What have they got, MacArdal? The garrison."

"I'm told Masterson keeps a force of two hundred. But for *guns*, four score of harquebus, is all."

"And what have I?"

"Reckoning in all that have cleared away off home, you've still upwards of a hundred and thirty of them. That's a fair few guns over them. And maybe two hundred and fifty bowmen." With that, Shane got to his feet. He raised his outstretched right hand above his head. As he slowly moved it from right to left the men fell silent in the camp.

"Boys! I know ye's have earned this wee rest, and well earned it too. But barely a league to the north of us –barely one league from this spot– there's a garrison full of sallowjacks in St. Patrick's Cathedral. And they're not there to pray! I'm told they've a fresh herd of kine in from the Pale, and I'm afeared there's a terrible danger that the wolves might get them tonight!" This was greeted by laughter and sharp whistles. "Tell me this- Tell me this, boys! Are yez up for a bit of crack?" There was a mighty roar, and the men were whooping and howling like wolves.

It wasn't long before Shane's cavalry were amassed. They arrayed themselves in raggedy formation, still laughing and frisking, but raring to go. With their guns slung over their shoulders, they charged off into the night, galloping through the hills after O'Neill.

There was no mistaking the sharp bite in the air. The autumnal spell was cast, with its bracing chill to quicken the blood. Even the horses felt it, as they thundered over the hard ground. A crisp October wind was whistling down the glens, shaking boughs and branches bare, and tossing burnished leaves to twirl and tumble on the night air. The big yellow moon was rising over the far mountain of Slieve Gullion, casting a coppery lustre and blue shadows over the dark Ulster hills. This was the 'moon of the stubblefields', and its light was said to have queer powers. Perhaps it was the wild starry night, or the time, or the season, but the men were restless, and the blood was up.

SHANE O'NEILL

After a spirited ride of some three miles, O'Neill's cavalry slowed to a trot as a tight jumble of glistening thatched rooves took their shape in the moonlight ahead. Above the low gables, the cathedral fortress on the hill loomed darkly against the starry sky. Although Armagh could boast its official rank of 'city' by virtue of its cathedral, at this time it comprised little more than a wee village. Twice in the last six years it had been burnt to the ground by Sussex, and, thus far, only this small puzzle of streets had managed to restore for itself the dignity of limewash and thatch. As his cavalry trotted silently through its muddy lanes without so much as a dog's bark to be heard, Shane was a bit disquieted. Here and there, curious faces peered out of doorways to watch this passing cavalcade, so one of his captains inquired of them as to the eerie quiet. He was told that the English soldiers had poisoned all the dogs of the town, a measure taken to stifle any warning of their own stealthy maneuvers.

The garrison's cattle could be seen dozing on the hillslope below the citadel, corralled by a bulky stone fence that skirted the foot of Drumsallock Hill. O'Neill led his men into the shadows of a ruined friary nearby. Only the peak of the cathedral's roof could be seen from here, and the top of the belltower. The church had been heavily fortified, its belltower bricked and shielded to serve for a sentry post, so the men were obliged to keep to the shadows. The night did not fail them there. For all its great size, the harvest moon was still barely over the horizon, leaving the low ground and hollows 'as black as the pooka's hole'.

Cattleraiding was scarcely a novel venture to these men, and they came with the needful to hand. Since the garrison's livestock was guarded by vicious English mastiffs, several lads were sent ahead with with collops of raw meat to keep them busy and quiet. A crew was then dispatched to pick a breach in the stone wall. As it was built without mortar, this was a simple task, a matter of tossing the stones quietly aside, until a gap was achieved. If even one steer could fit through it, those behind would begin to thrust and heave forward, until they toppled a great gaping breach in the wall, and the stampede would be on.

SHANE O'NEILL

Shane's plan was well devised, unburdened by complexities. He sent out a band of his men ready to rustle the stampeding cattle off into the hills, once they broke through the wall. Since the full force of the ward would undoubtedly sally forth after them, he placed a strong contingent behind the next rise waiting to ambush them. His main force he hid in the dark wooded swale just beside Drumsallock hill. The gunners in this hollow would await the garrison's departure, and then surprise the defenceless fort. If the ward should return, these were the boys that could hold it. In the meantime, they bided the time in silence, and loaded their weapons. The harquebus was a matchlock gun, so it had a few inches of tow dangling beside the trigger, a slow fuse that must stay lit. A small iron pot, filled with live embers made its way through the ranks, furnishing the tiny glow for these 'matches', and the guns were ready.

O'Neill watched with his men in the dark wooded hollow, and the minutes stretched endlessly on as they listened for the sounds of the cattlebreak. Only the rustle of the wind could be heard, snatching and scattering the crisp dry leaves from the boughs overhead. It whistled through gaunt bare limbs here and there, gnarled branches that creaked and shook under bright patches of starry sky. Horses were blowing, and clopping impatiently, rustling the dry crackly leaf bed beneath them. As Shane considered the breaching of the wall, he reflected that no fence he had ever seen, however sturdy or stout, could hold against a herd of steers once the cattle sensed that they had the power to break through. A lesson there for the Irishry, perhaps...

His horse bridled a bit when a startled curlew rose up with a scream, flapping noisily off into the night. As its cry faded on the wind, a great stir could at last be heard from the cattle on the hill, and, over it, the frantic barking and yelping of the mastiffs. Now a frenzy of lowing and bellowing moved through the herd like a mighty wave, and they staggered up from their rest. With a deep rumble, the oxen lurched and thrashed forward, and the whole hillside seemed to move. The groaning mass of shaggy longhorn cattle stamped and butted, moving slowly at first, then quickening to a thunderous rampage over the tumbled wall.

SHANE O'NEILL

In their dark hollow nearby, the Tirowen boys rejoiced quietly, with stifled whoops, and fists in the air. But as yet, no troops had emerged from the garrison.

Shane galloped back to the friary ruins for a better vantage point to watch the chase begin. He cast his sharp gaze over the hulking cathedral fortress, searching for signs of the impending response. The gothic windows had been mostly bricked up, leaving only the arched tops, which e'er this had been dark. He could now discern helmets glistening faintly by torchlight, as soldiers jostled to see the shadowy spectacle below. Their full supply of beeves, the last of their prized oxen were escaping into the night.

At length the great rumbling din subsided, leaving a fraught silence that lingered for a small eternity. There was a palpable air of disbelief and shock; within the fortress, at what had befallen them, but also in the dark hollow below, where there was a growing realization that the English ward would not be sallying forth to retrieve the herd. Clearly the little snare had been detected, and spirits sank in disappointment. But not for long. Soon there were smirks and stifled laughter when some of the Tirowen boys started to howl like wolves. The hollow against the hill proved quite sonorous, and the wolf cries resounded in the air. Their deft mimicry, despite its mischievous intent, cast an eerie pall over the quiet. So much so, that the garrison's mastiffs began to bay and whimper, taking up a loud plaintive wail. When Shane's men heard this, they roared with laughter, an explosion of mirth that resounded in the night, offering a galling affront to the English ward. The indignant soldiers shouted down from the cathedral's windows, hurling the most poisonous epithets that they could call to mind.

"Irish dogs, howling in the dark! Come out, ye cowering curs! Skulking taigs! Milk-livered Irish cowards! Hairy Bog savages!"

The Tirowenmen emerged slowly from the trees. Up from the shadows they came, silent as spectres, to gather on the brow of a low rise where they boldly faced the ward under the bright moonlight. The English voices from the lofty citadel fell silent, and into that silence Shane O'Neill called to them. "Come get your kine, Masterson! What

SHANE O'NEILL

have you to fear?" When no answer was forthcoming, he turned to his men and laughed. There now began a war of words, as Shane's men commenced to shout, roaring out their jibes, taunting and baiting the garrison with all the invective they could muster. "Saxon Cowards! Fetch your cattle, you trembling knaves! Sallow Jack is up a tree! Will you leave them to the wolves then, yellow Johnny? Come out if yez durst, and fetch your kine! The wicked wolves have them snatched under your noses!" Most of the lads were showing off their English, competing to amuse their mates, as much as to humiliate their foes. Some were tossing out whatever bits of English came to mind, and one fellow drew a mighty laugh with, "The sheep's in the meadow and the cow's in the corn!" Eventually, the slagging match wound itself down, and Shane called out to his men, in English, for the sake of the garrison troops.

"Let us away now, boys, to feast! We'll have us a fine feed of roasted beef!" With that, he reared and wheeled his mount, galloping off with his troops at his heels. They left behind them a bitter English garrison on a desolate hill, without provisions, and without honour. The howling of Irish wolves could be heard fading on the night wind.

Through a haze of mizzling rain, the lofty keep of Ross Castle loomed darkly above, with its crown of jagged merlins nearly lost in the grey billowing sky. Below, along the misty shore of Lough Sheelin, ghostly ranks of pines stood to attention as the motley troop of cavalry made its way past, up the muddy slope to the castle gate. A squawking of rooks announced their arrival, and the horsemen filed quickly into the ward, clattering over the cobbles, until the sharp cry of 'Company halt!' brought all to stillness.

Waiting there before them was another company, already in formation, and, at the sound of this new arrival, they were joined by several officers who emerged from the keep. The darker, taller officer was bedecked in splendid military regalia, and capped with a large red plume. He was surely Sir Frauncis Asgard, at whose behest they were assembled. From his place back in the ranks, Donagh O'Tighe recognized the youngest of them as Christopher Nugent, the Baron of Delvin and Lord of this castle. He was all of seventeen, and he had but recently come into his estate and title. He seemed a devout lad when he had called upon the Primate in Drogheda little less than a year ago, but since his father's death he was said to have been made a ward of the Deputy, Lord Sussex. Who could know what 'compromises' might be demanded of the boy in order to inherit? Even through the disguise of rugged livery and the stubbly beard, Nugent might easily recognize the renegade archbishop. After some moments of uneasy deliberation, Donagh had almost convinced himself that the young baron was unlikely to betray him. Nevertheless, he was thankful for the misty cover afforded him by this grey drizzly day. Another blessing in disguise.

The troop's commander trotted forward to report to Asgard. Young Tom Fleming it was. Master Robert had taken himself off to Tirowen to report to Shane O'Neill of the Primate's escape, and of his destination. Indeed, Lord Slane had mustered his troop of light-horse as bidden, but he had enlisted a few 'older recruits', including O'Tighe, the very quarry of the hunt. "We'll run with the hare, and hunt with the hounds!" he had said. Donagh reflected that it was a policy well known to such families of mixed blood, who so artfully straddled both worlds. With the rigours of the 'reformation' intensifying daily, such a position seemed less and less tenable. Black James had professed himself loyal to the Crown, but yet devoted firstly to the Holy Mother Church. Donagh blessed him for that, and for this devious gambit as well, and yet he knew he would breathe a fair bit easier once he was across that lough, and out of the English Pale.

Beside him were two stalwart lads, McNulty and Keegan, who were sworn to see him safely all the way back to his home in Adare, and there was some comfort in that. O'Tighe felt his nerves playing at him now, and so he prayed silently as he watched the officers confer. A stout woman suddenly appeared at the castle arch, her head coifed in rolls of linen in the Irish fashion, and she began waving and gesticulating in his direction. He caught his breath and looked to each side, to see what might be the object of her sudden fuss. As nothing was amiss, he was the all the more alarmed. Donogh then turned back, and looking up at the wall behind him, he smiled to see it was only three young boys marching and swaggering along the wall. They were frisking about with sticks over their shoulders in mock military drills, arousing the concern and ire of their nursemaid. he mused to himself that life goes on, with its silly larks and rollicks and vanities, even in times of woeful peril. The woman folded her shawl about her and started down to retrieve her charges with an angry stride.

After mounting his charger, Captain Asgard trotted out now before the company, flanked by his officers. Two attendants quickly rushed to his side, and hoisted a light fringed canopy over him that flapped and dripped, but provided him some shelter from the misty rain. He opened a scroll, and thundered forth his edict, helped in no small measure by the sonorous stone walls of the castle ward.

"We the Lords Justices and Council do by this our proclamation strictly charge and command all Mayors, Justices of the Peace, sheriffs, bailiffs of liberties, constables and other officers whatsoever within this Kingdom," Asgard here raised his eyes to the company, adding, "and most *emphatically* this yeoman cavalry here assembled', to make diligent search and inquiry to seize upon and secure the person of the titular Popish Bishop Donatus O'Teige, who remains at large to the great terror of her Majesty's good subjects, and to the endangerment of the peace of this Kingdom. The said titular Popish Bishop is relieved, harboured, and concealed by persons evilly affected to her Majesty's Government, contrary to law, and so likewise must all and every person and persons who are aiding and assisting in rescuing the aforesaid agent of Rome be apprehended, and so they shall be proceeded against with the utmost severity of law."

Donagh was suddenly aware that the nursemaid had stopped beside him, and was scowling sternly at the children, motioning with her finger for them to come. He inadvertently caught her eye, and she looked up and shook her head with an exasperated sigh.

SHANE O'NEILL

"And for the better discovering and apprehending of the said impostor, We the Lords Justices and Council do hereby promise the several rewards following: Whosoever shall apprehend the said titular Popish Bishop, or shall discover where he is, at any place within this Kingdom, shall have and receive the sum of *fifty pounds sterling* as a recompense and gratuity for the same, over and above all sums they are entitled to by virtue of any former law or proclamation. Whosoever shall apprehend those found to be aiding the usurper, shall receive the sum of *twenty pounds* for so doing, which sum shall be paid by the Clerk of the Council or his deputy." He quickly furled the scroll, and looked out over his mustered troops. "Her Majesty expects that every man jack of you will stand to, until we shall capture this brazen impostor! This militia is encharged to guard each gate and sally-port of the pale along this northwestern frontier, and to search all papist friaries and other like resorts of those ill-affected to the civil order of this realm. Following my conferral and briefing, your captains will assign and commission you accordingly." With that the officers trotted back to the Keep for their briefing, leaving the 'popish impostor' quite stunned. It was all most unsettling.

The sound of a child's whimpering shook Donogh from his troubled reveries. He looked down from his mount to see the nursemaid standing there with a young boy firmly in hand, but she was peering up at him with her mouth open. He froze in horror. Then, remembering the sly advisements of Master Robert, he turned his head and hoiked, loud and gruff, and spat. He turned back to her now, his lip curled up in a grin to flash the blackened tooth that he had laboured on for just such a moment. The woman huffed and yanked her shawl tighter, and strode off with the child. Donagh could feel his heart in his gullet, and he drew a deep breath. He looked over to McNulty and Keegan, who were nodding. "Good on ya, boy! Fair play to you!"

Tom Fleming was not long in returning. He had suggested to Asgard that the renegade might well attempt to cross lough Sheelin into O'Reilly's Country to get himself back to Armagh. This was deemed sound reasoning, and he was ordered to put a patrol on it. The young

SHANE O'NEILL

Baron came down loughside, and requisitioned them several light craft, a large cockboat and two small skiffs. He looked directly at O'Tighe several times with no glimmer of recognition, which heartened the cleric immensely, for it attested to the credibility of his worrisome disguise. When he had gone, Tom Fleming manned the smaller boats and sent them off to watch the east shore. He put five in the cockboat, a rather sizable crew for such a mission, but he knew that the boat would be lighter of three once it reached the shore at Finea. Only five miles to the west. A short jaunt to begin a long journey.

The boat was launched with no word of blessing. The only token of farewell was a sly nod and a wink from Captain Fleming. And as they rowed off into the west, leaving the English Pale behind, the sky could be seen brightening ahead over the far Curlew Mountains, another good sign, which surely merited a little prayer of thanksgiving.

"Good my Lord Mayor, our time is scant, and our business most pressing!" Sussex lowered his voice to the soft forbearing tones of mockery. "You may tender such regrets and excuses as may please you, but you shall see to the dispersal of that crowd. Forthwith!" The portly little man blushed and blinked, but moved not, being sorely flustered, so the Deputy assumed a more coaxing manner. "If their matters be so grave and urgent as to warrant the attention of the Lord Deputy, wherefore came they not to me in Dublin? These 'urgent' suits afforded them leisure to await my arrival in Dundalk, and so might they bide some while more. I shall see *only* the delegation of your Council. And Captain Smyth!" Sussex' dark eyes flared as he looked to his officers. "Where the devil is he?"

"Smith is below, my Lord." A young adjutant took a single resounding march-step from his post at the window. "Just now I saw him tethering his mount in the courtyard. I'll fetch him up to you." At Sussex' nod, he swiftly disappeared, making a clatter on the wooden stair. Sussex turned his smoldering eyes back upon the stout little Lord Mayor, his brows arched imperiously.

The Mayor's tiny eyes went wide, his fleshy lips parting again and again as he made to speak. His wagging chins set his broad ruffed collar to stir, so that he looked like nothing so much as a fish gasping on a platter. At last he swallowed, and stammered, "Indeed, your Lordship. Indeed, how dare they to presume so upon your office! I shall dismiss them at once!" He bustled off down the stair then, pressing his arm tightly over the heavy golden chain of office that was sliding from atop his belly. His few attendants followed noisily on his heels. The Lord Deputy sighed and shook his head after them, and his Marshall, Sir George Stanley, laughed aloud.

"Poor fellow! He has promised to serve you up to his patrons, and now he must turn them away! Belike they will devour *him*." As no smile was forthcoming, he took up the business at hand. "But what of young Captain Smith? What's *his* part in this?"

"I sent him up to O'Neill."

"To parlay?" The Deputy pulled a heavy oak chair from the table and turned it out to the room. He sat wearily in it, then drew himself up straight, raising his chin and peering down his sharp nose.

"What? Nay, Mercury's errand. A messenger only. O'Neill is quite taken with him. His vanity is soothed, I should think, to receive Lord Smith's nephew as his courier."

"Smith?" An older gentleman, bald and bellied and bushy-browed, turned from his idle musing at the window upon hearing this name. "Is this the young squire who put about that screed last year, pressing you to ban the rhymers? A cogent case he made! Quite sound. *The poets* are the true wellspring of venom in this land, a menace to-"

"That was his cousin, *Thomas* Smith, the apothecary." Sussex cut in sharply, impatient of such digression, but now George Stanley's interest was piqued.

"Indeed, the cousin! Bottle Smith' they call him. *He* is said to be the natural *son* of Lord Thomas Smith, whereby he learned his pharmacopeia and letters. Young John is not the scholar he is, though he is nimble-witted enough."

"The *natural* son?" The baldy gent nodded slowly to Sussex, with a sly squint. "Aye, well, he's not the first lord's bastard to be shunted off to Ireland."

"In this instance, most providential, as it happens. Smith is the *only* apothecary *in* this godforsaken fen. He knows his banes and his potions." The Deputy's voice lowered portentously. "And he has never *failed* me." Sir George Stanley winked.

"Lord Thomas is a busy 'smith' indeed. Methinks I do hear the ping and clang of his hammer and tongs in Ulster...But is the Irish iron so hot for the striking?" Sussex replied tersely.

"The house of Smith has taken a keen interest in Ulster of late." His vague response did not close the matter. Sir George persisted with a loud conspiratorial whisper.

"His plan seems to me quite mad!"

"I supposed when he was sent to Paris, I might hear no more of it, but his meddling persists." The other gentleman, Master Barron, now spoke up.

"What plan do you speak of, my lord, if I might so enquire?" Sussex sighed, and replied wearily.

"Sir Thomas has a grand design for an utopian colony in the Ardes, just to the north of here." Sir George elaborated with a good deal more zest.

"Oh, a grand settlement! That would be crowned withal by a great city to be called...Elizabetha!"

"Elizabeeetha? In the wilds of Ulster? Fools' folly! He is hunting unicorns!" Marshall Stanley laughed.

"He is as like to make civil the wild Americas! Will her Majesty be induced to grant approval? Indeed, to grant him the vast *estates* he will require?" Sussex' dark eyes flashed as he slowly shook his head with palpable relief.

"By a merciful stroke of divine Providence, he was denied. Her Majesty dismissed his wild conceit as inconceivable *–for so long as O'Neill*

SHANE O'NEILL

lives..."

"I see..." The older gent looked to Marshall Stanley, whose sly smirk promised further illucidation.

"Ah...'for so long *as*...' And so they come forth, his busy minions and gets, even to the gates of Ulster in Dundalk-" It was the hasty tramp of boots on the stair that silenced him, a silence that held, and creaked with expectation, until Captain SmIth appeared in the shadowy stairwell.

"Your Lordship." He was a slight fellow of medium height, his pallid face framed by thin blond locks, and a wispy reddish tuft at the end of his chin. His lips were pursed, and his brows raised expectantly.

"Captain Smith. How did you fare in Tyrone?" The young man's pale green eyes darted apprehensively, disdainfully perhaps, to the Deputy's officers, prompting Sussex to continue. "I believe you are acquainted with Sir George Stanley, the Marshall of her Majesties forces. This is Master Edward Baron, a sheriff of Dublin. You may speak free, John. What says O'Neill?"

"The Lord of the bogs will attend you presently. He will be at the Moyry pass tonight at the rise of the moon. Below the stone pillar. As to your entreaties, he deigned not to entrust me with his reply, but he would save his words for your ears alone."

"We will ride out this eventide. The moon is full. Mayhap this parlay will keep him from his raids and plunders for a night. But tell me, how did he receive my lure? Will he rise to the bait?"

"Oh, he is no fish -but a randy riggish goat that did slaver and drool at the merest mention of Lady Frances! I did shame to utter her name before him, for, like a debauched satyr, it seemed to convulse him in lewd and bestial transports. After much gibbering in Irish, he assailed me with such vulgar and dissolute queries about her ladyship, your sister, as I dare not recount before you."

"Fie! The wretched swine!" Old Master Baron harrumphed. "For her fair name to cross such lips! So foul and rank-"

"We must forbear." Sussex paused him with a raised hand. "Though it stinks ill, this bodes well! But what news of the Romish bishop? The petender, O'Teige? Is he in Ulster?"

SHANE O'NEILL

"I think not, in truth, for there was much agitation there over wild rumours of his capture. I heard, even, a report that he was beheaded in Dublin. He must perforce be elsewhere."

"In England such inference could be safely drawn, but the Irish are a devious lot, well schooled in guile and deception." Sussex looked to Sir George, who nodded trenchantly.

"And much given to histrionical effusions!"

"O'Neill was overmuch curious as to her Majesty's health, so word of her illness has come to him, doubtless from London. Is there news of -"

"Only that she is recovering her health."

"May God mend her swiftly for England's sake!" Smlth slipped the strapped leather bag from his shoulder, and took from it a packet of sealed letters. "He has his votaries at Court, it would seem, and keeps with them a vigourous correspondence. He bids me journey there now with these letters and his gifts for the queen and her ministers." Sussex took the bundle eagerly, and perused the markings of address.

"Dudley, of course...her Majesty, and Lord Cecil. Ha! The affrontery! To curry her grace and favour, even as he sunders her convenants." Sussex tilted his head back, taking close account of the young captain. "And he sends *you* as envoy to London...You have won a fair measure of his trust! Good."

"That is a simple but disagreeable task. To soothe his boundless vanity, I am obliged to stand agape, in feigned wonderment and awe before his boggy ostentations. And yet, in our dealings, I rejoin his sallies with sharpness. He has a taste for salt and banter."

"What 'gifts' does he send?"

"To glorify his petitions and plaints, he bestows upon her Majesty a splendid black Araby stallion. And so in likewise to Lord Robert Dudley, sending a present of two horses, two hawks, and two greyhounds, that his lordship might be a means for his favour with the Queen. I have them stabled at dockside. As to Lord Cecil, he sends him a present of a horse, a fine bay stallion."

Sussex nodded, and laughed quietly to himself. He flashed a sinister smile to George Stanley, and turned back to Smith. "You must take pains

SHANE O'NEILL

to present this gift discretely to the Lord Secretary, without arousing those cautions that give rise to scruples. If fortune smiles, he will accept it." He looked again to Stanley. "A bribe to compromise his oath and office! The very *whisper* of such malfeasance could o'erturn his policy, loosing those purse-strings to provide me the troops and arms to take Ulster. O'Neill's gifthorse might prove his *own* undoing. I might soon undertake to relieve Maguire and O'Donnell in their distress. Did you hear aught of them?"

"I *spoke* to them. I was present at O'Neill's lodge at Fathan when Maguire, O'Hanlon, O'Reilly and the rest were made to pledge fealty to O'Neill. I witnessed the solemnities, wherein each was obliged to kneel abjectly under his sword. There was much gibberjabbering in Irish, but, mark you, my lord, I was told that this oath held *no word* of 'her Majesty,' or of duties owed unto the sovereign. O'Neill was all! Thereafter, he repaired northwards to Benburb Castle, bidding me to take ship at Dundalk on his embassage to London."

"You spoke to Maguire, say you?"

"It was then I chanced to confer with them, Maguire, O'Reilly, and the rest. Upon seeing O'Neill so proudly departed, and not having received from you that help which they long had hoped on...they did forthwith burst out in so large, unseemly, and so lamentable talk! Yea, in effect cursing him that would believe *any* promise for the Queen's Highness, either by mouth or letter. O'Hanlon openly swore it were better to serve the worst Irishman of Ulster, than to trust in the Queen. Maguire spoke the same, and complained bitterly of his losses, 'both at the coming in of the tide, and going out of the same.'

"And so Lord Cecil's foolish parsimony has cost her Majesty the last of her loyal adherents in Ulster!"

"Oh, but they are not lost. O'Reilly, Maguire, and Con O'Donnell remain in her Majesty's service in despite of their losses. Maguire bids me tell you even that he has procured Turlagh Lynagh O'Neill-the second person in Tyrone- to forsake John O'Neill!" Smith reached again into his satchel and proffered a crumpled parchment." Here is a dispatch in his hand, and Maguire has scratched his own message below."

SHANE O'NEILL

"But this is astounding." Sussex turned to Stanley and Baron. "His cousin, a turbulent rogue! He was a very hellion during O'Neill's absence at Court...harrying the Pale and firing all the country round. From whence proceeds this new found devotion to the Queen?"

"I hold it but little wonder." Marshall Stanley frowned and shrugged his broad shoulders. "He has proved himself a bitter rival, and so wherefore would he not make common cause with John O'Neill's enemies?" Sussex read in silence for some moments, and then continued aloud.

> "You shall understand the cause that I did not meddle with your doings in years past. The first cause was that my father was once engaged to serve the King's Deputy to his great losses. The other cause is that I see no other man in the north of Ireland holding *your* part except my lord Maguire and Con O'Donnell, and I promise you that all Ireland does give them more mockery, seeing that there was no Irishman that ever meddled with Englishmen, but it was to their great loss and shame. I promise you that all Ireland does take an example how negligent you be about your servants' great losses."

The Deputy looked up, displaying an indignant scowl, his dark eyes flaring. "God's hooks! He is proud as O'Neill, and as defiant in his yielding. Maguire's postscript follows." He read on.

> "Turlagh Lynnagh O'Neill will cleave to the Queen all the days of his life unless your lordship forsake him, wherefore I shall desire you, as you do love your honour, to help him at his need, or else never look that no man in Ireland will give credence to what an Englishman is saying all the days of their life."

"If this be genuine, -now coupled with the pledge of MacDonnell and his redshanks to swell our ranks, we shall soon prevail in our call for troops and arms. And so our wars may at last commence." The Deputy raised his head and halted perfectly still while churchbells tolled out the

SHANE O'NEILL

hour. "I have yet to instruct the Council!"

"They are assembled below, my Lord."

"How now, Captain Smith? What more wonders have you in your bag? Is there aught more to report?"

"Nay, that is all of news, my Lord. A ship for Chester sails on the evening tide. What would you?"

"There remains yet ample time for that. Bide your hour. I shall read O'Neill's letters presently, and furnish you a proper 'addendum' to take withal." Sussex leered slyly at his Marshall and sheriff. "-Lest O'Neill has o'erlooked, perchance, some *trifling items* for the Queen's consideration... Come now, that we may dispose of these few matters below." With that, he followed his adjutant down the stair, and all followed.

At this thunderous clatter on the stair, the six burgesses and the Lord Mayor sprang to their feet around the broad table. There were several attendants standing behind, and a young footsoldier standing at attention by the fire. On the Deputy's arrival the councilors bowed, and the Mayor's attendant pulled out for him a grand throne-like chair. Sussex, however, held his place at the doorway, leaving most of his entourage huddled behind him in the stairwell.

"Alas, good my Lord Mayor, and sturdy yeomen of the Council, my time affords me not to take my seat amongst you, so pressing are the day's duties. As to those which concern this corporation...pray tell me, has a train of provisions and beeves been yet dispatched to replenish our beleaguered garrison at Armagh?"

"There was no need, my Lord, for the herd was restored unto them."

"Restored? By whom? We are told that Masterson did not pursue the raiders."

"Private James was at Armagh, my Lord. By your leave, he will recount for you what befell there."

"Very well. We will hear of it." The footsoldier took a step from the fireside, and saluted the Lord Deputy.

"Aye my Lord. Well sir, O'Neill surprised the ward by night, sir, and made off with all the oxen left for their provision. But Captain Masterson, he suspected some treason, sir, and he detained the soldiers

SHANE O'NEILL

from rescue-"

"Wherefore did he suspect this plot?"

"He was making ready to sally forth, and was close upon it, when he was bid hold, for the watch in the belfry had espied a vast number of matches aglow in the dark night. It was the tow of their matchlocks aflickering under the bare boughs in the grove just below the cathedral, for the Irish were mustered there, at the foot of the hill. More nor a hundred of them there was. And so, suspecting some treason, he detained us from rescue. This were no blunder, for belike O'Neill was hoping, you see, that we would issue forth to rescue them. And so, cutting between the ward and the fort, he meant to slay the ward and capture the fort. It was the Captain saved the day! Then the taigs came on again and railed at us, and bade us in English come like cowards, if we durst, to fetch our kine. The next day, Masterson sent six of us to O'Neill to demand restitution. He weren't hard to find, what with the trodden trail of that herd. He said they were *wolves* had taken the kine! And the matches we saw were but wolves' eyes! He was fair tickled by his jape, sir, and he said it more nor once. E'en so, he restored all, save five or six beeves which he said the wolves had eaten. Right jolly he was, with his fleering grin, well pleased with himself an' all."

"I do not doubt it! I do not doubt it...God's blood! All to pull my beard, the *whole* cursed escapade! A scurrilous jackanapes! Yet more of his strut and swagger!" Sussex sighed bitterly, and quickly settled with some measure of calm. He cast his stern eye over the assembled councilors before him. "And so the ward is replenished with no further cost accruing to the good burghers of Dundalk...Has Council seen fit, then, to honour our request? We did entreat you to levy a tallage, a cess to be exacted from all merchants here to garrison the town. Have you raised the sum?" Sussex peered sharply at the Lord Mayor, who averted his gaze by turning to one of his councilors, prompting him to reply.

"Alas, it was not possible, my Lord Deputy. The motion did not pass council, such was the uproar it did stir among the townspeople!"

"You prefer, then, to pay the black rents to O'Neill? Very well. We are bound, even now, for the gap of the North to parley with him. Shall I tell him of your frugal concerns?" He cast his accusing glare from face to face around the table. "Prithee, O'Neill, do cease your predations upon Dundalk, for the townsfolk can scarce afford to provide for their defense.' He will surely be moved to pity, and grant clemency withal! Oh, a wise council sits in Dundalk! A most prudent course they have chosen." He looked over his shoulder to his entourage, and then turned his fiery gaze back upon the abashed faces around the table. "That is all my business here. Good day, gentlemen." He strode then out into the courtyard with anger on his heels, followed by his officers. Sir George Stanley hastened to his side.

"A sound rebuke, my Lord, and sorely deserved. They are fools."

"Fools they are not! They know that I shall be obliged to station a garrison here, whether they provide for it or not. I, sir, am the fool!"

"I'll no more on it. You may save you your breath, Lord Sussex. And you might have saved you a rigourous journey to this windy height, if *that* be all of your tidings. By the indentures of London, I was charged with the duty of ordering this province on her Majesty's behalf -a task made ever more difficult by your *incitement and encouragement of Maguire and O'Donnell*. Urging them to spurn their duties, and to challenge my rightful authority."

Although they had been wrangling for some time about his western campaign, Shane's demeanor was cool, his gaze, stern and resolute. The weary horse shifted under him, and he straightened his back and lifted his chin as he regarded the Deputy and his escort. Their helmets glistened silvery in the moonlight, and the ensign's broad pennant snapped sharply in the cold October wind that gusted through the mountain pass.

Further off down the road could be seen the dark glinting forms of a more sizeable force, some eighty archers and gunners. Sussex was

SHANE O'NEILL

leaning across to hear some whispered advisement from his Marshall, but Shane saw no reason to await their deliberations. "In any case, it is settled! I have taken Lifford castle. Maguire and the rest have submitted, and are reconciled to their duties. The Maguire's son will wed my daughter Moraed. There will be a co-mingling of the heart's blood, and soon enough we will both be grandsires 'round the one cradle. Amity is sewn, and peace shall prevail. And so you see, my Lord Deputy, *Ulster* is *ordered*. When will the garrison be removed from Armagh?"

"When you have fulfilled your solemn pledge to banish the Scots from the glens of Antrim! Until such time, the ward shall remain." The Deputy grimaced, and drew in his sharp tufted chin. "Dare you *speak* of the garrison? Will you turn our eyes to still *another* infraction of the covenants you signed? There again have you broken the peace. Moreover, we are informed that you did rob from her Majesty the costly provisions made to her troops at Armagh. An expense, I might add, occasioned by your own disloyalty."

"Ah, no! Not at'all, my Lord. That was wolves! Let your Englishmen be advised that there is yet great danger in the woods of Tirowen. Aye, they'd want to mind themselves, for there are savage packs of Irish wolves that bide here still!"

"Have a care, sirrah! These pranks will cost you dear."

"When my men came upon the herd astray in the wood, didn't I restore it unto the garrison? You can't ask better than that!"

"Fully five beeves were amissing."

"It's a pity, so, that they made food for wolves. They might have served to betoken some small repayment for the vast herds that Sir George Bagenel stole from me at the Newry while I was in London. Forty thousand head, and not forty kine returned! A theft in violation of all covenants, and no word of restitution. Your Masterson, I'm told, never so much as ventured forth to recover his cattle. Do not look to *me* if this dozy shepherd does not mind his flocks...Where is the Primate of Armagh?"

"Dr. Loftus is happily installed at Termonfeckin, where he thrives and tends his duties. He will be cheered to know of your concern."

SHANE O'NEILL

"O'Tighe. Where is he?"

"You think to befool me with such posturing. The whereabouts of that rogue are well known unto you. Of *that* I am certain. But be advised, O'Neill. His warrant is writ for treason. Whosoever shall help him will be charged with the same. You stand warned."

"He is no rogue. O'Tighe is a pious man who serves the people as he serves God."

"He is an illicit agent of the Bishop of Rome. He has set himself against the constituted authority of her Majesty's government, and whensoever he is apprehended he will be dealt condign punishment. We are charged with *ordering* this kingdom, and we shall do so as we see fit."

If you harm him...if you harm that holy man, you will sew such bitterness in this land as can only ripen in endless war and bloodshed. You will be reviled by all, within the Pale and without it. What then of your charge to order this kingdom in the Queen's name? To establish the Queen's *peace*? Such wickedness and villainy *you* may hold fitting, but it is a shameful affront to her Majesty's honour."

"This insolence of yours will have a price. You forget, sirrah, that your *sons* are in my keeping..." Sussex' Marshall cleared his throat, so the Deputy turned to confer briefly in whispers. Shane's eyes burned with loathing, but he watched in silence, resolving to amend *that* matter, the hostages...The Englishman looked up with his thin vague smile. "Let us, then, O'Neill, turn our labours to cultivating the Queen's peace. There is...*another* concern. You spoke but now of the betrothal of your daughter to Maguire's son, a measure to 'sew amity' in the province. Methinks this is sound policy, a foundation for peace." He nodded to his officers. "Some of these Irish ways betoken a natural wisdom by which we might conceivably be instructed to our profit." Sussex cleared his throat, and swallowed. He resumed in louder voice, with a painful-looking grin. "We are informed...we are informed that you have approached Lord Cecil to sanction your courtship of our own fair sister, and it will doubtless please you to know...that Frances has consented to see you at Ardbracken. *If* you be amenable. What say you, then? Will

SHANE O'NEILL

you pay a call to us in Dublin? No doubt your son and the other pledges would be cheered to see you at the Castle." At this, Shane licked his lips, and his eyes danced with wicked glee.

"Aye, Lady Frances Radcliffe! Most fetching! She has me fair bewitched, so she has. And you say, now, she has an eye for me, so. Ah!" Shane's mouth twisted in a lascivious grin, and he tipped a wink to McArdal, a captain at his side. "*There* lies fertile ground for to sew the seeds of amity! And the fine broad hips on her, wherein to plant them! Fine round hips to bear me strong Irish sons withal!" He turned his leering grin to the Deputy, and nodded slowly. "Aye. I shall be down to you...whenever I have things sorted here, your Honour. Meantimes I must regale her with tokens and favours. My messengers will be at your gate soon enough!"

"Do not tarry, O'Neill. A wise suitor would not leave his welcome grow cold. You know what women are!"

"Aye. That I do. What news of her Majesty's fevers? She is much in our prayers up here." Sussex' smile vanished, and he bristled visibly.

"The fevers are abated, and our good Queen is recovering apace."

"God bless her, that's grand! I'd hate to think what might befall the kingdom if she were taken from us. The line of succession is-"

"I assure you, she is beyond all peril!"

"Ah! That's a great comfort. A great comfort, entirely...And now I must away. Keep to the road, gentlemen, and you shall fare well. But I caution you be wary, for the moon is low still, and the pass is dark as pitch. You had best take heed, for it is well known and attested that there are Irish wolves in this defile! Vicious and ravenous! You'll not be safe until you reach the Pale."

"You may rest your wit, sir. Your jape and your impertinence are conceived, I assure you." With a hearty laugh, Shane wheeled his stallion, and faced for north, as his men did the same. They drew up to a quick halt, however, upon hearing a sharp call from Sussex. "O'Neill!" Shane wheeled his horse about to face him. "Have a care, O'Neill. If you follow your foolish pride, her Majesty will destroy you at the last!"

"Indeed, and I will, my Lord. I shall have a care! Tender my fond

SHANE O'NEILL

regards unto your sister!" With that, he and his men galloped off into the night. And if there was howling on wind in the lofty gap of Moyry that night, it would be small wonder indeed.

CHAPTER 20

In spite of the promising brightness in the western sky, the misty rain gave way to a fierce downpour as the intrepid little cockboat made its way across Lough Sheelin. The lough itself took on a menacing aspect in the storm, an air of wild desolation. The soft rustle of showers upon its lapping waters had become a sizzling din that overtook even the plash of oars, as the crew rowed fiercely on. Still, huddled under his cloak of frieze, the fugitive bishop was undaunted, simply relieved to be outside the English Pale. "I couldn't give a toss if it's coming down cobblers' knives! 'Tis only an aul squall of rain!' All the same, the lads were concerned when they caught him sniffling, so they wrapped a cape of grey sealskin over his shoulders. It was worn and shabby, but it had a fine cowl to keep the rain off. Spirits lifted, finally, as they rounded the reedy marsh at the mouth of the River Inny, for the strong current would sweep them the last mile or so downriver to the wee village of Finea.

Stepping up onto the ramshackle wharf, Donagh chided himself for the overwhelming charge of elation that was welling up within him, for it was certainly premature, considering the arduous and perilous journey that lay ahead. After the briefest reflection, he put it down to the compelling aura of 'crossing the water', with all its biblical precedents, the Jordan, the Red Sea, and even the River Styx!

Finea was home turf to young McNulty, and he quickly led the crew to his grand-uncle's cottage that was nearly within sight of the river. A black and white terrier came bounding up to greet him, barking with excitement, and sniffing and yelping at the crew behind him. After a mad dash through the pelting rain, the men followed McNulty into the warm and cozy, but exceedingly humble, stone cabin. There was a broody sow taking shelter within, whose less than fragrant scent nearly overtook the stout smell of rabbit stew and onions that were simmering in the hearth. An old man was tucked into a settle-bed, snoring away, with his long white beard out over the tattered quilt. A short untidy woman, with a mass of greying red hair, was tending her pots at the fire, and at the customary chorus of 'God save all within!' she quickly rose to her feet, wiping her hands on her apron.

"And God bless ye's, ye are all welcome. Down, Cush, down! There's no harm in him, excited is all." The dog whimpered, and slunk over to the fire, where he gave himself a furious shake, sending a shower in all directions. The woman laughed. "There's one of ye has some sense! Lie down with you now, doggie, and hisht!" She looked to McNulty and tisked. "Only our Dinny brought me word, there'd be nothing in the house! Get up til the fire with ye's. The lot of ye are drenched and drownded! There's a bit of stew here is near to ready." Her quick blue eyes sized the men up, and she approached O'Tighe. "This is a sorry place for the like of you, your Honour, but 'tis a mighty blessing to have you under our thatch!" She lowered her voice, and cast a quick glance at the old man in the bed. "Maybe you would bless Daddo before ye's are away, for I'm afraid he'll not be long in it."

"I will surely. It's a blessing to be under any thatch *this* day!"

The woman caught her breath sharply and nodded, by way of reply. "Oh, 'tis a fierce deluge, right enough!" She moved a rope-seated chair up to the fire. "Shamey, get the bowls from the press. Sit yourself down here, Your Reverence, and take your ease." McNulty set about helping her now, laying a broad dealboard over the small table, and setting out the wherewithal, and it wasn't long before they were seated around it, putting away a hearty supper. The auntie busied herself hanging their sopping cloaks over a rope that was stretched across the hearth, and she then returned to her post, standing over them at the table. She insisted that *she* would eat later, for it wasn't hunger that was troubling her, but curiosity. "What way are ye's bound from here, Shamey? Will ye take the river south, is it?" She saw looks being exchanged around the table. "Sure, ye needn't worry yourselves about Maura McCormack. I'd as soon give Daddo up to them, the heathen scoundrels!" It was McNulty who answered.

"It's a word to the neighbors, Maura, is where the danger lies. No-one imagines you'd go to the English. It's for the best if-"

"There's no loose tongue in *this* head, Seamus McNulty. I always got more news than I gave! This tongue holds a rake of secrets, and some that would interest *you* plenty, but there's devil a one could shake them out of me. Beggin' your pardon, your Reverence."

"I suppose that's true enough." He looked questioningly to the others, who nodded their assent. "No then, we'll not go south, Maura. Indeed we'll not *take* the River Inny, for it's all loops and twists. There's a fellow is bringing our horses here, from out of the Pale, and I expect he'll not be long in coming now. We're off to the west, then, bound for the Shannon, and we'll take *that* river nearly all the way to the sea." She put her hand up to her mouth, and drew a sharp breath.

"God bless you, you've a fierce journey to make! But ye'll not be riding into this storm, surely ye'll not!"

"The day will lift, please God. There's brightness in the West."

"Aye, well, I'll not be hanging out my wash just yet! I'll pack some provisions for your journey. I've a few hens' eggs boiled. And a jug of bonnyclabber, and oaten farls." She stilled suddenly, and after a moment's reflection, she looked to McNulty. "Will ye be going the Granard road? Or Ballyfarron way, is it?"

"Granard, I expect." At this, Maura again drew a sharp gasp, and raised her voice a touch.

"Ah, now -there's talk of a *power* of English, -sappers and soldiers I think, out on that same road. Just beyond Abbeylara they're raising some class of bawn or tower or such, so ye's would be safer on the Ballyfarron road." With that, the dog leapt up from his dozing, and began to bark excitedly at the door. "This will be him, I suppose?"

McNulty scrambled over and opened the door, and Cush bolted off noisily into the rain to advise and admonish the new arrival.

"Aye, it's Avishteen, right enough, with the horses."

"It's lashing still. In with him, so, Shamey. Would you ever reach me that wee bowl there?" Keegan looked up, to see whom she was talking to. "Unless you'd like a bit *more*, is it?"

"Ah, no. I've my fill taken, Ma'am. Thank you kindly!"

"Ah, good man!" McNulty stepped outside, past the torrent of rain that was pouring off the thatch, and then, just as quickly, stepped back inside.

"Aye, it's clearing in the West, alright. There's no great hurry on us. Only that we'd want to reach O'Farrell's Long Fort by nightfall."

"It's the Long Fort in Annally ye'll be stopping? Sure, wasn't there just a great wedding there, was it, aye, only three days ago. I suppose any gentry is cleared off by now, only for the lingerers and the malingerers. But they say the O'Farrell is staunch, and if what they say is true for them, he'll see ye's rightly. His daughter was wed on Sunday to the O'Kelly's son and heir." O'Tighe smiled brightly.

"Well, God love you, you're a great font of knowledge altogether!"

"Sure, 'tisn't much of news, but it's been all the go these weeks past with the 'auld ones' hereabouts, for the bride is known to be a great beauty. Ye'll find no English beyond in-" There was a sudden gust as the door opened again.

"God save all here!"

"God bless you, come in with you! Come in to the fire out of that downpour."

"Good man, Avishteen. Did they stop you?"

"Divil the one I saw, nor saw me either. For I walked the horses out, one by one, through the little Sheepsgate, and no guard was posted there! Would you credit that, now? Not a bother on me! We're grand." Maura blest herself hastily, and clapped her hands together.

"May the rest of your journey be so blest, your Honour!"

When the Primate had finished eating, Maura gently woke her father from his slumbers, so that his spiritual needs might be attended to. Once he got over his initial confusion at the outlandish apparel of the bishop, the old man was comforted to find such an exalted cleric there at his bedside. He couldn't help but feel that such an ending to his days augered well for the Hereafter. Although he was feeble, his mind was sharp, and he was gratified to be confessed and given Last Rites.

It was not long after that, that the showers lifted and the company parted their ways. Some rowed, and some rode; the boatcrew began the hard slog back upriver to Lough Sheelin, and the Primate and his two guards rode west, taking the northerly route, mindful of Maura's warning, and grateful for it. Thankfully, the ride was uneventful, and when they arrived shortly after dark, the welcome at Long Fort was 'princely' and warm. To forestall any difficulties owing to his disguise, Lord Slane had given Bishop O'Tighe 'papers' to present, a missive carefully worded so as to avoid incriminating himself. He simply asked that the reader extend all courtesy to the bearer, and, most importantly, that he credit his word. That was sufficient. After the Primate said Mass in the private chapel, they were feasted and well looked after by the O'Farrell.

As it happened, one of the lingering guests from the wedding there was the Cannon O'Kelly, a younger brother of the chieftain of that sept, and he undertook to escort them the next morning to Cloontuskert, near the west bank of the River Shannon. There the O'Kelly entertained them in high style, but in low profile, with a lavish private dinner, his best harper, and bardic recitations over fine Spanish wine. This chieftain maintained a brisk trade with the continent in pelts, and whiskeybaugh and such, sending boats and barges down the Shannon, and he suggested that his guests might avail of one that was soon bound for the port of Limerick. This they resolved to do, and after only one day's delay, they were on their way.

The skies were heavy that morning, but the gulls and terns were soaring, so there was a feeling that the day would hold. The O'Kelly accompanied his honoured guests to the riverbank to see them off. He paid them a fine price for their horses, and as he made his farewells, he bent the knee and kissed the bishop's hand just as though the blessed ring were shimmering there. With a catch in his throat, he ushered them aboard the well provisioned vessel. The boat iself was a small gandlow, a shallow-draughted cargoe barge, flat bottomed, with a mizzen mast and sail to traverse the lakes that they would encounter along the way. It was loaded to the gunnels with bundles of pelts and barrels of spirits, all to be traded with continental ships at the docks of Limerick. The O'Kelly's youngest son, Mihawl was aboard to man an oar, to act as coxswain, and to handle the trading at port when they reached their destination.

The river journey was no sooner underway, when they came to a jumble of rustic stoney cottages at the water's edge, and as they passed the headlands there, the Shannon opened up onto the broad grey expanse of Lough Ree. The sail was quickly hoisted, but the brisk November winds out of the South did not avail them, so the oarsmen set to, ploughing their way across the choppy waters of the lough. As it extended some seventeen miles in length, this promised to be a long haul without that gentle thrust of a river's current. Lough Ree stretches to five miles in width, but Mihawl kept them close along the eastern shore to avoid shallows.

The first nightfall found them on the isle of Inchcleraun, one of a number of monastic islands hidden away in the Shannon lakes. The Franciscan friary there was dissolved under Henry VIII, but the monks had returned under Mary Tudor's brief reign, and thus far it had escaped the attention of Elizabeth's rigorous Protestant regime. The Primate was acquainted with the abbot there, and a rapturous welcome was given him. Donagh was astounded at the peace and seclusion he found on Inchcleraun, and in his cot that night, he imagined living out his days there as a contemplative. Indeed, sleep eluded him, with all the worries and uncertainties that seemed to demand his attention in the darkness and solitude of the night. When the crescent moon eventually cast its blue shadows into the cell, he sighed peacefully, for there would be clear sailing in the morning, and he soon drifted off.

At first light, they set off again over the shimmering blue lough, with a cold northern wind behind their sail. As they headed south, Mihawl had them all searching the waters for a rock called Cloosa-loocogue, 'the mouse's ear', for it marked the safe mid-point between the eastern and westerly shoals. Indeed, he knew every isle and inlet of the Shannon, and each lurking danger, and he guided them skillfully between its shoals and reedy islands.

It took several days to sail the lough. When the winds shifted or died away, McNulty and Keegan took shifts at the oars with the rest. Amiable banter was the usual way of things, and Donagh was pleased with the lively and erudite company of Mihawl. The bishop occupied much of his time with prayer and reading. Cannon O'Kelly had given him a breviary and several books for the journey, including a tract on the rulings of the Council of Trent. Donagh grieved silently as he read them, for it was painfully clear that he would not be the man to implement those reforms. Still, the weather and the winds were fair, and brought them at last to the narrows of the River Shannon, with its strong current to carry them along.

Fortunately, winter flooding had raised the water to navigable levels, but in some places just barely, and the crew had to use poles to pick their way through the shoals and reeds and rocks. This was as yet an untamed waterway. When they reached Athlone, the ruins of a stone bridge and a series of eel weirs around it presented more harrowing difficulties. A long punt had gotten caught up in the weirs, and several boats were waiting to get through. This delay was rather unnerving as an English garrison was posted here. Several mounted English cavaliers and sappers were overseeing this snag in the river traffic, and all was being watched by a sentry in the Norman castle above the river. This delay gave rise to fervent silent prayers in one particular vessel.

When the offending hurdle was cleared, the boats slowly poled their way through under the watchful eyes of the soldiers. In his tattered sealskin coat, the by now bewhiskered Primate had nothing about him that would draw their attention, but perhaps due to his seniority among the crew, the officer addressed him directly, asking where they were bound. Donagh answered with a smile, in rough Irish, and Mihawl spoke up in English. "To market, my good fellow! To market in Limerick Town!" With that, they glided past, happy to see last of Athlone.

SHANE O'NEILL

"Christ Almighty! Sit your arse down here, Farleigh, til you hear this! The blessed Primate took himself off to *Desmond* -and he wouldn't come to us here because he didn't want 'to be bringing war into Ulster!' He's protecting *me*, sparing Shane O'Neill from an onslaught of the English legions!" Farleigh splashed brandywine into a wooden mug, and as he put it to his lips, he winked.

"God save us from the madness of saints!"

"Begod, that's the clergy! It's like trying to understand the mind of a woman!"

"Not *all* the clergy. Not Myler Magrath at any rate!" Farleigh sat, and turned his smile to Robert Fleming. "Myler's in Rome, and probably swindling the Borgias, or teaching Machiavelli's boys some new tricks. Poor O'Tighe is only an innocent!" He clapped him on the shoulder. "Master Robert is with us once again. Good man yourself! You've put aside your law practice, so, only to be run ragged with dispatches. Hermes on the hoof!"

"Aye, desperate times, indeed! You're standing it well, Farleigh O'Gneeve!" Robert's smile faded as he turned to the sullen face of Shane O'Neill. The chieftain shook his head in exasperation. He sat back, and folded his arms.

"They're only after him to get at me! No harm must come to that man!" Shane swigged from his goblet, and huffed. "For the love of God!...Does he not know that Desmond is London? Why the devil would he go there?"

"*Is* he?" Shane nodded meaningfully. "We'd no word of it, no. Well, O'Tighe was born there, in a village called Adare. The Bishop of Kildare found refuge there when he was driven out. His Grace thought he might teach with him until he could get a ship to Spain. And isn't the Papal Nuncio, himself, able to carry on in that same quarter?"

"By Christ, he was mad not to come to me! And to trust that Nuncio!

SHANE O'NEILL

David Wolfe is a conniving bastard, with his English Jesuits, and his poisonous letters to Rome." Farleigh sighed.

"That's no word of a lie, Shane O'Neill. Rather dreary prospects, I fear! A lamb in the care of a Wolfe!"

"And *teaching*? He's no need to linger down there. There are ships sailing out of Limerick every day! One of Desmond's captains must look after him, get him on board a blasted ship. I'll send word to Lady FitzGerald. No harm must come to him. But I've another mission for *you*, Fleming. I need a free hand to smite this thieving hoor of a Deputy, so I need to get my pledges out of Dublin Castle. And I want *you* to arrange it. I'll send you down with some word or other for Sussex, and you can bring my instructions to the boys. A message for the Deputy..." Shane's brow gathered as he pondered this, but the inspiration came to Farleigh.

"What about that spindly sister of his?"

"Aye, Lady Frances! I'll send her some token, and stall him off. No, then, I'll not! You'll bring her a gift, aye, but you'll tell him that I'll not be coming down, because I suspect a trap. He'll believe that, right enough, and you'll have his trust. That's when you'll blow a wee cloud of dust in his eyes. We'll spin a fine rope of hay for him. I want him completely bewildered as to what I'm *at* up here. You'll recount for him every lie that's on the wind, and swear to it! Are you able for it?"

"I am, of course!" Farleigh tipped his cup to Robert's, with a wink.

"He's a barrister. Sure, isn't that what lawyers are trained to do? Snaffle and baffle and bugger all!"

"Now, the boys know to be said by Thady O'Brien, and he knows the plan. He's been holding off his escape, just awaiting the signal-token from me. Sure, he's an old hand at this sort of thing. And you'll bring the swag to pull it off. To buy horses, and grease palms. For that you'll need to meet a wee fellow called Master Shortall at the castle. He's like yourself, with an Irish mother, though you wouldn't know by the cut of him." Shane drained his cup, and a sudden thought brought on a hearty laugh. "Ach, Farleigh! Wait til I tell you! Do you recall the clash at Armagh, and the coward, Wingfield, who fled the fray? Riding down his own men, trying to scarper. Well, in the end, he was demoted...He's now Constable of Dublin Castle -minding the hostages! When the lads have made their break for it, the Lord Deputy will be scratching his head to find a lower post for Wingfield!"

"A turnkey maybe!" Farleigh's eyes danced with merriment. Shane's eyes were narrowed in a sly squint.

"Aye, or shoveling shite!"

The next thirty mile stretch of the Shannon presented its own difficulties for O'Tighe and his crew. The river wound its way through low reedy meadows known as 'the callows,' fields that were under flood at this time of year. It was difficult to ascertain the actual path of the river itself, and young O'Kelly was grateful that the hindrance at Athlone had provided him with several boats to follow in a sure pathway through these uncertain waters.

At Banagher, about half way to Lough Derg, they came upon Cloghan Castle. In the early evening light, its high walls and square keep towered over the flooded callows, casting a beautiful reflection on the still waters below. The Franciscan monastery, just beside it there at Lusmagh, housed a number of old friends that Donagh O'Tighe wished to see, and so it was determined to stop for the night. The wayfaring bishop and his crew were warmly received by the O'Madden of Croghan, and they were feasted and entertained lavishly, providing a much-needed and most convivial respite from the rigours of their long river voyage. The friars had gotten word of the Primate's difficulties, and after all their prayers, they were greatly relieved to see him alive.

The O'Madden shared with O'Tighe his concerns regarding Fitzwilliam's scant but busy garrison upriver at Athlone, and recounted the latest encroachments of the ever-expanding English Pale. "Alas, your Reverence, you're not the only Irishman to come afoul of their greed and wickedness. On this side of the Shannon, the O'Moores and the

SHANE O'NEILL

Kavenaghs have been driven to the fern. Ninety of the O'Connors and thirty-five of the O'Byrnes are slain or executed, and English settlers descended upon their lands. Fitzwilliam's men were o'erheard in a tavern, those swilling and swaggering ruffians from the garrison, boasting of Sussex' plans. Would you credit this, now? Sussex will shire six new counties in Conaught. O'Farrell's Annally will be called 'Longford', Thomond will become 'Clare.' Black will be white, and up will be down!"

"They'll have to reckon with Shane O'Neill, before ever that comes to pass."

"Isn't it a gauntlet thrown down before him? The O'Neill is pledged in London to keep to Ulster only. They wish to provoke him, or to English all this place before he can stop them." The O'Madden was curious as to the Primate's plans, and O'Tighe, with no mention of Adare, told him simply that he would have recourse to the protection of Lord FitzGerald of Desmond. O'Madden appeared troubled by this.

"But sure, isn't Desmond in *London*? He'll be little use to you there!"

"Ah, no... It was in Maytime he sailed. He's surely returned e're this!"

"I've heard nothing of his return as yet, your Grace. Divil a word. There would be news of his arrival in these parts, if he were come."

"Ah, no, he went to London of his own accord, and if he's not back now, he will be so shortly. No worry of that, now!"

"Aye, your Grace, you have the right of it, I'm sure. Desmond is a mighty prince, and his protection will keep you safe. I'm thinking I detect the flavour of Desmond in your fine melodious speech, if I'm not mistaken?"

"You would, of course, for I was reared in those domains, right enough."

"It's a wise course to take, for all the dangers, for I'd say now, you couldn't get further from Dublin, and still be in Ireland! God and his blessed mother will see you safely there."

The O'Madden presented the Primate with a bejeweled chalice, which he was obliged to refuse. "Until Our Lord wills it otherwise, the only treasures that I may keep about me are those in my heart! What I *shall* require, though, is a credible but threadbare suit of clothes such as an itinerant schoolmaster might be known to wear." The chieftain put a servant to the task of finding something suitable, happy to oblige him in this humble request, and soon the feast was underway. It was a grand evening, with music and singing and spirits, and even the fugitive bishop took his 'noble call' and sang a plaintive stave or two. The morning came early, and after O'Tighe said mass in the tiny ancient chapel, they were on their way.

Once they had poled their way to the riverstream of the Shannon, the current was swift, and with such a force moving them, Donogh wondered was it was the hand of God, moving him to his destiny? There were no other buildings to be seen all along this stretch of the Callows; the seasonal flooding made such developments quite impossible, so nature was all. The rushlands filled the air with a pungent acrid smell of decay and growth. The raspy sound of the crake was everywhere to be heard, and herons called among the reeds. In the glassy shallows magnificent flocks of swans glided serenely. To the weary cleric such a sight was profoundly moving and comforting, for, as he thought, it attested to the endurance of the natural order and elemental beauty, regardless of the folly and wickedness of temporal powers.

A guttering candle on his desk left the chamber in near darkness, although it was barely four of the afternoon. The single narrow window above provided little help, awash, as it was, in the grey rains of a November storm. The Deputy fumbled through the press behind him, and at the sound of his secretary's footsteps, he turned to look. "Where are the blasted tapers?"

"Allow me, my Lord." The young man reached in and quickly produced two candles. He held their wicks to the flickering grate at the fireplace. "There's a gentleman awaits a private hearing, my Lord. An

SHANE O'NEILL

attorney out of Drogheda, name of Master Robert Fleming. Says he bears tidings from Shane O'Neill." As he ensconsed the fresh tapers at the desk, his inquiring eyes shone brightly, insistently, in their glow.

"Fleming? By all means. He is known to me. You may send him in."

"Yes, my Lord." He bowed his head perfunctorily and left the chamber.

Moments later, Master Robert appeared in the doorway. "Your Lordship!" He drew the heavy door closed behind him with a resounding thud, and leaned his back against it. His eyes darted around the shadowy chamber. The rain could be heard thrumming on the high window, like gravel dashed upon the pane. Suddenly, darting over to the far wall, he pulled back the arras that hung there. Finding nothing, his eyes were drawn next to a tall ornately carved press that stood open in the corner of the room. He bounded over to it, and swung the door shut to see behind it. Breathing heavily, the anxious visitor turned to the Lord Deputy.

"Are you *quite* satisfied, Master Fleming? I can assure you that we are very much alone. Now! Be so good as to state your business!" Sussex sat back in his throne-like chair, taking close account of his agitated guest as he stepped into the candlelight before him. Only now, he noticed that the young man carried a small wooden box bound with red ribbon.

"Begging your pardon, my Lord, but were my divulgences against Shane O'Neill to be discovered unto him, they would cost me my life!" His shadow loomed ever larger behind him as he approached the desk.

"That is a matter of no concern, as I shall not *disclose* your confidences. And, as you see, we are alone."

"Swear it so, my Lord, I prithee! Upon the Saviour's blood!" Sussex sighed impatiently, his brow beetling as he held up his right hand.

"Upon Christ's blood, then, I do so swear. I shan't divulge your report. Now! So please you, be seated, and say you your say." Robert sat then, and placed the small box upon the desk, as he slowly recounted Shane's message.

"A token from O'Neill to her Ladyship, your sister. Inside the casket is a golden locket, and there within is a lovelock of his hair. He sends word withal, that though he be unhappily detained, yet e'er long he shall call upon her here to court her, and to woo her, and to win her hand." Fleming jumped to his feet, and raised his voice. He spoke on in a heated rush. "And therein he lies! For I did hear him say out plain that he shall never be such fool as to come to *you* nor *any* governor in Dublin, for fear of capture! O'Neill hears report every day out of the Pale. He has planted spies even here amongst your staff, for *they it must be* did tell him that your sister was brought to Dublin *only to ensnare him!*"

"Who are these spies in my employ?" Sussex' cool demeanor was in stark contrast to that of his visitor. "Have you names?"

"Nay, I know not, my Lord. But he has word of your comings and goings, and all between. You were best to put trust in no man here. And even those loyal Irish captains who stand pledged to the Queen, they have covert 'understandings' with O'Neill, and will oftimes tip him word of your designs and intents. Even as they withhold from you *his* plans that are well beknownst to them."

"What plans, then?"

'They know that O'Neill means to keep Cullagh O'Donnell in perpetuity! The poor man languishes in his shackles, and is near unto death, as I am told, and O'Neill has cast those keys into Lough Neagh for wicked spite. He intends to wed his daughter Moraed to *Con* O'Donnell, who will then hold those lands under him."

"This cannot be so, for I know Con O'Donnell to be loyal, an honest liegeman of Her Majesty!"

"Alas, therein you are deceived."

"What of his mother?"

"His mother?" Robert was momentarily confounded. "Ah! The scotchwoman! She too is shackled, chained to O'Neill's bed, that he might use her at his will. And even her child is most cruelly fettered! The MacLeans will furnish O'Neill a legion of Gallowglass in ransom for her. He will send her back to the Isles, for he avows that he will wed only Lady Frances, your sister. But he would see her in Dundalk, for never will he come to Dublin." Robert looked away for a moment, to gather any stray thoughts. He shook his head. "Nay, then, that is all of my news."

"That is all? But what of the titular Primate, the papist impostor? Is he in Ulster?"

"Alas, I cannot say with certitude. Only a rumour -but a rumour that reached my ears in O'Neill's own court -that O'Teig bides in *Dublin*, hidden under your very nose!"

"Could it be so?"

"Alas, who can say? These wild Irish be liars all. Truth is hard come by in Ulster!"

After days of rowing, and a few cold nights moored among the reeds, the Primate and his crew reached the broad expanse of Lough Derg, a challenge that lay shimmering before them under the morning sun, nearly twenty five miles of sailing. Even so, they were heartened by a blustering northern wind that promised good headway as it filled their sturdy sail. The little gandlow moved swiftly over the lough, and after another night anchored in the shoals, they were blessed once again with a sweeping northern wind.

Indeed the hand of God was moving the little barge along nicely, and yet the Reverend Primate was quite unable to read, or indeed to pray. He was in some disquiet over the O'Madden's tidings regarding the Earl of Desmond. Why was he delayed in London? Perhaps it would be best to go to Lady FitzGerald for protection. She would surely oblige.

Certainly O'Tighe' Primacy was a great source of pride for the House of Desmond. It was the Earl's father who had sponsored him as a 'poor scholar' at Oxford, and afterwards sent him to Louvain to study theology. Desmond it was, who, in the years that followed, presented him to Shane O'Neill, who dispatched him off to Rome on a diplomatic mission that eventually won for him the pallium, and Holy See of

SHANE O'NEILL

Armagh. Donagh resolved to leave these worries to the Almighty, for surely His Divine Prividence was providing. Desmond would soon return, and his protection would stand.

As they crossed the broad expanse of Scariff Bay, a rising swell and a sharp blast of cold bitter wind caused some alarm, and soon a dark foreboding shadow swept over the lough before them, grim and desolate. Huge black clouds were massing and billowing across the northern sky. A fierce gale was driving this wind, this sharp wind that was thrusting them ever onward through the choppy waters of the lough. The mast was creaking as the swollen sail pulled the little gandlow, keeping it barely ahead of the storm. As the darkness gradually deepened around them, bolts of lightning flashed over the lough, with deafening thunderclaps that burst upon the ear. Winds roared under the ragged racing sky, and a fierce downpour soon bedimmed and blurred all behind them.

Just as these rains began to overtake them, they passed the headland of Aughinish, where the lough narrows to less than two miles across, and the current began to gather once again. At last the swell was settling. But suddenly they could hear the trip of a hail-shower galloping furiously up the bay, and in a trice they were assailed by hailstones big as walnuts, thumping in the sail and rattling on the timbers. It whipped the lough to a cauldron of bubbles that burst in sizzling white froth. Mercifully, the winds had begun to shift westerly now, and the flapping and snapping sail was hastily pulled in before much damage could come to it. As shoals on either side prevented a putting in, O'Kelly called his crew to oars, ordering them to 'lay on for bare life!'

The Primate's knuckles whitened as he clasped each bead of his rosary in turn, assailing the turbulent heavens with his prayers. At the back of his mind, however, the dark and malevolent force chasing them across the waters seemed to mirror the evil turn in his fortunes, and he wondered what grave sin in his past could account for it. The men rowed furiously through the downpour, and by and by the hail ceased, and the swell settled as the worst of the tempest drifted off to the East, leaving only cold pelting showers for them to endure. Eventually, after passing the endless shoals and marshy shores, the dim towering shape of the steeple of St. Flannan's Cathedral came into view, and they came to the crowded little harbour of Killaloe.

The scrape of the keel over the gritty shingle brought untold relief to the weary crew, for ultimately, they had outrun the black heart of the storm. No sooner was the vessel secured, than the men scrambled up through the lashing rain to a dockers' alehouse just beside the watergate of the town's walls. Although it was early afternoon, the place was thronged with rowdy mariners, all made idle by the storm. Drenched and exhausted, the newcomers were welcomed, and given seats nearest the hearth. The scruffy and sopping archbishop was as delighted as the rest to get his hands around a crock of whiskeybaugh, and soon all were revived and in high spirits.

The men around them were all roar and rattle, giving out against the times and tyrants, but the talk of the alehouse mostly concerned the recent local skirmishes in the 'succession dispute' among the O'Briens, the princes of Thomond. Like that of the O'Neill's, this row spanned several generations. In this instance a younger brother of the chieftain had turned Protestant and loyalist so as to acquire the earldom from the Crown, and most of the O'Briens were resisting this. The Bishop of Killaloe was Turlagh O'Brien, and he held vastly more sway among his people than the Earl of Thomond.

Donagh and his men were disheartened to learn that the bishop was not in residence this day, as he had gone off to Dromoland to intercede for his two sons who were in some difficulty. They were known scandalously as 'the Bishop's bastards', and they were the chiefest rebels of Thomond, a distinction they held only because their uncle, the arch-rebel Thady O'Brien, was imprisoned in Dublin Castle. The Primate was quick to point out that these bastard sons were born *before* Bishop O'Brien had been 'called to Christ.' As for lodgings, the men decided not to entrust the bishop's servants with O'Tighes identity, but to settle for the somewhat frowsy accommodations of the local inn.

The sky was grey and heavy the next morning, but the rains had ceased. The men got underway early for this last leg of their journey.

SHANE O'NEILL

Limerick was only fifteen miles away, but the roughest stretch of the Shannon lay just ahead. With a course impeded by rocks and rapids, the river falls nearly a hundred feet between Killaloe and Limericktown, and it was as well that the O'Kelly's son was an old hand at making this journey.

Just beyond O'Brien's Bridge, which was in tatters owing to the recent upheavals, portage was required for well over a mile in order to avoid the tumbling rapids and falls of Dunassa. As it happened however, there was an enterprising drayman known to Mihawl, who handled this portage with a team of oxen and a sturdy dray. The men trudged along behind as they made their way down the boreen at the river's edge, and they were happy enough to stretch their legs. Grey skies or no, the wild beauty of Dunassa was something to behold- even with a dry gullet and a sore head from the night before. Seeing the rough and treacherous waters that lay ahead, made worse this time by the early winter flooding, O'Kelly resolved to carry the boat several more miles before they launched again.

By and by the river split in two just above Limerick town, and they rowed along Shannonside, under a stoney arch of Thomond Bridge, past the towering grey walls and castle turrets of King's Island. This part of Limerick was called Englishtown, and below it stood the walls of the Irishtown settlement. Along the riverbank before the these ramparts, were the busy docks. It was easily seen why, since the days of Ptolemy, this place had been known as 'Limerick of the Ships.' Huge three-masters and galleons huddled by the shore, and many a ship lay at anchor in the middle of the harbour awaiting a berth. O'Kelly's small gandlow required no such delay, and he quickly put in to shore. He hired a small punt for the rest of the bishop's journey, and after a few lively farewell bumpers in a publichouse close to hand -and a quiet word of blessing, the wayfarers parted company.

The November sun was sinking behind a low bank of purple clouds over the far Atlantic, as McNulty and Keegan rowed those few miles along the southern shore of the estuary, and a fiery gash of glowing sunset sparkled and glistened on the waves before them. It was a beautiful gilded finish for their long journey to the sea. They hadn't long to wait before the tide swelled to let them travel the two miles up the River Maigue to the Primate's village of Adare. Donagh's last visit home had been some seven years earlier, but he had come that time in the Earl of Desmond's carriage. This time he could mark each unfamiliar edifice and each slight change along the river since his boyhood days, and such little things as he recalled brought a flood of memories, and a warm secure feeling, like a cozy turf fire when a storm is raging.

Although he had often written and sent money to his father, he seldom heard from home, and hadn't a notion of what to expect. The little lane of crumbly stone cottages was bedimmed by evening's blue shadows as the weary strangers approached, finally, O'Tighe's boyhood home. Dogs barked, and children peeked from doorways, and Donagh was thankful for the falling darkness. He knocked on the door, a thing he had never done, and he said a silent prayer that he would find all well within. He knocked again, and a familiar voice called, "Come in so, out of that!"

A tearful welcome was given him, and his father was greatly confounded by his shabby apparel, for there had been no word of his troubles as yet. When he had explained all, his father simply nodded, closed his eyes, and blessed himself; such was the common understanding of the wretched state of the world. A widowed granddaughter was residing there with her two young boys. She was a fishmonger, and she soon arrived with a small cish of trout for the supper. Greatly excited by this unexpected arrival, she sent the boys off to fetch her uncles and her mother, but under strict orders to guard the secret of their illustrious visitor.

The family gathered. Donagh's sister, Nuala, was not as quiescent as their father when she heard all that had befallen him. She wept for him, and cursed the Nuncio for his treachery. The English were unspeakable, of course, but as a Catholic and a Limerickman, Wolfe's crime was held to be immeasurably worse. After they had eaten, a bottle of wine appeared, and helped to cheer the company, as they recounted their news and not-so-news. Donagh was truly happy to be back among his

SHANE O'NEILL

family, and much relieved to find that the only dire story was his own. McNulty and Keegan stayed the night, with a warm welcome and fulsome praise, for they had completed their task and delivered the Primate safely home.

Nearly a week had passed since Master Robert's call at Dublin Castle, perhaps the longest week the young Ulster hostages had ever known. Night by night, the waning crescent moon dwindled further, as by and by each piece of the scheme fell into place. From clay impressions, counterfeit keys were forged; operatives both within and without the castle were pledged to their parts, and now, at the darkling of the moon, all was in readiness.

High up in the Bermingham Tower, the warden's oil lamp cast it's faint glow through a narrow window. All other windows were dark. But in the middle of the courtyard one fire burned brightly, and, as the night was bitter cold, a number of the sentry guards stood huddled around it, passing the long hours in idle banter. They did not see the four dim figures emerging from the tower, or creeping furtively along the south wall.

A house of timber and cladding was being built just there, new lodgings for the constable, and it was only a short scamper, really, from the tower to the shadowy recesses behind this gaping structure. The lads were pleased to see shovels and picks, which might serve if it came to trouble, and they nearly laughed aloud when they saw a tall ladder left leaning against the back gable. Such woeful indiscipline! For *their* part, precautions had been taken. A fellow disciple of O'Neill outside the castle had been engaged to secure the closed drawbridge, by jamming a stout pole through the links of its great staple chains, insuring that any attempt at pursuit would be severely delayed.

By way of signal, Thady O'Brien tossed a brick over the castlewall, where it splashed in the River Poddle, which served as a moat on that side of the castle. Upon this signal, a knotted rope was thrown over the wall by the co-conspirators on the other side. This took several tries, and as it happened, the rope finally fell tangled in its knots, half way down, causing some agitation among the lads. Thady put his finger to his lips, and, with a sly and merry glint in his eyes, nodded toward the ladder behind them. It would reach up above the snag. One by one, now, they made their way over the wall, and swam across the narrow river where their horses were waiting. When they were at last assembled, the six horsemen galloped off over the sheep-meadows, and on to a safehouse where they would get dry clothing and provisions. From there they would ride south into the Wicklow Mountains.

In the morning, the Lord Deputy's chamber was a pit of seething fury. Outside his door stood a queue of yeomen guards who had been summoned to account for themselves. Inside, Lord Sussex hissed, and fumed and raged at the unfortunate constable, Wingfield, blaming him for the negligence and folly of his unguarded lodgings, and for the treachery in his ranks. Several guards within the tower had been bound and gagged, yes, but as the shackles had been found with new keys intact, it was evident that collusion was involved.

Apart from facing the Queen's inevitable wrath, Sussex now had to contend with an O'Neill unbridled by vulnerable hostages, and the chief disturber of the West now loosed to resume the dynastic wars of the O'Briens. He dispatched a message off to the Earl of Thomond that his cousin Thady O'Brien has escaped confinement, and also to his own brother Henry at Maryborough in Leix. "...Alas, Pandora's box is spilled out once again, unleashing troubles to beset us both North and South! Thady O'Brien must not be let cross the Shannon. Indeed, you must capture this miscreant before he will combine with his adherents in Limerick. He is an arch-rebel and traitor, as evil a man as any in Ireland, but for Shane O'Neill!"

Early in the morning McNulty and Keegan departed with the

SHANE O'NEILL

Primate's heartfelt blessing. After a prayer at his mother's grave, Donagh set off for the Augustinian Priory where, according to his brother, the deprived bishop, Leverous, was holding his school. The brother had also provided him a rather shabby, but warm, cloak against the autumn chill. Braving the blustery November winds, he made his way through narrow crooked lanes, amid the cluster of stone cottages that was known even then as the Shanbally, or 'oldtown.' Donagh was relieved that he need not venture into the newer village below the Abbey, for there was said to be a strong English presence there of late, with huge Tudor cottages going up. He crossed over the Mague by way of an old wooden bridge that was buttressed upon a tiny midstream island, and after passing under the gnarled and leafless boughs of an ancient apple orchard, he stood before the open gates of the 'Black Abbey', as it was known to him.

In his youth, schooling had been held at the Franciscan Friary back beyond the castle, so this place, with its high walls and gothic arches, was not familiar to him. Fortunately, he could hear gusts of male voices droning on the wind, in the sullen tones of recitation, and this led him easily to the tall lancet windows of the schoolroom. He heard a sharp command in English rise over the Latin drone from inside. "Eyes forward, boys! Carry on!" Squinting against his own reflection, he peered in to see if Leverous was within, but evidently, he had been spotted, for a voice called out from behind him, in Irish.

"My good fellow, I'm afraid you're too early entirely. You'll get soup and bread round at the east gable -but *not* before the midday!" There was no mistaking the tall spare form, the chisled features, now sharpened and lined by his three score and some odd years. Bishop Leverous wore the simple black cassock of a curate, and a three pointed biretta over his wavy grey hair. It was nearly twenty years since Donagh had seen him, although they had never actually met. Theirs was an acquaintance comprised solely of correspondence. "Did you hear me, then? What's on you, man?"

"Dr. Leverous, you must pardon my outlandish appearance. I am Donagh O'Tighe...in such state as my travels have left me, alas." The other bishop stared in disbelief.

SHANE O'NEILL

"You're alive!" He blessed himself quickly, then, and stepped forward, bending his knee. "My Lord Primate! Blessed be God in his infinite mercy! You are most welcome here!" Donagh held out the back of his fist, as from habit, and then splayed his ringless fingers, and shook his head.

"Alas, I've been stripped of such vanities. It's a story all too familiar to your own good self, I'm afraid." Leverous glanced at the window where some boys were watching. He flashed his eyes, and they quickly turned away. He rose to his feet.

"Come you, Your Grace. It seems the winter is here even before the snows of Advent this year. Let us step inside, out of this bitter wind." His Irish had the lilt of his native Kildare, and its use brought an informality and an easy intimacy unknown to English speaking clerics.

They stepped into a long hallway with a glistening floor that reeked with fresh size. Leverous stopped, absently pressing a finger to his lips. He looked up. "One moment, your Grace." He crossed the hall, opened a heavy creaking door, and disappeared inside. After a moment he emerged, but turned back again. "*What* say you? Nay...that he might proctor my class for some few hours. I shall be in my study chamber. Be so good as to send word when the Nuncio returns."

He closed the door and nodded to O'Tighe, leading him down the hallway. "You've been very much in my prayers, your Grace. Both by night and by day. I must own, I feared the worse!" They walked along an arcade then, and entered a nicely appointed study of oak and dusty velvets. The weak November sun spilled in through narrow mullioned windows. Leverous strode directly to the fire, tossed on a few sods of turf, and stoked it noisily. He nodded to a decanter on his desk. "Will you take a sherry?"

"I'll not. Sure I'm barely out of my cot." Donagh smiled, and shook his head. "When *you* were deprived, it's little I thought...Ah, life is a queer fellow." At a nod from his confrere, he sat in the ornate leathern chair behind the desk.

"Savage times. And worse to come, I expect." Leverous sat now, still and silent. Donagh thought that his kindly eyes held boundless sorrow.

SHANE O'NEILL

Leverous tisked, and smiled weakly. "And I thought you were a mendicant!" A flicker of wariness darkened those eyes. "Are you come to confer with the Nuncio? I can think of little else that would bring you to such a place as this."

"Sure, I was *born* in this village, in the shanbally across the river. I was schooled here with the grey friars, in the 'poor abbey." The inquisitive crook in the brow of his host was unremitting. "I've come to seek the protection of Desmond, for he was ever my patron. I was a 'poor scholar' at Oxford, you see, endowed by his Lordship's father. It was Desmond who educated me." Leverous looked away for a moment, as a shadow of worry crossed his brow, and he rid his throat.

"An Oxford man? I'm an alumnus myself, back in '23. But surely the Divinities there would have been heretical by then? What way would-"

"That's true, but I was graduated in '36, only two years after King Harry broke with Rome. And it was not Divinities I *did* there, but law! Oh, indeed. I was going for Law -I suppose to help the Earl in his endless wrangles with the Crown." He sighed. "But the Law was perverted from that time, as *you* would know, by their *endless* twisting –to appease the voracious lusts and whims of that cruel gluttonous king! Prisoners boiled in oil, wives beheaded, and all under the aegis of Law. And it was *English* law." Donagh crooked his brow and winked. "It's little use going to law with the Devil, when the court is in Hell! Ah, no...A life of useless and vain disquisitions...I knew then that the work to be undertaken was spiritual. In any event I was called to God's work, and Lord FitzGerald again stood by me. He sent me off to study in Rome at Capranica. I made myself of service there by pressing for O'Neill's causes among the Curia. Alas, now once again, I find I must call upon his assistance."

"But your Grace...Your Grace, it grieves me to tell you...his Lordship, the Earl, is in the Tower of London!" Donagh closed his eyes tight, and he lowered his head, as one wounded. "I'm sorry. Word has just come down to us from Lady FitzGerald. She is distraught and quite inconsolable. She's left Askeaton for the little castle at Lough Gur, where she's given herself over to constant prayer and penitence."

"The tower! Lord Desmond!" The Primate spoke barely above a

whisper. "Such wickedness...Did they trouble themselves to name a crime?"

"They clapped him in irons some weeks ago, for he refused to sign Lord Cecil's oath to institute the Common Prayer here, and to close the friary at Dunraven. Alas, it's little protection he can offer you!"

"My God what times are these? Things as certain and solid as cathedrals in flitters. Marble icons in chips and shards. Doctrines, saints, and tablets of stone hurled into the fray like the first war in Heaven, Lucifer's revolt."

"Aye, the Earl of Desmond in chains, and the Lord Primate a fugitive..."

"Sure, isn't that the way of it? The honest man is an outcast in such times. He must be so, for the powers of state are consumed by avarice; a web of lies and heresy is spun to mask their greed. And the greater the lie, the more we are called upon to affirm its truth. Oaths must be sworn, and heads must be lopped. Such times, indeed."

"They say that you are the first Irishman to hold the Primacy at Armagh in two hundred years. Indeed, I was the first Irishman to be named to the bishopric of Kildare in *four* hundred years. A terrible price has been paid. The both of us driven out...Is it not a queer thing...is it not a queer thing that *even in its apostasy*, England has increased its dominion over the Catholic Church in Ireland?"

"There's a great deal of truth in what you say. At every turn, the Irish speaking clergy are swept aside. All preferments for the Old English."

"In this very school, Fr. Creagh was enforcing the cingulum! An innovation he brought from St. Saviours in Limerick City."

"What the divil is a *cingulum*?"

"It's a thick straw collar. Any lad caught speaking Irish will have it round his neck, and he must wear it until he catches another lad speaking Irish."

"A very cunning device, that. Sure, who would be up to them? Teach them to shun the Irish, and to turn informer in the one go! I'm shocked to hear that, now. I must take that up with the Nuncio. It's a pity I'll not be here longer."

SHANE O'NEILL

"What will you do?"

"Exile, I fear. Lord Slane has promised a ship to Spain. I had thought I might stay here until then, perhaps teach..." He saw that Leverous's brow was gathering doubtfully. "I don't want to put *you* in the briars, now! But the Earl's dominion seems to afford some safety about *this* place. Your cassock, your collar, they are not concealed. The Nuncio manages to-"

"The Nuncio's brother, Nicholas, is *bailiff* here. They are scions of the Wolfes of Ballyphillip. My assistant, Fr.Creagh, is a nephew of the Lord Mayor of Limerick! The Creagh's own half of the newtown in Adare and a good share of Limerick-"

"Sure, I remember them of old."

"They are English bred castle-Catholics, both, and they *are* protected, aye! But their safety owes little to Lord Desmond's favour."

"But the priory is unmolested. Could I not teach, so? Until I can take ship? In the guise of an itinerant schoolmaster, perhaps..."

"Right enough, now...my assistant Fr. Creagh is away off to Rome; the Nuncio is putting him forward for an Episcopal appointment. So your services here would not go amiss; *that* much is true. But I'm quite sure the Nuncio will be apposed." Leverous huffed, and grimaced, as he tried to find the right words. "My Lord Primate, Fr. Wolfe is most severe and unbending in what he perceives to be his duties...*Surely* you are aware that he blames *you* for many of his difficulties with the Crown. Your Grace, I fear you may be in grave danger here. And Lord FitzGerald's absence could provide a free hand to those who would undo you."

"I have had my difficulties with David Wolfe." O'Tighe smiled patiently, and there was a knowing twinkle in his eye. "As the Pope's emissary, he has overstepped me in many important matters. But I know he is a good and holy man, and we are both of us toiling to keep the light of Christ burning in Ireland through these dark times. I'm sure we can come to some amity, once once we are met face to face. He is devout and sincere, and does his utmost, surely, according to his lights...But he knows little of the Ireland beyond the walls and pales of their cities. As he is the Pope's legate, and I am the Primate of All Ireland, *is it not* my *duty* to share with him what-"

"Your Grace, you *must* hear me out. There are things you must know. After you were installed in your Primacy and sent to Armagh, there was a great deal of intrigue in Rome. Some very powerful members of the curia opposed your appointment. After you received the pallium, this faction was quite unreconciled to it, and they induced even Cardinal Morone, the *Cardinal Protector* of Ireland, to withdraw his approval. Because your-"

"But who? Who is this faction you speak of, if I might ask?"

"Cardinal Pole's adherents. As Ireland's Cardinal Protector, and Primate of England, Pole would *never* have permitted you such a position. It was only by his death, and his successor Morone's unversed...well, his indifference to their concerns, shall we say, that you were allowed to assume the Primacy. Because your preferment was based upon the nomination of Shane O'Neill, the Provincial of the Jesuits, Lainez, assailed the Holy Father, beseeching him to *undo* the appointment, and even to recall you to Rome! In the end, alas, Pope Pius relented to some degree. He resolved to send his Irish Jesuit, David Wolfe, back to Ireland, as a nuncio *in residence*, for the *sole* purpose of overriding your authority over the Irish Church! *That* is why he empowered him to make all further appointments. I heard this story *from the nuncio's own lips*. You shall find but little common ground, I promise you, with Davy Wolfe."

"He was deliberately sent to...? His Holiness *deliberately*...But where...where is *God's will* in all this?" Donagh fell silent, and when he looked up, he could see that his anguish was weighing heavily upon his friend. "I'm sorry; my poor wits are in disarray. And yet it explains so much..."

"Perhaps you would prefer not to *see* the Nuncio? I'll say nothing of your visit if you find you would rather-"

"Not at all, man. Ne'er a bit of it. I must speak to him, don't you see? The Almighty has brought me to this. I'm not the man to turn from the likes of Fr. Wolfe. We'll be reconciled yet!"

SHANE O'NEILL

"He'll be back by midday for his dinner."

"Perhaps I might...Is there e'er a private chapel here, where I might say Mass?"

"There is. There is, of course. Will you take the loan of a cassock? By the cut of you, now, I'd say one of mine would suit." He raised his brow, and lowered his tone confidentially. "And it would be *wise*, I think, for meeting with his Excellency."

"Tell me this, Dr. Leverous, for it's a queer thing. Why was he made nuncio without being elevated to bishop? I've ofttimes wondered."

"Indeed, your Grace, it was not to further humiliate you -although it certainly would appear so. His Holiness thought that Wolfe would be safer, and less conspicuous without such honours. If you'll come with me, my Lord Primate, there are proper robes in the Sacristy. Will you allow me to concelebrate?"

"That will be grand. I've not broken fast, as I was hoping for just such a chance." Donagh lowered his voice confidentially. "Thank you for telling me the way of it. Without putting a tooth in it. Sure, I was right about *you*, at least."

Mass was said, then, in the closed chapel, with white vestments, for as it happened, it was the feast of St. Martin of Tours, who was known to be an uncle of St. Patrick. Donagh felt strongly his mission as Patrick's successor, and he prayed to him for guidance. For all his worries, he felt in some way restored that morning, in some vital way, and he thought that it was more than the fine vestments, more than the cassock and collar that he had so missed. When the Mass was finished, there was word that Fr. Wolfe had returned, and the two bishops reported to his office without delay. Bishop Leverous went in first to tell of O'Tighe's arrival. Even through the heavy oak door, Donagh could hear the tension of raised voices.

Finally, the door opened, and a young ginger-haired priest ushered him into the chamber. It was a dark, airless room. Leverous stood off to the side, his hands folded demurely before him. Wolfe was seated behind his massive desk, in the black robes of a curate, distinguished only by a large golden crucifix suspended on his chest. His hair was nearly black and tightly clipped, as was his short jutty beard. Jutting too, were his dark brows, and under them his small brown eyes fixed gravely upon the man who stood before him, as he allowed the silence to tighten between them. After a long creaky moment had passed, he spoke.

"Dr. O'Tighe. Do you see, at last, what your unholy pride has wrought? Your willful defiance of the temporal authorities of this realm, your reckless disregard for the Holy Father's diplomatic obligations? Do you see, finally, where this sinful pride has taken you? You, who were *instructed in the English tongue*, raised up out of ignorance and squalor from the very lanes of this parish, to be ordained, and ultimately entrusted with the spiritual welfare of this island! Who turned your back upon the Prince of Peace, to embrace the foul arch-rebel of the North and his belligerent savages. To bless their very *onslaught* upon Her Majesty's civil forces!"

"Saving your presence, but those English forces invaded Tirowen after just such a blessing from Dr. Curwen, the English Archbishop of Dublin."

Wolfe raised his brows and glared, still and silent, for a long moment. "Nay, then...You do *not* see! You most emphatically do *not* see!" His fiery eyes demanded another response, a penitent response.

"I am listening, your Excellency."

"You listen, but you do not attend! Your riotous tantrum has induced Her Magesty to appoint an heretical Protestant Primate to the see of Armagh! Causing *untold* difficulties for His Holiness. Difficulties that fall to *me* to resolve. Nay, you cannot conceive of the suffering your insolence shall bring to the faithful of this realm. For you are blinded by pride! And if you be suffering for your sin, perhaps that is God's will, for the heavy burden of blame falls squarely upon your shoulders. Look at you! Your beard is unkempt, your face lined and weather-whipped. You have been haled from your diocese. You are reduced to a sneaking felon, cringing for fear of condine punishment, hoping to draw others into your-"

"I might remind you, Your Excellency, that your own presence here is *every bit as illegal*. As an *agent of Rome-*"

"Silence!" Wolfe struck the desk with the heel of his hand. "That very *fact* is attributable to your own disloyalty! We shall be persecuted because *you* have chosen to cloak your Irish rebellion in the robes of the Holy Mother Church! You are an archbishop, and yet I see before me a grinning savage woodkern, with a dagger beneath his mantle. Why do you come? Why have you betaken yourself here to me? Have you come to bring down upon *my* head the forces of the state? Such a betrayal of a Papal legate would be an assault upon the Holy Father himself. What do you expect of me, Donatus O'Tighe?"

"A brief refuge, only. I had thought to await passage to Spain. There is talk of an Irish college, perhaps, in Alcala. I could be of some use to the Holy Father there, I should think. Or perchance to Rome, if-"

"You will find no welcome in Rome. Indeed, e'er long I expect you shall find yourself 'extra curiam.' Steps are being taken..." The nuncio's head was cocked back arrogantly, and there was a flash of triumph in his dark eyes. "You appear to be unchastened. Unheedful of the grievousness of your offences. Your very demeanor bespeaks the same pride that brought you to this pretty pass. And now *I* must decide what to do with you..." Leverous took a step forward.

"Your Exellency, since Richard Creagh has departed for Rome, I have dire need of an assistant. If it so please you, Dr. O'Tighe might take upon himself those duties, until his transport to the continent can be arranged. If he were attired in lay apparel, as an itinerant schoolmaster, there would be little question raised of his presence here." He looked to Donagh.

"So long as *my name* be withheld, there would be little danger."

"Mayhap... Should such an arrangement prove expedient. I shall bethink me further of this. Since he is come, he shall stay for such time as is meet. Father O'Brien, be so good as to show our guest to Father Creagh's former rooms. I need to speak to Dr. Leverous." The Nuncio's tone was suddenly casual, as his glance fell upon Donagh. "Dinner will be served at noonday. I should advise prayer, and repentance." Leverous nodded assuringly to Donagh, and so rather than attempt any rebuttal, he simply bowed his head.

"Indeed I shall pray most fervently. Your Excellency."

With that, the young priest led him into the hall, closing the massive door behind them. He offered his hand to the Primate, and when Donagh took it, he closed his other hand over it, and spoke earnestly in Irish. "God bless you, your Lordship! I must beseech you for your blessing, for I have sore need of it. After witnessing that spectacle just now! I swear, now, for my sins, I wanted to *strike* him. After *all* your troubles, such dog's abuse for you! A shower of spite! Words sharp as hailstones! For the holy successor of Patrick!"

"I thank you for your concern, Father, but-"

"Dermot O'Brien, your Grace." He squeezed O'Tighe's hand, and released it, and the two men started off down the hall.

"Dermot, then. But we must govern our tongues, with respect to the Holy Father's envoy to Ireland. I hope to soften his heart a bit, you see, over these few weeks. Perhaps Dr. Leverous and I can bring him 'round. In any event, there's no use nurturing such feelings, and letting them get the better of you."

"Aye, just so. Sure, I've sins enough without holding murder to my heart. But I've seen things here, Your Grace. If it was the Pope himself who set this Wolfe among us, it is the Queen's whistle that cocks his ear! This is no safe refuge for you. Divil a bit of it. You should have recourse to my uncle, the Bishop of Killaloe, I'm thinking, for it's the O'Briens would lay down their lives to guard and to keep you."

"The O'Briens have war enough on their hands, as I hear it, without bringing Lord Sussex' armies down upon them! But you must give over your fretting. Put your mind at rest now, Dermot, and let us trust in the Almighty."

Donagh was shown his rooms then, which were capacious, and very simply, albeit richly, appointed, doubtless by the Creaghs, who were wealthy merchants in the city. There was a towering statue of the Sacred Heart, and the troubled Primate flinted a candle before it, and knelt to pray. He tried to think of ways of reaching the nuncio, but no inspiration was forthcoming. After a time, he donned his tattered tweeds again and resolved simply to hope for the best. At midday dinner, however, Donagh was further distressed to find himself being introduced to staff by his own name. This casual disregard for the stipulation he had made, to say nothing of the grave dangers facing him, left him perplexed and uneasy. Leverous had been called away, and it seemed there was no recourse but to think anew, perhaps to make some new plan. He stepped outside and ambled down to watch the river flow, and to ponder the matter. The day had gone grey, with a soft mist falling. A hopeless sky, and little under it to lift his heart.

Some hours later, as the weary Lord Primate was meditating in chapel, he was shaken from his revery by the heavy clank and footfall of soldiery marching up the aisle behind him. He looked up to see helmeted guards moving into the chancel before him, brandishing halberds. From behind them appeared the bailiff, richly attired and wearing his chain of office. A man of medium height, his long black hair curled over the high ruffs of his collar, and as he strode forward, O'Tighe could not help noticing that his dark brows jutted precisely as did those of the Nuncio. This surely was his brother Nicholas, and, just as surely, the Papal Nuncio had betrayed him. "On your feet!" Donagh rose from his kneeling, feeling somewhat unsteady. His mind was in turmoil. To be captured in chapel, even as he prayed to the Virgin for help!

"Are you Donatus O'Tighe?"

"I am. I am Donagh O'Tighe, the successor of St. Patrick, and the anointed Primate of All Ireland. And by what authority do you dare to enter into this house of God to seize my person?"

"I am the Bailiff of Limerick, and I arrest you in the Queen's name, for usurping the primatial office in defiance of the lawful government of this realm."

"Have you a warrant to that effect?"

"Let there be no talk of warrants! You must hold your tongue, and come your ways! Else it shall be the worse for you! Bind his wrists."

Donagh made the sign of the cross, and as he held his hands forth, a soldier tethered them with a rough leather cord. He was led out into the courtyard where an agitated crowd had gathered. The Nuncio was nowhere to be seen. The young curate, Fr. O'Brien was at the back of the crowd, dispatching several stout lads to hurry into the Shanbally with word of this dark deed to muster the people.

The bailiff proclaimed that the bishop was lawfully apprehended, and he warned and threatened the people lest they should try to interfere. Donagh, his wrists bound, was hoisted up onto the back of a sturdy grey mare, and a burly helmeted soldier took the reins, leading him on foot out through the gates. Some of the young scholars fell in behind them, calling down curses upon the soldiery in fine Anglo Saxon English. Behind them, the bailiff followed on his black stallion, and trailing him two-abreast, the company of soldiers trotted after. As the horsemen clattered over the narrow wooden bridge on the Limerick road, a crowd could be seen gathering up ahead in the Shanbally.

As the grim cavalcade approached, the 'Balliers' closed in on both sides, and began pegging clods and stones at the soldiers. No sooner had the trouble commenced, when a heavy sod struck the soldier who held the Primate's reins, and in his fury, he picked it up and hurled it back at the crowd, striking a woman. She shrieked like a banshee, and the crowd surged. As he went to retrieve the reins, Donagh gave his guard a mighty kick to his shoulder, toppling him into the ditch, and he bolted off down a narrow lane, clinging fiercely to the horse's mane. The crowd cheered as they moved in to block the narrow passage. A savage struggle now ensued as the soldiers tried to clear the way, giving Donagh time enough to disappear around a corner into the jumble of cottage lanes. As he galloped through the lanes, he could hear the shouts and calls of his pursuers, and even the din of those ructions he had left in his wake.

Although it had been nearly forty years, Donagh remembered these lanes. He had walked them often on his way to the Greyfriars, and he soon made his way to an old packtrail that wound its way through an ancient forest, a forest that stretched for miles and miles to the East.

When the last sounds had faded, he stopped to catch his breath, and to take stock of what had just occurred. He clenched in his teeth the leather cord that bound his wrists, grunting and growling as he slowly loosened each twist of its knot. And as he did so, he marveled at that sudden mad burst of frenzy that had betaken him, and he recalled his own savage roar when he thrashed the guard into the ditch. Perhaps it was the swelling anger of the crowd that had sparked his own passions. Aye, or perhaps even the sword of the Archangel Michael that had awoken this fury in his heart, but he had prevailed! Now he must decide upon a destination.

This did not take long. He resolved to make his way to Lough Gur, for Leverous had said that Lady FitzGerald, his erstwhile patroness, was in residence there. Her little castle was sequestered in a lonely glen, hardly more than ten miles off to the South-east. The Limerick authorities would never think to search for him there. Finally, the last twist of the knot gave way, and the Prelate was unbound. He closed his eyes and blessed himself. Night was already beginning to fall, purpling the western clouds, and casting wisps of pink over the wintergrey sky. Donagh took up the reins, put his heels to the flanks, and galloped off into the gloaming, through the gaunt bare wood.

CHAPTER 21

The night was cold, and colder still for Donagh O'Tighe, as he galloped into the bitter wind. A further hindrance was the darkness, and for much of the journey, he had to trust the keen eyes of his swift grey mare. The unremitting clouds left the paths as black as the hobs of hell, but the sure-footed steed never slackened. Still, Donagh lost his way more than once, having to choose between unfamiliar roads and boreens. When at last the clouds scattered, moonlight spilled over the wild hills, lighting the ways, and lifting the heart of the weary Primate. On he traveled, and after the long hours of hard riding, Donagh thrilled to see, through the bare briary limbs of a blackthorn hedge, the crescent moon shimmering over the waters of Lough Gur. The high hill of Knockadoon loomed over all, and there beside it towered the Black Castle.

Donagh had no idea of the hour, but he was relieved to see that the castle's narrow windows were as yet aglow. The square Norman keep and the high hill beside it were nearly surrounded by the lough, but for a narrow causeway guarded by an imposing gatehouse. At the sight of it, O'Tighe realized that he had not yet considered how he would present himself. Certainly he did not wish to entrust his identity to these guards, and his shabby garments would hardly mark him as gentry to be entertained at such an hour. After brief reflection, he proceeded to the gates, where he announced himself, in an English manner, as one bearing a private communication from Lord Slane for her ladyship, the Countess. He was ushered in, and led by the porter to a small salon, which was, thankfully, snug and warm, with a glowing turf fire. The weary fugitive sank into a highbacked wooden armchair beside the fire, and in spite of the discomfort, was nearly dozing when he heard the clank and squeak of the great door opening.

Donagh rose to his feet with some difficulty, for his legs felt chapped and raw from the arduous ride. Indeed, he had not ridden so hard in a score of years, and his bones ached from the ordeal. Lady FitzGerald appeared at the doorway, flanked by two Dominican nuns in their habits of brown and white. All wore looks of concern. Although the Earl of Desmond was a young man of thirty, his wife the Countess was near in age to Donagh, and wisps of grey shone in her auburn hair that had been let down for the night. Her collar and ruffs, too, had been discarded, and her long velvet robe was unadorned. Donagh was surprised to see that her beauty was hardly diminished by the years. "Is it news of my husband? I am told that you bear tidings from Lord Slane." Her eyes suddenly lit with recognition. "*Father Donagh*? Your Grace, could it be you?" She drew a sharp breath, and clasped her hand to her bosom.

"Indeed, Lady Joan, you will forgive me my outlandish attire, but I am obliged to conceal my identity, for the Lord Deputy's forces are-"

"Yes, yes, of course! Word has come to us of your- Saints be praised that you are all in one piece!" She blessed herself, and the nuns followed suit. "Come! Come! Let us to the withdrawing chamber. And you must eat!"

"My Lady, so please you, let there be no mention of my name or office before your household or guests! I stand in gravest danger of discovery. Perhaps you will just call me Donagh."

"Just as you wish, Donagh." She led him into a grand drawing room, sumptuously furnished, and sent instructions to the cook to prepare a meal for her guest. When the Primate had obliged the two nuns with his solemn blessing, they excused themselves to retire for the night. The Countess seated him in a soft leather chair adjacent to the majestic hearth, with its blazing and snapping fire of logs. She poured from a silver tankard, and handed to him a sparkling goblet.

"Mulled claret. It's still quite warm, and 'twill do you good! Lovely and soothing..." Donagh took a sip, as she seated herself across from him. "Alas, you've come at an evil hour, for my husband is not here. Indeed, he is withheld this night in the Tower of London!" Her eyes flared, and she regarded him closely to see his reaction to her news.

"I've only just heard *this morning*." His brow furrowed in disbelief, for the morning seemed so very long ago. "Another dreadful outrage. How did it come to pass?"

"It was the bold antics of Shane O'Neill, I think, for as he so flaunted his defiance in London, my Gerald felt compelled to match him. He was charged before Council with openly flouting the reformation, since he has refused to dissolve the abbeys and friaries here in Desmond. Gerald answered contumaciously, of course, and when called to order he refused to apologize. Thereupon he was thrown into the Tower. Oh, he is hot tempered and spirited, as you *know*, I am sure."

"He was, always. I recall him so even as young lad."

"Only yesterday I had a letter from her Majesty, complaining of his opprobrious conduct. She speaks *lightly* of his imprisonment, insisting that he will profit by such measures. She tells me not to worry myself, and charges me to keep order until his return. But I am not deceived. I do not *trust* them! There are English lords who covet these estates, and they will stop at nothing. I do not forget my first husband, who entrusted his life to them at a dinner table." She blessed herself, and her blue eyes glistened as she gazed sadly into the fire. The Primate sighed, and shook his head.

"God rest his immortal soul! That was a ghastly business."

Before she married young FitzGerald, she was the widow of the Earl of Ormonde, who was poisoned at Ely Palace in London with fully sixteen of his retinue. It was her son Black Tom, Earl of Ormonde, who had accompanied Shane as far as Dublin when he repaired to the Queen in London. Her son and her husband were the same age, and most bitter enemies. Apart from the longstanding rivalry between the houses of

SHANE O'NEILL

Ormonde and Desmond, Black Tom had refused to render up the dowry upon his mother's remarriage, a bone of unabating contention.

"I'll not desist! I shall assail her with letters and pleadings until he is come home to me." Lady Joan cocked her head and raised her brows, looking intently to her forlorn guest in the firelight. "And I shall not forsake you. I know that it was my husband who first sent you to his cousin, Shane O'Neill. Whom you have supported -to your most bitter cost! But, you see -you *must* see, *as* it is the very issue of *conformity* that has my husband imprisoned in the Tower, it could do grievous harm to his fortunes were you to be found sheltering here. You shall stay the night, of course. You will be quite safe. But tomorrow, the surveyor general Walter Cowley and Oliver Sutton will call in the afternoon, and my confessor, Father Goode will be-"

"Father Goode? I don't know of him."

"A very holy man! And a wonderful confessor. It was the Papal Nuncio himself sent him out to me. A young Jesuit from Glastonbury." Her face lit with sudden inspiration. "Perhaps he could help you!"

"Lady Joan, you *must* promise me that you'll not mention my arrival to him. We don't want to burden Father Goode with a grave moral dilemma, by asking him to compromise himself on my behalf. You see, the Jesuits are quite loyal to the Lord Deputy, and he would be under tremendous pressure to give me up to the bailiff." Having considered the matter deeply, Donagh realized that he could not divulge the Nuncio's betrayal. He needed help, and such a revelation would present his patrons with the daunting predicament of choosing either to side with the powerful representative of the Pope, or to take the part of a deposed and fugitive bishop, apparently reviled by both Rome and London. No, he could hardly accuse the Papal Legate. Such an indiscretion would be disastrous. The Countess was perplexed, but obliging.

"But he is a priest of- Of course, as you say, your Grace. -No, it's '*Donagh*' I must say. Oh, such times! I shall say nothing of your whereabouts. To anyone!" She sipped from her goblet, and again her face was suffused with the light of fresh inspiration. "The Abbey! Well, of course. You must go to the Franciscans! In Little Friarstown. It's *just*

SHANE O'NEILL

beyond the hill of Knockfennell across the lough. It is quite sequestered -and unknown, I should think, to the English. Or *overlooked* by them, in any case, since Queen Mary restored it."

"I'd overlooked it myself, truth to tell. I'll go down to them in the morning. Aye, a quiet refuge where I might pray, tucked away in the hills. That will suit me grand, now."

"Splendid. But, Donagh, you must recount for me these travails that have brought you to my door. However did you manage to escape from Drogheda? And your journey! I'm sure it must be a woeful tale, but I long to hear all!"

The morning was bright and gusty, and if the trees were bare, the hills were lush wintergreen and the lough was a brilliant blue. Fortunately it was no more than a short jaunt to his destination, for Donagh's legs felt even more sore and chafed than they had the night before, and he could hardly sit the horse. He had only to ride around the lough and over the hill on his heroic grey mare. He had taken to calling it 'Lia Macha', after Cúchulainn's legendary steed. It means 'Macha's Grey', and it was for that pagan goddess, Macha, that his beloved Armagh was named. As he trotted along, he was struck as never before by the haunting beauty of Lough Gur and its wild unshorn hills. Where the bridal path turned away from the lough at the foot of Knockfennell, he saw in the middle of the path ahead, a roe stag and his doe. They stood, still as the trees, watching his approach, and when he had slowed to a halt, they suddenly bounded off up the hill. For just that moment, the perils and troubles of his life seemed to vanish. Perhaps this would be a place of renewal.

The abbey was nestled among the trees beside the river Comogue. It was known to its rustic neighbors as Ballynebrahirbeg, and it was indeed

SHANE O'NEILL

a small friary. The tiny stone chapel had a slate roof and high gable walls, with a square belltower. Adjacent to it stood a long, low, thatched building of unmortared stone. As Donagh approached, he saw that it had an open arcade facing the river, graced with Roman arches. The abbot was a stout and smiley fellow, one of the FitzGibbon clan who had originally endowed the abbey. He listened intently to O'Tighe's story, and then fell to his knees, thanking the Almighty that it had fallen his lot to be of assistance to such a holy personage as the Lord Primate. He pledged to keep the secret, and they determined that their new friar would be known simply as Brother Donagh.

Apart from the abbot, only a dozen monks resided in the little monastery, which immediately called to Donagh's mind the twelve apostles. It was a delight to don the brown robes, and to say Mass once again in the tiny chapel. He soon settled in to the quiet life of devotions and prayer, and as the days went by, he felt safe enough to restore his tonsure and trim his beard. It seemed to him ironic that, in the past, when beset by the cares of his high office, he had idly imagined just such a retreat as a balm for his soul.

Once he had recovered from the rigours of his escape, Donagh enjoyed his walks in the mornings, and he was drawn to the astounding array of antiquities thereabouts. The great Wheel of Crom Dubh, a circle of standing stones beside the lough, and the nearby dolmens and cairns attested to power of pagan Ireland.

St. Patrick had come here, to this very place, to conquer it. As his successor, 'Brother Donagh' began to make regular devotions at his shrines, which abounded in that dictrict. Patrick was known to have baptized multitudes at Knockpatrick, where a ruined church bore his name. Beside it was a holy well dedicated to him. Here he was said to have left a golden chalice. A Druid priest attempted to poison St Patrick, but by the grace of this sacred well, the saint discovered the poison. Three drops fell from the cup into the well, and, in that instant, its waters turned crimson as blood. Patrick was spared, and the druid cursed him. It is said that from that time the lough demands the heart of a Christian every seven years. The humbled bishop found these tales diverting, and, in truth, he had need of diversion, for always in the back of his mind was a feeling that in places unknown to him, perhaps far away, great powers were conspiring in his ruin.

Not so very far away, at the Black Castle, Lady Desmond, attended by her confessor, Father Goode, was finishing her midday vespers in the tiny FitzGerald chapel.

"...Oh Mother of the Word Incarnate, despise not my petitions, but in thy mercy, hear and answer us. As it was in the beginning, is now, and ever shall be, world without end. Amen." The priest got to his feet and offered a bracing hand to the Countess. She accepted it, and rose from the velveted prie-dieu. The white tile floor at their feet suddenly shimmered with an array of colours cast by a brightening of the tall stained glass window above, drawing their eyes to it. Lady Desmond smiled brightly at her confessor. He nodded solemnly as he stepped back to allow her to lead their exit. Did he actually see her at all? A curious sort of men, these priests. But for his three-cornered biretta, he was really no taller than she. She had seen him without it once, quite unawares, and she noted that, although he was hardly thirty-five, his sandy locks were thinning above. She wondered, idly, if it might be vanity that kept his hat so firmly in place. She suddenly took note of her trail of thought, now, and smiled at her *own* vanity. The priest followed her to the back, where she daintily dipped her fingers in the holywater font, and blessed herself as she emerged into the hallway.

"The sun has come out, Father, to brighten your journey home! I'm so grateful to you for coming. I find such solace in your visits, always. When shall I expect you again?" She picked up a small brass bell and jangled it smartly.

"Alas, Your Ladyship, my mornings are now consigned to this tutelage in Adare, and, truly, that place is so wracked by upheaval after all that befell there, that I dare not promise. But *if* I can be spared, I shall call tomorrow in the afternoon!"

"Oh, it is all too horrid! For the blessed Primate to be hunted so!"

"Such a great pity...that he allowed himself to be drawn in by O'Neill and the northern savages. How astounding it is, that a misplaced compassion could so gain mastery over his natural virtue, as to undo all his good works! I do truly pity him. For he *will* be caught. Of course, the Lord Deputy was severely embarrassed by the escape, and has mobilized new regiments in the district to find him out." A young servant entered the hall, and bowed.

"Yes, m'Lady?"

"Father Goode is ready to depart. Please ask Jack to draw his carriage 'round."

"So I shall, m'Lady" He hurried off quietly down the hall.

"Well, promise me you'll not trouble yourself about it! You really mustn't. The Lord knows, you have concerns enough of your own. But remember always...that God is with you, and he will see your husband safely home!"

"Perhaps you would like to take a seat, your reverence?"

"No, I shan't. I shall await my carriage outside, to enjoy the fine prospect of the lake in sunshine!"

"God be with you, Father!"

"Bless you, Lady Desmond."

The porter assisted him with his cloak, and opened the great door for him. Upon hearing the clop of horses from the gatehouse below, he followed the cleric outside. More visitors. Unexpected, this time. The English priest stepped out of the shadows into the brilliant day, but he did not venture far from the door, as his curiosity was peaked. He stood, imposing, despite his diminutive stature, in his long black gabardine cloak, and his three cornered biretta. His hands folded before him, he gazed out over the lough, which was as still and shiny as a looking glass.

The two riders cantered up to the great arched threshold, and halted. They were a wild looking pair, and Fr. Goode took care to observe them indirectly, while he appeared to be preoccupied with prayer. Both men were bearded, with tousled hair down over their foreheads in the Irish fashion. The taller one was garbed in gentle attire, while the other wore a shaggy mantle of frieze. They were conversing in Irish as they looked over to observe the priest. One of them called out a greeting in English.

"Good day til ye, Father!" The accent was unmistakably northern. Father Goode smiled broadly, and nodded a silent greeting, lest his English speech should be revealed. He continued to move his lips as though lost in prayer. "Aye. Say one for *me*, Father." The men dismounted, and a young groom rushed up to take their reins. "We'll not be long now, lad, but a wee feed of oats would do them a power of good! Good man!" The porter asked them their business, and the tall fellow answered. "We bear a message for the Countess of Desmond."

"Do you, so? A message from whom?"

"From the O'Neill, Lord of Tirowen!"

The great door opened, and the men were ushered in, just as the priest's elegant carriage appeared through the gate. Father Good reflected that, had these northern envoys seen it, they might have been a bit more discrete, and he would not be departing with such momentous news.

It was barely after dawn when Donagh was awakened by a loud thumping on the door of his little cell. "Brother Donagh! Brother Donagh!" He recognized the voice, and he sat up immediately.

"Come in, Father Abbot! Come in. What has happened?" The door swung open, and the stout monk charged into the room. His face was flushed, and he was in a hectic state.

"Oh, your Grace! The English army is upon us! On every side! There are scores of them. Whatever shall we do at all?" Donagh put his feet on the floor, and sat on the edge of the bed.

"What is to be done is past doing. There is naught to be done,

SHANE O'NEILL

Father, except to surrender myself, and leave my fate to the mercy of God." He got to his feet and set about donning his monastic robe. The abbot was breathing heavily and he appeared to be on the verge of tears.

"There is a cave under Knockfennell that leads to the lough...But how could you reach it? They seem to be everywhere and-"

"Have they called me out?"

"Not a word from them as yet, Your Grace. They are deploying still, surrounding the abbey. Oh, the Devil is abroad early this day!"

"There is a bishop's mitre in the sacristy..." He looked inquiringly to the abbot.

"Twas left here by my uncle, the Archbishop of Cashel. Will I fetch it for you, your Grace?"

"Do, Father, please. And bring me a chasuble, but not the best of them, for you'll not see it again."

"Aye, Your Grace, aye. May the Lord protect you this day!" With that, he scurried out the door. Donagh put on him his sturdy brogues, and his heavy woolen breeches. He didn't want to think about what this day would bring, but he could at least guard himself against the weather. He knelt, and prayed for God to give him the strength to endure the trials to come. When the vestments were brought, he donned the chasuble and mitre. Some of these troops would be Irish, of course, some only pretending to embrace the 'reforms'. Even the bailiff, brother to the Papal Nuncio, was surely a secret Catholic. Donagh was determined to stir the conscience, to make clear the enormity of what was being done here.

When he was ready, he made his way to the door. Upon opening it, he could see the infantry arrayed before him, flanked by cavalry, all armed with sword or harquebus. All this might to subdue one peaceful man of God. Oh, the folly and wickedness of Man! He could hear glass breaking, and as he stepped out, his heart sank to see that the chapel was in flames. A plumed officer rode forward, and behind him could be seen the Bailiff of Limerick, Nicholas Wolfe, once again at the helm. But it was Donagh who spoke first.

"I am Donagh O'Tighe, the anointed Archbishop of Armagh, and

SHANE O'NEILL

Primate of All Ireland. I surrender myself this day into the custody of the Bailiff of Limerick, and I ask only that you spare this abbey and its friars. They knew naught of my true office, nor of the warrants issued for my capture! Harken to me now, you men who stand before me! Let it be known unto you that your hand in this foul deed here this morning constitutes a most grievous sin. And while, for *my* part, I forgive you for the harm done to my person, I must caution you to make your peace with Almighty God." He then raised his hand, and blessed them solemnly in the Roman rite. "In nomine patris, et filii, et spiritus sancti, sit benedicti. Amen."

In truth, everyone was puzzled that he was let finish his oration. Perhaps it was the surprising spectacle that he presented, and the curiosity it aroused. Nevertheless, at the sound of his 'Amen', sharp orders were called out, and he was quickly apprehended, and stripped. A guard struck the mitre from his head, and tore the white chasuble from his neck. The robe was ripped off his back, and his breeches and shoes were discarded. He was left his ragged linen braies, perhaps in deference to the presumed delicacies of the Bailiff's brother, the Nuncio. Donagh's wrists were bound once again, this time behind his back, and he was marched up to the Bailiff who was still mounted. This time no writ was read, for there was no crowd to be addressed or appeased. The plumed officer leaned in to quietly advise the bailiff, who then turned his eyes upon the Lord Primate giving loud answer. "Oh no... Not at all! This time he shall not ride. Since he *stole* the last horse that was afforded him, he shall *walk* to Limerick! If it takes him all the day, what matter? He shall soon have for himself an eternity of rest!

Thereupon, a rough noose was tied around the prelate's neck, providing a tether to the horseman behind him to further torment the prisoner. Donagh was shoved up before the troops, and made to march up the hill to the road, and onward, all the way to Limerick, a journey of more than twelve miles. When he slowed or stumbled, the tether was jerked, and he was prodded and goaded. This time some of the cavalry took up positions in front of him, to disperse or intimidate any crowds in the villages along the way.

SHANE O'NEILL

At last the Bailiff's procession reached Limerick city. As they entered Irishtown, passing under the portcullis of Kilmallock Gate, the bells of St. John's began to peal the Angelus, strangely heralding their arrival. Their exhausted prisoner murmured its hopeful Latin verses under his breath as he staggered along. "...Pour forth, we beseech thee, O Lord, Thy grace into our hearts, that we to whom the incarnation of Christ, Thy son, was made known by the message of an angel, may by His Passion and Cross be brought to the glory of His resurrection; through the same Christ our Lord. Amen."

Because of the uproar that followed the Primate's escape at Adare, there was no question among the populace as to the identity of this captive, and as they marched him up John Street, people hurled abuse at the Bailiff, and threw stones at the soldiery. The mood was dark and angry, but, at one point, the crowds roared with laughter when someone emptied a chamberpot from an upper window onto the last of the cavalcade. All the while, there were blessings in Irish for the holy Primate, and people made the sign of the cross as he passed.

Nicholas Wolfe was thankful that it was such a short ways to the towergate at the Thye Bridge, where they would pass into Englishtown. But when they approached it, he was stunned. Someone had loosed four wild horses, and they came charging over the narrow bridge into the procession, in the equally narrow street. Mayhem ensued. A yeoman guard who tried to stop them on the bridge was spun around like a top as they rushed past him. People were screaming as the crowds pressed back into doorways. In the crush, Donagh was pulled up short by the noose, and nearly choked to death.

The four arches of the old stone bridge supported a row of three-story Tudor houses, and from a number of these fluttered the 'George's Cross'. This charged symbol was enough to dissuade the heady Irish crowd from following any further. But when at last the grim procession crossed that bridge, the reception was no better! The 'Old English' inhabitants of King's Island were 'unreformed' in their religious allegiance, and, 'mere Irish' or not, they were outraged at this persecution of their papally appointed Lord Primate. Indeed, such a

SHANE O'NEILL

move by the Deputy seemed to herald a new offensive against Roman Catholics like themselves, perhaps ushering in a regime of severe persecuton. They were clearly incensed. The grim procession made its way up Mary Street, past Creagh's Lane, and under the arches of NewGate. All along the way, the soldiers had to endure the howls and catcalls of their own community. People were banging iron pots and lids at their windows above, and after what had transpired in Irishtown, the wary soldiers marched with their eyes raised to the windows and rooftops overhead.

The hurly-burly in the streets could be heard in the castle, where the Lord Mayer, Nicholas Whyte, was quietly departing. His Bailiff, Wolfe, had sent a runner ahead with news of the capture, giving him ample time to make arrangements. Henry Radcliffe, Lord Sussex' brother, was known to be stationed nearby at O'Brien's Bridge, where he hoped to apprehend that other escapee, Thady O'Brien, crossing the Shannon. Whyte lost no time sending off a messenger to summon Captain Radcliffe, and notify him of O'Tighe's capture. Surely he would wish to preside over the interrogation and chastisement of the 'deposed' bishop. The Lord Mayor, himself, was a prominent Roman Catholic, an uncle to the Nuncio's great friend Father Creagh, and he thought it best to distance himself from the unpopular proceedings.

Crowds from the High Street followed the procession down towards the river on Thomond Street. A small throng was already gathered before the huge drumtowers of the castle, singing the 'Stabat Mater Dolorosa', which recalled the suffering of Christ in the Stations of the Cross. It was thought to be apt for the dolorous ordeal of their beleagred Primate. The drawbridge had been raised about ten feet in the air, when the crowd got too close, but now, with the arrival of the Bailiff and his troop, its chains and gears clanked and rattled as it lowered into place. Stepping up onto it, Donagh stumbled, and the crowd gasped as one, with mournful cries. He staggered to his feet, and marched slowly on until he disappeared under the shadowy arch of the portcullis, and out of the cold November wind. For all his fear of what awaited him inside, he felt a strange relief at the end of his long road, wishing only to collapse.

He was led into the castleyard, and waited, shivering there, for what seemed to be an age while the Bailiff remonstrated angrily with other officials. He was peeved at the Lord Mayor's departure. Radcliffe had not yet arrived, so Donagh was bustled off to the southwest tower, at Shannonside, and shoved roughly inside. He stumbled again, descending the dark narrow cockle-stair, and he felt a sharp sting and the cold trickle of blood at his knee. He was kicked, then, and heaved into the dungeon. He cried out when his flesh was pinched in the rusty iron shackles, as they were clapped over his ankles.

The door creaked, and slammed shut with a resounding thud, and after the jangle and clank of the lock and key, all was silence. And darkness. And bone-chilling damp. The chamber stank of its weight of misery. Donagh felt a stinging in his nostrils from the fetid air around him. With each breath, he drew into his bosom those foul vapours reeking of piss, feces, mould, and rot. The straw under him was filthy and wet, but he could not move. He wasn't sure if his eyes were open or closed... Now, after listening to his own heavy breathing in the dark, he could hear the scurrying of rats. His chest heaved as again he tried to pray, but after a time, mercifully, exhaustion overcame him, and he drifted off.

Awakened by a fierce blow to his side, Donagh opened his eyes just as a grimy hobnail boot swung at his face. He flinched too late, and he could hear the crunch of broken teeth, as a profusion of warm blood spilled from his lips. "Get up, ye papish swine!" The burly Englishman towered over him, a dark silhouette against the flickering light of the doorway. He gave his charge another kick to the shin, and then snatched up the tether that was still tight around Donagh's chafed and bleeding neck. Choking, he staggered to his feet, and nearly passed out, then, with dizziness. He was puzzled to see that he had been unshackled. "Come you, now. There's a reckoning awaits you, filthy taig!" Donagh stumbled up the narrow winding stair, and staggered into the round chamber above. There an oil lamp cast its yellow glow upon several officers who were seated behind a long narrow table, and glistened on the helmets of the four guards who flanked them.

Before the table, in the centre of the room, a thick rope hung nearly to the floor, suspended over two broad beams above, and Donagh's gorge rose at the prospect of an imminent hanging. The stricken prelate was leaning against the rough stone wall, coughing and spluttering, and swallowing hot blood, but he managed to fill his lungs with the relatively fresh air of this ground floor chamber. He could see that the officer in the centre was the very image of Lord Sussex, but clearly younger and fully bearded. A Radcliffe, though, surely. The burly henchman shoved him out before the rope, as the smirking officers watched in silence. He stepped directly in front of Donagh, and grinned up into his face, with missing teeth, and rank breath that stank of spirits. His hair was greasy, and his leather jerkin looked to be caked with dried blood. His voice was low, and his tone was treacly and menacing.

"Goosie goosie gander, where shall I wander,
Upstairs, downstairs, and in my lady's chamber
There I met an old man, who wouldn't say his prayers!
I took him by the left leg, and *threw him down the   stairs!*"

With that, he kicked the legs out from under Donagh, who dropped to the floor. This brought on a roar of demonic laughter from his tormentor, with the others joining in. He loosed the tether from around the prisoner's neck, and tossed it aside. He then grabbed Donagh by the hair and pulled him up onto his feet again. With his hands bound behind his back, it was nearly impossible to rise and balance himself. Snatching up the rope that dangled from the beam, the henchman tied it to the leather cord that bound the Primate's wrists. Then, stepping around behind the table he clasped the other end of the rope where it hung, ran it through an iron ring that was bolted to the floor, and pulled it taut. He pulled it further, now, incrementally, as he chanted his doggerel, and each gasp and moan from the prisoner brought fresh laughter from his tormentors.

SHANE O'NEILL

"Uppity up the goosie goes...
High into the sky...
Uppity up he rose..."

Donagh was now suspended nearly a foot off the floor in sheer agony, his shoulders up over his ears, and his neck constrained, almost choking him. His one eye was nearly closed with swelling. Finally Captain Radcliffe spoke.

"Behold, gentlemen, the elusive agent of the Bishop of Rome! He shall not elude us again, I'll venture!"

"The other officers laughed, assenting with spirited 'aye's and 'yea's. Radcliffe now leveled upon the holy Primate the dark gimlet eyes of the inquisitor.

"Hark you, sirrah. Whatsoever shall befall you here is a fate of your own making. For, at any instant you might mitigate, or even perchance *obviate*, your punishment...by craving pardon of Her Most Gracious Majesty. Should you but renounce your false claim to office, and swear to the Oath of Supremacy, you might forgo this disagreeable business." He held up a leather-bound bible. "This Holy Bible, which you do profane with Roman creed, may yet prove to be your salvation! For though you be a rank traitor, and attainted so by law, you need only lay your hand upon it, and utter this oath for your deliverance." He laid the Bible at the front of the table, and held up a sheet of vellum, to read out from it.

"I, Donatus O'Teige, do utterly testify and declare in my conscience that the Queen's Highness is the *only* supreme governor of this realm, and of all other her Highness's dominions and countries, as well *in all spiritual or ecclesiastical* things or causes, as temporal, and that no foreign prince, *or prelate*, hath or ought to have any jurisdiction, power, preeminence or authority *ecclesiastical or spiritual* within this realm; So help me God, and by the contents of this Book." He looked up at the primate, who was turned nearly to the side now, as the rope had twisted. "Are you prepared to solemnly swear this oath?"

O'Tighe tried to lift his head, and he answered in a strained whisper.

SHANE O'NEILL

"I am sworn to Christ. And I shall not barter my Faith for life or liberties." The rope was suddenly let slip some inches with an abrupt halt, bringing a bolt of excruciating pain to his shoulder blades. He cried out, and there was shrill laughter at the table before him. Donagh firmly believed this to be the laughter of demons. Radcliffe spoke up over it.

"More's the pity! A hasty answer is least like to be a *right* answer. Still, we shall forbear a while, that you might have time to think again. 'Patience as will ripen grapes, and age a wine, will see thy wisdom grow in time!' As he grinned from side to side, delighted by his own drollery, there was more laughter, and then a piercing crack! Donagh felt the stinging lash of a whip upon his back, and shrieked in agony. He had not even realized that such a one was at his back. Radcliffe rose from his seat and fixed the cleric in his baleful glare. "If you will spurn the Queen's mercy, you shall feel her wrath." With that, he took up a roster of questions to be answered regarding other miscreants, and the papal agents labouring in the island. After each unsatisfactory reply, Donagh was whipped. The questions were endless. Again and again came the lash.

When Donagh awoke, he was lying on his side with his knees up, aching and chilled, yet feverish, and drenched in sweat. Every attempt to move brought sharp jolts of pain. His back was a sheet of fire, and even drawing a breath shot fierce pangs through his ribcage. The last clear memory he could call to mind was the endless flogging. It was some time before he brought himself to open his eyes. Only *one* would open, and when it did, he was surprised to see a rushlight burning in his cell. It was wedged between the planks of a tall wooden chair that was covered with cobwebs, and it cast flickering shadows over the ghastly chamber. There was a bowl of gruel, crusted over, at his side. He could see what he thought, at first, to be a sleeping dog, but upon closer inspection was a brown blanket heaped on the floor. Had it had been there all along, hidden in the darkness? He tried reaching for it, but he could raise his tremulous arm only a few inches, and his wrenched shoulder pulsed with fresh pain.

Could it be so? Yes! He could recall them asking of him, *demanding*

SHANE O'NEILL

he reveal, the whereabouts of the Papal Nuncio! *As if* such a thing were unknown to the Bailiff! All a cod! A fiction. None of this was really a matter of Faith or 'reforms.' Not at all. These ghoulish inquisitors were hardly followers of Christ. Only a man of no faith could suppose that such a proposition was a 'choice.' Not a Christian, no...No more than the grandees of Spain with their tortures -if such a thing be true. The crime, the *only* crime, was in not assenting to, not affirming, the fictions of the state. Withholding from them the inviolable sanctity of the conscience! Every class of barbarity could be countenanced, except the truth, for that is the one great threat to the powers of the world. All a cruel mummery! Our blessed Lord was crucified to redeem the world of such wickedness, and fifteen centuries on, the scribes and the Pharisees rule all.

The penalty for treason is death, and Donagh resolved now that he should embrace it as the will of God. But why, why had he escaped at Adare, only to be captured again at Lough Gur? Surely the Almighty had his reason, but Donagh could not bend his mind to it. It was, all of it, quite unfathomable. The good Lord would never have sent him into such a trap as David Wolfe's 'lair', unless...perhaps to chastise him, to prepare him for a Heavenly reward. To purge him of the pride of office? Perhaps God wished for him now a glorious martyrdom, and he had only to endure this pain before an eternity of sacred bliss...He would offer up each pang and pain for the salvation of souls, for the eternal redemption of his Irish fold.

In spite of the cold, he felt a raging fever burning within, and gruel or no, the very thought of food was appalling. Suddenly a faint sound gave him pause. He listened intently. The clip of footfall on the stone stair. Someone was approaching. A turnkey, most like. But they would need a stretcher to resume their torture. He was suddenly filled with remorse that he had not prayed since his waking. The key clanked and jangled in the door, and it creaked open.

A young helmeted guard stepped in carrying a wooden bowl. Donagh watched him with a wary eye, as he set aside the bowl of gruel, and put this new one in its place. Seeing, now, that the prisoner was watching him, the guard tisked. "You never *touched* it! Sure, if *ever* a man needed strength!" He was a Limerickman by his speech. As he bent over to look at Donagh's bloody back, he gasped. "Flayed to *ribbons*, it is! God save you!" He quickly took up the blanket and spread it carefully over him. "Eat this stirabout now, your honour, while 'tis hot." Donagh closed his eye, and shook his head ever so slightly. "Can you *talk*, your Lordship? Are you able?" Donagh coughed and swallowed, and then spoke in a hoarse whisper.

"What time of day is it at all?"

"Morning, it is. You slept all the day yesterday, I'd say. The guard couldn't rouse you, anyway, as *I* heard it. Captain Radcliffe is still here, waiting on new orders from Dublin, they say. There are people praying the Holy Rosary out before the gates for you! A whole crowd of them." He produced a small leathern flask, and pulled the cork from it. "Put a drop of this into you, now, Father, for 'twill do you no harm." He put it to Donagh's lips and helped him to sip at it. The patient coughed and spluttered, and grimaced at his pains. Still, he drew a measure of comfort from the warming spirits, as he felt them move like fire down his gullet. The guard nodded toward the oatmeal. "Eat that now, and build your strength, for you'd never know, and you might need it."

"What is your name, boy"

"They call me Jamey." A sudden look of alarm came over his features. "But don't be *askin'* after me!" He picked up the stale gruel, and hurried off, locking the door behind him. Donagh began to pray now. He thanked God that he was alive still, and he prayed for the souls of his tormentors. He prayed for Shane O'Neill, that he might deliver the country from all this savagery and predation. The long Latin prayers came easily to him, and he was comforted by that. If his body was in wrack and ruin, his faculties were seemingly intact. Another blessing to thankful for.

Donagh drifted between prayer and sleep as the hours, and perhaps days, passed in the darkness of the cell. Indeed, after the rushlight had guttered, time was meaningless. He was soon able to lift his arms, albeit painfully, and was relieved that his shoulders evidently were not broken, but sprained. The itching was a constant scourge. But the fever was unabating, and this, surely, was the most perilous assault to his health. He tried to eat a bit of porridge, but he couldn't stomach it, and it was so difficult, for his mouth was swollen and raw, with jagged broken teeth. And also because he was filthy now. He had soiled himself, and the stench was repugnant to him. His back was stinging and burning so, that he was unable to lie upon it, and whichever way he lay, his bones ached. Always, the question of what would happen next loomed in the darkness around him. Most especially when a key jangled at the lock. A succession of different guards came and went, Englishmen mostly, muttering angrily about the stench, as they put down their bowl of gruel, or can of water.

After what seemed to be several days, the drowsy prisoner was awakened by a quick heavy tramp of boots on the stair. There was more than one in it, surely. He blessed himself slowly, with a trembling hand. The keys clinked and jangled at the creaky lock, and the door scraped open. It was Jamey, and behind him a thin fellow, who was pushed aside by a powerful, low-sized man with a full dark beard.

"Oh, God save us! The poxy hoors! Sure, a murderer wouldn't get the like of it!"

That voice was well known to Donagh, and it filled his heart with courage and cheer. It was Thady O'Brien. He was thought to be in Dublin Castle, so, for an instant, Donagh wondered if he was dreaming. He spoke up in his rasping voice. "Ah, Thady, you're a wonder!" O'Brien approached, and gasped as he examined Donagh's bruised and swollen face.

"Oh, Jesus, the state of you! There had better be a hell, or these boys will have nowhere to go!" Jamey had procured the keys to O'Tighe's shackles, and he set about releasing him. Donagh made reply, just above a whisper.

"Oh, there is a Hell! No worry of that."

"We're come to get you *out* of this hell, Father Donagh." He had known him of old, and the older, more familiar, appellation is what came to hand. "We'll take you from this, now." They watched as Jamey

SHANE O'NEILL

unlocked the last of the two shackles, and Donagh put his hand to his nose, and grimaced.

"Augh! Mind yourself, now. I'm bemired, and filthy!" Thady grinned.

"Never *mind* the stink. You're not an angel, *yet*, Father!" The shackles were kicked aside now, and he tried to lift Donagh by his shoulders, but the poor bishop groaned with anguish.

"The ribs, ah, the ribs!"

"Shamey, is there aught to be found up there for a stretcher?" Jamey started to go, but was stopped short. "No, then. The chair! -Father, can you bend your legs?"

"I can. But I'm weak as a cat."

"Good on you." Jamey swiped the cobwebs from the chair, and brought it to him. "Hold that steady now!" He tipped the chair back and Jamey held it firm. Thady gave a nod to the other fellow. "Right, Mahon? Nice and gentle, so." They wrapped the blanket tightly around him, and, with grimaces and groans from the patient, they lifted him by the shoulder and knees until he was lying back onto the chair. "See is the way clear up there, lad." Jamey sprinted up the stair, and they followed slowly, and with great difficulty owing to the narrowness and the sharp curve of the cocklestair. When they reached the top, Jamey stuck his head back in at the door.

"Tis clear, alright. But hold yet! For there will be cloudcover in *moments*, now! They waited in the flickering candlelight, and a terrible commotion could be heard from afar. Donagh wondered at it, but he kept to his silent prayers. "Now, so." They carried the 'stretcher' out along the castle-wall no more than twenty feet, to a narrow sunken stairwell. As they maneuvred him down the steps, Donagh could hear the lapping waters of the Shannon. This was the tiny 'watergate' of King's Castle, and they had to wait when they reached the doorway, for moonlight was spilling through the clouds once again. Shouting, and the clatter of galloping horses, could be heard up on Thomond Bridge, which was less than forty yards away. Some sort of ructions were afoot at the Castle gates, surely. Thady tucked up the blanket around Donagh's neck.

SHANE O'NEILL

"Are you right?" Donagh nodded, and squinted inquisitively. Thady smiled. "That's *our* boys, now. A bit of a *diversionary* measure!" The bank had a few feet of muddy ground along the castle walls, and Donagh could see a long punt bobbing beside it, with a man aboard, standing. He wore a cowl, and held a long oar up like a staff, keeping the boat in place. The holy Primate shuddered upon seeing him, for he brought to mind the gruesome image of the ferryman, Charon, waiting at the River Styx. When the gap in the clouds had drifted by, they laid their ailing bishop in the boat, and slipped the oars into the water.

A cold wind whistled over the river, and, on seeing that Donagh was shivering, O'Brien laid his mantle overtop the blanket. The oarsmen were O'Briens too, nephews of Thady's, and Donagh knew them by reputation, for these were the 'Bishop's bastards'. After Thady introduced them to the Lord Primate, he said with a wink, 'Sure, it's the O'Briens are looking out for you! Like O'Neill, you see, we have our own people in King's Castle. Young Shamey is a cousin, and he's not the only one inside. Even Lady Desmond is one of ours, by her mother, Amy O'Brien!" He winked, and nodded with a turn of the head. He held his palm to Donagh's forehead for a few moments, and then spoke. "Ah, you'll be alright now, Donagheen. We'll have a doctor looking after you in Kilmallock." The tone was re-assuring, but Donagh's forehead was burning up. Thady did not like the look of him, shivering and sweating so. There was a rattle in his chest, and so often he was wincing with pain.

It was a comfort to know, at least, where they were headed. And Kilmallock was a sound choice. It was a walled town, well fortified, and still in the hands of the Earl of Desmond's forces. They would offer stout resistance, should the English pursue them there. Thady recounted for him his own escape in Dublin, and Robert Fleming's hand in it. He did not ask of Donagh's harrowing escape, as talking seemed to be such a strain for him. The 'bishop's bastards' told of their own exploits, and all this talk shortened the journey. To be safe, they kept to the Thomond side of the river, and with the help of a swift current, it was not long before they had passed the walls of Irishtown. Soon they spotted their signal fire on the far banks.

As they rowed into shore, the silhouettes of two men in Irish mantles could be seen before the firelight. Thady said that these were his wife's brothers, and they were waiting there with six horses. When they put in, the men helped to lay Donagh on the grass, and they hardly needed to be told that the Primate was not able for a horse. One of them spoke of a wagon he had seen up the road, and they galloped off to 'requisition' it. Upon its arrival, Thady was delighted to see that it was nearly full of straw. They laid the Primate into it, with blanket and coat, and covered him with straw. The signal fire was kicked hastily into the river, and they set off on the road to Kilmallock. The town is nine miles beyond Lough Gur by the same road, and with their precious cargo in the wagon it was a slow journey, so it was some time before they arrived.

The Desmond Castle towers over the walls of the town, and there was a faint glow from its high narrow windows. But just outside those walls, across the narrow winding Loobagh River, the Dominican Priory lay in darkness. Thady sent his nephew to rouse someone, and to find a stretcher or a plank. While the others tended to the Primate, he wheeled his horse, and galloped off into town to fetch the doctor. He had only to ride back across the little bridge to the friarsgate, and up to the Highroad, the one crooked thoroughfare that comprised the town. Just down from the castle was the stone townhouse of Doctor Éamon O'Hickey, chief physician to the Earl of Desmond. He was well known to Thady, for his family, since time out of mind, had been liegemen to the O'Briens. Indeed, his mother was the midwife who had brought Thady into the world. The lamps were burning still, and the doctor appeared at the door on the first knocking. He was eager to make the call. He donned his hat and cape, and the two men galloped up the lane.

When they arrived back at the priory, the Dominican monks were roused from their sleep, and bustling about the place like noontide. This was their esteemed Lord Primate, and, certainly, it was a momentous arrival. Beyond that, he was a beloved figure, and their concern was deep and abiding. If the perils and cruelty of the great world had suddenly burst upon their sweet refuge of prayer, these men would rally to the call. Their pristine white robes would soon be mired, but that was of no account to them, and they simply rolled up their sleeves.

Donagh was not yet cleansed, for the cauldron of water was still warming on the hearth. Nevertheless, the doctor looked him over, fore and aft, and emerged from the room with a countenance so grave as to instantly dash Thady's hopes. He was a serious dignified man, dry and droll, but this was a look of dread and woe beyond measure. His tone was quiet. "They are monsters. He has been savaged as by ghouls! Alas, Thady, I see little hope for the blessed man, but I shall do all in my power to save him. The ague has set in, with chills and sweats. His back is inflamed and festering with abscess. The ribs could heal, the muscles, the bones- but his lungs! He is wheezing, and the infestations! I shall bide awhile, now, and have a closer look once he is washed."

"What will you do, Éamon?"

"He's too weak for letting blood, but I have good leeches for those oozing welts on his back. The poisons must be drawn out." He shook his head and sighed. "He is so silent in his agony! He will need prayer."

"Oh, he's in the right place for prayer, to be sure. And when word of this escape gets about, there will be prayers pouring forth all over Ireland. The news of it will instill such hope in the people. It would such a pity, now, if..."

Thady sent one of his nephews up to Adare to fetch the Primate's sister, and to relieve his people with news of him, however dire. Beyond that, there was to be no word of the Primate's arrival let pass the threshold, for, as it was said, 'word will mover faster than wind.' The patient's cleansing was a long and arduous ordeal. His blanket and tattered undergarment had to be burned, and stinging 'turbentyne oil' was used to rid him of infestations of lice and fleas. Eventually the exhausted bishop was clean enough to lie on a bed of fresh linens, but he refused to sleep. At his ardent request, the Abbot administered the Blessed Sacrament to him, along with the rite of Last Anointing. Although this was said to be a 'precaution' only, Donagh took great solace in it, and before the abbot left the chamber, he was drousing.

The following day, the Primate's sister Nuala arrived, in a state of

SHANE O'NEILL

mournful desperation. It was lashing rain, but she would have no delay. She rode behind Mahon O'Brien on the crupper of his horse, cloaked in a heavy frieze mantle to shield her from the storm. After all her haste, when brought at last to his chamber, she declined to enter. Donagh was being leeched, and apart from her own squeemishness, she deemed it unfitting to intrude. Nuala was a plumpish woman, with dimpled cheeks and kindly blue eyes. Her hair was thick and grey, but it was piled up under a sort of wimple. When the doctor departed, she was brought in by Brother Cahal, who was tending the patient. As she approached her brother, despite a firm resolve to keep courage, she burst into tears.

"Ah, Donagheen, your lovely face! Divil scorch them for blaggards on the hottest flags of hell!" Nuala wiped her eyes with her sleeve, and took his hand and squeezed it. "God forgive me, now, Donagh, but such wickedness would take the heart out of you!" He made to answer in the thin whispy voice that was left him, but she was perplexed. "Beggin' your pardon, Donagh, love? Spare your voice, now. Don't be straining yourself." But he spoke again, and she leaned in to hear.

"We must thank the Almighty...for wasn't it a great mercy to deliver me from their chains? ...Two miracles, now...and if I will live, a third!" He was grateful that she had not seen him before his cleansing. He was wheezing now, and he started to cough, wincing with pain and holding his side. She gave him a linen that was there, and he hacked up terrible phlegm. Once he settled, he could see that despair had overtaken her features. The eyes, that only moments ago were agitated and quick, now had a listless glaze to them. She saw his look of concern, and smiled instantly. "The holy Dominicans! These are the boys will mend you, now! The Lord didn't pull you twice from the fire, only to let you go!" She mopped his brow, and then looked around her. She drew a chair up and sat beside him. She spoke to him of old times, and sunny days, and the mischief they'd gotten up to in the Ard-shanbally of Adare so long ago. Later Brother Cahal and another friar brought in a cot for her, since she would be keeping vigil.

Thady O'Brien called in to bid farewell. Kilmallock was, in ways, a safe place for him, but his presence there, he insisted, was like to bring the attentions of the English, and further imperil the holy Primate. His eyes glistened as he said a quick prayer with Donagh, and received his blessing. With their heartfelt 'Godspeed!', off he charged, out into the storm.

Later, when the Abbot returned, Donagh hushed him, for Nuala was snoring in the chair, with her rosary in her hands. She awoke then, all the same, and greeted the friar sheepishly. Not a brow was raised, of course. How could she not be tired, after that long hard journey to her brother's side? The Abbot read out the Litany of the Sacred Heart, and she voiced the responses for Donagh. In spite of his fondness for the ritual, the drone of it brought sleep to his eyes, and he, himself, was dozing before they finished.

The rains kept on for the next few days. Donagh was longing to see the sun shine again, but this was bleak November. Nuala got them to shift his bed over, so that he could see out the window, even if it was only gloom and rain. She helped to feed him his flummery, a sort of watery oatmeal, and she left his side only for calls of nature, when Brother Cahal would attend him, and for the Doctor's ministrations, of course.

Donagh's back was responding to the leeching, but even as it did, his lungs and fever had taken a turn for the worse. Doctor O'Hickey regretfully diagnosed this as pneumonia, and it was rapidly overtaking him. His pillow was sopping each morning, and he was shivering and coughing throughout the day. The sound of the Vespers and Gregorian hymns that could be heard from the Cloisters, were at least some comfort to him.

On the fourth day, the Cistersian Abbot from Holy Cross Abbey arrived, having been sent for. He came under guard bearing the sacred relic of the Holy Rood. It was said to be a fragment of the true cross, and it was brought to Donagh's cell that he might touch it, and by its veneration, receive God's grace. A special Benediction was performed there in his small chamber, the splendid golden monstrance held aloft, and hymns were chanted by monks who had crowded into the hallway. It was an uplifting and wondrous occasion for the holy Primate, and he was gratified, but humbled, of course, to have such attention lavished upon him. In spite of such spiritual graces as may have been imbued upon him, however, the day proved quite exhausting, and less than salubrious.

That evening, Donagh's condition deteriorated further. He woke with great pain after a short sleep, and was hacking and coughing up blood, and later he could not remember his prayers. He was drifting in and out of consciousness as his fever climbed. He spoke to Nuala now and again, but she could make little sense of his words. Only once, he spoke lucidly with great intensity, "They have pierced my hands and my feet; they have numbered all my bones…" This rather startled his sister, until Brother Cahal told her it was from a psalm. The rest was muttering, most of it in Irish. It continued so all the next day. When he was not grimacing and writhing in agony, he lay in a heavy torpor, his eyes glazed and dull. Nuala tried to engage him, but he was miles away, deep deep inside himself.

It was a long evening. Nuala sat in her chair as he slept, his lungs wheezing and rattling, and, although she was fingering her rosary, her thoughts were elsewhere. How unfair it all was. How cruel. 'The Lord chastises those he loves', the Abbot had said. Such a perverse carry-on did Him no credit, certainly! Who would chastise a loved one, only a bully? But isn't it a world of bullies? She sighed, and gazed sadly on her brother beside her. Oh, it's a lovely cozy little world until a young lad leaves the hearth, for then he is prey to wolves and blaggards. And the further afield he goes, the greater the danger. The higher he rises, the clearer the target, and the easier prey he becomes. She thanked God that her own boys had stayed on the land… The candle was burning lower and lower, and Nuala dozed in the chair. She awoke with a start. He had spoken. He had said something. "What is it, Donagh? What are you after saying, love?" She leaned in to hear.

"Is that the sun, is it?"

"What? The sun?" She saw, now, at the window, the moonlight streaming in, spilling over his coverlet. He was talking a kind of sense! "Ah, no, Donagheen. 'Tis the moonlight. The clouds are lifted, so. And, maybe you'll have your sun in the morning! That'll be grand, now." She looked at him, unsure if he had heard. "The *moon*, it is."

"Ah, St.Catherine's moon!" His voice was feeble and strange, but she was delighted at this sudden clarity of mind. She spoke a touch louder now.

"Aye, so it is, Donagh! Her feast was two days ago. The Advent is upon us now." She stood and went to the window. The stars could be seen, and the full moon shone over the hills. "It's lovely. St. Catherine's moon..." A queer gurgling sound made her turn suddenly, and she rushed to her brother's side. But he was gone.

In the morning, the sun did, indeed, shine, glistening on the dewy green beside the Abbey. The churchbells began to peel, sending a ruckus of jackdaws flitting from the high gables, and drawing a stream of alarmed and curious townsfolk out from the friarsgate. Already a multitude had gathered, when the messenger galloped off into the hills, with his sad tale to tell. His journey would be a long and hard one, for he was bound to ride until he reached Tirowen.

CHAPTER 22

It was a sad Christmas all over Ireland. Word of this horrible deed was on the wind, a wind that wafted through every village, crossroads, and lonely glen, making one heart of all the people. They saw a saintly man, put to death for his adherence to the Church of Rome, a devotion shared by nearly all the Irish, from castle to cottage. If he was guilty, so then were they. The Holy Primate's end was seen to mark a new low for the English, even after all that had befallen the Irish since King Henry's break with Rome. And Rome? The Holy See was curiously silent after this brazen affront...

There was silence, too, from Dublin Castle. Lord Sussex, and, indeed, all the lordlings and hirelings of the Tudor imperium, were determined not to acknowledge the 'incident' in any way. The man was an impostor, a usurper whose appointment had never been recognized by the queen, and consequently his demise was held to be of no account whatsoever. Privately, it was deemed fortunate, and even exonerating, that the prisoner did not die in custody. The Lord Deputy was simply relieved that the matter was closed. His attentions were now solely directed upon securing authorization and support for a renewed military campaign against the arch-rebel of the North.

In Tirowen, the depths of winter were darkened all the more by this new sorrow, but at Benburb Castle, there was blazing fury. Shane felt this blow keenly, for he well knew that the Primate's loyalty to him had cost the holy man his life. He raged and roared for two days, and finally ordered his captains to "sally forth, and fire the Pale!" The Dean of Armagh arrived just then to see the camp stirring, making ready for the raids. He found Shane and his captains lingering over their cups amidst the casks and barrels of the castle's Buttery.

"Ah, no! Shane O'Neill, you must call down this mad foray! Do you hear me? Now is not the hour to cast aside all our painstaking diplomacy. It is a time for reflection, cold blooded reflection!" The cleric, attired in his black soutane and tri-corned biretta, stood stock still in the doorway, his tall dark form silhouetted in the failing light of a January afternoon. At his commanding tones, the faces of his brothers and a few other captains looked up uneasily around the table. Shane's bleary eyes glistened in the flickering glow of a candlebranch.

"Tortured he was! To the death! As saintly a man as- only that he was Irish! Will I reason with such savages? I'll burn them out! Ash and cinders from Dundalk to Dublin! They'll think the gates of Hell have burst asunder!"

"Have sense, man! Sure, isn't that what Sussex wants? A shiny key to the treasury that has been shut to him this long while!" The priest huffed, and closed the door. He walked slowly towards O'Neill, and stood over him with arms crossed. He lowered his tone, but spoke on with authority. "Rage and grieve as you must, Shane, within these castle walls. And then let your fiery wits to cool, and *meet* his hellish challenge. Rise to it. Match him for guile and craft, and you will best him."

"Guile and craft?' Christ Almighty, the man is dead, Terence. Tortured to death! This is hardly a game."

"It *is* a game! To Sussex, it is a deadly game, and it is a game that you must win."

"Sit down with you, for Christ's sake." Shane drank from his goblet, and wine was poured for the new arrival. The Dean's brothers, captains of Shane's army, were most deferential to his high office, and would confine themselves to listening in such company. Already they had slid over to make a place for him on the rough wooden form. He seated himself now, and waited for Shane to speak. "A game is it? This '*statecraft*'? Perhaps 'churchcraft' is a game too, hah? It may be there are too *many* cursed games, and too many crafty players! I am *not* a man for playing, Terence, I'm a man for fighting! Am a courtier? To sit at the Lord Deputy's knee, trifling with rooks and pawns while he has murdered my bishop?"

"Will you tumble the board, then? In a vain fury? Or will you ponder its disposition, and *deftly move* like a champion? Indeed, he has taken your bishop. You must put forth another."

"Put forth another?"

"Appoint a *new* Primate. O'Tighe's death leaves that greedy English swine Loftus as sole claimant to the Primacy of Ireland." The Dean's face tightened in a sour frown, and his head shivered with disgust. "A pampered little godling! A heretic who has taken the Queen's fancy, named to the chair of St. Patrick! If that is let stand, you have lost your Ecclesiastical Prerogative. You must name a Catholic to the See, and then prevail upon the Holy Father to install him." He lowered his voice and his head, then, and peered up at Shane, with a sharp admonishment. "And you'd best do it smart and quick, while you are yet Lord of Ulster. For, once you have 'torched the Pale to ashes', you will be little more than a brigand!" Shane grinned now, brows aloft, but his eyes narrowed slyly, accusingly.

"Ahhh...*I* see what you're at... Is it your *own* nest you're feathering now, your Reverence? Will you take up his crozier so soon? I never knew you to be ambitious, e'er this."

"I don't give a toss for honours, and well you know the truth of that. But, as Dean of Armagh, the duties of Primate shall fall to *me*. Once again to weigh upon *my* shoulders!" Terence glanced suddenly at the abashed faces of his brothers "Ah, choose whom you will, O'Neill, but do not tarry, else you'll forfeit the privilege."

"True enough. The duties shall fall to you. '*Spiritual* Guardian of the See', the Pope called you last time. Aye, aye... Just as you say, Terence. You have the right of it. As oft before...The Primacy must come to you as well..."

"Call down your men, Shane. There is much to done, and we must be about it!"

"You *sound* like the Primate, right enough. Am I to be said by the Dean, now?"

"Look you to your wits, then. And be said by them."

"Éamon, tell the boys to fall out. There will be no raids this night." Éamon Donnelly leapt to his feet.

"Aye, O'Neill. So I will, now." He hastened off with his news. Shane turned back to Dean Donnelly with a baleful glare.

"This will mean letters. More letters. Letters to Myler in Rome, to Cardinal Moroni, to the Pope, Mary Stuart, and her thieving uncle, the Cardinal of Lorraine. By Christ, all this once again!" He shook his head with a sigh. "But let it be as you say. It must be done. Let the ink to flow!" He drank from his goblet and noticed, as he set it before him, that all heads were turned to Katherine, who had appeared at the Buttery door. She was heavy with child, but smartly attired in deep velvets. Her face was bright, and her eyes were big.

"Did I hear rightly? Ye's are not away off then?" She stepped lightly over to Shane's side.

"The Dean reckons there are wiser moves to be made."

"Thanks be to God, then, for a spark of sense! The poor man was a saint, Shane, and a *martyred* saint. That's a sacred and holy thing! Vengeance and bloodshed would rob him of that. Your foster-brother is a wise man..." She draped her arms over his shoulders and kissed the crown of his head. "And so are you, my love, to listen to him!" She smiled sadly at the Dean.

"Lady Katherine." He nodded.

"Oh, Father, it's all so wicked!" She clapped her hand over her mouth, and shook her head. "To think of the poor soul, driven through a blaze of pain, thrashed and flailed. It's monstrous! And they would count themselves Christians, these English, and descant piously on 'doctrine' and 'conformity'. It would chill the blood of an eel, so it would!" Shane's grey eyes narrowed, as he peered through the candlelight. His voice was a low rumble.

"I'll make them sup sorrow yet. No fear of that!" The Dean brightened his tone in reply.

"In due course. In due course...'Don't show your teeth til you are ready to bite!' It was my father told us that; do you recall it? When you were still a beardless boy. And there's wisdom in it. You must bide your hour til Europe is acalmed, and the Catholic princes can take your part!"

"Oh? And when will that be? More vain hopes and fancies! Will I toss buttons down a holy well? Help from the Continent!"

"Only a fool would discount it. Who could foretell the shifts and turns of the winds of war? Just don't hoist your sail til they are with you, that's all. It's the warrior spirit in you is impatient, Shane O'Neill. But hold, man! A Prince must bide his hour for Providence."

"The nod from God! A man would be a long time waiting for that."

Katherine laughed softly at that. "The nod from God', indeed..." She tossed her hair, and then clapped her hands softly together. "Right! And what is this 'wiser move', then? What are you resolved to do?"

"I'll name our 'Terence Danyell' here to the Primacy. And assail the powers of Rome to get him the pallium. Elizabeth cannot have preferment. She is a heretic." Katherine looked horrified.

"But surely- But will that not place you in grave peril, Father? After what they've done to Archbishop O'Tighe?" The Dean tossed a glance to Shane, and then a smile to Kat.

"I think not. The Queen's ministers are well used to me, by this time. I advise and 'inform' them, as Shane would have me to do. They think me a sort of agent in the Court of O'Neill for them!" He met her wide eyes with a sly wink. "There is nothing writ in four Gospels against a bit of deft diplomacy." Katherine squinted, as she puzzled over this news.

"And what of this Papal Nuncio in Limerick? Will he support you?"

"Most certainly not!" The Dean looked to Shane to ellucidate.

"To the devil with Wolfe; we'll outflank him! It must be a fait accompli before he is any the wiser. Our Myler is in Rome. I'll put him onto it." The priest cast a furtive glance at Katherine's prominent belly.

"Is he making any progress in the...little matter of the annulment?"

SHANE O'NEILL

Shane laughed heartily now, perhaps at his friend's discomfort.

"Ah, yes. My Countess is swelling like a broodmare! And like a broodmare, she'll soon be *unfit for the ride!*" He threw his arms around where her waist had been, and she slapped his paw smartly.

"It's *your riding* has me so, you great beast! Saving your presence, Father." She pulled herself away from him, a blush rising at her white neck, and infusing her cheeks. "God forgive me, but he's wild as a colt. The manners of a buccaneer! Seeing guests in the *Buttery!*" She tisked. "*That* for you now!" Shane knocked back a draught of wine, and held out his goblet for the servant to fill. He pushed his chair back noisily from the table.

"Myler tells me he's making some headway there in the Vatican States. Attending upon the Cardinals of the Rota, one by one. He'll bring them 'round, to be sure. But my Katherine is due in three months time, and we'll never have the parchment by then." Kat looked up sheepishly at the priest.

"Another wee'un born on the wrong side of the sheets..." She shrieked now, as Shane pulled her down onto his lap with a hearty laugh.

"But the only cure for love is marriage! And I'm suffering something fierce, Father. So we'd best procure that parchment soon!" The Dean raised his palm in caution.

"Ah, now...We'll get the child christened, and, when the dispensation comes through, we'll put it all rightly. A fine stately wedding with a High Mass." Shane, nodded, and lowered his voice confidentially.

"Myler writes that I have enemies in Rome. Even though that English Cardinal Pole is dead, his faction persists. They are busy still, he says. And he'll have the divil's own work-" He saw the Dean's brow arch suddenly. "He'll have *Trojan labour* on his hands to get 'round them. But isn't it grand that I have my little chessman in place. Myler is already there to take this up! And to begin before the opposition is roused." The Dean nodded, smiling.

"Most Providential, indeed."

SHANE O'NEILL

"How fares your Mistress since last I called?" The Lord Secretary smiled hopefully, as he stepped into the dim vestibule. His sister-in-law quickly raised her finger to her lips, her eyes wide.

"Hushhhh, Sir William. Hush you!" The air was stuffy, but not charged with the usual pungence of vinegar, or other such medical vapours, and that, certainly, boded well. She replied in a loud whisper. "Her fevers are slaked, and *not* like to return, unless I miss my mark. She is haler now, these two days past, and her pulse is strong. -But still she is most needful of her *rest*! The vexing business of State is no-"

"Mary Sidney!" From within, a familiar voice rang out. "Is Lord Cecil come? Cease your huggermuggery, and leave him to enter! We would speak to him... And draw back these draperies!" Sir William made his way into the darkened chamber, as Mary proceeded to part the heavy drapes, spilling winter sunlight across the floor. Behind a curtain of lace, Elizabeth was sitting up in her huge canopy bed. Her face was drawn, her eyes rimmed with red, and her fair skin covered, here and there, with squares of oily white gauze. "Cecil! You are come. And long enough about it! Sit now, and rest your gouty bones here beside us." He settled himself in the tall chair, and placed his folios and scrolls on a small bedside table that was already cluttered with correspondence and books. He smiled assuringly.

"Her Majesty seems to be much improved! England may take right good cheer to know that her sovereign Queen is mending apace!"

"There will be little of cheer whilst yet that deadly plague rages through our kingdom!"

"The pestilence is chiefly confined to London, for the which we must thank kind Providence. But here at Greenwich, the air, though it be wintry and sharp, is sweet and wholesome. And look you, how it restores you to your health!"

"Therein we do take heart, Cecil, for we perceive our frail limbs to grow the stronger with each new morn! Mark you, this stalking plague, gathering all by his grim scythe, has not carried off *our immortal soul*, and therefore are we grateful. Oh! But part you these lacy cobwebs, and you shall see what ravages he has left *behind* him. Mary!" Mary Sidney dutifully drew back the lace bed curtain, and withdrew, leaving them to their business.

"Nay. Nay, her majesty's splendor and beauty are not so easy vanquished! Some radiance is there that I saw not when last I called. And morn shall follow blessed morn, til *all* shall stand restored." Elizabeth closed her eyes and sighed, bitterly.

"And month shall follow blessed month..."

"Though patience is a virtue little favoured to Princes, still, kind Nature must take her course, and will heed neither scolding nor praise."

"Nor must Princes heed such folly! And so, to matter. Lord Sussex' dispatch?"

"Indeed. I am daily beseeched by Lord FitzWilliam for his leave to return to Dublin. How would your Majesty bid me reply?"

"We have bethought us this matter by night and by day, since last we spoke. Now we are mired in the French wars, yet still must we keep watch behind. For, ever and always, at our back there skulks this rabid mangy cur, this Ireland! We had hoped O'Neill would keep his promise to war upon the Scots, for whomsoever of them should get the better, we would get the best! Alas, Lord Sussex assures us that he has reneged upon that solemn pledge. He warns that no greater danger has been in Ireland than these present perils. If this be so, we had best take heed. We have read us the piteous letters of Maguire, and by them see that O'Neill is a foul traitor. An ungrateful wretch, whose fevered mind is cankered with ambition! 'Enough', we say! Whilst yet he lives he is a temptation to Mary Stuart. Indeed, our spies within his ranks tell of letters from her, *advising* and inciting him!" Her eyes flared, and she spoke slowly, deliberately. "We shall see him dead and done!"

"But *two* wars, your Highness?" In spite of his vehement objections to another Irish campaign, Cecil gave a measured response. He was aware of rumours that O'Neill had bribed him to oppose such a venture.

SHANE O'NEILL

Rather than call attention a certain gift-horse, he thought it wise to simply appeal to the Queen's frugality. "Those few coppers in your treasure not snatched off to the French wars, will be picked clean to fight O'Neill. There shall be little left you but straw and dust!" The Queen shook her head slowly, with just a hint of a smile on her tight lips.

"This 'peril' that the Lord Deputy decries is no multitude...Nay, it is but *one man*. We need not send legions to subdue one man. There are more *frugal* means at hand." Cecil raised his brows in rapt inquiry. "We have writ to Lord Ormonde, who, though he holds by the reformed Faith, is Irish, and trusted by O'Neill. We have asked him to find some more 'expedient' device."

"Lord Ormonde? Alas, I have his letter here, my Lady. Though he be a man of no tender conscience, still he has abjured. And, if I might say, in some state of pique." He opened a folio, and thumbed through the parchments.

"God's teeth! Have we no captains sound and true? Well then, read us what is writ!"

"Ah, here it is. 'The clause in the Queen's letter seems to me most strange. I will never use treachery to any, for it will touch her Highness's honour too much, and mine own credit withal. Whosoever gave the Queen advice thus to write to me, is fitter to execute such base services than I am."

"Hah! Black Tom Butler would wax indignant? The guileless lambkin! 'Twould rend the heart!"

"Though he be both Protestant and loyal, oh, I do not wonder that he has no stomach for such deeds! Her Majesty was too young to recall it, but the Earl will be mindful that his own father, with all his vast retinue, was poisoned at Ely Palace, when he was but a lad. Such a request would sit ill with him. Alas, it was *indeed* a bad advisement."

"It was *Lord Sussex* who so advised us! And were he fitter to the task, we should not have troubled the Earl of Ormond." She turned her head away, silently calculating. At length, she looked sharply to Lord Cecil, and spoke loudly, decisively. "Let Sussex have his war, then. Aye, but let him pay its cost! You may tell the Lord Deputy that he must raise his troops within the Pale, and levy a goodly tax there to provision them. We shall send to Dublin but *one* ship of munitions and artillery. But one! Beyond that, he shall have only our fond prayers!"

There was jubilation in Dublin Castle upon receipt of the Queen's directive. Although Lord Sussex was disappointed in its terms, he was undaunted by them. After all, he had managed to cobble together a broad and formidable alliance of Irish forces. He had the promises of Lord Kildare, Lord Ormonde, O'Brien of Thomond, and Clanrickard to supply contingents of troops. In Ulster itself, Con O'Donnell and Maguire anxiously awaited support to renew their resistance to O'Neill. Shane's cousin Turlagh Lynnach O'Neill was poised to attack from within, and James MacDonnell had pledged his Scots galloglass. Bands of 'kern', barefoot Irish warriors, from the lowest orders of the Irishry, would make up the rest. Sussex was aware that Irish troops fighting for the Crown were notoriously unreliable, but with such a broad spectrum of support, he felt quite assured of victory.

He immediately appointed commissioners for each county to levy the needed supplies: money for soldiers' pay, and two months of victuals to feed them, chiefly wheat malt and horsemeat. Cartage was difficult and costly, so provisions and stores would have to be shipped to the Newry, where pack ponies could convey them to the garrison at Armagh. Also aboard the ships would be five hundred labourers, hired to cut a pass through the wood between Dundalk and Armagh. There were troops to be raised, and bands of Kern enlisted to aid them.

The "enterprise for the expulsion of Shane O'Neill", however, proved a more difficult task than the Lord Deputy had supposed, even in his gloomiest estimations. Indeed, it was fraught with snares and setbacks. Firstly, and perhaps most devastating, the one and only munitions ship sank, wrecked on the bar, in Dublin Bay. All hands perished, but two. Additional levies would be required to replace the arms.

There was fury in the Pale at all these new levies. Suppliers protested that they had not been paid for such provisions for three years. It was widely believed that this general hosting was concocted to satisfy the Lord Deputy's private grudge against O'Neill. To these Palesmen, the squabbles of the wild Irish out in the lands beyond the Pale were of no concern, and the imposition of fees and cesses to interfere in such matters was an insufferable burden. A delegation famously declared to Sussex that they would 'rather be hanged in their doorways than pay up.'

Raising troops was exceedingly difficult, with soldiers pay several years in arrear, and the army near to mutiny. When called upon to muster, the five Irish Earls stalled and prevaricated. Kildare, who was naturally disinclined to attack his kinsman, claimed to be 'unwell' and unfit for the rigours of such a campaign. He induced Ormonde, still vexed by the Queen's dishonourable request, to hold out as well. As disappointments mounted, Sussex came to suspect a conspiracy in the Irish Privy Council "to keep O'Neill from falling".

On the feast of St. Patrick, an edict was published forth on the newly acquired printing press in Dublin Castle. It proclaimed Shane O'Neill traitor, and called upon "all Her Majesty's loyal subjects that have been by his tyranny forced to aid him in his rebellious doings, to return to Her Majesty's dutiful service." An offer of amnesty for repentant rebels. Shane received word out of the Pale regularly on these developments, and he laughed when presented with one of these broadsheets. To the exasperation of his captains, he evinced little concern over this pending invasion. His perception of the 'military prowess' of Lord Sussex allayed all fears, and he weighed his military options with equanimity, and an enigmatic smile. "The Viceroy cannot have war unless I choose to give him war, but he *can and he shall* lose his army."

At last the Viceroy's army began to move, ill-equipped and ill-tempered. Lord Sussex assembled his motley forces at Dundalk, and led them through the great pass of the North. They were no sooner in Ulster, when the clashing elements within his ranks came to blows.

SHANE O'NEILL

Kittyn's kern, 'the scourge of Wexford' came afoul of some Scots galloglass, and blood was spilt. Several wagons of wounded had to be sent back to Dundalk.

Upon reaching Armagh, supplies were laid in at the garrisoned cathedral, but two days later the army was obliged to march the long road back to the Newry to retrieve stores and munitions that had been left behind. After several days there, they advanced once again to Armagh, to await the arrival of Scots from Antrim. Instead, Captain Pierce of Carrickfergus arrived with letters from James MacDonnell. He spoke of a renewal of the bloodfeud with the MacLeans in the Isles, and said he could send no more gallowglass until certain matters were rectified. He wanted the earldom of Antrim granted in writing, as well as restitution for the murder of his two kinsmen by the Englishman Brereton, who had fled to England. Such conditions promised endless delay, and were likely intended to do so. Still more foot-dragging.

For lack of an enemy to meet upon the field, Sussex went after Shane's vast herds of cattle, but only managed to take what would sustain his troops. For his part, O'Neill set his men to harry and hinder the army, with little skirmishes here and there. He laid a small ambush in the wood near Armagh. Sussex' men were cutting wood that day, when they were surprised by a small contingent of Shane's men. The Deputy issued forth with his company, chasing the 'rebels' for three or four miles to a lough where O'Neill was waiting. His harquebus lay in ambush there, and they fired off five or six volleys, slaying nearly twenty before disappearing into the bracken. The army returned to camp, with the sporadic arrows of Shane's kern whistling through the trees.

On the 12th of April, Sussex sent young Captain John Smith to O'Neill to request a parley. He returned three nights later with word of Shane's consent to talks, and bearing a great deal of information on the 'rebel' army, including the news that the Chieftain was celebrating the birth of another son. Nothing seems to have come of this parley, however, for the English broke camp that night, and the following day made a foray into O'Neill's lands beyond the Blackwater. There, they captured two hundred cattle and sheep and then made the long march

SHANE O'NEILL

back to Armagh. Sussex now set his men to work shoring up the defenses of the cathedral garrison. Trenches were dug, and walls fortified.

Several days later, apparently being left with no recourse but cattle-reaving, the Viceroy led another foray, this time into the Trough Mountains in the district of Monaghan, said to be the strongest fastness in Ulster. Aided by his Irish scouts, he took a prey of two thousand from O'Neill's secluded herds, and brought them back to provision the garrison at Armagh. Upon his return, a messenger arrived from Turlagh O'Neill, with a story of a 'victory' over Shane at an unnamed lough, but when Turlagh was commanded to combine forces and report to Sussex, he failed to appear.

After sunset on the 22nd of April, the eve of the feast of St. George, the Lord Deputy donned his robes of St. George, and flourished the Cloth of Estate. He spent the following day keeping the Festival of the Garter royally in his tent. Outside, in the lashing rain, O'Neill's boys crept up on the camp and stole the 300 pack horses. Perhaps the dragon-slaying patron of England took a dim view of the Deputy's ill-timed devotions. Certainly Her Majesty did, when presented with this feeble excuse.

After three weeks of this inglorious campaign, the army's provisions were at an end. Some cattle had been filched, and the Blackwater had been crossed for but a few hours. Crestfallen, the army lumbered its way back to Dundalk, where Lord Sussex harangued the Council once again for supplies. He dashed a letter off to Cecil, bitterly bemoaning his plight, and blaming all but himself. "I have been commanded to the field, and have not one penny of money; I must lead forth an army, and have no commission; I must continue in the field, and I see not how I shall be victualled; I must fortify, and have no working tools. I cannot get a man to serve the Queen, nor a peck of corn to feed the army!" In his exasperation, the Lord Deputy was compelled to hire a band of eighty woodkern out of his own pocket. He was prepared to go to any lengths to redeem himself after this disastrous first assault.

SHANE O'NEILL

As Sussex' army retreated into the Pale, Shane hastened home to Benburb Castle, where Katherine presented him with 'another wee manchild, braw and bonny.' With Armagh serving as a garrison, the christening was held at the Cathedral of Clogher, and O'Neill's cavalcade and carriage rolled over the Tirowen hills for the great day. The honours were performed by the Dean of Armagh, but a High Mass and lavish hospitality were offered by Bishop MacArdle of Clogher. His brother was one of Shane's trusted captains, and he himself was the other of Shane's preferments that had been honoured by the Pope, along with O'Tighe. He, likewise, was troubled by the Nuncio's efforts to unseat him, efforts that he had thus far managed to resist.

The boy was christened 'Art O'Neill'after a brother of Shane's who was rheumy and inclined to illness, but was greatly please by the honour. After the splendid ceremony graced with the dulcet chanting of a choir of nuns, a great feast was held. Shane spoke lightly of the English incursion, with a nod to local pride. "Yellow Johnny made a bold march, but he turned on his heels before he came up against the men of Clogher!" He called upon Farleigh O'Gneeve to pay tribute with his new poem for the occasion.

"The words of a dead King carry but little weight in the Court or in the alehouse; it's seldom he'll be quoted. But his Poet's words shall echo from ear to ear 'til the Day of Truth!" Into the thundering ovation, Farleigh stepped forward.

"Unless...unless the King's *deeds* miscarry, and his nation falls! For history tells that a conquered people's very *tongue* may vanish; the Poet's words then are but airy nothing, dark cyphers scratched upon a page, and all is lost. It is the *deeds of Kings* that shape the world to come!" He gestured to the ornate cradle. "And the *sons* of Kings bring to us hope." Farleigh stood over the cradle, raised his arms aloft, his palms to the heavens, and his eyes blazed as he intoned his somewhat druidical benediction.

"God bless this heart that beats anew,

SHANE O'NEILL

Send to him your blessings.
Let the cold North Wind, bring him strength;
The warm South Wind, bring him gentleness;
The the dry East Wind, bring him wisdom;
The the moist West Wind, bring him love;
Fire, forge his heart for valour,
Water, tickle him with mirth.
Oh, bless this child with all
The treasures of the Earth!
The Sun to bring him beauty,
The Moon to bring him grace.
Lord, shower your abundance
Upon this tiny face.
This face and form
Begotten of
Millennia of love.
This creature created
Of bloodline blossoming
From womb to womb,
Of essence mated
By maid and groom
Fused in fiery love,
To lodge their store
Within the core
Of every pore
And atomy of flesh,
Flesh
Breathed to life
With a *soul*,
A soul summoned fresh
by Love,
From the molten light
Of the Almighty
God above!"

SHANE O'NEILL

Sussex remained in Dundalk for a fortnight, frantically calling in supplies and promises. By the beginning of June, he had managed, through the kind offices of Lord Cecil, to acquire both the indentures for peerage requested by the MacDonnell, and a written promise of punishment for the English murderer Brereton. Sussex was confident now that he would soon see a large contingent from the Scots. Lord Desmond had been released from the Tower, and returned to Ireland with the stipulation that he assist in the Northern Campaign. Kildare finally acceded to a Royal command to muster, as did Lord Ormonde, albeit unwillingly. On June 14th, the long line of soldiery and wagons emerged from the gates of Dundalk.

After reaching Armagh, the army marched north, guided into the heart of O'Neill's country by a brother of Art O'Hagan, Shane's chief Brehon. An older brother, this was, who had been passed over for that high office. Ambitious and embittered, he and his son served as spies for Sussex. It was he who had reported of Mary Stuart's letter to Shane.

The English army crossed the Blackwater at Brantry, fully expecting to lay siege to Dungannon Castle. Indeed they were lumbered with several canons for that very purpose. Upon their arrival, however, they found it empty and undefended. This was both astonishing and vexing. What was O'Neill's intention? Sussex thought to raze the castle, but he had convinced himself that this time he would run his quarry to ground, and ultimately install one of the Baron's heirs in that very place to be Earl of Tyrone.

He sent yet another messenger to the elusive Turlagh Lynnach, instructing him to appear the next day where they would be camped beyond the hill of Tullahogue. Instead, Turlagh sent back a messenger, who was swiftly dispatched with the Deputy's strict orders that he should repair to him without delay. Two small bands of gallowglass arrived from the MacDonnell, another crushing disappointment for the Deputy, for they bore a letter promising only more excuses from their

SHANE O'NEILL

chieftain.

There was great excitement when Sussex' scouts discovered Shane O'Neill's camp less than two miles away "with his whole power, and his cattle, in a very strong fastness." The Deputy promptly sent his footmen, kern, and galloglass charging into the pass, surprising Shane's men, who quickly disappeared into the woods to fire upon them in the open clearing. One of Sussex' horsemen, a renegade O'Neill called Cormack, was shot in the back, and the English captain of footmen was slain. After several hours of skirmishing, Sussex won the pass, slaying but three of Shane's men, and he "expulsed the remainder to their bogs, hanching and killing mares and ponies which the kern would have taken for spoil." The spies, Seamus O'Hagan and his son, fell in the midst of the fighting, and, while the son managed to escape, the old man was captured by O'Neill's men. The names of several informers were beaten out of him before he was executed for his treachery. All of this transpired within sight of the O'Hagan's fabled hill of Tullahogue.

The Lord Deputy was becoming increasingly apprehensive about Turlagh Lynnach's commitment to the enterprise. This time he sent out a lieutenant with cavalry to meet with the 'Queen's O'Neill', but he was not to be found. As time wore on, it became apparent to Sussex that he had been deluded as to the real intentions of this deceitful 'rogue' O'Neill.

The English troops marched on then through a long pass in the wood for two miles and came upon a great plain by Lough Neagh. Sussex' Marshal, with a few light horsemen, discovered nearly eighty of Shane's kine which he seized, killing four or five of his men, and taking two prisoners. These captives reported that the same morning, sixty of the Deputy's Irish footmen, belonging to the slain Cormack O'Neill, had deserted at Lough Neagh to join with Shane.

And so it went, one day very like the next. Shane bristled, but said nothing when word came that Sorley MacDonnell's promised contingent of gallowglass would not be forthcoming. This betrayal would not be forgotten. He divided up his army into small bands, and carried on this strategy of attrition, harassing the invading army, and then melting

SHANE O'NEILL

away into the hinterlands. There were small ambushes, and skirmishes, but never a full-on engagement.

Ulster was the last uncharted place in Europe. Maps of that time, so accurate elsewhere, were wildly distorted in their depiction of this Northern province. Lord Sussex, now without guides, advanced his fluttering standard into the wilds of Tirowen in pursuit of the elusive enemy, who appeared to be everywhere and nowhere. It was the sort of spring so unseasonably cold that it was known as a 'blackthorn winter', and the Ulster skies did their part, obliging Shane with a relentless deluge of rain. Before long, just as he expected, a virulent plague of dysentery had spread through the English army, leaving Sussex burdened with the sick as well as the wounded. By July, he had gotten as far as Clogher, but with supplies dwindling, the Viceroy was compelled to march southwards again with a hungry and a weary army. Shane followed close on his heels, cutting off stragglers here and there, harrying the English even in retreat.

When at last the Deputy's forces re-entered the gates of Dundalk, the skies behind them were billowing black smoke, for O'Neill's farewell gesture was to raid the Pale and burn its outlying villages. Lord Sussex, bilious by this time, and resentful of the 'mean and disobliging yeomen' thereabout, refused to provide for their defense. He wrote to Lord Cecil that "the Englishry of the Pale" were secretly desirous that the rebellion should not be quelled, and that he had been forced to abandon the expedition against O'Neill as being "but a Sisyphus' labour".

A messenger was sent to Shane requesting him to meet with Lord Kildare and Lord Ormond to open negotiations for terms of peace. He had won! The Queen was suing for peace. He assented. He stipulated, however, that it be a private parley in sworn secrecy. The Earls, for their part, agreed not to divulge his statements except to the Lord Lieutenant, and such of the Council as he could name. And so, with a small

SHANE O'NEILL

company of horsemen, the two Lords came to Benburb.

Shane was at first obdurate, "demanding all and granting naught". He hinted to Ormonde of a secret pact with his rival, Desmond, implying that it would be in his own interest to conciliate him. Kildare advised him privately, that Sir Robert Dudley was working quietly on his behalf in London, and that if he would but spare the Queen her dignity, and make only such proposals 'as in matter and manner were worthy of a loving subject', he might attain all that could be claimed by an O'Neill.

Mindful that he had not yet confronted the full might of her armies, Shane agreed to sue for the Queen's pardon. He sent Robert Fleming off to London with a letter bearing his most abject and effusive apology, and his promise for the future to be Her Majesty's true and faithful servant. On the same parchment, however, he drew strict limits as to the terms of this 'servitude', explaining that "he cannot govern his subjects otherwise than by the statutes and ordinances of his predecessors, since neither he nor they are skilled in the Queen's. An abject refusal to accept English law!"

Sir Robert Dudley had, indeed, been working his way with the Queen, mostly to affect the ruin of Lord Sussex, but all to O'Neill's benefit. He had *his* man Sir Thomas Cusack appointed Lord Chancellor of Ireland, (FitzWilliam resuming his post as Lord Justice), in order to 'oversee' the hearings about Lord Sussex' malfeasance in office. And while Sussex was mired in the bogs of Ulster, Cusack came to London.

The Queen, sorely pressed by dire financial straits, and an escalating war in France, was at last resigned "to come to an end of the war of Ulster by agreement rather than by force.' It was at this auspicious hour that Sir Thomas Cusack arrived with his ambitious scheme 'for the peaceable settlement of Ireland', and Her Majesty was easily won over. Henceforth, the four provinces would be ruled separately, with only Leinster under the direct control of the Viceroy. In the Queen's name, O'Neill would rule the north, O'Brien the west, and the south would be commanded by the newly chastened Desmond. Cusack convinced Queen Elizabeth that peace would result from such an arrangement, and he was granted full authority to conciliate the Irish earls by whatever means to secure their cooperation.

In August, Sussex received a weighty dispatch from Her Majesty entitled "Orders meet to be taken with Shane O'Neill in eschewing of more trouble." He was livid, breathing fire and fury at this betrayal from London, but as always, he waited for his temper to abate before putting quill to parchment. He begged the Queen to reconsider, pleading for 'fixity of purpose', that the reins of government might not be 'tossing to and fro, entangled in a labyrinth, losing one year what was holden in another!' He put forward his own plan for 'peaceful settlement'. The first thing to be done was to expel Shane, to divide Tirowen into three shires, to build a strong town at Armagh, and 'to install there a martial president of English birth.'

Queen Elizabeth wrote to him a terse reply, noting that the expulsion of Shane O'Neill was the very task he had proven himself incapable of carrying out. "You have failed; your failure has been a direct encouragement to the disaffected. As you have confessed yourself powerless to carry matters with a high hand, there is nothing for it but to temporize."

Sussex was devastated. But, curiously, there was another sealed letter from Her Majesty among the dispatch. This was a short missive in the Queen's hand, expressing her abhorrence at yielding to the vile traitor, and suggesting that perhaps matters needn't be carried with a high hand. She said that unless he find and execute some covert device to rid her of this hellion, 'Shane O'Neill shall take all! ...Such essays be all times dangerous, for the cup bearer must be afforded some preservative measure, that whatsoever betide the drinker's draught, the carrier takes no bane thereby. Mark slow your course, make swift your deed!" Her tone was intimate, written without the royal 'we', and, fearful of discovery in her incitement to murder, she directed him to dispose of the letter, alluding to the Roman god of fire. "Let this memorial be only committed to Vulcan's base keeping, without any longer abode than the reading thereof. Yea, and with no mention made thereof to any other wight! I charge as I may command you- Seem not have had but the Secretary's letter.

SHANE O'NEILL

Your loving Mistress,

Elizabeth R"

Sussex took the letter between his fingers as if the touch of it burned his blood, and stepped over to the smouldering grate. He stirred the embers to a fresh blaze, and dropped it upon the flames. His lips curled into a tight little smile as he watched it blacken and crumple to ash.

SHANE O'NEILL

CHAPTER 23

Although it was an evening in high summer, darkness was gathering early, and the glowering skies cast a queer greenish tinge over the shops and stalls of Castle Street. The downpour had ceased, and Dubliners were venturing forth, stepping cautiously over the greasy cobbles, the puddles and mire left in its wake. Lord Sussex nodded sternly to the odd few who doffed their caps to him. His attention, for the most part, was engaged by his companion, a rustic fellow in doublet and hose, who bobbed up and down alongside him with a loping stride.

The man's long unraked hair was swept back revealing a very pale forehead, for James O'Hagan, the 'informant', was more accustomed to sporting the shaggy Irish glib down over his eyes. A full beard, too, that was but recently shorn, had left its pallid margin around his weathered nose and cheeks. The new doublet and silken trunks were betrayed by wrinkled hose, bobbed with darning, and points hanging untied. His hands were fidgety, and he cast many a quick glance over his shoulder as he spoke. The thick northern 'brogue' obliged Sussex to listen intently. "I said...I say I told him I could surely put you in the way of some information and advisements, on the ways and habits above in Benburb...so as ye'll have no bungling when you go to...to..."

"Help him towards his 'quietus.'" This brought forth a nervous laugh from the Ulsterman.

"Aye, 'his quietus', that's a good'un. Well, *I'll* breathe a bit more quiet when 'tis done, I'll tell ye that for naught!" A roll of drumfare drew their gaze up towards High Street, where a regiment of cavalry, evidently down from Dundalk, was making its way back to the Castle barracks. Sussex halted to await the passage of a carriage that obstructed his view.

"This will be Marshal Stanley with the last of them -although his arrival was not expected until tomorrow. Perhaps he bears some news." The two men hurried on, and stopped at the gate of Christchurch Yard, just as the Marshal took sight of them. Stanley raised his hand, and his captain called the troop to a halt. He trotted his mount over to the Viceroy, who called out to him. "You are early, Marshal. I trust the North is quiet?"

"Quiet enough, my Lord. The burghers of Dundalk are joyful of this hard bought peace, since it is not *they* who shall pay its cost. Cusack is gone to Benburb Castle to parley for-"

"Even *there* is he amiss!" The Deputy scowled bitterly. "O'Neill should have been obliged to come in to the Gap of the North!"

"O'Neill will not be summoned. But young Fleming, the barrister, is returned from London. He will meet Cusack at the Gap, and escort him hence." Stanley smiled bitterly. "Oh, that is but the start! From this, it will be O'Neill's way in all things!"

"Perhaps not. These mad indentures do not yet bear the Queen's signature. Who knows what might befall O'Neill ere the Great Seal of the Realm be affixed to them." The Marshal's eyes flashed with sudden interest, causing Lord Sussex to immediately regret his indiscretion. "Carry on, then, Marshal. Your men are drenched, and weary of the journey. God save the Queen."

"God save her Majesty." He rejoined his regiment, and with a roll of the drums, the cavalcade moved on. Sussex and his Irish spy turned off Bothe Street to cross through Christchurch Green. O'Hagan was eager to earn his shilling with 'advisements'.

"Now, the thing of it is, your Honour...Divil a bit of good it'd do you to poison Shane O'Neill's victuals. You'd only send a few beggars off to their eternal reward. For ever and all times, the first portions of his meal are sent out to the beggars at his gates. 'Tis all done with a great show of virtue, of course, but in truth, he's minding his gullet against the likes of yourself." Sussex' brow raised, as he nodded slowly.

"Well considered. But I have chosen to target his wine. The superfluity of *wine* which he daily uses with his pernicious counselors."

"Aye, just so. Still...Ye'd want to mind ye don't slay Lady Katherine intil the bargain, or ye'll have the Scots howling for your blood, and *another* war on your hands."

"But the Countess is known to be a lady of sober habits. Am I to understand that she is like to partake in his toping?"

"Ach, she'd sip the odd wee flute of wine, but then...she's not so long out of childbed, and she mightn't..."

"Indeed. The concubine. To baptize the *second* bastard from a union where no marriage is possible! And still they scorn the reformed church! Godless savages I know them to be, and yet I am confounded." Sussex shook his head and sighed. "I suppose she may bear but little blame, for he keeps her shackled in gyves and chains." O'Hagan grimaced and drew his head back.

"Are ye joking me?" He laughed. "Ach, it's the O'Donnells be saying *that*, but they're not fool enough to believe it! There's divil-all chains on *that* wee woman! She near to rules the roost!" Sussex halted and spoke with sudden sharpness.

"Tush! Govern your tongue, you fool! *You*'d best not tell such fanciful tales, lest you'll find yourself outcast on *both* sides of the pale. The woman was abducted. She is a captive." He glared for a moment, and then resumed his brisk pace across the green in silence, considering the matter. At length he spoke, in a subdued, if agitated, tone. "But tell me, then, *and tell no other*... If there *be* no shackles, wherefore is she not back with her people in Mull? Is she so mad as to *cleave* to this savage who tossed aside his wife?"

"Katherine wouldn't come that. 'At least' she says, 'Moya O'Donnell left with her head on her shoulders -the differ to Anne Boleyn and the rest.' Aye, she's as proud as a cat with two tails." O'Hagan's face now assumed a look of pained forbearance as he weighed his next revelation, drawing a breath through his clenched teeth. "I'll tell you this, as well, your Lordship, because I'm an honest man, and your loyal servant. You can measure the worth of O'Neill's submission by Katherine MacLean. If she believed his oath to Elizabeth was worth a ha'penny she'd have slit his throat. She'd be in Scotland, with or without her childer. She hates the English. And she schemes for Scotch Mary."

"But he has outraged Mary Stuart's Court with this scandal. He keeps a prisoner of her husband. And yet the woman *stays*..." O'Hagan winked, and lowered his voice confidentially.

"She stays for the horn. Shane and Katherine are like flint and steel, d'ye see. Hard and cold. But when they come together there's fire. All their raging and blustering only stokes the fires below."

"Only a rutting beast could o'erlook the torture of her husband!"

"Aye, well...Blood may be thicker nor water- but it thins out a bit when heated." Sussex tisked and frowned, but O'Hagan grinned slyly. "Oh, you may well wonder at it, for ye English are a calm lot, but the Gaelic women are hot blooded."

The Lord Deputy stepped into the shadows under a low archway, and, with echoing footfall, he quickly descended the eleven steps into a dark narrow passage below the Cathedral. His bewildered companion followed close on his heels. "What place is this, your Honour?"

"This is an expedient, albeit *gloomy*, little pathway into Trinity Lane. It is known to Dublinfolk as 'Hell'. And so, ere long you might boast you have been through Hell!" No trace of a smile accompanied this 'jest'. The air was dank, and there was puddling from the day's showers. A dark figure stepped out of the murky shadows up ahead, a silhouette with arms folded. His stance was crooked, with one leg bearing his weight, and his chin was cocked arrogantly, so that Sussex knew him in an instant. As they approached the man, Lord Sussex addressed him tersely. "You are late." The reply was breezy.

"Alas, I was detained." On seeing the bristling arch of Sussex' brow, he continued. "I deemed it more prudent to await you here." He shrugged, adding under his breath. "We are *met*." They, all three, stepped quickly up the steps, and halted under a low archway to avail of the grey evening light. The Viceroy presented his companion.

"Captain Smith, this is O'Hagan. As he is privy to the usages in the household of-"

"Indeed I know the man! -from O'Neill's retinue; oft did he slip to me a crumpled missive for your Lordship from out his rustic mantle. Though, in truth, my eyes were deceived by this new-gotten attire. He goes like a proper Englishman now!" A single brow arched, as his glance shifted to the man's hose. "Or *nearly* so."

"Ach, O'Neill has his spies abroad too, so he does. And I'd not fancy having my throat slit, like as they done til my father, the rotten hoors!"

Sussex frowned, and then nodded to Smith to proceed. They came out into the little laneway known as Trinity Lane. It was less than twelve feet wide, a cramped little passage that led from Skinners Row to Winetavern Street. Shops were shuttered along the lane, owing to the late hour, but there were a few children about, clamouring after a boy as he rolled a barrel-hoop with his stick. Captain John nodded toward the top to the lane. "It's up here." He turned his eyes to the Deputy, and assumed a challenging tone. "All are saying now that O'Neill has won, that he will no longer be answerable to the Viceroy in Dublin!"

"Are they indeed? *That* foolish concession was granted him last year. Since London, he treats directly with her Majesty - and these busy-headed knaves at court. Dudley and the rest...his devious brother-in-law Harry Sidney..." Captain John smiled, always delighted to instruct the Lord Deputy with his savvy counsel.

"Sidney is no fool. And he knows Shane of old. I'd wager he's sowing salt in your fields. Wants his old post back."

"Pah! Sir Harry would sooner covet a banishment to wild America! Dublin is a *bog*, and were he posted here in my stead, I would rejoice exceeding. Yay, though 'twould astonish the petty lords here about, the mean and trifling matters of this isle signify *nothing* in the affairs of states." The captain nodded to large draywagon up ahead.

"It's just beyond this, your Lordship, t'other side of the King's Head. Master Thomas is expecting you." Several young lads were unloading barrels for the alehouse, blocking the laneway, but Captain John led his companions, singly, through the tight space along the far wall. They saw before them now a modest wooden signboard bearing the moniker 'T. Smith Apothecary', the only such shop in Dublin. The facade was shuttered, but Smith quickly found the door to be unlocked, and he held it open for Lord Sussex. He, however, was detained by the Irishman. Apparently O'Hagan had taken exception to the Lord Deputy's remark.

"Aye, well, Ireland must signify greatly to *someone*! Doesn't O'Neill get letters from the great Courts of Europe? Medicis, and Guises, and Stuarts, and the lot. Sure, hasn't he sent an agent off to the Pope in Rome!" Sussex turned abruptly to his 'informant'.

"How now? What is his new business with Rome?" The Viceroy's tone was sharp, and it drew a timid reply.

"I...I couldn't say rightly...but I think he's looking to get what they call a Papal Order- some class of lordship from the Pope." Sussex' thin lips twisted in a sour smirk.

"I do not doubt it. Mayhap the Bishop of Rome will find in him a suitable candidate for his sordid and debauched Curia. It shouldn't surprise me if he made of him a Cardinal! -We will hear more of *this* anon." With that, he followed Captain Smith into the cluttered little shop.

The air was musty, and the shop was dark, but for an oil lamp flickering on the broad low counter, and a long shaft of light from the door which stood ajar. The low planked ceiling was studded with hooks and nails, from which hung tangled roots, and 'cullings of simples', assorted bunches of dried and drying herbs. The walls were nowhere visible, lined as they were with over-laden shelves, bearing canisters, pots, bottles of every size and form, and jars of musty seeds and pungent powders. There were coils of packthread and twine, bladders and bones, dried fishes, tortoise shells, pelts and lizard-skins. Beside the till was a human skull with a goose-feather quill lodged in the eye-socket, and behind it sat a mortar and pestle containing partially ground roots and herbs. From the beam overhead, there hung a dried alligator, belly up, the very symbol of the Apothecary's trade. It had been acquired as a customary 'token' from one of Smith's suppliers. The captain gave three sharp raps on the counter. Almost immediately, a curtain in the back parted, and Thomas Smith appeared, wearing a skullcap, and a stained white smock over his finery. His hands were raised before him. As he approached, a tiny sickle could be seen in one, and in the other, a single sprig of herbage.

"Ah, my Lord Sussex! I am so greatly honoured by your visit! And most gratified that I might once *again* do you a service!" He was a robust man, near to Sussex in age, but more youthful in appearance, in spite of his thinning pate. He was darker and taller than his young cousin John; indeed, he bore him little resemblance, apart from certain inflections and turns of speech, which marked them both as Essexmen. He stepped briskly in behind the counter, dispatched his tool to its drawer, and placed the sprig of herbs in the mortar. He raised the wick of the greasy lamp until its glow cast sufficient light, and then straightened up and smiled. His teeth glistened yellow in the lamp's radiance, and a quivering shadow loomed above, as his dark eyes fixed intently upon the Deputy. "Now! If I might enquire...it is precipitous, I know, but you will forgive me...Is any word yet come from Her Majesty regarding my treatise?"

"Nay, Master Thomas, not as yet. But the *Lord Secretary* has read it. And he commends it highly. So highly, indeed, that I would venture to say that your advisements regarding the Irish rhymers may soon find their way into the policy of the realm! Her Majesty's duties draw heavily upon her time, of course, but she shall read it, and discuss your proposals with the Privy Council."

"The bards *must* be banned! If there is to be peace in the realm, the bards must be banned. These lying poets are very poison to the commonweal, for it is *they* who chiefly spur the rebels to their wicked-"

"I assure you, I am fully versed in your argument!" The Deputy's abrupt tone forestalled the impending tirade.

"Of course, your Lordship. But I beseech you, there be many *other* ill-usages in this realm that might be redressed if your honours will give ear unto me. And if it may stand with her Majesty's pleasure that I should make *further* recommendings how this savage people may be punished –chastised- to cause them to leave their vile fashions, I will, -*if* it be her pleasure, show by what means they may be remedied."

"Indeed, you would appear to possess remedies and cures for all ailments of the body, and the body politic as well. In due course, I am sure the Lord Secretary will hear of your advisements. He is mindful of your labours in establishing the new Dublin mint, as well as your physics and potions. But my business today is of quite another nature. It is not a cure, but a poison that is required of you."

"Betimes the poison *is* the cure! Indeed, my Lord, I *know* why you are here, the order of your business, and I do commend you on the wisdom of your course. Cousin John has informed me of all." There was a sudden shriek and shouting in the street from the children, as they scampered by the open door. The captain spoke quietly, as he strode back to the door.

"Shall I latch it?"

"Nay, John. Let you and the Irishman bide without, presently. Give us leave, that his Lordship and I might have a quiet word." The two men stepped out into the dusk-dimmed lane. Thomas Smith smiled weakly at the Deputy. "A small matter. A delicate matter, perhaps." He blew sharply at the shelf beside him, raising a little cloud of mites, and motes, and atomies that swirled in the lamplight. Alas, as you see, Lord Sussex, my wares serve only to gather dust. A shop...barely able to sustain itself! The Irish-born, hereabouts, are wont to use the ministry of their leeches and suchlike. They do spurn the wisdom of our English science -much to *my* cost... My Lord, I was paid but little for founding the Dublin mint. Precious few of its coins have found my purse! Now I have wrought such a sly device as will solve the Northern Wars for you, as surely as night follows day -or 'death follows life', perhaps. And so it shall be Her Majesty's to have, and to use for her worthy ends. But...I *must* have promise of a stipend for my service."

"You shall have a goodly fee."

"A stipend -*yearly*. She must endow me thusly, or Dublin shall be *without* an apothecary. She will need send another in my place, incurring costs far beyond a modest pension."

SHANE O'NEILL

"Oh, very well, then. You shall have it. And now, perchance, we would *see* this device!" He turned to the door and bade his two hirelings to return, as his obliging host disappeared into the back of the shop. Moments later, the curtains parted, and Smith re-emerged, carrying aloft a tierce, a middling-sized oaken cask. In his other hand was a scantling for it, which he laid on the counter. He rested the cask snugly upon it, and proceeded to extract the bung from the topmost stave, as is done to allow air for a free flow. Next, he removed the bung from the front head of the cask, and quickly inserted the wooden spigot. He took from a shelf a dusty glass, wiped it with his smock, and decanted a small amount of red wine into it. He took a fair sip, and offered the rest to Sussex.

"A fine Rhenish. Perhaps you will taste of it?"

Perplexed, but amenable, the Lord Deputy accepted it, and took a swallow. He nodded amiably, his brows raised in expectation of further revelation. But Smith said nothing. With a wry smile, he removed the spigot, and replaced the bungs. He quickly turned the barrel until another plug appeared along the bilge. He now set about reversing the position of the cask on its scantling, bringing the other end to the fore. Sussex noted instantly that there was another bunghole. One at each end. Most curious! Smith removed the stoppers and tapped the keg once again. He took the glass from Sussex, swallowed what remained, and wiped it again on his smock. As he tilted it to the spigot, his eyes were fixed upon the Deputy, who was quite surprised to see clear water splashing into the glass.

"Ahhh! *Two* chambers within! Most cunning. But to what *end*, precisely?" Thomas Smith smiled darkly.

"O'Neill's end. Precisely! The bearer of this cask –It *is* John, is it not?" Sussex' nodded.

"He shall bring it as my token to honour the new Treaty of Peace. '*Eternal* peace', let us hope. O'Neill will be feasting in his hall to celebrate it." Master Thomas smirked again, marking the Deputy's drollery, and continued.

"Upon presenting it, John must tap it firstly at this end. See you, it is marked by this notch along the quarter-hoop -the safe end. He shall make a grand show of quaffing the first cup, and then filling it to the brim, that he might continue to tope with them after the switch is made. He must *then* contrive to remove the cask to another place, and tap it this time at the other – the *lethal* end. For in place of this water will be a most costly wine, laced with a most deadly bane!" Sussex' dark eyes glistened with relish of his impending triumph.

"Well contrived! An artful ruse. Methinks you are not an apothecary, but a wizard. And shrewd one." Smith bowed immodestly.

"And so O'Neill and his ministers might be *easily* induced to drink freely of it!"

"To a certainty." Sussex turned now to his hirelings, and noted a dubious squint on the Irishman's face. "How now? What say you, then? What cautions do you advise for Captain Smith?"

"Aye. Aye, a sound plan, right enough. Present it to O'Neill at his table, and fill his cup first with the safe wine. Make a wild boast of its cost! A rare French wine. He'll be gaggin' for it, -But don't let the cask go to the *buttery*, for the butler is a crafty hoor, and he might hoard it there for himself. There does be always a long sideboard just behind O'Neill's table. Set it out on *that*, then, so as you can turn it about, without anyone being the wiser. Ah...But they'd want to be 'well on' at this point, so you can sidestep the servants. There's my only caution...Howandever, let me tell ye this! This 'bane', as you call it. -It best be *powerful* to fell a man of so strong a make as O'Neill!"

"It would poison the blackest poison. Who so drinks of it shall die." Captain John tutted.

"Just so he who delivers it *does not*! With all of these mad Irish savages dropping, and clutching their bellies, just how might I affect my escape? Surely they will seize me! Did you spare a thought for Cousin John?"

"Nay, then. Fear not on *that* account. This is a *slow* poison, concocted of hemlock with the mawseed of poppy, so that the drinker will swoon. The Irishman is right, John. You must arrive at a late hour...when O'Neill's wits are sodden and his cautions sleep. Having drunk of it, he will grow drowsy, and when at length the bane has worked its way, it will seem sottish ebriety has brought him sleep. The company, most like, will finish the draught, for naught will be suspect til the morning. O'Neill and his councilors, if they imbibe this, will never awaken. You might easily slip away into the night, long before the bane is detected." There was silence as Captain Smith stepped slowly around behind the counter to join his cousin. He nodded thoughtfully to him, and then his steely eyes shifted to Lord Sussex. The glow from the oil-lamp, on its low counter, cast strange shadows on the four solemn faces gathered above it, imparting a vaguely ghoulish aspect to the company. After a pause, he spoke.

"And for my part in this...?"

"Her Majesty will be gracious. There will be new titles to grant in Ulster. And land and estates."

"Estates in Ulster? Aye, six foot by two foot -with a fine herd of maggots!"

"Pah! Such fears are baseless. There will be a ship awaiting you at the wharf in Dundalk to spirit you safe away to England. Once quiet is restored, you might easily return. With O'Neill dead, Lord Thomas Smith shall be gratified with leave to build his colony in Ulster. His great city of Elizabetha shall rise there."

"And *pleased* he shall be...But what is that to me?" The Captain's admonishing tone reminded Sussex that neither of these men had openly acknowledged their kinship to Lord Smith, or their interest in his scheme.

"Once you have dispatched O'Neill's soul to Eternity, there will be a great rejoicing in the land. And nowhere more exultant than in the Royal Court! But doubtless that is naught to you. A man of so little ambition..."

"One hundred fifty marks of land to me and to my heirs. Not in Ulster, nay. In Kildare, secure within the Pale."

"So be it."

SHANE O'NEILL

After the initial parley with Kildare and Ormonde, Shane dispatched Master Robert off to Cusack in Dublin. The courier was hard at it for weeks, setting off with demands and returning with offers. Shane even pressed for Terence Danyell to assume the Primacy, knowing that the Crown's approval would simplify matters in Rome. Clause by clause, concession after concession, the 'Treaty of Drumcree' was draughted, a document virtually dictated by O'Neill. Fleming was then obliged to take all to a Royal Commission in London for more deliberations. At last he returned to Ireland, and made his way back to Benburb Castle, bearing good tidings. He sent his account of what transpired there to Lord Cecil.

"My humble duty remembered to your Honour. Immediately upon my arrival here in Ireland, I took my journey unto O'Neill, and declared him of the Queen's clemency and inclination towards him, and how gracious she was to him, and how Sir Thomas Cusack has come; whereof he and all his people being then present were wonderful glad, and rejoiced. The messengers of the O'Briens, the O'Connors, and the O'Moore's were attending him for to have them upon his peace. He said that both he and they would serve the queen, and that he would be their means unto the Queen's majesty, if they would be good and gracious, and they, understanding his meaning, departed.

My arrival proved a cause of much relief to my Lord O'Neill, for on the day appointed, his country assembled and came unto him, greatly troubled, as our ship's landing in Dundalk was as yet unknown to them. The people said, "We understand that this peace which was concluded is but a delay and tracting of time to bring more power upon you!" And they desired him to shift for himself. But O'Neill said that 'Sir Thomas Cusack and Robert Fleming are with the queen, and

SHANE O'NEILL

would not tarry so long, lest it was beyond their power. Perhaps the wind does not serve.' Thus he assured his people to have faith. The Dean of Armagh was likewise present, having been asked by the Chancellor Cusack to remain in the North until his return, and his wholesome good counsel and advice unto them did much, and was a great stay.

One week hence, when O'Neill perceived that Lord Cusack was in readiness to set off from the Pale, he appointed a place, and sent me forth to escort him. The two lords were joyfully met at O'Neill's camp at Drumcree, and after they had concluded the peace, with O'Neill being sworn for the true performance thereof, his gentlemen and the best of his country who were present were called by the Chancellor to take the like oath as O'Neill did. 'Nay!' said O'Neill, 'Sir Thomas, do not give them their oath so, but let me give it them. 'You shall swear' said O'Neill, 'if ever I break upon the Queen's majesty of anything that I have here promised, or granted to Sir Cusack in her Majesty's behalf, that you shall not only give me your good advices and counsels not to do so, but also to maintain the Queen's majesty against me, and to do the uttermost that you can against me for the destruction of my person.' Then he himself did hold the book to swear every man after that sort. After that was done, both he, and as many as was present, were so glad and joyful that it is not possible to declare!

Assuring your honour that it is the best peace, and tended most for the Queen's honour, that ever was! The people here lifted up their hands and rejoiced in God, and praised so inwardly for the Queen's majesty, and for Sir Thomas Cusack, that you would marvel it has so rejoiced men's hearts, and put them in great quietness.

Yours to serve Her Most Royal Highness,
Master Robert Fleming"

Cusack had greeted Shane warmly, and won him over immediately

SHANE O'NEILL

by addressing him as 'Lord Tyrone', his father's title. He assured him that mere formalities were all that remained to delay his investiture. Indeed, the Chancellor bore nothing but good news. The garrison at Armagh would be removed on the Feast of All Saints. Shane had only to enter into a bond for £1,000. to the Queen, if he failed to perform his promise of restoring the Cathedral to divine service, a task which he was most anxious to undertake.

Still more gratifying, and surprising, were the Queen's orders that Terence Danyell be made Archbishop of Armagh and Primate, with Adam Loftus to be transferred to Dublin. The Queen's choice of a Catholic would be highly regarded in Rome! And closing up a lingering point of contention, Shane was not to be held answerable for the murder of Brian, son of the late Baron of Dungannon. Regarding Shane's prisoner, O'Donnell, the treaty confirmed that Cullagh's son should pay all things which his father had promised to 'Lord O'Neill' for his release. As to the controversies with O'Reilly, and Maguire, it was ordained that they should henceforth pay to O'Neill whatsoever they were accustomed to pay to his predecessors. All that was required of Shane was that he cease his alliances with the MacDonnell Scots, a turn of policy that he was already determined upon, since they had failed him in this campaign.

> "Her Majesty receives Shane O'Neill to her gracious favour, and pardons all his offences; he shall remain captain and governor of his territory or province of Tyrone, and shall have the name and title of O'Neill, and all the jurisdiction and preeminences which his ancestors possessed, with the service and homage of the vassal captains, and other chieftains of the O'Neill country, and he shall be created Earl of Tyrone."

There was wild jubilation in Ulster, and a great feasting was called for Michaelmas to celebrate the Peace. Invitations were sent to Sir Thomas Cusack and Lord Sussex to attend, and to accommodate them, the festivities were held in Shane's lodge at Fathan, near to the Pale.

SHANE O'NEILL

Katherine was blissful at the prospect of genuine peace, and this promise of non-interference from London was a thing 'out of all ken and reckoning!' With little Art but half the year old, and Hugh barely weaned, Kat had only recently divulged to Shane that she was with child yet again. Since her heart was set on a 'fine brood of bairns', she was joyful, of course, but still... Hardly had she got her maidenly shape back, and now it was to begin all over again! These festivities at Michaelmas would be a sorely needed respite, a bit of conviviality and glamour -if she could manage it, before she was 'all belly and bubs' again. And so, she made the journey down with her two infants in tow to preside as hostess, and she beamed with radiant joy as she received the excited guests in her lovely Parisian gown.

Indeed, it was a lavish affair, with wax blazing to the doorposts, and such a profusion of viands and drinks as to astonish the great crowd that assembled. The rustic hall was decked with late summer flowers, and festive garlands hung from the great racks of antlers up in the gables. Nearly all the chieftains of Ulster attended, with the finest poets, harpers, and pipers to regale them. Cusack had sent his apologies, but hope was held that the Lord Deputy would attend. As the evening wore on, however, such hopes dimmed, and it was nearly ten o'clock when his impish messenger arrived. Captain Smith bowed to Shane, and when the hall had stilled, he read out a rather terse greeting from his master, which Robert Fleming was obliged to put into Irish for the company assembled.

"From the Earl of Sussex, Lord Lieutenant, to John, admitted by the Queen's Commissioners to the name of 'O'Neill.'" This brought an indignant gasp from the company, but he pressed on. "We have received your letters, and seen what has been concluded between the Commissioners and you. We will observe the same. We have given audience to your men, and made answer to them. The war is now ended, and our former friendship remains. Lord Sussex, at Ardbracken."

This was followed by a stunned silence, and then an agitated murmur rose like a gust of wind through the hall, for the perceived insult had struck such a discordant note in the proceedings. Shane

SHANE O'NEILL

stood, bringing all to a hush. "He's an honest fellow, the Deputy. It's easy seen that our 'former friendship!' remains *former*, as kind as kin, and warm as winter! And if he's not smiling over the harsh terms I've won, well...we'll take it in good heart!" Laughter filled the hall, restoring the easy harmony of the banquet. Captain Smith nudged his page to the fore, presenting a cask in his arms before O'Neill's table, and then spoke up over the chatter of the heady crowd.

"Indeed, such hasty words, inked upon a page, can scarce convey his Lordship's heartfelt cordiality and cheer upon this long-sought Day of Peace. To that end, he sends a token of this cask of wine, a first pressing of Chateau LaFite, the finest and *most costly* in his cellar at Ardbracken! He bids us toast the Accords on this Feast of St. Michael, who is known unto us as both angel and warrior!" The gift was greeted with applause. Shane was pleased with the precious wine, and Smith saw to it that it flowed lavishly for one and all. Katherine had finished a goblet of claret, and she abjured now, lest another should weaken her resolve for an early night. The music was still blazing in the hall, with revelers whirling in set-dances and clapping time, as Kat bid a few quiet 'good-nights'. She slipped off then, to nurse her babe, and round her long exhausting day with sleep. But there was a brutal morning to come, and early it came.

It was well before cockcrow when the fraught and shrill alarum resounded through the great lodge. Cries of 'Treachery!' and 'Poison!' filled the air. Most of the women, the abstainers, and those of moderate habits had drifted off long before, and it was the servants who raised the cry. Instead of the usual high-spirited madness among the late tipplers, too many at the head-table had nodded off or swooned, and the rest were flagging. When the servants found themselves unable to rouse them, the horror of what was unfolding became evident, and they rushed to awaken the household.

Two physicians, O'Sheil and O'Cassidy, were first called from their beds, and they quickly appeared in their disheveled black smocks, and began firing orders. The ale and spirits drinkers, some still reveling, were dismissed noisily to the camp below, with a few wobbly fellows oxtered out the door. Servants were dispatched to the kitchen to heat water, and

SHANE O'NEILL

to fetch hot mustard powder for an emetic. Funnels and tubs were called for, and buckets of cold well-water. Doctor O'Sheil attended Shane, while O'Cassidy attempted to make order out of the rapidly developing pandemonium, as frenzied wives and kindred flooded into the hall. Old Bríd Donnelly put a stop to the women's keening, and enlisted their aid for her make-shift hospice. They helped her administer the emetic to those woozy revelers who were still on their feet. Gillie and a few other young striplings were passed out over a table, but a cold dousing roused them enough to take their mustard, and spill their guts, like the others. The rustic hall, that had but a while ago been the scene of a lavish and decorous feast, was now filled with ghastly sounds and noxious smells.

The Dean of Armagh had departed early with his coterie of Franciscans, but the chaplain was in residence, and, roused from his bed, he moved quickly among the afflicted, administering Last Rites to those who were not responding. Lady Katherine, garbed in a hooded cloak of deepest blue, moved swiftly through the crowd with her long raking stride. Her feet were bare, and the rushes on the floor were sodden and cold, with the sops and spills of a long night, but she never felt it. She heard, now, the shrill whine of Shane's wolfhounds, yelping and baying plaintively, and she shivered. As the throng parted before her, she found Shane stretched still upon the table, with a solemn crowd of teary onlookers gathered over him. Katherine uttered a wild shriek, thinking him to be dead. Doctor O'Sheil assured her that he was breathing yet, but neither his cold water, nor vigorous slaps could bring the chieftain round. She nodded silently, her slender fingers clapped over her open mouth. There was terror in her eyes. The doctor bade Father O'Loan to hold off just yet with his holy oils, until all curative procedures had been tried.

Fearing that Shane might choke in his sleep on the emetic, O'Sheil quickly ruled that out. Instead, he set about trying to induce vomiting by tickling the back of his throat with a hackelfeather, plucked from someone's cap. Katherine insisted on helping, and she cradled Shane's head over the end of the table as the doctor plied his quill. She was horrified at the seeming desperation of such a trifling measure, and she prayed fervently under her breath. As the long moments passed, though, her face drained of all tension, her thoughts vanishing in a hopeless torpor.

"Now!" The doctor's cry jolted Kat to her senses. Shane was at last responding! His eyelids barely flickered, but he heaved suddenly, gushing copious amounts of cloudy wine onto the flags below. Once more O'Sheil induced him to spill forth, and then he shook him and dashed cold water in his face. Still he was unable to rouse him. The doctor looked to Katherine, and he ventured to say that 'most of the poison must surely be out.' Only now did she collapse in tears.

Farleigh O'Gneeve, in a state of mild inebriation, was among the throng watching over these ministrations. He cursed the English, and the foolishness of the young, who ever spurn his warnings and cautions. He, of course, had refused to partake of the English Deputy's wine. "Bedamned the cost! Bedamned the vintage! Perhaps now they will listen to a hoary old man and his hard-bought sense!" Fergus O'Kane was beside him, soft in drink, but not befuddled.

"He was too free with that brazen wee whelp, that English knave Smith! By Christ, I will *have* that bitch's bastard! I'll pay him on the bones for his wine!"

"The Devil mince his bones!" Farleigh spat contemptuously. "It was Sussex, damn his blood! More of his villiany! I'll curse him to the seventh generation!"

The voices of the crowd surged now as Shane was carried off, his hounds pattering along beside, barking and whimpering. The grey of morning was at the windows, a sombre wet morning, though the braziers still flickered against the walls. Brίd Donnelly led the doctor and the stretcher-bearers up to a chamber with a four-poster, where, the doctor assured her and Katherine that he would sleep it off. "Fear not, my Ladies. All will be well yet. If *that much wine* was in him still, there's damned little that could have dispersed into his blood. He's a strong man, and a bit of sleep will see him right, surely." Kat nodded, her eyes vacant, over-whelmed with distress, but Brίd glared incredulously. Her white-knuckled fist was clasped firmly to her bosom.

SHANE O'NEILL

"But surely to God, Doctor! He made piss of a fair few flagons ere this! The Dear knows *how* much poison has gotten intil him!"

"It's in God's hands now." O'Sheil glanced warily at Shane, nodded, and turned to the chamber door. Bríd crossed herself quickly.

"Aye, so it is. There's Father O'Loan is out there with his oils and his unctions. Would you ever send him in, Doctor?"

"I will, then. I must help Doctor O'Cassidy see to the other victims."

"You must surely. God bless the work." One of the wolfhounds was up on his hind legs at the bed, sniffing and licking his master. "Hup! Hup! Get down out of that, Scohaun!" She hit him a swat, and he slunk off, mewling quietly. A servant was tending the fire, which was just kindling to a blaze. "Take those beasts out intil yon hallway; they're underfoot! And ye may take up your station outside the door." When he had shooed the dogs out and gone, Bríd turned about to Katherine. She shook her head and sighed wearily. "A Last Anointing -only a precaution..." Kat's thin voice replied.

"Tis little good *that* will do!" Bríd rounded on her in horror and disbelief.

"God forgive you!" She tisked then, and spoke gently. "Sure, you don't know what you'd be saying; you're in tatters. As taut as a bowstring! Sit ye down here now, and rest yourself." She pushed a chair closer to the bed, and settled Katherine into it. "For his immortal *soul* it is! And sure, there's no tellin'. There's quare powers in them same oils. More nor the doctor's tonics, maybe!" Bríd put her hand to Shane's forehead, and after a long moment, she tisked again. When the priest appeared at the door, she rushed to welcome him. "Not a stir, since, Father. He's the color of ashes and his breath is crosswise in his chest, God help him. And he's drownded in sweat. Oh Father, you must bless this place afore ye go! The devil himself has been under our roof."

When the Last Rites had been administered, and the blessed candles snuffed, Fr. O'Loan slipped the narrow purple stole from his neck. He kissed it hastily, and tucked it into his black case with the rest of his accoutrements. He took Bríd's trembling white hand, and gently squeezed it.

SHANE O'NEILL

"Hopefully, now, he'll take this sacrament *again*, many long years hence. It isn't final." As the priest turned to go, he winked. "Say a wee prayer. God's help is nearer than the door."

"Oh, he'll not die for want of prayers!" When he had disappeared, Bríd looked to Katherine, who met her gaze and spoke with the full of her voice.

"He'll *not* die. He'd have done by now."

"Please God, you're right!" Brid was gladdened to see Katherine taking heart, and she blessed herself swiftly again, with a silent 'Thanks be to God'. Off she bustled then to manage the troubled household. Katherine got no more sleep, but kept a vigil through the long day at Shane's bedside, nursing her babe, or stitching idly at her needlepoint. The thought of actually losing Shane, with another baby on the way was too terrifying to face, and she struggled to keep her mind on more comforting matters. 'He has only to awaken', she thought, 'and he has won all!' Now and then she would shake his shoulder and beckon him from his slumbers, but to no avail. She listened to the rain on the thatch, and to the crackle of the wood fire in the hearth. She tried to keep her spirits up.

"No, he'll not die." She sighed, and spoke in a small voice to the sad rustling rain. "Ach, he'll not, surely. He'd have died ere this, if his heart were poisoned." But, whatever might he do now? And what of this Treaty? Would there be war again? All the rest of her life, she knew, depended upon whatever was to happen in this room...

Brid Donnelly was in and out through the day, to mop his brow, and to bring news. It was held a wondrous and hopeful sign that none of the others had died. There were a few that were still under, the way of Shane, and some were feverish and pained, but none had died. And surely he would over it yet. The cask had been examined, and the 'device' of the poisoner discovered, causing a great fury in the Hall. None of the chieftains had departed; all were awaiting news of Shane's fate. Éamon Donnelly had galloped off to fetch for the Dean, and when he arrived he urged caution, and patience 'for the unfolding of God's holy will.' He looked in on Katherine and Shane, and then returned to lead a

SHANE O'NEILL

rosary in the camp. It was well after lamplight when the crisis lifted.

A gentle knock at the door roused Katherine from her dozing in the chair. A servant inquired if she would join the Dean and others below for an evening supper. She declined, and dismissing him, she rose, and yawned, and then stood over to the fire. There was a fresh log of bog fir burning brightly, throwing shadows about the room. A distant growl of thunder made her aware of the ever-falling rain, and the scrawking of rooks below, and the snap of the fire... Suddenly it struck her that she did not hear the wheezing sound of Shane's slumbering, and she rushed to the bed. She sighed with relief to see that he was breathing, quietly now, and laying her hand to his brow, she found it was no longer clammy and cold!

Though it was well before her customary bedtime, Katherine stripped off and nestled in beside her man, embracing him in her warmth. Her breathing soon slowed to match his slumbering pace, and, though her mind was beset by legions of worries, she drifted off to sleep. The fire was nearly embers when her troubled dream dissolved in the growing awareness of a deep murmur at her side. She opened her eyes to the flickering shadows above from the flagging fire, and she strained to make out the indistinct, but spirited mumbling of the man beside her. Little sense to be gotten there! She started up, and shook him vigorously, but he did not respond. "Shane! Shane!" He moaned, now, and that was new, but still she could not waken him.

A falling brand of burning fir took Katherine's eye to the fire. She rose quickly, and donned her blue cloak. She lit a candle at the drowsing fire, and held it up to Shane for a proper look-see. A certain hopeful twitch in his brow sent her off to get assistance, but upon opening the door, she was nearly toppled by Shane's wolfhounds as they rushed to his side. The footman jumped to his feet at this commotion, whereupon he heard Katherine's trembling voice. "Bid the doctor and the Dean come at once! I think the O'Neill is beginning to stir!"

The yelping hounds bounded up onto the bed, licking the face of their recumbent master. Kat stalked over, about to banish them, but seeing that they were trying to rouse him, she stood back to watch. God

SHANE O'NEILL

willing, they might succeed! The tone of his palaver was anxious now, and soon his head was tossing under the slobbering of the hounds. At last his eyes opened, and he raised his hand to shield his face. He pushed them away, and strove to rise, but collapsed back onto the pillow. Kat shooed the hounds down off the bed, as Shane looked about him in confusion. The dogs barked merrily now, with their ears aloft, and their tails awag. O'Neill propped himself up on his arm, and opened his eyes wide, but he was still unable to dispel the mist in his head.

Just then, through the low doorway, the Dean, the doctor, and a number of Shane's intimates crowded into the chamber. There was an awkward silence, born of astonishment and expectation. Shane squinted, and peered at the faces before him. Finally the doctor spoke. "O'Neill? Shane O'Neill! Do you hear me?"

"Hah?" Shane closed his eyes and opened them again. O'Sheil repeated his question, louder and slower. This time Shane nodded. The doctor returned the nod, and, with a grave demeanor, he resumed his inquiries.

"O'Neill...do you see me once? Or do you see me twice?"

"I see you once. And that's *enough!*" There was a mighty laugh now at this gruff reply, a laugh that savored of sweet relief. Shane stared at the lot of them. "Christ Almighty!" His voice was hoarse, but strong. "What in the name of thundering Jasus is *this*? Hah?" Farleigh clapped his hands and rubbed them together.

"By the Powers! You're back with the living!" Katherine, teary eyed, stepped in, and, gently stroking Shane's damp disheveled hair, she spoke softly.

"Ach, Shane, love! Don't be blaspheming, now! All the night, and all the day, only til now, you were clay-cold, and near-as-no-matter to quitting this world altogether! *Poisoned* you were! Father O'Loan is after anointing you, forehead to foot, with his Last Rites." There was a long pause while Shane's grey eyes filled with memory and understanding, and as he nodded slowly, under his arched brow, they took on the shrewd look that was familiar to all.

"Let him save his holy oils for Sussex! It's *he* will have need of them!

SHANE O'NEILL

I'll wet my sword on his black heart ere the year is out!" This brought an approving cheer. Shane shifted himself suddenly, dropping his feet to the floor, but he nearly fell over, so unsteady was he still. This brought a gasp from the company who rushed in to support him. Bríd pulled up the blanket smartly for him to cover his nakedness, but Katherine tossed his frieze mantle across the bed to her. She tucked it over his shoulders.

"Sit over til the fire, now, Shane, love, where you can gather your wits and your strength." She turned to an attendant. "Fetch him a bowl of broth, and a wee oaten farl; there's divil-all in him to hold him up. Sure, an empty sack will not stand!" A hefty chair was pushed noisily over to the fireside, and Shane was settled into it. "Ye must be that bit queezy after the-" Bríd stopped at the doctor's approach.

"What way are you now, O'Neill? Are you pained?"

"Ach... I'm grand, sure." His hand was at the back of his head, and he saw the doctor noting it. "Ah...just a little...crown of pain about my temples." Shane cleared his throat, and spat hard into the fire. He raised his palm to O'Shiel. "I'm fine! I'll be the better, when Sussex is the worse!" O'Kane laughed low, and chimed in.

"And that poxy little swine, Smith!"

"Augh!" Shane shook his head. "Smith is no more than a messenger. His message was poison. And it came signed and sealed by the Earl of Sussex..." Farleigh stepped into the firelight.

"Aye, and 'tis well for *you* he made a guts of it! 'Tis well for the lot of us. We might have had a score of corpses to bury this day, all for we trusted the English and their fine words of 'peace'!" O'Kane nodded trenchantly.

"An Englishman's word is not worth a cuckoo's spittle! Farleigh is right, O'Neill. It's only for that poisoner's bungling that we have you in our midst this night!" Katherine had stepped in behind Shane. Her cheeks glistened but her eyes were dry now. She laid her hand on his shoulder.

"Shane is alive by the grace of Almighty God! He has the strength of a spring tide in him! And It would take a better man than Sussex to lay him low. Even with treachery." The Brehon O'Hagan spoke up now.

SHANE O'NEILL

"There's no man here will dispute *that*, Lady Katherine. Sure, we all speak of Sussex, for well we know it was *he* sent the wine. Aye. But *you may be sure* it was done upon the Queen's word! She is King Henry's own daughter for spite and divilry!" Farleigh concurred, in a booming voice.

"She is a venomous viper! As pitiless and vengeful as the wife of Zeus!" The Brehon O'Hagan nodded, and continued on.

"These orders came from London! How could it be else?" His challenging glance was met by a growl of assent all round. "At least they have finally torn off the mask of high-mindedness! Pomp and honour! trumpets and flash! And foul treachery behind it all! *There* is the 'majesty' of England!" After a brief pause, O'Kane voiced his little addendum.

"Aye, they're majestic alright, and 'valiant' too. *Poison* -the sword of the coward!" Shane looked to O'Hagan, nodding. His eyes narrowed, with a guileful arch of the brow.

"This 'pageantry and flourish'... That's their master stroke! They're a crowd of cutthroats, but the people honour them, for they trouble themselves to observe all these 'niceties of form'. Even the sordid business of a hanging, they dress it with a wee drumroll. There's a great deal to learn from these crafty hoors..." But Farleigh pished at the notion. Loudly.

"A noble deed does not need a flourish of trumpets! That is all dumbshow for ninnies. Fine for England, but where would you find such fools in Ulster? You want to mind the lessons you'd take from the like of *them*. It isn't trumpets or other such trumpery will answer an assassin's tilt, but fire and sword!" Shane laughed softly, darkly.

"You may set your mind at ease, Farleigh O'Gneeve, for their will be smoke rising over the Pale soon enough!" O'Neill's eyes smouldered as his gaze swept over the cheering company before him, but his dark grin vanished when he beheld the disapproving countenance of the silent Dean of Armagh. "Holy Christ! What is it now, Turlagh? What would you have me do? Will I crave a Royal Pardon for waking up?" The others stepped aside from the tall stern cleric, now, giving him the floor. He

SHANE O'NEILL

stood with arms folded, looking grave and commanding in his long black soutane, with the short black cape about his broad shoulders.

"Not at all, man! But you must see this for what it is, Shane. Your awakening this night is another *defeat* for Sussex. Another victory for O'Neill! This move by Sussex is was mark of *sheer desperation*. It is a Parthian shot from a vanquished foe. *And*...a measure of just how much you have won! Those legal 'niceties' you spoke of- the proprieties, strictures, the decorum of governance- they can be mighty weapons for you now. For it is *the Viceroy* himself who has transgressed them! And *all* touching the Queen's honour whereby she derives her authority. She will *have* to disavow this treachery. She will be forced to call Sussex to account. But, most crucially, she will have to hold by the terms you have won, and afix to them her Royal Seal, a thing, it is clear, she never intended to do. I tell you, O'Neill, this poison will stand against her in the Councils of Europe! And, *if* you do not forfeit your victory, *if* you do not let it dissolve in smoke above the Pale, she will come to rue this dark crime. And you will have reason to be glad of it!

CHAPTER 24

"Nothing of the kind, your Majesty! No, no, no, I assure you, my lord King Philip prays *only* for your welfare and weal -*wherein* are tied his *own* fortunes!" His Grace, the Ambassador, looked furtively over his shoulder, and lowered his voice, assuming a tone of deepest confidence. "Since France and Scotland are lately bound in alliance, were England brought low...Spain might stand to lose the Netherlands..." Elizabeth responded to his raised brows with an acquiescent nod, and he smiled slyly. "Wherefore, then, should not His Majesty covet England's favour, and bid you prosper?"

"And you may assure your prince that we dearly prize his kindly solicitude for our welfare, and do so return in kind!" Her voice raised in pitch to strike a final cordial note, without betraying her intended irony. The Spanish Ambassador, however, chose to ignore the implied dismissal.

"But, yet, this poison attempt has unsettled much of Catholic Europe. Princes and states must adhere to law, else the common subjects will forsake it. As you avouch your Viceroy Lord Sussex innocent in the matter, we must perforce accept him so. And still, if you can assure his Majesty that the true miscreant will be pursued and brought to justice, it will go far in calming the clamour of his uneasy subjects."

"You may tell King Philip that we do share his concern, and for that reason we shall recall Lord Sussex to London. Though he be not complicit in this foul deed, nor yet did he prevent it and preserve the public order as was his charge. Sir Nicholas Arnolde shall assume his duties, and he is sworn to find out the poisoner and bring him to charges."

"That should not prove difficult, your Highness, for the poisoner is widely known to be one 'Captain John Smith' who serves as an emissary for Lord Sussex. And so it is only natural that-"

"*It is only natural* that a Magistrate shall determine in the matter, and not the vain caprice of rumour-mongers!" The Queen sprung to her feet, with fire in her eyes. "We would you commend us to your sovereign King Philip. You may withdraw!" DeQuadra held his gaze upon her for just a moment longer than could be deemed proper, and, with the barest trace of a smirk on his lips, he bowed.

"Your Majesty." With that, he turned and took his leave, followed by his two attendants.

"The *insolent* wrrrretch!" Elizabeth shook her fists at her side, and cried to the heavens, "God's wounds!! They come like crows to carrion! And my Lord Sussex! He shall answer for this blunder! He lets his spite to rule his wits, and so are we chided and admonished by every menial envoy to this Court." She began to pace with a heavy stalking step, turning her skirts, and shouting. "God's teeth! What *induced* him to embrace such folly? To imperil our very honour! Has he taken leave of his feeble wits? To undertake so *reckless*! And to *then* miscarry! A wanton boldshow- botched and bungled!" She stopped and turned to Cecil, with sudden malicious glee. "We should deliver him up, and t'would serve him sweet justice!"

"Indeed, your Highness, he has o'er-reached himself to the very brink! And he shall rue it. O'Neill will doubtless swagger and swell in this martyr's crown that Sussex has bestowed upon his head! Alas! I much fear we shall be compelled now to ratify those ill-conceived

SHANE O'NEILL

indentures..."

"*That* we shall do!" Elizabeth seated herself once again. Tilting her head back, she looked to Cecil's astounded face, and added, portentously, with mounting stridor, "*When* they have been *amended* to uphold the Queen's honour!"

On the Feast of All Hallows, nearly every blessed soul in Armagh was gathered on the heights around the Cathedral to watch the English Garrison take their leave. The air was crisp and invigorating, and the sally grove at the foot of Drumsallock was a blaze of rust and gold under the October sun. The crowd was merry with the exuberance of the holiday, heightened by giddy relief at the spectacle of this long awaited departure. There was also a great swell of triumphal pride, for the O'Neill had prevailed after all! "We'll see their backs!" he had promised, and now, with a roll of the drums, they were marching away in full retreat. A gleeful crowd. Here and there a huddle of musicians struck up their tunes, and dancers whirled around them, just as on a fairday!

Shane O'Neill and his horsemen were gathered on a low rise below the citadel, a site that could hardly fail to call to mind, for the Garrison, the 'war of words' on the night of the great cattle-raid the previous autumn. This time, however, by virtue of 'victor's largesse', the Tirowenmen were under strict orders to stifle their 'last laugh', even if there was no stopping the quiet snigger, and the fleering grin. At the sound of a sudden cheer behind him, Shane turned to see the Dean of Armagh approaching on his fine grey hunter, with two attendants in black clerical garb trotting after. On seeing Shane, O'Donnelly kicked his heels to the flanks, and galloped up beside him.

"They are going, then!"

"So they are! We're holding here, so as to avoid incident. I wouldn't like to see this fine day marred. You'll soon have your Cathedral back!"

SHANE O'NEILL

"I will."

"You had the right of it, as usual, Turlagh. This is all owing to a wee cask of Chateau LaFite. Her bungling assassin has shamed her into honouring the Accords!"

"Those Accords are not sealed! And there's little honour to be seen as yet! Have they commenced the trial of Smith?"

"Not at all, man! The Lord Chancellor Cusack has writ me a fine dispatch. You'll want to read it! He has even recounted her Majesty's words for my edification! A grand effusion of blather and fuss! He confides that she took a weakness when she was told of the deed. Collapsed with the vapors -no doubt because it had miscarried!"

"And what of the Nuncio?" Shane's voice deepened with concern.

"There's been divil-all word. Nor from our Myler in Rome!" The Dean nodded gravely.

"I've a letter arrived last night from Wolfe. It's just as we expected; he is taking measures to oppose us. We'll need-"

Suddenly there arose a great cheer on the hill. The final wagon was loaded full, and its wheels at last lurched forward to join the rest, creaking and grumbling along behind the line of sullen Infantry, as they marched off to the east! The jubilant crowd parted now before O'Neill and his men, who trotted jauntily up the hill to the great doors of the Cathedral. Behind Shane and his soon-to-be Primate, rode his officers and his chief mason, MacAteer, followed by a contingent of stonemasons, joiners, and artisans, all eager to commence their work. After dismounting, they ascended the stone steps, where Shane turned and spoke briefly to the crowd of 'a new beginning'. They would salvage and repair the Cathedral, he said, and restore ere long all that had been lost in Ulster. And holy Armagh would once again shine forth as a great city of learning!

The damage that had been wrought inside the ancient church exceeded everyone's expectation. The nave was a jumble of makeshift wooden structures, mostly for billeting, with smashed bunks piled into corners. The shattered stained-glass windows had been bricked up, but for their lancet peeks, and there were rickety catwalks up along these

SHANE O'NEILL

'gunports'. Several brick fireplaces had been constructed. The Sacristy, having served as galley and scullery, was verminous and infested with rats. The altar had been gutted to accommodate long planked tables and forms for mess. All *that* was as expected. But the deliberate desecration within the holy edifice was shocking. Precious statuary was smashed, saints beheaded, and the few paintings that remained of the blessed virgin had been marred and 'used for profane purposes'. Priestly garments and vestments, too, had been defiled. All were aghast.

The men were still reeling from these discoveries, when a breathless curate called them outside to inspect the Cathedral Close, where Shane's forefathers, the Kings of Ulster, were interred. The churchyard was a shambles. The stone-cross monuments were hacked and smashed, and a row of privies had been dug beside them! Shane's face flushed with rage upon seeing this, an anger that left him speechless, and the Dean wisely coaxed him into adjourning to his office at a nearby friary. The masons and artisans were left to plan the restoration. The chieftain and his hard-riding Dean galloped over the hills, and oaths were flying as Shane vented his fury over the defiling of those sacred graves.

At the Drumadd friary, O'Donnelly firstly decanted for the chieftain a generous measure of Port, to put him in better heart. Then he showed to Shane the letter he had received from the Papal Nuncio. In it, Wolfe castigated him for 'having *accepted* the elevation to Primacy by an heretical Queen', a thing he knew most explicitly had *not* been done. But here was a clear indication of the line of deliberate distortion that would already have reached Rome. Wolfe wrote that he would certainly *not* provide a commendatory letter for the Dean as Shane O'Neill had requested. He had himself put forward a worthy candidate, already in Rome. This was none other than his Limerick colleague and friend, Fr. William Creagh. He cautioned the Dean to spurn the traitorous designs of the Northern chieftain, and to beware his wiles, lest he should be led into heresy. Although he had clearly acquired 'fine English and education', he must not forfeit eternal salvation for earthly ambitions unbecoming his merit! The letter did little to sooth Shane's temper.

"By Christ! The cunning scoundrel! All that Myler has said of Rome

SHANE O'NEILL

must surely be true, if the Pope has taken this slimy serpent to his bosom! A jumped up sallowjack from the englishtown of Limerick! I've not heard back from Myler this while, but he'd best be hard at it!"

"But surely we *knew* that David Wolfe would oppose me!"

"The Pope should be saying a Te Deum for what I have accomplished! I have induced the Queen to deny a protestant heretic his claim to the Primacy of Ireland! In favour of a *Roman Catholic*! Brought an end to rival claimants for the See! By Christ! What more could he ask?"

"That is what they must hear! To counter this poison out of Limerick. More letters. We need to dispatch more letters. The Papal Legate, Morone, is away at the Council of Trent. He was appointed to oversee all our Episcopal candidatures. We must enlist his aid. He could over-ride his Deputy in Rome. And he could render the Nuncio powerless!" In spite of these resolutions, he saw utter dejection in O'Neill's eyes, and thought to venture a more promising note. "We don't know! Perhaps Myler Magrath is making some headway there. His letter is bound to come soon, please God!"

"Aye, please God! T'would please *me* well enough!"

"It's the Chancellor's letter that I should like to see. You've brought it with you?"

"I have, aye." Shane extracted the much-folded missive from a small leather pouch, and handed it to the cleric. "They've captured John Smith, and they suppose I should be thankful of that!" O'Donnelly moved to the window. The glory had departed from the weather, and the room was fairly dim. He stood with his back to the sombre light, reading down the page. "Och, read it out, man! I think it must surely be meant for my amusement!" The Dean laughed quietly at this, glad of O'Neill's restored humour, and giving due credit to the fine Portwine for it. He cleared his throat, and obliged him.

"Her Majesty has directed me to look into the matter very closely; She begs *you* to produce every proof in your possession that might assist in the detection both of the party himself, and of all others that were anywise thereto consenting; to the intent none might escape that were parties thereunto." The Dean raised his eyes and laughed. "You *might* produce the hundred-odd witnesses who *saw* it!"

"I've sent down the double cask. But, sure, it doesn't bear 'Ardbracken' writ large in golden letters, so it will hardly stand as evidence!" O'Donnelly nodded, and with a wry smile, he continued on.

"Herewith are her very words unto the Lord Deputy Sussex: 'We have given commandment to show you how much it grieves us to think that any such horrible attempt should be used, as is alleged by Shane O'Neill, to have been attempted by Thomas Smith to kill him by poison; we doubt not but you have, as reason is, committed the said Smith to prison, and proceeded to the just trial thereof; for it behooves us, for all good and honourable respects, to have the fault severely punished! And so we will and charge you.' And thereby, O'Neill, you may see some measure of the distress suffered by our most noble Queen for your own sake!" He peered up at Shane to see his response.

"And *I* thinking it was *myself* was aggrieved! Ah, God love her! She'll need to find a new poisoner now!" The Dean grinned, and read on.

"To mine own self she has writ thusly: 'We assure you the indignation which we conceive of this fact, being told with some probability by you, together with certain other causes of suspicion which O'Neill has gathered, has wrought no small effect in us to incline us to bear with divers things unorderly passed. And to trust to that which you have, on his behalf, promised hereafter in time to come."

"What in the name of God does *that* mean?" The Dean drew in a big breath, as he shook his head, and then huffed, short and quick.

"She trusts the Chancellor to wriggle her out of it. But why does she say *'Thomas'* Smith? Was it not John Smith?"

"She's too distressed and concerned to learn his name. Or perhaps he has a partner. Perhaps it was Lord Thomas *hooring* Smith! Och, damn the wee messenger! And damn his trial! For Christ's sake! Lord Sussex attempted to slaughter a score of my councilors, and myself! Upon the Queen's orders! What care I for their judicial jackacting!"

"It's astounding! No more than a charade. They lie. They *know* you're aware of it. But always they demand complicity in the lie!"

SHANE O'NEILL

"*That* is a thing they'll not get from Shane O'Neill. The trial is a fraud! Let them go to the Devil!"

When Shane returned to Benburb Castle, he was surprised and relieved to find that Myler Magrath's letter was waiting for him among the scrolls and folios on his great desk. The letter was in Irish, and his secretary, Garret Fleming, read it out to him, as was his practice. Shane sat in his massive chair of carved oak, sipping at a goblet of Port, and nodding slowly here and there at the monk's tidings.

"O'Neill, My Lord and brother,

I pray this letter finds you well, and enjoying the fruits of your triumph over the enemies of our people.

Were the Pope and his Curia truly guided by spiritual concerns, my mission in Rome would be brief and undemanding -but Mary pity us! -in the bustling halls of this Vatican Palace, political intrigue is all. It differs not one whit from machinations of the English Court in Whitehall of recent memory. So much so, that it behooves me to request of you more silver for 'gifts'. These 'princes of the church' are not to be swayed by trifles. It is Rome of the Caesars still, and politics is foremost. I suppose putting our foster brother Turlagh forward is 'a brilliant stroke of policy', in that light, but as he is a wise and a devout man, loyal to the Pontiff and yet acceptable to England's heretical Queen, his preferment *should* require little exhortation or blandishment. But that is precisely what will be needed, and you may be assured that I shall do all in my power towards that end. And if intrigue be the way of it, I shall not be found wanting!

As you surmised, Wolfe is busy about procuring the office for his own client. That is, another scion of a wealthy Old-English merchant family out of Limerick, a Fr. William Creagh. What we did *not* expect, is that Creagh has been piously pursuing the episcopal seat of Armagh

SHANE O'NEILL

since his arrival in Rome in early October of last year, nearly two months prior to Archbishop O'Tighe's martyrdom -May God rest his soul! While affecting humility and reticence, Creagh arrived with letters from Wolfe and his Jesuits urging the Holy Father to deprive O'Tighe of his See and Primacy, and to recall him to Rome. Wasn't it a great boon to him, that Donagh was called to God just then, with the ready assistance of English Inquisitors in his own city of Limerick? I am making discreet inquiries in this regard, and I'll keep you apprised.

Creagh has the full might of the Jesuits behind him, which, I assure you, is formidable indeed. I was surprised to learn that our man David Wolfe is a protégé of Ignatious Loyola, the Order's founder! I am told, also, that the Provincial, Lainez, has censured our friend Bishop Dequadra in London for his letter advocating the Dean's preferment. King Philip then directed him to spurn such overtures from 'seditious Irish lords'. Now, I find that he has been recalled to Spain! Such is the power they wield!

Father Creagh is loathed by the Irish hereabout, for he is aloof to them. He consorts generally with the English Catholics who abide in great numbers here to press their cause. He keeps four servants, and there are two Jesuits ever at his side: another Limerickman, Fr. Edmond Daniel that was one time Éamon O'Donnell, and is said to be a cousin of David Wolfe. The other is a priest from Somerset called Fr. Goode. This man never ceases to disparage the mere Irish, although he speaks familiarly of Limerick, and of the Countess of Desmond with whom, evidently, he has had some dealing.

Creagh, himself, is a wispy ascetic little fellow with eyes like a nun, who eschews both meat and wine. A dreary Catholic puritan! He speaks of 'the northern savages', and of the supreme duty of loyalty to the Queen. If he prevails, may God forbid, we shall soon have an enemy of our own beloved Church of Rome!

As to the causes that brought me to the Eternal City; I feel certain that you will have your annulment, barring interference. The cause for delay is the enactment of rigorous new strictures by the Council of Trent, but Cardinal Morone himself assured me that the Pope would like

SHANE O'NEILL

to gratify you in this matter. Possibly, I fear, to soften a denial of your brother's claim for the See of Down and Connor. The objection is his age, and again, they are loath to be seen in breach of the new solemn enactments of the Council, but I'll wager that Creagh had a hand in this. I will continue to press his cause.

I must close, and dispatch this letter, for my courier sails upon the next tide.

> Your loving brother in Christ,
> to serve your command,
> Father Myler Magrath, Rome

Sombre grey clouds blanketed the heavens on Christmas morning, and snow was falling upon the ancient cathedral. Perched on its lofty height, against the white hill and the frosty winds that blew, its high gables loomed dark and imposing over the town of Armagh. But as the crowds approached, they were cheered to see that its windows, so long bedimmed, shone with warm yellow candle-glow to welcome them back, to welcome them home.

The short spire above was still only a conical wooden frame, and scaffolding towered against its walls, but St. Patrick's 'battered aul fane' had been deemed sufficiently ready to house the Blessed Sacrament, and to be restored to Divine Service in time for the holy feastday. Ulster's chieftains, and gentry, had all journeyed over the far hills to join the faithful of Armagh for the re-consecration of the fabled church.

A solemn procession began the rites, and St. Patrick's 'Bell of the Testament' was rung to the four winds. Holy Benediction followed, and the ancient ritual, the fervid congregation, the array of flickering candles, the spicy redolence of wafting incense, and the strains of gentle music all conspired to infuse the vaulted temple with a powerful and ethereal spirit. Most transporting was the music, for in the freshly painted choir-loft, the Augustinian nuns of Fertagh and the Franciscan friars of Drumadd mingled their voices in sweet Gregorian hymns -and hymns older still! They were led by their distinguished Chanter, Fr Patrick Dorell, under the guidance of two venerable old monks, Rualán and Niclás MacGillamurry.

The musical brothers were known locally as 'the last of the Culdees', for their order numbered no more than eight votaries. The Culdees were the original holy order founded by St. Patrick himself, who recruited heavily from the Druids. It was they who illuminated the splendid manuscripts during the Dark Ages, and their ways had changed but little since. Rome had forsaken this Celtic rule in the twelfth century in favour of the continental orders, and these unyielding few at Armagh were the very last in Ireland. Their specialty was music, in its purest Irish tradition, and the Christmas renderings on this cold morning would be long remembered. The mysterious ancient airs, and the mellifluous voices intoning them, seemed to dispel from the vast chamber any vestiges of those dark powers so lately banished. All this made for an inspiring and uplifting celebration of High Mass, and, for the war-weary Ulsterfolk, the ancient ritual gave form and grandeur to their deep feelings of restoration and deliverance.For Shane O'Neill, the exultation over the Cathedral's recovery, a momentous occasion to be sure, was tempered by a sobering awareness of the tenuous nature of this peace. In Dublin, the windstorm of deliberations over Captain Smith continued to gust, 'all idle winds and hot air', it was said, 'that would soon blow over!' As no-one was dead, there could be no question of murder; as Smith claimed he acted alone, there could be no implication of the Lord Deputy. Outrage on the Continent, and even among such men of conscience as might be found in London, was counted for naught, and, notwithstanding the Dean's promising expectations, the Crown brazenly defied any attempts to uphold its dubious honour.

There was another troubling development. An emissary from the Lord Deputy had come to Benburb Castle that very week bearing the Indentures of Drumcree, signed, at last, and affixed with the great Seal of State. But there was roaring red fury when it was discovered that they

SHANE O'NEILL

bore little resemblance to the terms that Shane had accepted. Once again the Dean argued patience and forbearance. The balance of power that had dictated those terms still obtained, he advised. The Queen had agreed because she had little choice, and she would do so again for the same reason. His arguments prevailed as usual.

'Dean Terence Danyell', as he was known in London, wrote a lengthy dispatch to the Lord Secretary, closing with a concise account of how matters stood. "O'Neill intends to perform the peace concluded with the Lord Chancellor, but he finds fault that the Queen's letters patent do not agree with the articles of peace subscribed by him and Cusack; and he requires that they be confirmed as they were writ, verbatim. He requires, further, that his creation as Earl of Tyrone be accelerated." The Dean added that he would draw out of the Irish chronicles the pedigrees of the O'Neill, and send them forward to the Palace.

In addition to this, Shane dictated to his secretary a short letter for the Queen, requesting that she prevail upon the Pope to honour her appointment of a papist bishop to the Primacy of Ireland for the sake of peace and the unity of Christendom. He assured her that once he was created Earl of Tyrone, and Terence Danyell made Primate of All Ireland, she would have naught but peace and dutiful service in Ulster. Having thus replied to the altered Accords, O'Neill and his council could take their ease to partake in the revels of Christmastide. Clearly, nothing could be determined in these weighty matters until there was new word out of London.

The winter was fiercely cold. It was said that 'its like had not been seen nor heard of by any man living!' Shane spent the time with his counsellors, making plans to order the province. New Brehons were appointed to resume the quarterly circuit in time for St. Brigid's Feast. MacAteer and his army of stonemasons, having restored the Cathedral,

SHANE O'NEILL

would have plenty of work come spring. A new castle was to be erected at Fathan, to control the land passage to the Newry. And other sites were being considered. It would be a time for building.

With the long awaited relief of February's thaw, Shane O'Neill's thoughts turned to the West. Elizabeth's armies had gone; peace prevailed, and his cousin Black Hugh O'Donnell was urging Shane make good on his promise, the pledge to confer upon him the reins of power over his own people in the vast lands beyond the River Foyle. His half-brother Cullagh was still O'Neill's prisoner, pending arbitration according to the new treaty. He had, however, agreed to all of Shane's harsh terms: a ransom of jewels and plate, title to the long disputed peninsula of Inishowen, the release of his father, Manus O'Donnell, who was imprisoned in Lifford Castle, and, most importantly, the transfer to O'Neill of Lifford Castle itself. The possession of that strategic fortress would leave all of Tirconnell at Shane's feet.

In spite of Cullagh's orders, on this last demand his son refused to yield. Even forsaken, as he was, by the English at Drumcree, and even at the cost of his father's release, he would not relinquish the castle. Con's own ambitions were not to be discounted in this bold stand, for already he and his turbulent cousins were contending to usurp the chieftaincy from Cullagh.

Now word came out of Tirconnell that spurred Shane O'Neill's resolve to settle these matters decisively, and to bring his full force to bear upon the O'Donnell's dispute.

The warm winds of spring had not come soon enough for old Manus O'Donnell. The father of the warring half-brothers, Cullagh and Black Hugh, had died in the tower of Liffer Castle, where he had languished for eight years. A scholarly chieftain, Manus was lauded for having written 'The Life of St. Colmkille' in Latin. The man was for a time Shane's uncle, and he harboured a fondness for him.

In any event, Manus's death marked a turning point, and on hearing this news, Shane called a hosting of his troops. For nearly three years, Cullagh O'Donnell had languished in his dungeon on the isle of Inishdowal near the shores of Lough Neagh. Now, at last, O'Neill freed

SHANE O'NEILL

him of his shackles for the journey back to his Donegal home. But the weary chieftain was returned to his people shamefully, escorted by O'Neill, the man who had cuckolded him! Once Shane's formidable army crossed the Foyle, Cullagh was released to his people who were gathered at the ford of Lifford to await him. Among them was his cousin, the Archbishop of Killala, who had come to console and counsel him.

Black Hugh had kept abreast of the events at home, and among his warring nephews he had partisans who were willing to intrigue for him. Cullagh's son, Con O'Donnell considered himself the natural heir to the chieftaincy, and he had mustered his forces to attack a rival cousin, Hugh McHugh O'Donnell, who had taken possession of Donegal Castle. Con was unable to prevail in this until he convinced two other cousins, Ennahan and Con Mór, who were members of the garrison, to betray the castle into his hands. All went according to plan, and the garrison was surprised and easily vanquished. Thereupon, Con and his men celebrated their victory, as was customary, with a carouse of several days.

Now, in that betrayal, Ennahan and Con Mór were carrying out orders from Black Hugh, and sending him word of all that transpired within the walls. And so, in the midst of the merry debauch, when Con and the boys were footless drunk, the castle was once again surprised, this time by Shane O'Neill and Black Hugh O'Donnell. Ennahan and Con Mór opened the gates as before, and the victors became the vanquished. With this handy bit of double-dealing, Black Hugh was rid of both his young rivals, and Con O'Donnell took his father's place as Shane's prisoner. It was boasted by O'Neill that this was the second O'Donnell he had managed to take without a drop of bloodshed.

The young man had no choice now but to surrender Liffer Castle, and that he did, but his garrison would not comply. The importance of this castle lay in its command of the one and only place where Tirconnell could be entered from the east without boats. Upstream the Foyle is deep and turbulent, and below, the broad tidal estuary is treacherous, but Liffer is always fordable. Shane, having time at his

SHANE O'NEILL

disposal, laid siege to the fortress. He invested the place with a force so large that they stripped the country bare for miles around, and finally starved the garrison into surrendering the castle. Black Hugh put his own garrison within, and then assumed the chieftaincy of the O'Donnells, but with the addition of an oath of vassalage to the O'Neill. After due celebration, Shane rode eastwards with his army, satisfied that he had put an end to the turmoil, and secured the West of Ulster with a trusted ally at his back.

"We have surrendered LeHavre, with no promise of Calais! Let us hear no more of that swindling treaty! What other troubles have you, Cecil, to addle our head withal? What are these worrisome tidings you spoke of?" Accustomed to it as he was, Elizabeth's prickly mood made the Lord Secretary's duties exceedingly tiresome, and he replied with some apprehension.

"Throckmorton has writ also to say that the three Irish bishops who attended the Council at Trent-" Her eyes flashed fire. "Upon its dissolution they have appeared at the French Court, where -in despite of his most *ardent* reproval- they have been received with high honour. There they have accused your Highness of complicity in the poison attempt upon O'Neill, and raised *much stir* withal. He pleads for us to bind up these matters in a timely and beseeming fashion, lest they should further hinder his labours on your behalf."

"Irish bishops! Lying papish swine! See that they all three be captured upon their return, that they will answer for their treasonous slander! What of Smith's trial, then? Throckmorton is right. Justice must be swift, else tongues will wag, and fools will clamour."

"Indeed, your Highness. But *time* is also known to bind and mend." In spite of discomfort owing to his gout, he smiled reassuringly. "Sir Thomas Cusack writes to advise that strictest silence be our policy in the matter. Smith has endured imprisonment, lo, these four months now. He

SHANE O'NEILL

has wisely owned to his culpability, bearing sole guilt in the poisoning affair. But as no-one has *died*, there is no law to punish the offender other than by imprisonment, which O'Neill would little regard –He has said he cares not for the proceedings, except the party might be executed by death, and *that* the law does not suffer. And so as the matter being wisely pacified, it were well done to leave it."

"Leave it and do naught? *Naught* was done this morning, and naught was done yesterday, and still this matter is before us! Come, Cecil, what is to be done?"

"Mine own opinion is to enlarge him, forthwith, that he might hie unto England. That being done, the affair would give place to newer gossip on the wagging tongues of that kingdom, the sooner to be forgot!"

"That is wisely said, Lord Cecil." With a wincing frown, and a soft voice, Elizabeth suddenly chided him. "Will you cease this fidgeting! Why do you stand like a ninny, if your gout be ailing you? Sit you, dear Cecil, and be quick!"

"I thank you, m'Lady." He drew a chair up beside her desk and sat. "And has Lord Sussex conveyed *his* advisements as to Smith?"

"Lord Sussex remains indisposed at Ardbracken."

"He is out of temper. As *we* are out of patience. You may inform him that upon his return to Court, we shall appoint him to our Privy Council. That may soothe his wounded vanity, for therein lies his distemper. The ordering of that cursed kingdom has o'erstepped the grasp of many before him. And Arnolde is doing *little better*. How fares his scheme of temporizing with O'Neill?"

"There is much news out of Ulster, your Majesty. O'Neill has at last released Cullagh O'Donnell from bondage, upon terms mutually agreed. The-"

"We do rejoice to hear it! Arnolde's policy may yet bear fruit!"

"The Countess of Argyle has *not* been released, and it is said that she is yet again with child by O'Neill's usage, and nearing her time."

"She is a fool -if it be true that she devised her abduction! And he has befooled her again. Does she *know* that O'Neill seeks the hand of Frances Radcliffe? Oh, for a countess to bear such disgrace! Could she e'er be so witless?"

"Belike his pursuit of Lord Sussex' sister is unknown to her. But it is

SHANE O'NEILL

most queer. By those acquainted with her, she is counted very sober, wise, and no less subtle. She is not unlearned in the Latin tongue, speaks good French, and as is said, some little Italian. If it was a reckless fancy, she has surely come to rue it!"

"Is her husband restored then in his lands?"

"Nay, he is usurped. Shane O'Neill has led his army into Tirconnell, where he installed O'Donnell's brother Hugh as chieftain of his clan. He captured Cullagh's son Con, and now holds him prisoner in his father's stead. The Chief Justice makes little of this, saying that O'Neill is simply 'about the ordering of his province in her Majesty's name."

"Arnolde makes little of *much*! There is grave danger in letting O'Donnell's country fall under the power of O'Neill. We have yet to see if his good words are more than air!"

"If Black Hugh be true to his O'Donnell blood, he might be easy prized from O'Neill's keeping. His woeful brother, Cullagh, bereft of wife and wealth, has made his way to Dublin to seek redress. He is accompanied by his cousin, the papish Bishop of Killala." He nodded to his folio. "Arnolde gives full account of his supplications, *and* of the cold rejoinders they begot. He says that-"

"Nay, then, we would hear of it. *As* he has writ." Cecil withdrew the letter from his sheaf, and brought forth the second page of it.

"Upon his arrival, he was received with such outward marks of respect as were due his station, but Bishop O'Gallagher was stayed in an outer chamber. Crediting the Chancellor's good counsel, I gave O'Donnell naught but fair words, and a letter to O'Neill bidding him to use his new prisoner well. Still, he remonstrated with me, until it behooved me to make it plain to him of his position. I reminded him that no O'Donnell ever did come to the Governor for service, but only to crave assistance. His grandfather never came but to ask aid when banished by his son. And *that* son was in turn banished by his own self. As for the woeful tale of his usage at O'Neill's hands, I reminded him that he imprisoned his own father for eight years, offering him neither mercy nor clemency, nay, nor is *he* alive to make complaint of it. I spoke it plain that he has reaped what he has sewn, and now he can go to the

Turk." Elizabeth tisked. "Upon hearing my words, O'Donnell burst out into such a weeping as when he should speak he could not, until his interpreter was obliged to pray license to weep, and so went his way."

"Was this man not our loyal ally at the time of his misfortune?"

"Indeed, he was pledged to support our assault upon O'Neill, and was awaiting an earl's chain for his promise of service, your Majesty!"

"Arnolde was *ill*-advised! If we be seen to spurn our loyal captains when they are undone, we shall *have* no loyal captains!"

"Most like, he is trying to spare your Majesty the man's woeful entreaties at Court. He has forbid O'Donnell to come to England, but adds that the man is determined to go to the Queen with, or without, license, and if necessary, by way of Scotland."

"Let him tell O'Donnell that we would see him at Court, if it would do him some good -but that the causes between him and O'Neill must needs be tried in Ireland, and apart from our fond condolence, we do not see what he might gain by the journey."

"Shall I convey to the Lord Justice your Majesty's rebuke? -For his ill usage of a loyal captain?"

"Nay, we shall withhold such word. Some part of this was just deserts, and might serve to temper O'Donnell's *future* entreaties. But Arnolde listens too close to his Chancellor!" The Queen laid her palm across her brow, and closing her eyes against the world, she heaved a deep sigh. "-As mayhap *we* have done! For Cusack advised *us* that appeasing O'Neill would induce him to banish the Scots out of Ulster. Instead he has crushed our allies in the West!"

In March came the distressing, if by this time expected, news that the Nuncio's candidate, William Creagh, had been granted the Pallium in Rome. Both the See of Armagh, and the Primacy of Ireland were conferred upon him when he was consecrated in the Sistine Chapel on St. Patrick's Day, precisely as Donagh O'Tighe had been four years

SHANE O'NEILL

previously. Myler related that he himself had been appointed by Morone to be 'special assistant' to the new Primate, the Cardinal being unaware, of course, that the two men cordially loathed one another. Fr. Magrath assured O'Neill that this position could be advantageous in undermining any of Creagh's enactments that might adversely affect him. The news of Creagh's appointment was met with resentment in Armagh, where it was seen as repudiation of not only their beloved Dean, but of O'Neill himself.

Katherine was delivered of a third son 'in the lambing season', just as her two before had been. He was given the name 'Brian', and joyous celebration attended his Christening in the restored Cathedral of Armagh. Shane was overseeing the construction of his two new castles, so he was away to Inishdowell, or down to Fathan much of the time. Upon his insistence, Dean O'Donnelly, having duly sent to London Shane's pedigree from the chronicles, wrote twice more to the Lord Secretary. He inquired as to the delay in procedures for 'Lord O'Neill's peerage'. Cecil's reply was evasive, but in early summer Shane received the 'unofficial' response, by way of a letter from Sir Robert Dudley.

Dudley wrote to say that he now served on the Queen's Privy Council, and was hopeful of his own peerage, very likely before the Christmas. He advised Shane to do 'some notable service' to her Majesty, and suggested in the strongest terms that he fulfill his pledge to banish the Scots out of Ulster. Such 'evidence of good faith' would surely mend the pace of the proceedings, and earn for him a place in the House of Lords. As it happened, Shane was finding himself under increasing pressure from his own people to fulfill that pledge. The O'Kane and the MacQuillan had called upon him to honour the terms of their vassalage, and put a stop to the Scottish encroachment on their lands.

The very notion of keeping 'good faith' in a pledge made to his unsuccessful assassins was met with a bitter laugh. But the Scots settlement in the Route and the Glens was now the only part of Ulster not under O'Neill's control. The MacDonnells had proven themselves unreliable allies, and a useful tool in the predatory designs of the English. Always, he knew, a final reckoning with the English lay ahead, a battle beyond any thus far, hopefully with help from the Continent. The Scots were encumbering, a threat, always, to his course of action. With any inducements from London, these redshanks would double the Crown forces in such a clash. Perhaps now was the time to sweep them from the board. How auspicious that Katherine's father was at war with the MacDonnells, for that would prevent any 'connubial repercussions'. As for the English, they would likely assist, and reward him with his earldom. From this time, 'Dudley's request' would never be far from Shane's thoughts.

The change of regime in Dublin had inadvertently shaken loose some of the cozy arrangements that sustained local potentates and clerics, those who operated outside the officially sanctioned channels of power. Among those unsettled was the Papal Nuncio himself. Various compromised officials in Limerick, upon whom he depended, had been replaced or were superseded by appointees of Arnolde and Cusack, and the papal agent found himself in ever-deepening peril.

In May, the Pope issued a Bull, *Dum exquisita*, empowering Fr. David Wolfe and the new Primate to erect a Catholic university and seminary in Ireland with all the privileges of the Universities of Paris and Louvain. The Jesuit Provincial, Lainez, considering that the Church was free from proscription only in O'Neill's Ulster, ordered Fr. Wolfe to repair to the safety of that province, where he might carry out the Pope's wishes. With the gravest misgivings, for he was convinced of the 'savagery' of Ulster's Gaelic inhabitants, the Nuncio made his way north. Now, to wield his authority in Armagh without first presenting himself to Shane O'Neill would have been impolitic, not to say 'dangerous'. O'Neill's permission and help would be crucial. And so, on a lingering evening in late June, the Pope's envoy, with his several clerical attendants, called at the gates of Benburb Castle.

SHANE O'NEILL

Shane was taken quite by surprise when his extraordinary visitor was announced. He was entertaining his erstwhile messenger, Robert Fleming, who had just taken office as the new Lord Mayor of Drogheda, with all the Fleming brothers and Lord Slane joining the usual roster of guests. It was a jovial celebration, for Robert's election was due in no small part to his association with O'Neill, and marked a swell in support for the northern lord within the Pale. Drogheda, being staunchly Catholic, harboured a fierce resentment over what was perceived as the martyrdom of Primate O'Tighe.

Dinner had been cleared away by this time, and the convivial hum of voices stilled at the herald's stunning pronouncement. In the silence that followed, the approaching footsteps could be heard, until, there, before the great arched doorway stood the Papal Nuncio like a dark spectre in his black soutane, flanked by his attendants. His grim countenance was jarring, and the steely glare under his 'jutting' black brows seemed to suggest that he had discovered the company in some untoward business. All looked to Shane, and as he rose to his feet, they followed suit. The princely host smiled broadly, and extended his arms before him, saying in Irish, "We are honoured to welcome the representative of His Holiness, Pope Pius IV, into our company!" He added in Latin, "Please come, your Reverence, and take the place that is due you, here at our side!" This was followed by robust applause from the clearly relieved gathering

Fr. Wolfe nodded, and responded in Latin. "Allow me firstly to extend unto those present the Holy Father's most ardent blessing. 'In the name of the Father, and of the Son, and of the Holy Ghost. Amen." He then proceeded to the head table, while his attendants were seated among the Franciscans. The Dean of Armagh stepped forward to greet the Nuncio, and to usher him into O'Neill's presence. Shane called for food for the new guests, and gave a sharp wave to the crowd, at which they resumed their conversing, enlivened now by curiosity at this unexpected arrival. A goblet of wine was put before the Nuncio, which he cautiously accepted. On being introduced to Lady Katherine, Wolfe nodded, curling his tight lips in a mirthless smile, but he said nothing to her. He turned instead to Shane, and spoke sharply about the personal affairs of the Desmond FitzGerald.

"Perhaps, O'Neill, you would write to your cousin Garret of Desmond! He must be brought to his senses, and to his duties, for his profligate behavior threatens the peace of the whole province of Munster."

"What has Garret done now?"

"Since his return from the Tower of London, he has taken up with a young woman in *flagrant* adultery, causing his wife untold distress and heartache. Lady Joan worked unceasingly to effect his release from the Tower, and now he is flaunting this young mistress before her. A woman half her age! She is *inconsolable*, and her health is failing. Her son, Ormonde, is threatening war." He cast a glance at Katherine, cold and quick. "But, of course, you are hardly in a position to admonish him, or, indeed, to counsel him in such matters! A great pity! The untamed passions of the mighty are apt to bring great ruin unto the meek!"

"*Is* it a pity, then? Surely it is *your* duty to give spiritual counsel to Desmond! And just as surely, it is none of mine!" Wolfe was then asked of his journey, and the smallest of small-talk ensued, with sharp glances being exchanged around him. Finally Shane asked of him just what it was that had brought him into Ulster, and to this Wolfe replied, "Matters of education, principally, and the reforms of the Council of Trent. But certainly all of this will keep until the morrow. Perhaps you will accompany me to the Primatial Cathedral?"

When the Nuncio had finished his late supper, and listened patiently to several songs in Irish, he excused himself and retired. He left with Terence Danyell a copy of the Pope's Bull, which was eagerly accepted. Upon his departure, merriment was restored to the hall, with much speculation as to what David Wolfe's purpose might be. Farleigh suggested that he had come to gloat over his checkmate in the matter of the Primacy, and to sniff out the ground for his 'Wolfe in sheep's clothing', Archbishop Creagh. The new Primate was expected to leave Rome in the coming weeks.

On the following day, after a concelebrated Mass, the Nuncio

SHANE O'NEILL

inspected the restored Cathedral, flashing quick eyes into every corner under his taut black brows. "It's all very well, but it is quite bare of icons and blessed images -like a Protestant prayer hall! Are we to follow the heretics in this too?" Shane scowled, and looked to the Dean, who replied in an easy measured tone.

"Alas, all the blessed treasures of this church were destroyed and defiled by the English, your Reverence. I have asked that such statues as are hidden in the Pale might be secreted unto us here to glorify the Cathedral. Thus far we have acquired only the altar screen, and the Sacred Heart, and such as you see, but more will come. These things take time. I'm confident that the alter will be nicely adorned when Archbishop Creagh arrives."

They then proceeded out onto the steps of the Cathedral, and at last the Nuncio's business was broached. With a stern reprimand for both Shane and the Dean, Wolfe remonstrated about the Primatial dispute. Much to Father Wolfe's displeasure, it seems that matters were still moving forward in London to affect the transfer of the Protestant Primate Dr. Loftus to Dublin, and to appoint Terence Danyell to the See of Armagh. The Nuncio made no attempt to soften his words. "This heretical outrage must stop! It must stop! Are we to have the Babylonian Captivity here in Armagh? *Three* primates? One for Pope, one for Queen, and one for the petty-chieftain of the realm! You must disavow these measures at once! And make plain your adherence to the Holy Father's decision -*and* your acceptance of his *sole* authority to make it!" Terence looked to O'Neill, whose eyes were aflame, and he replied calmly.

"You have been misled, your Reverence, if you believe that the Queen of England or her ministers look to us in Armagh to decide such matters. However, if she *should* choose to remove Dr. Loftus from this See, for whatever misapprehensions she may hold, then there shall be but *one* Primate of All Ireland, as consecrated by the Holy Father in Rome. And *that* is a fortuity much to be desired. Neither I, nor Lord O'Neill, have voiced *any* misgivings as to the Pontiff's decision. On the contrary, I have-"

SHANE O'NEILL

"You have been *acting* as Primate in this Cathedral, and encouraging the laity to regard you as such! I have had reports!" "Indeed, I have been acting in his stead, as those are *precisely* my duties as Dean of Armagh. The Primate remains in Rome, and the Church's business must be attended to."

"Enough dissembling! I am aware that a Conge d'elire has been handed down to the Chapter of Armagh to anoint you, Terence Danyell, to the chair of Armagh, and the Primacy of Ireland!"

"It is true, Father Wolfe, that such has been sent to them. But the Chapter is resolved to ignore it, as a usurpation of a Papal prerogative. We have uttered no word here against the Holy Father's decision."

Shane uncrossed his arms, and stepped forward, towering over David Wolfe. "*I* will voice *my* objection to the Pope's decision. *You* are a *messenger*, Fr. Wolfe. -That *is* the precise meaning of the word 'nuncio'. The envoy of a foreign Prince *within* my realm, on my sufferance, and under *my* protection! But fear you not -for you will hear my objection as plainly as I can make it. His Holiness has appointed to the Irish Primacy a man who advocates loyalty to a *heretic*. And should that Queen prevail, Dr. Creagh will earn for himself a *martyrs crown* for his foolishness! Were it not for *my* resistance to the heretics, and my triumphs over their forces, there would *be no* place in Ireland where the Pope's ministry could be carried out, and *no* occasion for this discussion. Now, *in* his ignorance of Irish affairs, his Holiness has surely made his best effort at reaching a proper decision. His disastrous choice was made at *your* behest. And you, David Wolfe, have no such excuse to absolve you of your part in this."

"You dare to defy his Holiness!"

"I am the O'Neill. And I dare as I might. I am certainly prepared to defy a *messenger*, regardless of whomsoever has sent him to my door. Now, I shall spare you an apology, your *Reverence*. The Dean tells me that you have been sent *to seek my aid* in establishing a seminary here in my lands. If that be so, I will hear of it." David Wolfe stood stock-still and silent, breathing heavily through his nose, his 'jutty' brows twitching with suppressed fury. Terence spoke up, in a calm assured

SHANE O'NEILL

voice.

"Perhaps we had best adjourn to my office, where we can discuss the Holy Father's wishes. It is a bold initiative, your Reverence, and one that will be welcomed here in the capitol of Tirowen. Armagh has much to gain by such a plan!" He bowed respectfully to his superior, and led the two adversaries to a tiny office in the old Culdee priory just below the Churchyard wall at Castle Street. A curate set three goblets of portwine before them, but the Nuncio would have none of it. The men were seated, and as the Dean read it out, each clause of the Papal Bull was parsed and considered. Shane and Terence both found the document to be strangely naïve, but they were enthusiastic, if cautious, and things went smoothly until the matter of finance was raised. The university would be empowered to 'apply the revenues of *all* monasteries, and of benefices, and to make use of *all* ecclesiastical properties." When Shane questioned Wolfe on this point, he was told that these were 'hardly matters for his concern.'

"All of these revenues most properly belong to the Bishop of Rome, and are merely administered, as he suffers them to be, here within the diocese. This university is no local undertaking. Its purpose-"

"-Then why will local revenues be appropriated for it?"

"*Its purpose* is to provide training for priests to minister in *all* parts of her Majesty's kingdom where the Church is under proscription, in place of the Continental colleges."

"Training for *England*, is it?"

"For *all* parts of the kingdom. Including the English Pale of Ireland. His Holiness hopes to restore all the kingdom to the Holy Faith.""To restore *England* to the Church. *Ireland* has not *left* the Church. And how will English scholars fare in an Irish college? Will they learn the Irish, Fr. Wolfe?"

"What? Learn the *Irish*? Most certainly not. A *university* instructs in Latin. His Holiness is not proposing to conduct a bog-school in the Primatial City. And such a seminary will *not* graduate men ignorant of the King's English. It will be administered in English. You are aware of this, surely. And you suppose I do not know mockery when I hear it to

SHANE O'NEILL

my face!"

"Your 'English university' is a mockery to this holy city, Father Wolfe. Armagh has been the centre of learning in Ireland since St. Patrick established the Church here –*centuries* before we were able to convert the savages of England to the Holy Faith. Let you take your 'university', David Wolfe...and let you undertake to found it within the English Pale, where the writ of your sovereign Queen runs unchallenged. As you are her loyal subject to command, it is surely beneath you to defy her here among the outlaws of the North. Ah, no...Use the benefices of the Pale to found your university, or the treasure of Rome." The Nuncio's face was now contorted in undisguised loathing.

"I fear you have o'erstepped yourself *this* time, Shane O'Neill. You are in defiance of his Holiness, and you shall be shunned by the sovereigns of Europe! You shall answer for-"

"Get along with you, now, Messenger. You have delivered your message. You see, I too am beholden to my sovereign -*by solemn treaty*, and if you stay within my realm beyond tomorrow, I *may* be bound by conscience to turn you over to the Queen's deputies. You may convey my warmest regards to Pope Pius IV. Tell him I have restored the Blessed Cathedral that the English destroyed. It will be here for his Holy Primate when he comes to us from Rome. Archbishop Creagh will have the support of the O'Neill, *so long as* he confines himself to his religious duties. If he meddles in politics, and proves a traitor to my people, he will feel my wrath. Those are my words to carry with you. And *that* is the road south."

It was not until July that the new Primate, Dr. Creagh, set off from Rome for Ireland. He was accompanied by his two Jesuit companions, Fr. Edmund Daniel and Fr. William Goode, with four servants on heavily laden donkeys who trailed behind. Also at his side was his 'special assistant' in Ulster, Fr. Myler Magrath. The four horsemen were no more than fifteen miles outside of Rome, on the dusty road to Assisi, when Myler pulled up his reins and called the party to a halt. He had left important papers behind, he said, and would have to return. He promised to reconnoiter with the Primate at Louvain, the seminary in Belgium where Creagh had got his training. Despite the half-hearted appeals of his companions, who found this most curious, Myler would not be swayed, and he turned back. On seeing him galloping off to Rome, Creagh heaved an airy sigh, for, in truth, he was glad to be relieved of the Ulsterman's company, and the three could now converse more freely.

The papers in question were not Myler's. He took himself to the office of Cardinal Gonzaga, who acted as Morone's deputy while he was at Trent. Myler told him that there were papers needful to the Primate among Morone's folios. As expected, he was obliged. One letter of interest turned up, with words of a dubious, or possibly incriminating, character. This he tucked away for Shane. He did not, however, find what he wanted. In the end, he concluded that certain letters would be in the keeping of Creagh himself, to be ferreted out when the opportunity might present itself.

Myler had another affair to attend to, the one which he had not been at liberty to confide to William Creagh, the business of Lady Katherine's annulment. It would keep him in Rome for some time, but he was delighted to hear that this mission would be blessed with success. The Roman Rota had decided to grant the annulment, pending only formalities. Myler had further cause for joy, for his dealings with high-ranking Cardinals at this time brought promise of his own elevation to new dignities within the hierarchy.

By late summer, Shane had set his masons to work on two more castles. The island where he had kept O'Donnell, Inishdowell, offered not only a pleasant prospect, but also the added security of insularity, and in the event of a final clash with the Crown, it could serve as a more remote base of operations than Benburb. Due north of the great Lough, Drumtarsey Castle stood in ruins on the west bank of the Bann, overlooking the little village of Coleraine on the other side. O'Kane's people had been run off of those lands across the river, and new Scottish settlers were digging their heels in. These Scots watched uneasily, as the old O'Kane castle rose again from its ruins on the far bank, and Sorley MacDonnell posted a small sentry to keep a hawk's eye on the proceedings. It was possible that O'Neill was merely fortifying his northern frontier, as he was doing at Fathan in the South, but the rising battlements could have a darker meaning.

It was nearly September when Shane learned through Katherine of James MacDonnell's detainment in Edinburgh along with her father. The Duke of Argyle was attempting to press a settlement on the two warring chieftains. This would leave only Sorley to contend with in Ulster, and O'Neill decided it would be advantageous to strike swiftly, and surprise him. Even the weather was propitious, with a lingering dry spell, for the Bann was a difficult river to ford at the best of times. Dean Donnelly insisted, however, that Shane procure a written endorsement of the campaign from the Lord Justice before he commenced, lest Arnolde might feign indignation after the fact.

This precaution would mean a delay, but such perfidy was hardly beyond the administration, so Shane wrote to Arnolde and to the Privy Council of Dudley's 'request' from London. He said that as he could see no greater traitors or more dangerous rebels to the queen's authority than the Scots, he was 'disposed to inflict some signal punishment upon them.' Arnolde's reply was swift. Four days later Shane got word that he had the full support of her Majesty's Council, although they regretted being unable to offer him provisions out of Carickfergus, as he had requested. They would not contribute, but they would be most gratified to accept his victory over the Queen's enemies, or, as Shane said of the Queen, 'She'll glory in MacDonnell's defeat, but she'll begrudge *me* the

SHANE O'NEILL

victory!' In truth Arnolde and Cusack were most anxious for this assault, as it would vindicate their reversal of Sussex' policies.

Along the rocky coast of Antrim stand three high promontories, the headlands of Torr Head, Crockanore, and Benmore. On each of them Sorley kept a pyre in readiness for kindling. He had only to put the brand to them, and his signal fires would be seen in the Scottish isles across the Sea of Moyle. In six hour's time, a fleet of galleys filled with armed redshanks would reach the shore. To stay those brands, surprise would need to be a key element in the assault. As a precaution, Shane called his hosting in the far west of Tirowen at Castle Corcra, in the village of Lisglass on the River Srule.outside of Strabane. He assembled nearly a thousand men, and with no further delay, he led them forth to begin the fifty-mile journey east.

Barely a few miles had they put behind them, when the weather took a dark turn, and Shane cursed himself, *and* his cautious Dean, for having awaited Dublin's approval. Fierce rains set in, and the ride east proved daunting indeed as they wound their way through the hazel and scrub, along the rough horse-track that was known as 'the Northern Road'. The hours bore on, and the long line of cavalry encountered more and more runoff from the mountains, with the ways submerged under gushing streams, an ominous token of what lay ahead. Still the hooves of the thousand horses thundered over the rough terrain under the lash of teeming rain. Night was falling when at last O'Neill's weary legion approached the mighty river. Through the dark dripping wood came the unmistakable roar of the raging swell. The River Bann was in full flood, a seemingly insurmountable obstacle that would render all the day's hard riding a vain and bootless endeavor.

The army pitched camp beside Drumtarsey Castle, which was near to completion and roughly furnished. Waiting there was the chieftain Fergus O'Kane with his brothers, and in their company was the intrepid Dean of Armagh. They immediately accompanied Shane and his captains up onto the battlements to see what might be done.

Directly across from the castle, on the eastern bank of the river below the Scots, stood the ruins of an old Dominican Friary. All were agreed that it was the right place, the only place, to get a foothold across the raging waters. The ruins themselves were not without meaning. The Dominicans had been driven out by the English in '42, after Conn

SHANE O'NEILL

O'Neill was defeated at Bellahoe, and, for Shane, its crumbling walls were a prickly reminder of his father's disgrace. Just beyond these ruins was the new Scotch settlement, where there was no movement to be seen but the low drift of smoke from the chimneys as it dissolved in the grey rain. Not a stir. All were likely huddled by their fires, waiting for the deluge to subside. By the look of things, the Scots were unaware of the mighty host across the river. Night was falling, and the O'Neill and his men repaired to the warm fire of the great hearth below.

A number of the local fishermen thereabouts, kinsmen of the O'Kane, had gathered at the castle. These men stood to regain their lands, and they were eager to cast in their lot with O'Neill's men. The river was fierce wide here, they said, nigh on a quarter mile across, and wider still in the surging flood. Only boats could make a crossing. They had 'naught but wee cots', small hide-bound coracles for fishing, but with luck, they would have all night to transport the army. There were close on to thirty boats, and it was determined that even now, as dusk turned to dark, they would begin ferrying the troops across the river by twos and threes. If the storm should lift in the night, 'please God', the river would fall quickly, and the rest of the army might ford it in the morning.

The humble flotilla had managed three crossings by morning, and the dim and drizzly day was heralded by gunfire, as a barrage of harquebus attacked the friary ward. Evidently O'Neill's forces had been noted upon their arrival, and runners had been sent off to raise the alarum, for here was Sorley Buí's force of nearly seven hundred newly arrived. They descended upon Shane's advance forces, who were now trapped in the ruins by the raging swell. The Tirowenmen battled bravely for hours to hold their ground. Dean Danyell's account told of ninety casualties that morning. He said, "The Scots attacked the outpost like madmen! They lost many men, but succeeded in killing all the defenders, save the few who swam the flood." Sorley MacDonnell himself was wounded in the shoulder. With all hope of surprise lost, and little hope of crossing the Bann, Shane brought his army north, where he laid waste to a scatter of Scottish settlements that found themselves on

SHANE O'NEILL

the wrong side of the river. He then made for home.

Sir Thomas Cusack penned a rapturous account of Shane's doings for Cecil, praising him lavishly for his commendable work on the Queen's behalf. This consisted of his having swept with fire and sword over those stray Scottish settlements west of the Bann, all of which he described in the very terms that had been used to recount O'Neill's 'outrages' against the Maguire only a year before. Indeed, now that he was 'the Queen's O'Neill', the customary reports of his savagery gave place to a glowing picture of the dutiful liege, who fed the poor at his gates before he took meat. Shane himself made little of the setback at Coleraine, ascribing it not to the prowess of the Scots, but to the elements of Nature. But spring would not be long in coming, and, 'come weather mild, or weather wild,' he would drive them to the sea!

SHANE O'NEILL

CHAPTER 25

"Oh, indeed, there is much amiss, Lord Sussex, but t'were best to temper somewhat these complaints to Council. You are but newly welcomed home, and I will commend you this caution." Cecil lowered his voice, peering up from his paperwork. "For the present, her Majesty is loath to hear ill of Sir Arnold. She holds hope still that the governor's temporizing will bear fruit."

"Ireland yields no other fruits to her governors than disgrace at home! I stand but the latest to attest this woeful truth"

"Come, Good Thomas. There is no disgrace in being summoned to sit in Council. I should think *relief* would attend such a promotion! Should you but refrain from this shrill tirade in Council, her Majesty is disposed to confer upon you the high dignity of lord-chamberlain. Now. Won't you be so good as to take a seat?"

"Thank you, m'Lord." Sussex seated himself before the Lord Secretary's immense desk, which was arrayed with carefully sorted sheaves and letters. "But the Council cannot counsel wisely if they be blind to the willful impolicy of Arnold's government. He has sought to defame all English-born ministers, to subvert all measures that have born goodly effect, surrendered on all counts to the Queen's enemies, whereby great disorders have arisen! And greater peril may ensue!"

SHANE O'NEILL

"But yet there is quietness in the North under O'Neill's rule-"

"*If* he be *unhampered* in his villainy, his villainy shall proceed in quietude. But such is not *peace*! And if the North be in quiet, the midlands are in an uproar, with great stirs risen in the English Pale by the FitzGeralds, the O'Connors, and the O'Mores of Leix and Offaly. All are giddy at the fall of Sussex! The loyal are undone, and the rebels ascendant! Wherefore would they keep peace? In the West, Thady O'Brien and his brother assail the Earl of Thomond for the captaincy of their sept, and now Desmond is at their side. The Earls of Ormond and Desmond are on evil terms, with war sure to follow -and it is Arnold's favour of Desmond stands cause."

"*They* have been at odds since Desmond wed Ormond's mother. Indeed, that rancor has smouldered for generations!"

"But hark my warning! For I tell you, my Lord, it is *about* to kindle! South, and East, and West, the O'Tooles, the O'Byrnes, the O'Reillys, the Kavanaghs, and other loose people must needs be suppressed! As her Majesty's soldiers remain unpaid, the expedition against them will be neither honourable nor profitable to the Queen. My brother, Sir Henry, and Marshal Stanley pursue them, with but little support from Arnold and Cusack, and they regret that such matters grow so chargeable unto her Majesty's purse. All for Arnold's 'temporizing', Arnold's '*tampering*'! Now, 40,000 pounds will not suffice to restore Ireland to the tranquility it was in but two years ago!" Cecil sat back in his great chair, with a challenging smile.

"The Earl of Kildare writes to *commend* Sir Arnold, and gives good report of the midlands campaign. He is most fulsome in his praise!"

"Wherefore would he do else? Kildare has come to favour in Dublin! Indeed, *all* those now within the Castle are minions of the Queen's favorite, and all my supporters turned away. Robert Dudley has captured the Irish government! To pursue his own nefarious designs! His faction wields all power there. And now, this ambitious stablemaster is made - *Chancellor of Oxford*?' Cecil nodded trenchantly. "And created Earl of Leicester, and so is eligible to wed the Queen. Heaven forfend! I fear that golden chain about his neck is but prelude to a crown!" This assertion brought a laugh from the Lord Secretary.

"Paaah! If it be a crown, 'twill be a *Scotch* crown, with a sceptre of thistles." He continued in an amiable confidential tone. "Good my Lord Sussex, you have been away from Court! Dudley is raised up, like a worm baited to a hook, so to lure and catch Mary Stuart. The Queen has made an earl of him only that she might offer him to her cousin, that ill-luck may attend them both! He *cannot* wed her Majesty. Nay, not since poor Amy took her spill at Cumnor Place." He lowered his voice still further. "It has been 'whispered in shadowy inns' that it was the *Crown* she tripped upon, and sent it rolling 'cross the board, never to fall within his grasp again. The misfortunate woman was dying of a virulent cancer in any event, so she was but hastened to her end. A deft and artful device to hobble the horsemaster! And, of course, to protect the common weal. But who could be so devious?"

"Walsingham."

"Who can say? Not I. Nay, nor you. But, as for Ireland, if it be Dudley's conniving responsible for the northern quietude, her Majesty will hold it to his credit! She will hear *only* good report. The Dean Terence Danyell tells of peace and order in Ulster, with all kinds of husbandry and sowing of wheat. And the Chancellor Cusack roundly concurs. He is rapturous in his letter...if it be not mislaid." He found it close to hand, atop a small stack of correspondence, and read from it with an ironic glee. "Ah! 'Because of the Dean's preaching and Shane's ordering, that part of the country is much the more reduced to good order, so that no other part of the country is so well ordered at present, whereas every man may live by his own, in such sort as merchant-men and all others may pass through the country with their merchandise or any other thing without fear of robbing, by day and night, which is rare to hear the like!"

"We must be thankful that such tall tales be rare!"

"And so too, our newly fledged 'Lord of Leceister' quotes his chaplain at Oxford in praise of O'Neill." He quickly produced another missive, the next in the pile. 'Shane orders the North so properly', he says, 'that if any subject could prove the loss of money or goods before

SHANE O'NEILL

his Brehons in Tirowen, he would surely force the robber to restitution, or *at his own cost* redeem the harm to the loser's contentation!' *All* this, my Lord, her Majesty accounts as owing to the overturn of *your* policy there. So have a care! She will be gainsaid only to your cost, to your *further* grievous cost! Now that O'Neill has engaged the Scots, Arnolde is proved aright, and all that went before is folly."

"The Scots! A piffling little skirmish! At Coleraine?" He looked in disbelief to the Lord Secretary's nod. "His army most explicitly failed to cross the Rubicon! He turned at the Bann, and fled north to harry a few far-flung *cottiers*. 'Engaged the Scots' say you?"

"Blood was spilt - Danyell tells of ninety casualties for O'Neill -such as will beget more bloodshed come the spring. Arnold assures her Majesty that the war is commenced, and bides only the turn of season. Cusack is most keen for the war –but I think he wields his quill with a wont of discretion not proper to a Chancellor." Cecil methodically plucked out two more letters from a shief. His eyes skimmed down the page. "I am with all the wild Irish at the same point I am at with bears and banddogs when I see them fight; so that they fight earnestly indeed, and tug the other well, I care not who have the worse." He looked up to Sussex, expectantly.

"Even as I loathe him, I could ne'er dispute such words!"

"That is not to say that *I* could leave them unchallenged! List you- 'Your letter shows you to be of the opinion that many wise men are, from the which *I do not dissent*, being as an Englishman. But being as a Christian man, I cannot without some perplexity enjoy of such cruelties." Sussex laughed, and wagged his finger at the Lord Secretary.

"Ah ha! And still you 'do not dissent'. Nor, indeed, do you disown your *enjoyment* of these cruelties; only that you do so with 'perplexity'. A masterful quibble, with just a sting of rebuke! Doubtless Cusack's head is spinning still! His words are merely boldshow, an echo to Nicholas Bacon, who lauded Elizabeth's princely policy to weaken the Irish by division and disunion. Cusack's *own* policy is to *strengthen* them! -By yielding all and sounding quick retreat. Even the harbours of Ireland are perilous on his watch." Cecil nodded.

SHANE O'NEILL

"The accursed pirates!"

"Pirates *everywhere* off the coast -since my displacement. In Dublin Bay itself, ships are preyed upon by sea-rovers that lurk in great numbers on Lambay Island. The havens of Cork and Kerry are *full* of English pirates, who keep a roaring trade with Irish chieftains in their booty." Sussex' eyes lit with sudden alarm. "You *know*, I suppose, that Stukeley is in Kinsale?"

"Lusty Stukeley is back on the Irish coast? Nay, I had no word of it."

"I heard it from Captain Phettyplace, the buccaneer –Stukeley has with him an armed ship of 400 tons like the Man o'War! He calls it devilishly 'The White Dove'! On it he keeps a hundred tall soldiers, besides mariners! And what, I must ask, does my Lord make of *that*?"

"The colony is abandoned." At Sussex' look of wide-eyed wonderment, he explained. "Nigh on two years ago, her Majesty was induced to embrace Stukeley's mad scheme for a colony in Florida. I'm sure the prospect of *his absence from Court* highly commended the scheme to her. He staged an elaborate –and costly- naval pageant for the queen, a mock battle on the Thames before the royal barge, to show her Grace the thrilling pleasures that can be got fighting the turbaned infidels, with playing of drums and trumpets and all. In the face of her ailing treasury, my efforts to dissuade her came to naught. She relented, even unto granting him five ships for his fleet of privateers, demanding only a half share of the booty. Evidently the colony is in shambles, and the Spanish have run him off! And now, the Crown is assailed by France, and Spain, and Portugal to make restitution for his countless plunders. - Is he *lately* seen at Kinsale?"

"I spake with Phettyplace but two days before I sailed."

"I shall instruct the Admiralty to dispatch a fleet to capture him. There are charges aplenty, and he shall answer for them on the dock -or the gibbet- if we are to quell the complaints from the Spanish King." Sussex folded his arms, and added to his tale with smug satisfaction.

"Furthermore...Phettyplace swears that Stukeley sent a shipment of arms to Shane O'Neill at Carlingford, through the local chief Maginnis."

"Does he? Does he, indeed?"

SHANE O'NEILL

"Doubtless it was done *in quietude*."

"Belike Phettyplace is *himself* the source of that shipment! Queen Mary of Scots is relentless in pursuing the demands of the Wigtown merchants for restitution of *their* ship. It was looted in Carlingford Lough by O'Neill's men, and Maginnis, and such. And *Phettyplace* was named to be among them! We can but hope that his sighting of Thomas Stukeley is not willful misdirection. But *if* it be true, e'er long, the rogue may meet the rope!"

The new Primate and his retinue finally departed Rome. He endured two months of hard travel to reach the port of Antwerp. On the journey north from Innsbruck, he was stricken with fever, and obliged to rest for a week in Augsburg before moving on to Cologne. It was a harrowing ordeal, as the plague was a constant menace all through the Germanic States and even in the Lowlands. Dr. Creagh lingered for a time at Louvain among old friends, scholars and Jesuits, as he awaited his wayward assistant's arrival from Rome. Among the English exiles in his company there was John Clement, physician and former tutor to the children of (St.) Thomas More. Richard held a banquet for his former colleagues, at which he appeared for the first time in his canonicals of powdery blue cambric. It was a pleasant interlude from his arduous journey, and staved off for a time his growing sense of unease regarding what lay ahead.

Several letters reached the Primate in Louvain, including a rather curious one from Cardinal Morone's secretary, Fr. Polanco. In it, he commended the industry and diligence of Creagh's assistant, Fr. Magrath.

"This native Ulsterman will be of great usefulness to your Excellency as a suffragan bishop'. Fr. Magrath has gone to endless trouble to locate the documents relating to your appointment in the Roman files, and is now on his way to present them to you in Louvain." As such papers were neither requested nor required, nor had the Primate heard anything of Magrath being made a bishop, he wondered at this news, but supposed hopefully that it was merely a misunderstanding.

Upon his arrival in Antwerp, Dr. Creagh happened upon six Irish sailors on their way to Mass, a most providential meeting, for they told him that they were sailing for Ireland within the week! Such auspicious harmony of purpose surely signaled divine guidance and protection, and this bolstered Richard's courage. Fully three weeks later, on October 18th, the ship set sail for Ireland with Fr. Creagh, Fr. Good, Fr. Daniel, and their three servants on board.

The Primate's Jesuit companions had both been enlisted to help him set up the new university in Armagh, and that mission occupied their thoughts and prayers as they embarked on the voyage. The galleon had barely put to sea, however, when the skies darkened ominously, and the seas swelled. Soon fierce tempests and contrary winds, despite the passengers' most ardent supplications to the Almighty, drove the vessel ashore at Dover.

Creagh was grievously shaken by the ordeal, for it called to mind the very incident that had inspired him to enter the priesthood. In his prior career as a merchant it happened that, as he was about to return from a trading expedition from Spain, he slipped into a dockside chapel to say a prayer. A Mass was in progress, and he stayed until the last Blessing, whereon he found his ship had sailed without him. While it was still in sight, the vessel was struck by violent gusting of wind and foundered with all hands on board. The 'miracle' of his being spared that day had imparted to him an overwhelming sense of destiny. And a wariness of sea voyages.

Creagh refused to wait in Dover with the others for clear sailing, vowing that he would never board that vessel again. He told of a premonition of 'the occurrence of some evil to him' should he take that voyage. He resolved, instead, to accompany two merchants in their hired carriage who were bound for London. From there, he proposed to set out for Chester, where he could surely find a ship to cross the Irish

SHANE O'NEILL

Sea for Dublin. With him he took his white pallium, several documents attesting to his conferral, his hoard of twenty-seven sacred relics, balsam for sacramental chrism used in annointing, and six robes of blue camlet. All that his servant could not carry, the bulk of his belongings, were left aboard in the care of Fr. Good who declined to accompany him for fear that, as an Englishman, he would be recognized in London.

Good and Daniel were obliged to wait another three weeks for the voyage to resume, but when at last the winds availed, the crew did not! The Irish mariners had likely reached unfavourable conclusions about the attitude and intentions of this Jesuit, for, although they had been first encountered on their way to Mass, they refused now to take aboard this man who was 'an Englishman and a priest'. The captain instructed Fr. Good to find some other means of following his Superior to Ireland. Creagh's baggage was released to him, and a small sum was given him for his journey.

As they passed through Kent, Richard Creagh's merchant friends made a brief stop in Rochester, and while they were about their business there, he struck up with an Irish beggar, a poor scholar named Florry O'More. The Primate hired him on as a second servant, and the young fellow was soon perched atop the coach as it rolled on along the road to London. Once there, 'Sir William Creagh' took lodgings for the three in Broad Street at the sign of 'The Three Cups', and spent several days exploring the great city. Like any pilgrim, he headed for the spires of Westminster Abbey and St. Paul's Cathedral, and was rapt with wonder at the grandeur of the metropolis.

Nonetheless, Richard found the city troubling, for the talk everywhere was of the arraignment of the Bishop of London for *praemunire*, that is to say, upholding the claims of a foreign court over those of the Crown. The issue was Rome, of course, and he was himself liable to such charges. After three days, with deep foreboding, the weary Prelate took to the road again, bound not for Chester, but for the port of Bristol with his two manservants. More storms and adverse winds detained him there through mid-December, but, at last, a week before Christmas, his ship came to anchor at Howth Head on the northern

SHANE O'NEILL

headland above Dublin Bay.

The two Jesuits, meanwhile, had set out for London on foot, with their servants, much encumbered with the Primate's belongings. They were nearly three weeks behind him. Irish contacts in London gave word that Creagh had set off for Chester, for Richard had deemed it prudent to conceal his true destination. This precaution sent the reverend fathers off on a fool's errand, eight days of wintry footslogging, only to find in Chester no trace of their quarry. It was five weeks before a ship could be got to Dublin. The two arrived penniless and exhausted, and it was here they parted ways. Fr. Daniel headed west to Limerick to report to his cousin, the Nuncio, and Fr. Good set off for Armagh, hoping to meet Dr. Creagh at his ultimate destination.

On the fourth of January, a bitterly cold and snowy day, Fr. Good, accompanied by his servant, called at the Cathedral of Armagh, asking for Dr. Creagh. Dean Danyell was summoned, and greeted the Englishman warmly, but could give him no word of the new Primate's whereabouts. The Jesuit was disconsolate at this turn, although he was somewhat relieved to encounter, finally, in this vast wasteland, a man with the King's English. After a trencher of stew at the fireside, and a short rest, Father Good was provided a fresh cloak and a swift horse, and the Dean accompanied him to Benburb Castle to call upon Shane O'Neill.

It was late afternoon when they were ushered into Shane's keep. As there were two days left of the Christmas, the chamber was bedecked with holly and ivy. O'Neill was seated at the fireside with Katherine and his children. There was her young brood of three, as always, and Shane's eldest daughter, Moraed, who was visiting with her new husband, the son of the Maguire. The two lads Éamon and Turlagh were playing 'fidhcheall', a native Irish form of chess, with its silver against gold. Introductions were made, and Fr. Good reluctantly accepted a flagon of mulled cider, as he cast a hawk's eye about the room. He smiled tightly at the young children and asked them about Jesus and the manger, but as they had no English, they giggled and looked to their mother. Shane tipped a wink to young Éamon, and he answered for them in bright

SHANE O'NEILL

Latin. The English priest 'corrected' his Latin, but that was the end of the catechizing. When the priest had given the children his blessing, their nurse shepherded them off, leaving the elders to their business.

Shane explained that he had gotten neither word nor warning of the coming of Dr. Creagh, and that he thought it likely that he had been delayed, that Fr. Good had simply beaten him to the post. He suggested that the priest stay until they could get news of the Primate's whereabouts. With that, he dispatched a messenger to Fleming, the Lord Mayor of Drogheda, who was usually first with news from the Pale. Good was filled with dread that Creagh had been captured in England before he ever reached Chester, and he regretted, now, having departed without him. Even in his remorse, however, he could not forbear to correct Shane's Latin usages. The Dean quickly advised the visitor that such forms were proper in Ireland, where Latin was more widely known and used than in England. This was met with a frown and a 'tisk'.

Father Good recounted the difficult journey from Rome, and then began explaining to O'Neill, as to a child, about the Pope's new university in Ulster. The proud Jesuit was surprised to find that Wolfe had preceded him, and was certainly taken aback to hear that the seminary would have to be established not in Ulster, but in the Pale, or in the city of Limerick, either of which seemed quite impossible. He himself was to be Rector of this university, and he was greatly affronted.

Shane assured him that Richard Creagh would be welcomed in his See, but he repeated the warning he had given the Nuncio regarding political interference. The wary priest could see that if there would be a welcome for the Primate, it would be a chilly one. Indeed, he took a decidedly dim view of what he regarded as the insolence of a petty chieftain, who bore hostility towards the shining beacons of both Rome and London. He determined to leave the next morning for Limerick.

Pleading exhaustion then, Good retired early, leaving the others to ponder over the fate of the new Primate. But before he snuffed his candle that night, he scratched a long entry into his journal, enumerating the bestial and brutish ways of Ulster, and declaiming the rudeness of O'Neill's court. While he noted that so many of the Irish

SHANE O'NEILL

spoke Latin as a second tongue, he lamented that 'their Latin, even in those who would like to be considered learned, is most barbarous and disagreeable, if you do not make the same grammatical mistakes and use incongruous forms of speech'. Displeased with his accommodations, he declared that the natives 'are unaccustomed to the use of bread, wine, beer, or beds.' He could abide there no longer but was 'bound for Limerick, away from these barbarous parts, and must make [his] perilous way through deserted places, savage people extremely hostile to the English, woods, wolves, marshes, snow, frost, hunger, and thirst.'

The dour Jesuit was given a horse the following morning, and with his servant he departed after saying a low Mass in the chapel. He was not so very long gone when the messenger returned from Drogheda with his momentous news. Fleming's sources were privy to confidential information in the Pale, and the messenger gave a full accounting of what had befallen the new Primate.

Richard Creagh, on his arrival in Ireland, had made his way north, and three days after Christmas he reached a Franciscan Friary near Dundalk, where he announced his presence and proceeded to celebrate Mass. No sooner had the last bells jangled, and the Primate pronounced "Ite Missa est," than the doors burst open to the sudden rumble and clank of marching troops. They advanced swiftly up the aisles, and Creagh was seized unceremoniously with barely a word spoken. His two attendants were identified and taken. It was only then that the commander appeared. It was Sir Nicholas Bagenal, the squire of vast holdings in the Newry, and a former Marshal of the Queen's forces.

As Creagh was being shackled, he commenced to pray loudly and tearfully in English, his pale green eyes glistening, luminous, in a kind of rapture that infused his pallid visage with an aura of sacred passion. The friars began to pray with him in a mesmeric chant. All was suddenly overtaken by the crash and crack of halberds and swords upon the altar. The altar-screen, statues, candlesticks, and tabernacle were rent and smashed. The sacred hosts that remained in the chalice were cast onto the tiles and trampled underfoot. Creagh was taken to Dundalk, to await the arrival of Bagenal's brother.

SHANE O'NEILL

A vociferous opponent of Rome, *Sir Ralph* Bagenal would glory in the capture as a victory over the dark powers of Satan. The Captain himself was satisfied with a badly needed victory to bolster his flagging military career. He had lost the Marshalcy under Queen Mary's brief Catholic reign, and this prize capture might help him to regain it. His zealous brother, distrustful of the accommodating policies of Arnolde and Cusack, insisted upon accompanying the Captain to Dublin to see that the miscreant was prosecuted with due severity. The brothers Bagenal, then, delivered Dr. Creagh and his two servants to Dublin Castle, where they were imprisoned.

It was said that the Primate had been betrayed by 'one of the country', and Fleming's messenger intimated that it was a monk from Armagh, a partisan of O'Neill and the Dean, that had tipped the word to Bagenel's men who happened to be patrolling the area. It was as well, perhaps, that Father Good had departed by this, for O'Neill's hall was the one, the only, place in all Ireland where this woeful tale was met with boisterous laughter! It was held to be a sorely needed lesson for the new Primate on the value of loyalty to England, and on the reward that such folly would beget!

The winter was cold and bleak, more white than wet, but Ulster was at peace, and it was a time for mending and building. The word from the South was of turmoil, and before the warm winds of spring would blow, Shane was to lose an important ally. On the second of January, Lady Joan of Desmond died at Askeaton, as some said, of a broken heart. After her unremitting efforts had managed to secure the release of her young husband from the Tower of London, the bold Garret had taken up with a young one, flaunting her shamelessly before his wife. Lady Joan languished in her humiliation, and succumbed ultimately to despair. His paramour was Eleanor Butler, a cousin, no less, of his bitter enemy and stepson, the Earl of Ormonde. Black Tom was overtaken by grief and fury to see his mother so ill-used, and without Lady Joan to keep the peace, war was inevitable. Before the month was out, Garret brazenly married his young bride Eleanor, and armies marched.

The pretext for the clash was provided by a dependent of Desmond. This vassal, holding territories along their mutual border, suddenly renounced his fealty to Garret, and declared his allegiance to Ormonde. Black Tom was behind this, a deliberate move calculated to make Garret attack first, so as to effect the Earl's ruin. Garret FitzGerald duly mustered his forces at the Black Castle of Lough Gur, and marched them east into the Decies of Waterford to coerce his rebellious leigeman. Ormonde mobilised his men to intercept the Geraldines at Affane, a ford over the River Finisk in the foothills of the Knockmealdowns, and there the battle was enjoined. In the fiery exchange, Ormonde's brother hit Desmond in the right hip with a musket-shot, cracking his thigh-bone and toppling him from his mount. With their captain fallen, the Geraldine forces were soon routed, and the Butlers pursued them to the bank of the Finisk. About 300 Geraldines perished, many of them drowned as they were intercepted by armed boats in crossing the river.

As the captive earl, Garret FitzGerald, was being carried shoulder-high from the field, his enemy, Black Tom Butler, rode up and taunted him jubilantly, "Ah, the great Lord Desmond! Where is *now* the great Lord Desmond?" Whereupon, Garret retorted, "Where, but in his *proper* place? On the necks of the Butlers!" The simple exchange was never to be forgotten.

Affane is said to have been the last battle fought between two private armies in the British Isles. Each side flourished the standard of their dynasty, and that defiance of Royal authority infuriated Elizabeth. "The Queen's sword," she said, "shall touch the guilty. And no other shall be drawn!" As the House of Ormonde shared her kinship through the Boleyn line, there was little question as to who would bear the blame. Garrett was arrested, brought before the Privy Council on a litter, and imprisoned once again in the Tower of London. John of Desmond, his brother, assumed command of the vast earldom. He would prove a

SHANE O'NEILL

far less dependable ally to Shane O'Neill.

For three weeks Richard Creagh was held in Dublin Castle, and, as Bagenal suspected, the Viceroy Arnolde was inclined towards leniency. This Sir Ralph Bagenal would not abide, and he railed in Council against papal supremacy and the evil designs of the Council of Trent. He wrote immediately to the Royal Court, and managed to effect the Primate's transfer to London on a false promise of 'mere legal formalities and an expeditious release'.

Creagh was initially held in comfortable quarters within Sir Robert Dudley's manse, but after an 'unsatisfactory' first interrogation by Lord Cecil, he was marched from Westminster under guard, and confined in the grimmest dungeon in the Tower, known as 'the whale's belly'. For a month he languished in the dark cell, sleeping on damp straw. Due to the efforts of a sympathetic guard, he was moved, then, to a cell with a high narrow window to avail of such murky light and air as might reach him there.

The Primate underwent three more interrogations there. In each of these, Creagh was forthright and unguarded, and some less charitably inclined might say 'indiscreet', as he named everyone in any way involved with Roman Catholic resistance. When asked, "where does the Nuncio commonly keep in Ireland?" he reported, "he does secretly come to Limerick, and has been this past summer in Tirowen with Shane O'Neill." He felt that if they but knew of his deep and abiding loyalty to the Crown, the authorities would leave him unhindered in his work, and therefore responded candidly about his mission in the written statements. He was cunning enough, however, to suggest that the next papal appointment might not be so loyal as he.

"I was sent by obedience to Ireland...and sent for to dwell and serve among barbarous, wild, and incivil folks in

SHANE O'NEILL

Ulster, having nobody before me there that ever beforetime I was acquainted with. The Pope thought convenient to send some kind of letter with me to Shane O'Neill, with a letter also for a pension to be given to his brother on the bishopric that the priest aforesaid [Magrath] requested in Rome for the said brother, which priest feigned to come at once with me to Ireland, but tarried nevertheless there.

I knew not whether Shane O'Neill should repute me for his foe, or for his friend, firstly because he had made persuasions in Rome and at Trent for to have that Archbishopric of Armagh for his foster brother, who is Dean there. And secondly, because I made not my devoir in Rome in procuring the bishopric of Down and Connor for Shane's brother, a young man unlearned, ignorant of English, not passing 23 years old.

If O'Neill or any other should give some help for erection of some schools wherein youth should be brought up in some good manners and beginnings of learning, I should wish it; thinking earnestly that long ago they should have forsaken their barbarous wildness, cruelty, and ferocity, if their youth were brought up in knowledge of their duty towards God and their princes. As for erection of any university, I am not so ignorant but that I know it cannot be done without the aid and authority of the Queen's Majesty. As for any other friendship or conversation with the Ulstermen, I intended to shun it while they should live that are brought up in such all kinds of iniquities, murders, adulteries, drunkenness, robbing, stealing, foreswearing, and other like, without any punishment to be spoken of.

My poor power, from my youth hitherto was always spent to serve the Crown of England, as of nature and duty I was bound, knowing –and also declaring in diverse places- the joyful life that Irishmen have under England, if they were good and true in themselves. Howbeit, if I should die today, and on my death the Archbishopric of Armagh should be procured from Rome for

SHANE O'NEILL

some *other* of that country, may it be for one to whom God give grace to be true to his natural Queen and Crown of England, whom the Lord God maintain now and ever."

Given his rhapsodic nature, the rigours of his confinement brought Creagh to a pitch of feverish piety, and he was most often rapt in prayer or lost in transports of penitential extacy. In the latter end of March he was moved to a more comfortable cell, reflecting a shift in the attitude and intentions of Lord Cecil towards his prisoner, but the Primate's spirits were not acalmed. He later recounted the last days of this incarceration in terms that reflect his state of mind. Firstly he recalled being disturbed by the sight of a bird that flew into his cell. Unable to make its way back out through the bars, the bird plumed its feathers and then escaped through the window. The next night while he slept, a 'loud Pentecostal noise' emanated from his room, and in the morning he found 'signs of a disturbance'.

The following night Creagh's dreams were most queer and vivid. The dead to whom he had granted a special indulgence appeared there in his cell, and led him out of the Tower. Upon waking, he knelt and said his office, but was unable to finish, so distracted was he by thoughts of escape. He rose from his knees, and tried the door of his cell. With utter amazement, he found it to be unlocked. He quickly rolled his spare tunic in a bundle, clutched it under his oxter, and faced the door that stood ajar before him. Terrified now at the actual prospect of escape, Creagh froze, and considered what might befall him should he be caught, perhaps harsher confinement. Or torture. But the signs, the portents of Divine guidance were compelling, and he could only proceed through the open door. He spoke later of being 'led like St. Peter' through the unfamiliar passageways, wherein he encountered seven more doors that each yielded to his touch. At the Tower's gate, however, the hulking, but jovial, Beefeaters demanded of him a password.

As Creagh later recalled, the curious question posed was "Hoy, mate! Where is your butt? Show forth your butt!' meaning a target for archery (presumably!). Creagh was tongue-tied, with no answer to give, but the guard laughed, and said it was bundled under his arm. He was then asked whose servant he was, and he named a priest of high birth who was held under easy restraint. The jocular guardsmen laughed again, "Very well! Be off then!" and so he was let pass through the high gate. The Primate spent three fearful days skulking about the city. To avoid detection, he spoke French when spoken to. Creagh's hair and beard were so fair as to be called white, and he felt most fortunate in that the description given forth of the escapee's 'white beard' was apt to lead any pursuers to look for an old man. Finally he managed to board a ship for the Lowlands, posing as a French merchant.

Richard Creagh's colleagues in Louvain were immediately aware of a great change in his demeanor. He seemed inspirited with 'extraordinary holiness' after his miraculous deliverance, and bore the aura of a saint. They little suspected that the 'miracle' might be the result of Lord Cecil having prevailed in Council, where he had proposed to loose upon O'Neill the enmity of Rome. A dewy-eyed impassioned adversary blessed by a fresh miracle, to sway from Shane O'Neill the credulous Irish peasantry! The monarchs of Europe would have little regard for a 'Catholic champion' who was at odds with the Pope! Creagh's imprisonment was initially conceived as a gratification for O'Neill and Dean Danyell, but now Elizabeth decided that to set Shane against the Pope might be worth the sacrifice of dignity that would attend such an escape. The resolution occasioned a good deal of jesting in the Privy Council, but it was suggested in deadly earnest that perhaps both O'Neill and Terence Danyell might yet embrace the Reformation!

Shane celebrated Easter in his new castle at Fathan with Katherine and the children. The Countess was busying herself overseeing the furnishing of the Hall and living chambers, mostly to take her mind off the grim business that was afoot, for this was no quiet holiday. O'Neill

SHANE O'NEILL

was marshalling his forces for war. Word had come that both her uncles, James MacDonnell and Alastair, were away in Kintyre, leaving only Sorley and Aengus in the Glens. Upon hearing this, Shane summoned his vassal chiefs to muster their men for a speedy hosting. The time was come to finish the war he had begun the previous autumn.

The campaign had been deftly plotted through the winter, a plan that demanded a precision of timing, and a coordination of movement, that could withstand no unforeseen setbacks. The blood was up, and readiness was all. Only the singularity of purpose, and the dauntless spirit of Shane O'Neill could drive his men forward to effect each turn and tick of its exactitude.

On the morning of Easter Monday at first light, Shane marched his men, eighteen hundred of them, the sixteen miles from Fathan through the Fews to Dromore, and there they rested. On the Wednesday, they cut twelve miles of road through the 'fast gnarly wood' of Killultagh, a pass so broad 'that ten men may go in a rank'. The following day Shane reached Gallantry at the northeastern tip of Lough Neagh. There he began to rebuild the old fortress of Edenduffcarrick up from its ruins to serve as an outpost. He was awaiting the forces of the Clandeboy O'Neills, a kindred sept, who would join them there. With lashings of manpower, this task took only a few days, and at noon on Sunday, all was ready. Leaving a small garrison behind him, Shane led his freshly gathered forces, now numbering twenty-three hundred, out to meet the enemy.

Sorley Buí MacDonnell had concentrated his defences along the Bann to the west, expecting Shane to come once again by way of Coleraine. Now, alerted by his scouts, he rushed to man the pass at Knockboy, the sole gateway to the Glens of Antrim and the Route. Shane needed to capture this pass before the Scots' could set aflame the great signal-pyres to alert the boys in Cantyre. As his men spilled into the narrow defile, the Scots swept down on them, but O'Neill bore on, 'killing a goodly number', while 'the rest were fain to take the Bogs and Woods'. By the first glimmer of morning Shane had taken the pass, and held Sorley's camp at Cloughdonaghy.

SHANE O'NEILL

Shane split his forces now, for the next 'piece' to be taken was James MacDonnell's lavish coastal fortress at Redcave. This would entail a furious race against time, the gallop of O'Neill's horses, against the oarsmen of MacDonnell's galleys rowing across the Sea of Moyle. Shane knew that the moment that Sorley was dislodged from the pass of Knockboy, those signal fires would be blazing, and he would have but twelve hours to prevail. For, barring ill winds, that would be the time needed for the summoning and transport of the highland Redshanks from Kintyre. Five and twenty miles of rough country lay between Cloughdonaghy and Redcave, to be marched in four hour's time. There would be little more than one hour, then, to capture James MacDonnell's fortress before that chieftain's mighty fleet rowed into the bay. Shane sent a large force off to take Redcave under the command of his cousin, Turlagh Lynach O'Neill, while he led his main force due north to Sorley's town of Ballycastle.

Turlagh's men were able for the task. Upon reaching the bay, they assailed the battlements with fire and fury, and slaughtered all within. Bands of them roved out to sack the adjoining lands of Glenariff to the south. When the fleet of galleys from Scotland hove into view at midday, they saw the fortress engulfed in flames, and quickly changed their course. North to Ballycastle they rowed with new fury, to join forces with Sorley Buí before it might prove too late.

Shane pitched camp that night just below Cushendun, where news reached him of the taking of Redcave. The following morning was Mayday, or 'Béaltaine', and, following the ancient custom of the quarterfeast, upon breaking camp, O'Neill's cavalry galloped their horses between two bonfires, to imbue them with the all the fire and fortune of the day. They marched north then across the moors without opposition to Ballycastle, which, Shane was surprised to find, had been abandoned. His scouts reported that James MacDonnell's redshanks, after making landfall at Cushendun, had joined forces with Sorley Bui, who had retreated to a position close by.

Massed upon the heights above the vale of Glenshesk, the Scots force now numbered some twelve hundred redshanks. Although it was

SHANE O'NEILL

high ground, Shane found it curious that the MacDonnell should choose such a position. The wily Scots Chieftain, however, had left behind him his brother Alastair to muster additional forces in the Isles, and his immanent arrival was expected, hopefully to come at O'Neill's back from the sea.

What James did not know was that Alastair's first contingent of six hundred reinforcements would never arrive. They had been turned back! The feud in Katherine's family proved fortuitous for Shane this day. Because of James MacDonnell's feud with her father, Hector MacLean, these MacGregor redshanks were blocked by their Lord, the Earl of Argyle, from coming to James' aid, blocked from the MacDonnell galleys, and from the burgh of Ayr. They were forced to land at the English-held port of Carrickfergus, where Captain Pierce ordered them home to Scotland!

Shane moved his army then, to stake out his position in the vale of Glenshesk. That night the two armies were encamped barely a mile apart. There were neither campfires nor tents, but half the men rolled themselves in their plaids or mantles in the damp rough fields. The others stood a wary watch, listening to the cold sea wind that keened through the darkness. The warriors were under arms by the first blush of dawn, drawn up in full battle array. Shane's harquebus were placed center, three hundred of them. On each side of them were stout gallowglass, with coats of chain-mail to their knees, and battle-axes at their shoulders. His cavalry stood at either flank, and to their rear were a thousand woodkern, a forest of spears, with lances and halberds aloft. As he was riding in the Queen's name, or declared to be so, Shane was clad in his scarlet tunic, but the bristly grey wolf-pelt over his shoulders told a different story. He galloped out before his troops, and wheeled his horse to face them.

"Where is the man who will not spill blood when his home is taken? I see him not here before me! Where the man will turn his back when his brother is driven to the fern? I see him not! I see before me the fighting men of Ulster! We shall drive these ravenous strangers before us, and put paid to their predations in our land. Not for England! Not for

SHANE O'NEILL

Scotland are the lands of Ulster! Let you steel yourselves now, men of Ireland, and fire your blood like warriors of the Red Branch! This is not a place or time for words. Forward, now. We shall wet our swords this day in the red blood of ClanDonnell!"

Shane swung about now, and trotted a few slow paces forward. He held aloft his sword, and shouted, "Red hand to victory!" The men cheered wildly, and, as their pipers struck up a war-march, they began to move as one up the broad slope of Glenshesk. Above them the clansmen stood ready, with claymores and axes to hand, as their own pipers skirled metal into their blood. When O'Neill's gunners got close enough, he shouted "Leadshot, boys! Let it rip!" and a volley poured forth into MacDonnell's centre, cutting a large swath through his line as warriors toppled. Swinging their heavy battle-axes, Shane's gallowglass hacked their way through the ranks under a cloud of smoke. Pikes and swords clashed in a shower of blood. Then, just as the Scots began to waver, Shane loosed his cavalry upon them, and they came charging into the fray. With fierce cries and war-whoops, his men crashed onward to rip, and pierce, and hack, and cleave the flesh and iron before them. Under this frenzied onslaught, the Highlanders fell in great numbers. Through the smoke, James MacDonnell could be seen rallying his clansmen.

He was a man well beyond his warrior years, and although his helmet hid the locks of grey, his claymore was no longer swift. He charged at one of Shane's burly gallowglass, and in the clash, his sword fell from his hand and a sword pierced his shoulder and breast. The chieftain toppled from his horse onto the bloody grass. The Lord of the Isles had fallen! Such is the power of a captain in war, that with his fall, the Scots began to lose heart, and the battle would soon become a rout.

Down the glenside, Sorley Buí was still at grips with the foe, slashing wildly into the enemy's phalanx in the havoc of a last desperate charge. His mauled ranks recoiled, and surged again in the onrush of battle-fury. But O'Neill's line was unbroken. As they advanced, Shane's right flank rolled forward in a powerful sweep to encircle the ClanDonnell Scots. And now an ever-tightening ring of slaughter and carnage closed in upon Sorley, until at last he was taken prisoner, one of the six hundred

SHANE O'NEILL

captured on that fateful day. When the guns ceased, the strange silence was broken by a lone piper's mournful dirge on the wind, and the lonely screech of gulls and curlews. Then began the frenzied scrawk and caw of huge daws and crows that decended upon the dead and dying. Seven hundred Scots lay stretched upon the blood-sodden slopes of Glenshesk. The rest had fled to their galleys to man the last ditch at the castle of Dunluce.

Thirteen ensigns and banners were taken, and captured were nineteen sons of the Scottish nobility, along with Sorley Buí and the grievously wounded Lord of the Isles, James MacDonnell. Their brother, known as Aengus the contentious, lay among the slain. Shane took the prisoners to Ballycastle, where he made his camp. Here he laid down his sword, and dispatched a letter to Dublin Castle. In crisp Latin, he recounted the furiously fought battle, taking due care to accredit the Deity, and his prickly patroness as well. "But God, best and greatest, of his mere grace, and for the welfare of her Majesty the Queen, gave us the victory against them...Glory be to God, such was the result of these my services undertaken for her Majesty." To his powerful patron Dudley, 'Lord Leicester' now, he sent off Aengus MacDonnell's prized black steed.

The following morning, in tragic irony for the Scots, the galleys of MacDonnell's brother, Alastair, with nine hundred more reinforcements, finally made landfall on Raghlin Island, only two miles out from Ballycastle. Had they arrived but one day earlier, they would have swelled the Scottish host, and possibly changed the fortunes of the day! The story that had reached the island was of slaughter, that both James and Sorley were dead, that O'Neill had taken all. On hearing this doleful tale, Alastair in his despair, manned his galleys again, and put to sea for home. But the war was not over, and there would be no help now for the Scots at Dunseverick, or Dunluce.

O'Neill marched north with his prisoners. Dunseverick, reputed to be one of the three oldest castles in Ireland, was only a few miles on. It was an O'Kane Fortress that the Scots had taken. Only a small ward had been left to defend it, and it quickly fell to O'Neill. Fergus manned the

SHANE O'NEILL

castle with his O'Kanes, and then the army moved on to the next great citadel.

The majestic Castle of Dunluce stands perched on a craggy promontory, separated by a chasm from the rocky coast. Below, in that deep defile, lay the Mermaid's Cave, a vast cavern reaching more than a hundred yards beneath the castle itself. As the cave is sixty feet high, the sea moves through this channel with an unearthly roar. The castle was known to be impregnable, and indeed, it was –from the outside. Sorley Buí had taken it by stealth, only seven years prior to this. His brother Colla had wed the daughter of the McQuillan chief who owned it, and when Colla died, Sorley seized the castle from his widow during the funeral. It was now the Scots' last bastion in Ulster.

A ward of barely fifty manned the castle, and from atop its towered walls, their sentry kept watch. They watched the flames lick the night sky over Redcave, and after the smoke had cleared over Glenshesk they sighted the galleys arriving from Cushendun, galleys bearing nearly two hundred weary survivors of the battle. The drawbridge slowly lowered across the chasm, and the ranks of bloodied warriors staggered across it with their woeful tale weighing heavily upon them. A gory tale of savage slaughter, a taking of hostages, and a killing of prisoners. There were no clear tidings of the final overthrow, but both James and Sorley Buí were assumed to be dead.

The highest-ranking of the new arrivals was Sorley's cousin, Gillaspick MacDonnell, and he quickly took command of the castle. He was a solid man of medium stature, ruddy and quick. His bristly short hair was silvery grey, well before its time, and he had a long broad nose and closely-set eyes of lightest grey that conspired to give him a wolf-like appearance. He was a bitter man, whose thwarted ambitions, as he thought, owed to the murder of his father when he was young. It was his father and uncle who had been murdered by the English adventurer, Brereton with impunity. Although dour by nature, Gillaspick shook the men from their dreary silence, firing orders down the line to prepare for a siege, getting in stores of food and fresh water. He was delighted to learn that, if needed, more supplies could be got in from Raghlin Island

SHANE O'NEILL

under cover of night, by means of a sea-cave stair below the castle. Gillaspick stationed his men upon the battlements, in the towers, and at the firing loops, in full confidence of holding fast.

For all the gloom in the castle, the skies above were glorious blue, and as the day stretched on, the victorious skirl of pipes could be heard on the wind. Soon the long trailing line of O'Neill's army could be seen approaching along the coast road. The troops were ragged now, and depleted in their numbers, but boisterous and triumphal, with chanting and singing. They made their encampment just over the green ridge, beyond range of bow or musket, and it was not long before Shane had them assembled in battle ranks, facing the castle. When all was in order, he rode out before his lines. Beside him his ensign flourished the Red Hand banner, and at his other side was a burly chieftain with a long red beard. Shane reached the edge of the chasm, where he halted, and called out to the men behind the parapet high above.

"I am Shane O'Neill! Beside me is Rory, Chief of the MacQuillans who is rightful owner of this castle! Let you surrender it now, and all will be spared!" From his height on the battlements, Gillaspick glowered, and called out his reply.

"I am Gillaspick, son of Gillaspick MacDonnell, whose murderer your Queen does shield from justice. Stand away, MacQuillan! MacDonnell is not one of your like, for what MacDonnell holds, MacDonnell will keep! And I shall yield to no man!" Shane huffed, and called out once again.

"List me, now! I have hostages! Of the noblest blood of Scotland, I hold twenty! Among them is the Lord of the Isles, who is gravely wounded. And with him is his brother, Sorley Buí MacDonnell. Surrender now, and all shall be spared!" There was a pause above, and several figures disappeared from the parapet, which was thought to be a hopeful sign. Then the captain re-appeared and spoke again.

"It shall never be said that Gillaspick will bring disgrace upon his lord MacDonnell, by surrender for his sake! Have a care, O'Neill! For ClanDonnell shall avenge any harm done unto him, or unto the rest of our noble sons! Be off now, Shane O'Neill, to your English Queen!

SHANE O'NEILL

Dunluce shall withstand. And I shall take no terms!" He stepped back again from the parapet, and a flaming arrow was loosed from the drum-tower, clattering on the rocks before O'Neill's black steed.

Shane turned his horse, and the three men trotted back to their lines. Firing commenced now, as a barrage of artillery was unleashed against the battlements. Hails of musket-fire poured upon the defiant archers who were perched over the gaps of the parapet, and, within moments, one of them took a screaming fall into the deep chasm. Showers of burning arrows flew over those walls, but a great deal of shot, both arrows and lead, simply raised dust against the stone battlements and tumbled into the abyss. There was harquebus firing from the castle's loops, and casualties on both sides were mounting.

After a time, the barrage suddenly ceased, leaving an eerie silence. The MacQuillan chieftain rode forward holding aloft a white flag. After him marched four tall gallowglass in their conical helmets and chain-mail, and staggering along between them, a thick rope about his neck, was Sorley Buí MacDonnell. He was easily recognized, even from the high ramparts, by his flaxen hair. His wrists were bound, and his mouth gagged. More men followed behind with a rough beam on their shoulders, and long spades. Sorley was pushed to the front, nearly to the brink of the ravine. Now Shane O'Neill came forward on his black charger. All along the parapet, Scots could be seen looking down with grave concern. O'Neill called out to the battlements.

"Here is the Captain of the Glens, Sorley Buí MacDonnell, as great a warrior as any in Scotland, and here he shall stay! Here he shall stay until you lower this bridge, and raise your gates. If you be a worthy captain, Gillaspick, put aside your folly, lest he shall perish! Nor food nor drink shall pass his lips until you relinquish the Castle of Dunluce!" Shane nodded to the men, who struck their spades in the earth. In a trice, they had dug a small deep hole, and slid the beam into it for a tall stake. When it was secure, Sorely was stripped to the waist, and bound to the stake. O'Neill stepped his charger over to Sorley then, and before he trotted off, he said something heard by none but the prisoner. Terse and simple were his words.

SHANE O'NEILL

"Enough have died. Let there be an end to it.' Sorley understood. He had been given the choice to submit, and had refused, costing many a man his life. Now a price would be paid. Both of these men were seasoned in war, and bred to its cruelties. Once the sword is drawn, all doubt, all softness is banished from the mind. 'Nature peers through the eyes of the cat, and he will seize his prey.' These men had no misgivings about the chance of battle, nor did they expect mercy of their friend, for by the warriors' code, the bonds of fellowship must break under the supreme burden of duty. Shane's eldest brother, Phelim Caoch, was killed in battle by a MacDonnell's lance; this man was wed to Shane's sister. But such things held no place in his reckoning. Sorley was the same, and as he faced what was before him, his only fear was that he might cry out, or weaken, to disgrace the honour of a warrior's death."

However long the days of May, by and by night fell, and the strange deep bellowing roar of the sea cave seemed to grow the louder for it. There was drinking in the camp, for Shane had resolved that time and Sorley's thirst would wage the fight. In the castle the men were restless and uneasy. The next two days seemed endless, as the men looked on to watch Sorley's decline. Surely a few days of fasting would not bring him low, but a parching thirst was a kind of torture. The men knew that, but for his gag, Sorley would exhort them to stand the siege, to hold the fortress, and none voiced this more loudly than their captain, Gillaspick. But all knew that the Ulster colony had been vanquished, that this small rock was only a token, for it would soon be abandoned, and they would be back in the Isles. If Sorley died, would James be next? And what of this Gillaspick who is so filled with fire against O'Neill?

By the third day there was open talk among the men. All knew that Gillaspick's grandfather had been Chieftain, and that he harboured ambitions to stand upon the stone. If James and Sorley perished here, it would be upon his insistence, and likely for his own ends. As the men looked down from the battlements, Sorley was slumped on his ropes, and huge scald-crow settled on his shoulder like Cúchulain of old at his moment of death. A sudden scream of sea-mews was chilling, and the men looked to each other with shared resolve.

SHANE O'NEILL

Gillaspick had kept watch through the night, and he was sleeping now, when the strange sound awakened him. A grinding clattering rumble below! As his wits gathered, he heard a resounding thud, and he knew that the drawbridge had been lowered. Both seething rage and trembling fear now gripped his heart, as he bolted up from his cot, and soon he was spitting curses as he scurried down the dark cocklestair. He had no doubts about what had taken place, nor about what might befall him, should he be taken by O'Neill.

As he made his way through the castle, Gillaspick could hear the raucous jubilation as the MacQuillans took possession once again. Quickly he found the hidden stair, and descended to the Mermaid's Cave below. There he found a galley ready to push off, and jumped aboard. As the ship put out for Raghlin Island, the enormity of the moment shook this man to his marrow. The last outpost in Ulster relinquished! This shameful defeat of his clan was new fire for the smouldering embers of his father's unavenged murder. But his eyes burned with seething hatred for only one man. Gillaspick MacDonnell cursed Shane O'Neill then, and swore that he would wreck vengeance upon him before ever he should breath his last!

CHAPTER 26

"Huzzah and hallelujah! Let the bells of victory peal! Send him in and quick!" Seated in her Presence Chamber, Elizabeth beamed at her Lord Secretary and Sir Harry Sidney, her brows arched in smug triumph, all her doubtful measures vindicated. On hearing the approach of footfall, she crowed, "Ah, the lively step of good tidings! We have had *too* much of those sluggish messengers of woe!"

As the great doors opened, a voice rang out. "Captain William Pierce, Chief Constable of Carrickfegus in Ulster." Pierce, 'a tall, burly man with a big brown beard', was well known to the Queen. It was said that in her youth he had 'rescued her from the rage and fury of her sister, Queen Mary, by conveying her privately away', and his position in Ulster was owing to her gratitiude. As he entered, Cecil leaned in with a quiet advisement.

"O'Neill requested to use Pierce's garrison at Carrickfegus, your Majesty. I refused, of course, but instructed Pierce to replenish him with a small quantity of supplies, a token amount, and to send a scout to accompany him that he might report of the battle." Elizabeth clapped her hands together and outspread them in joyous welcome.

"Captain Pierce! We rejoice to see you hearty and hail, ever our gallant protector! Are they banished out of Ireland then? Mary's wild legions? How many remain in Ireland?"

"Seven hundred Scots remain. -Not *in* Ireland, but under it! The rest have fled to the isles"!

SHANE O'NEILL

"Oh, these are tidings! How did O'Neill complish this rout?"

"He firstly toppled the fortress at Redcave, and wasted the country 'round. He moved then to Sorley Buí's own fort at Ballycastle. The Scots appeared in force, and on the second of May the great battle was joined in Glenshesk. A bloody affair, great losses on both sides. But by night, the day belonged to O'Neill! Seven hundred killed, and James and Sorley in chains. James is gravely wounded. O'Neill followed hard on this, destroying all their castles along the coast. He captured Dunluce Castle by threatening to kill Sorley before its gates. He is still east of the Bann, restoring the wild Irish to their lands." The Queen turned with a smirk to Cecil.

"And Lord Sussex avowed O'Neill would never banish them!" Sidney could not resist concurring.

"A thing *he* failed to do for six years!" Pierce continued his account.

"MacDonnell made offer to O'Neill of all his goods -cattle, herds, and lands in Ireland and Scotland, pleading with Shane for his bare liberty, but O'Neill refused -on the grounds that he was but the Queen's officer, and the quarrel was none of his." Cecil spoke quietly.

"I shall instruct Arnolde to send a special man to O Neill to practise with him for the recovery of James MacDonnell and his brother into the possession and keeping of your Majesty."

"They will fetch a tidy sum from their cousin, Mary Stuart!" Elizabeth clapped her hands together tightly and shook them at her breast. "Mary's Irish intrigues have come to naught! Oh, by heavens! We do rejoice to hear it!" With a knowing nod to Sidney, she offered firm instruction to the Yorkshireman. "James's brother-" She looked questioningly to Cecil.

"Alastair"

"*Alastair* will thirst for vengeance against O'Neill. See that you give him good words of sympathy, Captain Pierce. And reasonable entertainment. His spite against O'Neill may prove a useful tool in time to come!"

"Just so, your Majesty. In time to come. Now the Scots are cleared out, mayhap her Highness will consider Sir Thomas Smith's plan for a

SHANE O'NEILL

proper English colony there. I have furnished a report for you, at his request, with advisements as to its placement. Might I leave it with his Lordship?" Under her breath, Elizabeth gave a quick word to Cecil, and he spoke out.

"We thank you Captain Pierce. I should like to read it. When you have finished the writing of your battle report you may see the bursar. I shall consult with you further e'er you depart."

"Aye, my Lord, E'en so, I must leave ye this caution. There is great unease in Carrickfergus and Dundalk... for since O'Neill is become overlord of O'Donnell's country in the West, there is now but *one* power in all Ulster. O'Neill's sway is complete. And he will likely take more than her Majesty would give! Your Majesty's name is no more reverenced, nor your letters of commandment obeyed within Ulster than they would be in the kingdom of France! My soldiers are much dismayed. For while O'Neill's banner is the Queen's, still his manner is a king's. He demanded even that -"

"Gods Teeth!" The Queen exploded with sudden rage. "Not for one *moment* are we let rejoice! O'Neill is our captain! Tell *that* to your quaking soldiers!"

"Aye, your Majesty!" Pierce bowed, and turned to depart.

"William."

"Your Highness?"

"Sweet William. You are *no* courtier! But a blunt and honest soldier, too loyal to let your caution bide its proper hour. We do commend you your good service! We would you make known to Lord Cecil all these cautions anon, when his time affords! For now you may withdraw, with our fondest gratitude."

"God save you, your Majesty!" With a bow, then, he took his leave. Elizabeth was anxious to dispel the note of unease over O'Neill's triumph. She smiled to her ministers and exulted.

"O'Neill is broke with Mary! And France! *Never* to be restored! And her Scots gone back into Scotland!" The two men matched her smile, but Cecil ventured a new concern.

"He has done this your bidding, M'lady. He'll expect now to be elevated to Earl." The Queen's smile vanished.

SHANE O'NEILL

"Let him live in expectation, and he will need act in compliance." A sharp glance from Cecil prompted Sidney to speak.

"And yet, Sir William has struck near the mark. O'Neill has vanquished your Scots, and as his further compliance is demanded, mayhap your Majesty will gratify him in the matter of *Stukeley*..." Elizabeth froze, then looked from one to the other in disbelief.

"Stukeley! In a pig's eye shall we countenance such folly! He is our prisoner! Stukeley is a faithless beast, rather than a man! A blaggard, and a *pirate*! Nay! At long last he is captured! In the Tower sits he. And if justice be served, soon to tread the flags of Hell before the Prince of Darkness that he has so faithfully, so unstintingly served! And will you have us unleash him then to swagger in Ireland, and conspire with rebels there? What rash folly is this?" Sidney was undaunted.

"Oh, he is a rakehell, whom no prince in his proper mind would support! But yet I know no man, if the Queen would have peace with O'Neill, that better could please him, nor no man, if her Highness would have *war*, that more would annoy him! Now, neither do I desire it, nor persuade it, but in truth I would consent to it!"

Elizabeth shook her head, speechless, until she looked to Cecil, and exclaimed, "Oh, here is one for Bedlam!" On seeing that Cecil was about to demur, she quickly added, "Nay, *two*! Two for Bedlam!" The Lord Secretary met her jibe with an ingratiating smile.

"I fear we are all Bedlam bound, if O'Neill's rampage begins anew. And here is a frugal means of gratifying him, perhaps, in lieu of granting him peerage! Shane O'Neill has writ from his camp in Stukeley's favour, doubtless at the rogue's urging," Cecil paused his hand in mid-air for a moment's reflection. "Master Stukeley was his '*intimate* friend', he writes, who had shown him 'all his love' while he was stayed in London, and he begs your Majesty to show her 'clemency and favour' to a subject who, by his behavior in the past, had made him realize the 'magnificence and glory of her rule!' He begs this in return for his service against MacDonnell, and will write further, but is at present so much occupied with the expulsion of the Scots. Unless your Majesty is prepared to grant him his peerage, he will, I think, require some gratification. T'would soothe his vanity to o'erturn the ruin of his friend."

"Pardon *Stukeley*! The man is a *pirate*; of life dissolute, of expenses prodigal, of *no* substance on any account!" A fresh concern raised her pitch. "And *who* will assuage the Spanish Ambassador?" Sidney replied with sudden inspiration.

"The man himself! He could woo a lioness from her cubs. If he could soothe DeSilva's outrage, what miracle then might he not perform in taming O'Neill?" Elizabeth's thin lips pursed tightly, as she considered, and opened with a 'tisk'.

"*As* we are resolved *e'er long* to send *you* in Arnolde's place, Harry Sidney, to squire that wayward kingdom...we may venture you this folly. -*If* Stukeley can dissuade DeSilva from his ceaseless haranguing of our Ministers, we shall grant a stay of proceedings. -But no pardon! And you may have him for your envoy to O'Neill." Cecil quickly voiced his approval.

"A wise decision, your Majesty. O'Neill shall be a busy man from this! Now that he has vanquished his foes, he shall need to fight east and west to keep them in thrall!" Sidney thought it timely to broach other concerns.

"And while he is so engaged, we might contrive to seal the legal rat-holes that sheltered him at Court! Let us ban the Brehons and their Irish laws, that we might scotch *other* challenges to peerage." Elizabeth turned her questioning eyes to Cecil, who nodded assuringly.

"Their Brehon Law is barbaric! It does not countenance prisons, and will employ naught but 'fines' and 'ostrasization' to chastize the wrongdoer. A simple Royal edict, your Majesty." The Queen assented, and Lord Sidney chanced further business.

"The bards, too, stir up enmity among the people for civil order, and rail against your loyal subjects. *Never* would they be tolerated here in England."

The Queen turned back to her Lord Secretary. "Ah, your little screed! Indeed, we have read us 'Bottle Smith's Treatise', as you call it. Windy, we thought, but quite sound." Cecil quoted the poisoner's edict now, with great conviction, impressing her with its simplicity.

"No rhymer poet shall make verses to any one after God on earth except the Queen, under penalty of the forfeiture of all his goods." Elizabeth's head tilted to the side, considering, and then she snapped her verdict.

"Aye! We would do *well* to enact his proposals to ban these Irish bards and rhymers." She sighed. "Oh, would they were like unto our *own* bards, whose song is wholesome and sweet! And nurtures loyalty to their prince!"

"Indeed, your Majesty! So we shall do." Finding his mistress so thoroughly amenable, the Lord Secretary pressed on. "O'Neill has severed himself from Scotland and France -a propitious time, perhaps, to *enforce* the proscription of the Roman Mass, to outlaw the priests in Ireland. Unequivocally!" Elizabeth turned doubtfully to Sidney, but Cecil's coaxing did not slacken. "Your Majesty, there are black crows flocking across the channel! -These priests, who are beaten in England, will no doubt transfer the struggle to Ireland where they have so many partisans. And might create more! They go in great numbers, and not for any great learning the universities of Ireland shall show them, as I guess!" He looked to Sidney for support, but Sir Harry nodded only, so Cecil continued, raising his tone ominously. "Since those Irish bishops presented themselves at the court of France, Ireland is of great moment in the intrigues of the League of Catholic Powers!" Elizabeth raised her hand, and looked away for a moment's deliberation.

"This we shall do! Ban the Brehons and the rhymers, and proscribe the Papish priests. We shall see if O'Neill be loyal or no." Just then the bells began to peal in jubilation at the great victory of Glenshesk. The three looked at each other with slight discomfiture, and so the Queen raised her voice to match the joyous bells. "Still there is cause *enough* to lift our hearts! Mary is scotched in Ireland! And O'Neill's victory may prove his defeat!"

SHANE O'NEILL

Before Shane turned his army west, he oversaw the resettling of the Route and the Glens by the Irish who had been dispossessed of them. He marched his forces, then, back to Gallantry on the northeastern shore of Lough Neagh, and set up court in the castle of Edenduff Carrick. There he dismissed his western battalions, and assigned to Turlagh Lynach O'Neill the task of transporting the Scottish prisoners out to the west of Tirowen. Castle Corcragh, near Strabane, was their destination, a remote spot where they would be well out of reach of their Hebridian allies. One captive remained behind, however, for Shane resolved to keep Sorley Buí at his side, under guard, but as yet not imprisoned.

The massive round towers of Edenduff resounded still with the ring of hammers and trowels, as the restoration work continued. The castle overlooked the great inland sea of Lough Neagh, and Shane found letters awaiting him there, which had come in galleys from across the lough. Katherine's letter was first read. After some fretful solicitude for his safety and a plea for news of the wars, she announced joyfully that the annulment papers had arrived from Rome! "We must wed before summer's end, Shane, as soon as possible, lest upon your return I might might conceive again, and swell too stout for my new gown! Let us allow only so much delay as my people might need to travel from Scotland. All must be grand, in high style, with a High Mass in the Cathedral as Dean O'Donnelly promised. We shall have to invite not only my kindred, but all the nobility of Scotland, if ever we are to put an end to those ghastly rumours of 'poor wee Katherine' chained to a four-poster! I think you have the right of it, Shane, that it was *my* people put that story abroad to absolve me of my part in the wicked abduction, but let us have an end to it. The good Dean has advised for us the first Sunday in September after the early harvest is in, either the feast of St. Aidan, or the following Sunday on St. Fintan's. Send word at once, won't you, that I might dispatch my letters off to Duart without delay!"

There had been talk among the Scots prisoners of Mary Stuart's betrothal to 'her beardless and lady-faced English cousin' Lord Darnley,

SHANE O'NEILL

and Katherine had word of it. She wrote that she had received a long letter about it from Lady Jean Stewart, the wife of Lord Argyle -and Mary's half-sister. Shane was well pleased to hear her news! The Earl of Argyle, Mary's most ardent friend and her only Protestant supporter, was vehemently opposed to her marriage, and made no secret of it. The Queen, in her fury, had barred him from Court. Darnley, soon to be king, despised him, and as doors closed around him in Edinburgh, Archibald had been forced to beat a hasty retreat to the Highlands.

Queen Elizabeth had sent Sir Robert Dudley north in hopes that he might woo Mary, and she was infuriated when Darnley was chosen. Such a royal marriage, in defiance of Elizabeth's wishes, spelled an end to Argyle's long campaign for English support, and Shane saw in this a perfect opportunity to woo the powerful Highland Laird into an alliance. When messengers arrived from the Earl of Argyle and Queen Mary Stuart to offer ransom for James and Sorley MacDonnell, O'Neill took great care in crafting his response. Mary was furious, and would have to be assuaged, even if her own prospects looked precarious and doubtful.

Shane 'deeply regretted' that he was not at liberty to release the MacDonnells, as they were 'held in the Queen's custody', although this quibble had not prevented him from accepting vast sums from other Lairds to deliver up their sons and heirs. He dispatched Sir Patrick Dorrell, the old musical priest who served as Chanter of Armagh, to call on both Queen Mary and the Earl of Argyle with hawks and falcons, along with an invitation to attend his wedding. To Archibald he wrote a long letter in Gaelic, assuring him of a warm welcome and safe refuge -if need be- in Ulster, and of his ardent desire to assist the earl in any way until fresh winds would blow in Edinburgh. Shane was now Lord of Ulster, with or without Elizabeth's golden chain, and such an offer, he knew, would be held in high account.

When a messenger arrived from the Lord Justice Arnolde requesting to remove James and Sorley to Dublin Castle, Shane prevaricated, and ultimately refused to release them. He waxed indignant that, as the Queen's loyal captain in Ulster, his custody should be doubted! Still another courier came, this time from London, with letters from the Queen and Cecil, and Dudley –now styled Lord Leicester. Each of them insisted that Shane turn over his prisoners, and all ransom monies to Lord Arnolde. Shane adamantly refused this proposal, as the war had been undertaken at his own expense, and as captain and Lord of Ulster, directly answerable to Her Majesty under the Articles of Drumcree, he would not to be superseded by the hirelings in Dublin Castle.

Leicester wrote with cheer of the release of Tom Stukeley, and of her Majesty's especial regard for Shane's entreaties on his behalf. He wrote of the Queen's gratitude for his banishing of the Scots, and of the salutary effect it would have upon his prospects for a Peerage of the Realm. In his encouraging appeals, Dudley noted, by way of a hopeful example, that MacCarthy of Cork had been granted an Earldom that very day! He was now MacCarthy More, Baron of Valentia and Earl of Clancarr. This trivial bit of news had a scorching affect upon its reader, sending Shane into an unholy fury that nearly shook the foundations Edenduff Castle. "The lickspittle MacCarthy! That lumbering lumpish toady, groveling for any English churl on a horse! That cringing *oaf*? To be raised up over the O'Neill? Over the O'Neill! An exalted knave! A pismire! And what service has he done the Crown, but for licking boots? I have conquered the Scots, banished them to the Isles! But O'Neill must wait, and wait, and wait again! To be abased before the likes of ClanCarthy! This is a *deliberate* affront! A scurrilous mockery -one that they shall *rue* e'er long!"

With no further deliberation, Shane marshaled his forces, and set off for the Newry and Dundrum, those two remaining outposts of the English on his side of the Pale in Ulster. The small English garrisons both surrendered quickly, without loss of life, and were promptly cast out, to struggle back to the gates of Dundalk. Shane installed his own garrisons, for by the Treaty of Drumcree, he was acknowledged to be overlord of these lands, loyal to the Queen, and his Irishmen could just as well hold them for her Majesty as any Englishmen -all of this reasonable, by his lights, but sure to cause a great flurry and fury in the Royal Court.

SHANE O'NEILL

At Whitehall, the Privy Council was in clamorous session when the doors flew open and the Queen appeared, silencing the room and bringing all to their feet. After a chorus of 'Your Majesty!', Cecil drew back his chair, relinquishing his place at the head of the table. He smiled amiably.

"Mistress Ashley advised us that your Highness was unable to preside this afternoon, and so-"

"-And so you see that we are come after all. And feeling much restored." She took her seat, and nodded to the rest to do likewise. The others shifted down, allowing Cecil his place at her right hand. "And what is this order of business, so noisesome as to be heard beyond the chamber doors?"

"O'Neill, your Majesty. On the heel of his victory over the Scots, he has taken our castles at Dundrum and the Newry. He expelled your Majesty's garrisons, and has warded them with his own troops. He has driven Sir Nicholas Bagenal from his estates at Newry." The Queen was stunned.

"Bagenal, say you? O'Neill has driven off the new *lord-marshal of our royal army*? And manned our castles?" Cecil nodded solemnly. "God's teeth! The insolent *brute*! *This* is what comes of Arnolde's coddling. 'Aye and yea, and nary a nay!' We will have an end to it!" She turned her fiery eyes to Sidney. "You shall assume Arnolde's duties upon your arrival in Ireland! We shall have need of your cool head and keen eye, Harry Sidney, if we are to bring the grand disturber to heel."

"Your Majesty, I dare not ask my dear wife to bear this fresh burden atop the cumbersome load of debt we have accrued in your service in Wales. My plate and even my good wife's jewels are in pawn! I advised the Lord Secretary with a list of my conditions for-"

"A list that you have burdened *deliberately* with a cumbersome load of demands that we should never acquiesce to. Well, you are foiled, good Harry. We are purposed to allow that you keep your office of Lord Deputy of Wales, to augment your pay in Dublin. We shall

SHANE O'NEILL

grant you, too, those fresh troops you requested, 200 horse and 500 foot, in addition to those already in Dublin." After a moment of stunned silence, Sidney responded in an easy but cautionary tone.

"I would not go as *others* have gone- to twine ropes of sand and sea-slime to bind the Irish rebels with. I must bring a military chest of at least £10,000." The Queen nodded slowly to one side.

"This too, we are resigned to provide you. A new regimen for that cursed realm will be chargeable, it is true; but if you will give the people justice, and minister law among them -exercise the sword of the sovereign and *put away* the sword of the subject – we might have peace. And *incomes* where there is now endless costs." Sidney held his hands to his head, and then folded them as in prayer before her.

"Oh, would your Majesty but grant me leave to serve her in England, or in any place in the world else saving Ireland, it should be more joyous to me than-"

"You shall be joyful in Ireland -or you shall be *woeful* in Ireland, but *there* you shall be! I'll hear no more on it." Sidney shook his head, and then spoke softly but firmly.

"It is all very well to charge me with reducing that kingdom to order, but the question remains, what is to be done with O'Neill? Under the terms granted him at Drumcree, he is not *answerable* to the Viceroy, but directly to your Majesty. You must either give him his head, and lose that kingdom, or I must *take* his head, and establish the Queen's peace." Lord Cecil cleared his throat, and held up a parchment before him.

"Sir Thomas Cusack writes again to urge your Majesty to meet O'Neill's wishes regarding the restoration of the earldom. His appeal is re-echoed by Arnolde -like master like man- who has wrote thusly: 'If you use the opportunity to make O'Neill a good subject, he will hardly swerve hereafter. The Pale is poor and unable to defend itself. If he do fall out before the beginning of next summer there is neither outlaw, rebel, murderer, thief, nor any lewd or evil-disposed person -of whom God knows there is plenty swarming in every corner amongst the wild Irish, yea, and within our own border too, which would not join to do what mischief they might." Sidney's fist struck the table.

SHANE O'NEILL

"There again, it is the *threat* of O'Neill that commends his peerage!" Robert Dudley, Lord Leicester, had been silent until now, and he spoke out with a soothing tone and a smile for Elizabeth.

"And yet if he be gratified, he may *serve*, as Arnolde insists, and not swerve. He is right. O'Neill has kept your Majesty's terms. He vanquished the Scots. He has kept to the confines of Ulster. And he has encouraged husbandry and the growing of wheat. Tirowen is the most populous and most prosperous part of Ireland." Elizabeth turned to her Lord Secretary.

"Is this O'Neill's drunken boast or sober truth?" Cecil nodded, and looked up, his shaggy brows arched.

"It *is* widely reported, your Majesty. Even Lord Sussex wrote privately that over three hundred families did leave the civility of the Pale to live in O'Neill's country." Sidney bridled at this notion.

"Piffle! The reason for *that* is that O'Neill refuses to uphold the proscription of Papism in Ulster. As long as he is let to do so, the Catholics of the South will look to him for deliverance. And the powers of Europe will *see* in his defiance an unguarded gate to invade this kingdom. I must have either the troops and provisions to chastise him, or means to buy his loyalty with hopes or concessions." Leicester smiled at his brother-in-law.

"Aye, Harry, there is the crux of it. But O'Neill would make a better friend than foe. Though he be wild-headed, he is no fool! Since his pardon here at court he has prospered and advanced by his loyalty to the crown. Were he offered the title of earl that he covets so, he would be more like to *weed out* rebels than to cultivate them."

"What say you then, Harry Sidney?"

"It is true. With my experience the titles of our honours do rather weaken than strengthen the Irish chiefs of that country." Cecil turned again to advise the Queen beside him.

"When O'Neill holds by Rights Feudal, come there a time he should sink into rebellion, the Crown may legally confiscate all his holdings -and plant them with loyal Englishmen. No more talk of Brehon rights invested in the people. And we have Matthew's youngest boy biding with Lord Sidney at Penshurst, to put in his place."

"What age is the boy now, Lord Harry?"

"Hugh O'Neill is in his sixteenth year. He's become a fine Englishman, and has forgot the boggy habits of his kind. He is a boon companion to my young Philip. If John O'Neill forfeits in rebellion, patents could be drawn *anew* for Hugh O'Neill when he is of age."

"So be it done. We shall annul us the patents of King Henry to the bastard Matthew. Let the peerage be drawn up for John O'Ncill according to his father's grant for the succession to the estates and honours of Tyrone." Her eyes flashed, and she pointed her finger at Sidney. "But let *no word* of this reach O'Neill! ...Til he prove dutiful and true! If we can avoid the expense of war, 'twould be folly to burden our exchequer further. A vain and endless task, methinks, to drain the black Irish morass -fed *as it is* from the perennial fountains of Irish nature!"

A chorus of 'aye' and 'so be it' rumbled around the table, and Elizabeth spoke over it. "Henry Sidney, we shall grant you a season to make ready, but you shall sail before the onset of winter. Upon your arrival as Viceroy, you shall move Shane O'Neill to make his repair to you with safe conduct, to confer of such matters as have been promised him, and for the settling of good government of the North. He shall answer *all* disorders committed since the last pardon! Aye, as his proceeding against the Scots *without* advising the Governor of his intention! His using them as his captives, ransoming whom he listed, taking into his *own* possession their castles and countries, doing all things as though the countries and subjects were his own! And his entry into the Newry and Dundrum! If he be contrite, you may show him mercy and favour. But if O'Neill appear *not* dutiful, you shall forbear to deal, and proceed against him, that he might receive such as he deserves!"

SHANE O'NEILL

Low clouds were sailing by, white clouds, bright, and blithe and billowing, and a soft wind was moving in a kind of gladness over the lofty Cathedral hill at Armagh. The sally trees were sighing, the pale backs of their leaves flickering in the rustling breeze. Speckled thrushes, finches, and wrens in the bracken were darting and flitting, their tails aflutter; robins were warbling, and wagtails twittering, dispelling all traces of that faint air of sadness that is so wont to tinge the glory of a September day. Bright banners and pennants waved and whipped in the sprightly breeze, as throngs of well-wishers ambled and milled about below the Cathedral, waiting for the wedding party to emerge. The beech trees whispered expectantly overhead, and suddenly Shane's two hounds, Bran and Scohaun leapt to their feet with a shrill whine. And then the bells! The bells at last began to peal, casting a scatter of rooks and ravens to the sky. Finally the massive doors swung open, and into the sea of cheers and exultation, the grand procession came forth.

With a shrill blast, the bagpipers skirled a merry march to lead the way, led by the famed MacCrimmon, piper to the Campbells of Glenorchy. They were followed by seven young lassies, skipping barefooted in their light frocks, winsome and lithe, scattering rose petals from out their wee cishes before the bride and groom. Shane and laughing Katherine came slowly down the steps, waving to the heady crowds. Shane wore his scarlet doublet, and Kat was bedecked in a tartan gown of the MacLean reds, with a green bonnet sporting two pinion feathers that had once graced an eagle high atop Ben Mór! Behind them came her father, Hector Mór, and all her Macleans in the same fiery hues.

Shane's children followed, some full grown, and the wee ones in their nurses' arms, all in their most elegant finery. Next came Shane's brother Turlagh Donn, who was seldom seen owing to his precarious health, and Shane's nephew, Turlagh Brassalagh O'Neill, the son of his eldest and deceased brother Phelim Caoch. Turlagh Lynnach and other O'Neills of various branches walked shoulder to shoulder. Just behind were the O'Donnellys, Shane's foster family. Auld Bríd was smiling brightly, her eyes glistening, but her thoughts were mostly fretful, flitting above to Dungannon Castle, where her staff were preparing the Wedding Feast. In among the Donnelly brothers, and under their 'custody' for the day, was Katherine's tall flaxen-haired uncle, Sorley Buí MacDonnell. He walked along, sullen-faced, with a proud bearing, and he met no man's eyes.

The Highland gentry followed, led by the Earl of Argyle, sparkling in his bejeweled doublet and ruffs. His estranged wife, Jean Stewart had sent her apologies to Katherine, however, as she wished to avoid his company. There were lesser Campbells in his train wearing their gaelic plaids, including his cousins, Campbell of Carrick, and Campbell of Glenorchy. There was MacIvor, MacKinnon, MacKay, MacLeod, Stewart of Appin, MacNeil of Barra, and Gordon, all in an array of tartans, but with a flash of silver and jewels about them.

Farleigh headed the contingent of bards, which was considerable, as so many chieftains and lairds had brought their best. Argyle's illustrious MacEwen walked beside him, all of them peering about intently, and measuring phrases and rhymes for a possible rann to immortalize day's proceedings. Next came the Irish Gentry, the O'Hanlon, the O'Kane, Black Hugh O'Donnell, Fleming Lord Slane, and young Sir Robert, Lord Mayor of Drogheda, O'More, and O'Connor, and all the rest, barring only the FitzGeralds, for neither Kildare nor Desmond could attend. Following behind these were the clergy, mostly Franciscans, led by Shane's youngest brother, Father Hugh O'Neill.

Out in the churchyard, Shane's eldest son, Shane Óg, presented Katherine with a wreath of purple heather blossoms bound by a broad ribbon of black velvet, with a small spray of bright thistles in its bow. This introduced a sad and solemn note into the joyous proceedings, but one that could not be omitted. The crowd parted to let the wedding party through to the fresh grave of Katherine's uncle, the Laird James MacDonnell. He had died of his virulent battle-wounds only weeks before, and Shane had brought him from Castle Corcragh to be buried here at the restored Primatial Cathedral of Armagh. For the elder half of Shane's children, of course, this was their grandfather, and all honours were due him.

SHANE O'NEILL

Sorley Buí's eyes were moist as he kissed the bride upon her cheek, and he clasped a steadying hand upon her shoulder as she laid the wreath upon the chieftain's grave. A requiem prayer was intoned in Latin by the Dean of Armagh, who then spoke a few carefully chosen words 'to bind their hearts', suggesting that it was God's holy will to take James upon the battlefield, and that it might as easily been Shane or any of the rest 'under clay this day'. MacCrimmin piped a doleful air as all stood in silence. Upon its completion, a lively jig was commenced, and the merriment was resumed. When the good folks of Armagh had been attended to with libation and salutation, Shane and Katherine made their way to the waiting carriage, an elegant black and gilded coach with six white horses. It would bring them to the Castle of Dungannon little more than three leagues to the North traveling by the only stretch of proper coach-road in Ulster. Other carriages were boarded, steeds were mounted, and soon the progress was underway.

The long merry cavalcade passed under towering hedges, grown wild with elder and whitethorn, where sunlight fell in spangles across the road, but soon the ways were clear under a vast blue sky. September was going to gold, the hills dappled with a blaze of yellow gorse; the highroad was dry, and the air was laden with the sweet scent of hay. In the fields on either side, stooks of barley and oats stood ripening in the sun, and yellow hay-ricks towered over them, nearly ready for the haggard. Scythes and sickles halted now, as the grand procession came into view, and farmers and field-hands stood where they stopped in the stubblefields to take in the passing parade.

Upon the guests' arrival, the castle-yard was bustling with servants and dray-wagons, geese cackling, and fowl aflutter. Barrells thumpitty-thumping over the cobbles, clinking bottles, and hearty laughter all lent a frolicsome air to the imposing grey keep. As the day was so fine, many of the men lingered round a barrel of ale there under a festive canopy. Most of the women assembled in the Great Hall, where the chamberlain would assign to those newly arrived quarters in the castle, and servants to convey their baggage up for them.

Katherine and her sister Úna repaired immediately to her chamber to change their attire for the festivities. Lying across the bed was Kat's newest treasure, a blue gown of bright Florentine damask, it's bodice adorned with intense azure silk from the Via dei Tuscani which had been lavishly embroidered, and studded with precious stones. It's high puffed 'trumpet' sleeves were slashed over lavender satin. Upon seeing it, her sister gasped. "Och, Kassie, it's like a thing in Faeryland! Wait til our Julia gets an eyeful of it! She'll pass a stone!" Their elder sister was envious by custom, and they laughed at the prospect of her endeavoring to enjoy this lavish wedding. Úna and Mórag helped Katherine into her gown, and then she and her maidservant turned their attention to Úna. They had done their tartan duties for Hector Mór, and now the sisters could preen and primp to suit themselves. Kat was tugging at the back of her sister's bodice, while Mórag laced it up.

"This is a mite snug, Úna. Your Dónal Dhú is feeding you well, any rate!" Úna peered around at her, in wide-eyed wonder, and laughed.

"Are ye daft, is it? I'm as round as a May herring! And if I am, it's owing to naught but the night-fumblings of the 'dark Laird of Cameron'!"

"You're *never!*" Kat's eyes went wide, and her hands covered her mouth. Úna scrunched her head down into her shoulders, her blue eyes beaming with sly mirth, her voice a husky whisper.

"I'm two months dry now. Nary a flow, and the swell is on! Oh, there's a trout in the well, sure enough!" She laughed brightly. "Our Úna's been up the hill! I'll be next for the Chapel, it seems, now an heir is on the way!" The two sisters laughed and hugged, and laughed again. Kat tisked.

"And never a word!"

"It's *your* day, Kassie. I didn't like to-"

"The day is all the *merrier* for it! God bless you, girl!"

"Oh, I'm blessed rightly! And so are you! Begod, your Shane looked the right gallant today, in his crimson doublet! I thought it a bit wondrous, though, in fairness, for did you not tell me? Did you not tell me that he'll not abide courtly attire?"

"Aye well, he has no liking for it, and he bridled something fierce. But I brought him round. You see, he has a notion of coaxing Archibald to join in league with him against the English. And I told him that lordly attire would put him on a better footing with the Earl. 'Surely', I said, 'Argyle sees enough of shaggy aul bog-lords up in his Highlands.' That put the seal on it!" She laughed brightly. "Oh, I have my ways, girl!" There was a sudden knock on the chamber door, and Mórag opened it, just enough for a looksee.

"Aye?" Her young brother's voice could be heard.

"The O'Neill is on his way up, would ye ever tell your mistress?"

"Aye, then." At the close of the door, Kat dashed over to the looking glass. She brushed and tossed her hair quickly, pinched her cheeks, and put an elderberry to her lips to redden them. She looked up to Úna's laughing face.

"What? What has ye tickled so?"

"Oh, you're a howl, Kassie MacLean! *Three* childer you've borne this man, and still you want a keek in the glass afore you'll see him! A blushing bride, right enough, after all the madness!" When at length the door opened, they were greeted with merry bluster by the chief himself.

"Ohó! The bonny lasses of Mull -out from under their prickly plaids! There's danger afoot!" Katherine laughed gaily.

"Aye, you'd want to mind yourself -when you're outnumbered! Ach, there's *three* of us here, if truth be told!" Shane's eyes went wide with wonder. "No, then, it isn't me -*this* time! It's our Úna is on the nest!"

"Well, God bless the woman and the womb! Sound and healthy be the child!" Shane leaned in to Katherine, with a long loud sniff, and kissed her on the side of her neck. "And bless the bride -and her brood, too! Your aulfella is waiting on me down there, Kat, and I'd just as soon have you beside me!" The girls laughed, and Úna replied.

"Ach, aye, he's cantankerous, right enough. But I've never seen him in better humour! This marriage is a great boon to his fortunes, by his reckoning. And your defeat of the MacDonnells was a final blow for *his* side in the great feud over the Rhinns. You'd want to have heard him crowing!" She drew in her chin, and deepened her voice. 'MacDonnell's bonnet will nae be cocked sae high from this out!' he said. 'They'll need be more wary upon their keeping, now O'Neill has laid them low!" Katherine's hand was over her lips again, with sudden dismay.

"Och, surely that was before poor James met his death?"

"It *was*, aye. There's *none* wanted it to come to that, with our own kindred dying like sheep in a windy ditch. But Father will bless you for it, all the same. I'd say it's the *dowry* is on his mind the day!" Shane put his arm around Katherine.

"The dowry? Ah, divil take it! In your cheeks I have my dowry!" With that, he linked her, and swept her out the door, as she protested weakly.

"Och, hold off yet, Shane! I'm not ready!"

"Indeed, I say you are! Without another pucker or pat, you could set fleets asailing!"

Hector Mór MacLean was, indeed, in high spirits. A big ruddy fellow, he was, with white hair and hawk-like blue eyes that darted incessantly, tallying and reckoning, even as he laughed. His plaid mantle was pinned with a brooch of glittering precious stones, and his sporran was a glossy fur pouch made of the pelt of a sea-otter, richly garnished with silver ornament and studs. He greeted O'Neill with a hearty handshake, introduced his sons and daughters, and launched straightaway into the business of the dowry with a promise of two hundred mercenaries. "The finest gallowglass, of MacLeans, and MacKays, and MacLeods will be on the tide at the first whisper of a word from O'Neill!" When they had clapped hands and clinked a dram on this, his three young grandsons were presented to him, and he surprised everyone by unclasping his otterskin sporran, and producing from it suckets and sweets for the childer. It was understood by all that pressing matters of state, Queen Mary's marriage and the Chase-about Raid, would have to keep until after the feasting, lest they mar the merriment of the day.

A lavish feast was laid on, with the most rigourous formalities of seating and placement attended to by the chamberlain with his towering black staff. Blind Colm and several other harpers played at intervals to the strictest silence, but in between it was a merry crowd of stuffers and swillers, regaling themselves heartily on beef and mutton. The great wonder of the evening was a queer new vegetable from Spanish America. Several barrels of these 'prátaí' had been brought by

SHANE O'NEILL

Lord Slane as a token of thanks from his infamous nephew, Tom Stukeley, for Shane's intercession with the Queen on his behalf. A fellow sea-rover, John Hawkins, had brought the potato into Ireland only that spring at Youghal. The strange spuds were prepared much as turnips, but with buttermilk and scallions thrown in for flavour, and they were highly praised by the guests. Several raw potatoes were passed about as a curiosity, for indeed, there were a few doubters present who didn't believe in America, and here, at last, was incontravertible evidence!

It was later, after the delectation of songs and airs and odes, that serious matters were broached, when Shane asked the Earl of Argyll for his account of the newly quashed rebellion in Scotland. A small crowd gathered in around them at the head table to share in this stirring discourse, for these momentous events were still unfolding, and liable to bear upon all ties and rivalries in 'the three kingdoms'.

Archibald stood, so as to share his tale with the rest, his tall spare form towering over the table, his hazel-brown eyes suddenly somber and glistening. All eyes fixed upon him in the flickering candlelight. He cleared his throat, and reached out his hand. "Give us that tass of whiskeybaugh, man, for I've need of it." It was passed up to him, as others charged their tumblers. "Aye, slake! Slake, for you'll need it when I've told ye." The Earl took a nip of the spirits, and cleared his throat again. His face clouded, and he closed his lips very tightly. "Our good Queen Mary is a stubborn lass -*and small wonder*, for the line of Stewarts before her were none to yield neither. But the way of it was that the louder and quicker came the 'nays' to her foolish betrothal, the fiercer she set her heart upon Darnley. When she got wind of her brother James rising up to stop her, Mary rushed the nuptials through, and declared this lady-faced Englishman, Darnley, to be King of Scotland." This brought a disgusted grumble round the board. "It was then we took to the field, expecting to fight him. I joined my forces with James of Moray, to meet Darnley in the field, but the coward never appeared. In his place, Mary herself donned a helmet, and led her ranks in pursuit of our forces. Oh, she's a canny lass! And well she knew that we are loyal Scots, and would never face our rightful prince in battle. And so began the shameful 'chase-about' in the rain, whereby we crissed and crossed the braes and glens of Scotland, and never crossed our swords! Still, it was never cowardice, but honour that forestalled the clash! And after all the promises from London, English help was neither coming, nor yet to come! Aye, well, after word of London's betrayal, and of this rout in the hills, Edinburgh stood by Mary, and there was no rising up. James of Moray fled to England! And I? I made my way here to Ulster. And so sits Henry Lord Darnley upon the throne of Scotland, upon the Stone of Destiny -Aye, and well may we fear for that dear kingdom, and what *destiny* shall befall her!"

As he seated himself, his cousin, Grey Colin, Laird of Glenorchy stood, bringing the excited voices to a whisht. The craggy old man with the long grey beard stepped in before the company, raising his goblet high. "Not 'God save the King', nay! But 'God..save..the *Kingdom*!" The wry jest was in earnest, and the company called it, and clinked it with due reverence. Shane clapped Archibald on the shoulder.

"Have no doubt of your welcome here, Campbell. And let you bide as long as will suit you!"

"A few weeks, I expect -*I pray*- will suffice, til the damnable madness settles. Queen Mary holds Castle Campbell. She has signed the letters of horning, and I am outlawed. But I shall restore myself to her graces, I have no doubt. She needs me, for I am her *only* Protestant supporter. This wee sojourn may prove fortuitous, though. For, after all that has befallen Ulster -the slaughter at Glenshesk- there is great rancour betwixt the Gaels of Ireland and the Hebrides. And I shall do my uttermost to see to the binding up of those grievances."

"And so shall I! This very day the house of O'Neill has sworn to sacred bonds of kinship with MacLean of Mull! There's binding in that!"

"Aye, and there's a braw start!"

"So it is, Archibald, so it is. And as my wife's brother is wed to your sister Janet, you might well count me amongst your *kin* from this time."

SHANE O'NEILL

"By God you're right, *kinsman*! So I will." They raised their cups to that, and soon their voices dropped to a confidential level with talk of Katherine and family. The rest fell into boisterous discourse, then, mostly speculation as to Darnley and Mary's intentions. As Argyll and a few others were Protestant, remarks had to be finely honed and measured to avoid any fresh rows.

Shane informed Archibald that he'd had word from a well-placed source in London. One of Cecil's spies in up Edinburgh, a fellow called Rooksby, was reporting to Elizabeth that Mary Stuart said she 'intends to stir up trouble in Ireland' by supporting O'Neill, and then to invade England. What's more, she is seeking help from the Pope and Spain. Argyll had heard nothing of such plans, but he was quick to point out that he was no longer privy to such confidences. Nevertheless, he would get word of Rooksby's double-dealing to Mary, mindful that such a warning might help secure his pardon for the failed insurrection. At the same time, the Earl was quite stirred by this news of the Queen's intentions, and he felt that if it were true -if Mary had said such a thing- much indeed might come of it!

Later, in the course of the evening, Argyll casually mentioned, to the surprise of all, that Katherine's former husband, Cullagh O'Donnell was now dwelling at Inverary Castle, his family seat. "Aye, the poor wretch was spurned in London but for promises -promises that *none* believe- of a stipend and honours. In the meanwhile there is no man will trust him with one meal's meat! He came to my door, hard at heel, and quite bereft."

"And you welcomed him?" Shane's brows were furrowed.

"After a fashion, aye. Indebted, as I was, by his service in former days, I was obliged to take him under my roof. It's there I left him! I was away off to support Moray's rising. O'Donnell has blackened your name at Court, O'Neill, *that* I can tell you. He has recounted your cruelties in cot and castle from London to Argyll -a woeful tale, that would draw tears from a turk! I, *myself*, nearly expected to find Katherine in shackles!"

"He was dealt no worse in my dungeon nor the chastisement he meted out to my uncle, his father. Ah, damn his blood, the aul hoor is free to talk -lies or laments; 'tis nothing to me. Let his belly-aching console him, for *vengeance* he'll get none!"

"Aye. 'Tis little enough to soothe his ravaged pride, I suppose. He is idle, now, but for his brooding. He is quite ruined." Shane cocked his brow.

"But he *waits*..." Argyll nodded gravely.

"He waits, aye, for a turning of fortune's wheel."

"For a bad turn in the fortunes of O'Neill!" Farleigh appeared at Shane's shoulder like a spirit, with his confused white hair aglow in the candlelight. "Like many another! There's *many* a man waits for *that!*"

"There is." Young Sir Robert Fleming spoke up. "Isn't the Bastard's young son, Hugh O'Neill, waiting beyond in England for *his* chance to supplant you? They say he is nearly an Englishman by this." Farleigh's bright eyes rolled under his shaggy brows.

"God spare us *his* return! Huh! Another mincing 'Sir Barnaby' to chastise all about him!" This brought a bitter laugh from a few of the Irish, piquing the curiosity of the old greybeard, Glenorchy.

"Pray tell us, man, who is Sir Barnaby, then?" It was Shane who replied.

"The Baron of Ossory. It's a queer tale to tell, even in these mad times. After my father's defeat at Bellahoe in '39, the chieftain FitzPatrick -like many another chieftain, was made to surrender up his wee son and heir, Brían, to be reared in England. But *King Henry* took a liking to *this* boy." What's this he said?" He glanced over to Sir Robert.

"He said he was a '*proper* child', and one whom he 'much *tendereth!*'"

"He did. And so the boy was kept at Court as 'playmate' to his sickly snivelling son, Prince Edward. But he was *used* as his whipping boy!" Farleigh's face scrunched in a frown, and he shook his head.

"A perverse arrangement! Base and twisted, as only *they* could contrive! One that left its sordid mark upon him!" He looked back to Sir Robert, to elucidate.

"So it did. For later, as gentleman of the chamber, this 'Sir

SHANE O'NEILL

Barnaby' FitzPatrick returned to imprison his father and mother with most *unnatural* and extreme cruelty. -charging them with 'rebellion'. His cousins and kindred he punished wickedly. Cold hearted and brutal." This was met with shaking heads. Farleigh sighed with revulsion, and raised his voice.

"His own *sire*! And the mother that bore him! He has surpassed the English in his morbid revulsion of Irish ways and wonts." He harumphed, and raised a warning finger. "I'm telling you, this young O'Neill, the Bastard's son, who bides in their keeping may return one day, twisted in *just* such a way! Another 'white blackbird' who doesn't know his own!" Archibald twigged after a moment's puzzlement.

"A *white blackbird*? Och, I ken ye. Aye, just so!" Fleming ventured a metaphor of his own.

"Or a *vulture*, perhaps, biding his hour!" Shane laughed at this.

"A vulture, aye. A scrawny *vulture*. For I would *need* be dead and *carrion*, before ever he would dare set his foot in Ulster. A thing that shall never happen! He is the Queen's fond and foolish hope, no more. A measure of her desperation." Argyll sighed and tisked.

"Such a tale! An Irish whipping boy! The Gael to be lashed for the sins of the Saxon! Such depravity. Fie upon them."

"There you see, Archibald, how they would debase us. The Saxon would have us all, *all* our race, for 'whipping boy'. *If* we but let them!"

"Aye, they would have us in the one pot, Taig and Jock -and set a braw and bonny blaze *under* it! They regard us but little, in truth, yet they're wonderous fond of the land *beneath* us!" Shane held his burning gaze upon Argyll for a moment, and then spoke low and deep.

"If we fight *together*...we can best them!!"

"Och, go easy there, O'Neill. Draw down your topsail! I've woes enough these times with my *own* fair Queen! I didnae come to borrow troubles!" Archibald smiled then, and clapped his hand upon Shane's shoulder. "We shall talk yet. Time enough for that! But tell me this- You sent Sussex apacking, and now they say you'll soon see the back of Arnolde. Is it so?"

"It is. Now we're to lose Arnolde, it seems, the first Viceroy ever to suit me. A plain-dealing man with no turnings or windings. He would oftimes take my part with the Queen's Council. But she is sending Sidney back to us. 'Big Henry of the Beer', he's known on this side of the water."

"And how does that bode? Ill or well, foul or fair?"

"Oh, I have his measure -Sidney's a man will look you in the eye, and list you. The differ to Sussex, any rate!" But Farleigh O'Gneeve did not embrace such a hopeful prospect.

"Ah, there will be little enough difference once he takes up in Dublin Castle! When they assume the mantle of state, they embrace the darkness under it!"

"That may well be so." Shane nodded, his eyes hooded as he considered. "He may prove more iron-fisted than Sussex, for it was Sidney himself gave me a lesson in 'sovereignty', and the 'harsh measures it demands'. He was boasting in his cups one evening, when I was his unhappy guest in London. 'Firstly must you *break* a country with the broadsword!', he said, 'Then must you dole out power from the top, as you suffer chieftains to wield rapiers in your name.' He holds us to be fools here, for in Ireland, since the days of Tara, all power comes from below. Jealously guarded rights of chieftains, that will not yield to support a high king."

"There is wisdom there, right enough. And *trouble*, with it! Your stay at Court was a fine bit of schooling in their ways and wiles."

"Oh, I learned a share. 'Dissimulation is the art of kings, he said, "and he who does not know how to dissemble, is not fit to reign!' Lord Cecil, it was, pronounced that when I called him out on a lie. Would you credit that, now? He got that bit of wisdom, he said, from the great Emperor Charles V!" Farleigh's brows beetled at this.

"What is this '*dissimulation*', if it's no harm in asking?"

"Nothing more, nor less, than *lying*. They reckon it's a sin *not* to lie, if you've crown on your dome. Ah, but, sure, what's in a lie?" Shane shrugged casually, but he had asked the wrong party, for Farleigh, having put away a fair share of Jerez wine, was prepared to tell him. He tisked, and tugged at his long white beard.

"Oh, there is fierce power in words! Words are the corporal bodies that we give to thoughts as we conceive them. Thoughts are not born until they are wriggled from the heart to the brain into 'words'. Even if unuttered! Ergo, a lie is terrible because it debases this miracle. Words must come from the heart –not the head!" Argyll turned his wry smile to Shane.

"There ye be, you're told rightly! But who will tell *Elizabeth*? When does this new Viceroy come?"

"I've heard no word as yet of his sailing."

Farleigh, stirred with indignation, raised his arm and declaimed, "Well, may Lord Sidney have luck in his crossing! And may it be *bad* luck!" He clicked his thumbnail off his upper teeth, and held it out before him.

"Bad winds to him,
and foul seas to him,
and a shreiking and wailing on the shore after him!"

The Scots laughed heartily at this, but Shane cautioned them. "Oh, were you the mark of one of his maledictions, you'd have little enough cause for laughter! The curse of Farleigh O'Gneeve would scorch a man to ashes!"

The festivities grew more frolicsome as the evening wore on. The sprightly tunes and the liberal libation brought frisking and capering, and a merry din of laughter in the Great Hall. Katherine was in bright form, beguiling her guests and giving ear to their gossip, and Shane was ever bantering with the men, and cajoling them with coarse pleasantries. MacCrimmon's pipes skirled, and the Highland Fling was flung, with great kilted men twirling and lepping nimbly over their claymores.

Wedding gifts were then presented, publicly, by turns, with an air of amiable competition, a great deal of ostentation, and ever more fulsome praise for the great Lord of Ulster. In the end, though, there was little question as to which was the most splendid tribute. Shane's cousin, Black Hugh O'Donnell, stepped forward, and presented to the bride and groom the gift of an exquisitely carved wooden cup, ornamented with gems and silver fittings. It was an ancient and much revered heirloom. There were some present, however, who might have regarded this a bestowal of plunder. It had been seized by Black Hugh from the Maguire, one of the brutal consequences of that chieftain's hold-out against O'Neill's rule.

The bejeweled cup, which rests today in Dunvegan Castle, had been made for Neill Glúndubh, the progenitor of the O'Neills, in 950 AD. Although it was for over a century in the keeping of the Maguires, their claim to it had always been a matter of contention for their O'Neill overlords, whose very name was inherited from its original proprietor. The much coveted chalice now boasted a squarish golden 'lip-piece', newly fashioned for this occasion, with an inscription to commemorate the wedding of Katherine to the 'King O'Neill'. The relic caused a great deal of excitement in the hall, and added immeasurably to the grandeur of the occasion. It was praised highly by Argyll, who marveled at it's rich ornamentation and fanciful stylings. "A bonny Irish 'grail', but whimsical and queer! And where would you see the like of it? A mether on four wee legs, with tiny brogues on its feet. That's as Gaelic a treasure as the Gospel of Kells!" Farleigh winked and nodded.

"It's like a thing stolen from a faery mound! A fine thing it would be if they come looking for it!"

An elderly chieftain, the MacGuinness, begged leave to propose a toast with the goblet, and such was granted. The cup was filled to its golden brim with the choicest whiskeybaugh, and he held it on high. The chamberlain rapped his towering black staff thrice on the stone floor.

"Ho there, all! Let ye give ear to Art MacGuinness, Chief of Iveagh!" A hush fell on the instant, and the old man spoke out full.

"I'm an 'old spear' *these times*, boys, easy seen. Not as old as the Killeleigh bog, but nearly so... But if I *am*, I was as sharp, and as swift as *any* back in the day! I was out with Shane O'Neill's father at Bellahoe ford in '39. And I mind the day. And I *rue* the sorry end of it! But for *that* black day, Conn O'Neill would have borne the crown of High King of Ireland! And it's not the King of *Ulster*'s wedding we'd be

SHANE O'NEILL

tipping our cup to this day, but the King of Ireland's." There was cheering, and he lowered the cup to his breast. His bright eyes shone with ardor as he called those glory-days to mind, and his voice seemed to grow in strength. "The Geraldine League', as was called Kildare's confederation of Irish lords, they had their *deliberations*. And for that the O'Neill line has the strongest claim to the high kingship, they deemed that Conn Bacach would be crowned King of Ireland upon the Hill of Tara, as in days of old. Now, O'Neill had in his keeping a letter from Pope Paul III such as styled him 'King of Our Realm of Ireland'! Well, this was as good as tearing usunder the curséd Laudabiliter, whereby that English Pope had granted this island to the king of England. Alas, the defeat at Bellahoe put a stop to our march to Tara, and to the crowning of O'Neill as High King. But it was *that* resolve of the Irish people to crown O'Neill, and that alone, was the reason King Henry had himself named King of Ireland three years later. The first English king ever to do so! Aye, well, the English now are driven from Ulster, for we've claimed many a victory since Bellahoe, and each and *all* under the command of *Shane O'Neill!*" His emphatic mounting tone brought rapturous applause this time, and as MacGuinness raised aloft the chalice once more, all cups were lifted high. "And I'll say *this*... Aye, this I'll say, 'May God and his holy Mother bless this gladsome day for the bride Lady Katherine...and may *God save Shane O'Neill,* the King of Ulster- and *with the grace of God,* the *future* High King of Ireland!!"

The hall erupted in a thunderous ovation of "O'Neill abú!", and when Shane had drank from the golden mether, and passed it on, the crowd stilled expectantly. He stood, now, smiling so broadly that his eyes nearly closed. He nodded at MacGuinness, and winked with a merry eye.

"Ach, you old spears beat the Devil! It isn't '*some*' ye want, nor '*half*' ye want, for half is not half enough for ye! No, ye's are not easy pleased! But hold yet, for neither is Shane O'Neill! I'm not a man for stopping. And I say that '*enough*' will not suffice while there is *more* to be won!" He raised his hand to stop the cheers. "Now, 'tis not so long ago that I scratched my name to a treaty with London. A treaty that seemed like to promise fair, that seemed like to promise peace. Didn't it promise me the golden chain of my father's estate, the Earldom of Tyrone! Instead of a golden chain, what I got was black poison! What I got was a brittle peace that is like to shatter soon! Aye! For I've taken word off the wind that the English are girding for war. Even now, they're hammering out a new suit of battle-armour for Harry Sidney to wear, and I think it is not for talking. But, sure, what use is talking when I am wearied of their wiles? He will come. And when he comes- I will put him to the right-about!" There were cheers and whoops, and whistles now. "Bellahoe will look like a cockfight when I lock horns with 'Big Henry of the Beer'! For I have Ulstermen at my back, men hard as whipcord! And while there is more to be won, 'Old Spear', I'll not stop! Elizabeth Tudor might bid the winds to stop. She might bid the tides to cease. But Shane O'Neill will not be stopped! We'll drive the English to their ships, and O'Neill will stand upon the stone at Tara yet! So lay *that* to your hearts, ye pack of divils!"

Shane laughed, and the crowd roared, and the pipers raised a spirited march. What with the profusion of spirits, and high spirits, the men hoisted Shane onto their shoulders, and the giddy cheering throng carried him in a progress about the great hall. If this ballyhoo was sportive, it was earnest, and the men's hearts were in it. Their hearts were swelled with a rapturous pride in O'Neill's power, and with a mad fervor to drive him on towards that loftiest prize, the High Kingship of Ireland. Argyle and his lairds were amused, to be sure, but they were highly impressed by the princely display, and by the wild affection and reverence in which Shane was held by his people.

Argyll and the Hebridean chiefs stayed for some time. The Earl's journal marks his return to Glenorchy from O'Neill's wedding on the 17th of October. Campbell of Carrick did not arrive back until the 11th of November, so it was a lingering sojourn for all. Shane entertained his guests lavishly at Dungannon, with races, and hurling, and hunting, all followed by convivial feasting into the night at his lordly castle. There were contestings between the poets, the harpers, and the pipers, these last judged, of course, by the famed MacCrimmon, and O'Neill bestowed princely rewards upon the champions.

SHANE O'NEILL

While in Ulster, Archibald assumed the role that was customary to him in the Highlands, that of arbitrating disputes and feuds. Oftimes Shane and Sorley Buí would be seated on either side of him, as he tried to broker a proper peace, after the savagery of Glenshesk. In the end, he left Shane with a solemn promise of his assistance against the English, but his terms were not inconsiderable. Although O'Neill refused to release Sorley Buí, he was induced to allow the MacDonnells to resettle Ballycastle, and a few of the surrounding glens. Forbidden to them were the lands of O'Kane and MacQuillan, but even at that, such a concession would go hard with the Irish thereabout after all the blood spilled. All was, of course, contingent on their fighting beside Shane. In accordance with the Gaelic fashion of mending disputes, it was further agreed that a son and a daughter of the late chieftain, James MacDonald would be betrothed to a daughter and son borne to Shane by his Countess. Argyle's cousin, Campbell of Carrick, pledged to be gossip to their next child. All this was formalized, clapped up, and clinked proper, on the principle that 'there's no luck in a dry bargain!'

The one binding factor among all these Scots and Irish was an abiding hatred and mistrust of the English. From day to day, reports would come in from Shane's well placed spies, including news of London's perplexity over this mighty gathering in Tirowen. "The Scotch are going into Ireland in vast numbers," a missive warned. "Ten or twelve galleys lay upon the northern coast, well manned." One dispatch that vexed the Scots to a roiling fury concerned Fitzwilliam's merry report to Lord Cecil of James MacDonnell's death. "Praise God we have seen the last of that odious villain," he wrote,'whose airs and lewd practices I would also lay buried with him! And praise be that his Scotch kin lie mouldering in the glens, their tartans fluttering to the kites and crows." This put the lie to the crafty condolences of the English Ambassador in Edinburgh, Randolph, and served to strengthen the rather leery rapprochement with Shane.

When the last of the great square-rigged galleys was launched from the northern shore, and ploughing the waves toward Scotland, Shane's 'court' returned to the more modest fortress at Benburb. It was a time of quiet, a welcome repose for all, but with the certain knowledge that it was but an interlude. The change of regime in Dublin Castle loomed with its uncertainties, of course. But there was something more. Shane had been strangely moved by the grandeur of this occasion, with its fiery assemblage of Gaelic nobility. The heady exaltation, and the hue and cry for more, had left him with a new resolve, a resolve to push further, beyond the ramparts of the Black Pig's Dyke, to marshal the Irish of the South. He was determined that one day yet he should undertake his father's march to the Hill of Tara, there to set his foot upon the Stone of Destiny.

SHANE O'NEILL

CHAPTER 27

In early November, Myler Magrath returned from Rome. He firstly made his way to Armagh to confer with the Dean, who, he was surprised to learn, was in London. Dean Danyell had undertaken a diplomatic mission for Shane to smooth ruffled feathers at Court, and perhaps to further O'Neill's efforts to acquire the Queen's Primatial nomination for himself. As for O'Neill, he was off in the West, extending his domain by exacting tribute from the Connaught chieftainry. But in the Chancery at Armagh, a small office in the two-storied stone edifice known, improbably, as 'the Primate's Palace', Myler met with one keenly involved in his affairs.

Fr. Magrath's letters to the Dean from Rome had evidently been sent on to London, so Fr. Hugh O'Neill, Shane's impatient young brother, had gotten no word of what had come of his nomination to the See of Down and Conor. Myler's appearance now in episcopal robes and bishop's mitre, was enlightening, in a most jarring way. Myler explained to him that, due to measures newly passed at the Council of Trent, Fr. Hugh was ineligible by virtue of his age. He himself had been consecrated Bishop to that diocese, and would hold the chair for eight years, at which time Hugh, having reached his thirtieth year, would acquire the see. At Fr. Hugh's insistence, he was obliged to read out to him from the decree. "Pending his minority, the young man will be given a pension from the fruits of the void church that he may have the means to fit himself for future preferment." This 'pension' would consume nearly half of Myler's own salary, a provision most galling to the new bishop. Even so, the proviso did little to assuage the ambitious young cleric, and his fury was quite manifest. He regarded it, he said, as a betrayal, of himself, of Magrath's mission, and of Shane O'Neill, and he made threats as to what retribution 'his grace' might expect from the chieftain. Myler spoke roundly to him, reminding him that neither of them might dictate to the Holy Father in Rome, and abruptly took his leave.

The bishop rode the seven miles to Benburb Castle, then, to see how he would be received in Shane's absence. Lady Katherine gave him a warm, if troubled welcome. She congratulated him on his elevation, but at Myler's pressing, admitted that Shane was less than pleased. "Och, Myler -your Grace, when the news settles on him he'll come round. He knows that you can hardly gainsay the Pope in such matters! I think perhaps he's peeved that you'll no longer be at his side is all!" This prompted a new consideration. "But where *will* you be from this?"

"I'll be residing at Downpatrick." Noting Katherine's perplexed smile, he added, "East of the Newry. Kilclief Castle is my seat, a grand keep on the western headland of Strangford Lough." Lady O'Neill smiled brightly now.

"A new life for you!" Myler nodded, matching her cheerful countenance. Katherine looked at him now afresh, as though for the first time. He was all of forty-five years of age, but any might think him younger. He was quite dapper, really, for a cleric. His skin was fair and bright still, his blue eyes sharp. His black hair curled across a noble brow, fell in waves over his ears, and was cropped just below, with only a bit of grey about the temples to account for his years. His long sable brows curved down to frame his eyes. An aquiline nose, sharp but fine, and none too big. His beard betrayed his vanity, for it was a triple 'goat's chin' with three separate black tufts that joined below the jaw. He was attired in a powder blue surplice, and looked quite smart altogether. A certain devilish dignity attended his features that would often cause you to forget his calling. Katherine curtsied, smiling. "My Lord Bishop! Very grand! An honour *well* deserved, and long in coming!"

"You're kind, Lady Katherine, as ever, for that is your way. I'm making my way to Kilclief Castle this day, and, marry 'tis a pity, I must be off shortly."

"You'll not take supper with us?"

"Divil the stop I'll stay. I want to see the place before nightfall! Tell your husband that I was appointed suffragan bishop to the new Primate, Dr. Creagh, so –when he returns to Ireland, I'll be able to keep an *mindful* eye on his doings. I am well placed to do so. Aye. Tell *that* to Shane."

"Where *is* the Primate? Since ever he made his his 'bold escape'?"

"He's now in Madrid, consulting with King Philip. Creagh intends to return here by high summer, so he writes, aboard a merchant vessel."

"He will bring troubles with him, if all they say is true! Shane will be glad of your heedful watch over him. As for me, Myler -your Grace, I'll be forever beholden to you for procuring my annulment papers! And I'm only sorry that you could not be here for our wedding. It was a grand day! You were a long time away, and I'm sure it was no easy task to wrest those papers from Holy Roman Rota!"

"I had the devil's own job of it! The intrigue in the Vatican is little different from the Royal Court in London, but for the Italians -and the *age* of them!" Katherine laughed. "The Cardinals of the Rota are of such a decrepitude, that these matters of the heart are *inconceivable* to them! But they know wine! And they know silver! A man could lose his Faith in such a place." Katherine laughed again, clapping her hand up to her mouth. She shook her head.

"Both blunt and sharp is Myler's tongue' they say! You were well able for them! Tell me, what sort is the Pope? Kind or cross?"

"Both, by turns, like every mother's son." He winked. "For a Dominican, he is *gamesome* enough! -With three bastards to prove it..." Myler blessed himself and lowered his voice. "But kind or cross, he's not long *for* it! Upon my leaving, his Holiness was grievously ill, and there was much talk of who might replace him."

"My Shane will be glad of that -if it's ghoulish to say it! Please God, it will prove a fortuity for him!" Myler gave a slow nod, with a meaningful wink.

"I daresay it will!" Katherine blessed herself swiftly.

"God is good!"

"And he has a good mother!" Myler glanced to her belly, so big with child. "Yours has proven a fruitful union. God has surely blessed it!"

"He has, aye. This will be four! Hugh, Art, Brian, and the next little miracle to come!"

"God grant you a safe birth, my Lady! And now I will take my leave." With that, Myler took Katherine's hand and kissed it. She laughed.

"It's I should be kissing your ring, my Lord Bishop! Go you safe! And come you back when the O'Neill is returned."

On the 10th of November, the new Lord Deputy of Ireland set off from London under dark glowering skies that matched his mood. To the shrill accompaniment of fife and drums, Sir Harry stepped along on his white charger, leading a long train of followers and supplies in a stately parade through the city. Trotting along beside him, his standard bearer held aloft the scarlet pennant bearing the device of the Sidneys, the 'knotty cudgel'. It whipped and flapped in the blustery wet winds, as he emerged from under Newgate's portcullis to face the wintry hills ahead. The cavalcade struck forth, then, onto the Oxford road commencing an arduous journey that would take them far beyond the western shore.

After Sidney rode his many captains including the bold Tom Stukeley, who was delighted to see the last of the city's walls, and to savor the free air after the dank stench of her Majesty's dungeons. Trundling along behind him was the stylish Flemish carriage of Lady

SHANE O'NEILL

Mary Sidney with all her maids, and Stukeley's presence aroused lively gossip among them. Following was a line of packhorses that stretched far behind, heavily laden with chests, coffers, and portmanteaus holding all of Lord Sidney's most cherished possessions, books, plate, jewels, linen, robes, and the costliest wines of his cellar.

After three weeks of the hard road, the bedraggled travelers finally took sight of the sea at Chester. Sidney's crew had barely gotten their goods stowed aboard the two galleons, when a fierce storm swept in off the Irish Sea and battered the shore for nearly a week, leaving the party stranded. Wild winds and waves pummeled the harbour, demolishing the stone pier, and sinking every ship in the haven! Sir Harry and his wife were disconsolate. All their precious belongings lay at the bottom of Liverpool Bay, including seven of Sir Harry's finest horses. The Lord Deputy was quite unnerved by this 'froward beginning' to his business. He was convinced, and wrote as much to Cecil, that this tempest was begotten of witchcraft, a malevolent curse from the far shore!

By the 4th of December, the rains being somewhat diminished, the beleaguered Deputy and his weary train set off along the Welsh coastal road for Beaumaris. Even with their load lightened, Penmaenmawr was hard traveling, with only the roughest lodgings to be had. Given their numbers, simply finding a warm fire and dry shelter proved a nearly insurmountable task. Once at port, there was further delay procuring a ship, but at long last they put to sea, and the voyage was underway.

Just before the Christmas, two monks arrived at Benburb Castle from Downpatrick. Their ship had put in at Strangford Lough, and Bishop Magrath had sent them on to the O'Neill, for they carried momentous news. The Medici Pope had died. The new Pope was Pius V, Cardinal Ghislieri, a man renowned as the 'Grand Inquisitor'! He was a hard-liner regarding heresy, widely known to have pressed for the excommunication of Elizabeth Tudor. And now the decision was his to make! The news brought wild elation. Farleigh the poet declared to Shane that the constellations were moving into place for the unfolding of his destiny!

The monks also noted that Fr. David Wolfe's posting as Nuncio would officially end upon the death of the Pope. Unless his appointment were re-affirmed by Pius V, he would no longer be Nuncio! "Please God, it will not be!" Shane 'prayed' also that this 'Grand Inquisitor' Pope would keep his word and declare the Queen anathema, banishing her from the 'Faithful', and relinquishing all her subjects of their allegiance to her. As the greater part of her subjects held by the old religion, such a ruling would make a bedlam of her kingdom!

The Dean of Armagh was still in London conferring with the Queen, hopefully impressing her as the most suitable man to hold the Primatial See of Armagh. Indeed, the Papal appointee had not been seen for over for a year. Shane now felt confident that he could prevail upon the new Pope to name Terence Danyell to the chair of Patrick. A man who could openly serve there, and actually carry out his duties! There was great hope and wild rejoicing in Benburb Castle that Christmas.

The wintry seas were wild and raging. Again and again the bitter winds drove Sidney's galleon from its course, and it was not until the 15th day of January that the misty green headlands of Dublin Bay appeared over the bow. There were great sighs of relief onboard when finally the ship dropped anchor to moor in the crowded harbour at the old pier below Dalkey Castle. There the Viceroy's entourage were lodged for the night, properly, at long last! Sidney's first order of business, however, was to send a page galloping off to Dublin Castle, with a note advising the Lord Justice to prepare a state welcome for the morrow.

When his cavalcade reached Dames Gate just before noontide on the following day, the new Lord Deputy was greeted with fanfare and jubilation. Throngs of Dubliners cheered to have Sir Harry back; the unpopular tenure of his successor, Sussex, had cast a golden glow upon his memory, and the joy at this return was heartfelt. Flanked by the Lord Mayor, and his aldermen in their robes and chains of office, Sir Nicholas Arnolde gave his replacement a magnanimous welcoming oration.

One week later, blaring trumpets and an angelic choir at Christchurch Cathedral marked the solemn installation of the New Order. With the final notes of 'amen' ringing in the great vaulted heights, a bare tattoo of drums commenced, and Sir Harry Sidney proceeded slowly up the aisle. Before him, holding aloft the Sword of State, was his new Knight Marshal, Bagenal, who had won the office by his recent capture of 'the Pope's Primate', William Creagh. The Anglican Archbishop of Dublin, Hugh Curwan, administered the oath of office to the Lord Deputy, and then presided over a full Divine Service. Upon its conclusion, Sidney delivered "a most pithy, wise, and eloquent oration," and he was then conducted in state to the castle for a formal banquet. There the local gentry were presented, one by one, whereupon they knelt in homage, pledging their duty to her Majesty's Viceroy. For all the decorum and elegance of the evening, the truth was that Sidney had found himself presiding over a country as restless as the wintry seas around it.

As the evening settled in, the buzz of tattle and tidings rose ever louder, and the talk inevitably turned to those dark forces that were mustering beyond the high ramparts of the Pale, with wild speculation concerning the clash to come. Captain Stukeley fell in with Sir Nick Bagenal, whom he remembered from his days at Berwick in the Scottish campaign. On Tom's greeting him, the older gentleman eyed him coldly, saying, "Ah, the gilded villain! You have distinguished yourself as a *brigand*, I am told." But Stukeley only laughed, and as the wine flowed, the Marshal warmed to him, pouring forth his worries

SHANE O'NEILL

and woes. Behind each worry and woe was Tom's old friend, Shane O'Neill. Never had the country been in such disarray! "Only last autumn, O'Neill burst forth from his northern strongholds, and swept down like a tempest upon us! All the marchlands! Capturing all my vast estates! The Newry, Greencastle, Carlingford, all! I stand ruined. But for Sir Harry's pressing me to take on the Marshalcy, I should never be tempted to stay! Not another curséd day!" All of this was of more than passing interest to Stukely, who plied him with sympathy and wine, which he splashed to the brim.

"Bloody woes, man! Such utter ruin... 'Twould rend the heart! But, wherever would you go?"

"I would hie me back to Staffordshire, and gladly. Had I but the wherewithal! Only last spring, £6,000. those demesnes would have fetched me! Now they'd scarcely rate sixty! O'errun by rebels and savages. Worthless as cabbage leaves my deeds are now, tinder to light a candle!" This was merry music to Captain Stukeley, who possessed a keen ear for the rattle of loose ends, and the chance openings of Fortune's creaky gate. Already a grandiose notion was forming...

The Earl of Clanrickard was also present, with a tale more disturbing still. Shane O'Neill had ventured far beyond Ulster, and swept down upon the western province of Connaught. He camped in O'Rourke's country, in O'Conor Sligo's country, and in MacDermott's country for all of a week, demanding of those chieftains "the tribute due of auld time to them that were high kings of the realm!" He overawed them, and they quickly bowed to his will. He devastated O'Rourke's country, and, driving before him 4000 head of cattle, he returned in triumph to Tirowen.

Clanrickard's look was one of blank dismay as he recounted the deed. Upon being presented to the new Viceroy, he spoke words of solemn warning. "Pray, excuse me", he said, "for speaking plainly what I think. I assure you that O'Neill's move into the West bodes an ill likelihood for the realm! If it be not speedily looked unto, there shall be hazard to come, hazard as far out of her Majesty's hands as *ever* it was out of the hands of *any* of her predecessors in times beforepast. I beg you, look promptly to these things, or they will grow ere long to a worse end than any I dare bespeak!" Sidney was undaunted, and, truth be told, gratified to hear it! He had firmly resolved to wage war upon the rebel, and needed just such provocations as might convince her Majesty to undertake the expense.

Within the week, the Dean of Armagh arrived to confer with Sidney. He was returning from his gift-bearing mission to London. He called to welcome and advise, and to reassure the Viceroy as to O'Neill's intentions. Danyell, having learned little of Sidney's plans, was sent north with the Lord Deputy's 'request' to the chieftain for an expeditious meeting at Drogheda in the Pale. The sooner the forms and usages of diplomacy could be proven futile, the sooner might he have his war! But when Shane's prompt reply arrived, proposing the 5th of February at the Gap of the North, Sidney declared it 'too soon', and he insisted upon meeting in the Pale. Shane was equally adamant on that score. He wrote that his 'timorous and mistrustful people' would not suffer him to venture there, and recounted the several attempts upon his life made by 'previous' lord deputies. Shane demanded, further, that the Queen put her Royal seal to the treaties she had signed with him. Whatever the reason, Sidney was pleased to hold this written refusal, and he determined, then, to send Stukeley north. But that could wait.

The Lord Deputy lost no time in wielding his new broom, for he was determined that his should be truly a new order. He declared that there was no longer a single Irish-born servant of the Queen to be trusted, for 'every secret of the Castle reaches O'Neill by fall of night'. We simply 'cannot be guided in government by councillors of Irish broth! It is therefore meet that all unfit persons should be removed from their places, and sufficient persons of *English* birth be chosen to supply them.' The Privy Council was entirely re-staffed with Englishmen, and English sheriffs were appointed and renewed in every county. The troops he found 'beggar-like and insolent, oftimes allied with the Irish'. He set about striking from the rolls a vast number of Irish soldiers who had been enlisted in the companies.

After only a few weeks, Sir Harry sent off to London his brutal assessment, with a stirring exhortation to war. The Pale, he wrote, was "overwhelmed with vagabonds;" the English soldiers "worse than the people, so insolent as to be intolerable; so rooted in idleness as there was no hope by correction to amend them." In the South, since the Desmond wars, "a man might ride twenty or thirty miles and find no houses standing...In Ulster there tyrannizes the prince of pride. Lucifer was never more puffed up with pride and ambition than that O'Neill is. He is at present the only strong and rich man in Ireland; he could muster 1,000 horse and 4,000 foot. He could burn up to the gates of Dublin and return unfought. And he is the dangeroustest man, and most like to bring the whole estate of this land to subversion and subjugation -either to himself or to some foreign prince- that ever was in Ireland! No Attilla or Totile, no Vandal or Goth was ever more to be doubted for over-running Christendom, than this man is for over-running and bespoiling Ireland. If he be an angel from Heaven that will say that ever O'Neill will be a good subject ere he be thoroughly chastised –believe him not! But think him a spirit of error. Surely if the Queen does not chastise him in Ulster, he will chastise all hers out of Ireland!"

Lord Cecil took up Sidney's cause at Court, but could promise only further delays. "We do thoroughly take to heart the shame England has sustained by Irish disobedience; and we wish you fortuity and triumph in discharging this onerous task of repairing the disgrace received at the Chief Rebel's hands." The Queen could not yet bring herself to assent to the costs of the war, and so, at the risk of cruelly affronting a true and trusty servant, she sent her Chamberlain and kinsman, Sir Francis Knollys, to determine in the matter -and to limit expenditures. As her reason for so doing, she bewailed that 'the cost of levying troops in England was four times as great as it used to be'. Sidney was predictably furious, and turned his gaze from east to north. A letter was soon dispatched to inform O'Neill of the impending visit of his bosom friend Stukeley, noting, 'whose coming and speech we understand you so earnestly desire'. Time to see if 'the Seadog' was worth his salt!

To the Viceroy's consternation, Knolleys was as peaceable and parsimonious as the Queen. He was also astute and subtle. In Dublin

SHANE O'NEILL

Castle, he found himself among men of office and of the sword whose fortunes were 'more to be advanced by war and confiscations than by peace'. In his private correspondence with the Queen, he advised pacific measures, and decried the ambition and avarice of colonial officialdom, even as he encouraged Sidney's hopes. As winter melted into spring, the chances of mobilizing for a summer offensive seemed to be vanishing too. Sir Harry, thwarted, and ever more discomfited, fired off fervent pleas and frantic warnings, but nothing would persuade the Queen to open her purse. Nothing, that is, until the return of Tom Stukeley with word from the North!

Assured of a rapturous welcome, the new envoy had undertaken his mission with a light heart, and a great deal of excitement. On a blustery cold and wet spring day, accompanied by the amiable Mr. Justice Dowdall of the Queen's Irish Bench, Stukeley rode out from the high walls of Dundalk into the wilds of Ulster. In spite of the weather, he convinced his partner to veer from their course, and the two rode one league north of their destination for a quick detour. A hasty inspection of the Newry, those ruined estates of Bagenal that had so piqued Tom's interest! Suitably impressed, they turned south, and soon found O'Neill's new towerhouse in the dark dripping wood at Fathan.

It could be said, rather, that *they* were found. One of Shane's sentries intercepted them, a hulking gallowglass in a conical helmet and long chain-mail tunic, and led the pair through the sprawling encampment of the three-hundred-man guard. This was no easy task, for smoke from the campfires hung like a low cloud in the misty rain, obscuring their path, and it was some time before they could make out the towering form that was their destination. With a 'hup, ha!', they hastened on to the mighty stone keep.

A captain, one of the O'Donnelly brothers, greeted them, and settled them before the massive hearth. It was piled high with logs, licked by a few lurching remnants of fire, but after some spirited claps of a bellows, the flames blazed brightly. A torch was kindled, and ensconced on the wall. Once their sodden cloaks had been hung over pegs to drip on the hearthstone, Éamon O'Donnelly gave to each a cup of brandywine and bade them 'wait'. In the dark chamber, the jumble of shields and halberds along the walls glistened in the firelight, and the red hand of O'Neill seemed to be everywhere daubed, on doors, shields, and pennants. Rough voices could be heard, calling out in that dark tongue, and then heavy steps. The massive oak door creaked open a bit, and a deep familiar voice rang out from behind it, speaking in heavily brogued English.

"Fee Fi fo fum! I smell the blood of an English man! Be he alive or be he dead, I'll ground his bones to make my bread!" With a boisterous laugh, the door swung open, and there stood Shane O'Neill, a wild-haired buxom young woman under each arm. "Begod, ye mad hoor, ye! Well, ye're busted out of the brig, I see, anyroad!" Shane shook the girls by the shoulders gently, and released them. He cast a wary glance at Dowdall as the two men got to their feet. "And who's this you've brought with you? Your parole bondsman, I'll wager!" Stukeley laughed, and clapped a hand on the man's shoulder.

"You're near enough the mark, O'Neill! This is Sir James Dowdall," he said, and added with a significant look, "-*of* the Queen's Irish Bench." Shane shook his hand, and addressed the man in Latin.

"Dowdall... Are you anything to the Primate that *was*? Before our poor O'Tighe of blesséd memory?"

"Indeed. George, mine uncle. His memory is blesséd too, glory to his bones! And, like him, I am a Catholic. But, be of no doubt, I *serve my Queen*."

"So do we all! So do we all! She's a grand queen altogether -and a fine armful, I'll wager!"

"James is also a nephew of Sir Thomas Cusack, the Lord Chamberlain."

"Is he? Is he, now? Good man. Sorry to see him go." Tom Stukeley extended his hand, but Shane pulled him in for an embrace, hearty

SHANE O'NEILL

and swift. "By Christ, the pair of ye are wet as an otter's arse! Did you ride up from Dublin this morning? Put your boots to the fire, man!" He turned to the girls, saying in Irish, "Give a Christian a hand, now, and put a welcome before them." Dowdall raised a forfending hand and drew back a pace, much discomfited, but Tom stretched himself in the chair, and the girls tugged his boots off for him. He looked up to Shane's quizzical grin.

"*Ah*, Dublin? Nay, last night we lay at Castle Cooley, Sir Jame's estate in Dundalk. But, see you, this morning we strayed a piece from our path and betook ourselves out to the Newry. For a quick perusal of Bagenal's holdings. Or what *stands* of them."

"His holdings? Scarcely a *holdings,* if he doesn't *hold!*" Stukeley obliged with a laugh.

"Aye, I'm told that you drove poor Nicholas off his lands."

"*That* was no mighty feat! Divil-all ballads will come of it! He scampered off as we drew upon the place." Stukeley grinned.

"Do you *know*, Shane my hearty, that Bagenal is reinstated as Lord Marshal of the Queen's Forces?" Shane nodded, with a sly smirk.

"Ah, there's little comes to pass behind that high Pale that escapes the notice of Shane O'Neill. And *that* news sent *no* shivers up my spine, you may be sure!" He gave orders, then, to a pair of footmen in Irish, and they swiftly moved a cumbrous oak table across the flags up before the fire. They then opened several shuttered casements, to let the grey light into the chamber. Shane put his arm around one of the girls, whispered into her ear, and with that, the pair of them withdrew. As they did so, his two wolfhounds came bounding into the chamber. They did not bark, but sniffed and nuzzled at the strangers until Shane called them down. The men drew up to the table, and the hounds settled at their feet, panting and whimpering.

Shane regarded his two visitors. Dowdall, perhaps ten years his senior, was greying. He wore sober attire, drab and dark but for a short ruffed collar under his clean-shaven face. Stukeley's garb was sumptuous but muted, his tunic of dark umber velvet, intricately embroidered with deep blue. All of this served to underscore the bold flourishes, the double looped chain of gold, and the single earring.

SHANE O'NEILL

The chieftain smiled at them across the table.

"Ye will be perished by this. I've called for a bit of supper." Captain Tom nodded, smiling, and clanked his empty cup down before him.

"Hungry as a hawk!"

"No more nor myself! Divil damn the bite since early morn."

Dowdall concurred, as he took from his satchel a folded parchment. He extended it to O'Neill. "Herein you'll find the substance and matter of our expedition, my Lord O'Neill. A communication from her Majesty's Lord Deputy." Shane glanced at the crimson seal and swiftly set it to one side.

"Time enough. Time enough for such...things." He raised his eyes, and nodded, and a servant put down three goblets and filled them with white wine. "As you're so very partial to Sack, Thomas! A fine dry Sack from Spain. Will that suit *you*, Sir James?" Dowdall was rankled, indignant at his host's tossing aside of the Deputy's letter, but he swallowed down his anger, and presented a grim smile.

"Sack? Most decidedly so!" Shane turned to the Captain.

"Tell me this. What business was it betook you to the Newry this day? At Bagenal's behest, was it?"

"He proposes to sell it."

"Does he! He has only a lease to sell. A document that signifies nothing."

"Sir Nick is drawing on his three score years. It hardly astounds me that he is loathe to 'recommence', now he has lost all. He lately confided to me that, but for the Marshalcy, he is disposed to withdraw from Ireland, and return to Staffordshire whence he came."

"Ha! When he left that place, he was fleeing a murder charge!"

"Sir Nicholas?" Stukeley threw his head back and laughed. "'Pon my greeting him, the o'erweening prig put his nose in the air, and reproved me for a villain! A 'brigand', he named me. A murder charge! Do tell all!"

"Little enough to tell. He killed a man in a brawl in Leek, and fled to Ireland. He was a hired sword for my father, who for kindness' sake petitioned the King for Bagenal's pardon, and on his account it was granted him."

SHANE O'NEILL

"Ah! In like fashion to your *own* recent kindness on *my* behalf. Be assured I stand equally in your debt."

"Aye, well. I hope to Christ you'll not *requite the deed* in like fashion! Fifteen years ago... Aye, it was in '50. He got the Marshalcy from Queen Mary, and with it a 21 year lease on the Newry estate. From that day, he was a sore plague to my father, the Earl. He never ceased to harass him with warrants and predations. When I, myself, was held beyond in London, he robbed me of 4,000 kine from my herds. Bagenal is a jumped-up knave, a false-hearted marauder. These greedy and grasping churls who wash up on our eastern shore-" Shane stopped himself, considering his company. "But *you*, what is your interest in-"

"I wish to buy it. Sidney tells me I could acquire the Marshalcy with it. But yet must I know, will the Lord of Ulster have me for his neighbor? Therein lies the sticking point!" Shane nodded with a slow sly laugh. He turned sharply to the doorway where a servant had entered. At the footman's nod, he pushed his chair back, and stood.

"This will bear some pondering. But this I will say. You are the only Englishman I would suffer to hold it! ...were I of a mind to relinquish the place. Come, let us go up! My belly is empty as a drum!" He stopped and turned back, remembering just then to retrieve Sidney's letter. "As you've called of a Friday, you'll not mind- Ah, but sure you're both Catholics-" With a wry glance at Stukeley, he added, "*after* a fashion." The footman stood aside, and let the three men precede him up the narrow turnpike-stair, and the hounds scampered up at his heels.

The chamber above was lighter, and, as the walls of such towers are much thicker at the base, more spacious. It was adorned as a drawing room, save for stag's heads and shields on either side of the hearth. Lady Katherine had plenished it with draperies and tapestries, and a Persian carpet. Another lively fire was blazing, and before it in the centre stood a long trestle table. No trenchers here; it was set with bright delph that Shane had brought from London for just such diplomatic occasions as might arise.

The board was laden for a modest banquet. As for provender,

there was a silver platter of gillaroo trout and *'pullen'*, *a* fresh-water herring out of Lough Neagh. Beside it was a smaller dish, heaped with sautéed eel. Turnips, leeks, dulse, carrots, and a round loaf of brownbread completed the fare. In the middle of the lot was an ornate Venetian candelabra, a crowning touch of opulence that was belied only by a distinctly humble 'miscawn' of butter on a half-shell, that Shane ordered replaced immediately.

The board was set for five, and standing behind it, awaiting them, were two men, one of them a priest. Shane quickly introduced the guests to his chaplain, Fr. Broderick, and to his secretary, Neal MacKeever, whose presence he required at such meetings to act as witness, and to keep account of what was said. O'Neill then took his seat at the head of the table, and the others followed. 'Grace Before Meat' was intoned in Latin by the priest, and after a quick 'amen', they commenced their meal. For local pride, Shane boasted of the great wonder of 'pullen', and the guests heartily agreed as to its merit. He questioned Dowdall on his expectations of the new regime in Dublin, trying to discern if he were of Sussex' faction, but the judge proved an adept hand at the politic response.

Through the meal, Stukeley regaled the company with an accounting of his misadventure in the Florida expedition to everyone's great amusement. The chaplain and secretary spoke rarely, unless addressed, but both laughed freely, upholding the increasingly high spirits. When the plates had been cleared away, whiskeybaugh was poured, and Stukeley snatched it up eagerly.

"Ah! Spirits! Just the thing to warm my cold black heart!" Sir James abjured, but relented after coaxing, for he was anxious that the Lord Deputy's business should yet be taken up, and it wouldn't do if the company were befuddled. He resolved to linger over the '*one* only'. By this, the early spring dusk had settled to dark, and the mighty candelabra was lit.

The evening rolled along at a jostling pace, with seldom a pause, as spirits were consumed, and news of the Pale was parsed and puzzled over. The merits of 'Big Henry of the Beer" were extolled, mostly at the expense of Lord Sussex, whose tenure was thoroughly disparaged, with no noticeable dissent from Justice Dowdall. Sidney had stood gossip at the christening of Shane's son, Henry, and there was some hope that he would bring reason and candor to the dealings of state. At Shane's prompting, Stukeley recounted the hazardous journey from London, detailing the ordeal of the misfortunate Lord Deputy.

"He was fit to be tied," he said. "All his plate, the best of his cellar, and his prize horses, the lot! All for Davy Jones! 'A curse!' cried Sir Harry! 'A curse! This is naught but evil Irish sorcery!', for, in truth, the Lord Deputy -he harkins after prophesies and dreams!" This brought such a great laugh from the three Irishmen, that Shane was obliged to explain.

"It was our own Farleigh O'Gneeve laid that curse upon him! Wasn't I there! I heard him do it! There would be 'a wailing on the shore,' he said! And since ever he heard tell of the sinking, Farleigh's as proud as Lucifer's cat! There's divil a man will risk his temper now, for fear of his curse!" But Father Broderick pished at that.

"Sure, once news was out of Sidney's coming, he was cursed at many a fireside, you may be sure. And there's many a one is swaggering now on the head of it! Saving your presence, my Lord O'Neill, but the Almighty is not awaiting orders from that aul rhymster!" Shane's smile vanished, and the laughter faded with it. He turned his baleful glare to the priest.

"That aul 'rhymster'? There will be respect for poets in the Court of Shane O'Neill! That 'aul rhymster' is an *outlaw,* now, where *English* law holds sway. She has banned our bards. And even our very laws and judges!" He turned to Dowdall. "Did you hear of it? Christ, you're a magistrate, to be sure you heard of it! If Sidney's coming was cursed, it is small wonder! I did her bidding; I slaughtered the Scots, and this is how she repays me! They lie mouldering in the glens, their tartans fluttering to the kites and crows, and how many of my men with them? And all for the English Queen, with her 'golden chains' -of bondage." The two guests were astounded, and quite abashed at this sudden flare of temper. It certainly boded ill for their mission. In spite of that, Stukeley grinned.

SHANE O'NEILL

"Oho! This is a rum start!" Shane marked his guests' discomfort and drew down, though still a trifle heated.

"Well, I shall be their refuge! We'll draw poets from near and far to Tirowen, and they will sing her Majesty such praise as she deserves!" Stukeley laughed at this, glad of a chance to lighten the tone.

"'Tis well for her Majesty that she knows no Irish! Methinks there will be blistering satires here to scorch her ears!"

Shane grinned, and the tense chill was dispelled. In the brief silence, a shrill wind could be heard, and a sudden thrumming as it dashed rain against the thick panes of the windows. "That is the winter, bullying back!" He suddenly smacked his hands together, rubbing them vigorously. "Did you bring your rattlers, Captain Stukeley?"

"I am never without them! Ah! But Sir James is not a man for the dice."

"To your gaming, gentlemen! -If you will. Although I abstain from such diversions myself, I am no Puritan. Betimes I am known to play an innocent hand of trump or ruff. Nay, I am content to watch!"

"Not at all, Justice Dowdall. We'll forgo them, so. Thomas may yet be a neighbor of mine, and there will be many a chance to play." Shane turned to Stukeley. "But, tell me, man! What of your enlargement? Word up here was that you were for the gallows! And straightaway!"

"Aye, and but for *your* three letters, I *would have swung*! 'Twas only the testimonials of Shane O'Neill that sprung the gate! And...and pray *believe* me, I am much beholden for them! You see, I am rather taken up with the notion of living."

"'Twas little enough, I suppose... to spare the neck of a friend."

"To spare the neck of a friend with *neck* to spare, it would seem!" This unexpected little jest from the priest drew a laugh round the table, before Stukeley picked up his narration.

"Even having got your letters, Lord Cecil set before me a final hurdle to jump. And a high vault it was! He said I must needs sway the new Spanish Ambassador to withdraw his warrants, and to cease his

SHANE O'NEILL

bitter harangues. Or I could rot where I was."

"Pah! That for a challenge? To a slippery rogue the like of yourself? I'd have laid a fine wager on that! You could spin him for 'Hoodman Blind'! What was your shift, then?"

"I wet my cheeks, and pleaded with him that I am but a poor Catholic, and sadly martyred for it. I had *deliberately* foiled the Florida expedition, I told him, for the sake of the love I bear our dear King Philip! Nay, then, I went further! 'I am persecuted', I said, 'for that I hold common cause with the Prince of Ireland, O'Neill -who is so very staunch that he will lop the head of any English heretic that dares to tread beyond the Pale!" Shane laughed, but cautioned him.

"Mind that such lies do not reach the ears of Elizabeth, or you will earn your martyr's crown!" Dowdall nodded, and then tisked. Thricely.

"The Ambassador? You make too free, Tom Stukeley! Cecil's spies are all *about* him!" Shane concurred.

"And the Queen is none too fond of you as it is." Stukeley poured himself another dram of whiskeybaugh and knocked it back. He licked his lips, and laughed again.

"Hah! She knows not *what* to make of me! When I came into Greenwich to take leave of her -for her standard flew over my ships..." Laughing, he got to his feet. "In truth, I cut a dashing figure in that uniform. And her eyes were *full* of me! -Whatever our father should have thought of *that*! I spake boldly." He posed in the firelight, now, for a most antic rendition of his tale as he held forth. "Bold enough to tell her that I preferred to be the sovereign of a *mole-hill* than the highest subject of the greatest kingdom of Christendom! Moreover, I said that I was assured of being a prince before my death! 'I hope', said Elizabeth, 'I shall hear from you, when you are instated in your principality.' I bowed smartly, and said, 'I will write unto you.' 'In what language?' said the Queen, and so I returned, 'In the style of princes: 'To our dearest *sister*!' Well, say I, the paint on her cheeks did crackle, and I feared she might yet choke in her mighty ruff collar! I bowed again, and quick! Hoisted sail before she might change her mind! And blew on to the New World!" He arrived at this close with his tufted chin proudly raised, and his arm aloft in a grandiose posture that he held through the laughter of his companions. Shane winked at the others, and drew his head back to inspect his preening friend in the firelight, suddenly assuming a grave air.

"Begod, but ye're putting on flesh there, Thomas! You want to mind that!" Stukeley's brow shot up, and quickly gathered into a frown.

"What? Tush! Not so! Not so!!! I am lean and limber as a stripling youth!" At this peevish protest, the company burst forth in laughter. "Fie! You bait me, you Irish rogue! Devil roast your dirty hide!"

"Don't be cast down, Thomas! You stood in grave danger. There was nothing for it but to prick your vanity lest you might combust of it!"

"Dastard!" Stukeley laughed and filled their cups again. Shane shook his head.

"If you spoke *that* 'spake' to the Queen, it's small *wonder* she would have your blood!" Fr. Broderick ventured a question, now, with a smile.

"And where would *be* your kingdom then, Captain Stukeley? -If, indeed, it be of this world."

"This world? This world is a mighty globe aspinning, with uncharted lands barely peopled! -But for sparse bands of naked savages! I tell you I shall have my pick!" He looked to his host. "But it is here, firstly, I mean to wed. The flaxen-haired niece of Lady Kildare, Eleanor Somerset, do you recall her in London? She coaxed you out for a galliard at the Christmas revels."

"Aye, I'd not soon forget her. A fetching lass, comely and charming!"

"She resides now in Dublin, and keeps my company most regular. I shall wed her, I think, and settle here for a time. Settle *properly*! Enough of pulling the devil by the tail." Shane flashed him a devilish smirk.

"Aye, Thomas, 'tis plain to see, you stand in sore need of cherishing!" Dowdall cleared his throat, and smiled.

"*You* have wed, my Lord O'Neill -if the tale be true!" Eager to delve, Stukeley seized upon this with gusto.

SHANE O'NEILL

"Your Scotch Countess, so we are told in Dublin!"

"Aye, my Katherine from the Isles. A spirited beauty! With a temper to match her red hair! By Christ, she is fortune's own smile! She's borne me three fine sons who are growing fast as ferns, and now once again, she is heavy with child." Captain Tom lifted his cup to this.

"To your bonny bride, then! May she bear safe!" Sir James added to the toast.

"A long and fruitful marriage!" Their words were honoured with a clink and a drink. Stukeley's brown eyes kindled as a new and curious theme suggested itself.

"London is astounded that the Scotch lairds saw fit to attend you, after your slaughter of their kinsmen last summer! Contrary to Nature, they say. Passes all understanding! So bewildered are they at Court, that it is simply put down to the barbarous madness of the Gaels, both north and west!" Dowdall gave him a cautioning frown at such indiscretion, but he pressed on merrily. "I could not, myself, fathom the queer reasoning that would bring them to your door to honour you so, and even to partake of your cheer. It is held to be fact that you forged a treaty with Lord Argyll, and so there is new furor at Court! A pact against England!"

Shane was the astonished one now, to consider that Elizabeth knew of this! He sipped, and pensively rolled the liquor on his tongue. His sudden pang of unease was banished by a consoling thought; on St. Peter's chair sat a new Pope who was sworn to excommunicate Elizabeth, which would bring the princes of Europe to his aid. Perhaps the charade of loyalty was pointless now! No longer needful. Stukeley drank deep, and smirked at the abashed faces around him.

"Well, my Lord! Either the Scots be easy gulled, or I must bethink *you* a crafty wizard! The very Prince of Guile!" It was Fr. Broderick who replied.

"But wherefore should they hold 'Forgive thine enemies' to be barbarous madness? Is this their 'Reformed' Christian message?" Shane smiled.

"It is simply a measure of the turbulence of Scottish affairs. Both enmity and alliance are fleeting. See how quickly after the Chaseabout Rebellion Lord Argyll is restored to Queen Mary's graces! Hah? This murder of Rizzio by Darnley proved to her that Archibald was acting in her interest when he opposed the marriage. He was right, as she was wrong. Darnley is out, as Argyll is in. Ever shifting are the Scots!" It seemed that the squalid affair in the Scottish Court was on everyone's lips these times, and Dowdall's curiosity was piqued.

"Ah, but *was* it *Darnley* who murdered him? Stories abound, and you may have your choice!" Shane replied with assurance, leaving little room for conjecture.

"*He* it was! My Katherine had a letter from Lady Jean Stewart, the Queen's sister, who was there in the chamber." Sir James looked quite stunned.

"Then it was not James of Moray?" Shane shook his head.

"Oh, he is behind all the machinations of these Protestant lairds, and doubtless there are those in London behind *him*. But he was not present. Mary was dining with her ladies and her musician, this Rizzio. Darnley burst in upon them, drunk, with a pack of his debauched companions, Lord Ruthven and five others. Ruthven called the Queen a whore and a strumpet, and said that the child she carries is that of her Italian minstrel. When she rebuked them, they overturned the table and began stabbing him -*all* of them taking a hand, until he lay dead with *fifty-six* gaping wounds by the counting. When that table was o'erturned, Lady Jean it was, who caught up a candlebranch that had fallen into the drapery. But for that, they all might have perished!" The company evinced amazement at this, and the chaplain swiftly blessed himself. "I shouldn't doubt that Queen Elizabeth would wonder at the volatile Scots! But as for their coming *here* -let us say that they are fond of weddings, and my bride is a Scot." He nodded to an attendant who lavished more spirits around the table, with only Dowdall refusing. The judge placed his hand over his goblet. "Go on, Sir James, sure where is the harm? It will put you in better heart!"

"Nay, then, there is no better heart than mine, thank you all the same! It's my head that concerns me. It behoves us to discuss his

SHANE O'NEILL

Lordship's business, while we have yet the wits about us to do so!" Shane raised a dismissive hand.

"My wits are about me still, fear you not! I could drink spirits til I pissed punch, and be little the worse for it! Let it bide, now. Tomorrow is time enough for higgling and haggling over the demands and posturings of Elizabeth's menials! What we must do is to celebrate the deliverance of our friend here from an untimely end on the gallows!" He lifted his cup to propose a toast to this, but Stukeley interupted."

"Alas, Shane, I stand not yet in the clear!"

"What's this? But are you not after saying-?"

"Nay, I was granted leave, but not pardon. For all these tribulations, I am not acquitted. There stand charges from Portugal, and from the High Admiralty, yet to be determined." Shane was taken aback.

"But did you not say that it was the Queen herself who invested you with the fleet for your privateering?"

"Yea, but that bargain was clandestine. She swore she would disown me should I be caught out, and I could then expect the full rigour of the law! Once my identity was beknownst to the foreign Courts, she was bound to act."

"Ach! Crucified Christ! Is *that* how the wind sits? The gibbet beckons *still* for my bosom friend?" Stukeley stroked his beard, nodding solemnly.

"And the grave gapes *before* him, alas! You may see now wherefore it behoves me so to prove both useful and reformed the while I am in Ireland!" He held up his goblet, and winked. "When the bells of death do ring!" He took a hearty slug from it.

"What was that catch you used always to sing? One of those 'hey-nonny-nonnies' it was!"

"Ahhhh...nay, nay, I shan't!" Stukeley demurred with improbable shyness, but after a modest clamour around the table, he sipped of his whiskeybaugh, and cleared his throat.

SHANE O'NEILL

"Hey nonny no!
Men are fools that wish to die!
Is it not fine to dance and sing
when the bells of death do ring?
Is it not fine to swim in wine,
and turn upon the toe,
And sing hey nonny no,
when the winds do blow,
and the seas do flow?
Sing hey nonny no!
Then toast our girls, around we go,
Nor care which way the wars may blow,
We are no shakes, but jovial rakes,
Sing hey nonny no, hey ho!"

This was greeted with lively acclamation round the board, and Shane hoisted his goblet.

"Begod! If they hang you for singing, you'll die innocent!" This was met with merry laughter, but as Shane looked about the table, his tipsy eyes stopped on the long face of Justice Dowdall. "Christ, man, It can't be so dire as *that*! Sure, Thomas holds favour with the Lord Deputy, and highest favour!"

"But think, if my good Lord O'Neill might choose to turn from his unyielding defiance, and treat with the Queen's ministers! Why, peace would reign! And think you what credit would thereby accrue to our dear friend Captian Stukeley! Mayhap to save his pretty neck withal!" Dowdall had been waiting for such an opening to steer them to the business of their mission, but Shane found his tone irksome.

O'Neill snatched up the letter, and flicked off the hard wax seal. "*My* unyielding, is it? I shall find little enough of 'yielding' in these scratchings." He stood and stepped over to hold the letter before the candelabra. Although diminished by this hour in great gouts of cascading tallow, it's tapers blazed brightly still. He read the letter with singular composure. It was a deliberately peremptory summons to appear before the Lord Deputy in the Pale. Nothing more. Shane's eyes flashed to Dowdall.. "Let him come here if he would see me. Just as you have done. -But upon my condition." His deep voice resonated with authority, without betraying his anger. "I signed a treaty at Drumcree, beside the Queen's own signature, writ in her hand. A hard-won covenant. It is two years now, and *still* she will not grace it with her Royal Seal. Her hand means nothing; her word means nothing. And even her *oath* is proved meaningless. I will see the Lord Deputy when the Queen's Royal Seal is afixed to our sworn treaty, and not before." Shane held his composure, but his blood was up. Stukeley was abashed.

"O'Neill, my trusty friend, I pray you be not rash or hasty in your reply to the Lord Deputy. I cannot say the truth of it, but *there is rumour abroad* that papers are being drawn up for your peerage!" An old nerve was struck, and Shane replied with sharpness.

"You cannot say. No, but you will put wind to the rumour, if it suits you! That is a well blown tale!" The judge came to Stukeley's aid, in his best magisterial tone.

"If you but bend your knee, you might yet be dubbed upon the shoulder! Bend, now, O'Neill, and mayhap you shall rise the higher for it!"

"The dangling prize! A chain of gold! Bollocks to that! To the devil with their English honours!" Shane spit into the fire. Now a trifle heated himself, Stukeley's tone was brusque.

"You have yet to see the power this Queen commands, O'Neill! You *will* not withstand it, I assure you! Will you cast away your father's peerage, the earldom of Tyrone?"

"I am not ambitious for the abject title of earl; both my family and my birth raise me above it. I care not to be made an earl unless I may be better and higher than an earl, for I am in blood and power better than the best of them. And I will give place to *none*. She has made a wise earl of *MacCarthy Mór*. Pah!" He spat into the fire. "I *keep* as good a man as he! For the Queen, I confess she is my sovereign, yet I never made peace with her but at her own seeking. And it is yourselves that have broken it."

"But look you to your own vantage! Foolish pride will avail you naught! But *trust* will-"

"Who would you have me trust? I came unto the Earl of Sussex upon the safe-conduct of *two* Earls, and protection under the Great Seal -and he offered me the courtesy of a handlock! And therewith sent me into England. When I came *there* upon pardon and safe-conduct, and had done my business, and would have departed according the same, the Queen herself told me that, *indeed,* safe-conduct I *had* -to come safe and to go safe, but she had not told me *when*! And so there held me until I agreed to things- things so far against my honour and profit that *never* would I perform them whilst I live! *That* made me to make war! And if it were to do again I would do it. If Elizabeth your mistress be queen of England, I am O'Neill, King of Ulster. My ancestors before me were kings of Ulster and kings of Ireland. Ulster is mine and shall be mine! As for O'Donnell, he shall *never* come into his country! Nor Bagenal into the Newry. They are mine! With the sword I won them, and with the sword I will keep them!" He crumbled up the Deputy's letter, and flung it into the fire. "That is my answer. With those words you may commend me to my gossip, the Deputy." He stood, noisily pushing his chair back, and the servants snapped to. The others rose from their seats. He spoke gruffly. "I am for my couch now. They will show you to your quarters when you wish. Until the morrow, then." Dowdall had the temerity to speak up.

"My Lord O'Neill, we brought you 'Deputy's letters'. And by letters we look for answer, signed in your hand."

"That you shall have, and sealed." He cast a quick glance at his secretary. "Neal will see me in the morning. I bid you goodnight." With a heavy step, but a steady step, he took his leave. The two guests were quite dumfounded. Clearly they had failed in their diplomatic quest, that task that until mere moments before had appeared to bear every promise of success. The welcome, the cheer, the compatible spirited banter... Justice Dowdall was truly downcast, but Stukeley was strangely bitter. He now felt something akin to scorn for O'Neill. To have so overplayed his hand! For a man so adroit at dodging and parrying, to let his wiles desert him, his own anger and pride defeat

SHANE O'NEILL

him, it was repugnant to him, and unworthy, certainly, of the exalted stature in which he had held him. The wild boglord had cast his lot; let it fall as it might. Still, for his part, Stukeley was determined to wrest from him the Newry estates, and to prosper there when O'Neill was dust!

It was early when Shane awoke. He peered out the window to adjudge the time. The blue mist of morning was creeping through the dark wood below...like a memory slowly called to mind. The troublesome close of last night's discourse... Had he gone too far? He wondered for a moment if perhaps he hadn't taken a deal more spirits than his head would carry. No. He had said no more than the truth. If he cannot speak true before his own fire, how then can he rule Ulster? Farleigh was right. The constellations are moving into place. A new Pope, pledged to release Catholics from loyalty to the heretical Queen. All of Ulster under O'Neill's peace, and the greater part of Connaught under tribute. Surely nothing more could be obtained from Elizabeth by protestations of loyalty. There must be no retraction, no equivocation. The arrow is drawn, and so it must fly!

His secretary was presently summoned. MacKeever had seen fit to make careful note of Shane's trenchant response to the Deputy's command. On hearing it read out to him, Shane laughed darkly, and nodded. "Not a word taken from it, nor put to it, but only my signing. When the two envoys appeared, all was cordial, and even friendly, and they were quite surprised to see that Shane stood by his words of the night before. Although it was not yet noontide when they prepared to depart, Stukeley and Dowdall were obliged to drink a stirrup's cup for the road. Farewells were spoken, and the two men mounted and trotted down the path to take their leave.

Suddenly Shane hailed them back. He told Stukeley that he would indeed accept him in the Newry if he should purchase the estate. But he added sternly, "If you play me false, I shall play you cunning!" He was assured, and then reassured, of the Captain's undying gratitude and loyalty. He said simply, "Go safe," and turned his back. With that, Sidney's emissaries spurred their horses to a gallop, off down the road to Dundalk, bearing with them the fiery words of Shane O'Neill. The chieftain lingered before his door, the secretary at his side, and watched them disappear into the shadowy wood. After a silent moment, he spoke. "The storm is on...and all is hazzard."

"A false perjured and pernicious conspirer! God's wounds, We will have his head! We speak it to heaven!" Elizabeth smacked her fist on the table, and glared at her wary Councillors. "A stealthy *wolf* is more to be trusted! Look you how small effect our merciful dealing has wrought on his cankered and traitorous stomach!" Harry Sidney had seen fit to personally deliver O'Neill's bristling memorandum, that he might at last impel the Queen to open the royal purse. Glad now, of her fury, he sought to urge her on.

"Majesty, your name is no more reverenced, nor your letters of commandment obeyed within any place under his rule than it would be in the kingdom of France! The rebel *must* be be chastised before he-"

"His head! We will have his head!!" Elizabeth's knuckles whitened in her fierce grip on the letter before her. Her teeth clenched, her eyes narrowed, as she cast her burning gaze back upon the offending page. "After all his wiles! At last he shows his true colours above the parapet!" She looked up suddenly with great wonder. "Howe'er did you 'complish this?" Sidney drew himself up proudly.

"I considered how I might decypher him in the sensiblest and precisest manner that I could -which by *letters* I knew I should *never* do. For in the morning he is subtle, and then will he cause letters to be written either directly *otherwise* than he will do, or else so doubtfully as he may make what construction he list. And oft-times his secretary pens his letters in more dulcet form than ever he intends. But in the afternoon, when the wine is in, then he unfolds himself. In vino veritas! And then he shows himself what he is, and what he is like to attempt. Therefore I sent two gentlemen to him, that they might prize

SHANE O'NEILL

from him his true intentions. Thomas Stukeley and Justice Dowdall, both discreet, both faithful to the Queen, stout, and assured to me. And very well they did!" Elizabeth nodded, triumphantly.

"His treason, signed and sealed! Now we have him!" Sidney nodded trenchantly.

"Indeed, your Highness, now we must *get* him! Unless he be speedily put down, your Majesty shall lose Ireland as her sister lost Calais! Ireland would be no small loss to the English Crown, and it was never so like to be lost as now. O'Neill has already all Ulster, and if the French were eager for Calais, think you what the Irish be to recover their whole realm! I love no wars; but I had rather die than Ireland should be lost in my government! But I *must* have troops, Majesty! Scotland, France, the Netherlands, all your foes are beset and besieged by internal discord. Now! Now, might you safely turn from them to secure the western reaches of your realm."

"Nay, Mary Stuart, for all her troubles, did triumph over Moray's rebellion. There is peril enough yet in O'Neill's covenant with Argyll!" She pondered this silently for a moment, and with a barely perceptible nod, her countenance brightened. "But Mary is with child, and she will be loath to do battle until she has borne it!" She turned her fiery eyes back to the letter before her. After a brief moment, she glared up at him. "Hah! 'King of Ireland!' What rabid ecstasy is this? Bacchus has stolen his sodden wits!" It was the 'Queen's favorite', Leicester, who replied.

"When we dined at St. John's Head, O'Neill boasted that eighteen of his line had been 'high kings of Ireland.' And that his father was to be crowned King of Ireland at Tara by the Geraldine League -and *would have* been, had Lord Grey not crushed them in '39."

"And you said nothing to Council?"

"He was in his cups, and so given to jesting that I thought nothing of it." Elizabeth cried out, in fury.

"God's blood! That cursed island! We must be ever knitting a knot that is never tied!" Cecil sighed, then softly instructed.

"*If* that web be framed with rotten hurdles -though our loom is well nigh done, the work is new to begin. Alas, that is the sorry truth of it, my Lady." He smiled confidently now, and spoke with reassuring vigour. "Indeed, it was full time that Sir Henry went *into* Ireland, for he has found all out of joint there. But in all, no *true* peril, saving in Shane O'Neill. Oh, he boasts in his drunkenness that he will be king of Ulster; but I trust his head shall be from his shoulders before any crown can be made ready to make him king! –Or, I dare say, earl!" A certain cunning glint had returned to the Queen's gaze, and he cast a collusive eye to Sidney, who resumed his entreaties.

"If you would but hear me out, your Highness." Her brow arched regally, as Elizabeth set down the letter, and bestowed upon him finally her fullest attention. "We must look upon the problem anew. The Desmond-Ormonde feud has ravaged the South, making it quite manifest that bestowing power to the great Lords is of no avail. Let us, instead, scrutinize their ancient titles, whereupon we might seize their vast estates for Her Majesty's holdings. Confiscate! I say we must *welcome* insurrection, for only such will clear the way for plantations. And plantations there must be! Both civil and military colonies to inure the native inhabitants to our English common law and customs." This brought a vigorous rumble of approval from her Councillors, but the Queen was not convinced.

"Welcome insurrection? How now? What folly is this? Titles might yet stand under such a thing as scrutiny."

"Save for O'Neill, there is ne'er a one of these Irish captains will not yield unto me to procure his lands by her Majesty's letters patents. Once done, if they be found guilty of insurrection, those lands are forfeit to the Crown. Wherefore might we not rejoice in their rebellions? In the end it may be put to her Majesty's choice whether she will suffer this people, the natives, to inhabit there for their rent, or extirpate them and plant other people in it. The force which shall bring about the one shall do the other, and it may be done without any show that such a thing is meant!" The Queen's smile beamed brightly now, and applause erupted all around the table, ceasing only upon Elizabeth's reply.

"This were no folly, but counsel sage and sound." She raised her brows in expectation of more. "You have our ear, good Harry, what

SHANE O'NEILL

would you we do elsewise?

"The wisdoms that have obtained heretofore in the matter of Ireland have *not* subdued that nation to orderly governance. What then is to be done, is what has *not* been done. The Pale must encompass the whole of Ireland! All the wild lands must be shired into counties. It is our sufferance and remissness that gives the wild Irish heart! We make them proud by mewing up *ourselves* in walled towns, whilst they triumph abroad, and revel in the country as they please! To do this we must break them with the broadsword! And for that we must have troops! Your Majesty must needs reconcile herself to the cost of war, and consent to open her purse."

"His head would be worth a treasury! Aye, so shall you have them!" Her quick resolve as quickly vanished. "But Summer is upon us, and would be gone ere they set foot in Ireland!"

"In despite of that we must commence. We know that Argyll, with the whole force of the Western isles, will be with him ere summer's end -for that O'Neill offered him relief there in the time of his banishment. We dare not delay!"

"A winter war? You would empty our coffers before you *begin*!"

"It is far the best plan- as I have found to my cost. The Irish spring is cold. *Our* horses are stabled in winter and cannot bear the elements, nor the green food. The Irish horses are out all winter and only improve with each day." The Queen's head tilted back as she presented a sour smile.

"*And* the trifling matter of food?"

"Little harm can be done to young crops in spring, and the rebels find food everywhere. If we commence at harvest, we might destroy their fields of ripe corn, drive their herds into flooded woods and bogs, and *starve* the rebels in winter. We shall sweep through the province, and place troops in every fortress."

"And our scant purse must provision the army all the winter?"

"We have weighed us this consideration. A permanent settlement in the far North, your Highness. There is a small port-village called Derry, on the River Foyle. It is an ancient episcopal seat, and so boasts a cathedral which we might seize and fortify. That will serve most capably as an outpost where a large garrison with a full supply of warlike stores might be kept. Such a venture will furnish us with a base of command at O'Neill's western flank, so that we might close upon him from each side. As for food, were we to restore O'Donnell in his country, he could provide withal." Elizabeth held for a moment of absolute stillness, and then looked sharply to her Councillors.

"What say you, then, our trusty men and true?" There was a chorus of hearty assent, and the Queen turned to Sir Harry for his response.

"Give me but one thousand soldiers. Furnish them proper, and sail them to Derry. I will meet them from the South." Elizabeth gazed at the empty air before her, nodding slightly. After this pensive moment, she looked sharply to her advisors.

"Who shall be sent?" Leicester replied immediately.

"Who but Colonel Randolph! He is idle now, and will be of little use to you in Berwick!" Sidney was perplexed.

"The ambassador? Wherefore stands he idle in that place, with such mayhem in Edinburgh?" When no one spoke, Sir Robert explained.

"Queen Mary has newly banished him from Scotland. He was caught red-dripping handed, bribing the Protestant rebels to topple her crown, and so we are lost our most subtle intriguer!"

"Subtle?" Elizabeth swallowed a sour little laugh. "A bungler! To be caught out by such as *Mary*! But, indeed, he is able in the field, a wise commander. We shall send him hence!" There was a gabble of approval, and Sidney was joyful.

"I must commend her Majesty's wisdom, as always! Randolph will relish a military command, and I know of none better to lead the assault. Do you this, your Highness, and ere long O'Neill's head will festoon the battlements of Dublin Castle!" With that, the Queen stood, prompting the others to rise.

"So be it done. Bring all to readiness, and let us then this war to commence! We caution you to spare no rebel! For sake of charity and thrift, wars were best an' they be bloody and swift!"

SHANE O'NEILL

CHAPTER 28

As by custom, Shane O'Neill moved his court to Dungannon for some weeks at Eastertide. This year, however, the sojourn would provide little rest. Those delays from London that so immobilized Sidney proved a boon to Shane, and he set about bringing his forces to readiness for the coming war. Detachments were sent off east to fortify Dundrum Castle with 'brass artillery', and west, likewise, to his castle at Liffer on the River Foyle. Shane built up his army, and acquired new stores of munitions from the pirate, Phettyplace, at the port of Carlingford which was now safely out of reach of English patrols. To help with the expense, he expropriated the temporalities of the diocese of Armagh, albeit with the approval of the Chapter there. But his first priority in all these preparations was to call in help from wherever it might be got. Will Fleming was enlisted to share the demanding secretarial duties with Neal MacKeever, as masterly correspondence was of the utmost importance in this endeavor.

Through the ripply panes of a single narrow window, the glorious April sunshine had managed to breach the mighty walls of Dungannon Castle. It cast a sheen on all it touched, the deep velvet drapes, the brass fittings, and the ancient polished oak, imparting a hopeful air to the day's proceedings. Shane was sprawled in the majestic chair of carved oak, in what he still thought of as his father's study. Across the massive desk from him, Fleming's quill scratched its way industriously across a parchment, another fine page bound for the highest Courts of Europe. The chieftain sipped at his glass of portwine as he patiently looked on. Suddenly, the heavy plank door creaked open a pace, and Lady Katherine's head appeared. She spoke in a half whisper.

"Those two Franciscans below, waiting on your letters- they're being fed now, but the old one keeps an eye cocked on the hourglass. He says that their ship will sail on the evening tide. Are ye anyway near to-"

"Come in, come in out of that. We've the last of that dispatch here in hand. The others will go north or south." Katherine stepped briskly into the chamber looking quite fetching, even though she was well on in her term. Dressed smartly in russets and browns, her lustrous hair drawn up with bejeweled combs, she was the picture of elegance. "Give ear to this, now, Kat. He's only putting the tail on it."

"It's *Myler Magrath's* ear you want. Who is this bound for?"

"Myler be damned. It's for his own sake *that* cat purrs! This one is for Mary Stuart's uncle, the Cardinal of Lorraine." Fleming blew on the page, and looked up expectantly. Shane nodded, and he commenced reading out the letter.

> "To the most Reverend Cardinal Lorentino,
> We, Lord O'Neill, prince of the Irish of Ulster and defender of the Faith in Ireland, Salute You.
> We hope this letter finds you well in health and spirits, and we must own that it makes occasion for us to fondly recall a most singular incident. That was a hunting party in England with Lord Leicester, whereupon we were astonished to witness your brother, the Duc de Guise, transfix two stags with a single arrow! A mighty feat! We would you commend us to his Lordship!
> We make known to you that we have sent our letters to the Most Christian Prince, the King of France, requesting his Majesty to send us for our aid five or six thousand Frenchmen, well armed, for the expulsion of the English out of Ireland, for that the English are heretics, and schismatics, and enemies of Almighty God and of the Roman Church, as well as of the

French and the Irish. St.Lasarian predicted that the Catholic Church of Rome shall fall when the Faith has been destroyed in Ireland. And, as we have defended the Catholic Faith in Ireland according to our ability, and have followed the maxims of the Roman Pontiffs, we request you, in all becoming reverence and humility, to use your good offices to press the urgency of my cause to King Charles (since this is the opportune time, and all the Irish are in our council) that he would send to us the said number of Frenchmen for the expulsion of the said heretics from Ireland, and for the union of Ireland to the Crown of France. For *if* they be not sent now in the time of need, the armies of the heretic will vanquish us! If the Most Christian King will not help us, move the Pope to help us. I alone in this land sustain his cause.

Only the greatest haste will serve our urgent need. God grant us succour as we fight in his most righteous cause.

From Dungannon, xxv. April, 1566,

Misi O'Neill"

Both Shane and Will looked now to Lady Katherine for comment. "Och, aye, I'm sure that's grand. But did you not promise Ireland to Philip of Spain? And even to Mary?"

"Matter a damn! If they do this, it will be with the Pope's blessing, for the Holy Faith. And if they tried to claim this kingdom after, they would appear predatory and grasping before the world. How could they hold me to such an offer? Sure, who am I to be handing away kingdoms? But it casts me in the light of a loyal and holy crusader seeking their protection."

"Sure, who would be up to you? Well, it's a grand letter. If that will not do the job, then I'd say he was not minded to help you at all. So best to send it off, while the friars have yet time enough to reach their ship before it puts to sea. Have you the letter for King Charles?" Fleming nodded to a parchment near to hand.

"It's signed, but not as yet sealed." Katherine unfolded it, and read down the page silently. She then looked up at Shane with an arched brow of approval. She read on, aloud.

> "...Your Majesty's father, King Henry, in times past required the Lords of Ireland to join with him against the heretic Saxon, the enemies of Almighty God, the enemies of the Holy Church of Rome, your Majesty's enemies and mine. And yet God would not permit that alliance to be completed, notwithstanding the hatred borne to England by all of Irish blood, until your Majesty had become King in France, and I was Lord of Ireland. The time is come, however. The time is come, when we all are confederates in a common bond to drive the invader from our shores; and we now beseech your Majesty to send us six thousand well-armed men. If you will grant our request there will soon be no Englishman left alive among us, and we will be your Majesty's subjects evermore. Help us, we implore you, to expel the heretics and schismatics and to bring back our country to the Holy Roman see."

Katherine folded it and looked up. "Aye, 'tis nicely writ, Shane. Strong words, just where they're needed. Please God, it will bring you those legions! Now is the hour, it would seem!" Katherine leafed through the stack of sealed parchments. "Pope Pius V...King Philip, the Duc de Guise, the Duke of Alva, Catherine de Medici... Argyle?"

"He's stalling. Mary says the time not yet right."

"Mary is with child. If she can deliver aright, she'll bear the only true heir to the thrones of Scotland and England both. She'll want peace until then. But Archebald mightn't turn a deaf ear if you...if you would release my uncle..."

"A deaf ear? His hearing was fine when we clapped our oath! It was at *his* insistence I allowed the MacDonnells back into Ballycastle and the Glens. Having Sorley in my grip is all that prevents them from overrunning Antrim. Ah, no. I don't need them at my back again, breathing down my neck, so I don't."

"Ach Shane, it cuts my heart to see him languishing in that damp murky place."

SHANE O'NEILL

"*Don't* see him. I've forbidden you to go to Inishdowal."

"Aye, so you have. That sweetens the trip for me! Anyway, your towerhouse there is nearly complete. You'll be wanting me to plenish it soon, with new tapestries and the like."

"I've a mind to hold off on that yet. We may need to move the trappings and furnishment of Benburb up to this new wee castle, if help from the Continent is not forthcoming. -And should Argyll fail to make good his promise."

"God Almighty, what are you saying?"

"It may be my father had the right of it." Kat saw him look to Fleming, and she did the same. He nodded, unsurely.

"The *curse* is it?"

"Aye, it may be he was no dotard when he spoke it!" Katherine sighed, loud and quick, in exasperation.

"Will one of you ever tell me what this means?"

"My father, on his death-bed, was embittered of the English; he regretted having come to terms with them. He pronounced a curse upon all his posterity -if ever we should learn English, sow wheat, or build castles!"

"*Build castles?* But he owned this very keep!"

"Remorse, it was. Late-found wisdom. He reckoned that on capturing their castles, he should have leveled them, stone from stone. When I take them, I have had the great sense to man them with my own garrisons. Now, this is grand -so long as I'm able to *hold* them. But look you how long it took me to expel their ward from Armagh Cathedral once they were stuck in! The Da may have been right, in the end of the tale."

"But would you dismantle your own-"

"*They* cannot hold the land without fortresses, but *we* don't need them, for we have the people in every hollow and hill. If these letters fail me, *I may have to level Benburb and the rest*, and fight them in the wood. The thorny drumlins, the bogs, and the very rain will fight for us. And you and the wee'uns can take shelter in Fuanagall on Inishdowell. The island is impregnable." Seeing her so taken aback, Shane smiled softly. "A precaution is all. It surely will not come to that. I will rally the South, Desmond, Kildare, and the rest."

"*This* is the why and wherefore of Inishdowell?" She glared at him, and he shrugged. "You're a close one, Shane O'Neill! Well, please God, the letters will *not* fail! But they will do us little good where they lay! Let you sign that now, and we'll send them on their way!"

At the Inns-of-Court, on the north bank of the River Liffey, in a dusty little 'barrister's parlour' the deed was done. Signed and sealed was the deed whereby Sir Nicholas Bagenal sold to Stukeley all his interest in the office of Marshaldom, and the castles and manors that went with it. The terms were a good deal steeper than Thomas has anticipated, and in the end he had to stump up £3,000 of his ill-gotten hoard, but he counted it a bargain. In a letter to Lord Cecil, Sidney gave the transaction his full endorsement, heartily commending Stukeley's services to the Queen. Cecil, however, was astonished to hear of it, and even wondered publicly, if 'the knave had bewitched him!' Sidney's letter caused an 'uproar on all sides', a 'general misliking at Court', and fueled a barrage of invective from his rivals in the Palace. Her Majesty assailed the Lord Secretary with 'some very strange speeches', which he was at a loss to answer, except to suggest that Sidney must have some private compelling reasons of his own, 'more than did plainly appear'. She was not to be assuaged.

"We find it most strange that Thomas Stukeley should be used there in *any* service *at all*, considering the general discredit he remains in! -Not only in our own Realm, but in other countries abroad. Has Lord Harry forgot the grave charges still outstanding in the High Court of Admiralty? Nay, *this* folly we shall not brook! Master Stukeley shall return home at once! Let him clear himself -*if* he can!" The 'adventurer' had ventured too high. Her Majesty canceled the sale, impounded his funds as illicit spoils, and took him once again into custody. His overreaching had brought him to ruin, and

SHANE O'NEILL

nearly toppled his protector, Lord Sidney!

Indeed, it was a time of great trial for the Lord Deputy. In spite of all the promises, his appeals to London for supplies and troops availed him nothing. Prevarication, time and again. Word everywhere was that he had fallen from the Queen's graces, that she had spoken to his disparagement. His predecessor, the embittered Lord Sussex, had the Queen's ear, and her antipathy to Stukeley, coupled with her outrage over the Bagenal estates gave her a ready ear for such poison. Sidney wrote to her, declaring his grief at hearing that she had accredited the slander raised upon him by the Earl of Sussex. Furious at the turn events were taking, he urgently demanded that he be allowed to return and face his adversaries. He went so far, even, as to challenge Lord Sussex to a duel!

The Lord Deputy pleaded desperately for his brother-in-law and patron, Robert Dudley, to intercede for him at Court. "Her Majesty must send money in such sort as I may pay the garrison throughout! The wages must be paid. My dear Lord, press these things on the Queen, I pray you! By force or by fair means the Queen may have anything that she will in this country, if she will minister means accordingly, and with no great charge. If I have not money, and O'Neill make war, I will not promise to encounter with him until he come to Dublin. Give me money, and though I have but 500 to his 4000, I will chase him out of the Pale in forty-eight hours. If I may *not* have it, for the love you bear me, have me home again, for all will come to naught here, and before God and the world I will lay the fault on England, for there is none here!"

O'Neill was hardly the Lord Deputy's only concern. The Queen expected him to enforce her new restrictions on the bards and the Brehons, to prosecute papistry, to accomplish the Reformation of the Church, to restore the castles -Dublin, Kilmainham, and Carickfergus, and even to put down piracy! Though she was willing to lend a ship and a pinnace, she refused to provide a single sailor for the task, and she wanted the kingdom pacified with his present allotment of with 882 soldiers, and 300 kerne.

Of the Reformation, Sidney could report only that the churches of the Pale were going to wrack and ruin. No masses were allowed, 'but tithes were being paid to greedy ministers' of illusory congregations who did not trouble to repair them. He protested that "As for the Protestant religion, there is but small appearance of it, the churches being uncovered, the clergy scattered, and scarce the being of a god is known to these ignorant and barbaric people."

To implement the other royal decree, Lord Sidney issued a proclamation whereby his officers were 'straightly charged and commanded to execute by marshal law all manner of Bards, Rhymers, and Harpers', stating that "whosoever could seize a rhymer should spoil him, and have his goods without danger of Law." Irish lords and patrons were prohibited from rewarding the 'lewd rhymes' of bards, else they would be fined twice the amount they tendered for the poem, while the guilty poet would be fined and chastised. Sidney directed his forces to pursue such 'miscreants' to extremity.

None took up this order with more zeal than one Sergeant-Major Nicholas Malby. He thrashed and robbed several poets in Kilkenny, one later dying of his wounds, which caused a general outcry. The offense was such that the Irish bards threatened that they would 'rhyme Malby to death,' a threat that was taken quite seriously at the time. The poets were accused of inciting bitterness among the Irish, and enmity against the English gentry, while the bards contended that it was the English themselves who were busily earning the people's loathing.

Shane O'Neill was furious at this new cultural offensive, and he had a particular bone to pick. An Irish poet had written a vicious satire in Irish, promulgating all the slanderous lies about him from Dublin Castle, in order to give them currency among the Irish. The poem was signed 'Fear Ganainm' (man without a name), but Farleigh's bardic associates named him to be one O'Daley, and they said that he had been handsomely commissioned to write the piece by Lord Sussex. Shane demanded that the Deputy apply the strictures of his 'law' to his own crier. Sidney wrote diplomatically that 'should he be caught', O'Daly would receive due punishment. In his rage over the ban on Brehons and bards, Shane issued his own edict. Henceforth, all

SHANE O'NEILL

the English customs and ways creeping into Ulster from the Pale would be forbidden, and those caught promulgating them would be punished!

Beyond that, O'Neill was beset by problems far more pressing. Encountering frustrations not unlike Sidney's, he had as yet failed to procure any assurance of help from the Continent. A letter had come from Phillip II of Spain, affirming that O'Neill was the 'foremost Catholic champion', but it was painstakingly devoid of promises. Unbeknownst to Shane, his letter to King Charles IX had been captured by Cecil's spies en route to France. While the French Cardinals, uncles to Mary Stuart, had received Shane's entreaties to press for the King's support, and Mary was quite amenable, all was really contingent upon the Pope's response. And thus far, there had been only silence from Rome.

`As for domestic support, apart from the Earl of Kildare, who had admonished him, insisting that he capitulate and beg the Queen's pardon, Shane's Irish allies in the South were responding with amenable but evasive words. His cousin Garret, the Earl of Desmond, however, offered some hope. He was back in Ireland, after his imprisonment in the Tower, and he promised to beset the Deputy with diversionary troubles in the South when the time was right.

In late June, Mary Stuart bore a 'knave child' safe into the world, an heir to the throne who would one day -and that day not so far off, become James VI of Scotland. She now brought to bear all the pressure she could muster to compel Elizabeth to acknowledge him heir to the English throne as well. This offensive was countered by a stern rebuke from London for Mary's 'meddling in Ulster'. It was known that she had urged Argyll to favour O'Neill, and he had given word to Shane that he would return with troops before summer's end. Now, Mary found that she must insist upon caution, until the question of succession was settled.

Adding to this northern chill, Elizabeth's Council devised a ploy to sunder the cosy alliance between Argyll and O'Neill. Argyll was a staunch Protestant, and that was the card to play. The 'Reformed' Primate of Ireland, Adam Loftus, was directed to sound Argyll, and to impress upon him that the Papists were Shane's real supporters. He wrote to Archibald that it 'was reported' how O'Neill and Danyell of Armagh had sent to Mary Stuart a promise that if she should now set upon the Protestants, he, her Irish abettor, would 'find occupation' for the Earl of Argyle! Here was a lie that might not only sever all ties with O'Neill, but estrange the Earl from Mary as well!

When Shane got wind of this, he sent to Argyll his denial of having sent any such message to Mary. And, since Archbishop Loftus was so desirous to keep correspondence with Lord Argyll, he then sent counterfeit letters to him. Delivered by a messenger who had 'returned from Scotland', there came to the 'Queen's Primate' two letters purportedly from Hamilton, Duke of Chatelherault, and from the Earl of Argyle, desiring to know details of the English plans for making war on O'Neill. The counterfeit was good, apparently, but for the form of address, which was a usage not then current in Scotland, and Loftus's suspicions were aroused. To test the truth of this mission, the Primate dispatched a man of his own back to Argyll, upon whose return, the letters in question proved counterfeit. The incident angered and grievously offended The Earl of Argyll, and put his mission to Ulster very much in question.

In spite of his war footing, Shane wrote to the Queen once again on Stukeley's behalf, with a letter so gracious as to belie all the charges of barbarism being leveled at him. "Many of the nobles, magnates, and gentlemen of that kingdom treated me kindly and ingenuously, and namely one of the gentlemen of your realm, Master Thomas Stukeley, entertained me with his whole heart, and with all the favour he could. But I perceived that his whole intention, and the benevolence he showed me, tended to this: to show me the magnificence and the honour of your majesty and your realm. I cannot do less than with all my might requite him with love, the fervency of whose love I then enjoyed. But it has been lately shown me that you are persuaded that he has done something that offends you and your laws. If it be true, alas and alas!" He went on to beseech the Queen to examine Stukeley's case with equity, and to restore him to favour. But 'alas and alas,' for all his fine words, this time the endorsement of Elizabeth's greatest public enemy was of no benefit to Stukeley.

In June, only a week before the birth of Mary Stuart's 'wee prince', Katherine was delivered of her fourth child, a lass this time, and at her insistence, Bishop Myler Magrath was asked to preside at the Christening. He did the honours in the Cathedral at Armagh, and the child was christened Áilish, after Shane's mother. This was Myler's first meeting with Shane since his return from Rome, and he came not without trepidation. In spite of the merry occasion, he found the chieftain prickly and guarded, resentful of what he considered his usurped episcopal elevation, but also agitated by the mounting disappointments regarding foreign support. Myler had anticipated as much, and he wisely came well armed with good news.

There were rumours within the Curia that Pius V was preparing to excommunicate Elizabeth, even if little of substance could be offered to confirm it. As for the despised Papal Nuncio, Myler had received word from Primate Creagh in Spain that, while Wolfe's mission in Ireland had, indeed, been renewed, it was clearly in jeopardy! Creagh was greatly distressed that David Wolfe had 'alas!' become embroiled in scandal in Limerick City. It involved the Nuncio's 'personal' dealings with the inmates of a shelter for fallen women known as 'Mná Bochta', and it had given rise to a growing clamour for his recall to Rome.

This bit of news raised a howl of laughter, and instantly warmed the bishop's welcome. Beyond this, Myler could announce with certainty that the new Pope had gone so far as to request the Superior General of the Jesuits, Francis Borgia, to withdraw the order from Ireland! The Jesuits were leaving! Myler Magrath's trove of cheering news did much to brighten the Christening Celebration. Katherine was delighted to see the foster-brothers reconciled, and most especially that Myler had brought this badly needed hope to Shane.

In Dublin there was cheer as well, when Lord Harry's entreaties to the Queen were at last met with success. A letter arrived in midsummer informing him that he would soon receive the 1,000 men that he had originally been promised. Three hundred seasoned soldiers from Berwick, 100 men from London, and 600 more from the

SHANE O'NEILL

Western counties were to be placed under the experienced guidance of Colonel Randolph, at whose urging the Queen had finally relented. Moreover, two brigantines would be dispatched to guard the Scottish coast. Sidney was authorized to levy 200 horse and 200 foot in Ireland, and Her Majesty urged him to take the offensive. All would be underway immediately in order to invade the North before the harvests of August. "Upon this preparation here, we think that Shane O'Neill will grow into some heat, and perchance break his brickle peace, and therefore he is to be seen to as though you had open wars with him!"

In July, upon hearing this news, Shane called a hosting of his army, and made a sweep into the west to bolster his holdings there. He fortified his garrisons in O'Donnell's country, and drove Shane Maguire out of Fermanagh, installing in his place a younger brother who pledged support. Maguire arrived in Dublin on the 26th of July with his bitter tale, and informed Sidney that O'Neill would soon repair to the border with his whole force to invade the English Pale. The Lord Deputy quickly gathered an army of 1,500 foot and 600 horsemen, and hastened north to Dundalk.

Along the way he was met by a messenger who carried an 'insolent letter' from O'Neill, urging a convening of Parliament to determine in his causes, demanding that Maguire be turned over to him, and advising that he was sworn to give battle should Sidney's forces issue forth from Dundalk. After reaching the town, however, Sidney called his bluff, marching out to a hillfoot quite near to where O'Neill was encamped. There he remained until evening. Shane kept in his fastness, however, and no battle ensued, but for a few small skirmishes with woodkerne. On the second day, Sidney returned to repeat the challenge, 'but battle there was none'.

The Deputy returned to Dundalk. He was then forced to retire his army for want of provisions, uttering many a curse for the parsimony of his royal mistress. He determined to leave a sufficient ward to defend the place, but to withdraw the rest, lest they should quickly exhaust the town's meagre store of victuals. Evidently, O'Neill's demurral to engage his army led the Deputy to suppose that the town

SHANE O'NEILL

was safe, for he left his wife, Lady Mary, within its walls.

Within days of Sidney's departure, however, O'Neill rampaged through the outlying Pale, sacking and burning villages along the border. He then repaired to Dundalk and laid seige to the town itself. Shane had a force of several thousand, and he arrayed them in great numbers around all the gates of the town. Much of Dundalk was in a 'ruinous' state, but the walls were formidable, and the garrison well manned. Under the command of Captain Bryan FitzWilliams, brother of the Lord Justice, Dundalk withstood the siege for several weeks. The entrapment there of Lady Sidney, Leicester's sister, added a personal note to the distress of the Royal Court at news of this siege. It was Mary Sidney who had nursed the Queen through her perilous illness, and Elizabeth was gravely concerned for her safety, as was her brother, Dudley Lord Leicester.

O'Neill, as it happened, had many partisans within the town's walls. The local Catholics were as angry as he over a recent edict issued by the Mayor, banishing priests and friars, and imposing a burdensome fine on householders who abstained from Common Prayer Service. One of these Irishmen undertook to breach the town's defenses for the 'enemy without'. On a moonlit night a pair of white breeches were hung out over the high walls above a small sally port. This was a signal to Shane's men, who, upon finding that postern gate open, rushed through it into a narrow laneway. But the plan had been detected! And as they poured into the close, a barrage of harquebus fire was unleashed, killing eighteen of the Irish, the rest beating a hasty retreat.

This bloody rout was followed the very next day by the timely arrival of William Sarsfield, the Mayor of Dublin, who led a sizable contingent to relieve the beleaguered town. These troops, recruited from the weavers, barbers, and other members of the guilds of Dublin, bore much-needed provisions, and comprised sufficient numbers as to compel O'Neill to raise the siege after but one more day of battle. Upon their arrival, Sarsfield's troops broke through Shane's southern flank with fierce fighting, aided by a timely sortie from within the gates. The siege was lifted, and Lady Sidney was rescued. O'Neill

SHANE O'NEILL

departed then for Carickbradagh Castle in the Moyry Pass, marching off through the smouldering country, lands wasted and pillaged by his army. Behind him, to the delight of crows, and kites, and Englishmen, eighteen heads were left to grin hideously over the gates of Dundalk.

Back in Dublin, Sarsfield was knighted, and on the 3rd of August, Shane O'Neill was declared traitor. All his adherents were charged the same. A bounty of 1,000 marks was set for the capture of his head. Lord Sidney reported of the English triumph with the embellishment of numbers so typical of second-hand report, when verification is deemed irrelevant. "The Irish entered the town, but had such a welcome that the traitor lost there of his gentlemen, so many, as I was credibly informed, that there were fully seventeen of their horse litters filled with dead corpses. These he sent to be buried at Armagh. Those that he buried near the town, as some of them have confessed, were about the number of a hundred. Those that were slain within the walls do now garnish the gate with their heads, but such was the repulse as he could not procure any more of his men to follow the enterprise, and sure my Lord, it was manfully and honorably defended."

This engagement was a thing quite unprecedented for Shane O'Neill. A defeat! And if it was a jolt to Shane, and a wound to his pride, it was something more to his followers. Never having been vanquished, O'Neill had acquired an aura of invincibility that claimed their loyalty as if by divine ordinance. He was as certain as destiny or rain. They had never doubted the unfolding of his inexorable fortunes, and this defeat shook them to the core. As for Shane, he was now convinced beyond all doubt that if he would prevail against the might of England, he must get help. More letters and emissaries were dispatched to the Courts of Europe, to Argyll, and to his cousin in the South.

The Earl of Desmond, having only recently returned from his captivity in London, was detained once again in Dublin for determinations in the matter of his conflict with Ormond. This being the case, Shane sent a swift messenger to his brother, John of Desmond in Kilmallock, bearing a letter in Irish that called for a rising in Munster. A letter as succinct as it was brief!

SHANE O'NEILL

"...Now is the time or never to set against the English. Certify yourself that Englishmen have no other eye but only to subdue both English and Irish of Ireland, and I and you especially. And certify yourself also that those their Deputies, one after another, have broken peace and did not abide by the same. And assure yourself, also, that they had been with *you* ere this time but only for me! If Desmond fails or turns against his country, God will turn against him."

From Carickbradagh, Shane departed with his legions east to Carlingford, casting just the fleeting shadow of his power over the English settlement there before turning north. He marched on to Ballycastle to attempt a rapprochement with Alistair MacDonnell, the brother of Sorley and James. The Scots were somewhat daunted by his numbers, and Alistair was obliged to treat with him. He came forward with another Scot at his side, a surly glowering fellow whose countenance was familiar to Shane, but his name beyond recall. Alistair demanded firstly to know of Sorley's condition. Shane gave him assurance that his brother fared well in his keeping. For all his bitterness, this was Katherine's uncle, and he mustered the civility to ask after her and the children. He knew well Shane's reason for calling upon him, and he comported himself proudly, cold and canny. They stood this day, after all, at Bonamargy Friary, only a few miles from from Glenshesk, the scene of all the carnage barely one year earlier.

Shane wanted the MacDonnells' help against the English. He told of Argyll's promise, and of his expected arrival. He offered to deliver up Sorley Buí, and to cede to them all the lands of Clandeboy, all the geld kine of his country, and to give them pledge and assurance of his fidelity towards them. But Lord Sidney had been shrewd enough to foresee this, and had made his own pact with Alistair.

The Scot disavowed having any word of Argyll's coming, and he affected not to believe it. He listened to all Shane had to say. He turned then, to confer with the other man whom Shane now recognized as Gillaspick, the MacDonnell cousin who had defied him at Dunluce Castle. The two men once again faced O'Neill, smirking. Alistair narrowed his eyes and laughed to himself. "Clandeboy, and its geld kine! All *that* I shall have. And more, O'Neill. I have only to bide your undoing. When your head adorns a gate, we shall take us possession of *all* the Glens of Antrim. Time moves apace, Shane O'Neill, and that day draws ever nearer."

When his new set of pontifical documents and credentials arrived from Rome, Primate Creagh was at last ready to return to Ireland. There in the Spanish port of Cadiz, through the offices of the Jesuits, he had put in place a crucial line of correspondence between Rome and Ireland. A local Irishwoman was deputed to send the letters on by ship to certain entrusted merchants in Limerick, from whence the Nuncio, Wolfe, would direct them on to the new Primate in Armagh.

King Philip bestowed upon Dr. Creagh funds for his mission, enabling him to purchase books and objects for the adornment of the Cathedral there, and included 150 ducats for the hire of a ship to take him to Sligo. In view of all his misfortunes as a passenger on cargo ships, the wary prelate insisted on full control of the voyage and its itinerary. Once again, however, it seems the aspiring martyr was to be tested by God, and he was beset by perils. His travails were recounted by Wolfe, who lavished praise upon the beleaguered saint, and these new misfortunes simply burnished and added lustre to his ever more discernible halo.

Again the holy man had found himself 'at death's door' due to the treachery of an Irish crew. Wolfe posits that knowing, as they did, that Creagh had paid for the charter of the ship, these 'false brothers' assumed he was a wealthy man, and such was the cause of their

SHANE O'NEILL

venom. This leaves aside the political and cultural animosities that were bound to surface, given the Primate's staunch loyalty to the Crown, and his propensity to recommend it. Initially the crew's plan had been to throw him overboard, but for fear of a possible inquiry, they resorted to poisoning his drink. As he lay 'dying', one of the sailors repented of the deed, and confessed it to him, begging forgiveness. This being granted, the rest of his shipmates were then absolved, with the bishop's humble plea that he should be buried in Cantabria, if he should die at sea.

'Through the mercy of God,' however, a great tempest arose, and put the ship in peril of foundering in the Bay of Biscay. It was driven ashore in Brittany at Blavet, just beside (providentially) a priory of Franciscans. Creagh asked to be confessed by a priest, and the crew assented, fetching a friar to hear him. He confessed more than his own sins, however. Upon hearing what had transpired, the confessor inveigled the crew to hear Mass at the Priory, whereby they might bring back medical supplies to the ailing Lord Primate. A supper was provided, during which the ringleaders were captured and held, pending the delivery of the Archbishop. When Creagh was brought in, the plotters were released. Accepting his forgiveness once more, but declining to be confessed, the Irish crew put to sea. After two months of care, the Primate was fully recovered, and he hired another ship to sail from Nantes. Once again, 'unvanquished by evil', the pious prelate resumed his holy ordained mission 'to minister among the savages' of Ulster.

Bishop Myler Magrath, as requested, journeyed to Sligo to meet the Primate upon his expected arrival. Creagh's ship had docked a day early, so he was found waiting patiently, much encumbered with trunks and truck, and still attended by his faithful young servant Florry O'More, and one still younger called 'Seán beg'. Myler had brought his own servants, with horses and a dray, so it wasn't long before they were on the road east.

Their road took them through Maguire's country, and the devastation of O'Neill's last foray was everywhere evident, much to the Primate's distress. Shane had driven off the chieftain, an adherent of the Crown, and replaced him with his rebel brother, who happened to be married to Shane's daughter. Myler was first cousin to this Cúconnacht Maguire, and he determined to avail of his hospitality for the night's lodgings, mindful that such a Primatial visit would confer an implied imprimatur upon the new chieftain, and lend an additional air of legitimacy to his command. With Enniskillen ravaged, Maguire had taken up residence in a minor fortress at Tempo Deshell, and there it was that Myler led his company.

Shane's daughter Moraed greeted the illustrious visitors warmly, and apologized for the upheaval around them. Shane's two cousins from the West, Turlagh Lynach O'Neill and Black Hugh O'Donnell, were down to advise the new chieftain, and the evening's spirited discourse in the hall gave the Limerick prelate his first taste of the intricacies of the fiery contentions in Ulster. The tone and terms of discussion were very much tailored to his pious ears, of course, and lighter subjects were entertained as much as possible for civility's sake.

Turlagh, a widower, had made overtures to court Agnes, the newly widowed wife of James MacDonnell, and Black Hugh, having been rejected by Agnes, was openly wooing her raven-haired daughter, Fionnúla. The two men were about to ride east to Antrim to press their suits of marriage, and this brought them a share of teasing and trifling banter over their wine. Both the suitors were wished success with their lasses, of course, in hopes that such a match would help to heal the bitterness after the slaughter of Glenshesk. In any event, the two resolved to accompany the Primate into Tirowen, where he would be presented to Shane O'Neill.

Dr. Creagh and his escort would be spared any idle wandering, now, for Turlagh O'Neill had precise knowledge of his cousin's whereabouts. Apart from a token force of a hundred gallowglass from Mary Stuart, and two hundred more from Katherine's father, there was as yet little sign that any armies would be coming to Shane's aid, and he was digging in for a dogged resistance to the coming invasion. To that end he was fortifying a cranogue in the middle of a small lake some miles west of Armagh. The tiny islet of Glenaul was impregnable. Only a fleet of sturdy boats could take it, and, given its remoteness, they would need to be built on site. It was the safest place for O'Neill to store his plate and treasure, and that was the very task he was undertaking when his visitors arrived. Beside him in the murky cellar was his captain, Cormac MacArdal. Farleigh O'Gneeve had been brought along for diversion, and it was he that rushed in with the news.

"Thunder and shite! You'll never credit this, Shane O'Neill. You've a clutch of wild cocks roosting on the shore beyond, crowing and hullooing for you! And two of them are got up in red mitres and robes!"

"Christ almighty, what's this, then? I'm expecting Turlagh, alright. Is he among them?"

"He looks to be among them. And Black Hugh O'Donnell, if I'm not mistaken. And his mighty Reverence, Bishop Myler the Rogue, no less. The other one could only be that Englishtown hoor from Limerick, Bishop Creagh! What in the name of God is he doing *here*? By Crom the Crooked, you'd be as well to bring *Sidney* out here! Are they mad? Myler knows better than to trust that thieving little sallowjack. Where is the good of a hide-away, and they bringing spies into it?"

"Sure, how could he know his whereabouts, from one green hill to the next? He's as wise as 'hoodman blind', I'd say. Take it soft and easy, now, Farleigh. Come along so; I want to get a gawk at him!" Up they stepped, then, out into the blinding August sun. Under the shade of his hand, Shane saw across the water the curious aggregation of visitors, with the two scarlet robes fluttering on the shore. Only Turlagh was still seated on his mount, and his hand was aloft in greeting.

"Hoigh! O'Neill! We've brought you a wee gift from Rome!" Creagh had learned Irish, and he bristled at the tone of this 'introduction'. Shane's attendants scrambled into a couple of skiffs and set off to collect the guests beyond. The cranogue itself was a round islet, no more than ninety feet across, surrounded by a thick and thorny hedge and bearded with stakes and sharp wooden spikes.

SHANE O'NEILL

The sight of it confirmed for William Creagh the barbarity of the Ulster 'tribes' with whom he was now obliged to treat. When at length the boats approached the isle, the Primate had his palms raised to frame his chin, as he intoned a Latin prayer. His face was composed in a vague smile of blissful serenity with his eyes shut, and only when the boat thumped up against the moorings did he open them. He was helped up onto the small mossy landing then, and he did not turn his gaze to O'Neill until he got his crozier into his fist. The others held back, to give his arrival its due moment. Shane and Farleigh held their ground, taking him in.

William Creagh was roughly the same age as Shane. He was a slight fellow of medium height, sharp-featured, with a slightly boney countenance. His hair was wispy, and so fair as to be called white. His eyes were of palest grey, nearly suggesting blindness, and he was prone to blinking. He stood now facing Shane, with his gilded crook towering beside in his left hand, and with his right hand he signed a benediction thricely. He looked quite entranced and distant, and he spoke with a thin reedy voice.

"Pax vobiscum." Shane nodded at this.

"Pax tecum." The Primate now held his fist forth inviting Shane to kiss his golden ring. Shane affected not to see this, and, turning abruptly, called back to him. "Come, your Grace. A humble cranogue it is, but you'll have a princely welcome within!" The bishop turned sharply to the others to check any insolent smiles, and then strode forth up the slight embankment, each step buttressed by his lofty crozier. Shane led him past a tall wattled fence, and into the imposing roundhouse with its conical roof of thickly layered reed-thatch some thirty feet high. He murmured orders to an attendant, while another drew chairs out from a broad deal table, and bowed to the prelate. The rest of the party followed them in with hearty greetings, the servants withdrawing to the rough benches near the fire. Shane smiled warmly but warily as he turned again to the Primate. "Ah! What is *this* we have?" Creagh handed to him a sealed scroll.

"It is a letter of introduction -written unto you by His Holiness." Shane took it from him, and gestured towards a chair.

SHANE O'NEILL

"Won't you be seated, your Grace! After your long journey, aren't you due a rest? A wee drop of Cabernet Franc! Would that suit you?"

"It would not." Creagh sat. "*I* am not a votary of Bacchus. Howandever, a drink of water, now, would refresh me, for the day is rather close." A servant nodded, and withdrew.

"The boys are scorching a bit of trout for us. Fine trout, as fresh as this moment, for they'll be gathered up out of a cishawn in the lough." The bishop smiled and nodded his approval. He then settled his head back, and eyed the scroll in Shane's hand, raising an impatient brow."

"From the Pope, is it? The *new* Pope?"

"Indeed, my letters from Pius IV were confiscated. These were drawn anew." Shane unrolled the letter, and ambled over to the doorway, where sunlight was streaming in. He stood and read the missive, while wine was poured, and the others arranged themselves about the table with soft-spoken pleasantries. On finishing, he rolled it, and handed it off to a servant to pack away for him. He seated himself then, with an amiable smile.

"A fine letter, indeed. A 'defender of the Faith', he called me. And so I am. He has blessed my victories over the heretics." Creagh's mouth curled sourly. "You were a long time in coming to us, so you were, but at last you are here to take possession of your see!"

"-Of what remains of it!"

"Indeed, your Grace, what remains of it *remains*...because a great many Ulstermen have spilt their blood to protect it."

"Too much blood has been spilt! Come, come, O'Neill. Our good Lord has commanded us to peace. And we must endeavor to abide by his holy Word."

"I hope you have written as much in your *letters to Lord Cecil*. He is sending armies as we speak, and not for any peace, as *I* can discern." Creagh shot an accusing glance at his suffragan bishop, the only one who might know of his correspondence, as he supposed. "As I have written to his Holiness, you will be welcome here to administer your see, so long as you concern yourself with matters of Faith and morals - as is meet for a man of the cloth. If you will meddle in matters of State, you shall find yourself banished on *both* sides of the Pale."

SHANE O'NEILL

"I intend to follow the Gospel, and to 'render unto Caesar those things that are Caesar's, and unto God, the things that are God's.' But I shall bear witness to our Saviour's message of Peace."

"Just *who* is this Caesar that you serve? *That* we have *yet to see.*" Shane's stern visage lightened now. "One of our many bones of contention, Dr. Creagh. And we shall have time to chaw and tussle at them all I expect. But, sure, you've only just arrived. Perhaps if we try, we might find some matters wherein we are agreed. We both would seek the welfare and betterment of Ireland-" Shane realized as he spoke, that even the word 'Ireland' had a different meaning to the 'Englishtown prelate', and he resorted to simple social proprieties. You've not met my retinue! These are my captains, Cormac MacArdal, and Dualta O'Donnelly, both devout as any men you'll find in Christendom. And this is my chiefest bard, the reknowned poet, Farleigh O'Gneeve." The three men nodded amiably, but Farleigh spoke up.

"We have heard a great deal about you, your Eminence, and much of it wondrous! I thought perhaps you would have *walked* out to the island!" This drew a somewhat tentative laugh from the company, prompting Creagh to smile rather tightly, as he had no ready answer. Shane winked at Myler.

"Like *yourself*, your Grace, Farleigh O'Gneeve finds himself on the wrong side of English Law, for it is not only our priests that are proscribed now. They have outlawed our poets, and our judges as well!"

"That is most unfortunate. Perhaps if the poets would write for the glory of God, instead of the glory of their paymasters, they would then fare better with their sovereign!"

"*All art* attests to the glory of God! Ah, but you confuse our callings, your Lordship. Yours is to instruct of the Creator, *mine* to sing of Creation!" Farleigh's deft parry was met with a ripple of laughter, and bright smiles round the board." Creagh was insistent.

"You sing of more than *creation*! Indeed you sing of destruction. I have heard your rhymes on the lips of more than a few minstrels and vagabonds, harping on treason and villainy."

SHANE O'NEILL

"Indeed, I have given voice to my people's suffering under the yoke of English tyranny, and-"

"It is not a *yoke*, but a halter. A bridle to lead a wild and headstrong people out of depravity and sin –and ignorance. If we suffer, it is the will of God. 'He shall cast down the wicked! *And* the *proud!*" He leveled an accusing glare at Shane. "Pride goeth before a fall, O'Neill, and it is your pride that has brought war and calamity to your people. There would be no troops asailing, but for your defiance of the divinely ordained prince of this realm. *Divinely* ordained. It is God you defy! And his Holy Will. If he has seen fit to punish the people of Ireland for their sin, this we must accept as Christians. These evil times have befallen us because we have turned away from God. Lust and sloth, wrath and pride. We have been wicked and sinful and now God is chastising us! But this suffering is a *blessing*. A blessing to be joyous of, for it will purge our souls of the stain of sin, and with the remission of sin, redeem us to enter into eternal life. The Lord chastises those he loves!" At this point Myler Magrath was red in the face, but he strained to hold his temper in check.

"And are the English so virtuous then? So holy as to be the instruments of God's affliction to these Christian people? These same greedy English are *heretics*, while the Irish, Gael and Gall, hold true to our Holy Faith. To say the heretics are virtuous is *itself* heresy!"

"Indeed, the English *are* a virtuous people. A people of civility! And husbandry! –A people that have much to *teach* the Irish, who languish in ignorance in their filthy hovels. A people steeped in lewdness and deceit and corruption, and treachery and rebellion. I dare say it is a mercy that the Almighty has not sent a pestilence!"

"Aye, a plague!" Shane laughed bitterly. "That would avail them nicely in their greed. The Irish under churchyard clay, and the English settled in their place. It is a mercy, surely. We must be thankful."

"The English do not covet these Irish bogs. Albeit such scurrilous claims serve well those who would incite rebellion. In truth, they seek only to impose the Queen's peace for the *relief* of her Irish subjects – who suffer more from the exactions of squabbling bog-lords." The company was quite shocked by the insolence of this remark, and all expected a flare of temper as Shane stood abruptly, but he spoke calmly and sternly.

"I have word from friends in the Royal Court that you wrote to Queen Elizabeth from Spain. You beseeched her to allow you to take up your duties here as Primate. Perforce you believe her to *possess* such authority—She has emphatically *denied* you that permission. Why are you here?" Creagh was dumbfounded. He breathed heavily, but he spoke not. "You assent to the Queen's authority in the matter, and yet you defy her refusal. It is you, William Creagh who stands in rebellion. I grant her no such authority. Why are you here?"

"I am here to fill my office. Much of which you have usurped! I find my priests and friars are turned warriors, and are serving in your army. And whom are they armed to fight, but their rightful Sovereign! My own priests are joined in sinful rebellion."

"And fine Fenian fairplay to them! It is right and fitting for them to do so. For if my army fails against the invaders, it is these priests who will be driven to the bracken, hunted as outlaws. Why would they not take arms against it?"

"Because it is wicked and sinful! You have stolen my clergy. *And* you have stolen for your wars the temporalities of this Diocese!"

"That money was rendered up by the Chapter of Armagh for the selfsame reason. They know that if my armies do not prevail, they will be supplanted by heretics. I have stolen nothing." A servant appeared with a large tray laden with provender. He looked to O'Neill, who nodded. "And now, Dr. Creagh, you will partake of some fine gillaroo trout that I have sinfully stolen from this lough! These contentions will have to keep. They'll have to keep while we betake ourselves of nourishment and sustenance enough to wrangle them out after!" A bit of laughter now softened the hearts around the table, and even the Primate smiled freely. He rose.

"Indeed. Better feasting than fighting, I suppose. But I must pay a call of nature." He looked questioningly. Shane nodded to a servant.

"Round the back, your Grace. Kian will show you. We've not the amenities of Rome here, but we make do." When the Primate had disappeared through the sunny portal, looks of wonder passed around the table. Shane looked to Bishop Myler.

"Mother of God! *This* is what Rome sends to us?"

"It is blackest heresy to hold such heretics virtuous! His Holiness is fiercely opposed to them, and Creagh may o'erstep himself yet! If he stood before the Inquisition, he would find himself in a sore state! We need the Inquisition here in Ireland." Farleigh swallowed back his wine and thumped his cup down before him.

"The Inquisition? It's an atrocity, and a fool's folly. The truth has never needed, nor will it ever need, laws to uphold it. It exists

SHANE O'NEILL

regardless of what is said to the contrary. But, by the powers! Did you hear him? I'd like to take a puck at him myself! A wheeshy skimpy little wisp of a man! Hasn't enough spunk in him to-"

"He's bold enough in his *replies*." Shane smirked at the bard's roiling temper.

"An unhealthy caste of mind, that's what it is! He answers boldly, aye, but he seems to *revel* in weakness. He urges it on the people. Mark you- I will say *this*! A people who glory in suffering will suffer! I shudder to think what may befall this land under the crook of such a bishop! And under the spell of such a morbid and stifling creed." Myler raised his palm.

"It is not the creed, but a perversion of it. It is the creed in the service of English greed! His heart is poisoned against the Irish, and he serves only his kind." This brought a sudden burst from Black Hugh O'Donnell.

"By the sacred book, boys! I shame to hear this blackmouthing of a blessed bishop!" He glared at Myler. "Even from a *bishop*, God forgive ye! He is a holy man, and he will neither speak nor think like a warrior. For the love of God, *this* man is known to have miraculous powers! And the people are calling him a saint!" He tisked, and sighed as he shook his head with disgust. O'Donnell was considered fairly pious, but this outburst took the others by surprise. He was not known to be credulous, and Shane wondered now what was behind it.

The meal a was pleasant repast, despite the underlying discord. News and blessings from Shane's daughter Moraed were duly and cheerfully conveyed. And again there was needling of the two anxious suitors who would soon be off to the glens to woo their Scots ladies fair. Fionnúla, the formidable daughter of the MacDonnell, was known only as 'The Dark Daughter', and it was deemed fitting that she should be courted and wived by 'Black' Hugh. He was anxious to turn the talk from his affairs, so he entreated the Primate to recount his wondrous escape, and the other miraculous deliverances that had so captured the imagination of the people of Ireland. Both Hugh and Turlagh O'Neill seemed enraptured by these tales, while the rest exchanged sly glances of merriment.

After the supper, further discussions ensued on a more cordial note, but little common ground was discerned. Creagh's great passion was for the founding of a University at Armagh, where, as Shane pointed out, he hoped to train counter-reformation priests for England, and, to a large extent, *from* England. Such proposals had been rejected by Shane, and he was not inclined to reconsider. The Primate also wanted to hold a synod at Armagh for the priests of Ireland in order to implement the decrees of the Council of Trent. Shane obliged him in this, and then made three requests of his own. He had important papers for the King of Spain, and he wanted the Primate to take them to the Escorial, adding spiritual authority to his desperate plea for military aid against the heretics. Creagh was indignant. "Not for *that* did I journey to Ireland! No, but to carry out mine *own* mission -my papally appointed mission, to minister to the faithful here."

"If you will not undertake my embassage to King Philip, I must entreat you then to sign with me our urgent request for his help." Creagh's eyes closed, and he slowly shook his head. "By Christ! Look to your wit, man! Should the Queen's writ take ascendancy in Armagh, you will be unable to minister to *anyone* here! And, most like, you will find yourself once again shivering in the 'Whale's belly'!"

"If such be the will of God, so be it. But I will not be a party to treason."

"In the Pope's very letter, the letter that you yourself delivered to me from Rome, His Holiness blessed me for my victories against the forces of heresy. Will you gainsay the Holy Father? Do you condemn his words?"

"His Holiness is not a subject of Her Majesty, and so he cannot be held treasonous."

"By Christ, I'm wasting my breath with you. No, then. I have another request still, if it will not o'ertax your tender conscience. I'm sending my army to drive Pierce from Carrickfergus, and there is a priory of Franciscans there. I'll need you to bid them quit the place and withdraw, else they shall find themselves under heavy mortal fire." The Primate's eyes blinked several times and then closed in anguished silence. "It is the safety of your monks that must be seen to!"

"This, again, I cannot do. But I must bid you to stay your hand from such wickedness! For the sake of your immortal soul, O'Neill, you must refrain from these evil predations." Shane turned on his heel to withdraw, but there he stopped. He turned, and put to the Primate his last question, with a brusque demanding tone.

"Sunday is the Feast of the Assumption. Which Mass will be yours?"

"I will celebrate the High Mass at Ten of the forenoon. You'll be most welcome to-"

"Oh, you may be sure I'll be there. And with my captains, and my troops. If you are a Catholic, I expect you will exhort my men to fight for their Faith in the name of his Holiness, Pope Pius V."

"I am indeed a Catholic -and a Christian, Shane O'Neill. And I will call upon them to do their duties as soldiers of Christ."

Before Myler Magrath returned to his see at Downpatrick, he came privately to Shane with a copy of a letter he had found when rummaging in Cardinal Morone's office in the Vatican. It was addressed from 'David Wolf, S.J. Nuncio Hibernicus, to Giovanni, Cardinal Moroni'. Myler watched anxiously as Shane read it, and then he leaned in, and pointed further down the page. "No, here. Here is the evidence." Shane read aloud.

> "I would respectfully bid your Eminence to require of Magonigle and Creagh, in virtute obedientiae, information as to the conduct of Donat O'Taige, Archbishop of Armagh."

Shane looked up. Myler nodded. "It wasn't '*good* conduct' he had in mind. This shows plainly that he was undermining O'Tighe in Rome before he replaced him in office. But, look you now. *Here* is the one I'm after finding among his things as we traveled from Sligo these days past." He unfolded another parchment. "This one is from Pius IV, detailing his mission as Primate, and granting him special provisions of authority. Ahh. Here, look you." Shane read aloud.

> "As per your request, you are granted power to absolve from excommunication, censures and pains, subject to the imposition of salutary penance, those who were guilty, either as principals or as accessories, of the capture of Donat O'Taig, late Primate of Ireland, and also all such as have since laid violent hands, even to the effusion of blood, upon priests and other clerics."

Shane's grey eyes narrowed as he lifted them to Myler's eager and troubled scowl.

"So he's told by the Pope that he may absolve David Wolfe and his brother, the Bailiff, for their part in the capture and death of O'Tighe - who was then tortured and killed to make way for himself. He is an impious fraud! Sure, what is it, only murder!"

Sunday was lashing rain, but on its lofty eminence above the little lanes of Armagh, the Cathedral was crowded with over 600 of the Faithful to hear the new Primate's maiden sermon. The congregation was comprised, for the most part, of O'Neill's soldiery, with the chieftain and his officers standing foremost in the nave. Farleigh O'Gneeve was among them, attending, as he said, 'out of morbid curiosity'. Black Hugh, and Turlagh, having returned from their courting, were also to the fore. The air was charged with tension, for O'Neill, by his very presence, seemed to dare the Primate to defy him in his preaching. The Dean of Armagh stood beside Shane, in a not-so-subtle declaration of his position on the issues at hand.

The choir, under the direction of Father Patrick Dorrell, outdid themselves with his splendid choices of plainsong and ancient Irish liturgical music. Still, their plaintive strains cast a melancholy spell on some of those present. In truth, Shane was not alone in ruminating over the loss of Donagh O'Tighe, and the sorry consequences of it. Creagh's part in that pious man's cruel end, his abetting the Nuncio's betrayal of O'Tighe, was preying hard upon his mind, and it was really only now, during this High Mass, that O'Neill conceived his deadly hatred for the Primate.

For the Gradual of the Mass, the choir sang a spirited Allelujah, in keeping with the joyous feast of Our Lady, and the Gospel was taken from St. Luke's, the 'Magnificat' of the Blessed Virgin. The Primate kissed the blessed book, and ascended the pulpit stair. He began his sermon assuring the congregation that the Council of Trent had re-affirmed the doctrine of Mary's bodily assumption into Heaven, a teaching which was reviled by the Protestants. It looked, for a time, as though the new Primate would avoid the thorny issues posed by the presence of O'Neill's army in the nave before him.

At length, however, Creagh turned the narrative to his purpose. He expounded upon Mary's humility, her cheerful acceptance of suffering and sorrow, and the glorious reward this merited her, being taken up bodily into Heaven. Now, he brought out Romans 13: 1. "Let every soul be subject unto the higher powers. For there is no power but of God: the powers that be are ordained of God. Whosoever therefore resisted the power resisted the ordinance of God: and *they that resist shall receive to themselves damnation!*" He turned to Proverbs to bolster the authority of Elizabeth. "By *Me* kings reign, and prince's decree justice! By *Me* princes rule and nobles, even all the judges of the earth!" And with the help of St. Peter's letters to the Romans, he admonished the 'rebel' army to "Submit yourselves to every ordinance of man for the Lord's sake: whether it be to the king, as supreme; or unto governors, as unto them that are sent by him for the punishment of evildoers." As he spoke on, he was emboldened, his thin voice rising, shrill and loud, to fill the vaulted chamber. Having armed himself with 'God's word', he proceeded now to demand that the soldiers before him repent of their sinful rebellion, comparing it to Lucifer's revolt against God. Finally Shane stalked forward to the pulpit and roared.

SHANE O'NEILL

"Enough!" There was an audible gasp in the church. "Prelate! You have o'erstepped yourself! You betray your trust! Two years ago this cathedral was a filthy sty, defiled and profaned by these English forces you cherish so! Icons and holy images shattered and befouled with lewd and vile blasphemies! You stand with the conquerors of your people, and you betray Ireland! Just as you betrayed your predecessor Primate O'Tighe, even to his death! This army before you has a mission from the Holy Father in Rome to resist the armies of the heretics, and you, sirrah, are a traitor to the Church of Rome! You've forsaken your spiritual duties in order to espouse the political cause of London. No more of your treason! I'll hear no more of it. I shall tear down this temple and drive you out!" He turned about and called out to the startled faces before him. "Men! We are away" With that, he stalked out of the Cathedral, followed by his officers and troops.

Two of O'Neill's captains, however, did not follow him. Unnoticed in the stormy departure, both of Shane's cousins, Black Hugh O'Donnell, and Turlagh Lynagh O'Neill remained behind. When the Mass was ended, they knelt in the chancel before the shaken archbishop, repented of their sins, and were granted absolution for their sinful rebellion. They lost no time then, in mounting their steeds and galloping off into the West, before news of this might reach the O'Neill.

Four days later, after grave and painful deliberations, Shane returned with his forces to the Hill of Drumsallock. He sent a squad of men into the Cathedral to strip from it all valuables and blessed images to be stored at Glenaul for safekeeping. A warning was given, and out came the furious Primate, with his sacristan, and his attendants. He remonstrated with Shane, shouting up at him, for the chieftain remained mounted and silent. When the draycart had been filled with the treasures of the church, Shane ordered the brands lit. Finally he looked down on Primate Creagh, and spoke.

"There is no choice left me, your Grace. Though it goes hard with me -for 'twas my great and grand-sires built this church, I'll never again endanger my people by allowing an English garrison to lodge within these walls. By St. Malachy, and by the Crozier of St. Patrick, the holy fanes of Drumsallock Hill will be no shelter for English troops! When the wars are acalmed, I will build it up anew." He turned to the men with their flaming torches. "Set it ablaze. Topple the walls as you can. It must afford no shelter for Sidney's army!" The men stood dumbstruck. "What are ye waiting for? Get on with it! Put it to the torch. Every stick and stone of it." The roof was set ablaze, and one of the walls pulled down. Even though he was relishing the Primate's fury and distress, it was painful for Shane to see all the fine work of his artisans going to ashes. Still, in war, he told himself, one must divest of *all* encumbrance!

Creagh and his boys had rushed back into the Sacristy, presumably to salvage vestments. But he appeared now in his white surplice, his crozier aloft, and his servant, Florry O'More carrying a tray with bell, book, and lighted candle. His intention was clear to all. The Primate took up his long thin purple stole, kissed it, and draped it round his neck. He rang the bell thricely, and, with his hand on the holy book, he called out the solemn order of excommunication upon Shane O'Neill. This caused great consternation among Shane's captains, and in his ranks, but he only laughed. "Haven't I letters from the Pope authorizing my wars, naming me 'Defender of the Faith'?" The Dean was concerned, if he was not.

"It's that *very* standing that he threatens. There is grave danger in this, Shane O'Neill!"

"This little man will be exposed for what he is, a traitor and a heretic!"

"It is the Primatial Cathedral. His Holiness will surely misconstrue this as sacrilege."

"Is it not sacrilege to make a dung-hole barracks of it? Christ! I'll soon have to raze my *own* castles -before we come to clash! That will make the reason for all this clear enough to the Pontiff." There was a loud crash, as a burning crossbeam fell within the Cathedral, and they both turned their gaze to the flaming church and the burgeoning plume of black smoke above it. They saw the Primate, now, moving slowly towards them, holding forth his crucifix, and tolling his bell. An uneasy murmur arose among the men behind. The wind shifted now, bringing the dark smoke billowing down around the Primate, as the bell clanged and the candle flickered, and the prelate intoned his Latin hex of damnation yet again. Dean Donnelly turned back to Shane with a look of deepest doubt, but the chieftain would hear no more.

"Ah, no! I stand well with Rome! And by Christ, I'll not be daunted by the curse of this prickly wee ghost out of Englishtown!" He raised his right hand aloft, bringing his men to silence. "Let the curser be acursed! We fight in the name of Pope Pius! And upon his word! We will vanquish the heretics, and send them back to England! Now, men. Away!" O'Neill wheeled his mount, and galloped off down the hill, raising a thunder of hooves behind him.

CHAPTER 29

If the winds of war were blowing, they were as yet ill winds for all. A financial bind brought unexpected delay, and Lord Cecil was obliged to send Sir Thomas Gresham to Antwerp to to procure a 'respite of payment' for the Queen's outstanding debt there. The Secretary was even required to pledge his own credit for the seemingly small sum of £1,100. When Col. Randolph and his legion finally departed from Bristol, they were fully a month behind schedule. They sailed in the face of foul and adverse winds that kept them buffeted on the raging seas until O'Neill had all his harvests safely in.

On the 17th of September, when news reached Sidney that Randolph's fleet had made landfall on the northern coast beside Lough Foyle, his 3,000 troops were ready and waiting. The bugles blew, and the drums tattooed, and he marched his long lines of cavalry and infantry out of Drogheda along the northern road.

Word of this approaching army brought great consternation to O'Neill's war council. His appeals for support had all come to naught. Summer had ended with still no sign of Argyll's promised regiments. The sharp letter summoning John of Desmond to his side had been spurned. Whereas Garrett, the Earl, on such a call to duty, would have stood to, his ambitious brother did not. Upon reading Shane's message, John FitzGerald, supposing that O'Neill would likely have the worst of it, repaired to Sidney 'with none of his followers' following. Angling to supplant his brother, as it might be surmised, he professed loyalty to the queen and accepted a posting on the border of the Pale. He was to guard the outlying Pale with the help of Lords Dunboyne, Power, and Delvin, all of them Catholics formerly allied to O'Neill. Shane had no choice now, if he would prevent a second occupation, but to raze the many castles in Ulster which he could no longer hope to hold with advantage. Dark plumes of smoke rose ominously from many points along the northern horizon.

At the Viceroy's side as he advanced northward with the Earl of Kildare were the two aged chieftains, Cullagh O'Donnell and the deposed Maguire. In spite of their advanced age, they would brave the campaign, hoping to be restored to their domains. After halting four days on the Louth border to await the arrival of supplies, Sidney marched to Armagh to find the Cathedral devastated, and the city wasted. He was hardly bereft, for he intended to take Benburb Castle nearby, and that would serve just as nicely for a garrison. But firstly, there was another matter to be attended to.

The Lord Deputy and his long ranks of soldiers moved on swiftly, purposefully, then, through nine miles of wild country until he came to the secluded little lough of Glenaul. The prickly cranogue could be seen rising out of the middle of the lake, barely a hundred paces from shore. The conical thatched fortress was clearly manned, with archers and gunners poised round its spiky walls, ready to defend it. Having had 'reports' that O'Neill had hidden his money, plate, and treasure in this primitive stronghold, Sidney was determined to take it.

A rude pontoon bridge was promptly constructed with planks and barrels, and a party advanced to the assault. But as the soldiers scrambled onto the planks, their two fuel kegs submerged, destroying the combustibles with which it was intended to burn the hedge and stockade. Flaming arrows set the thatched roundhouse ablaze at one point, but it was swiftly doused with buckets. Heavy fire from the besieged Irish did not let up, and the fight raged on. Sidney sustained great losses, and finally, on seeing a number of his men drown, and knowing that the only recourse would be to stay and build boats, he resolved to lose no more time or men. He quickly withdrew his troops and departed, to the galling sound of cheering from out on the lough.

SHANE O'NEILL

The Blackwater was now very low and easily crossed, a further vindication for Sidney's autumn campaign. In previous expeditions undertaken in springtime, all the provisions had been exhausted while waiting for the river to become fordable, so this was most gratifying. As he approached O'Neill's chief castle at Benburb, the Deputy was shocked to find it a smouldering ruin. A puzzling, and somewhat disconcerting, discovery! If he failed to leave a garrison, these wild hills would be virtually unchanged after the passing through of his great army. All that had *been* would yet be! That very thought lay behind Shane O'Neill's devilish smirk, as he looked on from the nearby wood. Clad in a tunic of chainmail, with a wolfskin over his shoulders, his grey eyes watched coldly the movements of his enemy. He and his army were never far away from these invaders. Now and then he would show his forces along a distant ridge, and then melt back into the fastness, but always he would shadow them. Time after time, Sidney would find his sentries dead. Scouts would not return, or an arrow might suddenly come whirring through the bracken to take out stragglers in his ranks.

In the vicinity of Clogher, Sidney found "pleasant fields and villages so well tended as no Irish country in the realm was like it." But the dwellings were abandoned. The people were in hiding along with their harvest, just as Shane had instructed. The Deputy encamped there, and sent forth squadrons to burn whatever corn had not been taken in for twenty-four miles around.

The evening sun lay hidden behind a shroud of black smoke as the pillagers returned to camp. Kildare, lagging in the rear with his horsemen, was attacked by O'Neill, and had a narrow escape of it. From out the great wood, Shane's men charged on horse and foot with a barrage of 'leadshot and Scottish arrows'. A battle ensued with casualties on both sides, until Sidney's main force arrived in pursuit. But the Tirowenmen slipped off into the wilds. 'Tirowen among the bushes!' Such was the Lord Deputy's complaint of O'Neill's army throughout the campaign, "that they could never be drawn to any such place where any good could be done upon them!"

It was near Omagh that the old chieftain, Shane Maguire, died in

SHANE O'NEILL

camp, just weeks before he was to be restored to his own. Among the hills near Castlederg, Shane 'showed himself in the rear with a great host', and riding at his side, Sidney was outraged to see the Bishop of Clogher! Kildare told him that it should be no great wonder, for this bishop, Con MacArdall, was the brother of one of O'Neill's highest captains, Cormac MacArdall. He had acquired his mitre in Rome on the very same day as Donagh O'Tighe, and he was of the same stripe, both of them having been nominated by O'Neill. Sidney took stern note of the warring bishop for a report to Council. But as for O'Neill, he was perplexed. With all his great host, Shane had not ventured even to skirmish this time, though the English troops were caught on highly unfavourable ground.

Near at hand, the mighty fortress of Omagh Castle was held by O'Neill's men. Inspite of this, Sidney chose not to besiege it. Provisions were too low, he reported. "We were scanting sore. For that we wanted men to win it, if the like men would keep it. And winning it, it was to no *purpose* to keep it, and leaving it, no harm can come of it." A strange war was this, for neither army seemed pressed to engage!

The rains of October flooded the ways and the rivers until they were virtually impassable. When the English army was struggling to cross the Derg, O'Neill showed himself on a height, his men ordered in battle array. An ominous sight it was! But then, as Sidney reports, he "broke his order and retired into his fastness." Shane's captains were anxious to attack, but he was convinced that the rain was doing his work for him. As Sidney's victuals diminished, or perhaps with the inevitable onset of pestilence, they would surely see the last of him.

At the ford of Liffer, Sidney found that strategic castle a rubble, dismantled stone from stone. On a ridge just to the north, however, could be seen Colonel Edward Randolph and his troop of horse awaiting him under Elizabeth's fluttering standard. Sir Harry was elated to finally effect this rendezvous with Randolph. As fording the mighty swollen river was out of the question, the two commanders turned their long weary ranks northward, on to the new settlement at Derry. After watching the last of the English march off, Shane turned his back to them and faced for O'Reilly's country. He would have a go at the turncoat John of Desmond, who had been sacking the Breffni borderlands. Just beyond them, the Pale lay open to attack, where he would get his own back with fire and sword.

From the eastern bank of the Foyle where Sidney halted his lines, Randolph's entrenchment could be seen across the river. The fleet was gone, but the colonel had been left a command of seven companies of foot and a troop of horse, comprising over 1,000 men, including 300 gunners. They had expelled the clergy from St. Columbkille's Abbey, driven off the Irish inhabitants, and taken for themselves the town of Derry. Having pillaged the cabins and chapels, they were now busy fortifying the Garrison, building walls and ramparts. One small pinnace had been left behind by the flotilla, and that sufficed to effect the crossing of Sidney's army, albeit slow and piecemeal, taking many trips across.

Only the O'Dogherty and his brother, the Bishop of Derry, were on hand to pay homage to Sidney, for none of the O'Donnells had appeared to welcome back their aged chieftain. Among his people he was considered disgraced and cuckolded, and his treatment of his father had earned him little sympathy. A small ceremony was held in which Cullagh O'Donnell signed over to the Lord Deputy the 'city of Derry and all its dwellings and stone houses.' He also pledged that he would provide for the English Garrison, a promise that was received doubtfully in light of his nowhere-to-be-seen supporters. Such was the Lord Deputy's mission now, to repossess O'Donnell of his castles and estates. To that end, Sir Harry took the lion's share of the newly arrived provisions, and left Randolph with six weeks rations for his six companies to hold the fort.

The army set off then, and marched twenty miles west to Raphoe, another episcopal seat. Sidney conferred with the Bishop of Raphoe, a protegé of Nuncio Wolfe, who naturally sent word forth for all the chieftains of Tirconnell to come and submit themselves. Bishop Magonigle assured them that Sidney would not interfere in the matter of religion, so long as they swore allegiance to the Queen. At his call, there very quickly assembled a gathering of chieftains who so swore, and joined with the Lord Deputy's progression. Notable among them were the two MacSwineys, the O'Boyle, the O'Gallagher, and even the bishop himself rode along beside them.

Over the Barnesmore gap, and through the hills of Tirconnell, they made their way toward Donegal Castle, encountering no opposition. The few castles along the way surrendered immediately. Sidney was serene in his glory, unaware that this docile compliance was simply the Irish way of accommodating a temporary nuisance. 'When a big wind blows, open the doors!' It was assumed that once this massive army disappeared over the hills, it might well be forgotten!

At length the mighty host reached Donegal town, where the castle was surrendered to the Lord Deputy by none other than the usurper himself, Black Hugh O'Donnell. He affected great joy at his half-brother's return, and promised to serve him faithfully. Sidney then delivered the fortress up to old Cullagh O'Donnell in the Queen's name by letters patent. This fine keep had been Cullagh's home with Lady Katherine, and entering it brought a sudden flood of tears to the old man. It was the close of a long and arduous ordeal, ending years of exile. He chose to stay on there, and bade the others farewell.

Black Hugh now joined the Deputy's progress, and they moved on to Ballyshannon, which was also rendered up without resistance. After crossing the Erne by way of boats, they came to Belleek Castle. They found it abandoned by Shane's garrison, who had made some attempt to burn it. Sidney gave the castle over to Black Hugh O'Donnell to hold of the Queen, along with Castle Finn, where he would now reside as a loyal vassal to Cullagh. Since the old Maguire chieftain was dead, Sidney summoned Cúchonnacht Maguire to make his submission here at Beleek Castle. He duly appeared, paid obeisance to the Lord Deputy, and was allowed to hold his lands of the Queen. Had Sidney known of his marriage to Shane's daughter, he might not have so readily accepted his oath of fealty.

The Lord Deputy recommenced his triumphal march now, unopposed, into Connaught, demanding the fealty of local lords including the O'Connor Sligo. This he received as readily as had Shane only a year before. Sidney then marched his men through the 'craggy

SHANE O'NEILL

Curlew Mountains' to Boyle, and on through Roscommon to Athlone. The bridge across the Shannon was in ruins, and it was necessary to cross by swimming, whereby some baggage horses were lost. The Deputy swore that he would build a proper bridge there once the Queen's peace was restored.

After his long arduous march, Sidney reached Dublin in early November. He wrote to her Majesty boasting that, "like as by this journey your Majesty hath recovered to your obedience all of Tirconnell, a country of seventy miles in length and forty eight miles in breadth. The service of 1,000 now are restored to O'Donnell, and so united and confirmed in love towards him, as they be ready to follow him whithersoever he shall lead them! So is your Majesty's name grown in no small veneration among the Irishry, who now see cause to appeal to your justice!"

Her Majesty, however, was something less than pleased. She had gotten 'reports' from confidants among the Deputy's captains. He had shirked an opportunity to capture O'Neill's treasure at Glenaul; he had left Omagh Castle to the rebels without so much as attempting to oust them. He had settled for a 'tip of the bonnet' from the miscreant Irish lords along his path, and taken no hostages. He had failed to engage or even to encounter Shane O'Neill! O'Neill, moreover, had been busy the while, ravaging the Pale, quite undeterred by the forces levied to defend it. The garrison in Dundalk alone had sustained a loss of more than 200 men.

O'Neill, by now, had withdrawn to Fathan Castle in the fews, which stood unscathed. Though only a few miles from the Pale, it had thus far escaped Sidney's attention. Shane was out in the encampment with his captains, Dualta and MacArdall, when he got word of the arrival of two monks from Derry. They were brought to him, and with a 'God save the O'Neill', the two quickly introduced themselves. The elder bearded friar, MacMenamin, gave forth their news.

"Twas Father Crilly sent us to you, my Lord O'Neill, for as he reckoned you ought know that the old chieftain Cullagh O'Donnell is lately dead." They both swiftly crossed themselves. Shane smiled darkly.

"Dead, is it? Hah! Bless*é*d tidings, indeed! What befell him, then?"

"Sidney's forces drove your men from all O'Donnell's castles, and reinstated Cullagh over his country. And he-"

"Och, don't I know that!"

"Well, the aul man was no sooner back in power, when... He was riding towards Derry with supplies for the English ward -just between Ballyheen and the Church of Hath. In the midst of all his cavalry he was, and without the slightest starting, stumbling, shying, or prancing of his horse, he tumbled to the ground! Auld Cullagh was seized with a fit, there where he lay, which soon carried him off! He lived just long enough to call his chief clansmen around him, and make them all pledge to serve the Queen. His brother Hugh that they call 'Black Hugh' was taken to the stone at Kilmacrennan. He is now the O'Donnell."

"By Christ! The aul hoor has gone west! He was long enough about it! When did *this* come to pass?"

"Only a day or so ago."

"The 26th day of October, it was," the other monk interjected. Friar MacMenamin nodded.

"The people swear it was the hand of God struck aul Cullagh from his horse. Didn't he let the English expell the priests and monks, and shatter the holy statues? O'Donnell was punished for profaning the Cathedral with heretics and soldiers."

"Where is Father Crilly?"

"He's at Kilodonal Abbey, just above Ramelton. We were all of us driven out of the abbey in Derry, and he was among those that got the lash. T'was shockin', so it was. The townsfolk are now huddled in the bogside, outside the town, and Friar Corr and I minister to them there."

"And what of Randolph's settlement? I'm told he has 600 men."

SHANE O'NEILL

"Aye, near enough to that, I'd say-"

"What way are they fixed?" Shane sighed impatiently. "What do you know of this Randolph? What sort is he?"

"Aye, well..." The friar assumed a coaxing tone, wary of disappointing, but determined to tell it out straight. "They are not *badly* fixed, for he minds his troops any rate, that they have shirts, kerseycloth, canvas and leather. Food and forage are forthcoming when needful. They're never idle, but he keeps them busy always at the building and masonry when not in the field, the way that they'd be in good fighting trim. A wise captain, so. But Randolph is without regard or reckon for the Irish there! No more nor for brute beasts. It's they who are subjected always to deeds of cruelty. He permits his soldiers every excess of riot and spoilation! And they would be worse only for Hugh O'Donnell bringing them their supplies!"

"What? Black Hugh is provisioning the English?"

"Aye, so he is. And for his pains, the Queen has promised to dub him Earl of Tirconnell!"

"By Christ! He'll see his maker ere ever he sees an earl's chain!" Shane turned his fiery glare to Dualta O'Donnelly, who nodded and spat.

"Aye, but, sure, wouldn't that just be the way of it, Shane? If Black Hugh is to get the support of his people, he'll have to take *you* on! They know he's your cousin, and he'll want to prove he's his own man, and one of them."

"Prove it with treachery! It was I put him over his people. I'll not have that Derry Garrison at my back. And Black Hugh hiding behind them. They are the source of his boldness. And insolence! As soon as we've made ready, we'll face for Derry, and I'll put paid to this Colonel Randoph!"

The gusting of November winds, and the patter of rain on the snapping canvas of his pavilion tent took Lord Sidney's notice now, as he waited patiently at his field desk. A candle flickered, and the quill was still poised in his hand over a letter, but the arrival of a surprising visitor had taken him from his labours. The tent flap opened, and the dark dripping form of Black Hugh O'Donnell appeared.

"Your Lordship!"

"O'Donnell! What ill tidings have taken you from your keep in Tirconnell? Are you driven hence?"

"The castle is safe. But there's great peril in Derry, my Lord. Peril that warrants your speedy return. Colonel Randolph is dead."

"Fie! What new calamity is this? Not a fortnight is past since I left him -with sturdy battalions and six weeks of provisions!" Sidney laid aside his quill, and turned his chair to face his visitor.

"O'Neill it was. He crossed the Foyle at Liffer, where he attacked the sappers and pulled down their newly begun battlements. He then rode with his force of eight hundred to the stockade at Derry. He paraded fore and aft for two days, brandishing his colours before the gates. In a wood barely a league from the fortress he was encamped, plotting to attack the fort. And at daybreak, on the twelfth of November, he was surprised by Randolph and O'Doherty, who were guided out to the camp by a loyal priest. Randolph set upon O'Neill's horsemen and slew his footmen in great numbers, but then, leading a bit more forwardly than readily followed, he charged into the thickest of it. The Colonel was thereby overthrown and slain! Alas, his fall saved many of the rebel's lives, for while the soldiers sought to rescue his lifeless body, O'Neill's men had leisure to flee. Still, O'Neill lost most of his best footmen, as well Galloglass as shot, and many of his Scots lost faith in him and left his service from that day. Barely a hundred of the garrison have died as yet –apart from the Colonel himself, though many are sore wounded. Whereas O'Neill lost three hundred and more! Not reckoning for the wounded, more than twice our casualties. To put it rightly, we won the day...but there's many a day to come. The officers bade me to hasten your return." Sidney's brows beetled over his incredulous glare.

"Are other curriers gone forth with this news?"

"Only myself, your Lordship. I came to you straightaway."

"We must amend these tidings. There was but *one* casualty of the

Queen's own ranks. One! A few score of wounded, and a gallant Colonel slain in a signal victory. By his heroic sacrifice, Her Majesty's garrison stands. The tale is in the telling, O'Donnell. And *so*, by God, is the war!"

"I take your meaning, my Lord. A victory, with but one slain." The Deputy shook his head and sighed.

"Even so, these are hellish tidings! So rash and headlong for such a shrewd captain as Randolph! Do you tell me that he allowed O'Neill to goad him forth at the glint of his colours?"

"Aye, your Lordship. He said it was for the Queen's honour." The Deputy lowered his head with a sigh, and laid a hand across his brow.

"God's wounds! Like the heated bull, he let his eyes to rule his wits, and we are lost a worthy captain." After a moment's pause, he looked up, and spoke with impatience. "Nay, nay...I cannot return as yet. I will send Edward Saintloo in my stead. Derry is well provisioned and fortified."

"The men hold that it is vulnerable and cut off."

"Not so! Not while you hold Donegal and the rest of Tirconnell. You must return with Saintloo. O'Neill will not venture a direct assault. He is like to a swarm of gnats! Ever a bother and vexation -but always in flight, never still to meet a blow. We made a two months progress through Ulster and wasted Tirowen, trod upon the smoking rubble of his castle, and the Grand Disturber stayed only at our heels." O'Donnell made a sour grin.

"And his people call him Shane the Proud."

"A proud tongue, but a craven heart. He skulks like a wolf. From dawn to dark he never gave over to skirmish, and upon our turning he would vanish. And this coward, I am told, demands tribute as High King of Ireland!"

"His pride is a madness! I have as much of my grandfather's blood as he, yet I am not so proud as to challenge her Majesty's crown. But yet-"

"It was your good fortune not to come by the *name* of O'Neill! That name will soon be proscribed, for it is a spell to raise the devil!"

"But to challenge the Crown! He's *that cunning*, your Honour. He would ne'er wax so bold unless he was assured of aid forthcoming. I'll warrant there are armies under sail from France or Spain! He must be crushed before ever they reach Ireland."

"Fool's folly! Nay, *there* you are wide amiss! These foreign princes are liberal with promises- but *not* with armies. Nay...nay, they relish the troubles he stirs for the Queen -It binds her hands and empties her purse while it costs them naught." Sidney straightened his back and beckoned. "Guard!" The flap was brushed aside, and a tall sentry snapped to attention.

"Sir!"

"Call Captain Saintloo to my tent." With a quick salute, the man disappeared. "Aye. He is the best I might send...to replace the good Colonel. Blast it! There was none better! *Edward Randolph* dead! Had Mary Stuart not banished him from Court, he would be among the quick yet, conniving like the Machievell in Edinburgh. More is the pity!" Black Hugh cleared his throat, and ventured another matter, nearer his heart.

"Has the Queen sent any news of my peerage, your Lordship?"

"Eh? What?" Sidney rose to his feet indignantly. "Harken unto me, Hugh O'Donnell. But hold fast to those countries that were lately delivered unto you, sirrah, else you may gain title and lose place!" He heaved a quick sigh of disgust, and took his seat once again. "An earldom? There never has been a more miserable realm than this wretched isle. God spare me, I would liefer be in England, and there to beg my bread or labour at stones, than *here* to be a lord!"

Shane had withstood the invasion. He had forestalled, he thought, the great slaughter that a direct confrontation would have engendered. There was a reason behind that queer policy of evasion. All this time O'Neill was anxiously awaiting word of the new Pope excommunicating Queen Elizabeth, for then surely the European armies would come to his aid. He had determined that he must by no means diminish his great numbers before that, lest he should not merit their support when came the crucial hour. But this stratagem had its price, and a dear price it was!

How crushing and dispiriting for his men to find themselves taking up the enemy's labours! Laying waste to O'Neill's castles, and even torching the newly restored, and highly cherished Cathedral of Armagh. The endless skulking in the wildwoods. For such a force as they! And now the defeats! O'Neill was undeniably bested in his siege of Dundalk, and now once again at Derry. Shane held it a victory to have robbed Elizabeth of her one skillful commander, but it was he who had sustained the great share of casualties, and most tellingly, the Garrison remained. Several companies of Scots deserted him after that day, and this boded ominously for the disaffected among his troops. Doubt had entered his ranks. There was grumbling. Shane noted a sluggishness in the carrying out of his orders, and his response was fury. He imposed a sharper, more severe command, with brutal punishments that could only provoke further disaffection.

On Shane's return from Derry, sad news awaited him. His elder brother, Art Crosach O'Neill, had died of his tumorous ailments. It was a dull morning, threatening rain. Rooks and daws squawked indignantly high above the churchyard of St. Patrick's where O'Neill's people were gathered, and the charred ruins of the Cathedral cast their own gloomy pall over the large crowd. Katherine and her brood were at Shane's side. His brother, Fr. Hugh, had said a High Requem in the chapel at Drumadd, but Dean Danyell was pledged to officiate at the burial. As there was no sign of him, Shane told Hugh to get on with it. The prayers were barely underway when the Dean came galloping up the hill, and to the surprise of all, trotting up after him was the Primate, William Creagh.

The Archbishop was attired in black vestments, arrayed with both mitre and crozier to proclaim the dignity of his office. He came firstly to Shane, expressing in low tones his condolences on the loss of his brother, and Shane thanked him for coming. Katherine did the same, but more effusively, so anxious was she to heal the dire enmity between them. No other business was broached, but O'Neill was glad of this olive branch, a seemingly magnanimous gesture, after all that had happened. Creagh took his place, then, and intoned the Latin prayers over the coffin. At the words, 'ashes to ashes and dust to dust', clods of earth resounded on the wooden box, and with the last strike of the spade, the Primate gave the final blessing. "May his soul and the souls of all the faithful departed through the mercy of God rest in peace."

"Amen," sang the mourners, and then a keen started up among the women of Art O'Neill's household with a wailing and chanting of 'ólagáns'. Creagh looked upon them with abject horror, and after a moment, he raised his crozier and called out over their voices.

"Hold your peace, I say! You do his blessed soul *no honour* with these pagan shrieks and moans! Stop, I say! Death is a joy to the Christian, and a calamity to the heathen!" It was only when Dean Danyell added his call for silence to the Primate's interdiction that the keening subsided.

Shane felt it incumbent upon himself to requite the Primate's gesture by approaching him, and he did so with a warm sad smile. "It is a terrible thing, your Grace, to let harsh words fly, and to leave discord and rancour in the very air. It unsettles the people, and sets a poor example for them when the mighty cannot reconcile themselves in peace." With a flutter of his lids, and a stern demeanor, Creagh replied.

"Have you, Shane O'Neill, made such a reconciliation? Are you prepared to turn away from your unlawful rebellion? For I cannot absolve you of this grievous sin, while yet you persist in leading my fold into peril of eternal damnation. There can be no"

"Oh, but I must have absolution, your Grace!" Shane's grey eyes narrowed with loathing, his face flushed with rage, but his voice did not betray his fury. "You see, I'm only just returned from Tirconnell, where I hanged an ordained priest! His spying for Colonel Randolph left several hundred of my men dead, and so I hanged him from a tree." Creagh's eyes fluttered once again, and he gasped audibly as he quickly blessed himself.

"You hanged a *priest*! May God forgive you! But certainly *I* cannot. I cannot grant you absolution, Shane O'Neill, for only His Holiness, the Pope, can absolve a man of such a grievous and wicked sin as killing a priest!"

"Oh, but that's not quite true... *Is* it, your Grace? I have had word from Rome that the Pope granted you *just* such powers when you undertook your mission here. Could you have forgotten a papal mandate to forgive the killing of ordained clergy? Sure, even I can recall it. I have it off word for word. The Pope gave you leave 'to absolve those who were guilty, either as principals or as accessories of the capture of Donat O'Tighe, late Primate of Ireland, and *also* all such as have since laid violent hands, even to the effusion of blood, upon priests.' So you do have that power, your Grace." Creagh mouth was open, and his eyes wide with horror. "You have it, and you have *used* it to absolve the Nuncio David Wolfe and his brother the Bailiff of their part in the murder of the very man whose Holy Office you had usurped. Oh, to be sure, you have such power." The Primate collected himself, and raised his chin to an arrogant tilt.

"I know not *what* you're speaking of. I know nothing of this!" Despite the iron composure of his features, Creagh's eyes were blinking frantically. Shane smirked.

"Indeed, you do. And I suggest that you come to terms with me before the wide world knows of your perfidy."

"I fear you are quite mad, Shane O'Neill. Your wickedness and pride have blighted your wits, and you must beg God's forgiveness! Aye, and pray for his holy redeeming grace! I must go." After a few steps, he turned and called. "Such is the gratitude I would expect from a man of such o'erweening pride, from one...one who *glories* to be in league with Satan! May God forgive you." He looked to the crowd with beatific sorrow in his pale little eyes. "This man will lead you to eternal damnation!" He raised a tremulous arm to point at Shane. "*If* you value your immortal souls-" He stopped himself, and stood silent a moment, then he turned and stalked off down the hill, stabbing the ground before him with his lofty glittering crozier. Katherine, teary-eyed, begged Shane to go after him and soothe him, regardless of the right or wrong of it. But O'Neill stepped forward only to call after him.

"Go on then! I hanged the priest from a tree, your Grace. That's what happens to spies, be they monks, or priests...or *bishops!*"

Even more than the recent defeats, the Tirowen men were troubled by the Primate's excommunication of Shane, a shocking spectacle that they had witnessed themselves. The holy man, widely rumoured to be a saint blessed with mystical powers, was held in awe by the people both high and low. As word went forth through the hills of this second clash in the churchyard, grave doubt was cast upon the chieftain. So it was that the very factors that made O'Neill so eagerly await the Queen's excommunication were coming into play against himself! Elizabeth and Cecil had played a trump in abetting Creagh's 'miraculous' escape, and setting him down in the very heart of O'Neill's domain. Dean Danyell recognized the gravity of the situation, and he badgered Shane to reconcile with the Primate for the sake of his army's morale. But O'Neill would not hear of it. He loathed the Primate, he said, more than the Queen of England!

In December, the Protestant 'Reformed' Primate, Loftus, from his manor in Dublin, also pronounced O'Neill anathema for burning 'his' cathedral. Once again Shane only laughed. "And how can Loftus excommunicate a man who never belonged to his religion? That greedy hoor may curse me as long and as black as he please, so long as I stand well at Rome. Surely, to be excommunicated by a heretic is to be counted at one with God! I might be disposed to thank him for the blessing!"

SHANE O'NEILL

Winter settled in with its short days, drizzly and raw, but for the first time it brought no relief from the rigours of war. Shane was beleaguered now on all sides. In the West by Black Hugh, In the North by the Derry Garrison, and from the Pale Sidney sent out marauding companies to ravage his lands. To the East, Captain Pierce out of Carrickfergus was raiding cattle.

Also out of the East, the bitter Alistair MacDonnell with a thousand fresh reinforcements from the Isles was rampaging, not only to avenge Glenshesk, but also to requite a substantial payment from Sidney. If his brother was Shane's hostage, it did little to stay him, for he was confident that Shane would never kill Sorley Buí. His hosts swept across the River Bann, taking great preys of cattle. He slew more than sixty of Shane's footmen and horsemen in one raid and, by his own written account, "burnt all the country, killing many wives and bairns." Queen Elizabeth quite approved his letter, 'from a hand more used to a claymore than a quill.' She said he "had well served in preying upon Shane!" With trouble in every direction, O'Neill found himself greatly straightened, but as Constable Pierce lamented, "the whole country stuck fast to him."

As Armagh lay in ruins, the monks had taken shelter in the little friary at Drumadd nearby. On the 16th of December, when Shane was off in the West, a shocking incident took place that signaled a new level of depravity in the official English efforts to 'reform the Church'. Three monks were abroad in the town, ministering to those who were attempting to dig out and rebuild. A party of the Queen's soldiers, 'under the leadership of a certain Donald', came upon them. They seized Fr. Rory MacConvill, Fr. Con MacCourt, and Fr. Fergal MacWard. The soldiers stripped the friars naked, and flogged them through the ravaged streets of Armagh until they all three died beneath the lash. That such an outrage could occur so deep within Tirowen shook the people to the very heart, and gave grim proof against the power of the O'Neill to protect them.

With Armagh laid waste, and the country wracked by warfare, Primate Creagh was in a quandary as to where he might go. Leaving

SHANE O'NEILL

Ulster was impossible, for he was liable to arrest elsewhere, and so, with Dean Danyell's guidance he set himself up in a small priory at Dunavally in the parish of Loughgall, four miles north of Armagh. He was eager, still, to conduct his synod of reform. Again relying on Danyell's advice, he called his synod for January, to be held in the priory of Dungiven, under the protection of the O'Kane. Since the murder of the three monks, there was a growing disquietude among the people, a restiveness that brought the Dean once again to Shane's door. He demanded that O'Neill attempt to reconcile with the Primate. The people's fears, he insisted, must be allayed or they will surely turn from him! Shane relented, finally, and invited the Primate to attend his Christmas festivities in the castle at Fathan.

The weather on Christmas Day was hardly auspicious. Under the bare black winterwood of the Fews, a sharp and bitter rain pelted away at the last remnants of an early snow. The stable was filled with shivering horses, and drifting smoke hung low around the chimneys of Shane's towerhouse at Fathan. From inside, the skirl of pipes could be heard as Primate Creagh trotted up the path after his two servants, Florry and Seán beg. A drenched and dripping groom dashed out to take their horses, and the three were quickly ushered into the keep.

When Dr. Creagh divested himself of his cowled mantle, his arrival was met with some surprise, for he had sent no response to Shane's invitation. He wore a cassock and stole of greyish blue cambric with a tri-cornered biretta to match, in place of his usual opulent mitre. Nor, indeed, was his awe-inspiring bejeweled crozier to be seen. He was led up the twisting turnpike-stair, but he paused at the top to await the end of a jaunty and rollicking dance. Three brawny youngfellows leapt, and whirled, and pounded the floor to the wild rhythm of a frolicsome tune. When the applause and lusty 'whoops' subsided, the Primate was announced and welcomed into the chamber. But the raucous din gave way now to a troubled murmur. This arrival was truly a cause for great wonder, since, for many of those present, Creagh had last been seen with bell, book, and candle, pronouncing damnation upon their host!

The large chamber was festooned with holly and ivy, and a roaring fire blazed in the massive hearth. Mulled ale and Christmas punch were set out for the guests, but a flagon of wellwater quickly appeared for the bishop. He looked askance at the gingerbread and other dainties, but he managed to effect a fairly convincing smile for his host. The gathering was mostly men, Shane's paladins and foremost captains. His main forces were several miles away. The O'Hanlon, a nearby chieftain, had sent his regrets when told that the Primate might attend, as he feared that 'reports to the English' of his presence there would have repercussions. Katherine had refused to come down, for her dear infant, Áilish, was still a 'busy wee bundle', as well as the boys, to say nothing of the inherent danger of leaving the island in such troubled times.

With a rather awkward formality, Dr. Creagh inquired after the health of Shane's daughter, and of Lady O'Neill's health as well. He spoke then of the upheaval in the province, and informed Shane of his plans for the synod of bishops at Dungiven under the protection of the O'Kane. He announced proudly that the Nuncio, David Wolfe, would be attending, and was to arrive on or about the Feast of the Epiphany. Shane looked slyly to the Dean, who shook his head sternly to deter him from mentioning Wolfe's lusty little scandal in Limerick. Creagh spoke on in lofty tones, noting that 'David has the Holy Father's ear in all matters,' implying that a proper welcome was due him.

The prelate was not altogether surprised to see that Bishop Myler Magrath was on hand, although he accounted it an insolence, considering Shane's present standing with the Diocese. They were cordial nonetheless, apart from occasional chilling pauses. Shane's chaplain, Broderick, was present, as were the Donnelly brothers. The dinner passed uneventfully, with the conversation confined to pleasantries. Since nearly any topic was liable to lead to a clash, the atmosphere was subdued, and the underlying tensions led to a good deal of wine being consumed. All of which was noted scrupulously by the taciturn guest of honour. Eventually the talk turned to the new Pope, and the Primate found his voice. He took pains to assure all that Pius V would never consider excommunicating Queen Elizabeth. The very notion, he said, was risible!

SHANE O'NEILL

"And yet she is an avowed heretic!" Despite his firmest resolve, Shane was unable to hold his tongue. "And, if I am a sinner itself, I am a devout Catholic. I have dedicated myself to the cause of His Holiness, but yet you have not hesitated to excommunicate –to *publicly* excommunicate *me* before my entire army." Dean Danyell winced and frowned to halt him, but Shane would not be led. "In the spirit of Christmas, your Grace, mightn't you see your way clear to lifting your curse of damnation upon me? I will see that you will be well used in Ulster! And, upon my oath, you shall have your church as honourably as any archbishop ever had since holy Patrick!"

"Alas, I cannot undo what is done, whilst yet you defy the will of God. This I made quite plain to you at Armagh. *When* you have proven yourself faithful, you shall be admitted to the company of the Faithful."

"And to whom were *you* 'faithful' when you informed the English of Ulster's treasury at Glenaul? Was ever there such treachery from a bishop of Armagh? Not since the snakes were driven from Ireland have we seen the likes of you!" In his surprise, Creagh stared blankly for a long moment, and then wagged his head slowly from side to side.

"It was not I, O'Neill, who led the Deputy there. Nay, not I. Perhaps Hugh O'Donnell or Turlagh O'Neill. I count it one of the most blesséd triumphs granted unto me by our Lord, that my humble preachments were able to sway those two noble captains from unlawful rebellion! They have both of them repented and reconciled themselves unto God and to His appointed Prince." Shane's laugh was dark and gleeful, and quite stunned the prelate.

"Oh, it grieves me to snatch suckets from a child, your Grace...but it was *not* your preaching that brought them to heel –to *Lord Sidney's* heel! No, then, it was something a bit more carnal than 'duty, honour, and grace' that induced them to betray me. My wife had a letter from her sister that cast a most revealing light upon their miraculous 'Damascan' conversion. My two lovelorn cousins are of late wooing the widow and daughter of the Laird James MacDonnell, both of whom hold me responsible for his death in battle. They are kindred to my wife, Lady Katherine. Fionnúla, 'the Dark Daughter', as they call her, has made Black Hugh and Turlagh pledge to wreak vengeance upon me. Neither she nor her mother, she avows, will wed them whilst yet I live. So, perhaps your powers of oration are not so wondrous as your modesty bids you to believe."

"Our Heavenly Father works in mysterious ways. I can only hope, if it *was* love that occasioned their change of heart, that my words served at least to bolster their resolve to forsake your sinful rebellion!" Dean Danyell stepped in and turned the talk to the Primate's lodgings in Dunavally, and how his Eminence was getting on there. News from the South was discussed, and there was speculation as to fresh troubles in that quarter that promised to bring new pressure to bear upon Sidney. Sleet pattered relentlessly against the thick glass windows, and icy droplets hissed in the fire, as thunder rumbled from afar. Although the early dusk had yet to settle, an abundance of candles were lit. There were songs and recitations, but eventually the talk found its way back to contentious matters. It was Creagh 'the meek and mild' who took the offensive, shaking his head sadly and tisking with feigned pity.

"It is said that your home at Benburb is in ruins. Indeed, yours is a sorrowful lot this Christmastide, Shane O'Neill. And where is your good wife on this holy feast?"

"She is safe with her children from the murderous-"

"On *'Inishdowell'*?" Creagh's pale eyes at once glared and blinked, as he pounced, with triumph in his thin reedy voice. "Tell me *this* O'Neill. Why do you give scandal by naming your home 'the Devil's Island'? Do you so openly embrace Lucifer? It is a scandal to the Faithful, and an abasement of your noble office." Shane shot a glance to Myler, a flash of wicked glee. "And I am *also* told that your castle there is named Fuanagall 'Hatred of the English!' How can you even *pretend* to be a man of peace when..." Shane's burst of exultant laughter brought the bishop to silence. Most looked on apprehensively, but Myler Magrath joined in the mirth. Shane drained his goblet, and addressed his prickly guest.

"Would you *ever*, for the love of God, let a splink of sense into that skull of yours? You listen *only* to my enemies. You preside as Bishop of

Armagh, where you know *nothing* of the place or the people, but give ear only to the English who would undo them!" He leaned in now, and spoke slowly, explaining as to a pathetic child. "In Irish, the Blackwater is known as the River *Dowell*. The island near to its mouth in Lough Neagh is 'inish' - *the island*, of the *'Dowell.'* As for Fuanagall, it was a simple jest, initially. A jape! In Irish, you see, it rhymes with Donegal: 'doonagall, foonagall." Creagh shook his head, still perplexed, and turned to Dean Danyell for clarification, but it was Bishop Magrath who explained.

"When old Cullagh O'Donnell was a prisoner there, Shane told him, 'you're not in *Dún* na nGall now. You're in *Fuah* na nGall!' It's not the *'fort* of the English', but *'loathing* of the English!' The people found the name amusing and it stuck. A bit of sport is all."

"People in these parts are fond of a jest, your Grace. Still, for the enemies of my people, such trifling nonsense is brandished as testimony to my diabolical evil, the evil of one who refuses to surrender Ulster into their greedy hands. My wife bides in that island-keep for safety from the murderous bands of English that have been set loose upon us. Tell me *this*, your Grace. How ever will you have your synod of priests, when the Crown forces are torturing them to death in the streets of Armagh?"

"We may look to *you* for the cause of *that* tragedy! You have cloaked your murderous rebellion in the borrowed raiments of the Catholic Church. It is small wonder that they equate our Roman Faith with sedition." Myler, emboldened by a fair share of brandywine, could not let this pass.

"And *you* use the cloak and crozier of your office to advance the conquest of this realm by that heretical Queen! Only a heretic could countenance the slaying of holy friars, and lay blame at the door of the *one* prince in Christendom who is defending our Holy Faith. *You*, Creagh! You are a heretic!" It was just then that Shane leapt to his feet, raising his hand aloft abruptly.

"Whisht! Hold your *whisht!*" A silence fell immediately, and in that hush could be heard the wind and sleet, and something else. It was a hunter's horn, a trenchant warning from the sentry of the

SHANE O'NEILL

enemy's approach! A young guard from the parapet burst in, and rushed up to inform O'Neill of the alarum, and of the advance of a vast army in the far hills. After a quick exchange, Shane looked to the Primate with murderous venom. "You *wrote* to Sidney!" Creagh froze, in silent panic, and looked away. His face was ashen. "By Christ, you *did*! You whore's get! Christmas Day, and we have Judas in our midst!" He stalked over to his captains, Dualta O'Donnelly and his brothers for a quick conferral, and then turned to the guests. "We'll have to scarper. We're riding for- No!" He turned again for hasty words, and then pointed to the Primate. "We will firstly bid farewell to the Primate Iscariot, and when he is gone, we'll betake us *elsewhere*, lest he inform upon us once again to his English friends." He then redirected his arm, pointing towards the door. "Go! Get you gone and quick! Or I'll re-arrange your scrawny bones for you! You're a whited sepulchre! Be gone with you, heretic! Hump off back to Englishtown!"

Creagh blessed himself, trembling, and with the wan and sorrowful smile of a pious martyr, he hurried off with his two attendants. When they had disappeared, O'Neill fired orders to the company to move out. They would join the rest of his forces at Carrickbradagh Castle, three leagues away.

Primate William Creagh had, indeed, written to Sidney with details of this meeting with Shane, requesting orders from him.

> "...And now before we should speak unto O'Neill, we thought but to know of your lordship's will, and what you shall will us to do. Therein we shall, by God's leave, do the best we can... If it be your lordship's pleasure, you will not disdain to write to us firstly whether it should please your lordship that we should have our old service in our churches. We would know if you would suffer our said churches to be up for that use, so that the said Lord O'Neill should destroy no more churches." Lest there should be no doubt as to whom he served, he closed with:
>
> From Dunavally near Loughgall,
>
> By your lordship to command in what we can lawfully

SHANE O'NEILL

execute,
RICHARD Archbishop Armagh

Sir Henry Sidney boasted of this incident twenty years later in his memoir, a narrative that served to give to himself the last word as to what transpired, and to define for the ages the merit of his accomplishments. "I shortened his Christmas, and made an end of mine own with abundance of his good provision, but not *provided* for such an unbidden guest as I was."

Only four days later, on the 29th of December, 1566, Shane signified by letter to Sydney that he was prepared to settle for peace, but only if they would stand by the articles he had signed with Cusack. If the Queen would affix to them her seal, he would abide by them. The Lord Deputy considered the option of bringing him to such terms. He wrote to the Privy Council asking if he might sue for peace. Even after his campaign through Ulster, he wrote, O'Neill was still a power, and could muster 4,000 foot and 700 horse, but he would have no peace save on the terms of Drumcree.

The Queen was livid. She replied to the Viceroy, ordering him "to employ his whole care and consideration as to how O'Neill, who has now manifested himself so contemptuous a traitor, may be utterly extirpated!" In Sidney's reply to Cecil, however, he doubted the wisdom of such extremity.

"Her majesty means such a total extirpation of the rebel and his people so as there shall never be an O'Neill more! She proposes either to bring the people to the just rule of English law, or to banish them quite and unpeople the soil, followed by establishing colonies. Although this course is quite feasible and optable, yet it will take time and money, for in that case look for no sound friendship at any Irishman's hand, for each will think his staff standeth next to the door!"

SHANE O'NEILL

The Primate sequestered himself in his remote priory at Dunavally, engrossed in prayer and correspondence. The heavy snow freshly blanketing the hills only made him feel safer from the turbulence beyond them. The arrival of the Papal Nuncio on the feast of Twelfthnight brought him great relief, and a pleasant surprise, too, for he came accompanied by Creagh's brother. Civilized company at last! His brother and his dearest confrere! Here were two companionable souls who shared his English and his Englishtown sensibilities! Creagh recounted to them his harrowing months among the Ulster savages, and most particularly he apprized Wolfe of the outrageous charges that O'Neill had leveled at them over that grave in the churchyard regarding O'Tighe. Both men agreed that silence was the only prudent course. And they comforted themselves with the certain knowledge that if O'Neill should pursue the matter, it could only serve to further discredit him. Clearly no one would believe it.

The two clerics then discussed the growing suppression of the Church outside of Ulster, as well as their plans for the synod at Dungiven. Creagh relished hearing news of home. Davy Wolfe had brought to him several letters from Limerick and Rome, and the Primate was delighted to learn that his widowed sister was to be wed in the spring. Immediately, he resolved to attend, and prayed that circumstances would prove amenable. Hopefully, Desmond's offensive in that district would be crushed by then.

The letters from Rome mostly concerned the predicament of the Nuncio himself. The Primate was willing to absolve Wolfe of his 'sins of the flesh' involving the residents of Mná Bochta, the hostel for fallen women. "We may take solace in that He who shall pass judgment upon our tally of sins, is He that formed us in frailty." Even so, he did not spare him a chastening penance, or wearying sermons about giving scandal and the solemn duties of holy office. Officially, of course, the scandal would not be acknowledged, for the sake of the spiritual well-being of their Irish pastorate. Indeed, as a 'show of confidence,' in brazen defiance of the 'foul rumour-mongers,' the Primate appointed David Wolfe 'Vicar General of Ireland.' Dr. Creagh penned for the Nuncio a sterling testimonial on his behalf for Rome, as well as letters to the Pope castigating Shane O'Neill, of whom he wrote, "He is addicted to venery. A persevering votary of Bacchus!" He also berated the Bishop of Down and Conor, Dr. Myler Magrath.

Myler, as it happens, was also busy with his quill in these snowbound days by the fire. He took it upon himself to forge a letter to the Pope purportedly from William Creagh! In a ruse to get the Primate recalled to Rome, he copied from purloined notes in Creagh's own hand, and wrote a letter in which many uncanonical measures were recommended. The forgery contained, as it was later said, "horrible things and evil counsels most foreign to the Primate's nature." Myler quoted all the most offensive utterances of his superior, and took pains to point up Creagh's deferral to the heretical Queen of England, wherein he required her approval before he would even attempt to carry out any Papal orders. In all of this Magrath felt justified, as he firmly believed the Primate to be a supporter of heresy, and a grave danger to his see.

At Dungiven Priory, the Synod of Northern Bishops was convened to implement the decrees of the Council of Trent. The only real contention arose over the 'alleged' transgressions of David Wolfe at the women's shelter. The accuser was none other than the 'disputed' Bishop of Clogher, Dr. Con MacArdall. As a partisan and protegé of O'Neill, his own standing had for years been under relentless attack by the Nuncio through his patrons in Rome. MacArdall also accused Wolfe of complicity in the capture of the late Primate O'Tighe, but, apart from Bishop Magrath, he found little support. The bishops closed ranks and censured MacArdall, imposing upon him a fine of 200 cows, thus putting an end to the matter of Mná Bochta.

In February, Shane was dealt a devastating blow when he got word that Fergus O'Kane, the feisty warrior chieftain, had gone over. He had presented himself to Colonel St. Loo in Derry, along with several of Shane's captains, and had sworn his allegiance to the Queen. There had been words between him and the O'Neill, of course. He had

SHANE O'NEILL

bristled under his orders, and been called sharply to account under Shane's increasingly brutal command. In truth, O'Neill's volatile temper, under the mounting pressures of the war, caused some among his captains to fear for his soundness of mind. Still, given the O'Kane's hatred of the English, it was inconceivable that he might forsake the cause! It was assumed that he had simply lost faith in their chances of prevailing over the English forces, but Shane was suspicious that other factors might be at play.

Things became clearer when Myler Magrath was consulted. It seems that during the Northern Synod in O'Kane's own town of Dungiven, Creagh and numerous other bishops had assailed the chieftain with threats of eternal damnation, imploring him to cease his rebellion. Not only his soul was imperiled, but his holdings as well. "When O'Neill is vanquished," they said, "you shall be driven to the wastelands, bereft of all!" The loss of O'Kane was a staggering jolt, one that threatened the resolve and mettle of Shane's army.

Through these winter months, O'Neill had only to contend with the Derry Garrison and his Irish and Scottish foes, for Sidney's main forces were needed elsewhere. Shane's cousin Garret, the feisty Earl of Desmond had finally been released from Dublin Castle, and, unlike his perfidious brother, he answered Shane's call to battle with a compelling diversion, prompting Sidney to write, "But the Devil never sleeps! For now the Earl of Ormond has plied the Queen with such complaints against me, that her Majesty wrote earnestly to me, touching hurts done to him and his by Desmond, as I am forced to leave my northern actions against O'Neill, alas, and address me southward against Desmond."

In spite of Sidney's withdrawal, it was a grueling winter for Shane's men, an agonizing bone-chilling campaign in bog and bracken, among the drumlins and bare woods of Tirowen. O'Neill split his army into several brigades, each off to repel the incursions of his various foes. It was a war without a front, of vicious raids and counter-raids, a wearying war of attrition. As spring brought its relief, however, fewer inroads were being made upon him, particularly from the garrison at Derry. Even so, the very presence of that ward was a vexation, a galling wound to his pride.

At the end of March Friar MacMenamin, the rustic monk from Derry, paid another call to Shane's camp in the Wood of Glenconkeen. With him was a raggedy young lackey, peering out from under a shaggy glib of dark hair, and grinning devilishly as the monk recounted the dire plight of that English garrison.

"Once Randolph was killed, St. Loo never made a fist of it. He made a right guts of it, in truth. Things went from bad to worse, til it's a roaring disaster now! The rations gave out quick enough and disease crept in. November it was, those cold murky days, when the plague first appeared and struck down the strongest among them. 'The flux!' they said. It's torn through them like a blaze through the heather! Decimated them! D'ye see, they foolishly made their encampment over the burial ground, and the miasma has done its work!"

"And good *enough* for them!" Shane turned to Dualta, his next in command. "They are ghouls. Desecrating yet another blessèd graveyard. Farleigh is right! It's a *deliberate* affront. Not only to debase us, but to efface every remnant of our people from the land!" O'Donnelly nodded.

"Why would anyone disturb such a place? Armagh Churchyard was purposely defiled as well. He's right. There's something behind it." The monk agreed.

"Aye, it wouldn't be done lightly, I'm thinking. But they're billeted over the crypt of the ancient monastery, and the vapours from the charnel-house, they say, do rise in the night and choke the slumbering soldiers! Betwixt the dead, and the dying, and them as run off...there's now scarcely two hundred able men out of all the legion that came!" Shane gave a thunderous clap, and rubbed his hands together. The monk's eyes glistened with zeal.

"That's the spirits of the place, the holy saints, coming to your aid!"

"It is, surely! And their own English foolishness as well!"

"True for you, O'Neill! Wait til ye hear. Come Christmastide, there was a ship arrived with provision, but sure, through some fool's blunder, the beans had been to *Florida* and back! And the corn was rotten for them! Our people thereabouts are charging them fierce prices for victuals -and fair play to them. But those soldiers are lucky to get bread and peas! Their vicar was giving out to me about it!"

"The vicar? He says more than his prayers, I'll warrant."

"Och, aye, he does, surely. Their clothes are in flitters from the constant torrents hereabout, and he comes into the Irish districts searching for friezecloth and the like. Their entrenching tools failed them, he says, for they've twenty dozen battered spades and shovels, and no good left in any of them. In January St. Loo made a raid upon the O'Kanes across the river and brought off a vast herd of cattle, but little good it did them. The boys drove most of them off into the hills. The Vicar says there is talk in London of removing the garrison to Coleraine, or to Strangford even, but sure, that place is in your hands, as I hear tell."

"It is, to be sure, Father. But what of the entrenchment itself? Does he speak of it?" MacManemin scratched his tonsured head.

"Ah, he was giving out about the rats, aye...and storage room they've none, for the cathedral is filled with their munitions, and they're down to-"

"The church is filled with munitions?"

"It is, aye. The Temple Mór." He sighed and blessed himself. "That sacred place is now a keep for gunpowder, leaden bullets, towmatch, guns and pikes. Bad cess to them! I'd say but you could-"

"Are there any Irish within the town?"

"There's not, no. Our crowd are all driven off. But we're near enough, like, in the bogside."

"Traders? Doctors? Who is let come through the gates?"

"No *Irish*, any rate." His servant tugged at his sleeve, and whispered.

"Father, them O'Friel boys-"

"Oh, aye. There's a few young lads helping the farrier in the forge."

"*In the forge*? Is the forge *near* to the cathedral?"

"Tis only just beside it."

"Aaah...*Is* it, so? Come along then, Friar, and our boyo here as well. Ye'll be famished, I suppose, after your hard ride. By Christ! You did well to come! Taking Colonel Randolph from them was a greater blow than ever I had hoped!" The lad grinned, and the monk nodded sagely.

"You've only to leave the rest to Providence!"

"Perhaps, Friar. And perhaps we might help Him along yet..."

In early spring the bitter news arrived that Desmond had been captured at Kilmallock, and was once again imprisoned. His ambitious brother John, had been knighted. It was widely supposed that this victory would free the Lord Deputy's hand to turn his attentions northward once again. If this turn was a disappointment for Shane, it was exceedingly good news for the Primate, as it made possible his visit to Limerick City. In April he undertook the arduous journey home to officiate at his sister's wedding. It would be a lavish affair; Creagh's people being wealthy merchants, and his sister was marrying into just such another family. In spite of the attendant perils, he longed to see his people, and to walk again among the denizens of King's Island, in an Ireland that was familiar and comprehensible to him. Because of the dangers he was sure to encounter, both David Wolfe and the Primate's brother insisted upon accompanying him.

The three set off then, along with Creagh's faithful servant Florry, arriving in Sligo in time to concelebrate a High Mass for Palm Sunday. There Creagh conferred with the bishops of Elphin and Raphoe, who endeavored to convince him to take ship to Limerick, rather than risk the perils of traveling through Connaught. The English presence there had risen sharply over the last year, and the suppression of the church had taken a vicious turn. Given his calamitous history with ships, Creagh would not hear of such a plan. Instead, he accepted an invitation to celebrate Easter Mass the following week at a friary in Mayo, and, stubbornly over-riding their protests, he sent his brother and the Nuncio on ahead to Limerick City.

From Moyne Priory, on Easter Monday, Creagh travelled south

SHANE O'NEILL

with a party of Franciscans. When they had gotten as far as Kinelea, despite the Primate's objections, the monks insisted upon calling at the castle of the O'Shaughnessy, as was ever their custom, to request alms. Wary of being discovered, Creagh waited outside the gates. After a time he ambled down the lane, murmuring the prayers of his breviary. It happened that a group of Limerickmen bound for the castle passed him on the lane, and they hailed him cheerfully. Richard recognized them, but in his terror he gave no acknowledgement to their greeting. They were of course offended, and did not fail to remark the bishop's rudeness when they met with O'Shaughnessy, alerting him to the Primate's presence there.

The chieftain, by some stroke of ill fortune, had a most ambitious brother, Dermot O'Shaughnessy, who had lately returned from London, where he had served as a guard for Sir Robert Dudley. This was a man who had made friends at Court, and with his 'keen eye for main chance', he lost no time in seizing the Primate's person. And so, on this last day of April, William Creagh was arrested once again, and taken to Dublin Castle where he would stand trial, not only for his escape in London, but also, most ironically, for 'conspiring against the Crown with Shane O'Neill!'

For his efforts, the bold Dermot received a fulsome letter of gratitude signed by her Majesty, as well as title to the family's estates in Gort, supplanting his brother, the stated heir. He did not live long to enjoy his ill-gotten gains, however. Only a few years later he murdered his nephew in a dispute over the estate, and later died of a wound incurred in the fray.

Just a slip of a moon shone through the leafy wood of Glenconkeen, and a mild May breeze whispered above the tents and fires of O'Neill's encampment. Shane and his captains were seated round a blazing fire with methers of ale sloshing to and fro, as they listened to a tall white-haired priest who stood before the fire. Only a few moments before, a sentry had galloped into camp escorting the priest to see the chieftain, a sure sign of news. And news it was, joyous relief after a long harsh winter! Suddenly a wild cheer rose up among them to pierce the stillness of the wood, echoed by the shrill screech of startled nightbirds.

"All of them perished! Blown into the next world, and answering now only to their captain, Lucifer!" Father Crilly blessed himself. "Safe be the telling!" Shane was exultant.

"Oh ho! By the Powers! It's just as Farleigh said! The stars have turned! The Englishtown Primate, and the Derry Garrison *both* banished in the one week!" Shane looked triumphally to his foster brother. Dualta O'Donnelly's eyes narrowed, and his dark brows rose in a crafty sort of grin.

"So it is! The tide is turned for you, O'Neill! There's the *lot* of them- blown to hell!" Shane tipped him a wink, and looked back to the priest, eager for his words.

"Heaven or Hell, I couldn't say. But the fortress is demolished. And it was St. Columbkille *himself* that has freed his town of those impious divils!"

"Good on you Shane!" Con MacArdall shook his fist before him. "If they commanded the field, you took their commander! And their fortress too!" Shane raised his palm..

"Aye. Let the man speak, for the love of God!" He looked up to the priest. "What way did it happen, Father? Tell it out, now, without stopping or staying."

"The townsfolk of Derry all have the one story, and let *that* avouch for the truth of it. 'Twas *this* way it fell out. The English took to storing their magazine in the church itself, and the people attest that holy St. Columbkille took onto himself the shape of a *huge wolf*, with bristling hair and eyes like embers. He came boldly out of the oak grove, and into the town. They say he entered the iron barriers, emitting from his mouth a shower of sparks –the like as you'd see fly from a red-hot iron when 'tis struck. The bristling beast proceeded to the place where the powder was stored. Roaring fiercely, and breathing sparks and fire into it, he set off the great combustion!"

SHANE O'NEILL

"Cawboom!!!!" Someone bellowed, and set off a great uproar of laughing and cheering. "Oh ho, boys! Cut her loose! Huroo! Pwillaloo!" A few of them howled like wolves. Shane's excited hounds joined in, yelping and shouldering one another, and they began to bay on a high shrill note. O'Neill raised a commanding hand, and the reeraw subsided, but he was laughing still.

"A *wolf* it was? A fire-breathing bitch of a wolf!" MacArdall put a shielding palm up beside his mouth, for a mock-whisper.

"Be the divil's tail, I think you may *know* that wolf, Shane O'Neill!" He was teary-eyed with mirth. "Never let a wolf near the poitín, boys. They be breathin' fire! Sure maybe he let go with an ill wind!" His own laugh was even louder than the rest. Fr. Crilly took up his tale again as soon as he could make himself heard.

"Now I'll not attest to a wolf or no –although I'd say it's no lie. But *this* much can't be denied, that the gunpowder suddenly took fire. The English who were in the church were burnt up, and those patrolling nearby were struck with the shot and the burning tiles, and *killed*, God rest their immortal souls. Those who fled up the town, or into the water were caught by the flying debris! There were pieces flung *five hundred paces* from the town!" A rollicking cheer erupted. Shane added his jest to the tumult.

"St. Columbkille is a mighty rebel! Fair play to him and his whiskey breath!" Father Crilly waited again for a settling.

"Those that were left took to their boats, and I'm told they made for Carrickfergus, although there were close on seventy-five of them did a hard march up along the Foyle to your cousin Turlagh Lynagh - and found a *warm welcome* before them!"

"And he my Tanist, sworn upon the stone to uphold me!" Shane spat into the fire. "I'll do for him! He'll be sorted soon enough!" MacArdall was tipsy, and fired up.

"These thievin' English won't be messin' with our saints after that!" The priest shook his head, and gently raised his palm in protest.

"Aaaah no, sure, they wouldn't give in to *that*! They said there was a wind up, and it was sparks from the nearby forge that blew into the church. They say there was never a wolf." Shane nodded cunningly.

"Oh, I know a few wee *forge-stokers* who are *sly as wolves*...and when they get the wind up -Clear the way!" The priest was perplexed, but the merriment was unabated, and Shane raised his voice now in deadly earnest.

"Right boys! There's Randolph gone, and the Derry Garrison gone! And Black Hugh O'Donnell next to go. He has no Garrison now to hide behind! I'm ringed round with foes on every side, but I'll break the circle at its weakest point, and *that* is Black Hugh. We'll take him down before the English come back north. Christ, I don't need help from France or Spain to sort *him* out." Again, a cheer arose, and at the first sign of its fading, the priest spoke again.

"Shane O'Neill, now, I can't avouch for this story either, no more nor the fiery wolf, but we got some word..."

"What is it man?"

"Well, tis only a '*He* told *me* that *he* was told', but a priest back from Galway told of a Frenchman off a ship who said that the Pope has excommunicated Elizabeth." He blessed himself again. Shane laughed.

"By the powers, the ships will be sailing soon! The tide has turned!" He held up his dripping mether. "And we'll be there to meet it! We'll give O'Donnell a dose of lead. And *he'll* not wake up two days later!" This was met with a roar of approval. He quaffed his ale, and turned to Dualta O'Donnelly, lowering his voice a trifle. "Tomorrow, you'll bid my captains to make ready. Send a few scout up to O'Donnell's country to find his position. I'll need to pay a call out to Inishdowell, now we're so near. But upon my return to camp, we march on Tirconnell!"

SHANE O'NEILL

CHAPTER 30

A day of the days it was, a bright May morning. Spangles of sunlight danced on the rippling blue lough, and glinted off the white wings of gulls that soared and screamed overhead. The few fleecy clouds that drifted afar served only to glorify the brilliant blue expanse beyond. By smooth rhythmic strokes, the four oarsmen glided O'Neill's boat swiftly over the shining waters toward a lush wooded island that lay within a mile of shore. Up in the stern sat Shane O'Neill, his arms drawn tightly around each of the two hounds that were settled uneasily on either side of him. A bevy of white swans had caught their eye, and Bran and Scohaun whimpered and strained as the boat drew ever nearer the isle of Inishdowell. If truth be told, for all the fine day and joyful homecoming, Shane felt a spark of restiveness too.

Waiting just above the gravelly shingle were four tall guardsmen in chainmail tunics. Shane's young son Turleigh stood boldly beside them, with a bow on his arm, a sheaf of arrows over one shoulder, a brace of rabbits slung over the other, and a proud smile for his Da. As the boat scraped up onto the slip, Shane stood, and the hounds bolted. They plashed their way up onto the land, where they shook a mighty spatter in all directions, and raced off along the shore to bark at the swans. O'Neill gave his boy a ferocious hug and tousled his black hair. Turleigh was nearly nine, and he strongly favoured his father for features and hair. He spoke excitedly of his mastery of the bow, and boasted that he was provisioning Shane's guard, since Lady

SHANE O'NEILL

Katherine was not partial to rabbit.

From one of these guards, Shane learned that Farleigh the Poet was stopping nearby at Art O'Hagan's rath on the hill of Tullahogue, and he sent him off to fetch the pair of them. A sharp whistle, then, and his hounds soon appeared, bounding out of the bracken to trot along behind as O'Neill and his son ambled up the shady path. Presently they came upon a round stone tower, wider than it was high, that stood amid a sea of bluebells now in high Spring, and as they stepped through them the air was abuzz with flitting bees.

The little rounded door was open, its heavy iron-gate wide ajar, and the prisoner, Sorley Buí MacDonnell, was more than likely to be found colloguing with his niece above at Fuanagall. He had the run of the island by day, under the watchful eye of a formidable guard. Shane and Turleigh rambled on then toward Fuanagall, the boy pleading earnestly to go off to the wars, and Shane counseling patience and reason, with a good measure of praise.

The boy told his father of the island lore he'd learned from the monks who often visited the island from Ardboe. It seems Inishdowell had served as a retreat for St.Patrick, and there was a stone near the castle called 'Patrick's rest' for there it was that the saint would repose and meditate. The great wonder, though, was a strange rock formation, a submerged ridge in the lough that formed an underwater bridge from the island to the shore. It was known as 'Patrick's causeway', and it could be easily seen in early summer, for it was less than two feet below the surface of the water. You could walk across the lough, and look miraculous doing it, just as St.Patrick had so long ago!

The thorns were all in flower, and the sun slanted through the trees so that the blossoms were incandescent. The earth smelt rich and pure with the sap of spring, a pungent scent of exuberant growth, although the pulse of summer was already throbbing in the mossy green wood. Birds were warbling and twittering, bluebottles buzzing, crickets chirping, and the sounds of war were many long leagues away.

The isle of Inishdowell is small and round, barely eight acres of dense forest. At its very centre, in a sunlit glade, the square towerhouse of Fuanagall stood three stories high, and its crow's step gable could be seen just above the trees. As Shane and his son reached the edge of the shadowy wood, a score of hares darted among the fern frisking madly about, and the hounds set off after them, barking and snarling. The whole glade was astir with their lepping and diving, yelping and yowling, and the boy chasing after them. For all that, Shane lingered at the edge of the clearing to regard his wee castle, and he was fair pleased to look on it. He had conceived it, commanded it into being, and there it stood, solid and regal and secluded.

At the sound of this ruckus, Lady Katherine and her uncle emerged through the gate of the Castle close, with Sorley's guard, and her maidservants, who had the young childer in tow. On catching sight of the hounds, they gave a cheer, and quickly spotted Shane striding in from the wood. Katherine's auburn hair was a blaze of red in the sunlight, and a white May blossom adorned it. Her frock was powdery blue, with a lavender chemise that shone over her bodice and under the broad slashed sleeves. On her arm was a small basket, for she had only now been gathering 'simples' in her garden. Her face was flushed and her eyes shone with teary joy.

"Mother of God! Here's your Daddy home!" She called out as he approached,"Here's a sight! Are you home to me, Shane O'Neill?"

"Aye, until the morning comes! With the first chirp of the sparrow, I'll be on the march again, but I've only good news to tell!" He took her in his arms, and after a rather passionate embrace, he greeted Sorley, and lifted, in turn, each of his wee sons high into the sky. Art was four, and he had a firm grip on his mother's skirts as he peeked around from behind her. He pulled back when Shane went for him, and giggled wildly as he was lifted onto his father's shoulders. "Is it *shy* you are? Shy of your aul Daddy?" Art grinned and giggled, and Katherine laughed.

"Aye! He's shy but willin', like an ass eating thistles! Och, he does be bold enough with his *Mammy*! Will you ever tell us, Shane O'Neill? What are these fine tidings you've brought, then?" Shane made a short narration of the Primate's capture, and of the annihilation of the

SHANE O'NEILL

English Garrison at Derry, and there was rapturous joy at this turn in his fortunes.

They retired then to the withdrawing room above in the castle, which was slightly dank for the fire had only just been lit. Kat delighted in showing her husband all her adornments and furnishings. The chambers were smaller than those at Benburb, and she had sent for the finest pieces out of Dungannon Castle, lest they be destroyed in the war, so the chamber possessed an elegance quite unknown to Benburb. Even the marble of Achilles from London was on display. All of this won Shane's approval, and he said that he was pleased to see his wife in such high heart, for the move from Benburb Castle had weighed heavily upon her. Katherine sighed, and looked from one to the other.

"It's a lonely place, in truth, and I should be lost without my poor uncle, but the wee'uns are safe here, and happy." Seeing her husband's look of concern, she brightened her tone. "Och, I'm grand! I'm an island lass, so I am, and it suits me well enough." A wry smile came to her lips. "At least I might rule my own hearth in this place without auld Bríd leering over my shoulder. God bless her, but she was tart with me from the first." She looked to her uncle's inquisitive squint. "Shane's auntie has gone back to mind her auld father. Truth be told, I heard her say she didn't fancy being a 'castaway' here in the Lough!"

The babe in Katherine's arms gurgled, so she cooed at her, and rocked her gently. "Who's this has come to see my wee Áilish? Do ye not know your Daddy? Sure, I hardly know him myself these times." Kat gently handed the baby over to Shane, and Áilish's big blue eyes opened wide. Shane went to tickle her with his beard, and she let out a mighty bawl that succeeded in getting her safely back into her mother's arms. Peace was quickly restored when Katherine gave suck to the child, and to secure the peace, the boys were sent off with their nurse. Wine appeared, and the three settled back to take their ease, and to sift and weigh the affairs of the day.

Shane spoke of Alastair MacDonnell's cold rebuff to his offers of conciliation. Sorley huffed and pished.

"Och, man alive, did ye reckon he would kiss ye? It was not only our James we lost to you, but Aengus as well, and there was less than a year betwixt him and Alistair." He sighed, and looked to Katherine. "Och, ye should well ken by *this* -that's the way of the clan MacDonnell. Kick one, and we all limp!"

"It was a MacDonnell's spear that slew my brother Phelim, but I have buried him. I accounted it bygone when I allowed you to wed my sister, for I knew we were best to put such things behind us. The living must live, and Alastair must turn his face to the fore! Aye, but I'll tell you this, if Alastair was aloof, his cousin was riled with spite and spleen, He was-"

"Gillaspick? Was Gillaspick riding with him?"

"Aye, that was he. Girning and grumbling!" Sorley nodded, and instructed with a sly smirk.

"Och, well, have sense, man! Alastair couldnae be civil to you with *Gillaspick* at his shoulder! That's a man covets the lairdship, d'ye see! If Alastair didnae show a hard face to you, it would be thrown up til him afore the rest. A vengeful surly scoundrel is Gillaspick. His father was killt by the English, and his teeth are on edge ever since." Katherine spoke now, in a soft tone, for she was nursing her 'wee lass-bairn.'

"All that may yet be of no account, Shane, for if Argyll comes in with you, Alistair will have little choice. He is bound to follow the Campbell. I sent your letter off to Archibald a fortnight ago with your brother. Aye, Fr. Hugh and the auld priest, the chanter of Armagh, they're gone to Inverary this while now. Armed with gifts! I came upon your father's dress robes in an old trunk when I was unpacking here. The splendid garments he got of King Harry. I know well you're sworn against wearing them, so I sent them off to Archibald. They will befit him well, I should think, for he's tall and spare like your father, and the Duke is partial to such English finery. And-"

"He's welcome to them. By Christ, she's a sound wee woman is your niece!" Shane winked at Sorley, about to make some jest, but Kat was not finished.

"That's not the whole of it, Shane..." She swallowed, and there was apprehension in her eyes. "I sent to him the O'Neill Cup!" Shane looked stunned. "Little good will that goblet do us if we lose this war! Archibald admired it so at our wedding, and the four wee legs on it. Do you not remember? And I thought it was a fitting token to call to his mind that day, and the *pledges* he made that day. He knows he is beholden to you for aiding him in his time of banishment. He wrote as much when he promised to come last summer. But for all this upheaval in Scotland, I'm sure he would have come. Mary needs him now in her black hour, but all that could change in a trice."

"You did rightly, Kat. And you must write him again, with news of the English banished out of Derry. Tell him I am riding high, and want only his swift support. Please God, he will hold by his word." Shane nodded to Sorley. "And when your brother Alastair has lain aside his enmity, you'll go your road, back to poor Mary. I'm sure my sister is pining for your return. By Christ, you know yourself, man. It's none of it as we would wish it, but what is needful must be." The baby was drowsing now, and Katherine gave her over to Mórag with instructions to settle her in the cradle above, and to keep close. She could not help but follow her to the door, and when the footman had closed it, she turned with a smile, and spoke out in full voice.

"Well, saints be praised! The loss of his Garrison will be a great blow to Sidney! And now you are riding high again, those deserters will have cause for remorse! O'Kane and his cock-lairdies."

"Divil choke him, and his remorse." Shane spat in the fire. "The lot of them! Turlagh and Black Hugh. Craven dogs all of them!" Sorley looked up at Katherine.

"Och, he right, too, so he is. Regrets or no, O'Kane willnae be at O'Neill's side again. A man can only turn coat the 'wanst!" Shane nodded.

"His people will put him aside if they judge the war to be with me. And that will be a message to all, when his son is at my side. If the wind will only stay in my sails now, they will all rue their treachery."

"Please God, an' it will!" Kat blessed herself quickly for luck.

"I'll set out tomorrow to put a deal of remorse on Black Hugh O'Donnell, and some manners into the bargain! He has but little support among his people, so that will be no great task. I'll pack him off to Hell." Shane looked darkly into the fire for a long moment, and Kat was concerned.

"But could we not leave the wars now, Shane, for this one day! Tomorrow will come soon enough." He nodded, and brightened.

"So it will. And, by God, it's a grand day altogether." He held up his goblet and the attendant replenished their wine. The talk then turned to lighter concerns, news of their older children, both Shane's and Sorley's, and Katherine slipped out to fetch her 'latest needlepoint opus', as she called it.

On her return, Shane smiled devilishly, for he noted that she had done some primping, with even a touch of elderberry to her lips, and certainly not for the sake of her uncle. The men admired her craftwork, a fanciful unicorn among thistles in rich vivid hues. "Begod, she has clever hands, that one. Anything she turns them to is bright and elegant! She's a wonder, so she is!" Katherine, blushing a bit, took it over to a tall oak press to bestow it. She moved gracefully with a swinging of her hips under her frock. Her bosom was hoisted provocatively over her tight bodice, and Shane's glistening eyes followed her intently, like a cat with a bird. She had regained her fine form since the birthing, but she was rounder and softer yet. Her uncle could scarcely help noticing Shane's rapt regard of his wife, and he felt suddenly intrusive, a beholder where he oughtn't, so he made his excuses, and promised to see them at supper.

As the heavy oak door closed and clanked, Katherine faced her husband, and caught sight of a familiar glint in his eyes. She smiled secretly, turning her face away, and she took up an airy manner. "Such a grand day. You'll be wanting to enjoy the fine afternoon with your sons, I suppose." She sighed. "You're nearly a stranger to them."

"Time enough for that. It's a long afternoon ahead of us."

"Aye, long indeed. Hours and hours of it. However will you pass the time?"

"This castle was barely rooved, the last I saw of it. Firstly you must show me the bedchamber. I want to see what adornments and flourishes you've contrived up there."

"Och, well...no great wonders there, my pet. Mostly what was above in Benburb, apart from the new lace curtains on my bedstead, and a few wee pillows." She sighed as she threw a coy glance at him, and looked quickly away again, but not before he had seen the devilish gleam in her eye. He got to his feet and stood over her where she sat.

"Curtains is it? By Christ, *this* I've got to see. They had better be comely or there will be trouble! Get up with you, wee woman, for I've a mind to see that bedstead now. I've some business there." Katherine abandoned her airs with a billowing laugh.

"Indeed, your Lordship, I wouldn't like to refuse you, for I know you're a divil for frippery and lacy frills." She took his hand and rose, and as she met his gaze her smile faded. Kat sighed gently and her eyes wandered over his face, soft with desire. He took her in his arms, then, and caressed her, and when they had kissed, she smiled again impishly. "Come, then, you great beast! You'll not wait for the shades of night, but you'll have your way, for that was ever the way of you!" They retired to their chamber above, and presently the door opened again. Out flew the cat, Pishogue, landing on her feet with her dignity unruffled.

Katherine's head lay soft upon her husband's sweaty chest, which was still heaving. She listened to his heart thumping, and wondered how to say what was troubling her, but say it she would. "You were very rough, Shane... I only pray to God I'm not bruised."

Was I?" He shifted, but she stayed where she was, without looking at him. Her voice was low and intimate.

"You were. It was not a bit like you. It was like there was someone else in your skin. I don't know were you there at all." His hand swept across his brow, drawing away a damp lock of hair, and he heaved a sigh.

"Christ, I'm sorry. I lost the head of me. Are you hurted?"

"I'm not, no. But I'm shaken." He drew his arm tight over her, and kissed the top of her head. He whispered to her.

"I'm sorry, my darling one. My fawn of the wood."

"You were like a battering tempest, like there was a rage driving you. I saw it in your eyes earlier. What is on you, Shane O'Neill? What is ailing you?"

"There's divil-all on me. I'm not rested proper, maybe, and it's an age since I held you, many rough months in the bog and bracken." Katherine sat up now against the bolster. She composed herself, and gently faced her husband.

"I know you're not a man that's easily cast down. Nothing daunts or dashes you. But, open your heart to me, Shane O'Neill. There's some darkness there, some corner of your mind ever smouldering. Let you speak it out." After a moment, he swung his feet round to the floor, and sat up heavily on the tousled bed, his back to her. There was silence now, and he appeared to sink gloomily into his own thoughts. On hearing her sigh, he turned and raised his eyes to her.

"Christ, I don't know, Kat. I couldn't say rightly. I'm unsettled in my thoughts. I'm beset by treachery and betrayal til I am nettled to the very soul! I've never known the like of it. Black Hugh, and Turlagh, both cousin to me, and Fergus O'Kane who can't abide the Saxons is gone over to them. Even the O'Hanlon has left my camp. And there is some sourness and confusion among the people. A change is come, and not a good one."

"As to your cousins, we know well it's the spite of Fionnúla MacDonnell is behind their turning, her thirst for revenge. And perhaps Turlagh covets the chieftainry. Did you not say that his father was one time heir to the office?"

"He was. He was my father's tanist, first in succession, but when Conn became an earl, the succession went to his son instead. Turlagh would be mindful of that, and bitter."

"So, how could it be elsewise? And you mustn't trouble yourself over these thick-headed bonnet-lairds, O'Kane and his like. He's more nor-"

"But they are my *mainstay*. If I lose them, the clan order, its whole tangle of obligations will unravel, and the hewers and tillers will follow after them. Even the poor are grumbling against me."

"The poor must take the world and the weather as it comes. There is nothing left them but to grumble. What came between yourself and O'Kane?"

"He reared up on me before my captains. These last months my word is challenged in court and in camp, and I'll not stomach it."

"But what was the bone you were snarling o'er?"

"A baker. And a noose!" Katherine's jaw dropped, and she uttered a barely discernible moan. After a moment, she spoke crisply.

"It's true then. They say that you hanged a man for baking bread, but it is so appalling I never believed it." His face darkened.

"For defying my word. *Not* for his curséd baking."

"If *this* be true, I would wonder at nothing!" She shook her head in disgust, and leveled an accusing gaze upon him.

"This jumped-up sallowjack from the Pale set up his bake-stall in Limavaddy, turning the people to his English ways-"

"The English have many *good* ways, and clever innovations that might yet prove a boon to the Irish!"

"So they have. But they *all* come to us with poison, glistening with poison! For every one of them is a tool and a weapon to extirpate us. To divest us of our ways and our oneness until we haven't a notion of who we are. Then they will sweep us from the land. I sent my men round to him twice, and told him the law, told him to hump off and peddle his Saxon wares in the Pale. We warned him that in O'Neill's country the word of O'Neill is the *last* word, and that if he defied me a second time, he would swing from a tree. The fool paid no heed, and so he *did*."

"Hanged for..."

"For defying my word. They've killed our poets. They want to kill our very tongue. Sidney has ordered stocks be built to shame our bards in the village squares! And I'll not have their English ways creeping into the countryside."

"You may have the right of it, but it was *savage*. Such a deed would only bear out the awful slanders of the Primate, and the Deputy. You must not let your temper have mastery of you, Shane

O'Neill. I know you are sorely tried, but you must not let them make a stone of your heart!"

"Savage? Let you go to Dundalk to see the eighteen heads spiked over the gates, heads of young Irishmen, and you'll tell me who the savages are. Never was there seen severed heads over *my* gate. No, nor over any other Irish gate since the time of Conor mac Nessa and Cúchulain. But as for his hanging, I didn't scruple to do it. This churl was inviting others to defy me in my country, and I stretched his neck for him...the way others might know to the better."

"But the people, high and low, will turn from you if they believe you to be a tyrant."

"The people are turning because they believed I was losing the war. Now the Garrison is shattered and routed, and when I am victorious, the people will turn again to me. The people! They blow like thistledown on the wind. That is my one task, my *only* task –to rise victorious. And if I have to kill a hundred such churls to have my word honoured in Ulster, I'll do it, and I'll not care a rotten straw about it." The assurance with which he had spoken, and the silence that was spreading around them now made Katherine wary. He was clearly bereft of help in his 'life or death' struggle with the English. Even with the garrison obliterated, defeat seemed, for the first time, a real possibility. If Shane O'Neill should lose heart...

"I've written again to Mary, that she might prevail upon her uncles and the Pope to send armies. God grant us this rumour is true, and he has excommunicated Elizabeth. That would set ships asailing! They all proclaim you their Catholic champion, and yet they begrudge you help. It's little wonder you're heart-sore."

"None of them, nary a one, has honoured his promise."

"It would seem so, but you mustn't feel so beggared. When he was finally able, did not your cousin, the Earl of Desmond, rise up in the South, just as you asked of him?"

"Aye, I'll grant you that. Desmond gave Sidney all the trouble in his power until they imprisoned him again. But his brother John betrayed me."

"He is craven."

"He's like an ale-house dog; he'll go a piece of the road with anyone. When I've set the Deputy back on his heels, John of Desmond will change his standard again."

"And Mary Stuart sent a hundred of her guard!" She saw a dismissive smirk pass across Shane's features. "Aye, barely a token, of course. My father sent twice that, but his was a dowry. A high price for you to make an honest woman of me!"

"I'd have married you with an inch of candle! Sure, you know that." Shane looked at her a long moment, his eyes glistening. "What would become of you, if I were slain? And the boys?" Katherine started, and blessed herself quickly.

"What puts a question like that on your tongue?" He rid his throat.

"Chance of war. Nothing more nor that. Where would you go?"

"I don't know rightly...Back to my people, I suppose."

"Promise me this, Kat...that the boys will stay in Ulster. If they would rule after me, they must be proper Irishmen, born and bred. They could be put in fosterage, as I was, with the Donnellys, O'Hagan, or any of Clan Fergus. Promise me, so."

"I will, Shane. I'll make that pledge to you, and you must pledge to me that I'll never need to keep it, that you'll keep a fierce grip on your immortal soul, and come safe to me when the wars are ended!" He nodded.

"No fear of that. I'll give you my word, and I'll *keep* it, if others won't."

"I shall owe a tall candle to Our Lady when you do." He lay back down beside her, and put his arms about her. As they lay there in silence, Katherine smiled, for Pishogue could be heard scratching at the door.

.After a grand but intimate feasting under the mighty stags' antlers of the Great Hall, Lady Katherine bustled her small coterie of guests into the more genteel environs of the Withdrawing Chamber, with its Persian carpet and Greek statue. Blind Colm was there, to regale them with his harp. Her uncle, Sorley Buí, if somewhat taciturn in company, added to the small group of Shane's intimates. O'Hagan had brought with him his son Owen Óg, formerly a secretary to Shane. Both they and the poet were a bit soft in drink, having been summoned from a Christening, and their hostess was hoping that wine, rather than spirits, would keep a chivalrous restraint on the evening's discourse. Farleigh hoisted his goblet, and as a servant replenished it, he winked at O'Hagan. "Divil's cure to you! Here's Jerez wine, a Spanish sherry now, to set our blood into a livelier motion after that fine feast! It's a pity, now, it's only a pity the good Primate Creagh could not be with us on such a night." O'Hagan took up his theme with a wry smile.

"He's with his own sort in Dublin Castle, where the ways and manners will be more to his liking! He's well out of it now, any rate, where he'll not be riled and tormented by that fierce Chieftain of the *savage* northern tribes!" He nodded to Shane, who laughed.

"Aye, I had him in a fair lather! And the eyelids aflutter, like a mole in the sunlight!" Kat drew a sharp breath.

"Stop! I thought he would burst into flames! Standing over your brother's grave, and the two of you girning at each other like a pair of pipers! I could see the sort he is!" Farleigh scrunched up his ruddy features.

"A shivering priestling, with a shepherd's crook and no *sheep*! That's the sort he is." Katherine tisked.

"Och, he is a weak man is Creagh. Sure, a whisper would go through him."

"Aye, but he is *peevish*," Shane added. "And just when he looks to be at his most diffident, he is about to sting. Like a wasp!"

"Just so! Like a nest of hornets!" Farleigh shook his head. "The man is a woeful menace. With his grim smile. The little pink eyes of him peering out out at you, his mind flying like a weaver's shuttle, and his ears cocked, waiting for some infraction, for a chance to *pounce*.

And the disdainful *airs* of him! He is as lordly to the Irish as he is servile to the English!"

"And malicious!" Owen Óg urged him on.

"It is the malice of one who thinks himself a pious saint who has been robbed of his halo. An aspiring martyr! He is a martyr to his own torturesome *vanity!*"

"And a martyr to his Saxon scruples!" Shane raised his goblet. "Thanks be to God, that is him *gone*! Here's to his going! Soon to be locked up once again in the Whale's Belly! Oh ho, we are well shut of him!" The company cheered and clinked and quaffed, but Farleigh held back. He regretted having to be a doomsayer, but he knew that he was obliged to raise his ominous warning.

"Perhaps not so well as you suppose!" The others turned to him with surprise. "Creagh is once again to glory in an ecstasy of mortification. And you may be sure that the priests will howl, til they stir the people into a pious frenzy for their sainted Primate! And the whole piteous passion-play will lend more thunder to that solemn Damnation he leveled upon *your own good self*! I'm afraid we are not shut of him at all! I fear Creagh may prove a greater peril to you in his dungeon, Shane O'Neill, for it will elevate him in the eyes of the people."

"*Do* you? Let you save your fear for what is fearsome! I've no fear of that little man, in or out of his shackles. He has sown the wind, let him reap the whirlwind of his slavish devotion to the English. Now he is in their grip, he might learn something of their nature, and repent his foolishness." Farleigh was unmoved.

"He will learn nothing. The zealous are beyond such things as learning." Katherine sounded a more hopeful note.

"And if he is locked away, might Dean Donnelly not be named at last to the Primacy?" Shane shook his head gravely.

"Their only interest in Donnelly was that they suppose they can control me through him. That was the Dean's trump. That is why Sidney threw his support behind him, along with most of the Court. But now I'm in the field, the Queen is determined to crush me. And should she succeed, they would have little need of him. Perhaps when

I have cleared the field..."

"But Elizabeth will *have to* name a new Primate for Armagh." O'Hagan relished his news of intrigue. "The Queen's Primate, Loftus, is a greedy man, so I am told. Since he can get nothing from Armagh, he wants the revenues of Dublin, and he'll shift Bishop Curwen to get it. Sir Robert Fleming hears everything as Lord Mayor of Drogheda, and he says that Loftus is panting after the see of the Metropolis, and he is even putting rumours abroad that Curwan is a *sodomite!*" This news brought a peel of bright laughter.

"Och, there's nothing would surprise me!" O'Neill drained his cup. "And *he's* just the boy to know! But it is the Pope's word that matters, finally, and he'll surely not replace such a martyr to the cause as Dicky Creagh. He is worth more to Rome now that he is languishing in the heretic's dungeon."

"But will they *keep* him there?" Kat tisked. "The charges are laughable."

"They're charging Creagh with colluding with me in Treason against the Queen! It's inconceivable that they believe it. But, laughable or no, there's no man can prove himself innocent. He could be *found* innocent if they wish to loose him upon me once again. Time will tell its tale. At least this will put an end to his spying and intriguing." More wine was poured, and the talk moved on to more trivial matters.

Some time later, Katherine was talking to Blind Colm, and Farleigh bent his keen eye for a moment upon her. He looked up to see Shane regarding him, and he tipped him a nod. "The handsomest woman for shape or build, or colour or countenance. And *grace* with it! *And* she is no *fluttery* woman!" He had raised his voice, and Kat turned, smiling. Sorely spat into the fire, and Farleigh turned to him, so he spoke.

"Our Scots lassies are none for fluttering! If they're braw and bonnie, they're sound and canny too!" Farleigh considered a jest about their unfortunate Queen, but he thought better of it. Mary's brash and flighty ways were hardly a matter for levity after all the mayhem they had brought. But Lady Katherine, he knew, was a great source of knowledge about the ructions and upheavals in the Scottish Court, so he made inquiry of their 'braw and bonnie Queen'.

"I had a long letter from Lady Jean Stewart, Mary's sister –and indeed, a spate of them since. She stood proxy for Queen Elizabeth at the Christening of wee Prince James in Sterling, just before the Christmas. She says that-"

"*Elizabeth* was Godmother?" Shane was taken aback.

"She was, aye. The King of France was Godfather."

"But she is a *heretic*! By what pious 'shuffle-the-bróg' do thy justify *that*, I'd like to know?"

"*She* has not been formally 'excommunicated' -unlike *some*! Or had not been so last December, any rate." O'Hagan took up Shane's part.

"Please God she has been *since* then! But the godparents' pledge is to raise the child in the true Faith. A Faith which she has emphatically denied." Katherine shook her head, and looked smartly at the pair of them.

"Och, don't be coy. There's neither of you came down in the last shower! The Pope will *always* indulge the mighty Princes of powerful kingdoms! And well ye ken as much! Mary is struggling now to have Elizabeth name wee James as her successor to the throne of England, so for her to stand gossip to the child is accounted a very laudable first step. Poor Mary, I don't know what will become of her! And now!" She blessed herself quickly. "It is a dreadful affair, beyond all!"

"Shadow of God! What has befallen the poor woman now?" Farleigh glanced uneasily at Sorley Buí in his plaid phillamore. "You wouldn't know what to believe of the pandemonium in Scotland..." Sorley spoke pointedly, eyeing his niece.

"So you would not...for them that kens best, *says least*!" But Kat took no heed.

"Mary's sister kens it all, and she doesn't spare ink in her letters." Farleigh prompted her again.

"They say that kingdom is in an uproar since the Queen's husband was blown to the high heavens in Edinburgh."

"No, then, it wasn't quite so. Her husband, Darnley, was

convalescing at Kirk o' Fields –He was down with *the pox* after all his whoring. And he was plotting to usurp her crown, so while Mary was out, the house was indeed blasted to bits -but not Darnley, for he had leapt out the window! He'd gotten as far as the orchard, where his naked body was discovered. He had been smothered to death. Mary's consort, the Earl of Bothwell was found innocent at the proceedings, but there's none can say as much without a smirk. And now, Bothwell has abducted her! And I am told they shall soon wed. My sister writes that Mary was *willingly* abducted!" Farleigh's eyes shone with mischief.

"Ah! One can only surmise that this is the Scotch way of courting! For *that* sounds rightly familiar, if truth be told." Katherine trilled a little laugh.

"Aye, our Úna said as much! That Mary was stealing a page from my book! But however will it end? Bothwell divorced his 'wife of one year' for her. He's a Protestant, and she'll have a Protestant wedding!"

"She'll get no more Catholic support, from Pope nor Prince. Mary's power is fled with her honour!" O'Hagan cocked his brows and nodded to Shane. "There are some saying...there are some saying that Shane O'Neill has missed his chance! That Mary can no longer help him."

"I have heard what is said, and I've heard who has said it." Shane's cagey smirk invited no questions, and Farleigh's Jerez wine at last got the better of his discretion.

"Scotland is a pretty parcel of enmity these times! And it's Mary Stuart's foolishness has brought it to this pass! Whatever *possessed* her to marry such a fop? A pretty scoundrel!" The words stung a bit, but Kat kept her composure.

"Mary has a wild heart. But a pure one. And she is young."

"Unless there is soon a turning in her sad tale, she has cost O'Neill the hosting of Argyll's five legions!" Katherine tisked at Farleigh, and tossed her hair.

"Her Grace Mary cannot be held accountable for these Religious Wars. They are the doing of men. Wild eyed zealots and such! Across the width and breadth of Europe there are such wars. They owe nothing to Mary Stuart." The chief Brehon, standing between them, sided with the Defense.

"Lady Katherine is right. Since ever she arrived in Scotland, the poor lass has been mired in the wars of parsons and priests, trapped in the gloomy maze of casuistry such men call 'Faith'."

"Religious wars? They have divil-all to do with Faith or God. It is *power* that is disputed, not doctrine." Old Farleigh lowered his voice, and extended his long boney finger in a pedagogical flourish. "The power of the state! In each principality every man must have the one story, word by word, with the powers that be. That is the tip and the tail of the matter. And woe betide any who don't sing from the one hymnbook! A man must know only what his betters know, or what they would have him to believe. Thus was it ever, since the time of the Garden! Tell me this! What was the sin that won us death and damnation?" His watery eyes roved imperiously across the faces before him. "It was eating of the fruit of *forbidden knowledge*!" Art O'Hagan grinned.

"You sound very like a Protestant, Farleigh O'Gneeve!"

"Divil a fear of *that*! I'd protest them too! And where they rule, the story is little different, if it is not worse. When the drummer drums, we must march in step!" With that, a little arpeggio was sounded on the harp, and eyes turned to Blind Colm. Farleigh was about to continue, but Katherine allayed him with a smile.

"And when the harper strikes, we must hush!" At the Lady's "Whisht, now", MacCuarta commenced his playing, and was accorded the rapt attention of all. He played a slow air, and then sang a lovely mournful ballad. This was followed by a sprightly jig that ended with a hearty ovation. There was light banter after, and Katherine asked O'Hagan about the Christening he had come from, but the talk soon found its way back to the current wrangles of the war, and the various positions and evasions taken by the lords and chieftains known to them. Even her uncle found Lord Argyll to be inscrutable, although Katherine was inclined to trust him. "My sister writes that Archibald is coaxing Agnes and Fionnúla to accept the betrothal of Turlagh and Black Hugh, and to forego their vengeance against my Shane. But the

SHANE O'NEILL

Dark Daughter will have her way of it. And O'Donnell is set upon avenging her father. Úna has it that when Black Hugh was asked by Sidney what it was had severed his ties to O'Neill, he said it was 'a matter touching a lady's honour!" Farleigh harrumphed at this.

"Her honour? *That* is the only part of a woman that he would *not* touch!" Dark laughter followed, and the treachery of this man 'whose mother was an O'Neill' was noted and wondered over. Shane spat into the fire.

"It is not for his hair, but for his *heart* that he is called Black Hugh. Give me a cutlass, and I'll see if it be black or no! He's made another raid into Tirowen, ravaged all the country adjacent to Strabane. Tomorrow I'm for Tirconnell to put a fine end to his marriage prospects." O'Hagan struck his hands together and rubbed them vigorously.

"And right you are, Shane O'Neill. You must strike now, while the winds veer and the tide is running to your will! Smite him rightly, or every dog and divil will be at the same tricks. With Derry gone, he has no English to hide behind, and when he is layed low, the West will be clear." Farleigh smiled and nodded.

"And then it will be Lord Sidney's to begin once again, without a pace of ground taken! Not an inch of sod, for all his great offensive!" He raised his goblet of sherry." To a swift settling of the West!" They clinked and drank deep to the next victory. Afterwords, O'Hagan absently touched three fingers to his temple, and huffed.

"*Who's* this it was?" He looked up, with a troubled countenance. "The priest at the Christening is after telling me that Bishop Myler is in some dire peril of losing all! What has happened him? Do you know of this?" Shane nodded.

"He's told you no lie. Myler has landed in the briars, rightly. He was caught out in his forged letter to the Pope! He was endeavoring to get Creagh recalled to Rome, but the ruse has misfired, God help him."

"But I saw him only days ago. And he said nothing to me of this! Divil a word!" Farleigh shrugged.

"A man will be a long time abroad before he brings back a bad report of himself!" The judge pressed on.

"But what will become of his bishopric, his episcopal appointment?"

"He's to stand before a tribunal in Rome."

"Merciful God! They'll crucify him. Those shifty wheedly old Romans of the Curia?" Shane shook his head.

"They are no strangers to intrigue. Perhaps he might convince them of Creagh's heresy." Farleigh's eyes went wide at this.

"Divil a bit of it! And Creagh in an English dungeon? True it may be, but it does not befit the tale they are telling. They'll not hear a word against their Englishtown martyr. Mary pity poor Myler! They will *ate* him! Without salt!" Shane sighed with resignation.

"Trying to be hopeful, I was. But I fear you're right. He will be humbled to the dust. It was *I* told Myler to give it a go. I read it. A perfect forgery, I thought. And he put nothing in the letter that wasn't the God's truth about that blasted heretic."

'Twas *yourself* who was blasted!" O'Hagan lowered his voice. "For the love of God, don't own to any *part* in it, or you'll never get your excommunication lifted. Has there been any word on *that*?"

"No, then, the Dean has heard nothing back from his letters. But the Curia moves slowly. They are ancient, decrepit aul 'princes of the Church', and they are quite indifferent to the concerns of this far-flung island. In truth, we send precious little silver their way."

"Please God Myler will be able for them!" O'Hagan's son blessed himself. Shane gave a sidling nod.

"Divil a fear. He knows how many beans make five, does our Myler Magrath."

More airs and songs followed as the night wore on, and Farleigh gave a spirited rendition of his new verses decrying that English ban on the Irish bards, an interdiction that was being enforced in those parts of Ireland not under O'Neill's protection.

"Woe betide the bold bard
Who plies his father's art
Among the soft sons of Banva!

SHANE O'NEILL

Such duties shall pass no longer
From sire to son
In the cold green hills of Ireland.
No threads of learning shall be woven,
Our noble pedigrees shall not be told,
Nor shall pleasing patterns of poetry
Be moulded and fashioned as of old
to stir the noble heart
In the ancient metres or our art,
Since Brehon rule is sundered
And Saxon law laid down,
To rend the tender threads of
Éire's slender gown!
To tear her lavish raiments
Wrought of rhyme and reverie!
Ireland's woes!
An edict read in every part
In clacking Saxon prose!
To ban her graceful verse,
And what is worse,
To outlaw those...
Who compose."

Farleigh's ode was warmly received, and, for all the sherry that had passed his lips, he had never faltered. He was, nevertheless, in a heightened state, effusive and fantastical. Lady Katherine appeared at his side and took his hand into her hers.

"A bonny wee poem! Och, Farleigh O'Gneeve you are a joy. Even with your great tally of years, you are embroiled in creation! Bright as a forge fire!"

"Ah! But nothing is so fecund as womankind. *You*, my Lady, have brought forth worthy new scions to the House of O'Neill, and Queen Mary has born a son to save the Stewart line –Indeed, she may have buried the Tudors! Ah, the woman's womb! Where the world is made anew! Our Milesian tribe is gone awry since Patrick consigned Breegia and Danú to the outer darkness to bewail their fates. Éire and Fodhla and Banva are banished, and nothing shall stand aright until their return. The goddess must be restored to her place, her rightful place, in the Pantheon!"

"Do we not have the Mother of God? She is not a god, of course, but she is rendered such devotion as-"

"Mary is no goddess! She is 'obedience' beveiled in blue. And little more. Cool and placid in her seven sorrows, as if hewn from marble." Farleigh's eyes glistened in the firelight, and he cast his glance now upon the Grecian marble that stood beside the hearth, and sighed.

"Magnificent! Oh, the Greeks were the lads for it!"

"It's a Florentine copy only, I'm afraid. But it was carved and sculpted with the same artistry as the ancients possessed."

"The mastery of it! The soul exultant! It is precisely as I say. Art is *extravagant*. It is not mean and crimped!"

"Shane, did you not say that Farleigh had no liking for such things? It isn't a poem, you said, but only a *statue*." Farleigh spluttered.

"Only a statue? I never said such a foolish thing!" Shane smiled.

"You did, surely, and more than *that* you said. In London."

"Ah, well of course! Who could make sense of the world in such a place? No, it's much more than a statue. It *'tis* a poem, now I come to look upon it...And eloquent in its making, as in its message! It calls to mind our sublime Irish philosopher, Ian Duns Scotus, and his notions on the genesis of 'self.' What is life, after all, but a distillation of the spirit, a whittling down of our elements!" The poet turned his eyes from Shane, and settled his gaze on the Greek hero, speaking as in a reverie. "You, I -we commence with *infinite* possibility, making choices by the hour, by the day, discarding 'that' for 'this', feeding appetites that devour you, learning skills that become you, collecting wounds and hurts, and scars that define you. Each choice is irrevocable –narrowing the very scope of self, delineating you, carving away at the marble, chipping away all that *isn't* you, until at last the chiseled soul is laid bare in cold stone. Immoveable, unalterable, staring blankly impassively at Eternity, at the fate that's cut out for you, at the only fate possible for this hewn immutable rock that is ultimately you! Standing there among the disowned shards and dust of what might have been. Of *who* might have been!" Farleigh became aware of the looks of wonder on Shane and Katherine, and he closed his eyes, and nodded slowly. He opened them and pointed his long finger at the marble icon. "And here! Here stands Achilles, with his one flaw! One chip awry and he is shattered to dust! So stand we all!"

O'Neill and his wife were left quite speechless. And strangely disquieted. The three gazed at the ancient hero in the shifting shadows of the flickering fire. Smiling, the Brehon O'Hagan approached them a bit unsteadily with an expression of good-humoured ferosity.

"Tell me this, O'Neill. With all your grandeur here at Fuanagall, how comes it that you have no mechanical clock to tick away the hours for you between the late and early?" Shane looked up, and grinned.

"We have the Pleiades in the night sky to tell the hour. It was good enough for the Greeks!" Farleigh drew his fingers through his long white beard.

"Aye. The Pleiades. 'The Starry Herd', as *we* have it! When they wend their way down the heavens into the Sperrins, it is time to retire! What need have we for such foolishness as clocks? The belly will never fail to tell you when it's time to eat!" Katherine took the nod from Shane.

"Aye, well. Those celestial cattle will be down the mountains by this. The nights are short enough at Maytide, and Shane must be away at first light." The old poet drew a long face. He shook his head and sighed.

"So soon away! Always moving, as the restless spheres..."

"Aye, *rest* is what is wanted. The servants will take you aloft to your rest." Farleigh drained his cup, and leveled his gaze once again upon Achilles.

"Ah, the Greeks...the glory...the grandeur of the Age!" Katherine regarded him, his pale eyes shining in some ecstasy of contemplation.

"Will there ever come such times again, Farleigh O'Gneeve? For civilization and learning?"

"Ah? Who can say? A tale only time may tell. But this, this, I will tell you. The good that *is* is better than the best that was!"

CHAPTER 31

The grey glimmer of dawn gave way to a sullen morning, and few were stirring at Fuanagall when Shane slipped away. Katherine's farewell was warm but cheerful. This was in keeping with custom, for a tearful send-off was regarded as bad luck when departing for battle. They embraced at the slip, and then both turned their backs and parted. O'Neill stepped aboard a small lake galley, fully manned, and set out for his fort at Maghery on the southern shore. And if Katherine watched his crossing from the shadow of the wood, and murmured a wee prayer, what harm in that?

Shane's small convoy was awaiting him with his black stallion, Macanillar (son of the eagle), and they were soon galloping up the path along the western shore of Lough Neagh. They forded the Ballinderry at the tiny clachen of Coagh, and skirted Slieve Gallon by a trail through the braes. It was not long before they reached O'Neill's camp in the fastness of Glenconkeen. Shane's marshal, Dualta, reported that he had over 1,500 mobilized, and with his runners abroad, they could expect to pick up another 500 from contingents that would be joining their force along the route.

In the van were Shane's 'homeguard' troops of ClanFergus, the O'Quinns, O'Devlins, and O'Mallons, with the O'Donnellys and O'Hagans, each sept led by its chieftain or his son. After them came his lieges, the MacMahons, MacCaghwells, MacCanns, MacCrossans, MacRorys, O'Cannons, O'Corrs, O'Gormleys, O'Hamills, O'Kellys, O'Loans, O'Teaneys and O'Tomeltys, and the rest. Every clan bound to render up a muster of warriors when word came down. Crops were planted by this, and the harvest would be long in coming, so men were at the ready.

O'Neill and Dualta led the way, with O'Devlin the sword-bearer, and MacCaffrey the standard-bearer, on either side, the Red Hand pennant waving softly in the gentle May breeze. Shane's officers followed: Séamus, Éamonn, and Manus O'Donnelly, Cormac MacArdal, MacKenna, and the rest, as well as two of Shane's young sons, Shane óg, and Henry. At the blast of a 'hunter's horn', the long train of horse and infantry set forth, with all its pack-wagons behind, going by tracks and byways to an ancient drove road that followed the Ballinderry west, and then wended its way through the Sperrin Mountains to Omagh. From there, it would shadow the course of the River Strule up to Strabane.

The vast column of warriors snaked its way through sheepstrewn hillsides bristling with yellow gorse and purpled with heather, here and there coming upon a huddle of cabins, or a few straggling cottages. They marched past naked fields and dun bog, where channels of bogwater gleamed with inky brightness, and gulls screamed overhead. Through rough stoney glens they slogged, and wide barren crags. As the day wore on, fleeting sunlight shone through the grey clouds to catch the rills and streams on the lofty Sperrin slopes so that they sparkled like gems from afar. Indeed, hearts were light, for no great battle was expected. It was a show of force to put some order on Tirconnell, and to chastise its errant chieftain. Shane and his Marshal discussed what should be done once Black Hugh was settled, and they agreed that on the return east, they should put manners on Turlagh Lynnach at Dunnalong Castle on the Foyle.

O'Neill's two legions forded the River Foyle at Liffer where Shane's scouts were awaiting him, as planned, with word of O'Donnell's position. Black Hugh was not in residence at Castle Finn, but away up at his holdings above Letterkenny in Ardingary. The last rays of the sun were streaking the rosy clouds in the West, so the army made camp. It was thought best to allow their mounts rest and fodder, and get a fresh start in the morning. They had before them another thirteen-mile stretch from the Foyle to the Swilly estuary.

Thankfully the next morning was clear, and the Tirowenmen set off early, plodding the northwesterly path towards Letterkenny. Soon could be seen the Derryveagh Mountains far ahead, with the lofty summit of Sleeve Errigal jutting starkly against the sky to mark the way. After the fourth hour of hard march, the roaring river could at last be heard, and the men quickened their pace. Upon mounting the brow of a hill by and by, O'Neill saw the mighty River Swilly in flood, and there before him lay the great ford of Farsetmore. He called his army to halt on that far slope, where they would be hidden for those few hours to wait upon the tide.

By mid-afternoon the Swilly had ebbed sufficiently to be forded. By now it was clear that the crossing would be uncontested, as no activity was seen across the river. Shane's scouts reported that Black Hugh was at his small fort two miles beyond the ford with his eldest son Hugh MacHugh O'Donnell. He commanded a complement of little more than one hundred and thirty men, his personal guard. Black Hugh had his spies and scouts too, however, and he was informed of the coming assault. In desperation, he had sent runners off to three powerful septs of gallowglass MacSweenys, but as they were not wholly resigned to his chieftaincy, it was very much in question whether they would respond in time, or indeed at all. Hugh had made bitter enemies here during his long alliance with O'Neill, and he could expect to find little support among his own people.

From a dark cove at the edge of the wood, three of O'Donnell's scouts watched the crossing commence. Farsetmore was a much-storied rivercrossing, and its name recalled for these men tales of a battle in 1098, when Tirconnell defeated the invading Tirowenmen. Here also, in 1392, a standoff with Tirowen had won for Tirconnell an age of peace and independence. But now! Here was come the enemy once again, surging across the river with none to stop them!

Down the dark mucky sandbanks they came, with gulls screaming overhead. Hundreds of horsemen splashed forth through the streaming waters of the wide channel. Lances aloft, bedecked in glistening chainmail and iron 'skulls', they made a fearsome sight! Next came the infantry, four abreast, shouting fierce battle cries and cheering. O'Donnell's scouts kept careful tally as the long train of warriors continued to file over the brow of the hill. They staggered down the wet gushy banks under the frenzy of screeching and swooping sea-birds. After them came the camp followers, and when finally the long train of pack-wagons trundled across, one of the scouts mounted, and galloped off to report the numbers to O'Donnell. It was a mighty crossing to behold, and strangely, suddenly, it seemed to Shane as ultimate as the Rubicon, or the Styx itself. Already the waters were beginning to swell and foam as the salty sea rolled back in from the estuary.

With only eighty horsemen and fifty infantry at his command, Black Hugh could neither contest the crossing, nor hold his fort, but he was determined to resist. He sent his son Hugh Óg down with his four score of horsemen to skirmish with the enemy, a brave undertaking with two thousand arrayed against him. But the move would give his father time to draw his forces back to a moor secluded among the bogs and bracken called Magherennan, where they would be out of O'Neill's reach until reinforcements could arrive.

Black Hugh's fate was truly in the hands of his enemies, with O'Neill before, and none to save him but those bitter galloglass regiments of his brother's that he had so harshly vanquished in the past. No doubt St.Colmbkille, the patron of Tirconnell, was besieged with prayer by O'Donnell's crew as that perilous day wore on. Indeed, alongside Hugh's standard bearer was the MacRoarty, brandishing the sacred relic of the O'Donnells known as 'the Cathach' [KAH hagh] , the ornate gilt and bejeweled box that once contained Colmbkille's psalter. It was held to bestow mystical powers on the forces of Tirconnell, and its presence did a great deal to put heart into these woefully outnumbered men.

Hugh's meagre band engaged the vanguard of O'Neill's cavalry at Aghanunshin hill, where he fought bitterly to cover his father's retreat. But no sooner had he got word that Black Hugh's men had safely withdrawn to the scrubland, than he disengaged his men, and slipped off to join them. Hugh's cousin Neil O'Donnell had fallen, as had O'Donlevy, the son of his chief physician, and most tragically for morale, the MacRoarty was slain, and the precious Cathach had fallen into the hands of the enemy! The men were consoled with a reminder that the ancient reliquary carried a curse for any who unrightfully held it.

O'Neill called his men back to camp, where already the fires were burning, and the tents and pavilions were rising on the sward near the river. O'Donnell, he supposed, was likely brooding and licking his sores. Tomorrow would be time enough to settle him. Shane had lost men as well. The noble son of the MacMahon of Monaghan was mourned around the fires, as was the O'Devlin's son, and other less illustrious horsemen. The camp was bustling, with two thousand men from so many parts of Ulster. It is little wonder they took no notice of two strangers in their midst. Who would know a Tirconnell man among the lads of Tirowen?

"What say you? Damnation! Slow you down, and draw a breath for yourself! Now. Where are they pitched?" The shorter of the two, a thick-set fellow with a tousled glib of black hair hanging over his eyes, swallowed hard and replied.

"They are encamped in the meadow of Cloonarra beside the River. More nor eighteen hundred of them!" The other shook his head.

"*Two thousand*, there are. And about forty besides. I tallied them at the ford. Aye, it's the meadow just below Aghanunshin Hill. We moved all through the camp, from fire to fire. I was in holy terror of comin' up agin renegades from our own crowd. There's some Gallaghers have gone over to them. There was food goin', but we never ett, for if we once broke bread with them we couldn't hardly betray-"

"Give over your yammering! I don't need a report on the state of your belly! I'll slit it open and fill it for you!" Black Hugh turned to the other scout. "What of his sentries?"

"We only counted twelve, but near as I reckon they're mostly on the north and east side of the hill. If you come round the riverside of Aghanunshin, he's mostly unguarded. And the slope would be in your favour. Their weapons are stacked beside the pack-wagons! Beggin' your pardon, Hugh O'Donnell, but they've captured the holy Cathach!" He blessed himself swiftly.

"Aye, we know that. The MacRoarty is slain."

"God be with his soul. Those renegade Gallaghers told O'Neill's men of the curse of Colmbkille that comes with the relic upon any but the rightful holder, and the talk round the fires is uneasy. They reckon Shane O'Neill is damned doubly to Hell, betwixt the holy Primate and St. Colmbkille, and there's a fair bit of grumbling!"

"So he is. Twice blasted. The Devil's own demon!"

"We got to the middle of the camp, the great fire before Shane O'Neill's tent. There's a *massive* torch blazing away -thicker nor a man's body! About sixty-"

"I know his bloody torch!" O'Donnell raised his fist to his mouth, the knuckles white, and his jaw taut. "Christ! Where are these mad MacSweenys!"

"It's what I *heard* there, you need to know, my Leige. About sixty Galloglass were milling about. When O'Neill retired for the night, their captain come out of his tent and gave them word that you had less than two hundred. And that you'd moved back up here intil the bogs, and they all reckoned you'd be gone in the morning! So they broke out barrels of whiskeybaugh, and they were tearing intil it! There was more nor a few in a quare state when we left!" Black Hugh's eyes flickered with sudden hope.

"He thinks we're on the run from him!"

"So they say, aye. Your man made a wager you'd scarper, and no one took it up. They said there'd be no battle in the morning, but only hunting us into the mountains. And they fell to roistering -all through the camp! Even his *sentries* were huddled around methers, and quaffing like the rest!"

"We could *do* it! But surprise would be *all*. If these MacSweeney regiments arrive in time! Is there *still* no sign?" His aide, a burly captain with a long ginger beard, shook his head.

"They've not come as yet. No fear, but! They've got to be here right soon. Macartan got their pledge, but they had yet to muster. Three septs of them. Morrough's axes, MacSweeny Fanad, and Mulmurry's clans." Black Hugh's dark eyes gleamed in the firelight.

"That should make us nearly five hundred strong. I swear we could do it! We've about four hours of darkness left. If they come before dawn we'll rush O'Neill's camp. The tide will be raging by then, and they with their backs to it! We'll run their horses off, and sweep them before us. Go on then! Fill your bellies and put word through the camp. And any hoor that swallows spirits this night will taste my sword!"

A shrill death-screach, like the scream of a hare in a snare, broke the stillness of the grey morning twilight. A roar of frenzied battle-cries followed, and a thunder of hooves swept through the wakening camp as startled, groggy men rose and scrambled to their defense. Tents were trampled over, and heads cracked and lopped as hundreds of warriors, three septs of MacSweeny's gallowglass, splattered their way through the encampment swinging their long battleaxes. O'Donnell's infantry too, ran through with flaming brands, firing the tents, and wagons, heavily laden munitions wagons that soon exploded. Billowing smoke added to the murk of the misty dawn, and shadowy figures were running in all directions. Of those on foot, it was scarcely possible to discern your own from the enemy. Now could be heard the sound of harquebus fire, the clash of steel, and spears and arrows whirring blindly through the smoke.

Shane emerged from his pavilion with a look of grim determination. With his personal guard, a phalanx of his own gallowglass warriors, he charged into the thick of it, hoping to rally his men around him. But O'Donnell's yelping cavalry were everywhere by

SHANE O'NEILL

this. Having picked off Shane's sentries, they had managed to descend upon the camp before arousing the alarum. Weapons had been stacked, and were now inaccessible; Tirowenmen were being slaughtered before they could arm themselves. Men quaking, heads bloodied, stumbled through the billowing smoke, trying to outrun the onslaught. Some took cover behind overturned wagons, but it availed them little, for these bands of axe-wielding horsemen moved like a sickle of death slaying all before.

The last shadows of night were giving way to a drear misty morning, and through the billowing shades Shane thrashed his way forward, clashing swords with the charging warriors. At the sound of a heavy thudding gallop, he turned to see a horseman charging, nearly upon him! With his sword out before him, he rushed madly into the oncoming stallion so that it reeled and threw its rider to the ground. Before the burly gallowglass could find his feet, Shane plunged his sword through the man's beard into his neck, and then commandeered his battleaxe. He thrust its long shaft upright into the damp ground, where it stood the height of a man, then, his hands free of it, he leapt up and mounted the red spattered white steed.

As Shane retrieved the axe, a scatter of his own kerne came running past, fleeing the Tirconnell horde. Shane gave out a savage roar. "Turn on your heels, and stand the ground, ye bloodless cowards! Stand to, ye hoors ye!" With the shaft of the axe, he tripped up one who was rushing past. He pointed his blade down at the timorous man. "Get up! Or have you the spine to stand? *Up*, worm!" The raggedy kerne looked up with terror in his eyes.

"It's only a slaughter! The horses are driven off! They have our arms! It's holy slaughter!" An arrow pierced the ground, inches from him, and as Shane reeled his horse to meet the enemy, the kerne scrambled off toward the river. Shane raised his axe, and swinging it wildly, he charged into an oncoming line of O'Donnell's archers, taking down several in short order. A light drizzle of chill rain had set in on the brisk morning wind, and it was tamping the smoke so that he could see over it now. He made a bloody path through the enemy's lines, until an arrow pierced the neck of his steed, and down it crashed with an anguished whinnying groan.

Following the sound of fierce fighting, Shane made his way on foot to the core of the clash, a bold stand being made by his men under Dualta O'Donnelly, and he fell in with them. They were fighting bravely, but MacSweeney Fanad's host was pouring down the side of Aghanunshin hill upon them, with the advantage of the slope. None of the Tirowenmen could fathom what was happening. It seemed that half of Tirconnell had appeared out of nowhere. In truth, they were beset by a force of little more than five hundred, a mere quarter of their number, but they knew nothing of that. The fighting seemed to go on for ages, but in truth it was still early morn, with O'Neill's ranks ever and always being pushed back toward the river. When Shane's Marshal, Dualta O'Donnelly, was slain, the men seemed to lose heart. Then another exploding wagon brought smoke in acrid clouds rolling into the whelter of combat, and they turned and fled toward the banks of Farsetmore, pursued by the thundering horsemen of Fanad.

Shane, coughing and spluttering, ran blindly through the vaporous fog, with ghostly shapes of men and horses appearing and fading like phantoms. At length an insistent breeze from off the river brought him clear of it. His throat burned, and his eyes were streaming and stinging from smoke. He found himself staggering through bracken and trees, and even over the din of battle, he could hear that the Swilly was in raging flood. The roar of the river melded with the shrill cries of men, and gulls, and curlews. The crack of harquebus fire, the rumble of hooves, and those distant screams all rang in his ears, but still he could hear someone calling his name.

"Hoigh! O'Neill! The men said you were kilt!" It was his captain, Cormac MacArdal, hallooing him through the brake of thorns and bracken along the riverbank. "By Christ, I tell you we're destroyed! Come up, til you see!" He was waving him over. Shane's wiped his burning eyes with the back of his wrist, for his hands were begrimed and bloody. He sheathed his sword, and tottered heavily up the path. MacArdal turned to a pair of men beside him. "Well, *bring* them, so. And whatever horses can be found!" He greeted Shane with a fierce grip of the hand, and spoke low. "Christ, the Divil is rampaging this

SHANE O'NEILL

day! The gates of Hell are torn asunder! There's no crossing!" He led him through to the clearing. "Here with you, man. Set your eyes on *that!*"

Shane stepped up onto a small rocky precipice, and squinted to take in the scope of the cataclysm. In the vast tragic scene, he could discern the thrashing and flailing arms in the churning waters, and the hundreds of corpses being bourne on the tide out into Lough Swilly. His gorge rose in his throat at this ghastly sight, and he swallowed hard and groaned. He had to lower his gaze, and he stared blankly now at the dark waters below, the swirling rime of froth and jetsom gathered by the flood along the bank, and the dark swaying tangles clinging to the white rocks. He stood transfixed, still and silent, his breath heaving, and his clenched fists trembling at his side. Cormac shook his head, coughed up and spat. He sniffed loudly.

"They were...they all...the waters were already rising, and they tried to ford it. But the sea flows in fast and deep here. The first few score of them made it across, but...All these hundreds of men! Christ, there must be six, seven hundred, drowned! Swept out to sea. Lord God, have mercy! The torrent has taken them all. O'Donnell drove them down the banks, men well known to him, who once fought at his side..." He crossed himself. His voice quavered. "My Conor and Donagh died in the field; may God take their blesséd souls to his bosom! And O'Hagan's youngest, I saw him go down. But these poor lot! And the O'Quinns, and O'Devlin's boys -" Shane turned sharply to him, with a sudden look of terror.

"But my-"

"Your lads are safe, O'Neill. Henry and Shane Óg, I sent them off with McKenna. But there will be weeping at every hearth from Lough Neagh to Lough Swilly. All Perished! No more nor *fifty* made it across the Farset here. All swallowed up in the great waters!" Shane stood silent, the haggard ghost of ruin in his eyes. His spirit moaned as he beheld the grim spectacle before him. Again he heard his name voiced as from afar, voiced with concern. As MacArdal approached warily, Shane held his listless gaze on the surging river, and spoke in a rattling voice, barely above a whisper.

SHANE O'NEILL

"A black curse on this day. It's the Red Sea! Swallowed in the flood like the Pharaoh's armies!" Cormac went to pat him on the back, but Shane turned abruptly and grabbed him by the shoulders. He shook him violently, raging with tears. "Where were my *sentries*? Where? Where was my watch? Where were my *captains*?" He pushed him away, and seized his own head in his hands as if it would explode, roaring still. "God curse them all, then, for cowards and rogues! Let the fish feast on their rotten bones! We could have held the camp!" He was weeping now. He turned away and slunk to the ground, covering his face in his hands. MacArdal winced, and sighed heavily.

"Shane! Shane!" He raised his voice sharply. "O'Neill! Those renegade Gallaghers say we can cross a few miles upstream at Ahantarshy, or beyond at Scarriffhollis. I've been sending men up that way. A narrow crossing, only. We might gather across the river, and see what is to be done. O'Neill! Up with you, now! We've a few miles hard march. Are you right?" He took him by the oxter, and hoisted him to his feet. "Now! Let you stand. The way of a *king*."

"A king!" Shane laughed mirthlessly. "Aye a king! Lord of the Dead! Mighty commander of the dead! Hah? Oh, that *they* should be dead, and I treading the earth! Who will forgive me for *that*? Hah? We'll skulk off through the fern, so. Aye, then, Farleigh said it, and so it has. The tide has turned!"

It was early evening when the visitors found the encampment, a sombre grey evening of thin drifting rain. Following a hazy trail of blue smoke that wafted low over the treetops, Captain MacKenna led the small party of illustrious callers into a small glade in the Glenconkeen wood. The Chief Brehon O'Hagan had come to the camp searching for O'Neill, with the chieftain's secretary Neil MacKeever, his wife, Lady Katherine, and a small retinue of attendants. An untidy makeshift camp it was, mostly deserted, bestrewn with debris and the remains of wild game and fowl. Here and there a lean-to was pitched with smoke curling up into the misty rain. They came to a halt under the doubtful shelter of a broad dripping beech. MacKenna saw a bearded man stepping through the smoke, and called out to him.

"Where is the O'Neill? You there, hoigh!" As the man came forward he could see that it was Captain Cormac MacArdal.

"Ah, MacKenna! I hope to jaysus you've returned with supplies. And with good report! He near throttled the last bearer of bad news!"

"Supplies we've plenty. But as for news, I've nothing, Cormac, only more bad tidings. Is he no better?"

"Divil a bit. Ach, well, you've brought Lady Katherine; maybe that will put some heart in him. I thought you were off to Maghera."

"I'm just returned. I found these'ens at the ford two miles back looking for the camp." Katherine stepped her charger forward. Although the day was only seasonably cool, she was wrapped in frieze mantle, heavy with rain.

"We've journeyed from Inishdowell, Cormac. He's had my wits astray, waiting for word of him! The boys were back days ago. Will he see me?"

"Och, why would he not, Lady O'Neill? You'd put a glint in a blind man's eye, so you would. Allow me, m'Lady." He helped her to dismount, and nodded to the others. "O'Hagan. MacKeever. Begod ye are cuttin' it rough this weather. I suppose we're all close to the wind in these black times." O'Hagan nodded only. Katherine retrieved a small cloth bundle from the pannier of her mount, and turned to him once again. Some long red strands of hair flew across her face in the wind. Pushing them back, she held a hand to her head, she looked seriously at him, her eyes fretful.

"What way *is* he?" Cormac sighed, and then spoke plainly.

"He's as cross as a bag of weasels! Shane was never a tyrant before this. You'd wonder is he determined to become the monster they say he is. After all that drowned and died at Farsetmore, three of his sentries survived -and he hanged them! His Marshal, Dualta and two of his brothers were slain. He's lost his Donnellys, and he's heart-scalded. Most of his leigemen have broken ranks and scarpered,

SHANE O'NEILL

O'Corr, O'Gormley, O'More of the Fews. McMahon and MacCarron cleared off. And MacGuinness was gone this morning. He's raging something savage!" Katherine nodded as she listened, then shook her head slowly with resignation.

"I shouldn't wonder at that, for he's lost *all*! Terror and shame and anger are coursing each other through his soul. Where is he?"

"You'll get little sense out of him. You know, yourself, when the wine is in, the wits are out! He's beyond in that rushy shieling." MacArdal turned, and led them over to the primitive sod-walled shelter. It was three sided, facing upon an open fire. From within could be heard the strains of a harp. He motioned for them to wait, and stepping round the fire, he stooped to enter. They heard him calling sharply, "O'Neill!" There followed an indistinguishable but heated exchange, and then Shane's voice bellowed.

"Go on away to hell out of this! The lot of ye! Och, no, not yourself, man. Stay you, and give us that sad air again. These good people are here for my wake!" With that, two greasy-haired women stepped out round the fire, followed by three equally scruffy younger men, all of them dissolute in appearance. One of the women was clearly naked under her mantle, and she made bold eyes at Lady Katherine as she passed. Behind them stood Cormac, motioning them into the shadowy lair.

Disheveled, and woozy drunk, Shane was seated on the ground, his legs crossed under him like a turk. His tunic was stained and wrinkled, as were the threadbare grey hodden breeches he wore. He was bare-shinned, with brogans of rawhide on his feet. Staring sullenly into the fire, his unraked black hair swept back from his face, he appeared ruddy in the flickering light. It was an anguished countenance from which all hope had fled. His deeply sunken eyes were wild, swimming in inward agony. His broad shoulders were hunched. He was slumped forward, his arms locked before him, stingily hoarding his misery, as he murmured quietly in a broken voice. Katherine called to him.

"Shane!" At the sound of her voice he shuddered, and cocked his head to one side, gazing up at her vacantly. "Shane! Shane, my love, how are you faring?" After a long moment, he answered with a distant smile.

"Bad for my friend, good for my foe."

"You've no foes here, Shane O'Neill. Only friends." He looked at her now with sudden clarity and recognition. "You've heard then? The sea has swallowed up my army!" He turned to his harper. "Make a song out of *that*! *Days*, it is. It must be seven tides and more have washed their broken bodies over the piercing rocks by this! Hah?" He started to croon a low keen. "Och ochón ó! Och úllagán ó!" He thumped soundly on a mantle beside him that was spread over a couch of heather boughs. "Sit in, sit in!" MacKenna cleared off the top of a barrel for Katherine, and they all managed to seat themselves. Shane pushed a jug over to his secretary. "I'd say there's a gill of brandywine there. Take out your quill, Neil MacKeever, til we fire off a letter to God! I've a fair bit to say." Katherine untied her cloth parcel, and laid it out on the board before him.

"Eat something for yourself, Shane. Fine cheese, and fresh bread."

"Och, feasting or fasting, 'tis all the one now." He nodded, and handed a bottle to the Brehon, with a piercing look. "I see you've more black news for me. Well, *out* with it, O'Hagan! Hah? What did you hear from Fleming up in the Pale?" Owen cleared his throat.

"There'll be no troops from Spain this while. Or France. Those rumours were false. The Pope did not excommunicate Elizabeth."

"As yet!" Katherine added quickly.

"Oh ho! Well, long life to the poxy aul bastard! 'Tis only Catholics the like of *myself* he will see damned! Shane raised his cup. "Viva il bloody papa!" What else have ye got, ye hoor? Say it out! Some more wet kindling for my fire! They're all *gone*, Kat! Deserted me." He looked to O'Hagan again.

"Art MacBaron, the bastard's son has been taking preys. He is biding with Captain Pierce in Carrickfergus. Made off with a thousand head of steers in a raid yesterday.

"The worm is arisen from his mire. *There's* one who thinks me dead, or he would ne'er show his face! And the South! What of the South?"

SHANE O'NEILL

"There's none will move without a fleet from the Continent. Most of them have taken the field with Sidney. He's a cunning bastard. He has relaxed the penal measures in the Pale, promised the Catholics there will be no confiscations -so they've all fallen into ranks."

"Like sheep to shambles!" MacKenna added sorrowfully. O'Hagan sighed.

"Nevermind a *rising*- there are none in the South will so much as rise their *voice* now!"

"Wise men, very prudent," Shane replied, "tis the silent pigs that eat the meal!" Katherine tisked.

"Would you not be as well to eat the meal *yourself*!" She handed to him bread with cheese. "Go on, now, and get that inside you." She heaved a sigh. "They are sleekit cowards, the lot of them! When Shane O'Neill is put out of the way there will be confiscations aplenty!" After a slight hesitation, he ate voraciously, looking sternly to O'Hagan as he did so, prompting him to speak further.

"But, no, Shane, you'll get no help from the Irish of the Pale." O'Neill swigged his wine, and wiped his mouth on his sleeve.

"Aye! Irishmen with English tongues. 'White blackbirds' Farleigh calls them! Well, someone must tell them that they've a cuckoo in the nest! And they'll soon find themselves banished to the four winds! These English want to kill us all. They want our land, and ourselves under it!" Shane turned to his harper. "Give us a bloody dirge for Ireland, boy...for I think she's as dead as Shane O'Neill!" He set in keening once again. "Och óchón ó..." Katherine spoke tartly.

"There's always hope this side of the grave. Give over, now." The harper left off his playing. "Don't unman yourself, Shane O'Neill, for I can't bear to look on it. Now is the time for you to show your mettle. *Any* cock can crow atop the midden! An O'Neill must rise from the mightiest blow of the mightiest foe!"

"Ah, no, woman. *This* was no mighty foe. They tell me he had but a quarter of my numbers. Hundreds slain in the field, seven hundred of my men drowned! Maybe twelve hundred dead. Do you not see? It's all come to naught, and I am toppled. I have fallen."

"Even a four-footed beast will stumble. But he will rise back *up*!"

SHANE O'NEILL

"It is hard to rise with the weight of a slaughter hard upon your shoulders. On *me* it is! All of it. Every one of those deaths. I am the O'Neill. My *will* should have prevailed!" Katherine looked to the others with concern, then she replied roundly.

"Your *will*? Sure, that's daft. You can hoist the sails, my love, but you cannot raise the wind! We have but a half-share in our fate."

"And who will rally to my banner now? My truest captains are slain, Dualta and his brothers. Only Éamon remains of the Donnellys. My own foster brothers. I swam the river in my *pelt*, Kat! They hold me a coward. Slithering away from a slaughter. What mother in Ulster now will not hate me for that I'm not dead?"

"Are the *other* survivors cowards then? Eight hundred cowards? A mystical battle this, when only the cowards are left standing? Turn your mind from this, Shane O'Neill. And when you have resolved to rise and fight, then may you have my counsel!" This challenge seemed to get a rise out of Shane. MacKeever spoke softly.

"Lady Katherine is right. You're alive, O'Neill. It were best to put this from you now. It's a plan you should be making. Time enough for a wake when you're dead." Shane locked eyes with Katherine now, a piercing stare that faded and blurred with woozy fatigue. Suddenly he spat into the fire.

"Hah! I'll step out now til I make my water." Shane rose, and stepped unsteadily out round the fire. Looks were exchanged, but no one spoke. Katherine had her head cocked, listening. The rain had let up, no longer rustling in the thatch above. She listened until she could hear him purging himself outside, just as she had expected. Kat blessed herself quickly, and whispered.

"Thanks be to God! Maybe we'll get sense out of him yet. We can't let him bide here!" The others nodded, and partook of the cheese and bread until Shane emerged again from under the low lintel. His step was steadier, but his speech was rough. He settled himself, and took up a jug of wine.

"And where is this *God* vanished to? Hah? I was never meant to recover from that curse o' God poison! It's Lucifer's ruling the heavens and I've had nothing but thunderbolts ever since! Now I've the curse

SHANE O'NEILL

of Holy Columbkille down upon me." Shane drank greedily from a jug, and Katherine watched him with glistening eyes. She huffed loudly.

"Och, divil mend you, Shane O'Neill! Give *over* with that now, my love. And don't be drowning your wits! It's a *plan* we need to-"

"Oh, I've a plan! You think I've no plan?"

"There's hard choices in it, Shane, but I have some-"

"Shhhhhh! Hisht!" He put an unsteady finger to his lips, and made a loud show of 'whispering.' "Here's O'Neill's plan. I'll throw a halter 'round my neck, and present myself to the Lord Deputy. I'll join all the wise men round his banner. Beg him for mercy!"

"Don't greet the devil til he greets you! There may be a way, Shane O'Neill. Sidney is in no shape to resume his war. And I've not told you all. There is *more* to impart. Listen to me. Have you sense enough to listen?"

"I hear your sweet voice, my love!" His eyes were alert now for the first time, if there was still the taste of a smirk on his lips."The MacDonnells are back in Ballycastle. They've resettled it while you were off in Tirconnell. They've-"

"Ah *there's* good news, girl! Are they marching this way? Any more glad tidings? What about the Day of the Mountain? Is Doomsday come?" Katherine laughed a bit, in spite of herself.

"Well, your wits have not gone wandering altogether. They've not strayed *too* far, anyrate. Listen to me, Shane O'Neill. Put down your cup, and sup sense! There is news from Holyrood! Mary Stuart has been captured. The son she bore- James the Sixth of Scotland. The Lairds want her to abdicate the throne in favour of the infant."

"James the Sixth! A mewling little shite-arsed king, with dirty nappies and a crown!"

"List you now, Shane. Your brother is returned to us from Argyll. Father Hugh has brought a *reply* from him. Archebald sent word to Elizabeth that if she doesn't recognize wee Prince James as heir to the English throne, he will combine with you, and send troops and monies for a rising here. He told Hugh she is bound to *refuse*. She'll never accept his terms, he says, and he is sworn to be in Ireland shortly to help Shane O'Neill."

SHANE O'NEILL

"Christ, woman! What's this you're telling me?"

"Argyll and the MacDonnells will combine with you for a rising. He wants us to-"

"Combine with *what*? I have nothing! The fish are eating my army. Tell her, MacArdal!" Cormac shook his head sadly.

"We've little more nor three hundred. Mostly ClanFergus. What's left of it."

"They'll not know what you have. Archibald says he will go to Cushendun on the Antrim coast in two week's time. And you must meet him there. Alastair MacDonnell has agreed to treat with you, and Argyle has ordered him to fight beside you. I will go too. As a surety. You must free Sorley, and bring him with us. You may bring but fifty soldiers –so your *real* numbers will be unknown to them. What can you *give* them?"

"We killed seven hundred of their kin. What sort of promises will stop them slaughtering us?"

"Alistair is pledged for your safety. His word is good. This is my mother's brother. I believe him. And Sorley believes him. What can you give them?"

"I'll give them all the lands of Clandeboy. And the lands of the O'Kane. They can drive the McQuillens out of the Roe; they ran off on me too. And cattle. All the geld kine of Tirowen."

"And some soft words, and a pledge." O'Hagan looked to Katherine.

"Those are all such things as they covet. And the offer is *good*. These are my people, and they'll keep their word. They're bitter after Glenshesk, but their hatred of the English is abiding, and more compelling far than mere spite. Now that you have secured the help of Argyll, some of the Irish will surely come back in. Will they not?" Kat saw that Shane's gaze had cleared somewhat, and was glad of it. She looked to the others for support, and MacKenna obliged.

"Aye, Lady Katherine knows her people. If the Scots are anything, it's hard-nosed. Cunning and shrewd they are, saving your presence, M'Lady." Neil MacKeever agreed.

"True enough! If they stand to profit, they'll o'erlook any

SHANE O'NEILL

impediment. As to *our* lot, whatever of their qualms about *you*, they've not been won over to *Sidney*. If your star is rising again, they'll fear to be on the wrong side of you. And they know *well* what the English are at!" Shane shook his head.

"They don't. Lord Leicester told me that they plan to sever Tirowen into three shires, and to settle all our lands with English Protestants-even the great lough will be English. He tells of a map whereon is written a new name for Lough Neagh. It is called Lake Sidney!" Cormac spat into the fire.

"Lake Sidney! The low scoundrel!" Shane looked to O'Hagan.

"True for you, O'Neill. Our lot want to believe Sidney, and have *done* with it. They've no idea. Young Sir Robert Fleming confided to me that Sidney warned his Parliament of the Pale that the mere Irish are the common enemy of the Palesmen as much as of the English. 'A barbarous people,' he said, 'odious to God and man, that would lap *your* blood as greedily as ours!" Shane's eyes narrowed in a moment of cold reflection, and then he nodded.

"These chieftains are weary of war. They imagine that they can buy peace. 'Give them Shane O'Neill, and things will be as before.' But they are fools. They will be swept from the land!" Katherine spoke up, calm and clear.

"Shane, you must come back with me. We will be home before darkness settles if we set out now. Home to your children. Will you ride with us? Your sons are waiting on you there, Henry and Shane Óg. They hold you no coward. They say you fought bravely to the last. Will you come?" This news braced him all the more, so that he began to pluck up a kind of spirit.

"I will, aye. Maybe they've not gotten the best of me yet! *Sidney* has not bested me, anyrate. I made ruin of his plan! For every hurt the English have inflicted upon me, I have inflicted thrice over upon them!" And O'Donnell will regret that ever I stepped alive out of that slaughter!" There were smiles all round, and MacArdal clapped his hands together, and rubbed them eagerly.

"Good on you, Shane O'Neill. Stoutly said! That's the man we know!"

SHANE O'NEILL

"Aye, we'll face them square, and brave it out, hah? Farleigh is right! Like a stag of the wood, I must run always *into* the wind!" He got to his feet. "Sidney wants to make a holding of my lands. And whether God wills or no -it will be difficult while I'm alive. -Not without parting the souls from me and my bravest! We'll ride east now. To the island, so." He turned to his harper. "Come you. Strike us up something with life in it! "Hup! Ho!" The fellow struck up a lively jig then, as the others rose and stepped out into the brightening air. Shane strode across the field with a hearty gait very much akin to his usual swagger, and the bright flicker of hope in his eyes.

It was only the 29th of May, but it felt like a day in high summer, and, were it not for the fresh breeze off the Irish Sea, Myler Magrath would have accounted it 'sweltering.' The sky was patched with torn clouds, but they gave no appearance of impending rain. Indeed, the vagaries of the weather had been thoroughly assessed and debated by the bishop and his cousin, Con Maguire, by the time they reached the lofty drumtowers of the West Gate.

The pair of Gaelic nobles expected no delay, as their appearance was that of two prosperous gentlemen, with no indication of rank or clergy about them. But Myler considered now the posibility, and indeed the irony, of being captured as the 'feigned bishop of Down', the 'Pope's agent', on *this* of all days! His square white collar was open, in deference to the sultry weather, and lay limply across his dark velvet tunic. A single drop of sweat rolled down his forehead. After a farmer's wagon trundled noisily ahead under the portcullis, the two men rode slowly forward. Bishop Magrath effected an air of impatient forbearance, and was relieved to be waved on through by the bored guards, into the bustling town of Drogheda.

There was no talk between them now, only a few deep sighs from the bishop, as they clopped along past the busy Thursday stalls, making their way through the afternoon crowds in West Street. Myler was resolved to go through with this, and further talk would only unsettle him. As they approached the corner of Ship Street, they were pleased to see St. George's flag flapping in the breeze, confirming the presence of the Lord Deputy. Unlike the rows of thatched houses and shops thereabout, the Tholsel stood three stories high, with timber cladding, and a slate roof. Most civic business was conducted there. Myler reflected that this solemn business today could never be undone. But what odds that, when there was no alternative? His companion's sharp voice summoned him from his reverie.

"Rein up, Cousin! Halt here til we see." There were four horses tethered to the rail, each of a different hue, white, fiery bay, black, and pale." Myler gave a wry laugh.

"Begod, the riders of the Apocalypse are awaiting us! I might be struck down yet! Did you not say, Con, that Sidney was up to meet with Captain Pierce today?"

"I did, aye. Meeting him half way from Carrickfergus. But look you *there*. He's brought *friends*." As a wagon turned the corner, Myler could see a tall highlander standing about in full MacDonnell tartan, and a shirtless gillie tending his garron with a bag of oats. "It seems Pierce has a redshank escort! It's *just* as you said!" Myler nodded, brows arched, knowingly.

"So it is! And you may be sure that one of those mounts belongs to Alastair MacDonnell, who is within, striking a bargain for the betrayal of Shane O'Neill."

"A bargain? But Sidney has already set the price. A thousand marks! There are bills posted in Dublin. I've seen them."

"They'll get more nor that. A title to the Glens, I've no doubt."

"Will you warn O'Neill?"

"A bootless task *that* would be. O'Neill will not *heed* my warnings. I remonstrated with him, forewarned him of every twist and turn to come. Mary's pity! I thought surely Kildare would dissuade him from this madness! Shane paid a secret visit to him last week at Kilkea in Kildare. But FitzGerald gave him no such counsel, only more dreams of French fleets that will never sail. They are hopelessly deceived. The

SHANE O'NEILL

Pope cares nothing for this island! Shane O'Neill is determined to go to the Scots, and he is marching headlong into a trap. Bloodthirsty savages, who will have their revenge. O'Neill, O'Hagan, Kildare, not a tither of sense between them! Well, so. If they have all taken leave of their wits, I must take leave of *them*. And I can wait no longer! If I turn myself in to the Lord Deputy *after* Shane is dead it will be counted false, a desperate ploy to save myself. When he falls, *none* will stand, I tell you. There will be reprisals against *all* his followers."

"Could you not go to Rome? You've been summoned there, and you would be safe."

"I cannot face the tribunal in Rome! After the forged letter -a forged letter to *the Pope himself*, I'll surely lose my see. And I may be defrocked!" Con Maguire at last ventured his doleful warning, quietly, wistfully.

"Better your frock than your *immortal soul*." Myler laughed with sudden brightness.

"My soul? Nothing so dire! I would say, in spite of the four gospels were they laid on my palm, that Rome is every bit as corrupt as the Royal Court and their 'Reformed Church. Oh, I have seen inside that 'whited sepulchre' such vile putrefaction and rot! Rome has betrayed us in appointing Primate Creagh. And I will not be a martyr to their treachery."

"*I'll* not instruct you, Myler Magrath. No fear of that!"

"Who is to say? Perhaps I might do some good for our lot by ministering among the heretics. I've oftimes envied these 'reformed' Lord Bishops, with their phantom pastorates, and lavish temporalities. I may yet even take to me a wife!"

"You'd not be the first! But O'Neill. What will-"

"O'Neill begrudged me my elevation. He appropriated half my wage to indulge his pampered godling of a brother, and confiscated the other half for his wars. I owe him sweet divil-all! Even now, he offered me nothing when-" From the great doors of the Tholsel there suddenly emerged Captain Pierce, bulky and brown-bearded, with another officer and a Scots laird. Magrath dismounted in great haste. "Get you down, Con. I mustn't be seen here!" Maguire alighted swiftly from his horse.

"What harm if he should see you deserting his enemy?"

"Divil a bit. But I'd not have Alastair know that I've seen *him*! He would surely suppose that I'll warn Shane of his pact with Sidney." They stood in behind their horses, waiting for the Scots to mount up. "I was wrong! It isn't *Alastair* that's in it! I don't recognize the *tall one*, but the other is Alastair's cousin, the one they call Gillaspick. A sour surly knave he is, too! Ah! A bag of silver, no doubt!" The Scot was packing away a heavy sack into the pannier of his steed. Just then Lord Sidney appeared, and beckoned Captain Pierce back inside. When the doors shut behind him, Gilaspick and his captain delved in the pannier to examine their new-gotten stash, while the English officer laboured not to observe them.

Lord Harry Sidney spoke over his shoulder as he hastened to seat himself behind the massive desk. "Captain Pierce, I must bid you tarry for one moment more, while I write this brief billet to Alastair MacDonnell. More promises, of course. But this time in writing, a thing I have hitherto refused him. It may prove necessary to overcome his dainty highland scruples." Pierce stood patiently before the desk, watching the Deputy's quill flutter over the page by the flickering light. It was only a gouty stub of sallow candle that burned and spluttered on desk before him. "The Lordship...of...Antrim." He blew on the parchment, and looked up. "It would be worth a king's ransom to be *at last* rid of O'Neill. This campaign, for all its rigours, has brought me only the most bitter opprobrium at Court. Even a wayward spark in the forge at Derry is laid to my dereliction!"

"Indeed, your Lordship. To be Viceroy of this benighted isle!" Pierce shook his head and sighed. "A post honoured by all, but envied by none!"

"I fear it shall be my undoing. Vexing and wearisome and thankless! On Sunday I passed a gallstone the size of a nutmeg! This infuriating, ill-starred campaign! The *one* victory of note belongs to O'Donnell. But my vindication is at hand! O'Neill has baited the very trap that will ensnare him. The savage Scots will 'complish our ends, and shield the crown from all reproach!" Sidney carefully folded the letter. He snuffed the guttering candle, and dripped wax upon it to affix his seal. Pierce laughed gruffly.

"Let the bears and bandogs *to* it, what! They say O'Neill's wits are in disarray. He is certainly mad to venture among the Hebridians."

"Mad? He leaps into flames to allay a chill. Our part is but to stoke the fire. This redshank of yours, Gillaspick, is a smouldering ember! Red hot to avenge Glenshesk! We shall send him forthwith to Cushendun to warm this prickly welcome for O'Neill!"

"And he'll not be alone. I did as you bade me, my Lord. I sent a rogue name of Douglas up to Kintyre to fetch over a galley of wrathful Scots, those who burn to requite their own losses at Glenshesk. They will stand by Gillaspick. But I am concerned, your Lordship, for he cautions me that O'Neill will be under Alastair MacDonnell's solemn protection." Sidney rose noisily to his feet, and handed the note to Pierce.

"And *that* is why he shall carry this letter to Alastair, wherein I promise title to his lands in Antrim, and certain peerage. I've told him the *true* state of O'Neill's fortunes. I bid you withold this letter unless it prove needful. But vouchsafe *any* promise to draw him on. When O'Neill's head adorns my battlements these Scots will be easily expelled."

"I expect Alistair MacDonnell will do our bidding in this. He will be mindful that I have a hostage of his son at Carrickfergus. Let us pray for a good end to this business, that Lord Smith's English colony might soon be planted in Ulster. There is naught can be done without the fall of O'Neill!"

"Oh, he will fall! And when he falls, he will fall like Lucifer, never to rise! Godspeed!"

SHANE O'NEILL

Captain Pierce appeared again, and held a brief animated conferral with Gillaspick. Then Myler and Maguire watched the party mount up. Followed by their gillie, the four horsemen trotted slowly up towards St. Laurence Gate, off to the Antrim hills. Bishop Magrath's mouth twisted in a wry smile. "Ha! Behold the *pale* horse! I might have known! It's *Gillaspick* rides the pale horse!" Maguire nodded, sagely.

"Death! On his way to O'Neill."

"If he is, it is *O'Neill* has called him forth! It is none of *our* doing. Come, so. Bringing in a recusant papist bishop will stand you well with the Lord Deputy. A splendid feather in your cap!" They led their mounts up to the Tholsel's railing, and tethered them. Myler paused on the step, and closed his eyes tight for a moment, drawing a look of concern from his cousin.

"Do you wish to say a wee prayer first, your Grace? Or we could go back, maybe?" Myler sighed.

"Ah, no. We'll *not* go back. Our Blesséd Lord has brought me to this pass. For I have followed my conscience, and served the truth. I am *glad* to free my hands of this hopeless struggle against King and Pope. I shall read their recantation of Faith, renounce the error of Popery, and declare myself a loyal Protestant. From there, I shall work out my salvation as best I can. But I shall never regret this day. Never!" He opened the great doors, and held them for Maguire. "Come, you. In a tempest, it is a fool who spurns the open door!"

SHANE O'NEILL

CHAPTER 32

The little castle on the isle of Inishdowell was astir early the next morning, as O'Neill and his small entourage made ready for the sojourn to Cushendall. Most of the preparations had been seen to, with tents, gifts, and lavish provisions packed tightly into several narrow pack wagons that awaited the travelers at Maghery on the southern shore of the Lough.

As the boys, and even tiny Áilish, were staying behind, Katherine had endless last minute advisements for the nurse. After a hurried call to her garden, she slipped into her tiny chapel. There upon the marble altar, Our Lady stood serenely in her springtide glory of May blossoms. Her month was nearly over, but these fresh cuttings would see it out. Kat culled the few fading flowers, and when she was satisfied, she knelt for a fervent prayer. She blessed herself and left a tall white candle burning to waft her wishes heavenward. A safe journey, reconciliation, and a warm reception for Shane among her kith and kin!

When the galley docked at Maghery, all was in readiness. Shane's new Marshal, Éamon Ó Donnelly met him with a splendid guard of fifty. They were mounted and waiting, all fitted out gallantly, with the standard aloft and no less than five red hand pennants fluttering on the morning breeze. Shane, Katherine, Sorley Buí, Farleigh, Blind Colm, Neil MacKeever and several attendants were brought their mounts, and without delay the journey commenced. In high style then, they rode out, with Shane's two wolfhounds bounding happily along beside them

Katherine's ample green skirts were kilted high, for she could could ride with the best, and she had no regard for such 'daft lowland airs' as the side-saddle. As they trotted their way northward up the lough shore, the soft wind tumbled and tossed her blazing auburn locks, but her green riding bonnet, with its two eagle feathers, was pinned firmly in place. Her radiant smile this morning lifted spirits around her, even as it belied certain misgivings and doubts about the venture ahead.

The heavens did their part to hearten the company with a glorious day! A few mealy clouds drifted across a sky as blue as a thrush's egg. The lough sparkled, and the sun played on the fresh fluttering leaves that sheltered their path along the sedgy shore. It was the very crest of springtide, a lush dewy morning filled with promise.

Rather than ride on northwards through O'Kane's country, Shane crossed the River Bann at the ford of Toome, and followed the northern shore of Lough Neagh eastwards to Gallantry. The cavalcade made a grand spectacle, and after all the grim rumours since Farsetmore, people along the route were cheered to see such a gallant procession, and they showed it. The company stopped for the night at Shane's grand castle of Edenduff Carrick, a stay that would allow them to arrive in Cushendun at a suitable hour the next day -and well rested too. Sorley MacDonnell rode on ahead with two of Shane's scouts to announce their approach, and to certify that a proper welcome would be forthcoming.

Katherine was impressed and uplifted to see the restoration work on the mighty round towers of the castle. Her window looked out upon the northeastern 'corner' of the great lough, and she could not turn away from the resplendent red sunset over its gleaming waters. Enchanting though it was, it aroused a deep loneliness in her for her wee Áilisheen, and her three little rogues as well, who dwelt by the far far shore of the Lough.

Shane's small garrison managed to provide a lavish feast with little warning, and some local chieftains called to pay humble but hearty respects to the O'Neill. Kat was glad to see Shane comporting himself with that proud, swaggering, damn-your-eyes air that she loved so. He had cast off his wretchedness, thanks be to God, and he would surely be able to brazen it out with Alastair and the rest!

The next morning was clear again, cool enough to be called fresh, and the travelers took horse early. Katherine had reconsidered her habit, and opted for her mother's MacDonnell plaids, a politic gesture, in light of all that had passed, one that might help to soften the welcome before them. Farleigh O'Gneeve, too, was in full feather, attired in his high mantle of seven colours. Katherine thought best that he should arrive in all the splendour and dignity of his high calling. Shane, too, deferred to his wife's wisdom, with a royal blue tunic, and a brat of deep purple gabardine over his shoulders, clasped by a massive ornate brooch of ancient design and provenance. The effect was imposing and majestic, and went a long way to cloak his less than felicitous circumstances.

On such a day, the last of May, the prospect was pleasing in all directions as O'Neill and his cavalcade wended their way northward through crag and scree and dun bog. Over low hills of purple heather and golden whins they rode, crossing lush meadows and dark streams. They made for Ballymena, and struck eastwards from there into the Glens by way of Broughshane and Clogh. Through Glenariff they rode, beside the lofty Shleevenanee, where St. Patrick spent so many lonely hours of his youth minding sheep. All was fresh and exhilarating. As she passed under the shadow of Carncormach, Katherine rejoiced to be riding among these wild mountains, after her years in the tameness of those low wooded moors beside the Great Lough.

For whatever shadows might lie beneath, the talk was light and frothy, with sharp banter, and even the odd poetical outburst from Farleigh O'Gneeve. After Broughshane all were amazed to see, following on high, two circling eagles, which the poet proclaimed to be an omen of great good fortune! In truth, however, he was uneasy as to just what they portended for the days ahead. Oftimes the company rode in silence, with only the rhythmic beat of hooves to be heard, and the sigh of the wind on the heather. Shane could not but reflect on the irony of his mission. It was but two short years since he had ridden these paths in triumph, having vanquished the Scots in dreadful slaughter. Now he was profoundly at their mercy.

The noble escort high above followed O'Neill for many leagues. Indeed, the eagles never departed until the weary company reached the sea at Cushendall. There they were met with an escort sent by ClanDonnell. With a piper to pipe them in, a small detachment of kilted cavalry arrived to conduct them the last few miles up the coast. The skirl of the approaching chieftain could be heard for several leagues, and just before O'Neill came in sight of Cushendun, a blast of pipes was heard from that quarter taking up the march.   All this seemed to bode well, and Shane and his band arrived, smiling brightly, if uneasily, into the sea of crimson plaids. A thousand MacDonnells, gathered above the strand, closed ranks behind them as O'Neill's party passed into their midst. There was no cheering to be heard, only the skirling clamour of the pipes, with quizzical smiles and smirks to greet them from the throngs on every side.

A row of twelve long galleys lined the strand, with bare masts spiring above at odd angles, skewed according as they had settled in the sand. Above the path a number of round colourful pavilion tents made up the encampment, with pennants waving in the spirited sea breeze. Campfires smouldered here and there among the tents. At the north end of the strand, just below Castle Carra was the chief pavilion, and before it, standing above the crowd on a stack of sea trunks were Alastair and Sorley Buí MacDonnell. Beside them, glowering fiercely was their cousin Gillaspick. Surrounding them was a phalanx of hulking galloglass in their long chain-mail tunics and iron skulls. Nowhere to be seen, however, was the Earl of Argyll. Shane led his company slowly forward on his black charger, and halted before their host, waiting some few moments until the last blast of the pipers' tune had sounded. Sorley MacDonnell raised his right arm, and into the ringing silence, he spoke.

"I am a Gael. I am a MacDonnell so I am a Scot. I alone of my brothers was born in Antrim, so I am an Irishman. I am fierce proud of my people this day -for the princely welcome they have put before

SHANE O'NEILL

Shane O'Neill. He held me prisoner these two years past, since the deaths of my brothers in his assault at Glenshesk. Although I was well done-by in his custody, it might be said that there is no man here has greater cause to hate him -that there is no man here has greater cause to call vengeance upon him. But there is a *greater cause*. Sixty years ago we lost the Lordship of the isles. Without O'Neill to fight the English we would soon be banished again. Our holy Faith and our ways lost forever. It is right that ClanDonnell should stand with O'Neill -for our noble blood is truly mingled. All of Shane O'Neill's issue are come of MacDonnell stock -the elder ones from my niece, Catriana, daughter of our late Chief, and the younger from my niece Lady O'Neill, daughter of our late sister Mary. Shane O'Neill's sister is my wife, and my sons are of his blood. He offers us-" Gillaspick stepped forward.

"And what of the blood of *our* brothers and sons, of their bones mouldering at Glenshesk! Will he walk among us? Will we let him walk among us?" There was a gasp from the crowd, and an ominous dark murmur, but as Gillaspick went to draw his sword, several gallowglass guards seized him, pulled him down and dragged him off. Sorley was chief of the Antrim MacDonnells, beloved, and newly welcomed home. Alastair had stepped aside upon his return, and none would see him gainsaid by this grasping rival. O'Neill's hounds were barking, and the crowd was in an uproar. Sorley stilled them with a raised palm, and spoke on.

"Aye. He *shall* walk among us! For we are ClanDonnell and we will honour our pledge for his safety! While I've a plack in my sporan and a beast in the field, he shall find welcome under my roof, for even in my captivity, he used me well. We are one clan, and we are of one accord. Shane O'Neill is welcome!" There was a tentative cheer. "And we shall not regret it. For O'Neill brings to us possession of the castles and lands of Antrim -all of Clandeboy, Dunluce and Redcave. And great herds of kine he offers! If he has betrayed us in the past, we must mind that we betrayed him too, also at the bidding of the curséd English. 'Shane the Proud' he is called across this land. But he comes to us today not in pride -but with remorse for past wrongs, and with hope in our manhood. He comes before you this day *without his sword*. This is the bravest deed of the greatest warrior in Ireland. And all Clandonnell welcomes him!" There was a great cheer now, and a sigh of relief from Katherine, and the rest, too, if truth were told.

Shane raised his arm to speak, but had to wait for a hush, so boisterous was the cheering. He thanked the crowd profusely, and promised a new day for Ulster; he spoke of ties of blood and Faith, and of the English threat to all. This brought more spirited ovation, and soon the Tirowen contingent dismounted and repaired to the chief's pavilion. Sorley and Alastair excused themselves to deal with Gillaspick, and their raised voices could be heard from within, as the miscreant cousin was taken to task. Shane stood outside the tent to observe what he could. After a stern rebuke, Gillaspick, in his fury, stormed off with rather a large following, a troubling turn that boded ill for Sorley Buí's newly restored command.

The two brothers returned to their guests, and assured them that all was settled, that Gillaspick MacDonnell had gone back to his holdings in Lecale to brood and lick his wounds, as was ever his wont. Katherine and Shane were quite composed, and showed no sign of their great relief. They had brazened it out, and won for themselves a fine welcome. There was elation, as they were greeted giddily by a small group of Katherine's kindred. Shane asked as casually as possible as to Argyll's absence. He was surprised to learn that Alastair knew nothing of the Earl's promise to be there. If this was disturbing news, he never showed it. After a short rest and refreshment, Shane roused his men to go and set up camp.

Just up the boreen to the north they rode, past the tiny chapel of Cross Screen, to the higher ground of Ballyteerim. Here was a clachan, a cluster of cottages belonging to the local Irish, mostly MacNeills. And in a nearby greensward along the banks of the dark, tumbling, Altagore burn, Shane made his camp. In its centre was a lone standing stone, known as 'the Hag.' Farleigh looked askance at this ancient monolyth, and wondered if they might be settling where they oughtn't.

While younger hands raised the mighty tents, he made inquiries in the clachan. It was the 'shanvan', they said, an old woman who was turned to stone by the druid, Cahvadd, back in the days before time. The hagstone was said to be enchanted, and at its foot offerings of oatcakes and butter were left for the fairies. Farleigh's news brought only mild amusement from Shane and Katherine, who were concerned about their missing Earl of Argyll. They were delighted with the site, and its fine prospect of the beautiful bay. And they were still only a stone's cast from the MacDonnell encampment. "Let us pray that that auld lump of a stone is the least of our worries this day!"

There was a long stretch in the evening, now that June was come, and those golden hours were spent in sport and feasting. The aroma of roasting venison and beef from the open spits mingled with the briny sea air. On the strand, the Irish and Scots competed in caber tossing and archery. Musicians struck up their tunes, and the Highland fling was flung.

Above the north end of the strand stood a small castle that had been built by the local Irish sept of MacNeills, who had lost it to the MacDonnells some time back. The MacQuillans burnt it out during Shane's campaign against the Scots, and it was now being refitted and re-roofed, but in its small cobbled yard Alastair's chief pavillion was pitched. Here it was that Shane and his people dined. Bran and Scohaun settled themselves at their master's feet and gnawed on meaty bones that fell their way.

Although there were but few women in the encampment, apart from 'camp followers', several of Katherine's cousins were on hand. Alastair's youngest daughter, Maeve took delight in regaling Lady O'Neill with all the news of her MacDonnell kin, and Kat was thankful that she had worn their colors instead of her MacLean reds. She learned that her father had chosen this prickly time to plunder the isle of Gigha, a holding of her Aunt Agnes, the Laird's widow. Both she and her 'dark daughter' were furious. Maeve confided that Fionnúla was still refusing to wed Hugh O'Donnell, even after his great victory at Farsetmore, "because O'Neill lives still." She and her mother were both in an uproar over this talk of Alistair helping Shane against Black Hugh. Maeve had news of the Scottish Queen too. "Mary has wed!

SHANE O'NEILL

Wed the murderer of her husband, and wed by the Protestant rite! She will be forsaken by the great powers of Europe! And there is a great fury on the people." As to Argyll's whereabouts, alas, she had no news.

Shane talked amiably to Sorley and Alastair about their prospects against the English. He told them of Sidney's speech in the Parliament of the Pale, for young Sir Robert Fleming had given him a full report. The Deputy had warned the Palesmen that the Irish were the common enemy, "a sort of barbarous people," Sidney called them, "odious to God and man, that will lap your blood as greedily as ours!" Shane spoke passionately. He called it 'a war of race and tongue,' and pleaded that it could not be won unless the Gaels of Scotland and Ireland stand together. The two Scots nodded their assent, but said little. As to Shane's Irish foes, all agreed that Black Hugh's surprise attack had been a 'quare fluke', and that it would be no great task to take him down. Sorley remarked the irony that it was O'Donnell's very desperation that had driven him to his mad dawn charge. Had his numbers been greater, he would have met Shane in the field, and been easily vanquished.

The people rose at a leisurely hour the following morning, and made their way to a sloping sward above the strand for Sunday Mass. The priest from the chapel of Cross Screen celebrated the Mass, and as per O'Neill's advisement, he gave a spirited sermon on forgiveness. The Prodigal Son had indeed returned, and the lesson was reconciliation. Afterward the great multitude dispersed to their campfires to break fast. Another fine day it was, and before long the men had organized a game of hurling on the white strand. To the Scots, the game was called 'Shinty', and played by slightly different rules, but Sorley call down his judgment that as they were in Ireland, Irish rules must carry.

The crowd oohed and aahed as the lads leapt and scrambled wildly over the sand in a kind of ancient fieldhockey, their sticks ever flailing and clashing with a mighty thwack. Katherine had to squint to make out the shifting and surging rooly-booly before her, for the sun glistened so on the sea beyond. For the first time, she found herself praying against the Irish, for fear that a win would be begrudged, and add to the remnants of ill will that lingered under the wintry smiles of her people.

Above the hurlyburly, the sea mews reeled with piercing shrills. The match was a close one, and, towards the end, it grew quite heated, so fierce was the rivalry between the two camps. There was a powerful roar of distress when the Irish suddenly rallied and took three goals, two off the same stick! The Tirowenmen had their victory, just as the tide was starting to swell and tumble onto the foreshore sand. Indeed the Scots were not pleased, but the attention of all was quickly diverted by a new development.

Through the glint of the sun on the eastern waves, someone caught sight of a galley coming in from Kintyre. Shane and Katherine were uplifted at the prospect of the Earl of Argyll arriving at last, and prayed fervently that it would be so. His promise of 5,000 troops was the key to a proper resurgence for Shane. But as the ship's prow finally hove into view, a ClanDonald standard could be seen fluttering on the galley-mast above it. Had the Earl been aboard, his Campbell colours would have been aloft. The tide was fairly high by this, and after a short wait the galley was able to beach itself alongside the rest. As the ranks of tartaned warriors disembarked, striding through the shallows, it was clear that this was a further company of the MacDonnell hosts. They said they were reinforcements, pledged to fight for Alastair. They were surprised and pleased to find Sorley Buí released from his bondage, and restored to his chieftainry.

Katherine was alarmed to see who was leading this band, for it was Randal Macdonnell, brother of the vindictive Gillaspick. He stopped for a time on the strand, conferring with his uncles, Sorley and Alastair. Sorley glanced over to Shane and Katherine several times, further piquing their curiosity. As the newcomers filed past O'Neill, they did not meet his glance. Some were grim-faced, and more were smiling after a fashion –dark smiles belied by eyes as hard as stone.

After a time, Randal and Alastair walked off together, and Sorley strode up the shore to the O'Neills. He assured Katherine that there

SHANE O'NEILL

was nothing to fret about. It was only a new contingent of recruits, under his own command. But they had brought news of Argyll. Archibald was in Kintyre, stopping with his sister Agnes, the widow of the chief. She and her 'dark daughter' were detaining him, prevailing upon him to forsake this alliance with O'Neill, and Sorley thought it best to intervene.

Sorley was concerned by Randal's news that his wife was ill, and he was determined on a plan. He would go to Kintyre that very afternoon to see his family after his long captivity, comfort his ailing wife, and he would then call upon Argyll. He was sure he could wrest him from his sister's keeping, and squire him back to Cushendall by Tuesday at the latest. In the meantime they should take their ease, and enjoy the lovely weather that gave every promise of holding. Alastair would look after them. Katherine tried to convince Sorley to stay and send a messenger, but Shane agreed with her Uncle. He would stand a better chance of actually returning with the Earl, and 'poor Mary' would certainly be the better for seeing him.

It was not long before Sorley's departure was underway, as he put to sea in one of the smaller galleys. The hills of Kintyre could be seen across the waters, and it was held no great journey to any of the MacDonnell seamen. Katherine and Shane walked the half-mile back up to their camp at Ballyteerim. She insisted they call in at the wee chapel of Cross Screen, for the priest had told her that it housed a fragment of the True Cross. Indeed, it's name means 'shrine of the cross.' They admired the tiny relic, and both of them knelt in solemn prayer. Katherine was uneasy in Sorley's absence, the grim newcomers adding to her worries, and indeed, to her prayers. Shane would admit to no such worries, but he tried to call to mind the words of the 'Prayer Before a Crucifix,' that had been given him by the Jesuit Spanish Ambassador in London.

> "...to contemplate Thy five most precious wounds,
> having before mine eyes that which David,
> the prophet, long ago spoke concerning Thee,
> 'They have pierced My hands and My feet,

they have numbered all My bones."

When they reached the rise of Ballyteerim, Katherine lingered to watch her uncle's galley out on the Sea of Moyle. What a relief it would be to see him return with Argyll's standard aloft! She sighed, and made her way back to camp, thankful at least for the fine weather. Before her, in the west, rose the gentle slope of Cushleake Mountain with a few bright wispy clouds billowing above. She arrived to find Farleigh conferring excitedly with Shane. He had been in the Clachan, ferreting out local lore and points of interest, and so the afternoon was spent on horseback, visiting each 'wee station' in its turn. Shane's trusty scribe, Neil MacKeever rode along with the three of them, and Farleigh brought a young fellow from the clachan who was not short of words for each dolman, or stone circle they encountered.

At the foot of a mossy hill, beside the Glenann River they payed a call to an ancient cairn known to be the burial place of the legendary Oisín, son of Finn MacCoole, and Farleigh regaled them with many a twist and turn of that hallowed tale. It seems that Oisín, after spending what he thought were three years in Tír na n-Óg (the land of youth), returned to find that three hundred years had passed, and all his warrior friends of the Fianna were long since gone to dust. He had been bidden to remain astride his steed, for if ever he touched the ground, he would suffer the decrepitude of those three centuries. Helping someone in need, of course, Oisín stumbled from the horse, and quickly withered into a feeble old man. It was then St. Patrick tried to convert him to the new Faith, but he argued that if his pagan friends were not to be found in Heaven, he had no wish to be there! 'The old ways, and those dear to him, could not be tossed aside for this dreary Christian heaven!' That this glen should be a resting place for ancient heroes, and even for the cross of Christ, struck Katherine as ominous, but for all her worries, she found the day enchanting.

The evening was spent in feasting with Alastair and the rest. Randal MacDonnell was there, but his newcomers were not in evidence. And if there were still some awkward chills in the air, and prickly exchanges, the feast passed without incident. This was a great relief to all, and Katherine decided to do as Shane did, and busy her mind with hope and conjecture about the Earl of Argyll's impending arrival, and the power and advantage his five legions would bring.

The cool grey morning was unexpected. A wind was up, the tents flapping and snapping. The sea was dark, with lines of white foam marching to shore and breaking upon the strand. When the old poet emerged from his tent, he was struck to stillness at the sight before him. It was only a scaldy crow resting atop the 'hagstone', but to Farleigh it was an ill omen, and boded dire misfortune for the prince of Ulster! The huge black bird had its back to him as he watched, but it turned of a sudden, taking wing with a great screech. It flew directly at him, and he raised his hands to his face, but he could feel the beat of its great wings as it soared up just over his head. Farleigh turned and looked up, but there was no sign of the huge bird. The old man was badly shaken. He was ever mindful of that dreadful vision he had beheld in London, and now he was powerless to turn the O'Neill from his course.

Shane was washing up when Farleigh found him, where the dark Altagore stream foamed and tumbled over its mossy stones, but the chieftain cut short his warnings, and dismissed them. These were "no more than illusions brought of fear", he said, and he told the old man that, as this was the one and only recourse fate had left him, he must bide. "I will face what is to be faced," he said, "and I will trust what wisdom I have, and what strength is in my heart. Put these fears from you, old man. Argyll will come, and all will be well!" He forbade him to tell Lady Katherine of the scaldcrow, or of his dark vision.

The Lady herself began her day feeling light and aery, in spite of the dull skies. She felt reassured after having put the night past without incident, even in Sorley's absence. But then she chided herself for this elation, for not pining for her bairns. Now of course, she ached for the children as though they had been torn from her flesh. Still, a dark shadow had been lifted, and missing her wee-uns was a sight better than fretting with fear of her own people. There was smoke rising from the ClanDonald campfires below, and a lone piper could be heard. On Shane's word, they all made their way down for the tournaments.

After a hearty repast in the chief pavilion, the O'Neills ambled down to the strand to cheer on their archers. Of course, Katherine could not help but turn her gaze out to sea in search of some sign of her uncle's galley. But on such a grey morning, with perhaps a smirr of rain drifting between the two shores, only the hazy outline of the Mull of Kintyre could be seen on the dim horizon. Thankfully, she found the games quite diverting. The Irish fared well with the longbow, the top honours going to Éamon O'Donnelly, but the Scots bested them with the crossbow. Afterward there was a javelin tourney, and a kind of jousting on the white strand. Pipers piped, dancers danced, and a festive air prevailed. Katherine noted that her cousin Randal was nowhere to be seen, nor, indeed, was his gloomy band in evidence.

Before the games had ended, O'Neill and a few chosen men of his escort joined Alastair in a hunt up in the woods of Glendun. Under some very welcome, but tentative late-afternoon sunshine, they coursed through the mossy wood, with Bran and Scohaun loping and lepping along beside Shane's black Barbary charger.

Kat spent the afternoon with her two cousins, Maeve and Máiri. They listened eagerly to her details of Queen Mary's ordeals, and she winkled news and tattle out of them concerning Agnes and the Dark Daughter. Agnes was 'nigh unto betrothed' to Shane's cousin Turlagh Lynnach O'Neill, but Fionnúla was bound 'neither to wed nor court' Black Hugh until Shane was under clay, and her father avenged. Kat shuddered to hear this, but she kept her composure, and even laughed it off boldly. Randal MacDonnell had brought word, they said, that Argyll had severely fined Kat's father, MacLean of Duart, for his assault upon the isle of Gigha, but Agnes was not appeased. She was raging, they said, and there would be more trouble on the head of it.

It was well on in the evening when the lingering sun disappeared behind the Antrim Mountains, sending up its despairing rays of gold through the purple clouds in the West. There would be no moon. As shadows deepened, smoke from the campfires wafted here and there between the pavilions, with the aroma of succulent venison from the day's kill. There was great feasting in the chief pavilion, where Shane

SHANE O'NEILL

and Lady Katherine were seated beside Alastair at the table of honour, with Farleigh O'Gneeve, Éamon O'Donnelly, and Neal MacKeever alongside them. Bran and Scohaun were on the prowl, happily scampering along among the tables, foraging for meaty scraps.

On this sojourn, for the first time in his life, Shane had asked his guard to stand down, that he might underscore the great trust he held in his host's word, and his absolute dependance upon the honour of ClanDonald. From the very first it had impressed them, and by this, good faith seemed to be the order of things. Katherine smiled easily this night, and she looked stunning in her pale blue gown, with its lavender bodice. Alastair's harper struck some lovely airs as the guests dined and chatted, and the wavering smokey light of tallow dips and rush-lamps cast long shadows against the billowing panels of the huge tent.

After the meal, Alastair challenged his Irish guests to a singing match with the men of the isles. He had fine singers to twist the slow Scottish airs, and the choppy lilting melodies of their boatsongs. Farleigh had recruited a local lad, an O'Drean, who was as good as their best, but the victory went to Blind Colm who rendered one of his heart-breaking ballads. The trophy was a drinking horn with gilded fittings and two tiny 'crow's legs' to steady it, and the singer was delighted to find that it was full to the brim with whiskeybaugh. Several of Alastair's poets recited over the delicate strains of a harp, and were cheered boisterously. But the fiery verse of Farleigh O'Gneeve was known through the Highlands, and many here were awaiting his latest bequest from the heights of Parnassus.

Farleigh rose, and nearly stumbled over Shane's hounds who were dozing on the cobbles over their fleshy venison bones. The bard was in his glory, attired in his cloak of seven colours, and he gave a long and impassioned ode, pleading for unity between the two peoples, finishing with a dire warning. His still-vibrant voice sounded clearly in the rapt silence, with only the restless sea whispering behind him.

> "...We have let the wave crash through
> that swept on board this foreign crew,

that that pierced the noble prow,
that broke the slender bow
of the galleon of the Gael.
Now,
lash and toss of tempest rage
have gathered in a surging wave
that towers dark above our tattered sail.
English hoards on every side,
and more ashore with every tide.
The Gael will soon be swept from sight
if the sons of Míl will not unite
and forsake their enmity!
It is right to man the fight,
to ply our swords
against the Saxon hoards!
And drive them to the Sea!"

A strange silence followed this verse, with the last quavering notes of Farleigh's voice ringing in the air. All but he were aware that during the bard's recitation, many men had slipped silently into the pavilion, men who stood listening in the shadows. After a seeming eternity, Alastair MacDonnell stood to applaud, and an ovation rose around him. He thanked Farleigh, and asked the O'Neill to speak 'on this grand occasion, sealing the bonds of alliance!' As Shane stepped forward, he saw that Gillaspick had returned. Like a shadow materializing at Alastair's side, that baleful presence stood watching him with his arms folded. Shane waited briefly to see if he would be once again banished, but Alastair gave no sign of surprise or concern at his presence.

Around the walls of the tent, the shadowy followers of Gillaspick lurked, darkly brooding, with sidelong glances at their captain. All of this Shane saw, and though his flood of thoughts was hot and strong within him, his composure never faltered. He appealed to the company present, keeping a glinty eye on Gillaspick, a challenging glare perhaps. His voice rang out with power and passion.

SHANE O'NEILL

"Fine words! Fine straight words to hear in these twisted times! For this day, in this land, our poet Farleigh O'Gneeve is a felon. And his finely crafted words are a *crime*. That is the law out of London. Sorley MacDonnell, when he welcomed me here these two days agone, was right to say that our cause is *greater* now. The stakes are higher now, and past wrongs must be laid to rest if we are to prosper, and even to survive in the coming days. Let there be no more strife betwixt tartan and broadcloth! All such rancour must be consigned to the past. I have been in the chambers of power in London, and I am here to tell you. This queen seeks to build a new England here on our lands -and to settle it with Englishmen. This second England will hold no place for a Gael -Irish *or* Scots! They have outlawed our tongue, and our laws, and our dress, and our Holy Faith. Queen Elizabeth has declared herself paramount over our souls as well as our bodies...and if-"

"And what of the bodies of our dead? Of our beloved? Do we forget them?" Gillaspick strode forward, breathing rage, with his arm raised high. "Can they be 'laid to rest' while yet their killer feasts with our chieftains? This Irishman was last among us trampling on the bodies of our slain. Fathers and brothers and-"

Some near the front tried to shout him down, but now those dark ranks in the back shuffled slowly forward murmuring, "Glenshesk! Glenshesk! Glenshesk!" Others called out over them.

"There's Scottish blood on your 'red hand'!"

"Murderer!"

"You betrayed us once!"

"We were Gaels at Glenshesk!"

They were soon on every side. Katherine called to Alastair to cast out these disrupters, but even she knew that he was in no position to do so. All were mindful that it was he who had arrived late for that battle of Glenshesk. Instead of landing his thousand warriors to protect Dunluce Castle, he had left Rathlin Island, and sailed away home, leaving Gillaspick to man the ill-fated defense. "Glenshesk! Glenshesk! Glenshesk!"

Farleigh had made his way back to his seat, only to discover that

SHANE O'NEILL

Shane's wolfhounds, Bran and Scohaun were not drowsing, but dead! Poisoned! Éamon slipped out to fetch Shane's swordsmen who were feasting in another tent. But no sooner did he step from the tent, than he was seized and run through with a broadsword! Katherine was standing, trying vainly to be heard, trying to call her people to order. It was Alastair's voice that brought them to an uneasy silence.

"Hould your voices! Och, let us hear the man out! What says O'Neill to this?"

"A fool I was! Like *your own* lairds many's the time, I was cozened by English lies, by English threats. I ask you to forgive me -for that I am contrite, and I came to you -to this place- on your promise of safety! The sacred word of ClanDonald was-"

"Hut! None of your whillywhas!" Gillaspick roared over him. "Let his folly in coming be upon his own head!" He waved his fist, and snarled through his teeth. "We must e'en do as we're done by!" Shane's voice rang out.

"But we have a *chance* now! Argyle is on his way with money and troops. Five legions of troops! Queen Mary of Scotland bids us to rise together against-"

"Queen Mary is finished! Even now she has fled, hunted by the lairds of Scotland, with her murderous husband, Bothwell the heretic, at her side. When she is captured she will be made to abdicate in favour of her bairn, who will be James the Sixth! And *he*- He has been acknowledged by Elizabeth as heir to the *English* throne as well! She has acceded to Argyll's demand. So the Earl of Argyll will *nae* be coming to your rescue, O'Neill!" Katherine strode forward.

"That's a lie! He's not been named! Before the throne of Almighty God I would swear it! James has *not* been named heir, and Argyll is on his way! *You* will answer to him, Gillaspick MacDonnell, and soon!"

"It's true as Gospel, my lass! I hold the letter here! Brought yesterday by my brother Randal." He handed his letter to Alastair, who opened it solemnly, and read it in silence. But it said nothing of the Royal succession. It was the note from Sidney, promising the Earldom to the MacDonnells, at last, in ink and parchment. Gillaspick again appealed to the crowd. His nostrils flaring, he shouted out to

SHANE O'NEILL

them. "Elizabeth has *acceded* to Lord Argyle's demand. James is the right heir. And Lord Argyll willnae be coming to ride with O'Neill!" All eyes were on Alastair. He looked up from the letter, and slowly nodded his assent. "So you see, it's gods-truth!" The crowd was closing in around Shane, and Katherine was being held back from him, as Gillaspick's harsh voice rose menacingly. "So there will *be* no rising! - The only rising is here and now. We'll carve a feast for worms! Wet your dirks -for *Glenshesk!*"

There was a moment of fraught silence, and then a big raw-boned glowering man drew out his claymore with a thin high-pitched skreak of steel. Suddenly they all fell upon Shane with dirks and swords. Katherine shrieked and screamed and struggled, as blade after blade pierced him, hacked him, with great gouts of blood gushing forth. But when at last the assassins backed away from his ravaged bloody corpse, she collapsed in a swoon.

The din of raging voices died away, giving place to the sound of a fierce slaughter that could be heard outside on the wind, where the Scots had set upon Shane's guard. In a camp of a thousand enemies, the fifty Irishmen stood little chance. Katherine, in her swoon, was stretched out upon a rough wooden form. Neal MacKeever the scribe lay hacked to pieces on the stones. Even Blind Colm had been killed. Farleigh O'Gneeve stood in the midst of the carnage, struck still as stone, his breath heaving, his eyes tearing, as he watched Shane's blood tracing its crimson web among the cobbles. Those grey eyes, glassy and still. It was his dreadful vision come to pass! As for the Scots, none dare raise their sword against a reknowned bard, and of all the company from Tirowen, only he and Lady Katherine were spared.

On the shore below the hill of Knockacully Katherine stood alone in the grey morning, waiting beside her small bundle. Waiting to go home. Her brooding eyes gazed out over the dark sea, with just a faint sullen hope that she might see her uncle's galley across the waves. Deep within, she was certain of his betrayal. These kindred were lost to her now, as surely as was her husband. Sorley had likely known all along that Argyll was not coming; perhaps his wife Mary had not been ill, but he had simply chosen to absent himself, that the slaughter might take its course. Perhaps from the very first it had all been a trap. She had led Shane into this deadly snare, and she would never forgive herself this side of time!

How strange it was. Everything that had mattered yesterday meant nothing now –save for her children. All those worries... Nothing more than shards of a shattered future to be swept away. One *night...one* moonless night... Oh, the wickedness of night! Men would turn to bestial depravity when the heavens were dark, as though God could not see them. After their murderous spree, Shane's camp was looted and torched! All of it lay in ashes. His body was wrapped in a filthy kern's shirt, and flung into a pit in the old churchyard of Cross Screen. And what of her wee prayers in that chapel? Were they just pennies tossed in a well? Did they go unheard, uttered into a void? Like the ship that was never to come? She blessed herself quickly now, and said an 'Ave' for her husband's eternal soul.

A Seagull screamed overhead, and curlews were calling and calling inconsolably. Katherine brushed back her windblown hair, and as she turned, three horsemen could be seen coming along the shore path from Alastair's camp. There was no mistaking Farleigh once he waved his bonnet in the air, his long white hair aflutter on the wind. With him were two of her uncle's young gillies. They halted beside her, and the old poet dismounted. He embraced Katherine without speaking. The pair of gillies quietly left a mount for 'Lady O'Neill', and rode off together on the one horse. Katherine sniffed.

"Oh, Farleigh!" He stepped back and looked at her sadly. Under her hooded grey cloak, she was still attired in the pale blue gown, spattered with dark blood as it was. He sighed deeply, and cast a glance across the waters to the vague grey shapes of the far isles.

"Will you go home, then?"

"Home? Och, home is my bairns, now. But, oh, Farleigh, to be *home*... I can nearly see it across the waters." She shaded her eyes with her delicate hand, and gazed wistfully out to sea. "There's snow lies on

SHANE O'NEILL

the hills of Jura...glistening white! And rain or mist will not remove it... Och, no, I'll not return to Duart. I'll journey with you back to Inishdowell -to wee Áilish and my sons." There was a wicker creel on the flank of Farleigh's horse, and Blind Colm's harp could be seen sticking up out of it. He packed Katherine's bundles in under it, and bound it tightly with a broken brass wire from the harp.

"If we ride to Edenduff Carrick, a galley will take us across the lough to your island, and spare us the hard ride." He turned to her, his brows raised in warning. "The boys will be in some peril now, Lady Katherine. Turlagh Lynagh will go to the stone, surely, and he'll lose no time doing it. And the Baron's son Hugh will be coming of age beyond in England. There will be more contention, but none of them will want to abide the rivalry of the sons of Shane O'Neill. For *they* will have the people's heart. The boys will not be safe!"

"I'll take them into hiding, so. I pledged to...to their father that I'll not take them from Ulster. My Hugh and Brian and Art. Scottish blood pulses through their hearts, and when they're grown they could unite the Irish and Scots of Ulster against the English –if we have not all been driven from the land."

"It is shameful for us to leave him here. These are your kindred. Would they not..." Katherine shook her head sadly.

"We'll not be let carry his body back to Tirowen. I pleaded and pleaded to no avail. So long as James MacDonnell's bones lie in far-off Armagh, they say, my Shane will lie..." Her face flushed red, and she swallowed hard. "Those lips I've kissed a thousand times will moulder in the..." A flood of tears came forth, and the old man embraced her once again. She sniffed and swallowed. "Oh Farleigh, I was sorrowing all the night! But my tears will not stay the worms from his eyes -those eyes that kindled so when he came to me!" She regarded Farleigh's eyes, the bleak hollow look of them, such utter desolation. She wiped her cheeks with a sleeve. "Have you no tears? No words? What way are you, Farleigh? How do you feel?"

"Like an inside without an outside...Aware of nothing but the dull chatter of birds."

SHANE O'NEILL

"Oh, Farleigh, you must not let them rain ruin on your good heart! You must return to the darkness of your wee cave and make a poem. There is solace in poetry."

"Poetry. There's nothing in it but *words*. The great poets are like dogs blown up with scent -snarling in the empty straw...Ah no, my lass. I'm finished. A brown leaf shaking in the cold spring air. I'll follow O'Neill into the clay, as my fathers followed his."

"You don't mean that, Farleigh O'Gneeve. It is your grief gaining mastery of you.

"Grief itself is vanity." His shaggy brow knitted as he shook his head with wonder. "It's all but the twinkling of an eye, this '*time,*' this 'life.' My father is dead nearly thirty years and it might be yesterday. We who grieve will not be long after." Another low roll of thunder rumbled from afar. Katherine cleared her throat.

"We'll face for home now." Farleigh didn't stir, but for a deep sigh. He spoke listlessly, as one thinking aloud.

"O'Neill's great hall is cairn of stones. Benburb will never rise from its ashes. Thorns, and a blight of thistles, own it now." Katherine hiked up her skirts, and mounted her horse. The old man was still staring out over the dark sea. She used the full of her voice.

"We'd best make our way, Farleigh. There's a storm rumbling in the West, and we've a long journey ahead, God help us."

"God? The gods have vanished. One by one the stars are slipping from the heavens. The constellations dissolve star by star into the glowering void. And here are we, left between a bare ridge of grass - and the proud fury of the heavens. What shall we do then but trudge on? And hope ...for hope."

"I have hope, Farleigh O'Gneeve. Were it not for hope the heart would break. While I have my sons, I have hope the wrongs shall be righted yet! And as for God, He is there still. Just look to the sky. You'll see no sun this day. But it is there -blazing brightly behind the clouds, as surely as God is there. And my Shane is with him now." Farleigh nodded.

"Ach, pay no mind to a weary auld man! You have the right of it, of course. You must keep the high heart! Death is part of life, and it

SHANE O'NEILL

must have its due. What's this Homer said? 'Every living creature is the more beautiful because it is doomed.' Aye, t'was Homer said that. A blossom that could not wilt could never possess the beauty of things mortal. And he was no fool! True beauty is ephemeral. Moments are precious because they are fleeting. Death has taken our Shane O'Neill, and we must bide, and be thankful that he was ours for a time. Such is life. You, Lady Katherine, will never be more lovely than you are now. Even in your grief. For time moves apace."

"Aye. And so must we. We mustn't *tarry*, now, Farleigh. Let us be off." The old poet looked about him with a swift turn of the head, and assumed a more purposeful air. With just a bit of struggle he managed to mount his steed, and the two began to trot slowly down the shorepath in silence, lost in their thoughts. Farleigh would survive. His words would sustain him. And she had her brood to raise now, howsoever she might manage it. At Cushendall, they turned from the sea onto the drover's track that winds through Glenballyeamon, but Katherine halted on the rise, and turned for a last look back at the sea. Farleigh saw that her cheeks were wet and raw.

"Ach, give over your weeping, my wee girl! Time writes its tale, and all the tears of the world cannot erase a single word of what has passed." Katherine sniffed.

"Aye, time's tale...Shane is only a story now. A lost hero..." She wiped more tears from her eyes and looked again out to sea, where rows of white breakers rolled in on the dark tide. Farleigh followed her gaze.

"Oh, aye...The mightiest waves froth and foam into nothingness upon the strand. One by one they come to nothing."

"No, not *nothing*. Never nothing. Shane *was* a hero, like Cúchulain of old. And ere he died he tossed his banner to the wind. The poets will sing of him. And others will follow. And one day...one day, one shall prevail!" A deep rumble of thunder turned their eyes to the darkening skies far in the West, and they rode on undaunted through the sorrowful glen, to meet the gathering storm.

FINIS

SHANE O'NEILL

EPILOGUE

After two nights of triumphal revelry, led by the swaggering, and gloating Gillaspick, the Scots at Cushendun welcomed the return of Sorley Buí MacDonnell. Alastair repaired immediately to Kintyre, while Gillaspick and his followers departed for Lecale. Sorley mustered his forces and retook his town of BallyCastle, as well as his fortress at Dunaneeny.

Upon hearing that the Scots had cleared off, Captain Pierce stole forth from Carrickfergus with a small detachment. They made straight for the churchyard of Cross Screen, dragged Shane's corpse from its pit, and set about the grisly business of hacking off his head. The bloody severed head was boded on a spear, and brandished high before the Yorkshireman's triumphant procession down to Drogheda. There the ghoulish trophy was received rapturously by the Lord Deputy, who paid out to Captain Pierce the price he had set: the princely sum of one thousand marks.

Lord Sidney's military campaign had been a dismal failure, but now at last the 'Grand Disturber' was vanquished! This operation, the third assassination attempt upon O'Neill, had been carried off to its mortal conclusion, salvaging the Viceroy's flagging reputation at Court. Shane O'Neill's head was 'pickled in a pipkin', and then gibbetted on a pole over the battlements of Dublin Castle. There it would remain for three years as a warning to any man who might resist the English Emperium.

Sorley Buí MacDonnell sent dispatches to Captain Pierce and to

SHANE O'NEILL

Sidney demanding payment of promises due, only to be disappointed. Regardless of what had been signed on parchment, Queen Elizabeth wrote to Sidney from Richmond on July 7th, urging that the Scots should be "largely rewarded for their part in the deed." She added, however, that if they refused to return to Scotland, they must be speedily expelled by force. Here was yet another English betrayal, one that would be met by a strengthening of ties between the Scots and Irish. The Earl of Argyll hosted a double wedding on Rathlin Island for his sister and his niece. The widow Agnes wed Shane's successor, Turlagh Lynagh O'Neill, and her 'Dark Daughter, Fionnúla, happily gave herself in marriage to Black Hugh O'Donnell, now that her father was avenged.

Only one week after Shane's murder, Queen Elizabeth wrote to the Deputy that she wished to proceed with Lord Smith's plan for an English colony in the Ards peninsula of Ulster. Sidney, in his reply, is already dissembling as to the nature of this assassination, but he makes quite plain the predatory intentions of the Crown. He laments wistfully, "I would the rebel had been taken (alive), that he might have received his just desert, and that he might have been compelled to admit so much as would have gained the Queen's majesty more land than Tyrone is worth. He might have been induced to disclose the whole conspiracy in which the Earls of Desmond, Kildare, and other owners of very broad lands, were believed to be implicated." They knew of O'Neill's recent clandestine visit to the Earl of Kildare at Kilkea, but the object of this concern was to to dispossess the Irish gentry, and steal their estates. In any event, Sidney arrested Shane's cousin, the Earl of Desmond, forfeited his bond for £20,000, and dispatched him to spend the next five years languishing in the Tower of London.

Queen Mary Stuart of Scotland was captured within weeks of Shane's death by her Protestant lairds, and was forced to abdicate in favour of her infant son. She fled to England where she was captured, giving rise to 'the Revolt of the Northern Earls', in which English Catholic gentry rose to support her. After all the desperate pleas from Ireland, it was the plight of these English nobles that induced the

SHANE O'NEILL

Pope to at last excommunicate Queen Elizabeth, and deprive her of the allegiance of her Catholic subjects.

This Papal bull came in early 1570, less than three years after Shane O'Neill's death, and as he had expected, it lit the fires of rebellion in Ireland. When Garret, the Earl of Desmond, was let return in 1572, he threw off his English clothes, donned Irish attire, and joined in full rebellion with his brother, and his uncle, FitzMaurice. Unfortunately, without O'Neill's northern forces, the Desmond Rebellion was doomed to fail, a disaster in which Shane's English protegé Thomas Stukeley played a prominent but ignoble part.

In her gratitude for Sidney's dispatch of her 'chiefest rebel', Elizabeth had acquiesced in the matter of Stukeley's advancement. He was given large holdings and the captainship of Wexford. When the Rebellion broke out, however, his personal ambitions led him to side with the rebels, who sent him off to Rome to procure help from the Continent. Stukeley presented himself boldly in the Vatican States as the 'Duke of Leinster.' "It was incredible," as (the English historian) Thomas Fuller recounted, "how quickly he wrought himself into the favour of the Court, into the chamber, yea closet, yea bosom of Pope Pius Quintus. The Pope entered eagerly into all his plans. He gave him a high title, creating him Baron of Ross, Viscount Murrough, Earl of Wexford and Marques of Leinster, and furnished him with eight hundred men to be paid by the King of Spain for his Irish expedition. For the first time, the Pope granted to the Irish a Bull authorizing them to fight for the recovery of their independence.

Unfortunately, Tom Stukeley's diplomatic success was undone by his vaulting ambition. On his return journey to Ireland, he put into the port of Lisbon where the King of Portugal was busily preparing for an expedition against Morocco. Stukeley agreed to accompany him against the Moors on the promise of a larger supply of soldiers, ducats, and honours when the war was concluded. This was a flagrant betrayal of his mission for Ireland. In the fatal battle of Alcazar, he and most of his papal conscripts perished, leaving Desmond's rebels to suffer defeat, and vast confiscations of land by the Crown.

In the aftermath of O'Neill's death, most of Shane's enemies

SHANE O'NEILL

prospered, while his supporters came to ruin. His poisoner, the apothecary, Thomas 'Bottle' Smith, became Lord Mayor of Dublin in 1591, and laid the foundation stone for Trinity College. Lord Smith got his English colony in the Ards. It lasted only a few years until his Irish servants rose up and murdered his son. Many chieftains, like MacMahon, who had wavered or withheld their support from O'Neill, found themselves under increasing pressure from London, and were driven to futile revolt, only to be hanged. Changing circumstances, like the Pope's excommunication of Queen Elizabeth, drew some of Shane's most ardent enemies into open rebellion -most notably, the Catholic Church.

With the loss of their powerful protector, O'Neill, the Catholic Church in Ireland faced a severe crackdown from Dublin Castle. The Primate, Richard Creagh, was imprisoned, having been taken one month before Shane's demise. Ironically, the nuncio, David Wolfe had the most reason to regret the loss of Shane, for he was captured the following autumn. He was betrayed in the manner of Donagh O'Tighe in Carrickfergus, and taken by Captain Pierce. Subjected to the full rigours of torture in his cell in Dublin Castle, he undoubtedly had cause to repent certain misdeeds relating to that Primate's capture. The deposed Bishop Leverous visited Wolfe in his cell, and he was appalled by the conditions. He wrote that he was driven away by the stench.

When the Pope excommunicated Elizabeth in 1570, releasing Catholics from loyalty to their sovereign, they became de facto enemies of the state. This unleashed a reign of terror and persecution that was to last until Catholic Emancipation in 1829. With the capture of the Nuncio, the Jesuits decided to abort their mission to Ireland altogether. The Church was now in full rebellion against the Crown, and it was thought best to keep the Order clear of it. Fr. Good and Fr. Daniel were recalled to the continent. Fr. Daniel managed to raise money in Portugal to free Fr. Wolfe, but on his return to Ireland, he was captured carrying papal letters for Fitzmaurice, the leader of the Desmond Rebellion. Fr. Edmund Daniel was hanged, drawn, and

SHANE O'NEILL

quartered by the English on October 25th, 1572.

Fr. Daniel's funds provided the bribes and pay-offs to effect the nuncio's deliverance. A somewhat chastened David Wolfe, was rescued from Dublin Castle by none other than Thomas Stukeley. Like the nuncio, the English adventurer had, by this, thrown in his lot with the Irish rebels. But if Wolfe was now a rebel, he held little public favour. He was known to have taken bribes as Papal Nuncio, and it was held that he had 'foresworn himself', promising to conform to the Queen's laws, whence the severity of his confinement had been relaxed enough to make the escape possible.

On Sept. 17th, 1573, Wolfe boarded a Portugese ship with a child. It was also commonly reported in Ireland that Father David had carnal knowledge of a niece, and from this there had been offspring. Wolfe claimed that the child with him was Fitzmaurice's son to be educated at Lisbon, but it was widely believed to be his own son.

Fr. Wolfe went to Rome to lobby for help, and finally got six ships and 500 men from Spain. They landed at Smerwick Harbour, near Dingle, and were immediately surrounded by English forces under Lord Deputy Grey. Although promised honourable terms upon their surrender to Sir Walter Raleigh, they were mercilessly slaughtered. The new Provincial of the Jesuits blamed Wolfe for this massacre, and he was severely censured. In defiance of his orders, he had 'attached himself to the court of a secular prince', that being FitzMaurice of Desmond. Wolfe's failure to disengage himself from political and diplomatic involvement resulted in his dismissal from the Society of Jesus in 1577. He returned to Ireland as a layman, and lived at Kilquane, across the Shannon from Limerick, with his uncle, who was Dean of the Limerick Diocese. He died the following summer. David Wolfe had extended himself valiantly in the Irish cause, but his conversion had come too late. The North could not help, for, thanks in some measure to his own efforts, the power of O'Neill was no more.

Perhaps, in his prison cell, Primate Creagh also came to repent his loyalty to the Crown, although nothing in his various testimonies indicates so. In spite of his unyielding dedication to English rule in Ireland, from the time of his capture a month before O'Neill's death,

SHANE O'NEILL

he languished in the Tower of London. Ultimately, after long years of suffering, he was poisoned by his captors. He died on October 14, 1585.

As for Dean Danyell, the last surviving of the O'Donnelly brothers, little more than a month after Shane's death, the Queen actually authorized his appointment to the Chair of Armagh. The Dean wrote to Cecil on the 5th of October, accepting the Primacy. As he refused to take the Oath of Supremacy, however, the appointment never took effect. It is likely that he had intended to continue to administer the diocese and the Primatial jurisdiction in Creagh's name, where Rome was concerned, but without the interference of a rival 'Reformed' Primate. Terence Danyell continued to serve as a mediator between the Crown and Shane's successor, Turlagh. He died Dean, not Archbishop, of Armagh. A copy of his last will and testament dated the 10th of August 1585 survives, in which he left eleven pounds towards the re-building of the Cathedral of Armagh.

The wily Franciscan, Father Myler Magrath, went on to perhaps the most scandalous religious career in the history of Ireland. As per his request, he was appointed by Queen Elizabeth to be the first Protestant bishop of Clogher, which was his home diocese. When his former friends realized that he had recanted and now served the Queen, he found himself reviled and shunned. Once again upon his request, he was translated to Cashel in Tipperary, a grand and glorious see, with sumptuous accommodations. Still not satisfied, he contrived to procure five other Protestant sees, all of which provided rich livings, and held them all simultaneously!

He wed Anna O'Meara in 1575, but because she never changed her faith, she considered herself no more than a concubine. She stoutly refused 'to eat fleshmeat' with him on Fridays, but Miler coolly assured her that such abstinence would avail her nothing. She might just as well enjoy her meat, he assured her, because she was certain to go to hell anyway for being married to him! All of their nine children were raised Catholic, somewhat unusual, perhaps, for a Protestant bishop.

A famed Catholic noble of the period, the Sullivan Beare, wrote that Anna was in the habit of sheltering Catholic bishops and priests from the English priest hunters. One of these was Darby Creagh the Catholic Bishop of Cork and Cloyne. Myler's letter to his wife from London is preserved to this day.

> "To my loving wife Anny mo ghrádh,
>
> Loving Wife, I have already resolved you touching my cousin Bishop Darby Creagh, and I desire you now to cause his friends to send him out of the whole country if they may, or if not, to send my orders, for there is such search to be made for him, that unless he be wise, he shall be taken. You must send from my house all the priests that you are wont to have, use well my gossip Malachy, for that I did as much as I was able to bring him out of his trouble here. Accomplish the contents of my other letters, and burn this letter presently, and all the letters that you know of yourself. Fail not of this, as you love me and yourself!
>
> From Greenwich this 26th June, 1592,
>
> Your loving husband, Myler"

Not only was Bishop Magrath unfaithful to the Government that promoted and patronized him, but he appears to have done more than anyone to prevent the spread of Protestantism in Ireland. He accomplished this by enriching himself and his children so scandalously with the spoil of the Dioceses of Cashel, Lismore, Emly, and Waterford. He lived the high life, undermining the Reformation until 1620, when he became bed ridden and sought absolution from the Pope to return to the Faith. It was granted, and he died at Cashel towards the end of 1622 in his hundredth year, a Catholic in good standing. In spite of this 'deathbed conversion', he was buried in state at Cashel, with the following somewhat cryptic inscription:

SHANE O'NEILL

"The Verse of Myler Magrath, Archbishop of Cashel
to the Traveller:
> There had come in times of old to Down as his first station
> The most holy Patrick, the great glory of our land;
> Succeeding him, would that I had been as holy as he!
> So of Down at first I was the prelate;
> But England, behind thy sceptre for fifty years
> I worshipped, I pleased thy chiefs in times of noisy wars.
> Here where I am laid I am not. I am where I am not;
> Nor am I in both places, but I am in each place;
> It is the Lord who judges me.
> Let him who stands beware lest he fall!"

For all the good he did, Myler Magrath was reviled as a rogue by both 'traditions' in Ireland, by the Protestants because he made a mockery of their Church, and by Catholics because he refused to sacrifice himself as a victim to the war of orthodoxies that raged about him. Indeed, it might well be said of him that he never stood, so he never fell.

As for Primate Donagh O'Tighe, the continued ascendancy of the 'Inter-Anglico' (English-speaking) wing of the Roman Catholic Church in Ireland over the 'Inter-Hibernico' (Irish-speaking) sector insured that he would be not only forgotten, but virtually erased from history. Many listings of the Primates of Armagh omit his name entirely. Every account in English says only that he died at the end of 1562. The Irish historian Seagháin Ó Loinsigh (?1599-?1675) recounted the bare facts of his arrests, subsequent escapes, and death in his history of the Irish Church, 'De Praesulibus Hiberniae', a book in medieval Latin that shockingly remains untranslated. Ó Loinsigh tells us that O'Tighe died taking shelter with the ecclesiastics at Kilmallock, "his body being still, as they say, free from corruption." This assertion of the miraculous indicates that he was still revered as a martyr and saint nearly a hundred years after his death.

SHANE O'NEILL

The poet, Farleigh O'Gneeve (Fearfhlatha O'Gnímh) was actually somewhat younger than here depicted, and he, like Myler Magrath, lived a full century. His bardic poems passionately decry Ireland's ruin, and his legacy includes such famous odes as 'The Downfall of the Gael', and 'The Death of Ireland'.

Katherine took her children to Shane's nephew, Turlagh Brasselagh O'Neill, where they spent the next eight years in hiding on his vast domains to the south of Lough Neagh. In the early spring of 1575, the Earl of Argyle once again took it upon himself to arrange her marriage. She was wed this time to John Stewart of Appin, from a cadet branch of the Royal Family. He was a staunch Catholic, and one of Argyll's most trusted advisers. The boys were of an age now where she could leave them in fosterage with their O'Neill cousins. With young Áilish, then, she went to live in the majestic Castle Stalker, the stronghold of the Stewarts of Appin. Doubtless she was glad to be back among her people, where she might share once again her sister Úna's company. Her sons would spend many a summer with her there, forming important Scottish alliances. Katherine was widowed again in 1596, and we know that she was alive in 1605, by a written reference of her son, Brian MacShane O'Neill visiting her that year in Scotland.

All of Shane's many sons led turbulent lives, struggling to claim their birthright, the chieftainry of Tirowen. Queen Elizabeth was soon exasperated with Turlagh Lynnach O'Neill, and only a year after Shane's death she sent over young Hugh O'Neill, the Baron's son. This anglicized young man was created Earl of Tyrone, the title so craved by Shane. But after his careful upbringing in Lord Sidney's household, Hugh O'Neill was to disappoint the Queen. He allied himself with Red Hugh O'Donnell, the son of Black Hugh and the Dark Daughter of MacDonnell. He reverted to his Irish ways, and at the end of Elizabeth's reign, he led the Irish in their next long struggle for freedom, the Nine Years War.

SHANE O'NEILL

Nearly two years after Shane's murder, Sir Henry Sidney drafted the bill for 'the Attainder of Shane O'Neill', and had it passed by Parliament. It was the simplest and most effective way of confiscating all his lands and rights of lordship, and the lands and lordships of those other Ulster clans who had pledged allegiance to him. It was a crafty move, for after steadfastly refusing to recognize Shane's claims to overlordship of the other Ulster septs, now upon his death the English chose to honour all such claims to the fullest, in order to confiscate most of Ulster's lands for the Crown. They disinherited Shane's sons, and outlawed the very name of O'Neill.

"The name of O'Neill, with the manner and ceremonies of his creation, and all the superiorities, titles, dignities, preeminences, jurisdictions, authorities, rules, tributes and expenses, used, claimed, usurped, or taken by any O'Neill as by right of that name...of any of the lords, captains, or people of Ulster, and all manner of offices given by the said O'Neill, shall from henceforth cease, end, and be utterly abolished and extinct forever."

Attached to the actual bill (most unusually) was a concocted story, purporting to detail the circumstances of Shane's death, but serving to conceal the part played by the government in his assassination. We are told of a drunken quarrel in which O'Neill boasts that he should marry Agnes, the widow of James MacDonnell, and of the Scots' growing fury until they rise to slay him. Such a story, of course, confirmed the public perception of both the Irish and the Scots as drunken barbarians. The preposterous tale, however, could only deceive a public unaware of Shane's marriage to Katherine MacLean, and of her presence at the feast. They must also be oblivious to the fact that Agnes was the grandmother of half of Shane's own children. It has, nevertheless, been repeated and quoted by virtually every historian who has ventured to recount Shane's untimely end. [apart from Prof. Ciarán Brady who discredited the story] When the attainder appeared, two years on, Elizabeth had reneged on her promises to the MacDonnells, and this version of events left them very

SHANE O'NEILL

much free of such obligations.

The displacement of the Irish language over the course of the 19th century brought with it an historical and cultural amnesia. Bardic poetry was forgotten, as was Shane O'Neill's valiant stand against the English conquest. The revival movements at the end of the century reinterpreted the history for a mostly English speaking Ireland, but as these nationalists were fervent Catholics, Shane O'Neill was largely disowned. The irregularities of his personal life were considered scandalous, and the time-honoured slanders of his enemies, however ridiculous, were enough to strike him from the rolls of Ireland's heroes. Claims of Shane's 'barbarity' are belied by English accounts of his visit to London where he was held to be 'a man of mark', by his voluminous correspondence in Latin and Irish, and by the predatory nature of the English conquest itself. His life was consumed in resistance to the very extirpation of his people, as is bourne out in the subsequent ruin and subjugation of Ireland.

Many of today's historians tell us that Shane had no concept of Ireland as a nation, but fought only for his self-aggrandizement, that the bards heart-wrenching appeals were only 'formulaic poetic devices.' But the poems speak for themselves, and so, quite plainly, does Shane O'Neill. His letters to the Princes of Europe make very clear his understanding and his aspirations for Ireland. The Geraldine League's election of Shane's father to be High King of Ireland left little doubt as to a nationalist agenda, as did O'Neill's insistence upon using the Irish language, and his protection of Irish custom.

The character and power of Shane O'Neill so threatened the English conquest of Ireland that he was slandered and vilified beyond recognition. 'History' branded him a monster, with the implication that his people, who cherished him, were no better. Shane O'Neill's heroic defiance established a pattern of resistance that for all its defeats proved to be unstoppable. Through centuries of oppression, every Irish generation "asserted their right to national freedom and sovereignty." His legacy of resistance culminated in the establishment of the Republic of Ireland, and lingers in the aspirations of Irish sovereignty that still rumble in the hills and laneways of Ulster to this

SHANE O'NEILL

day. It is fortunate that, after decades of bloodshed in our own times, the 'Good Friday Agreement' has served to channel those aspirations into a political process that may one day resolve the conflict between these two nations. Perhaps one day Shane O'Neill will be accorded his rightful place in Ireland's history.

SHANE O'NEILL

ABOUT THE AUTHOR

Heretofore, Brian Mallon is known prinipally as a film and stage actor by trade. He wrote a one-man show, 'Secrets of the Celtic Heart,' that was directed by Ellen Burstyn, and won a 'Best Play Dramalogue Award.' He speaks Irish (Gaelic) and Welsh, and has translated a good deal of poetry from those languages.

As it was Friar Turlough O'Mealláin who wrote the famous journal of the 1641 Catholic Rebellion, following Eoghan Rua O'Neill and Sir Phelim O'Neill, he is not the first of his line to chronicle the O'Neills.

SHANE O'NEILL

Printed in Great Britain
by Amazon